OF
LOVE
AND
LIFE

OF LOVE AND LIFE

Three novels selected and condensed
by Reader's Digest

CONDENSED BOOKS DIVISION

The Reader's Digest Association Limited, London

The Reader's Digest Association Limited
11 Westferry Circus, Canary Wharf, London E14 4HE

www.readersdigest.co.uk

ISBN 0-276-42668-1

CONTENTS

Artistic Licence

Katie Fforde

When Thea first meets Ben Jonson she has her feet in a rubbish bin. Not quite the romantic introduction she might have hoped for, but one that sums up Thea's life perfectly. Nothing is going right for her—her house is full of students who abuse her kindness, and her part-time job is about as interesting as watching paint dry. So when her friend Molly bullies her into coming along on an art appreciation course in Provence, Thea allows herself to be persuaded. Who knows, she might lose her heart to a handsome artist—and then Ben Jonson's opinion of her won't matter a bit . . .

Chapter One

THEA WAS STANDING in the rubbish bin, trying to crush its contents enough to get the lid on, when she heard people approaching down the hallway. They were talking.

'Come into the kitchen and excuse the mess, it's always a tip,' she heard as she crushed a pizza box beneath her heels.

Petal, her youngest and most demanding lodger, followed by a man Thea had never seen before, entered the kitchen.

'Hi, Thea! What are you doing in there?' Petal said, curious but not interested enough to hear the answer. 'This is my Uncle Ben. Oh, that's my phone.'

Thea tried to step out of the waste bin without falling over, as Petal, having dived on her mobile phone like a gull on a fast-food leftover, went out of the room, talking hard.

The bin teetered and the heel of one of Thea's shoes caught round the loop of a drinks can holder and she began to lose her balance. For an instant she had an image of herself lying prostrate on the floor, surrounded by eggshells, banana skins and coffee grounds. She put out a hand, groping for something to hold on to.

The stranger, seeing her predicament, crossed the room and caught the flailing hand and then her body.

Maybe, if she hadn't been in such a bad mood, she could have seen the funny side and laughed up at him. As it was, she blushed furiously while he supported her, unwilling to see if he was laughing at her.

'Thank you so much,' she muttered to the bin, as she rammed the lid back on. 'What a ridiculous thing to have happened.'

Petal quite often managed to make Thea feel more disagreeable than the most caricatured seaside landlady and she felt very tempted to tell her so-called uncle that it was all Petal's fault; she had promised to get some new bin liners, having used up Thea's entire roll. But that would be petty, and it was bad enough to appear bad-tempered and ridiculous in front of strangers without being small-minded as well.

'That's OK,' he said. 'It could happen to anyone.'

To anyone foolish enough to climb into a rubbish bin, she thought, but didn't say. Thea struggled to get her usual good humour back, but it was difficult. He was tall and dark, with deep-set eyes, and it was easy to take his serious demeanour as disapproval. She wished she could tell him to go and wait for Petal in the hall, but she was chronically hospitable, unable to have people in her house, however uninvited, without offering them food or drink. 'Would you like a cup of coffee? Tea?' She slid the kettle to the hot part of the Rayburn.

'I don't think we're staying. I just came with Petal to collect some things.'

'Does that mean Petal is taking her artwork home at last?'

This was such good news that Thea smiled widely. She would be able to get into the attic, her bedroom and the bathroom, without tripping over the component parts of a dragon, a princess and a castle, all made of papier-mâché and covered with Thea's bin bags. 'You might as well have some tea. She'll be ages.'

Perhaps her glee was rather too much of a contrast from the grumpy woman he'd helped out of a rubbish bin because the man frowned. 'I can't stay long. I've got to get back tonight.'

'Suit yourself, but if I don't have something my tongue will cleave permanently to the roof of my mouth.'

'Then, thank you,' he said, looking surprised.

Her euphoria faded a little. Petal's Uncle Ben appeared to have no social skills. Why didn't he comment on the filthy weather or something?

'Do you have far to get back to?'

'Well, after I've dropped off Petal's things, I've got to get back to London.'

That would take him at least three hours. Thea found an unchipped mug and put a tea bag in it.

At that moment the phone rang. Thea manoeuvred her way across the untidy kitchen and picked it up. It was an old and dear friend who liked a good half-hour per phone call—if she was in a hurry. Thea talked to her for a couple of minutes, then took evasive action. She picked up a box of matches and a candle, kept there for the purpose, and lit the candle. Then she reached out into the hallway and held it under the smoke alarm. The alarm shrieked obligingly. 'Darling,' she told her friend. 'I've got to go. Something's on fire!'

'Sorry,' she said to Petal's uncle, who was looking at her with stunned amazement. 'That always works. Although I do worry that I'll *have* a fire one day as a punishment. Now, where were we? Tea!'

'I really mustn't be long and I was supposed to call in on Molly—er—Petal's aunt, too.'

As she poured boiling water into mugs, Thea glanced over her shoulder. 'Molly Pickford? I know her. It's through her I got Petal.' Thea sighed as she wondered why she'd let herself in for having Petal as a lodger. Molly had insisted that her goddaughter and niece would be quiet and reliable, and able to pay the rent. While the last bit was true, Molly had forgotten to mention that Petal was extremely demanding. Thea often thought that even if she paid twice as much, Petal still wouldn't be worth it.

'Milk? Sugar?' She handed her guest a mug, with suitable additions. 'Are you related to Molly, too? Petal referred to you as her uncle, but it doesn't necessarily follow that you are.'

Usually, by this time, Thea would have got over her feeling of awkwardness at being caught with her kitchen at its worst, but as he kept looking around him like a character in a science-fiction movie beamed down onto a strange planet, she felt obliged to distract him with questions she didn't want to know the answers to.

'We're some sort of cousins. You'd have to ask Molly how many times removed we are. She loves that kind of detail.'

Thea warmed to him a little. She picked up a pile of papers from a chair and indicated he should sit down. 'Sorry, I didn't catch your surname?'

'Probably because Petal didn't tell you it. It's Jonson, without an "h". Ben Jonson.'

'Like the poet?'

'Yes.'

His slight surprise that she should have heard of the sixteenth-century poet annoyed her. 'I love his poems, especially the one he wrote about his son.' She bit her lip. '"His best bit of poetry—"'

'He said "piece", actually. "His best piece of poetry".'

Thea's irritation returned. 'Well, I knew it was something like that. You'd better sit down; Petal might be hours. Now, I hope you don't mind if I get on with my cooking? In a moment of madness I agreed to give my lodgers an evening meal.'

'Every night?'

'Not Fridays or Saturdays—they're usually out, or home for the weekend—but I always do a big meal on Sunday.' It was Sunday now and Thea had been making a bolognese sauce for lasagne on and off all day. Silently, she urged Petal to come back before she felt obliged to invite her uncle to supper. The lasagne might stretch, but the salad wouldn't. 'Please sit down, you're making the place look untidy.'

She didn't turn round to see if he realised she'd made a little joke; she was almost sure he had no sense of humour.

Petal came back into the room, still talking: 'Must go, see ya, doll.' Almost the moment she had disconnected, the house telephone went. 'Oh,' said Petal, breezily, 'that'll be for me.'

Thea took a gulp of tea, wishing it were red wine. Soon, Thea's other lodgers would arrive back from their weekend haunts, and the kitchen would be more crowded and cooking would be more difficult.

'I do wish Petal would get off the phone,' said Ben and Thea together. They looked at each other and Ben smiled.

It transformed him, but as Petal hung up the phone at that moment, Thea looked away before she could work out why. When she looked back again the smile had gone.

'Oh, Thea,' said Petal, 'Aunt Molly's coming over later.'

'Oh God, why?' Too late, Thea realised that this must have sounded extremely rude. 'I mean, I'm just so busy at the moment. Do you know why?'

'Some art appreciation tour or something. On Wednesday.'

'Well, I'm free on Wednesday—I'll give her a ring later. Save her the trouble of coming over.' It was more to save Thea the trouble of sanitising the kitchen. Molly would be voluble on the subject of Thea's standards of tidiness and hygiene.

Petal frowned. 'She said something about France. Aunt Molly wants you to go to France with her. On Wednesday.'

Thea put down her mug. 'Molly can't possibly be asking me to go to France with her on Wednesday.'

'Yes! Her mate's broken her leg or something, so she needs someone to go with. I told her you were probably up for it.' Petal, bored with a subject that didn't involve her, turned to her uncle. 'Oh, I'm glad you've got some tea. It'll take me ages to find the stuff in the attic, it's so full of junk.' She looked at the crowded table, the crockery-covered worktops, the Welsh dresser buried under paper. 'This house is always so untidy.'

'So would yours be if it were full of lodgers who can't put a mug in the dishwasher, let alone run a tap and wash it,' said Thea. 'And I hope you're going to take everything off the landing. At least the stuff in the attic is out of sight.'

Momentarily abashed, Petal said, 'Sorry, Thea, but you don't nag us enough. If you don't nag people, they just don't clear up. When I move into a flat people are just not going to leave their stuff all over the place!' Petal marched out of the room, stiff with resolution, leaving Thea limp and without it.

'So Petal drives you mad?' asked Ben.

'Is it that obvious? Well, only sometimes.' She tasted the bolognese sauce. 'I mean, I love her really. She's very decorative, and great fun and great to go shopping with.'

She was aware that if only she were a less indulgent landlady she wouldn't be so walked on by her lodgers. But she was new to the trade and hadn't learned how to make rules and stick to them. 'You wouldn't be a sweetie and grate some cheese for me?' she asked and then had to hide her giggle as she realised how inappropriate her endearment had been.

He raised an eyebrow. 'Since you ask so nicely, how can I refuse?' He took the cheese and the grater, and set to work.

'I wonder what Molly wants? I can't believe she really wants me to go to France on Wednesday. Even she . . .' she paused, suddenly realising she was about to criticise his cousin.

'Couldn't be that unreasonable?' he suggested, not giving anything away on how he felt about Molly.

'Not at all. I just meant that she's usually very organised.'

Petal came back just as Thea had levered the completed lasagne into the oven. Preceded by a large number of plastic sacks, Petal said, 'You really should clear out the attic, Thea. I can't believe you've got so many cardboard boxes. What on earth have you got in them?'

In fact, they were full of Thea's photographs and negatives, carefully indexed and catalogued, from when she was a student to the moment she gave up professional photography. But she had no intention of telling Petal that. 'The attic's probably a lot clearer now you've taken your work out of it, Petal,' she said.

In a minute Petal and her uncle would go away, and she could open the bottle of red wine that was hidden behind the bleach in the cupboard under the sink, the one place her lodgers would never look, however desperate for a drink they were.

Petal, oblivious to the acid in Thea's tone, looked about the kitchen. 'Don't you think you should tidy up, if Aunt Molly's coming?'

Thea would have liked to commit murder, but thought she'd better not. It would only add to the mess. 'I'm in the middle of cooking a meal, Petal.'

At that moment the doorbell rang. 'Answer it, will you?' Thea implored.

'But it'll be Aunt Molly, for you.' Petal was surprised Thea could ask such a thing of her. 'I'm really busy.'

'So am I!' said Thea, swooping round the worktops with a cloth.

'I'll get it,' Ben offered.

This was kind and, if he wanted to be even kinder, he would involve Molly in a lot of time-consuming chat upstairs in the hall, giving Thea valuable extra seconds to clean up.

Molly, whom she had met on her first day in Cheltenham, had been introduced by some distant relative of Thea's mother's. It was a very tenuous connection but Molly, who could be very kind, had followed it up immediately by inviting Thea for coffee. Thea, delighted to get away from the removal men, walked round in her old jeans and torn shirt. Molly, as always, was immaculately groomed and dressed, and had given her sherry, not coffee. She assumed that Thea's dishabille meant that she was 'arty' and had taken her under her wing. In the two and a half years that Thea had lived in Cheltenham the two women had spent quite a lot of time together. Now she entered Thea's kitchen, all benevolence, a good five minutes after she had rung the doorbell.

Thank you, Petal's uncle, thought Thea.

'Thea, sweetie!' Molly was brisk. 'I hope this isn't wildly inconvenient, but I wanted to come and tell you in person.'

'Tell me what, Molly?' asked Thea, after they had kissed.

'About the trip.' Molly pulled out a chair, regarded its seat dubiously and sat down. 'To Aix. In Provence. Should be lovely at this time of year. I was going with my pottery-class friend, but she's broken her leg. If I go on my own I'll have to pay the single room supplement. Come on,' she went on bracingly, as if Thea were refusing to go swimming because the water was cold. 'It's only for six days.'

'Take Derek.'

'Derek hates art and sightseeing. He is such a philistine.'

'But, Molly—it's terribly short notice.'

'Oh, I know it's sudden, but think how heavenly it would be. Early April is just my favourite time for Provence, before all the tourists get there.' Molly obviously hadn't noticed she was a tourist herself.

'I can't afford it, for a start.' Molly was, by Thea's standards, enormously rich. 'And really—'

'Oh, come on, Thea, be a bit spontaneous. Derek'll pay. It was his idea that I ask you, actually. He said you probably deserve a holiday for looking after Petal.'

Thea gave Derek a mental 'thank you' for understanding that his niece was not all joy. 'But, Molly, it would be far cheaper to pay the single room supplement.'

'Oh, I know. It's the company I want you for, really. I like to go with someone I know. Someone I can talk to.'

Personally, Thea liked to go on holiday with somebody she liked, and although she did like Molly, even the very best of friendships could founder in such conditions. And she wasn't sure that Molly qualified as 'very best'.

Thea decided to risk losing Molly's good opinion of her by producing her hidden wine. As Petal probably had the only decent corkscrew in her room, she had to prise the cork out with one that hurt her fingers. 'It's terribly generous of you, Molly, but I can't possibly accept. Have some of this. It's only a "bogoff" but really quite OK if you warm it up a bit first.'

'Bogoff?' Molly looked at her glass as if it contained nasty medicine.

'You know, buy one, get one free.'

Molly, appalled, didn't comment. '*Of course* you can come to France,' she said decisively. She picked up her glass, thought better of it and put it down again. 'Really, Derek can afford it and he's right, you deserve a break for looking after Petal.' The sound of banging and crashing indicated that Petal's artwork was nearing the front door. 'Can you get away at such short notice?'

Suddenly the thought of exchanging her lodgers and her boring part-time job for Provence in the spring was terribly attractive. And Molly, though bossy and overbearing, was fun.

Thea took a large sip of her wine and decided that it wasn't very nice. The wine in Provence was bound to be better. 'We're not particularly busy at the moment and I don't get holiday pay or anything. I don't think it would be a problem.'

'Super! You'll need comfortable shoes, an umbrella and a sunhat.'

Just then, Petal opened the kitchen door and shouted through it, 'Ben said thank you for the tea and sorry he can't say goodbye, but he's loading the car. And, Aunt Molly, he'll give you a ring as he hasn't time to call in now. 'Bye!' The kitchen door closed and then opened again. 'By the way, Thea, there are some clothes of mine in the tumble drier. If you could be an angel and hang them up for me?' Assuming that Thea would be an angel, Petal removed herself.

Thea regarded Molly. 'A sunhat?' The cold spring rain was lashing against the window and the tumble drier was full of Petal's clothes. 'I'd love to come, Molly.'

Thea's part-time job at a high-street photographer's was not one which was ever going to bring her much in the way of job satisfaction. Sending off other people's holiday snaps and handing them back twenty-four hours later was not intrinsically interesting. But because in a previous life she had been a photographer it had seemed natural. And while she often turned to the jobs pages in the local paper, she couldn't quite summon up the energy to find anything more challenging. She wasn't happy with her life, but hadn't the initiative to do anything much to change it. Perhaps an art appreciation tour in France would give her the necessary prod.

It would have been an overstatement to say that Thea's 'life' and the 'love of it' had both deserted her at the same time, but she had hoped that Conrad, the man in question, would turn into a partner—or even a husband.

She had been a photojournalist, just making her name, and what had happened was hurtful and humiliating, but the worst part was that her female photographer friends all told her it was her fault. They had bullied the story out of her after frog-marching her to a local pub where they decided they would straighten her out, accompanied by tequila slammers.

After they'd heard that she and Conrad had broken up, they moved on to the reason why. And, to a professional, hard-boiled woman, they condemned her as a naive amateur.

'I know,' she admitted, finishing her slammer. 'I've got so much egg on my face I can hardly see out.'

'I could do with egg like that,' said Zelda, a model who had moved round to the other side of the camera. 'How much did you get as a thank-you present?'

Thea repeated the amount, although they all knew perfectly well by now. 'I feel bad about accepting it, but Anna insisted. She told me that I'd given her much more than money could ever buy and that being generous involved receiving as well as giving. I thought it was rather sweet.'

The women's collective expression told Thea they found it rather nauseous, actually, but they didn't comment.

'So now what? You can upgrade your shoebox to a boot box. When you've got the bastard out, that is,' suggested one.

'What you should do is get some really fancy equipment that will earn you proper money.'

Elizabeth was career-minded and made Thea feel tired at the best of times. 'What I really want to do,' she said, preparing to duck from what was about to be thrown at her, 'is to buy a large house in Cheltenham and fill it with students.'

They were all too shocked to throw things.

'Why Cheltenham?' asked Elizabeth, in case there was something Thea knew about it that she didn't.

'Because I don't know anyone in Cheltenham. I can have a completely new start in life. Do something entirely different. Earn my living without having to hustle for work and lug half a ton of equipment around the place to do it.'

'But it's so stimulating! Not knowing where you're going to be working each day,' said Magenta. 'And you could always do studio work.'

'I could,' Thea agreed, 'and perhaps I might set up a studio, after a while, but now I want to hide away and lick my wounds.'

'You must have been hurt badly if you want to retire to the provinces,' Zelda said with a shudder. 'Have you ever been there?'

Thea nodded. 'I did some work at the literature festival once. There's a lovely parade of shops, with caryatids. I really fancy it. And yes, I was badly hurt. I don't think Conrad ever loved me. I just couldn't make him understand what he'd done wrong. It's put me right off men.'

'Don't they have men in Cheltenham?' asked Elizabeth.

'No, I don't think so. It's partly why I chose it.'

Everyone laughed, but they didn't manage to change her mind

throughout the course of the evening, and they did agree that she was way too naive for photojournalism.

'Well,' said Magenta, 'you can always come and stay if you want to come back and rejoin the world.'

'And you can come and stay with me, if you want to get away from it.'

'Thank you, darling. It sounds heaven,' Magenta replied, completely unconvinced.

Now, two and a half years on, her house was decorated and full of lodgers, and the lodgers were driving her mad.

Mostly, she enjoyed the kids. She didn't really mind hanging people's washing out, or taking it in if it was raining. And only a real cow could object to ironing something when someone was 'really, really late' and desperate for a white blouse for work.

But she was only thirty-five and was surrogate mother to people far too old to be her children. Those people, often away from home for the first time, were only too glad to find such a kindly, helpful person to listen to their problems and sew on their buttons in an emergency.

Thea felt she had gone from potentially successful photojournalist to mother of teenagers too quickly. She should have had a life in between. But when she had arrived from London, exhausted and emotionally bruised, 'a life' was the last thing she had wanted.

She hadn't intended to give up on men completely—at least, not for ever. She knew perfectly well that while Conrad was a shit, a lot of men were honourable and trustworthy. She had even gone out with a few of them since she'd moved out of London. It was a shame that these cardinal virtues seemed to go hand in hand with dullness and a love of obscure classical music.

Much to Petal's dismay, she had ended her relationship with one such just recently. Petal had been horrified: 'But, Thea, I know he's not very exciting, but he's *someone* and you shouldn't finish with one boy—I mean, man—before you've got another one. Otherwise you're on your own, manless and dateless! I mean, derr! How sad are you? You don't have to finish with a bloke because you don't share the same taste in music. Just bring him round to what you like!'

While Thea was certain that Petal could convert the most dedicated classical music scholar to 'techno', or 'drum'n'bass', she didn't feel she shared Petal's skills in manipulation. Molly, on the other hand, might even be able to teach Petal a thing or two about getting her own way.

Chapter Two

MOLLY'S HUSBAND, DEREK, well-trained and with the prospect of a week without Molly organising his life, had agreed to drive the two women to Gatwick. Molly took an elegant suitcase on wheels, and a fitted vanity case as hand luggage. Thea took a battered holdall, borrowed from one of her lodgers, and a large, flowery cotton handbag into which she could fit a huge amount. Molly would have made a list, and packed an outfit for every day and every evening, and numerous pairs of shoes. Thea had stuffed her bag with everything she owned that was navy-blue, so there was a hope of it blending in, if not exactly matching, and a pair of slightly less tatty shoes for evening than the trainers she was now wearing.

Derek and Molly arrived at Thea's at eight in the morning. Molly was in full make-up and looked marvellous. She regarded Thea with her lips pursed. 'Oh,' she said. 'Trainers.'

'You said I'd need comfortable shoes,' Thea reminded her.

'I know, but I meant . . . oh, well, never mind. Have you got a light mac and an umbrella?'

'I've got a cagoule but no umbrella,' said Thea firmly. 'I don't get on with them.' She hadn't got an E111 form either, or personal travel insurance, but she knew if she told Molly this she'd have a fit.

'Well, it's up to you. So, where's your case?'

'This is my case.'

Molly looked horrified. 'I wouldn't be able to go away for a night with only a bag that size. You do know that we eat out at restaurants every night?'

'I'll be fine.' Thea closed the front door behind her, wondering if agreeing to go on holiday with Molly hadn't been a dreadful mistake.

'We won't put our badges on until we're in the departure lounge,' said Molly after Derek had dropped them off. 'We don't want people identifying us too soon. You did get an identifying badge, didn't you?'

'Oh, yes,' agreed Thea, 'it's just that I've lost it. But if you've got yours, I can stand by you.'

Molly regarded Thea crossly. 'Honestly, Thea . . .' Just before Thea could respond Molly remembered that Thea had had only two days to get ready for this trip. 'Of course, it was terribly short notice and I'm really pleased you could come . . .'

Thea smiled. 'And I'm really pleased you asked me. I haven't been abroad for ages.'

'Oh goodness! You did check your passport hasn't expired, didn't you?'

'I must say,' said Thea, weak with relief that nothing wrong had been found with her passport, 'I'm looking forward to not having to think and just follow our tour guide like a sheep. It's been so hectic lately. It'll be restful to be told what to do.'

Molly never did anything like a sheep and wasn't good at being told what to do, but she did like a good fortnight in which to pack and have herself beautified, and couldn't possibly have got ready in the time available to Thea. 'It was a dreadful rush for you. But don't worry, I can lend you anything you've forgotten.'

'Thank you,' said Thea meekly, knowing she hadn't brought toothpaste and there would probably be other things.

'Shall we have coffee now, or after we've done the perfume?' suggested Molly.

'I need to buy a book—'

'Oh, no. You never get time to read on these holidays, you're kept far too busy.'

'So you've been on this type of tour a lot?'

'Yes, and our guide's such a nice man. You could say I was a bit of a Gerald groupie.' Molly giggled alarmingly.

'Oh, well, if you like it enough to come back, I expect I'll have a good time too.' Thea was trying to convince herself. 'What's the lecturer on Cézanne like?'

'I've no idea. I've never heard of him. But I dare say he'll be all right. They're very careful who they get. Now, come along, I want to get some cream for my eyes.' She peered at Thea. 'I expect you could do with some too. It's no good waiting for the wrinkles to appear before you do anything about them, you know.'

Thea smiled. 'I think I'll just cut along to the bookshop and meet you back here.'

Molly had put on her distinctive, stripy Tiger Tour badge as they stood by baggage reclaim at Marseille Airport. Thea began to spot other badges, and began to feel that she was going to be the baby of the party. Even Molly, though over fifty, was younger than most of this crowd. People began to smile tentatively at one another.

'You see why I wanted you to come.' Molly's stage whisper was guaranteed to reach the back of the stalls. 'Most of this lot are geriatric. I might have got latched on to by some old dear with incontinence pads who couldn't keep up.'

Thea hoped that the old dears were all stone-deaf. She smiled at a few people to detach herself from Molly's unkind remark.

'Right, troops,' said a tall, dark-haired man in his early fifties. 'Gather round while I give you a few instructions. I see some familiar faces, which is good, because you can help me keep the newcomers in order.'

Thea saw Molly smiling benignly. There were several other smiling faces too. They were obviously all Gerald groupies. Well, if he could keep Molly under control he must have something going for him. Poor old Derek was well under the thumb.

'And why aren't you wearing a badge, young lady?' Gerald asked Thea with an oily smile.

'I've lost it,' she told him somewhat defiantly.

'It's all right, Gerald, she's with me,' said Molly. 'You remember me? Molly Pickford?'

'Molly! Good to have you aboard again. Jolly good. Now, the *toilettes* are over in that direction, people, and the trolleys are over there.'

Thea could see people debating which was their greatest need and said, 'Shall I go and get a few trolleys and bring them over? Otherwise they'll all disappear.'

'Good idea. I'll stay here until we're all together again. Then we'll get onto the coach.'

The holiday had begun. And if Molly drove her mad, Thea comforted herself, she could always latch herself on to an old lady—there were plenty to choose from.

As Thea lay on the bed, watching Molly unpack, she realised that she hadn't shared a room with another girl since she had been on a school trip, when everyone had just lived out of their rucksacks.

At last Molly was ready. Her many clothes were neatly stacked in the wardrobe. Her underwear was in the chest of drawers. Her bath oil, shower gel, shampoo, conditioner and hairspray were lined up on the shelf in the bathroom. Bags of cotton wool balls and cotton wool pads were hung on all the available hooks, and her special linen cloth for her face was draped over the towel rail.

'Darling, where will you put all your stuff? Is that all you've got? Love, I know you are a lot younger than me, but you need a bit more than just a pot of Astral, surely? What about cleanser and toner?'

Thea, who was amazed at how much it took to make Molly look like Molly, felt she might as well come clean. 'I don't do much in the way of cleansing and toning. I just smear on some cream, wipe it off with loo paper and put a bit more on.'

Molly was horrified. 'I can't believe *anyone*, in this day and age, doesn't cleanse and tone.' She peered at Thea. 'Well, you seem to have got away with it so far, but it could rebound on you horribly. You have to take care of yourself, Thea.'

Before Molly could finish her thought, which Thea knew from experience was something along the lines of 'or you'll never find yourself a man', Thea broke in, 'I do have deodorant with moisturiser in it. It makes my armpits wonderfully soft and manageable.'

Molly pursed her lips. She was a natural matchmaker and, sensing this, when they first met, Thea had given her a very graphic and well-dramatised account of her breakup with Conrad. Otherwise, Thea had felt, Molly would be dragging single men out of the woodwork until, maddened, Thea put herself into a convent.

Now, Thea looked at her watch. 'We've got three-quarters of an hour before we have to meet downstairs for dinner.'

'Really? Oh my God! Do you mind if I have the bath first? What are you going to wear?'

Thea didn't have a lot of choice. 'Something navy-blue, I expect.'

Gerald was impatiently striding up and down the hotel foyer, waiting for the last of his flock to arrive, when they got downstairs. He wanted to march them off briskly to dinner. 'Late again, Molly! I thought I'd taught you a bit of punctuality when you were with me before.'

'It was my fault,' Thea began, sacrificing truth for her friend. But then she saw Molly bridling happily under Gerald's stern admonishment and realised she liked it. In any case, no one would believe that she had spent more than ten minutes doing herself up, when her hair was still slightly wet and her navy-blue skirt distinctly crumpled.

'Oh, Gerald, you're such a bully,' said Molly. 'I don't know why I come with you.'

As the party processed down the narrow street to the restaurant, Thea wondered if Molly would like it if Derek were as masterful as Gerald and decided she wouldn't. It was one thing to enjoy being bossed about by Gerald for six days, but quite another to live with someone you couldn't control.

'Well, I thought the bath was awfully small, for one,' said a woman who'd brought her husband with her, as they sat down.

'What was it like for two?' asked Thea under her breath.

Another Home Counties accent drifted across the clink of glasses. 'I looked and looked, but although they had everything else, they didn't have cards with "to my cleaning lady" on, so I had to just get her one with flowers.'

Thea was mesmerised and didn't at first hear her neighbour's kindly enquiry. 'Is this your first Tiger Tour?' She was certainly the wrong side of seventy-five but had a definite twinkle.

'Yes,' Molly answered for her. 'She's come with me.'

'I see,' said the old lady, sizing up Molly immediately. 'It's nice to have a younger companion when you're getting on.'

Molly opened her mouth to protest when the old woman went on, 'Just teasing, dear.' She gave Thea a roguish wink.

By the end of the evening Thea was feeling tired, but generally much more optimistic about the holiday. Not everyone was elderly, and the few who were seemed to make up for their years by their interest in each other and life in general. She yawned widely as they walked back to the hotel, and was asleep before Molly had finished her bedtime beauty routine.

After about an hour she woke up again. Molly snored, loudly and irregularly. Thea burrowed under the covers, wondering if she'd ever be able to get back to sleep.

Thea loved Aix-en-Provence. It was a charming town with beautiful fountains, old buildings and delightful cafés. It was a shame that she slept so badly at night because it meant she was prone to falling asleep on the coach. It wasn't that Thea didn't want to see yet another view of Mont Sainte-Victoire—she loved the mountain and fully appreciated Cézanne's apparent obsession with it—but she was tired.

On the fourth day the party gathered in a beautiful room in one of the ancient *hôtels* which had been taken over by the university. Old Tiger Tour hands got out notebooks and pens. It was time for the lecture on Cézanne.

Thea sat at the back, well away from Molly, with some of the older guests who might well nod off and not criticise her for doing the same.

The lecturer came in. Younger even than Thea, he was tall, dark and delicious. Thea sat up and decided not to fall asleep after all—ancient monuments had a beauty all their own, but so did well-built young men with blue eyes and curling eyelashes.

But his good looks did not make him a good speaker. He mumbled, he didn't smile and, unlike the masterful Gerald, he didn't bring his subjects to life with his brisk enthusiasm. Thea decided to nap after all. His voice—what she could hear of it—had an Irish lilt to it, which was pleasantly soporific.

After about ten minutes, Thea woke up and decided she wasn't going shopping with Molly that afternoon, which was designated 'free time'; she was going to have lunch instead.

She spent the rest of the lecture planning what she would say to Molly—'I'm going to return to my room and read a little Proust.' That would shut Molly up for a good ten seconds. She could, of course, just admit she was tired because she couldn't sleep and only wanted to sit outside a bar in the sun, but that would be unkind. Besides, Molly probably wouldn't believe she snored. She and Derek had separate bedrooms, but Thea have been given the impression it was because of Derek's bodily functions rather than Molly's.

By the time the lecture had finished Thea still hadn't come up with a story she thought Molly would wear. When she saw her edging along the seats towards her, Molly was already saying, 'We won't have lunch as such, just coffee later . . .'

What wasn't immediately obvious was that Molly wasn't talking to Thea, but to the woman behind her, who Thea remembered as Joan, a rather nice person from the Home Counties. She was nearer both in budget and age to Molly, and now it seemed she wanted someone to shop with.

'Are you set, Thea?'

'Actually, Molly, would you mind if I didn't join you? I'd like to take some photographs and I've got postcards to write.'

Molly took this almost without protest. 'Are you sure? Well, that's fine. Joan and I will have a lovely time.'

Thea felt like skipping as she set off on her own. Molly, at close quarters twenty-four hours a day, made her long for solitude.

She found an enchanting *place*, with an intimate little fountain and a charming-looking café with outside tables. She collapsed into a seat, ordered a beer and a salade niçoise, and took her book out of her bag.

'May I join you? I don't speak a word of French and I've a thirst on me which makes . . . my stomach thinks my throat's been cut.'

Thea looked up to see the beautiful, boring lecturer. He seemed so much less boring close up that she smiled. 'You could ask for a beer, couldn't you? I don't speak much French either.'

He helped himself to a chair at her table. 'I could, and I could probably order a cognac, but I should eat as well. I know that if you're not careful you can end up with entrails all over your lettuce. What are those?' He peered suspiciously at Thea's salad, which arrived at that moment. 'They put gizzards on salad here, you know.'

'Anchovies. It's a salade niçoise. Have it, it's delicious.'

'*Pour moi aussi*,' he said to the waiter, pointing at Thea's plate and glass. '*S'il vous plaît.*'

'You see, you can manage perfectly well.' Thea was beginning to enjoy herself. There were worse fates than sitting in the sun with an attractive man, eating and drinking.

'I can, but when I saw you sitting here, I thought, "Why walk past an attractive woman and eat on my own, when I at least recognise her and could inflict my company on her."' He held out his hand. 'Rory Devlin.'

Thea gave him hers. 'Thea Orville.'

'So what is a lovely young woman like you doing on a Tiger Tour?'

'Lapping up the culture and listening to lovely young men tell me about Cézanne.'

'I was shite, wasn't I? I've forgotten more about Cézanne than most of these people have ever known and I can't make him sound interesting.'

'And what most of the people listening knew about Cézanne could be written on the back of a postage stamp.'

He gave her a smile. 'You're a wicked, heartless woman, telling me the truth like that. So, what is it that you have in common with this bunch?'

'I came with Molly—the tall, handsome woman?'

'Oh, yes.'

'But actually, the others are dears. You wouldn't come on a tour like this if you were too stuffy or set in your ways.'

'I wouldn't say that. I gave a lecture last week to a bunch from another company. There was a woman there who was so damn bossy the others tried to bribe the coach driver to leave her behind.'

'You do these talks quite often, then?' She was surprised, since he was so bad at it.

He shook his head. 'I was offered my expenses and a bit of a fee, so I came early and took the opportunity to do some painting.'

'So you're an artist?'

'Yeah. What do you do?'

He obviously didn't want to talk about being an artist. It was unfortunate that she didn't much want to talk about being a landlady, or having been a photographer, either.

'The good thing about being on a tour with retired people is that, on the whole, no one asks you what you do, because they mostly don't do anything.'

'Is that a brush-off?'

'No. I just don't want to bore you.'

'I'm sure you couldn't do that if you tried. I, on the other hand, can do it at the drop of a hat. I saw you nodding off during my talk.'

Thea laughed. 'I'm dog-tired. Molly snores like a grampus.'

'And I'm shite at talking—we won't go into that again. I'm a much better painter.'

'I'm glad to hear it.'

He frowned. 'To punish you for that unkind comment I will make you tell me what you do.'

'OK, but here's your lunch.'

He picked up his knife and fork. 'Well?'

Thea sat back in her chair. 'I have a house full of students and a part-time job in a photographer's.'

He frowned. 'You're too young to be a landlady.'

'I like young people.'

'And the part-time job in the photographer's? That's some camera you've got there. You should be taking photographs, not putting them in envelopes.'

She looked down at her Leica M4. She had bought it for fifteen hundred pounds, secondhand. She loved it. 'Yes.'

'You're holding out on me.'

'Why shouldn't I? I don't tell my story to just anyone, you know.'

'I'll tell you mine if you'll tell me yours.'

He gave her the sort of smile which caused a reluctant awakening in the region of her libido. Thea had almost forgotten she still had a libido, it had been so long since she had allowed herself feelings.

'OK,' she said, 'you go first.'

He insisted on ordering cognac for them both before he started. Only when he had taken a large sip did he finally begin. 'Well, I was an art school whiz-kid. I went early and, at first, followed the party line. At that time anything representational was considered naff. Only abstract or conceptual work was thought worth anything.

'I did the conceptual stuff, the dustbins full of road kill, the giant aquarium with amputated limbs suspended in jelly. And I wrote statements about why I did what I did that would make you sick. Come the degree show, I did what I wanted. Paintings, drawings, of things you could recognise. I thought I'd be slated, but no, my degree show was a fantastic success. I was hailed as the next big thing and I met a beautiful woman who introduced me to the owner of a Cork Street gallery. So far, so fairy tale.'

He regarded Thea directly. 'Go on,' she said gently.

'To cut a very depressing story short, I got offered an exhibition, accompanied by as much hype as you like—and I blew it. I got completely wrecked before the show even started, and didn't stop drinking until I passed out. In the morning it turned out I'd insulted every major critic in the business and vomited over a major gossip columnist.'

'Oh dear.'

'Yes. So the critics trashed my work, and said I'd never come to anything and would end up painting greetings cards.'

Thea winced. 'What did you do?'

'I travelled for a bit and then settled in Ireland. Now I make a bit of a living painting people's dogs and horses. Sometimes their children. I like the dogs best. But I don't do frigging greetings cards.' He said this last so bitterly Thea could tell it still hurt. She put her hand on his wrist; there was nothing she could say to make anything better.

'I wouldn't have minded them telling the world I was a drunken slob, because that was true. But the work didn't change because I'd a few too many—OK, a lot too many. Now, what about you?'

She chuckled gently. 'I'm afraid my story hasn't got a happy ending either. I was a photographer, making my name, getting enough commissions to pay the mortgage.'

'What sort of work did you do?'

'I was a photojournalist. I took shots of famous people, sometimes abroad. I was just getting somewhere when—well, the shit happened.'

'What sort of shit?'

She took a breath. 'I had a boyfriend—a journo I'd met out in Africa. I thought he was a hero, risking his life to bring the stories of the oppressed to the world and I thought we were . . . well, I was about to sell my flat and move in with him.'

'And? He cheated on you?'

'Yes, though not with a woman. He stole something from me, an image, and tried to sell it and use it without my permission.'

'Would it have been the end of the world if he had sold it?'

'Yes. It was a very . . . a very sensitive photograph. I was only allowed to take it because the clients, who are extremely famous, trusted me. It wasn't for the general public to see.'

'Sorry, but if he didn't actually sell it, or make any money on a deal, what was the problem?'

Thea sighed. 'It was him selling—or trying to sell—something so private to people with the morals of tomcats. He disregarded the fact that it was my integrity that was on the line.'

Rory frowned, trying to understand. 'So was the picture published?'

'No, but no thanks to Conrad, and it took some persuading on my part to convince my clients that I hadn't had anything to do with trying to do a deal.'

'How did you manage it?'

'As soon as I found out what had happened, I advised them to get on-to their lawyers. I could prove that the image had been stolen.'

'How did Conrad get hold of it?'

'I lent him my laptop computer. The machine was running slowly and when clearing the recycle bin he came across a JPEG, a saved image, which carried the names of these celebs. He opened the file and got a full-page picture of someone very famous, very commercial, in glorious colour, in a very tasteful but erotic pose.'

'You mean, a naked woman?'

Thea nodded. 'The family wanted a series of special shots for their personal family album. I stayed with them for a week, taking shots of them eating breakfast, having a barbecue, that sort of stuff. Then one day the wife, whom I'd got to know quite well, wanted me to take a picture of her naked, wearing this special antique jewellery her husband had given her, in a copy of a pose in an old master they had. She told me later that she'd found a lump in her breast and was frightened she might have to have a mastectomy. She wanted her husband to have pictures of her in case. The lump turned out to be benign, but at the time she was frightened. Anyway, after I'd had them processed I gave her the negatives.'

'So how did the image get on your laptop if you were so careful?'

'She liked the colour shots, but she also wanted one in black and white. I told her I could take the colour out on the computer. When the job was done I deleted it, but forgot to empty the recycle bin.'

'So were they furious with you when you told them?'

'Initially, because the husband thought I might be trying to blackmail them, but his wife convinced him that was the last thing I'd do. She insisted that if I hadn't warned them, the picture would have been all round the European press. They gave me some money, out of gratitude. After I'd sold my flat in London and paid off the mortgage, I had enough to buy my house in Cheltenham and set up as a landlady.' Thea looked at her glass for a moment. 'I wouldn't have taken it, but she really wanted to give me something. Basically, because my life had been ruined because of that creep.'

Rory was silent for a few seconds. 'Men are bastards, that's the top and bottom of it.'

Thea sighed. 'Well, yes, I won't disagree with you there. But to be fair, I didn't *have* to give up photography. I'd just had enough of traipsing around the country with half a hundredweight of equipment hung round my neck.'

'So now you're a landlady, with a house full of lodgers. Doesn't sound very fulfilling.'

'Oh, it's all right. Mostly I like the kids. And it keeps me, just about.' She finished her brandy with a sigh.

'You don't sound like you've reached the happy ending to your story.'

'Happy endings don't exist in real life. It's all just compromise, isn't it?' She wanted him to agree with her, to tell her to ignore the yearning she felt when she wasn't fully occupied, the feeling that something was missing in her life. Then suddenly she chuckled. If he knew what she was thinking he would assume that what was missing was a man.

'What's funny?'

'Nothing—something just tickled my imagination.'

'And you're not going to tell me what?'

'No. Let me get you another brandy.'

'Only if you have one too. My mother warned me about beautiful women who ply me with alcohol.'

Thea really laughed now. 'I don't think it was the likes of me your mother had in mind.'

Rory regarded her with his head on one side. 'You're wasted being a student landlady—'

'—with a part-time job.'

'You need a proper life.'

'Like you've got one. Derr!' She sounded so like Petal that she laughed and realised at the same time that she was slightly drunk.

'No, I haven't. But between us we could make one.'

Thea suppressed more laughter. 'That sounds like an improper suggestion to me.'

His smile reflected hers. 'It could be, only to begin with I've got a proper one—at least, not one my mother could object to.'

'Which is?'

'Come to Ireland and look after me for a bit, have some time on your own to do some real photography, lap up the scenery, feel the wind in your hair and the sun on your face . . .'

'Do you write poetry in your spare time by any chance?'

'Now you're mocking me. I mean it. I could show you another life.'

'I'm sure you could, but why should I swap looking after student lodgers for looking after you?'

'Because there's only one of me, I'm very undemanding and I have a pregnant dog.'

Thea shook her head. 'Thanks, but no thanks. I'll have my holiday and go back to reality. You can't run away from yourself, you know.'

'But do you need to? Yourself seems in fine condition to me.'

He really was very attractive. His eyes were clear greeny blue, with maddeningly curly eyelashes. His hair was curly too and his mouth, large and generous, curled up at the edges.

'Well, it's sweet of you to ask me, but I couldn't possibly.'

He produced a battered notebook from his pocket. 'Here, I'll give you my address, in case you change your mind.' He scrawled something on a sheet and tore it out. 'You fly from Stansted to Knock. I'd pick you up from there. It's not far.'

'It's very kind of you, but I won't change my mind.'

'You never know. People do.'

She smiled a little wistfully. 'I think we should have a cup of coffee.'

'With another brandy?'

'Definitely not.'

He ordered the coffee and she shut her eyes and let the hot Provençal sunshine warm her face and chase away thoughts of lodgers.

'**O**h, it's you!' Molly's voice, strident with surprise, startled Thea into opening her eyes. Molly was frantically trying to disengage her arm from Gerald's, but because of the large bag she was holding she was finding it difficult. Molly had an odd expression, which on anyone else would have been guilt. There was no sign of Joan.

'Hello,' said Thea, 'come and join us, Molly. Where's Joan?' She was feeling a little sheepish herself. Sleeping with a strange man was always wrong, even if it was in full view of the public.

'We're having coffee,' said Rory. 'Can I order some for you?'

Molly glanced at Gerald, then regarded them with tight lips, obviously wondering if their sin was greater than her own. 'Joan felt tired and returned to the hotel for a nap. We went back later—to see if you wanted to join us for a patisserie,' she added quickly, in case Thea thought she'd gone to the hotel for any other reason. 'And you weren't there. I thought you were writing postcards?'

Molly's strange behaviour made Thea wonder if she and Gerald really *had* been up to something. 'No, I took a few photos and then felt like some lunch.'

Thea could tell that Molly was longing to ask if she'd arranged to meet Rory, or whether they'd met by chance.

Rory helped her out. 'And I was lucky enough to see Thea sitting here and persuaded her to order lunch for me, too. My French is rubbish, isn't it, Gerald?'

'Tiger Tours don't employ you for your languages,' said Gerald, pulling out a chair for Molly. 'Just as well, really, eh?' He laughed heartily.

Molly might have been one of a string of handsome, middle-aged ladies he dallied with on these tours. Maddening though her friend undoubtedly was, Thea didn't like the thought of her being used.

Gerald sat down and held up his hand. '*Garçon!*'

'I'll have a brandy,' said Rory quickly, 'and so will Thea.'

Thea was certain Gerald had no intention of ordering drinks for them as well as Molly, but as the waiter wrote it down on his pad, before looking expectantly at Molly, there was nothing he could do about it.

31

'I'll have a lemon tea, please, Gerald,' said Molly, 'if I may.'

'Certainly.' He turned to the waiter and ordered in French. He went on long enough to have ordered them an entire meal, more, Thea felt, to show off than because it was necessary.

She said to Molly, 'So, what did you buy? Did you get the shoes you wanted?'

'Yes, and a handbag.' Molly was torn between wanting to show off her loot and tell someone off—Rory for ordering brandy, or Thea for flirting with Rory. Possibly because she was in a dubious position herself, she got out a cardboard box. 'There—what do you think?'

Thea thought that another handbag and pair of shoes added to Molly's dozens made no difference to anything, but she murmured politely as the waiter arrived with their drinks.

Later, back at the hotel, Thea lay on her bed while Molly made up her face. She was still annoyed with Thea, although what about Thea wasn't sure. She questioned her about her lunch with Rory. 'Did you ask him to join you?'

'No, he just did. I think he was lonely. He's been in France painting and he wanted a little English company.'

'But he's not English, is he?'

'No, Irish. Is that eyeliner you're using?' Thea didn't care what Molly was doing to herself, but she was fed up with her questions.

'Yes. You have to be careful with it, or it looks dreadfully tarty.'

At last Molly was satisfied with her face, sprayed eau de toilette onto her wrists and glanced at her watch. 'Hell! It's nearly half past and you're not ready. Do hurry up. Gerald hates it if anyone's late.'

Fortunately, Thea's toilet took mere minutes.

'So sorry, Gerald,' said Molly as they appeared in the lobby, where he was counting heads. 'I am trying hard to be more punctual.' She glanced at Thea, managing to imply it was her fault.

'Well,' said Gerald, following her glance, 'I think we can agree that the effect was worth the wait.'

Thea smiled stiffly back at him, grateful that they would be going home the next day.

Derek wasn't waiting in arrivals, so Molly rang him on his mobile with hers. 'Oh. You're just parking? Well, thank goodness. I hate waiting around to be collected.' She punched in another number. 'Traffic, he says,' she told Thea as if she didn't believe his story. 'I'm just ringing my sister to see if there's any news.'

Thea smiled at departing Tiger Tourers as they made their way to their separate destinations. In spite of Molly she had really enjoyed Aix-en-Provence. She tuned out the bustle of the airport and let herself indulge in a little daydreaming, of Provençal sunshine and a certain lunch in a certain *place* in the company of a certain Irishman.

'Oh my God!' said Molly, ending her call. 'Your lodgers have had a party and they've left the place in a terrible state apparently. You'd better ring them, find out what's going on. Poor you, it sounds *dreadful*. Gate-crashers got in and there's vomit all up the stairs.'

Thea hadn't been looking forward to going home anyway; now the prospect seemed utterly dismal.

Molly tried to press her mobile phone into Thea's hand. 'Better to find out now than be greeted with a horrible surprise. Apparently you might have to have the whole house redecorated. And, Petal says, the washing machine's broken down. What a thing to go back to.' She wiggled the telephone helpfully. 'I know a firm of professional cleaners you could use. They'd only cost a couple of hundred pounds.'

Thea regarded Molly and all her previous indecisiveness fell away. She no longer felt like a sleepy sheep, following dozily along, obedient to every instruction to look up, or look down. It was obvious what she should do. 'Actually, Molly, I'm not going back. I'm not returning to a trashed house and a broken-down washing machine—the lodgers can sort it out for themselves. I'm going to extend my holiday.'

'What?' Molly was stunned. 'But how can you do that? How can you know your house is in a state and not do anything about it? Besides, you can't let Petal live in a house without a washing machine. I'm not sure it's even hygienic.'

'They can die of salmonella for all I care. It's *their* fault; they had the party. It's *their* gate-crashers who vomited up the stairs, *they* can fork out the two hundred quid for the cleaners. Why the hell should I do it?'

Molly gawped.

'Look, I know Cyril's going to Stansted. I'll go with him. *You* tell Petal to organise the cleaners, and that she can either ring up the repair man, or learn to use the launderette!'

And Thea picked up her bags and ran after the elderly veteran of ten Tiger Tours. She glanced back to see that Derek had now arrived, and that Molly was pointing in her direction, open-mouthed and horrified.

At Stansted, Thea rang Rory with a dry mouth. 'It's Thea, we met in France?'

'Oh, Thea, yes. Nice to hear you.'

At least he sounded as if he remembered her. 'You invited me to stay?' She must be mad! Rushing across the Irish Sea to stay with someone she'd only known a couple of hours.

'And you're coming?'

'Yes, if you're sure you don't mind.'

'I'll kill the fatted calf and put out the red carpet for you.'

Relief caused sweat to bead her forehead. 'It would be better if you met me at the airport. Is it miles from you?'

'Not at all. Only about an hour. What time do you get in?'

Elated, she ran to buy a ticket then fairly skipped off to the shops to buy some extra pants and socks. She spent a long time in the Ladies washing all parts of her uncovered by clothes—a girl did like to look her best, especially when she was chasing a younger man—then dithered between buying Rory a bottle of cognac, to remind him of Provence, or a bottle of Paddy Irish Whiskey. She settled on the whiskey, then, as clean and calm as possible, given that she was running away from home, she settled down to wait for her flight.

Chapter Three

WHEN HE SAW THEA, Rory opened his arms. Good manners insisted that Thea go into them and receive a very hearty kiss on what was nearly her mouth. She wasn't entirely reluctant. He was even more attractive than she remembered.

'Jaysus, Thea, it's good to see you. What changed your mind?' he asked, picking up her bags.

'My bossy friend Molly. She rang her sister and found out that there'd been a wild party at my house while I'd been away and told me I'd have to get professionals in to clean it up. So I decided to make a run for it.'

Thea paused. 'I am so glad to see you, Rory. You're never quite sure if people mean invitations issued on holiday.'

He made a horrified face. 'I wasn't on holiday. It was the hardest work I've ever done!' Then he gave her another kiss, this time definitely on her mouth, and although it was certainly pleasant, she did wonder if it meant he expected more than she was prepared to give on such brief acquaintance. Running away was one thing, but she didn't want to leap into bed with Rory before she'd had time to get to know him. Her morals were a lot harder to leave behind than her lodgers.

Seeing her doubts, he laughed. 'The car's this way.'

As she followed him, it occurred to Thea, somewhat belatedly, that the clothes she had thought suitable for a week in Provence were unlikely to be right for the west of Ireland. She snuggled into her fleece as he opened the door of a battered Land Rover.

'Do you get a lot of snow here?' It felt to Thea as if snow were imminent, with grey clouds tossing across the sky and flurries of icy rain throwing themselves at her.

'Not snow, hardly at all, we're too far west, but plenty of rain. It's what gives us the forty shades of green, after all.'

The Land Rover, for all its noisiness, had a very efficient heater, and as the scenery became pretty, she began to feel better.

'Mayo's mostly famous for Clew Bay and Croagh Patrick. It's a mountain which looks uncannily like a slag heap, but one day a year it's a place of pilgrimage and people walk up it, some of them in bare feet.' He smiled. 'If you look down to the left as we reach the top of this hill you'll see the bay.'

She looked. The sun suddenly pierced the cloud base, turning the sea to silver and tingeing the distant islands with gold. The beauty of it made her catch her breath. She sighed so deeply it became a yawn.

Rory glanced at her. 'You must be tired. But we're nearly there now. When you've got settled and had a drink, you'll feel better. And you've a choice of two bedrooms'—he shot her a look—'not including mine. You can choose which one you like best.'

'How kind.' Was he tactfully telling her that his bedroom wasn't an option for her, or that she had plenty of choice without having to sleep with him? She suddenly wished for a more misspent youth; she might be better at the subtext. The social niceties of running away with a man you didn't know were pretty much a mystery to her.

'Well.' He grinned at her. 'You won't be wanting to jump into bed with me until you've had a chance to check out how often I take a bath and things like that. Will you?'

His grin, his sympathetic understanding and the fact that the world was now tinged with pink and gold from the setting sun made her feel her mad impulse was justified.

It was a cottage, almost on top of the beach. A green lane ran down to where it hugged the ground, long and low with white walls, grey slate roof and a blue front door. She stood in the garden, looking at a gate framed by two thick, tall bushes, through which she could see the beach and the silver sea.

'The view's even better from my studio, on the hill up there.'

'I can see why you would want to live here. It's so beautiful.'

'Come inside. It's too chilly to be admiring the view from out here, when you get as good a one from the kitchen window.'

They were greeted by a huge, deep barking.

'Enough to put the fear of God into you,' said Rory. 'But she's a sweet thing, really. Ready to have puppies any day now.'

He opened the front door and a dog the size of a small sofa tottered out, unable to jump up because of her huge bulk. She greeted Thea with just as much enthusiasm as Rory.

'This is Lara. She's an English mastiff, but I've no idea what the puppies are going to be until I see them. Probably half collie. Come on, let's get you inside.'

The front door opened straight into the sitting room, which was wide and high, with a curved ceiling like a boathouse. There was a fireplace in which a turf fire smouldered in a welcoming manner, and bits of boat and fishing tackle hung on hooks high up, out of the way. There was no wall between the kitchen and the main room, so it had a feeling of space and light. There were windows on three sides.

'Now,' said Rory, 'would you like a cup of tea or a glass of whiskey, or both? I recommend both.'

Thea laughed. 'Both sounds greedy, but lovely.'

'You stay by the fire while I get that, then I'll give you the grand tour.' She looked about her. The kitchen she could already see, with its huge picture window facing towards the islands and, beyond them, distant mountains. There were three other doors off the main room and she hoped one of them concealed a bathroom.

She sat on a saggy old sofa, which was so soft that she seemed to sink to Australia in it. It was also covered with dog hairs and was obviously where the dog slept.

After regarding her with more than a hint of reproach, Lara sighed hugely, and heaved herself up beside Thea, squashing herself into the space that remained. She put her head on Thea's lap, an extremely heavy hint that if Thea sat on her sofa she would have to take the consequences. The weight was tremendous, but it was a pleasant feeling, warm, almost comfortable.

Rory produced a tray bearing a chipped brown teapot, a couple of mugs, two tumblers and a bottle of whiskey. A packet of sugar, crumpled and tea-stained, and a carton of milk were fitted on somehow. He set this down on the little table in front of the sofa. 'When you've a cup of tea in your hand I'll show you the bathroom and you can choose a bedroom. Do you have milk and sugar?'

'Just milk, please. Do you live here alone?' she went on, when he'd handed her a mug.

'Yup. There's a wee girl who comes in and keeps the house in as much order as she can. Otherwise it's just me. I live in the house and my studio's up the hill.'

'Will you let me see your work?'

He opened the bottle of whiskey, poured generous measures into the tumblers and handed one to Thea. 'I haven't shown anyone my work for so long that perhaps it's time I did. Slancha.'

'What did you say?'

'Slancha—it's spelt s-l-à-i-n-t-e, believe it or not.'

'Slancha.' She shuddered as the neat spirit went down.

'Oh God, did you want water in that? I haven't anything else except some red lemonade.'

'Red lemonade?'

'In Ireland it comes in two colours, red or white. You don't want any in your whiskey?' The idea seemed to horrify him.

She shook her head. 'No, this is fine just as it is.' She took a sip. 'More than fine, actually.'

The whiskey began to relax her immediately and she realised that at this rate, what with the fire, the dog and the drink, she'd fall asleep where she sat. She thought she'd better make conversation in an attempt to keep herself awake. 'Are there shops nearby?'

'Westport is about five miles away, but there's a little shop in the local village which sells everything. Can you drive?'

'Yes, but I'm not sure about the Land Rover. Why do you ask?'

'Well, it's just that I'm pretty unsociable during the day. It will be better if you can entertain yourself a bit. The Land Rover's easy enough when you get used to it, and there's no traffic here to speak of.'

'Do I have to drive to the shop?'

'It's three miles away. It would be your choice, but you don't have to do anything you don't want to.'

She felt a surge of warmth towards him, probably induced by hot tea and neat whiskey. 'It was kind of you to let me come at such short notice, when I said I wouldn't.'

'I like girls who can change their minds.'

'I'm hardly a girl. I'm thirty-five.'

She felt she had to tell him. While he could probably guess, she liked to be open about these things.

'Thirty-five is the perfect age for girls.'

'Is that so? So how old are you?'

'I'm twenty-eight, which is the perfect age for boys.'

'But too young for girls of thirty-five.'

'Would you like me to prove you wrong about that?'

Thea saw the glint in his eye, which told her not to push the point. 'I think I'll take your word for it.' Then, because she didn't want to close the door for ever, she added, 'For now . . .'

'Good things are worth waiting for,' he said.

Thea, in an attempt to change the mood, pushed at the dog's head and fought her way to the front of the sofa. 'I really should visit the bathroom. If you could tell me where it is.'

'Go through that door.' He pointed. 'And it's on the left. While you're there, take a look at the little bedroom. You might fancy it. It's got two single beds in it, one each side of the room. Very chaste.'

Thea ignored this remark but did inspect the room, which was pretty, but felt a bit chilly.

When she got back she found that Rory had refilled the glasses. She sat back down next to Lara, wondering if it was wise to drink so much on an empty stomach.

'You'll be wanting something to eat,' said Rory. 'Which presents a bit of a problem. I was going to eat at the pub.'

The thought of making herself look presentable and going out made her feel suddenly exhausted.

'On the other hand, you may not fancy a longish drive at this time of night when you've only just arrived.' He grinned. 'If I'd known you were coming, I'd have baked a cake . . .'

'I really am being a dreadful nuisance.'

'Not at all. I'm just not that much of a cook.'

Here was a situation she felt at home in. 'On the other hand, I'm an expert in making meals out of nothing. Why don't I have a poke around and see what I can come up with?' Thea got to her feet again, determined that Rory shouldn't regret her arrival.

'Excellent plan. I'll build up the fire. Did you want to sleep in the back bedroom?'

'What are the alternatives?'

'I'll show you.' He opened the door to the right of the front door and showed Thea a large room with a wonderful view of the sea. 'This is mine. It has a double bed, a goose-down duvet and goose-feather pillows, but I come as part of the package. I don't mind sharing, but I'm not giving it up entirely.'

'Right,' said Thea cautiously. 'And the other bedroom?'

It was on the left of the entrance. It had the same high, wood-lined ceiling as the sitting room, two single beds and a couple of wardrobes in it.

'The house belonged to my uncle. He didn't have children of his own, but he used it as a holiday cottage for his nieces and nephews. He left it to me when I told him I'd live in it all the time if he did. He was an artist.'

'Did he do these?' Thea indicated a pair of small seascapes in oil which hung over the beds. 'Or is that your work?'

'His. It's good, though, don't you think?'

'Mm. Did he do them here?'

'I should think so. I tend to work on a slightly larger scale.'

'Will you show me your work tomorrow?'

'Maybe. But now I'm going to show you the kitchen and all that it has to offer in the way of spaghetti, tinned custard and tomato ketchup. If you can find a meal in it I'll show you all the wonders of my kingdom.' He smiled into her eyes and she felt her libido stir. 'There's also a sack of potatoes and a hunk of cheese.'

They ate at the table in front of the fire. The dining table was entirely taken up with books and junk mail, a selection of dirty crockery and a large coil of rope.

'You're a grand cook!' said Rory. 'I'm glad I invited you.'

'Have some more pie.' She had boiled sliced potatoes and made them into a pie with tinned tomatoes, fried onions, eggs and milk, and covered it all with grated cheese.

'I will. I wouldn't have got anything half as nice at the pub. And don't worry about the washing-up. Susan will do it in the morning.'

Thea resolved to get up early and sort out the kitchen. She had a feeling that her lodgers didn't bother about clearing up their late-night snacks because they said, 'Thea will do it in the morning.' How were they managing? she wondered. Tomorrow she would ring them and tell them where she was. If she felt like it.

Wee Susan, from down the road, found the house surprisingly tidy when she appeared the next morning at about eleven. She was not overly delighted to see Thea, however, and not, Thea deduced, because the washing-up had been done. Susan had a crush on Rory the size of Croagh Patrick.

Rory gave Susan a friendly, easy smile, which confirmed he was not an over-exacting employer. 'Hello, Susan. Thea's come to stay for a bit. She's in the front bedroom, if you'd care to give it a bit of a once-over. Come on, Thea,' said Rory. 'I'll show you the studio while Susan gets on with the cleaning. You'd better borrow a coat.'

Thea tried to give Susan a sisterly smile, to show they were united by the oppression of lazy men, but Susan didn't respond. Perhaps I'll get her talking later, thought Thea, as she followed Rory up the hill.

The studio was a huge shed with windows from ceiling to floor. In April it was decidedly chilly, and it must have been really freezing in winter, for a wood-burning stove in the corner looked too small to make much impression on the place.

Thea moved towards a vast easel with a cloth over it. The painting beneath must have been the size of one of the walls in the cottage. Rory stepped in front of her.

'That's work in progress. No one sees that until it's finished. Over there are the kind of paintings that keep me in bread and butter. And whiskey.' He indicated a medium-sized painting of a horse.

It was an old-fashioned picture, representing someone's huge wealth, but it was beautifully painted. 'And is it a good likeness?' she asked, teasing him.

'Indeed it is. I could spend my life earning a very good living painting racehorses.' He made a face. 'My aunt, the widow of the uncle who left me the house, often asks me why I don't. The money's certain and painting is painting, isn't it?'

'No,' she said for him. 'One is a job and the other is your life.'

The look he gave her was more than reward for her understanding. She picked up a battered pewter mug and changed the subject, not wanting to have Rory make love to her there and then. 'Do you surround yourself with the things in your paintings, like Cézanne? Or was this just lying around?'

He sighed, accepting her decision. 'Women are all the same. Never satisfied until they have poked their pretty noses into every corner of a man's heart. Hell, Thea, you've come a long way to see me. You can see the paintings too. They're in the shed next door.'

'I don't suppose my nose is that pretty, just nosy.'

He took her chin and moved her head so the light shone on her fully. 'You do have a very fine nose, but it's your eyes which first caught my attention. It's their colour, pale, yellowy green with a dark circle round them.'

'Oh.' No one had ever commented on her eyes before, which was probably why she had run away to Ireland with an artist.

He kissed her lips, briefly, but firmly. Pleasantly.

'You probably want to get on and do some work,' she said, clearing her throat. 'Would it be all right if I had a look at what's in the shed?'

'Trust me to pick a woman who's more interested in my daubs than in me. Go and look then, and don't blame me if you don't like them.'

The paintings were stacked up along one wall. They were huge and there were no windows or electricity in the shed, so she opened the door to let in some light. When a shaft of silvery sunshine hit the first picture, Thea knew she would have to drag each one outside to have a proper look. They were stunning: beautiful, painterly landscapes, enormous rectangular views of the sea, the islands and the mountains. The quality of the light was superb; it glittered, making Thea believe that if she walked into the picture she would feel the brightness of the sun contrasting with the coldness of the air. He had done with paint what she could never have managed with a camera.

There were also still lifes and nudes. The painting was masterly, with hardly a brush stroke visible, the colours so intense they seemed liquid. She felt that if she stepped into their viscous depths she would emerge icy with sea water, or bloodstained. There were ten paintings in all and each one was different, each breathtakingly beautiful.

Thea was enraptured. This was not the work of an Impressionist, or a conceptual artist, but the work of a real, old-fashioned painter.

'It's one o'clock, haven't you seen enough yet?' Rory, coming up behind her, made her jump. She'd been so lost in his work that she'd completely forgotten about him.

'I don't think I can ever see enough of these paintings,' she said, aware that if she weren't careful she would start to cry.

Rory took her in his arms and held her tight. They stood together at the top of a windy hill overlooking Clew Bay, wrapped in each other's arms, overcome with an emotion neither of them recognised.

'I think you're probably a genius,' she said.

This time he kissed her passionately, deeply, bringing her already alerted senses to a peak of sensation. When he drew her down onto the grass she let him kiss her more. It was only when his fingers started to fiddle with the toggles on her borrowed duffle coat that she pushed away his hand and sat up. 'Not yet, Rory. You have to take it slower.'

Rory pushed his hand through his dark hair and shook his head. 'No one has seen my work for a long time. I got a bit carried away.'

'So did I. It's wonderful, fantastic work. If you showed those paintings in the right place you'd make your fortune. You've got to show it, Rory. It's selfish just to keep it here, hidden away.'

They were dazed, drunk with their discovery. They sat on the hill in silence, he shaking his head, she knowing she had to make him show his work if it was all she ever did in her life.

'But no one has ever wanted anything from me except a painting of their damned horses.'

'That's because no one knew you could do anything else.'

'It's only you who've liked them, though. You may be wrong. You may just have fallen in love with me and so with my work.'

'Rory, I haven't fallen in love with you, not yet. But I have definitely fallen in love with your work. Let me take some photographs and send them to someone. I know people at the art college in Cheltenham. They'll know who can tell you how good they are.' She hugged him again. 'I'm going back down to the house. Can I use your phone?'

It was rather a shame that, after all her proud boasting about knowing people, Thea had to call on Molly, who either knew, or would find out, who Thea needed to get in touch with. But Thea and Molly had parted on rather odd terms: Molly on the defensive—presumably about Gerald—and Thea . . . well, Thea had just upped and run away. If she hadn't felt so strongly about Rory's paintings, she would never have dared pick up the phone.

'Molly? It's Thea.'

'Thea! Are you all right? That man hasn't done anything dreadful to you, has he?'

Thea could tell that part of Molly wanted Rory to have loved and left her. Molly liked people to get their just deserts—not 'Death by Chocolate' when they deserved cold semolina.

'No, I'm fine. How are things your end?'

Thea held the phone a little away from her ear while Molly went on and on about the state of Thea's house, the washing-machine repair man and a thousand other irritations for which Thea should have taken responsibility. When the recriminations had slowed down she cut in. 'Molly, darling, I know I did a bad thing, but it's all right so far and I'm sure the kids are fine. Petal will sort them out. Now, Molly, I need your help. I can't think of who else to turn to.' Molly loved to be helpful and a little flattery would do no harm either.

'Well?'

'I think Rory may well be an artistic genius. I need someone to look at his work, but I don't know who. If I take some slides, can you think of whom I should send them to?'

Molly was silent for a few moments, a rare state of affairs Thea would normally have appreciated. Now it just made her nervous. 'I'll have to ring you back,' she said eventually. 'Have you got the number there? And the address? In the meantime, take some good photographs. I'll get onto David Knox, you know, head of fine art at the college? He'll tell me the right person.'

'Fabulous. Thank you, Molly, I knew I could rely on you.'

'Relying on me is one thing, but, Thea, you can't just run off . . .'

'Actually, Molly, I already have. Do you think you could be sweet and collect my rent for me, and pay it into my bank? You're a doll.' Thea rang off, thanking Petal for her unconscious lessons on how to manipulate people.

Susan came into the room just as Thea got off the phone. She was about twenty, with clear, freckled skin and hair which formed little ringlets round her hairline. Thea thought she would have been divinely pretty, had the girl not looked at her with such suspicion. 'I

43

hope you don't mind me staying. I'll try not to get in your way.'

'It's Rory I'm worried about. He doesn't often have people staying in the house. He likes to work undisturbed. Usually.'

Thea tried to look like someone who would never disturb Rory, not even if there was a fire.

'So, what do they call you, then?' said Susan. The 'and why are you here' was unspoken, but just as clear.

'I'm Thea. And I'll look after myself. I won't expect him to take me sightseeing or anything. And I'll try not to make more work for you.'

'I don't mind *work*.' Susan gave the word emphasis to make clear it was Thea she objected to, not extra washing-up.

Before she could start photographing the pictures, Thea had to get her film, which would either mean disturbing Rory, thus earning herself a stake through the heart from Susan, or struggling with the Land Rover.

Susan's pretty mouth tightened as Thea came into the kitchen, where she was drying the china Thea had washed the previous night.

'I'm going into town to get some film. Rory told me I could borrow the Land Rover. Do you want anything?'

'You're going to drive the Land Rover?'

'I was. Is it difficult?'

Susan considered, deciding whether to let Thea loose with the beast, or give her some pointers. 'It's a bit of bastard to drive,' she said at last.

Thea bit her lip. 'I really need the film. I want to take slides of Rory's paintings. I think he's really, really good. If I'm right, he may never have to paint a horse again.'

'Honestly? And what do you know about art?' This was a genuine question, not the sarcastic sneer it might have been.

'I haven't been formally trained, but I have a good eye.'

'And you say he could give up painting the horses?'

'If the right person sees the slides.'

Susan nodded. 'I've got to go in and do some shopping myself. I can take you in my car. When do you want to go?'

'Whenever it's convenient to you.'

'I finish here at two. I'll take you in then.'

'**S**o, how did you get on today?' Rory asked her, as he came down from his studio, paint-spattered but happy.

'I've got the film, but I won't start until tomorrow. The light's not good now, and if I get an early start I might get them done and off by the afternoon. What about you? Did you finish your horse?'

He made a face. 'I tell you what, the thought that I might never have to paint another one lent wings to my brush. Whiskey?'

'Yes, please.' Thea watched him pour the drinks. 'I bought some steak in town. Would you like oven chips or baked potatoes? I told Susan I would do the cooking while I was staying.'

'Fine by me. Did anyone ever tell you you're a lovely girl?'

She couldn't help responding to the twinkle in his eyes, but she tried not to show it. 'Does that mean oven chips?'

'It means whatever you want it to mean. Here's to your fine eyes.'

Thea concealed a little shiver of flattered excitement and took her drink into the kitchen. 'I'll get dinner started, then.'

'**W**ell, missus, is tonight the night we make passionate love under my goose-down duvet?'

The steak was eaten, the bits of fat fed to Lara, and the plates were pushed back. Rory was peeling apples and handing pieces to Thea, which she ate with some very good Irish blue cheese she had bought.

Like Eve, she took the apple and, like Eve, she was tempted. Almost everything was perfect. She liked Rory, she adored his work, and she found him extremely sexy. Perhaps it was the thought of making love with a complete stranger when she had had slightly too much to eat that was making her hesitate. Regretfully she put her hand on Rory's wrist. 'Would you think I was an awful tease if I said that it's still too soon? I just don't feel I know you well enough. I'm a bit of an old-fashioned girl, I suppose.'

Rory tipped the last of the bottle of wine into Thea's glass. 'Is that your final answer?'

Smiling gently, she nodded.

'Well, it's a blow. But I expect I can accept it in a manly way. I'll just take my broken heart to bed and sulk.'

'You don't have a broken heart and good things come to those who wait.'

'That sounds very like a promise to me.'

Thea bit her lip. It did indeed sound like a promise. 'You don't actually know that going to bed with me would be good.'

'Woman, that seems like a challenge. I've a good mind to carry you off and ravish you.'

45

Thea laughed. The joy of Rory was that he could be sexy without being threatening. '"Oh, what care I for your goose-feather bed . . ."' she sang merrily.

'You'll find out soon.'

'I'm looking forward to it, Rory, but I have to feel ready.'

'That's all right. It's just as well I'm not a raw lad who can't control his passions.'

'Away with you and your passions! I'll see you in the morning.'

The photography went well. The weather obliged and Rory took time off from his horse to help her drag the work in and out of the shed. When the major paintings were done, he said, 'I've got a whole lot of drawings in the loft of the cottage. Would you like to have a look at them, too?'

'I'd love to, but I've run out of film.'

'There's no need to photograph them. If anyone's remotely interested they can come and see them for themselves.'

Thea sensed his pessimism. Rory was by no means the first artist she had known who was arrogantly confident about his work one minute, defensive and apologetic the next. 'I know there's a lot riding on this, and I can't promise you anything, but I do think that eventually cream will rise to the top.'

'God, I hope you're right. Now, would you consider a little dalliance on the sofa in the studio? I've had the stove going all day and it's warm as toast in there.'

She smiled and pushed him away. 'I bought the most wonderful lamb chops yesterday. I thought I'd make you a chocolate sponge pudding for afters. Would you like that?'

'You're a hard woman, Thea, but I'll wait for you a little longer if you cook for me in the meantime.'

Thea frowned with mock disapproval. 'There are so many politically incorrect statements in there that I don't know where to start enlightening you. I'll just have to ignore them!'

The chocolate sponge pudding and the potatoes were in the oven, the kitchen was filled with a warm, chocolatey smell and Thea had had a shower. She could have done with some body moisturiser, and wished she travelled with as many beauty products as Molly did. She had not exactly prepared her body for seduction, but she did wonder if tonight she would have the courage to let Rory whisper Irish nothings to her until she followed him to bed.

She was preparing the lamb chops, when he came in and handed her a glass of whiskey. He raised his glass to her. 'To you, Thea. Thank you for coming.'

'Thank you for having me.'

'I haven't had you—' The 'yet' was unspoken.

This was showdown time. Thea took a deep breath and made her decision. But just as she was about to announce it there was a strange, high cry from Lara. 'What on earth's the matter?' asked Thea, her heart pounding with fright.

'Oh my God,' said Rory. 'I think the puppies are coming!'

They both moved quickly to Lara, who looked up at them, confused and distressed.

'It's all right,' said Rory gently. 'You're just having your pups.'

'It's a perfectly natural process,' Thea agreed.

Lara didn't seem convinced. 'Have you had puppies before?' Thea asked Rory, 'either personally or through another dog? She might need some help.'

A look of horror crossed his face. 'No. Lara is my first bitch. I haven't a clue what to do.' He backed away.

'Well, where do you think she should have them?' asked Thea. 'I mean, the sofa looks awfully cosy, but there'll be nowhere to sit for weeks and weeks.'

'I suppose we'd better have a box, though for the life of me I can't think what, short of an elephant, would come in a box big enough for Lara and her pups.'

'And I don't suppose you've had an elephant delivery for months.' Thea couldn't help feeling that Rory should have thought about this before.

'The service is a bit patchy, here in Ireland.'

'Well, let's push the sofa back from the fire and put newspapers and stuff down in front of it for now,' Thea decided. 'We can think where to put the pups later.'

'Sure, she's only a dog. She could have the pups in the shed if necessary. Then they'd be out of the way.'

Thea barely had time to give Rory a horrified look before there was a knock on the door.

'Who the hell is that?' demanded Rory.

As Thea was nearest, she opened the door.

Chapter Four

THEA THOUGHT SHE WAS suffering from some strange sort of hallucination. There on the doorstep stood Molly and, just behind her, Petal. Behind them loomed a large, dark man and a small boy.

'At last we've found it,' exclaimed Molly, pushing past Thea who, stunned, could only step out of the way.

'About time too! I'm starving,' said Petal, following Molly. 'They wouldn't let me play my music in the car. They are *so* not fair.'

'Who the hell are you lot?' demanded Rory as the man, whom Thea faintly recognised, came in with the small boy, who looked so like him that he could only be his son.

'I'm Ben Jonson,' said the man, holding out his hand to Rory. 'I'm sorry to barge in on you like this. I meant to come on my own.' He cast a despairing look at Molly and Petal. 'I've been trying to track you down for years.'

Lara gave another cry and began to move around the room as fast as her bulk would allow.

Thea, stepping aside and pulling Molly out of the way too, demanded, 'Molly! What are you doing here? And why did you bring Petal? I asked you to find a contact for me, not personally escort the Cavalry.'

'*I* came to look after Toby,' said Petal somewhat defiantly, and Thea noticed that she wasn't wearing make-up and didn't look her usual confident self.

'We were so worried about you,' explained Molly. 'I felt I had to come and see you were all right. When Ben said he'd heard of your artist, I thought it my duty—' Thea's look made her add, 'Oh, OK. I was *dying* of curiosity. I *had* to go with him and see what had happened to you.'

'And Toby came because he's dotty about Irish myths and legends. He's read a book about them,' said Petal, half proud, half mystified.

Thea turned to the little boy. Whoever else was to blame for this fiasco, it wasn't him. 'You must be Toby,' she said.

He nodded. He looked extremely tired and confused. 'Are *you* hungry?' Thea had little experience of small boys, but anyone under seventeen seemed to need to eat almost constantly. She wasn't sure when this kicked in, but thought she'd take a chance on it being at about seven. He could have some chocolate sponge pudding.

Toby looked around wonderingly. 'Not really.'

'I am. I'm starving,' said Petal again. 'Have you got a biscuit or any-thing? It's been *ghastly* at home. We got some people to clear up the sick, but the washing machine still doesn't work, although the man came and took a penny out of the filter. It cost ninety pounds, by the way, which you owe us, because he wouldn't go away until he'd got it. So, have you got any food?'

Any thought Thea had of offering Petal chocolate sponge dissolved. 'I've no idea, it's not my house. You'll have to ask Rory. Rory, this is Petal.'

Thea watched Rory make Petal wish she'd put on make-up. 'No bis-cuits,' he said, 'but would you like a drink? Irish whiskey, it would make a dead man get up and walk.'

'Not a good idea on an empty stomach, Petal,' said Thea.

'Why don't we all go down to the pub?' said Rory who, amused by Petal and interested by what Ben had said, had become more welcoming.

'You can't!' Thea objected. 'I don't mind not going to the pub, but I'm not going to have Lara's puppies by myself.'

'You mean, she's actually *having* them? Oh, yuk!' said Petal.

'Low blood-sugar level,' said Thea, relenting somewhat. 'Come and find something to eat, Petal.' Petal was enough of a handful when she was cheerful.

'It's so not fair!' Petal said the minute they were through the archway to the kitchen. 'I *did* want to come because home is crap at the moment, with no one there to look after us, and Piers dumped me and I didn't want to go out when I was single, because everyone would know.'

Thea's heart softened and she put a spoonful of sponge pudding in a bowl. 'Well, you'll have to go out some time, or you'll never get another boyfriend.'

'I know,' said Petal, with her mouth full. 'But I do think they might have told me that my phone wouldn't work in Ireland.'

'I don't suppose Molly's very phone aware.' Thea suddenly found herself on Petal's side. 'Otherwise they'd have rung and told me they were coming.'

'Oh, they did try, only they couldn't get through.'

A muttered curse from Rory told Thea that something was going on in the sitting room. She went to see.

Molly was looking tired and horror-stricken both at once, Rory seemed impatient and Ben Jonson was squatting down by Lara. Toby held on to his shoulder.

'Is she all right?' asked Thea.

'She's fine, but the first puppy is going to appear at any moment.'

The thought of trying to look after a dog having puppies with Petal and Molly in the room was more nightmare than bizarre dream. She knew they were both incredibly squeamish and would probably squeal louder than Lara. She caught Rory's eye and signalled 'Do something!' with every sinew.

He didn't respond. Either he found the thought of Petal and Molly screaming was amusing, or he couldn't do sign language.

She caught Ben watching her silent panic. 'Perhaps I should warn you, Molly,' he said. 'Whelping bitches can make an awful lot of mess. I don't suppose you'd like it and I expect Lara would appreciate a little peace as well.'

'What sort of mess?' asked Petal with horrified fascination.

'Oh, you know, blood, water, black slime. It stains everything it touches. Oh, look, she's having a contraction.'

Rory, obviously amused by the general expressions of horror, finally took the hint. 'Why don't I take everyone off to the pub? We can get a bite to eat there and Lara could have her pups quietly on her own.'

'You can't leave her on her own!' protested Thea.

'No,' Ben said, 'but the pub's a good idea. Rory, you take Molly and Petal while Thea and Toby and I see to the pups.'

'Right,' Thea said. She moved nearer to Rory so they could speak in private. 'And see if they do b & b—we can't put everyone up here.'

Rory went into his room to get a coat and Thea found herself being edged into a corner by Molly. 'Darling, I had to get you on your own, just for a moment. What I wanted to say is . . . I mean . . . there's no need for you to . . . you won't mention to Derek that I had a little flirtation with Gerald, will you?'

Thea really did wonder if she was awake—it was all so bizarre. 'Molly, we're in the middle of Ireland—well, on the edge of Ireland—Aix seems a lifetime ago. And I wouldn't dream of telling Derek about something I assumed was perfectly innocent.'

'Oh, it was! I just thought . . . I just wondered if you'd got the wrong end of the stick, that's all.'

Just as Thea realised that Molly had possibly come all the way to County Mayo merely to tell her there was nothing going on between her and Gerald, Petal screamed.

'That's it,' said Ben. 'Rory, take everyone away and let this poor dog have some quiet.'

He didn't actually raise his voice, but Molly instantly picked up her bag and her car keys.

'To the pub, then. Come along, Petal. At least they'll have a decent bathroom. Rory, you sit in front and direct me. Toby will want to stay with Daddy, I expect. Hurry up, Petal, Thea.'

'I'm not going,' said Thea firmly. Glad as she was of Ben's masterful stand, she didn't want him being masterful with her. 'I'm going to help with the puppies. After all, Lara knows me.'

A few moments later the house was almost empty and blissfully quiet. Ben, Toby and Thea watched Lara in silence for a few moments as she paced about.

'We'll need some newspapers and old sheets,' said Ben. 'And quickly.'

Thea, who had no real idea where to look, went to the airing cupboard and arrived back just in time to see a black bag full of puppy lying beside Lara, who was slumped on the ground.

Thea suddenly felt like crying. Watching Lara's huge tongue licking and licking, while the shape became more and more like a puppy made her feel very emotional. It even opened its little mouth and squeaked. At last Ben picked up the puppy and latched it on to Lara's huge flank, where it started suckling. It was dark brown with a few white patches.

'Oh, wow,' said Toby.

Ben smiled. 'It is a bit.'

'Will the others come now, too?'

Ben shook his head. 'It could be ages. Why don't you ask Thea if she can get you a snack, or something.'

Thea wiped away a rogue tear. 'I'll cook the lamb chops that Rory and I were going to have. I put a couple of potatoes in the oven ages ago and there's a chocolate sponge pudding if Petal's left us any.'

'Toby's a vegetarian.' Ben's expression seemed to chill slightly at the mention of the cosy meal Thea described.

'I can easily grate some cheese on the potato. Would you like that?'

Toby nodded. 'That would be very kind.'

51

'What about you?' Thea asked Ben. 'Are you a vegetarian?'

'No, I eat anything.' He gave her a grin, which was a little startling. 'It's very kind of you to look after us like this.'

'Not at all, I'm used to looking after people and if you look after Lara, it seems a fair deal.'

'Talking of which, did you find any old rags or sheets or anything?'

She was still clutching a lemon-coloured sheet she'd found in the airing cupboard. 'There's really nothing wrong with this, except it's a bit bobbly, but I can buy Rory another one.'

Ben produced a penknife, nicked the top of the sheet and ripped it in two. While he was draping the sofa as best he could, Thea asked, 'What do you think the father was?'

'As we're in the country, I expect it's a collie.' He looked up at Thea. 'Can you imagine, all the intelligence and energy of a collie wrapped up in something the size of Lara?'

Thea opened her eyes wide. 'I'd rather not—a baby elephant on speed.'

'On the other hand they might all take after their mother. The shepherd will say, "Come by," or something, and one of these chaps will amble up saying, "All right, all right, where's the fire? I'll be along in my own good time."'

Toby chuckled loudly and Thea giggled.

'And before you ask, no, we can't have one, Toby.'

'Aw, Dad!'

Ben laughed. 'Don't "Aw, Dad" me. You know we couldn't have a huge dog in London. And as it might be ages before the next pup, we might as well have a cup of tea and you could have your baked potato, Tobe.'

'I'll get it,' said Thea. 'I feel I should make Lara a cup, too, as she's just had a baby, and without swearing or anything.'

When Toby had eaten his meal, and there was no sign of more pups imminently, Thea said, 'I don't suppose you'd like to pop into bed? We could call you when Lara's next puppy starts coming. Whatever Ben thinks best.'

'Would you like to be woken, Toby, or would you prefer to find all the puppies born in the morning?' Ben asked.

'I'll see if I get to sleep. If I don't, I can watch the puppies, but if I do, I'll just see them in the morning.'

'I'll do you a hot-water bottle and show you the bed, then.'

Once Toby had been tucked up, Ben followed Thea into the kitchen. 'I'm sorry if our arrival spoiled your little *tête-à-tête* with Rory. You must have been all set for a romantic evening.'

'Well, we were. We were going to stare into each other's eyes while Lara had puppies around us.' She wanted to tell him they were going to make mad, passionate love on the floor, because he'd suddenly made her angry. She glared at him. 'I'm going to have a glass of wine. I think I need it.'

Ben's eyebrow flicked upwards, possibly asking what she'd done to deserve wine.

When the chops were beginning to heat up under the rather inefficient grill, Thea took her wine and went to join Ben. 'Did I gather that you already know Rory's work? He told me he hasn't exhibited since a disastrous time just after he got his degree.'

'I was at his show. It was stunning, though his behaviour was even more so and not in a good way. I haven't heard of him since.'

'So what is it you do, exactly?'

'Well, now I'm an art director in an advertising agency. Once I was head of an art college.'

'What made you change? The jobs sound rather different.'

Ben shrugged. 'I got married, we had Toby. My wife wanted something better than I could give her on my college salary, so I changed direction.'

'Are you—?'

'Still married? No. But being divorced is even more expensive. Two houses, a full-time nanny, the odd legal argument.'

There seemed to be a fair amount of bitterness attached to this statement. 'So you think Rory's work might be good?'

'It might be. But it's possible that it's a load of self-indulgent rubbish.'

'I don't think so, which is why I told Molly about it. I thought she'd know who I should send the slides to.'

'But you weren't expecting her to turn up, large as life, with a whole supporting cast?' There was a glimmer of a smile in this.

'No, I wasn't.' Her gaze narrowed. 'I suppose Molly said something which made you think my slides wouldn't be any good.'

He had the grace to look embarrassed. 'Toby and I had a trip to Ireland planned anyway. He's mad about Irish myths and legends. I think he secretly believes that he'll see a leprechaun. But I wouldn't have brought Molly and Petal if they hadn't made such a fuss about wanting to come. She said she really needed to see you about something, but personally I think she wanted to catch you and Rory in the act.'

'Huh!'

'But Molly's been very good to me over the years, and Toby likes her, so I indulged her and let Petal come. And I didn't know about the slides, so Toby and I would have turned up anyway.'

'Do you have Toby for holidays, then?'

There was an irritated pause. 'I have Toby all the time. His mother has him for the occasional weekend.'

'Oh.' Thea wanted to apologise for assuming Toby's mother would be his main carer, but she didn't know how.

'It is fairly unusual, even nowadays,' Ben went on, slightly less starchily.

Lara gave a little moan. Ben and Thea watched as a huge contraction rippled along her body.

Thea winced. 'What worries me is that we don't even have a tele-phone number for a vet, let alone know where one is.'

'We should try and find out about one. Oh. Here we go. Any minute now.' Lara got onto her haunches and strained.

'Should we get Toby?'

'I hope he's dropped off by now. It's been a tiring day.'

'I'll just check. I'd feel mean if he were awake and we'd promised to let him know.'

She found Toby fast asleep in her bed and sped back, arriving just as another black bag appeared. 'Toby's asleep,' she said, watching the puppy being shoved about by Lara's huge, rough tongue. 'It's amazing how they're just an amorphous mass and gradually take on puppy shape. It's as if Lara's a sculptor or something.'

'I think it's where the expression "licked into shape" comes from.' He looked up. 'If it's ready, we could eat. There's probably time.'

While he washed his hands, Thea cleared enough table for two plates and two glasses. She served up in the kitchen, adding a huge lump of butter to their shared potato. 'I hope they found somewhere nice to eat and stay,' she said, refilling her glass and waving the bottle questioningly over Ben's.

He indicated that he would like some. 'Yes. I don't think Molly's used to roughing it. Nor is Petal.'

'Well, after all this, I hope you like the paintings.'

'So do I.'

'What will you do? Buy them all?'

'I doubt if I'd be able to buy one, let alone the lot. No, I'll try to talk a London gallery into giving him a show. They're booked up years ahead, of course, but he'll just have to wait.'

Thea thought that while Rory might be prepared to wait a few days to get her into bed, it was unlikely he'd be willing to wait a few years for an exhibition, not when he'd just broken out of his artistic purdah.

Lara's labour went on through the night, with no sign of Rory and the others. She had had four puppies, and Thea had made three lots of tea, when a problem seemed to develop. Lara had been straining for some time, with no result. Suddenly she leapt onto the sofa with surprising swiftness and passed a lot of fluid all over the cushions.

'Oh,' said Thea.

'It's all right. It means the bag has burst inside her. It'll be a dry birth and the puppy might be breech. Ah, I can see something coming—it's a leg. Two legs.'

'Does that mean it's breech?'

'Yup.'

Lara gave a howl, which tore Thea's heart.

'Hold her head and reassure her while I try and get this little fella out.'

Thea held the head the size of a bucket and watched admiringly as Ben gently teased the little form through an opening which seemed too small for it. He murmured to Lara while he did it and, although she still whimpered, she seemed calmer.

'There we go.'

The puppy landed in Ben's hands and opened its mouth to squeak.

As Thea watched Ben give Lara the puppy to lick, she had a strange feeling that this moment was significant, as if she had learned some-thing extremely important, but had instantly forgotten what it was. She decided it was her hormones coming out in sympathy with Lara's.

Lara seemed fine, though, and the puppy, larger than the others, sucked strongly when Ben latched it on. 'Definitely a boy,' he said.

Thea mentally gave herself a shake. 'I think we need more tea.'

She thought about Ben, while adding to the pile of used tea bags on a saucer, about how he delivered that little pup. He was so strong and yet so gentle. Lots of women developed crushes on their vets and now she could see why. If they'd brought your beloved cat back to life you'd love them for ever in return.

By the time Thea brought the tea in, Ben had coaxed Lara back to her

55

place in front of the fire. He looked up at her and she noticed how dark his eyes were, how they had a hint of sadness in them, as Toby's had. It was something to do with Lara and the pups which made her want to take him in her arms, she realised. Having watched the miracle of child-birth, she felt the need to hug someone.

Thea sipped her tea. She was tired and anxious—all these strange feelings would go away in the morning.

She yawned loudly and Ben smiled. Thea smiled back. He had a wonderful smile, rare and special; you had to respond to it, however tired you were. 'How many more do you think she'll have?' she asked.

He ran his hands over Lara's flanks. 'I think there's at least one more in there, but I'm not experienced enough to be sure.'

While there were no more puppies imminent, they struggled to get the worst of the greeny black slime off the sofa.

'It'll need dry-cleaning,' said Ben.

Thea looked up. 'I expect Rory will just leave it. Where the hell is he, by the way?'

Ben gave her a look that managed to convey his opinion of Rory. 'We're managing perfectly well without him.'

'You're right. He'd probably get in the way.'

'So,' Ben went on. 'Did you and Rory meet on this holiday you went on, as Molly said? Or did you know him before?'

It sounded dreadful now. 'No, it was only on the holiday. I'm usually perfectly sensible and cautious—' She threw a glance in his direction to see if he believed her. 'But when I found out there'd been a party in my house, with gate-crashers and all sorts of hideous mess, I thought a week's holiday was just too short and I wanted to extend it a little.' Thea stopped. 'It does sound dreadfully irresponsible, now.'

'Oh, I don't know. If you'd just gone home and cleared up the mess I wouldn't have found out where Rory was.'

'Well, no, I suppose not. It was lucky Molly asked you about him.'

'That wasn't luck. When the head of the local college hadn't heard of him, I was next in line. The luck was that I'd remembered Rory. At the time I felt it was unfair that his work was slated because of his behaviour. He was the artist I'd been trying to track down for years.'

'Well, I think he's really good, too.'

Ben glanced at her as if them sharing an opinion was merely coincidence. 'I think Lara's going to have another puppy now.'

'Just in the nick of time, eh, Lara? Shall I put the kettle on?'

'No. I'm awash with tea. There's a good girl, another little bitch. If these were pedigrees they'd be worth a lot of money. It's not going to be easy finding homes for mongrels this size.'

'I expect I'll have one.'

'Have you any idea of the responsibilities involved in having a dog? They're not toys, you know.'

'I do know that, but I only work part-time. I could take care of a dog.' Thea's dormant maternal instincts had surfaced with all the force of a volcano.

Ben shrugged and turned his attention back to Lara. 'Come on, old lady. It's nearly three in the morning.'

'I suppose Rory must have decided to stay at the pub with the others.' This was a good thing. It meant Thea could sleep in his bed and she could put Ben in her room with Toby.

Lara's sides heaved. Another little pup appeared, much smaller than the others, and it didn't wriggle and squeak.

'Is it dead?'

Ben picked it up and started rubbing it roughly with the towel— Thea's towel—which she had produced earlier. 'It may not be, but it is a runt. Come on, little chap, take a breath!'

It did and a small cry emerged from its tiny mouth.

'That's the one I'm having,' said Thea with a catch in her voice.

'It may not survive. Don't get too attached to it.'

'Too late.' Thea realised she was crying.

Ben put his hand on her shoulder. 'Wait until tomorrow. See how it gets on. It may not last the night.'

Thea felt like emotional jelly. She wanted to lean into Ben and have him take her in his arms. For a moment it felt like he was going to, when the front door opened and in walked Rory, Molly and Petal.

'They didn't do b & b at the pub,' said Rory, slurring slightly, 'and the hotel was shut. So I brought them home. We've been wetting the babies' heads.' He staggered over to where he could see Lara and her pups. 'There, you see? I told you she'd be fine.'

Having no time to kick him, Thea turned her attention to Molly, whom she expected to be incandescent with fury.

In fact, she was also pretty merry. 'We had to get a taxi back,' she said gaily. 'We were all too drunk to drive.'

'I wasn't,' said Petal grumpily. 'Can I please go to bed now? The pub was full of old people, singing and dancing. It was gross.'

Thea, startled out of her emotional stupor, got to her feet. 'Have you got any bedding, Rory?'

'Don't know. Look in that cupboard.' He pointed to one in the corner of the sitting room, the last place anyone would put blankets. 'I'm going to my bed now. It's a double.' Then he opened his door and disappeared through it.

'If only I'd known about this cupboard before,' Thea muttered, as she sifted through old bed linen and blankets. None of it was in very good condition and most of it would have been fine for Lara.

'Oh, how sweet!' said Petal, who had discovered the puppies. 'Aren't they gorgeous?'

Thea had managed to find just about enough sheets and blankets for both beds in the back bedroom to be decently covered. Ignoring their complaints, she herded Molly and Petal into it and said firmly, 'No, there isn't any hot water. You'll have to wash in the morning.' Actually, she had no idea if there was hot water or not, but she wasn't having Molly and Petal fighting for the bathroom mirror at this time of night. No one else would have a cat in hell's chance of getting in before Christmas.

That left Ben. While Thea was sorting out worn blankets he tidied up the sitting room and made up the fire so it would stay in all night. He accepted his instructions about taking the other bed in Toby's room meekly. Thea could see now how tired he looked—a long journey, followed by Lara's puppies, plus a whole lot of baggage Thea could only guess at were etched under and around his eyes.

Alone in the sitting room, Thea was forced to face what she had known all along—unless she shared with Rory there was no bed left for her, the sofa having been scrubbed by Ben. 'Which leaves the bath,' she said to Lara. 'But not without as much bedding as I can scrounge.'

First, she tiptoed into Rory's room to see what she could scavenge. His bed, huge and comfortable, was very tempting, except that it had Rory in it. But she did find an old horse blanket draped over a chair, then, very bravely, she stole a pillow from under his snoring head and left the room.

A pair of old velvet curtains in the bottom of the airing cupboard were a good find, and a double sheet which was almost new and properly laundered. Suddenly exhausted, Thea just pulled out all the remaining bedding, which revealed a leaking paisley eiderdown, and carried it into the bathroom.

When Thea woke, it was eleven o'clock and Susan had let herself in the back door. She climbed out of the bath and stuffed her bedding back into the airing cupboard while Susan was in the kitchen. Then she went to say hello. 'Hi, Susan. Lara had her puppies last night.'

Susan's expression was radiant. 'Did she? How lovely! Where are they?'

'In front of the fire in the sitting room.'

Lara banged her tail hard on the floor, pleased to have her puppies admired.

'I told Rory he ought to be thinking about where she was to have them,' said Susan. 'They look so tiny, don't they? Look at that little one. I doubt he'll survive long.'

Thea instantly felt tears prick her eyes. 'Are you sure?'

'No, but he is little and you should probably—'

'Lara made a bit of a mess, I'm afraid,' Thea broke in before Susan could tell her to bump the puppy on the head. 'And one of the pups, that big one, was breech. Ben had to deliver it.'

Susan turned away from the little balloons which lay in a row by Lara's huge side. 'Ben? Who's Ben?'

Thea sighed. Perhaps now was as suitable a moment as any to tell Susan about the great visitation. 'Ben is some kind of relation of Molly's. Molly is a friend of mine and Petal's aunt. And Toby's Ben's son.'

'And they're all asleep? Here?'

Thea nodded.

'Mother of God, where did you find to put them?'

While Susan was tidying the kitchen, Toby appeared. He looked sweet and rumpled, and endearingly like his father.

'Hi, Toby. Come and see the pups.'

Toby knelt down at Lara's side. 'Look at that little tiny one,' he said.

Thea swallowed. 'He may not live very long. But he's my favourite.'

'Mine too,' Toby agreed.

Ben came into the room, dressed, but only half awake. Seeing him with his hair adrift made Thea put up her hand to her own. She discovered it had curled into knots at the base of her neck and badly needed brushing. She clawed at it with her fingers.

'Hello, Thea. Hi, Tobe. Admiring the puppies? The little one's still with us, I see.'

'That's mine and Thea's favourite,' said Toby firmly.

Ben gave Thea a look which told her never to lie to children about the chances of tiny puppies surviving. She looked back, trying to indicate that she hadn't. 'Has Lara been out yet?' he asked, when this silent altercation was over.

'She hasn't stirred,' Thea answered.

'She should relieve herself and she'll need breakfast, too.'

Thea opened the front door and called Lara. She wagged her tail but didn't move.

'You need something tasty to bribe her with,' Ben told her.

'Let's see what we can find in the kitchen and you can meet Susan. Susan, this is Ben and this is Toby. This is Susan. She looks after Rory. We need some food to make Lara go out. What is there?'

'Precious little.' Susan opened the fridge and peered inside. 'There's half a rasher of bacon she might as well have, as it won't feed a person.' Susan handed it to Ben.

He went over to where Lara lay.

'Come on, Lara, look what I've got for you.' Ben angled the bacon in front of her nose and she reared up to sniff it. Holding it out of her reach, he lured her to the front door, got her outside and only then let her have the bacon. Thea shut the door.

Through the window she saw Lara squat down, and then have a sniff about before charging back towards the door, demanding to be let in.

'Her food's in that sack, over there,' said Susan.

Ben inspected the sack in the disapproving way parents inspect boxes of cereal which are much advertised on television. 'She may need something with a bit more protein now she's got pups to feed.'

'You may all need something with a bit more protein in it, if you want breakfast,' said Susan.

'Is anyone else up?' asked Ben, when he'd fed Lara.

'No, and no sign that they'll be up soon.' Thea had put her ear to the keyhole and heard Molly's familiar snore, but nothing from Petal. 'I don't suppose Molly will want a cooked breakfast,' she began.

'Rory will,' said Susan.

Ben turned to Thea. 'Can you drive Rory's Land Rover?'

'I expect so.' But she wasn't keen.

'OK,' said Ben, seeing her lack of enthusiasm. 'We'll walk to the pub and fetch Molly's car. Then you can come with us and show me where the shops are.'

Thea felt unreasonably excited at the prospect of abandoning her sleeping, uninvited guests. Perhaps running away from people was becoming a habit. 'Susan, just tell anyone who appears that we've gone to buy breakfast,' she said gaily.

'You'd better buy lunch while you're there,' Susan told her. 'It's getting on for one o'clock already.'

Thea found Toby extremely useful in the supermarket. He was good at finding things, like fresh orange juice and Greek yoghurt for Molly and Petal, and croissants for Thea who felt she deserved a treat. 'He's a very efficient shopper,' she said to Ben as Toby spotted the dog food aisle and ran off.

'We neither of us like it much, so we get it done quickly.'

Thea didn't usually like shopping much either, but she had been enjoying this amble round an unfamiliar shop, looking at the different things that were available in Ireland. 'Oh, look,' she said, her spirits dampened by Ben's lack of pleasure, 'cooked chickens. I'll get one for lunch.'

There had been a slight tussle at the check-out. Ben had got out his wallet, assuming he was going to pay, but Thea had got in first. Her argument was that as they were all there because of her, the least she could do was buy breakfast. Ben had regarded her as if she were a rare species that he'd heard about but never thought to see.

They got back just as Rory came out of his bedroom. He was bare-chested and his lean, lightly muscled torso disappeared into a slender waist and flat stomach. A narrow band of dark hair led from his chest to the waistband of his jeans, where it disappeared. His arms were tanned and the hairs on his forearms were bleached by the sun. He yawned and brought his arms up behind his head. Thea saw Petal observe this from across the room and they exchanged glances. Yummy, they both thought.

Their moment of concord was swiftly over as Rory said, 'Hello, every-one. Jaysus, I've a headache!'

'So have I,' said Petal plaintively. 'Has anyone got any paracetamol.'

'Why are there no aspirins in the jungle?' said Toby to himself. 'Because the parrots eat 'em all.'

Diverted from Petal and Rory, Thea turned to Toby. 'I like that.'

'I didn't make it up. I heard it from someone at school.'

Thea nodded. 'Well, I expect Molly's got something for headaches. We've brought fresh orange juice for hangovers and all sorts of other things besides.'

Molly emerged from the bathroom, looking ready for whatever the day might bring. She was perfectly made up and Thea realised she must have got up the minute they left for her to be looking like this now.

'Good morning, everyone, Rory.' Molly averted her eyes from Rory's luscious torso; it was probably too much before breakfast.

'Molly . . .' Thea negotiated her way through people and furniture to her friend. She felt a rush of warmth towards her, for looking so good and for not complaining about anything. 'Good night?'

'Yes, darling. Now, who's going to show me these pups which caused so much commotion. Toby?'

Toby seemed to retreat, although he didn't move. 'They're over there.' He pointed to where Lara and the pups lay in front of the fire.

Thea wondered if he saw too much of his cousin. 'They may not want to be disturbed just now. What do you think, Rory?'

'Sure, I wouldn't know. But I do know that if I don't get a cup of coffee soon I won't be fit to live with.'

'I'll make it,' said Petal.

Susan, who had been in the kitchen watching the proceedings like a spear carrier in a play, decided to exit, left. 'I'll clean the bathroom then, if you folks have finished with it,' she said, having given Molly a look which told Thea that indeed, Molly had been in it for a long time.

'I'll cook breakfast,' Thea stated. 'Who wants eggs and bacon?'

'I do,' said Rory, 'and sausage and tomatoes and fried bread.' He gave Thea a grin which made her wonder why she didn't want to leap into bed with him. He was so delicious and cheerful. Ben seemed to have trouble finding his smile muscles.

At last everyone was settled round the table, and Thea was just relaxing into a bit of toast and marmalade, when Toby said, 'Thea, when I came to the bathroom to go to the loo last night, why were you asleep in the bath?' Everyone stopped crunching and swallowing, and looked at Thea.

'You slept in the bath?' Molly found her voice first. 'Why?'

'Jaysus, and there was half a perfectly good bed gone to waste,' said Rory. 'Was I too drunk to sleep with?'

'The answer to your question, Toby,' Thea told him, 'is that there wasn't anywhere else to sleep.' She felt colour creep up her neck and into her face. She was aware of Ben regarding her, but without turning to look at him she couldn't tell what sort of look it was.

'I'd like to see your pictures, if I may,' Ben said to Rory.

'Of course. I'd be glad to show them to you.'

'After breakfast, then.'

'Molly, what are you going to do while Ben sees Rory's pictures?' Thea asked.

'Oh, Molly,' said Rory, reaching his hand across the table. 'Are you not going to look at my work, then?'

'To be honest, Rory, if pictures aren't anything I can recognise, I really don't understand them. I think I'll do some telephoning and find a b & b instead. There's not room for us here.' Molly smiled back at Rory in a way which told Thea that last night, when they were downing pints of porter, or chasers of whiskey, Molly and Rory had become friends.

Led by Rory, Ben, Toby, Petal and Thea trooped up the hill to Rory's studio. He unlocked the shed, and he and Ben began dragging canvases out into the field. Thea didn't comment, but she felt their power again. They were breathtaking. And they were so enormous that no ordinary house could fit one through the door, either.

When they were all outside, leaning against bits of hill like huge, resting walkers admiring the view, Thea went back down the hill to look at them from a distance. She didn't want to hear Ben's opinion, or Petal's, or Rory's explanations. She just wanted to look at them.

Petal skidded down the hill to join her. 'Ben's very keen, but he says it's going to be hard to find somewhere to exhibit for a couple of years because they're so big. Rory says he's waited long enough, so he'll take them off to America where they understand "large".'

Thea felt instantly proprietorial. They were British pictures or, at least, Irish. They couldn't go to America to be exhibited.

'What do you think of them, Petal?'

'Amazing! They sort of blast you with colour and light, don't they?' Petal rubbed her arms, chilly in her sleeveless fleece. 'I'm cold. I think I'll go back to the house.'

Thea had stopped gazing at the work and was lying back on the scrub with her eyes shut. The sun was quite hot on her face. She was nearly asleep when Ben joined her. She sat up and tried to look intelligent.

'Well, they are good, that's for sure.'

'And you agree with me that they should be exhibited?'

'Yes, but where? London galleries are booked up for years ahead. He says he won't wait, but will ship them off to America. The gallery owner

KATIE FFORDE

he first showed with has a gallery in New York and might well show him
again, particularly now he's matured a bit.'

'But how will he afford to do that? He'd have to paint horses and dogs
for years to afford to get them to America.'

'Not if he sent slides to the right people. Someone would pay for
them to go.'

Thea's happiness threatened to vanish. She'd wanted Ben to like
Rory's work, she'd wanted the paintings to be as good as she felt they
were, but she did not want them to disappear to America. 'They're my
slides. Or they will be, when I get them back. I won't let him have them.'

Ben sighed. 'He can always take more slides, for God's sake.'

'But don't you want Britain to have them? Or Ireland?'

'Rory's not really Irish. He's just taken on an Irish personality because
he lives here. He was born in Liverpool.'

'Oh. Well, what has that got to do with anything?'

'Nothing, really. It just means he'd be happy to exhibit in England,
which makes it easier as I have contacts there.'

'But those contacts can't get us a show quickly enough?'

Ben shrugged. 'I can ask around, but it's unlikely. There's been a huge
surge of interest in art since Tate Modern opened and they're booked up
further ahead than ever.'

'Well, I'll tell you what. I'll have to open a gallery myself.'

Ben chuckled, assuming she was joking.

'I'm serious. I want to open an art gallery, to show Rory's work.' It
suddenly seemed so obvious that she wondered why she hadn't thought
of it before.

'You're mad! Do you know the sort of rents they charge for property
in London?'

'Who says the gallery has to be in London? I'll open a gallery in
Cheltenham, or somewhere like that. We'll make the Artylartary, or
whatever they're called, come to the provinces!'

Ben looked at her as if she were unhinged, but this didn't faze her—
she was getting used to it. 'I'll find premises near where I live and open a
gallery to show Rory's work. And if I like it, I'll keep it open and show
other people's work.'

The more she thought about it, the more she realised that this was
just the sort of project she needed. For the past two years she'd simply
been existing; this was something she could really throw herself into.

'You do realise,' he said eventually, having waited for Thea to start eating the grass and tearing her clothes, 'that it's unlikely you'll ever make any money?'

'Money is not the only thing in life.' She regarded him reproachfully. He should know that. 'I'll have my lodgers, who keep the house going. My day job earns me very little. I'd do better to run the gallery during the day and work in a bar at night.'

He frowned. 'When would you sleep?'

Thea shrugged. 'In the afternoons, when I'm sitting in my gallery and nobody comes?'

He smiled. 'So you have at least been in a small art gallery, then?'

'Yes. And before I make any commitment I will visit a lot more, talk to people, find out what's involved.'

His smile extended a little further and she saw he had small indentations in his cheeks. 'And all for the love of Rory?'

'It's his work I'm interested in. If he sends it to the States it'll be lost to Britain for ever. And in a way I feel I discovered him. Perhaps I want a little of his potential glory.'

'But how are you going to persuade him to hold back from the States? Why should he wait for you to set up your gallery in Long Shufflebottom, or whatever, where nobody may ever see his exhibition, when he could have a great big grand opening in some wonderful Manhattan loft in a matter of months, not years? I mean, if he has to wait for you to start a gallery from scratch, he might as well wait for a London gallery to have space.'

Thea felt a cloud pass over her enthusiasm and at the same time a breeze got up, making her feel chilly. 'No reason at all. I'll just have to convince him that he must. I know it's all a dream, really, but I've got to try, or I'll regret it for ever.'

Ben got to his feet and held out his hand to pull her up. 'I suppose that's true.'

By the time Thea was standing by Ben's side she felt more cheerful. She'd had a helping hand, literally. It must be a good omen.

Molly walked up to look at the work while it was still displayed outside the studio. Thea went with her, thinking she might need a rich patron. 'They're very good, aren't they, Molly?' she insisted, after Molly had inspected them in silence. 'Wouldn't you like one?'

'I can tell they're very well painted—our week in Aix has taught me that much—but they're so large. I've only got one small space in the hall, where the hunting prints run out, and another in the downstairs loo. Although I would like to help Rory out.'

'Well, I'm glad you think they're good, even if you can't buy one,' said Thea. She would tell Molly her grand plans later, when she'd spoken to Rory.

Molly had found a b & b nearby and announced that she and Petal would be staying in it. 'That means Thea won't have to sleep in the bath any more,' she announced, giving Thea an ambivalent look. 'What about you, Ben? Are you and Toby happy to stay here?' She didn't actually say that Thea needed chaperoning, but the implication was clear.

Ben glanced at Toby, who said, 'I'd like to be near the pups.'

'If that's all right with Rory, I think we'll stay put. It's only for a few days. We've planned to go down to the Burren later.'

Rory waved a liberal hand. 'You might as well hang around. I want to talk to you about the work, anyway. Now then. Who's coming out in the boat?'

'I will,' said Thea. She wanted to talk to him and the cottage was too small for conversation.

Molly and Petal shuddered in unison. Ben muttered something about 'life jackets'. 'We'll hang on here and look after the pups, and perhaps arrange to borrow some.'

Toby sighed resignedly.

'Suit yourselves. I'll show Thea the seals.'

Rory was adept in the water and the little vessel was soon speeding away towards the islands. Thea would have liked a life jacket herself, but she knew that Rory would think the idea feeble in the extreme.

'There are always seals on this island.' Rory pointed ahead to a lump of land. 'See? Those dark shapes?'

As they drew nearer, Thea watched, fascinated, as one by one the shapes slid into the sea and came swimming towards them, as if warning them off. They all had distinctive markings, and their huge liquid eyes were strangely glamorous in their round faces and shapeless bodies.

They watched until the seals had got bored and disappeared, when Thea said, 'Can we turn off the engine for a while? I want to talk to you. The house is so full of people that we might not get another opportunity.'

Rory switched off the engine. 'Speak. And tell me why you stole my pillow but didn't share my bed.'

'That's not what I want to talk about. This is serious, Rory. It's about your work. It's fabulous, you know that, and Ben's told you that you might have to wait a couple of years at least for a London show. So what I want is for you to wait for me to open an art gallery in the provinces and let me show your work. All of it, together, in one place. Your drawings and sketches too.'

'It sounds a grand idea, but how long will it take you to set up an art gallery? One year? Two? Now I've exposed my work to you lot, I want the world to see it.'

Thea realised he was lumping her in with Ben and Molly, Petal and Toby, when before it had been her and Rory, and a tiny part of her was sad. 'The world *will* see it. With Ben's contacts'—Thea wasn't quite sure what these were, but that didn't bother her. 'We'll get the art world to come to . . . to . . . wherever my gallery ends up being, to see your work. Mohammed coming to the mountain. Or is it the other way round?'

Rory grinned. It was a devastating grin, white teeth in a tanned face, with enough wickedness to turn any girl's heart. 'All right, m'darlin'. You've sold the idea, now give me a time frame.'

Thea watched him moving easily backwards and forwards as he pulled the boat through the water. 'How long can I have?'

'Three months, or I go to America. I already have a contact over there.' He shook his head. 'I must be mad! There I have a very lucrative bird in the hand and I'm turning it away for some harebrained chicken portion in a bush. It must be love.'

Thea swallowed. She knew perfectly well that Rory didn't love her, but he did want her and he might, not entirely unreasonably, expect a little something in return for his forbearance. 'Three months isn't very long to get an entirely new project going from scratch.'

'Tell you what, why don't you come to my American show instead, and I'll tell everyone you discovered me?'

'But I'm sure I'll manage. We'll need to get the drawings and sketches mounted and framed. Do you know someone who can do that?'

'Do you know someone who can give us a bit of a loan to pay for it? I already owe him money.'

'I'll sort that out,' said Thea, knowing she'd already got in far over her head. With luck she could ask Molly for the 'bit of a loan'.

'Good.' Rory shipped the oars. 'Now, Thea. Just a kiss to seal the deal.'

Thea allowed herself to be pulled into his arms. They were strong and his mouth was cold and firm. Very pleasant, really.

'So you're going to stay here, on your own, with Rory?' Molly was drying up glasses. Since Thea had told everyone of her plans to open an art gallery Molly had become an enthusiastic supporter. 'But won't that waste a lot of time?'

'I'd like to stay while the puppies are so little and while I organise getting his drawings framed. It's bound to be more expensive in England and, besides, I can't trust Rory to do it. He'll just forget and we must have them to show or no one will be able to afford to buy anything. And there's nothing much to lure me back home at the moment. Just a dirty house. I expect they've found someone to replace me at work.'

Thea didn't add that she had to keep Rory focused and away from the notion of sending her slides to his contact in America. She wasn't quite sure how she was going to do it.

'Three months really isn't enough,' said Molly, who'd argued at length and unsuccessfully for six. 'It takes longer than that to get a bathroom decorated.'

'I know, which is why I want you to go to estate agents and find out about suitable properties to rent. You can send details here—perhaps check some of them out for me. Please, Molly? I know it's a bit of a cheek to ask you but I don't know anyone else I could trust.' Who lived locally and who had time, she added silently.

'Oh, very well.' Molly hid her pleasure by folding up her tea towel. 'Now, what's Petal doing? We're going to go for a walk.'

Thea raised her brows in surprise. Petal didn't 'do' walking unless she was in a covered shopping mall. When Molly had gone she unfolded the tea towel, so it could dry.

Thea watched the party leave with regret. She hadn't asked them to come, but now she didn't want them to go. It was partly because she didn't want to be left with Rory, but mostly it was frustration. Now she'd decided to open an art gallery, she was anxious to leave her Irish idyll and do it, especially as she had so little time.

Rory stood behind her as they waved the car away. 'Well, Thea?' He turned her round and put his hands on her shoulders.

It was crunch time.

'Rory, you are one of the most attractive men I have ever met,' she began. 'And I must be completely mad not to make love to you right now, in front of the puppies.'

'I sense a "but" coming on.'

'I *am* completely mad. I don't want to make love to you, or for you to make love to me.'

He raised his eyebrows, but didn't seem particularly surprised. 'You mean you came to Ireland, to my house, with no intention of giving me what we both wanted? We did both want it, didn't we?'

It was important to tell him the truth, but not to give him any false impressions. 'When I came to Ireland I wanted a break from my humdrum life. I was terribly flattered by your interest. But when I saw your work, your paintings, I realised there was something more important than just wonderful sex.'

'Believe me, nothing is more important than wonderful sex.'

'Yes, there is. There's wonderful art. What I needed, and what I've now found thanks to you, is a mission, a project. I want to make you famous. I want your work to hang in all the important galleries. I want the world to see you, through me.'

He stood looking down at her. Then he sighed. 'Thea, now you've made your pretty speech, what about making me some lunch?'

A few minutes later, while Thea was in the kitchen chopping up vegetables for soup, she uttered a silent prayer of thanks to the sea, the islands and the mountains beyond, for having managed to pull it off. Many women, women she would respect and like, would have happily enjoyed Rory with simple animal pleasure, without feeling guilty, or used, or anything except happy. But she couldn't. You're a funny woman, Thea, she told herself.

In the following days Thea was very busy. First, they visited Rory's friend who framed the animal pictures. He agreed to mount and frame the drawings and sketches only if he was paid a deposit. 'I'm sorry, Thea,' he said with a sad twinkle, 'but this fella already owes me more money than you can shake a stick at.'

Thea wrote a large cheque. For the first time she regretted putting all her money into her house and not having a mortgage.

The slides arrived and, guiltily, she kept them to herself. She watched over the pups, made certain that Susan knew about Lara needing four times as much to eat as usual, and made sure there was plenty of nourishing food in Rory's cupboards. When she saw that Rory had a painting on the go, which would take up all his attention and not allow him to think about researching his American contact, she decided it was time to leave.

She handed him the book she had bought about rearing puppies. 'It tells you when to put them onto solids. In fact, it tells you everything. In eight weeks, a month less than the time I've got to get my gallery up and running'—she said this to rub in how unreasonable he was being—'I'll be back to collect my puppy. The little one.'

'Sure, he'll die, won't he?'

'If he dies, Rory, I'll . . . just don't let him die.'

She'd asked Susan to take her to the airport and she looked out of the window as they drove, partly excited but mostly terrified.

These are my last moments as a carefree, solvent woman, she thought. When I get home I've got to arrange loans, find premises, do things that grown-up people do. She sighed so deeply that Susan looked at her. Thea smiled quickly. 'Had a bit of a late night last night.'

'Oh. Had you?'

'Susan, you may not care about this one way or the other, but I might as well tell you. Rory and I haven't slept together. I'm only interested in his work.'

'You hadn't seen his work before you came.'

'I know. I was suffering from delusions. I thought I wanted a fling with a beautiful young man. What I wanted was a proper job.'

Chapter Five

WHEN THEA OPENED her front door she was bracing herself for chaos but the hall was much as usual—dusty, with the pictures hanging slightly askew on the walls—but there were no bags of rubbish blocking the door. Although this was a relief, Thea knew that it was just the tip of the iceberg. The kitchen might reveal the seven-eighths of mess below the surface.

But it didn't. Everything shone and everything was eerily missing, including the washing-up liquid.

There was a note on the table. *Dear Thea, I made them clear up. Hope you had a lovely time. How are the puppies?*

Thea suddenly felt very fond of Petal. How she'd managed to bully her other lodgers into producing this gleaming result she could only imagine, but she had and it had probably been very unpleasant for them. For her, coming back after a comparatively long journey, it was bliss.

The kettle was crammed into the cupboard with the saucepans, fairly easy to track down, and Thea filled it. Just then the telephone rang. Thea's heart lurched. She had been thinking about the puppies a lot during the journey from Ireland. Lara was a perfectly good mother, but the little one, known now as Little Chap, needed to be latched on for extra feeds. Susan would do it when she was there, but Rory was unlikely to remember. She couldn't face the thought of bad news.

The answering machine clicked on. 'It's Molly. I've looked at lots of properties for you, all hopeless. Give me a ring. By the way, Derek's thrilled I've got a new project.'

Thea sipped her tea contemplatively, relieved it wasn't Susan. Having Molly on your side was a very mixed blessing. She had bags of energy and enthusiasm and ideas, which was wonderful, but on the other hand she was so bossy that she was likely to take over completely.

When the phone rang again she answered it.

'Oh, hi,' said a slightly surprised-sounding deep male voice. 'I was expecting the machine. Ben Jonson here.'

'Oh, hello.' Thea felt her stomach give an unexpected little flip.

'I've got to be down your way to visit a client. I wondered if I could call in and talk to you? Next week?'

Thea was torn. She knew she would be very busy next week, but on the other hand she was surprised to find how much she wanted to see him. 'Well, of course.'

'I'm coming to talk you out of this ridiculous plan.'

Thea laughed, feeling suddenly light-hearted. 'Well, you can try.'

'How about Wednesday? I could meet you at the house.'

'Fine. I'll make some lunch.'

'Oh, don't do that.' The idea seemed to horrify him. 'We'll go out. See you on Wednesday, then. About eleven.'

His ending of the call was brisk, but nevertheless a smile was pulling at the corners of Thea's mouth.

The following Wednesday, when Thea opened the door to Ben, who was scarily prompt, she didn't know what to say. Really she should have told him immediately that he was completely wasting his time, she couldn't or wouldn't be talked out of her project. She settled for, 'Do you want to come in?'

He shook his head. 'I called in on Molly and she gave me all these.' He shook a sheaf of papers derisively. 'Apparently they're potential art galleries. I thought we'd go round them together, so you can see for yourself how totally impossible the whole project is.'

She felt she really should ask Ben why he thought he was helping her, when actually, it was nothing to do with him whether her gallery failed or not. But she didn't. Because she didn't want him to tell her she was absolutely right and turn round and go home. Her vision of him smacking his forehead with his hand as he realised his mistake made her smile.

Ben scowled, wondering why she was smiling, not wanting to ask. 'We can have lunch when we've got these out of the way.'

There was no denying it was fun. The first two were far too small and poky to display anything bigger than intimate watercolours, but the last space was much more encouraging—at least on paper.

It was in a small town about twelve miles away from Cheltenham, an area noticeably lacking in art galleries. She consulted the estate agent's details she had purloined from Ben.

'Why didn't I think of coming to this town in the first place? Property is cheaper.'

'I'm sure it is, but how are you going to get people in? I don't think this town is exactly a mecca for art.'

Thea was indignant. 'You'd be surprised! The surrounding villages are delightful—all sorts of artists and media types live in them, even if not in the town. They'll love having great art on their doorstep.'

He looked at her and sighed. He didn't say he thought she was doomed to disappointment, possibly because he knew enough about her by now to know that she wouldn't listen.

They walked down the hill and cut through a little alleyway.

'They call these laggars,' said Thea conversationally.

'Really? Where I come from they're slips. I suppose it's one of those words that never becomes a general term but just stays local.'

'So, where do you come from?'

'Wimbledon. It's got very smart recently.'

They located the property on a street corner, just by the station. Until recently it had been a building society, but before that it had been a prominent dress shop, with huge plate-glass windows on two sides.

'It's wonderful,' said Thea. 'It's so huge.'

'Let's go in before we get too carried away.'

While Ben struggled with the key, Thea wondered if he'd used the word 'we' in a patronising way, or if he meant 'both of us'. Naturally optimistic, she decided on the latter.

Inside, Thea was just as enthusiastic. There seemed so much space and light. Ben followed as she went into the largest room, exclaiming on the building's beauty. He didn't point out the grubby carpet, the dark beige walls or the dirt.

'It is a lovely space, you must admit that,' said Thea.

He nodded slightly, like a man bidding secretly at an auction.

'A pity there probably isn't enough wall space,' she went on.

Ben took a breath. 'You could block out the windows, if you needed to, with fibreboard.'

Thea turned to him, delighted. 'What a good idea!'

There were two other rooms, also with huge windows, and Thea began to feel more and more that this was the right property. 'Let's go downstairs,' she said, when she'd mentally found space for about half of Rory's huge works.

Downstairs was a basement. There were no windows, no natural light, and there was a suspiciously damp smell.

'It's the carpet,' said Ben. 'If you took it up and let some air get to it, it would probably be fine.'

'And there are no windows,' said Thea enthusiastically. 'We could put paintings on all four walls and prints in the corridor. We'd just need some good lighting. What's in there?'

There was a little kitchen and an office.

'This would be good for installations.' She indicated the office. 'And the kitchen's got potential.'

'As a kitchen,' said Ben firmly.

'And an office. I could put a desk in there.'

He was looking down at her and she sensed that he wanted to talk to her, in the way that headmistresses had often wanted to talk to her when she was at school. In other words, what he was going to say was not good news.

'Thea,' he began, putting a hand on her arm.

'Ben,' she said, taking it off. 'I think I know what you're going to say and I think it would be better if you said it somewhere else. Like a pub. There's one just across the road. I spotted it as we came in.'

'So,' she said, having taken a sip of her lager, still resolutely upbeat. 'You're going to tell me that I'm mad, that I can't possibly make an art gallery work without a private income, and that I should just let Rory's art go to the States and take up a useful hobby. But let me save you the bother—I know all that. I'm going to raise a mortgage on my house, put another lodger in to help cover the payments, and give this gallery my best shot. I'll give it two years and, if in that time I've made no money, I'll accept defeat. OK?'

He sipped his drink. 'Well, I was going to say a lot of that and I did come down here to talk you out of it, but I suppose I knew there was no point.'

Thea had been hoping for a brisk, impassioned argument. 'No,' she said quietly.

'So, while I think you're completely mad and doomed to failure, I will help you in any way I can. With contacts, stuff like that.'

Thea's mouth twitched. 'Not with the painting and decorating?'

His mouth twitched too, but was quickly controlled. 'I don't have a lot of time, but I expect I'll do a bit of that too, if I have to.'

Thea smiled properly and put out her hand. 'Of course you don't have to. And the contacts will be really useful—after all, any fool can slap on a few coats of emulsion.'

'Which you'll probably find is a good thing.'

'I'm sure I can get Petal and co. to help out. She got the other lodgers to clean the house beautifully, before I came back. I don't mean she actually did it herself, but she made the others.'

'Well, good for her. Perhaps she's growing up at last.'

'She takes after Molly. And Molly's mad keen to be involved, too.'

'Thea, I don't know how well you know Molly. I'm devoted to her myself but she is rather—'

'Forceful? Bossy? Yes, but I need someone like that. She's so positive. I think I can keep her in check.' She smiled. 'I'm so grateful for your help as well. Rory will be, too, I'm sure.'

'I'm not doing this for Rory!' He sounded unreasonably cross. 'I mean, much as I admire his work, I'm doing it—or I will be—because I admire you for having a dream and going for it.'

Thea gulped. To be admired by Ben, even for being crazy, was wonderful. And so, she realised, was Ben. Like the last clue in the crossword puzzle, it was so obvious when you knew the answer. Why she couldn't make love to Rory, why her heart beat faster when she heard Ben's voice on the phone, why she wanted him near her, even when he was saying negative things about her project. She was either in love, or had the most almighty crush. Either way, she had to say something, and quickly, or he might guess. 'I thought you thought I was mad,' she burbled. 'In fact, you said I was.'

'Yes, I do and you are, but I do admire you for it.'

'Oh.'

'And it will keep Molly out of mischief, too.'

She felt more in control of herself now, but he really did have lovely eyes. 'So I'll get a medal from the rest of the family?'

'Definitely.'

Thea smiled in what she hoped was an insouciant way. Without a mirror she couldn't check that she didn't just look simple.

Afterwards, when they'd called on the estate agents and told them Thea was interested in renting the property, Ben drove her home.

'Do you want to come in for tea or anything?' Thea asked. 'Or do you have to get back?'

Ben took a breath and looked firmly out of the windscreen. 'Listen, Thea, I feel it's only fair to tell you straight away that although I am attracted to you— I could hardly help it—I'm not into relationships.'

It took her a few moments to take in what he had said, but she still couldn't quite believe it. 'What?'

'I said, I'm not into relationships.'

A tide of pure anger began to force its way up from Thea's stomach to her face. She knew she was bright scarlet and that she must try to keep her feelings under control. If she let herself betray any emotion at all, she was likely to deck him.

'If you don't want a cup of tea,' she said, rigid with the effort of controlling herself, 'you only have to say no. You don't have to give me a whole lot of information I really have no interest in. Why on earth do you think I give a stuff about your dating habits?'

He appeared taken aback and she plunged on. 'But still, now I know, if ever I have an opportunity to pass it on to any woman mad enough to want to go out with you I certainly will.'

'I'm sorry. I've probably said too much—'

'You have. Way too much. Now, if you don't mind, I'm dying for a cup of tea, so I'll go.'

She had found her key, unlocked her door and got through it before Ben drove away. Once in the kitchen she stared at the whisky bottle for a long time before settling for tea. But she was glad she'd made the sober choice because five minutes later there was a knock on the door.

It was Ben. 'I've changed my mind. I *would* like a cup of tea.'

'Then you'd better come in.' Thea had had plenty of time to regret losing her temper. She followed Ben down the stairs to the kitchen. 'The kettle's just boiled, it won't take long.'

Ben stopped at the kitchen table and turned round to confront her. 'Actually, I don't care about the tea. I came back because I can't bear the thought of you trying to open a gallery without any sort of experience, or contacts, or anything. Whatever you think about me personally, you must let me help where I can.'

Having wanted to tear him limb from limb hadn't affected Thea's feelings for him at all. She shrugged. 'Then thank you. I would be very grateful for that.'

He scowled. 'You don't have to be grateful,' he said angrily and strode out of the room. She could hear that he took the stairs three at a time.

Meeting the owner of the prospective gallery's solicitor was not the boring but easy task she'd imagined it would be. The owner, it seemed, had been let down over matters of rent several times. Thus, he not only wanted Thea to sign a contract undertaking to rent the property for two years, whether the gallery was open or not, but he wanted three months' rent as a deposit. This amounted to approximately £6,000; money Thea had to have before she could sign the contract and get into the space to start decorating.

Thea was confident when she walked into the building society the following day. After all, she was a woman of property. It should be a simple matter of borrowing money against her house. The woman she spoke to was young, pretty and efficient. She was also firm. Thea could not have a mortgage unless she had a regular income. And she didn't think lodgers would count.

'Once you've got the money, of course, it's up to you how you pay it back. But we will need payslips and things to prove what you earn.'

When Thea got home she made an uncharacteristic raid on the bedrooms for dirty mugs. She rescued the corkscrew from Petal's bedroom yet again and decided to buy her one of her own. Then she remembered she had no money, and no prospective art gallery.

She thought about going back to the photographer's and asking them to write a letter, stating what she'd earned and implying she still earned it, so she could go to another building society, but decided against it. She had told them she wouldn't be coming back to work, but only after she'd got back from Ireland, when she'd already missed rather a lot of her scheduled days.

Instead, she put on the kettle and waited for it to boil. Something would occur to her. It had to, otherwise she'd have to ring Rory and tell him to take his pictures to America. And she would have to get a job that paid proper money.

Thea was still drinking her tea, or rather, sipping at the now cold liquid in her mug, when Molly rang. She definitely did not want to tell Molly her problems until she'd found a solution, but when Molly asked her how things were going, her 'fine' was a little forced.

'Good,' said Molly, not noticing, 'because I need a little favour. Ben's leaving Toby with us this afternoon while he goes to a job interview in Bristol and I'd forgotten we'd got to go out tonight. I was wondering—'

Even Molly had to breathe sometimes. 'If I could pop over and baby-sit?' murmured Thea, wondering why Ben hadn't mentioned changing his job to her.

'Oh, no, I wouldn't dream of asking you to do that. You must be far too busy with the gallery. I expect you're sitting there now, chewing your pencil, working out which picture to put where.'

Thea let out a sigh. 'If only that were what I was doing!'

This unaccustomed despondency penetrated even Molly's pressing concerns. 'Well, what *are* you doing?'

'Wondering how on earth to fund my gallery—at least, how to get some money quickly. Long term I could sell my house, buy something smaller in Stroud and do the gallery with the change. But I can't do any of that in the three months Rory's given me. Do you suppose, if I offered him my body, he might stretch it to four?'

'Oh, Thea!'

Realising she'd said far too much, Thea backtracked. 'It's only a temporary problem, Molly. It'll be all right. And if you want me to come over and baby-sit for Toby, that's fine.'

'Well, thank you, Thea, but I've already told Toby he's going to your house. I thought you wouldn't be able to come over, you see.'

'Well, I don't mind. I'd love to have Toby here, but what about Ben? Won't he be expecting to pick him up from you?'

'Ben's staying the weekend. It's some sort of team-building exercise. Although he hasn't definitely got the job, they want him to go along to see if he blends in.'

'How grizzly!'

'Actually he's very good at all that outward-bound stuff, so he'll be all right with that. But I was hoping you'd let Toby stay the night.'

'Well—it's not that I wouldn't love to have him, it's just where on earth could I put him? The house is full and so is my darkroom.'

'Toby says he's very good at sleeping on floors,' said Molly after a brief pause. 'And he wants to know how the puppies are.'

'They were fine last time I spoke to Susan.' She waited while Molly passed the message on. 'And he'll really be all right on the floor?'

'He says so.'

'Well, I dare say I can sort something out.'

While Thea was sorting out her bedroom so she could find a corner for Toby in it, she debated whether or not she should ring Rory and tell him that she couldn't open an art gallery in the time and that he might as well take his paintings to New York and have done with it. Somehow, she couldn't, not until she'd worried away at the problem a little longer and made absolutely sure she'd thought of everything.

Molly would probably have the odd £10,000 for emergencies, but she really didn't want her too involved.

But what was the alternative? The alternative was to give up the whole idea.

At last, Thea uncovered the sofa she knew was lying around somewhere in her bedroom. She could borrow Petal's sleeping-bag and Toby could sleep in that.

Seeing her house through Toby's eyes was a little unsettling. He eyed the clutter, the books lying in piles on the stairs, with eloquent silence. It was obvious his own house was very different. Masculine and spare, was Thea's guess. All this artistic student mess would probably put Ben right off. He was, after all, related to Petal and Molly, who were always complaining about it.

'Now, Toby. Are you hungry? I remember you're a vegetarian, so I could always do you a baked potato. But what about pizzas?'

'From the takeaway?'

'Well, no. From the frying pan.' Toby's eyes widened. 'It's quite easy,' she went on. 'You make a scone base, flatten it into the pan and cook it on both sides in olive oil. You can put anything you like on top—as long as I've got it, of course.'

Toby had a whale of a time. It was possible he'd never cooked using raw, basic ingredients before, thought Thea, although he had told her that he could use the microwave. 'Microwaves are a safe way for children to cook,' she said, 'but sometimes it's fun to do things from scratch.'

She had cleared the table, swathed Toby and herself in aprons and got out the flour. Very soon the cooks, the work surfaces and the floor were covered with a fine dusting of self-raising.

It was fortunate that Toby was as enthusiastic a washer-upper as he was a cook. Thea set him to it while she scraped the table.

'This is such fun!' said Toby, splashing water on the floor almost as fast as Thea could wipe it up again.

'Don't you ever do cooking with your mum?' Thea didn't know much about motherhood, but she certainly used to cook with her mother, when she was little.

'No, she doesn't like mess, much.'

'Well, no one actually likes it—it just happens. I don't suppose Ben is too keen on mess either.'

Toby shrugged. 'He doesn't mind it, I don't think, but we don't have much quality time.'

'Quality time? Oh.'

The flour on Toby, moistened with washing-up water, had now turned to glue. 'Mm. That's why we're downsizing. He's going for this job in Bristol. He should be able to get home a lot earlier and we can get rid of Margaret. My nanny. We should be able to find a nice little village where I could go to the local school rather than privately.'

Thea supposed it was the private education which made him so articulate. 'I see.'

'And it looks like Veronica's getting married again, so he wouldn't have to give her so much.'

'Veronica?'

'My mum. She doesn't like labels.' Toby frowned. 'I would quite like a mum, though.'

'You mean, you'd like your—Veronica—to be called Mum? But it doesn't really matter what you call someone, does it?'

Thea had missed the point completely. 'No, I mean a mum like my friend Edward's. She's always there after school. I would have gone to stay with them this weekend, only they've gone to see their granny. She makes cakes,' he added.

Thea would very much have liked to probe further, to find out Ben's feelings on all these topics, but she knew it would be wrong. Besides, Toby had given away lots of information already, without her having to torture him at all. She felt he deserved a reward. 'Well, we could make a cake, when we've done the pizzas.'

'Could we? Ace!'

Later, when Toby was licking out the chocolate cake bowl, Thea reflected it was a good thing he liked cooking.

'We have to wait until the cake's a bit cooler before we put the icing on, otherwise it'll fall off again,' said Thea. 'It's happened to me lots of times.'

'There's rather a lot of icing, isn't there?' Toby was a little embarrassed. The icing had got too wet and by the time it was the right consistency there was enough for a small wedding cake.

'Don't worry. We can freeze the rest and either use it next time anyone makes a cake, or I can eat it frozen, when I've got a chocolate craving on and haven't got any.'

'Oh. OK. Do you think it's cool enough now?'

'Not really, but put it on anyway. I can't wait much longer. You do the icing. I'll make tea. You need tea with chocolate cake, don't you find?'

Toby, who had no opinion on this, took the palette knife and started spreading.

Later, teeth brushed, but no other obvious washing done, Toby pulled Petal's sleeping-bag up over his shoulders and snuggled down on the sofa in Thea's room. 'Why are there so many black bags in here?' he asked.

'I'm halfway through sorting out all my clothes and getting rid of the ones that don't fit any more. I started before Christmas.'

'Veronica always does hers twice a year. Spring and autumn. She sends her clothes to an agency and gets money for them.'

'Oh.' Thea sent hers to jumble sales and, only if they were good enough, offered them to a charity shop.

'She says there's only any point in keeping really classic clothes that won't date.'

'You know a lot about it, Toby. Far more than me.'

Toby sighed. 'It's not very interesting, though, is it?'

'Well, different things interest different people. Will you be OK up here? I should have another go at the kitchen. Molly will be over in the morning and you know how tidy her house is.'

'Mm. Our house is always pretty tidy too.'

Thea's spirits sank a little. She had really enjoyed Toby's company and his presence had made her forget about her money worries. It hadn't stopped her thinking about his father, though.

'Yeah, well,' she said now. 'I'd better get downstairs or I'll have to take a chisel to the flour and water paste. I'll put the radio on, it'll probably be the news or something, but it may send you off to sleep. It always does me.'

Molly arrived promptly at ten o'clock as arranged. Seeing Toby sitting at the kitchen table eating pancakes, she looked at Thea. 'I hope you haven't been spoiling him.'

'Not at all. Toby and I like cooking, that's all. And I think it's important for men to learn the skills as well as women.'

As Molly had got through life perfectly well without cooking anything which hadn't come from Marks & Spencer's she lost interest. 'Well, can we go through to the sitting room? There's something I want to say to you.'

Molly had already refused coffee, so Thea lead the way somewhat glumly.

'Now, Thea, sweetie, I know you're not going to like this, but I've had an idea.'

Thea cringed into her favourite armchair.

'I want to put money into the gallery. Just until you're on your feet. Then, if you want to pay me back you can. Otherwise I can look on it as an investment.'

Thea didn't know how to answer. She was genuinely fond of Molly, but did she really want to be beholden to her, financially?

'Derek said you wouldn't want to do it, but he also said'—Molly paused—'that I was to tell you, that you were to tell him if I was getting too bossy.' She paused again. 'I know I can be.'

Thea suddenly felt overcome with gratitude and warmth. She went across to Molly and sat beside her on the sofa. 'Oh, Molly, it's so sweet of you. I don't know what to say.'

'I partly want to do it'—Molly cleared her throat—'because I've decided to stop going on Tiger Tours. That thing with Gerald, it was because I was bored, really. I realised that when you and Rory . . . I mean . . . you didn't have an affair with Rory, did you? Because you knew that you needed a project. I really admired that. Because Rory was—is—gorgeous. To turn down someone like that because there was something more important—it taught me that that was what I needed, a project I mean.'

'But what about Derek?'

'Derek said, "Go for it." You need the money and I've got it lying around in an account that's not paying much interest. Then Derek said it would keep me out of mischief and I suddenly worried that he'd found out about Gerald.'

'I'm sure he couldn't have done. There wasn't much to find out, was there?'

'No, but I could have made the most awful fool of myself.' Molly shook her head slightly. 'I won't interfere, I promise.'

Molly not interfering was like anyone else doing without oxygen, just not possible. So not an ideal business partner for someone, let alone for anyone who was so bad at saying no. But it was the answer to her problems. She could move into the gallery and start getting it ready. Thea made up her mind.

'I accept your very kind offer, Molly. It's really sweet of you and I'm very grateful.'

'But? I know there's a but, so you might as well tell me what it is.'

'I am going to be firm with you. I'm going to practise being businesslike. I'm going to tell it like it is and say no if I think you're wrong.'

'Well, of course.' Molly was pink. 'I never thought you'd accept. I thought I was just too domineering for you. Derek says I should go on a de-assertiveness course.'

Thea had a sudden insight into Molly's marriage; Derek probably let Molly do more or less what she wanted, but it was to him she turned when she needed help.

'I was thinking of going on a course in "how to say no", but I don't think we're either of us going to have time. I need you to help, Molly, just as long as you do what I want you to. It'll be my turn to be bossy!'

They were a good team. Thea signed papers and Molly signed cheques, and between them they put the fear of God into all the official bodies they had to deal with before Thea was given two sets of keys to what would be the gallery. She gave one to Molly as they drank a celebratory cup of coffee and Thea ate a celebratory cream cake.

Later, she rang Rory and told him the good news. He was worryingly ambivalent. 'Rory, you're not going to let me do all this gallery thing, borrow hundreds—no, thousands—of pounds, then just send your stuff to the States anyway?'

'Now, would I do a thing like that?'

His charm was less potent down the phone, but still evident. 'I do hope not, Rory, or I might have to firebomb your studio, or something,' said Thea mildly. 'I can't have you backing out now.'

'Now don't you go getting your knickers in a twist.' Thea winced at her least favourite expression. 'I'll let you have the first showing of my work, provided you've got space for it all.'

A finger of anxiety touched Thea for a moment; but she dismissed it. When Rory saw the gallery he wouldn't want his work shown anywhere else.

Once Thea had convinced Petal that organising the students to prepare the gallery for painting was the right and cool thing to do (helped in her decision by her new boyfriend who was hard up) Petal galvanised the troops wonderfully, making those without Saturday jobs give up their free day to Thea.

Molly, who had yet to shrug off her previous existence as a 'woman who lunched', was just going to drop an estate-car load, which amounted to four students, at the gallery. Thea's car was packed with an enormous sound system which Petal insisted was essential if any work was to be done; as many of her old clothes as she thought would cover the workers; mugs, coffee, a huge chocolate cake she had made in the night when she couldn't sleep; and a case of beers she planned to keep hidden until after the work was done. She also took her vacuum cleaner and Petal.

'You get everyone into painting gear while I make friends with the builders' merchants round the corner. I've opened an account there, so that'll mean I don't have to pay every time I go. We're going to be rigid about coffee breaks and only have them when we've seen real progress.'

Petal gave her a 'get a life' look and rolled her eyes. Thea frowned as she dumped Petal and the contents of her car onto the pavement. But as she drove away she looked in her rearview mirror and saw Petal organising a chain gang.

It took ages to buy the industrial-size tubs of paint, sugar soap, soft brooms, stiff brooms, rubber gloves and all the other myriad items she thought she'd need. All the while she consoled herself with the thought that Petal would have been making them get on. They couldn't do a lot, she realised, but they could start pulling up the carpet.

She had forgotten that they were mostly art students. First, they had had enormous fun dressing up in Thea's old clothes. Then they had put the music on loud enough to threaten the glass in the windows and pranced about, exclaiming over the wondrousness of the space. They had also found the chocolate cake, though not, thank goodness, the beer.

Thea turned off the music, realising that either Petal had let her down, or that she didn't have quite enough of Molly's genes. 'Right, you lot!' she shouted. 'I'll start paying you from the time you start work. We need to get this carpet up. And if this room isn't clear of carpet, walls and floor washed by five o'clock, no one gets paid and no one gets a lift back to town. Petal?' She hoped no one heard the note of pleading, which to her was only too clear.

At half past four Molly arrived, elegant as usual, to see if there was anything she could do.

If Thea hadn't been so filthy, she would have fallen on her neck in gratitude. 'Take this lot away,' she pleaded quietly, so 'this lot' wouldn't hear. 'They've been wonderful, but they can't agree what music to play, and there's nothing more they can do apart from painting and I don't want them doing that—they're art students.'

Molly managed to fit Petal and the sound system, as well as the four students into her estate car. Thea watched her drive past the window, everyone waving madly, with a sigh of relief. They were nice kids, but Thea had had enough young company. She wanted to have the place to herself, some calm, to give herself a rough idea how long it would take to get it into some sort of order.

The carpet was gone. The floor beneath washed, but otherwise in a bad way. She would have to hire a sander to get through the layers of dirt and stain. Then it would need lots of coats of varnish. She'd have to find something that was fairly quick-drying.

Downstairs, in the basement room, they had discovered the carpet was glued down. Thea had stopped them pulling it up until she found out if the glue would come off easily. The corner where they tried this indicated that only laborious scrubbing with a paint scraper would remove it, and with the prospect of varnishing the floor upstairs ahead of her, she tried to think of a plan B for the basement floor.

Now she was on her own she prowled around, exploring her territory. It felt good. It was still spacious and light, lighter without the carpet, and to her surprise it already felt like her space and she was happy to be there on her own.

She went down to the kitchen to make a cup of tea and, while she was in the kitchen waiting for the kettle to boil, she explored the cupboards and found a door she hadn't opened before. It was a little room, beyond the kitchen. There was a window in it, but it was too small to use as exhibition space. It was like a bedroom, really. Then she noticed the washbasin in the corner. If the worst came to the worst she could let her own room at home and live here.

Back in the kitchen, Thea decided to bring a sleeping-bag and pillow next time she came. Cheltenham seemed far away at the end of a long day and there would be many, many long days, though now, even if she'd had the sleeping-bag and pillow, the call of a bath would have lured her home.

At home she was annoyed, though not surprised, to discover there was no hot water when she felt the tank. She met Petal coming out of the bathroom looking pink and shiny, and irritatingly clean. 'I can't believe you lot have managed to use every drop of hot water,' snapped Thea.

This was so unlike the easy-going Thea that Petal tried to placate her. 'We borrowed a bottle of red wine from you. Would you like a glass?'

Thea sighed. Actually she yearned for one of Rory's tumblers of neat whiskey. 'Later, perhaps. Did you let the water out? Of your bath?'

'Er . . . no. I was just going to clean it now.'

Yeah, right, thought Thea.

'Then I'll get in your water.'

Petal shuddered at the thought.

Thea sighed and to soothe Petal's horror said, 'Thank you for getting everyone to work so hard today. You all did brilliantly.'

Petal smiled. 'We're sending for pizza. Shall we order you one?'

Thea nodded. 'That would be great.'

A few moments later she was lying in a lukewarm soup of orange-scented bath ballistics, baby oil and several other strange unguents with which Petal liked to anoint her body.

The phone rang just as she had finished slooshing herself and the now empty bath with clean, cold water.

She waited to see if the others would answer it before realising that they probably couldn't hear it over their music. Praying that it wasn't Molly wanting to discuss tactics, or anyone else who might take long, she wrapped herself in a towel and pattered across to her bedroom.

It was Rory. 'I'm about ten miles from you. I'm calling from a phone box. Are you at home to visitors?'

'Of course.' For anyone else she'd have said no, but Rory was different. Quickly Thea washed her ballistic-stiffened hair, pulled on clothes and rushed downstairs. Petal and the others had gone out, leaving Thea's pizza on the table.

'Thea! You smell like a flower garden and look even more appetising.'

Thea put her arms round Rory and hugged him. He reminded her of clear, light air and silver seas.

'Come in and let me get you a drink and some pizza. Can you stay for pizza? Bought in, I'm afraid, but quite edible. Do you want to stay the night?' Quite where she'd put him she didn't know, as it was unlikely a sofa in her bedroom would satisfy Rory. Then she became aware that Rory wasn't following her with his usual confidence.

'I've got something in the car to show you, bring you, really.'

'Paintings?' At least now she had space to store them, although she'd have to work out how to get them across to the gallery in her little car.

'No. I'm having those shipped. They should be here in a day or two. Puppies. And Lara. I need you to look after them for me.'

Rory moved to the back of the Land Rover. There was Lara and in front of her was a box of puppies. 'Rory! They've grown like mad.' Her heart leapt as she saw that all six were there; the little runt had made it this far. 'What are you doing dragging them all over the countryside? Bring them in before they get cold.'

Lara jumped down. She pattered down the road, then squatted and produced a wee the size of a garden pond.

Rory ignored this. 'It's May, you know, hardly the middle of winter.' He picked up the box of puppies. 'I'm off to London tomorrow. I'm hoping you'll look after them for me.'

Little black and white faces appeared over the top of the box, looking plaintively at Thea, who was staring at Rory in confusion and horror. Then she shut her mouth and ushered the party inside. 'Bring them down into the kitchen where at least we can talk.'

Lara settled herself in front of the Rayburn which, because of the huge hot-water demands of the household, was kept going summer and winter. She grinned happily up at Thea.

'I'll put the pups down here next to Lara.'

'Rory, I can't look after the puppies. I've just started work on the gallery. And anyway, they're far too young to be moved.'

'I know, but Susan's gone away somewhere and there's nowhere else I can leave them. I have to go to London. Sure, you wouldn't have me let them starve to death?'

Thea pursed her lips as she poured the wine. 'I don't suppose I should give you this. I'd better make some coffee.'

He took his glass of wine. 'Ah, don't be cross.' He grinned maddeningly. 'Although you do look lovely when you're angry.'

'Rory! Don't you know that saying that sort of thing is likely to get you something unpleasant and messy tipped over your head?'

'I thought I might get away with it with you, Thea.'

Thea couldn't be cross any longer. She was too tired. 'Well, let's get Lara fed. Are the pups on solid food yet?'

Rory shook his head. 'I've no idea. Susan's been doing them up to now.' He pulled out a chair and sat down. 'Have you any more wine?'

'When are you going to London?' asked Thea, having retrieved her secret bottle from behind the bleach.

'I'm planning to drive through the night. I can't cope with London traffic in daylight.'

That at least solved the problem of where he was to sleep. 'Well, don't drink any more alcohol.'

'Stop fussing, Thea, and sit down and let me look at you.'

When Lara was happily eating her supper out of the washing-up bowl, Thea sat and poured herself another glass of wine. 'So, why are you going to London?' His body language made her wonder if he was hiding something from her.

'To visit family. There's a whole lot of cousins and aunts and things I haven't seen for years. I want to catch up with them all.'

It sounded a perfectly valid explanation. So why wasn't she quite happy about it?

'Tell me', he said, 'how this gallery's going. What are the chances of it coming off? Sixty-forty? Or only evens.'

'What? Rory, how dare you!' She was laughing, but she was genuinely incensed by his lack of faith. 'Of course my gallery is going to come off. I have been through hoops getting the space, that's all. Which meant borrowing money from . . . someone.'

She realised just in time that if she mentioned Molly he would assume it didn't matter if Molly was paid back, because she was rich.

'I've spent all day pulling up carpets, washing floors, doing everything I can to make it into the most wonderful art gallery, and you suggest to me that it might not "come off"?'

Rory sighed. 'Jesus, Thea, you know how to give a fellow a hard time.'

'I am not giving you a hard time. I am telling it like it is. So I hope you haven't even the inkling of an idea about reneging on our deal.' She smiled. 'It was your work that inspired me. Your work which made me want to do it.'

Rory got up from the table, pushed past the chairs and put his arms round Thea. His hug turned to a kiss, chaste enough at first, but then he opened her mouth with his and kissed her properly.

Thea found herself responding. He was a wonderful kisser, his arms were firm and comforting, and she was tired, a little drunk and still angry. It was nice to be held and kissed, even though it was the cause of her anger who was kissing her.

He pushed his hand up under her shirt, caressing the skin of her waist and back. 'Come to bed with me.'

Thea reconnected with reality. 'No. You're an artist. A bloody good one, but I don't want to sleep with you.' She tried to pull away, but he wouldn't let her. 'Have you no morals?'

'I left them in my other coat. You're so lovely, Thea, and I want you so much. Give me one night in your arms and I'll take the puppies back to Ireland and let my family go hang.' He was getting more and more urgent, his hands up and down her body, running his fingers round the waistband of her jeans.

Thea pulled away more determinedly this time. 'Rory! Sit!'

Lara, who had been watching her master with interest, sat.

Rory sighed and sank back down into a chair. 'Come on, it's a good offer, isn't it? Sleep with me and I'll take the pups away.'

Thea watched him. Something about this situation wasn't quite as it seemed. It wasn't him trying to take her to bed that bothered her. There was something about this London trip which didn't ring true.

She gave him a friendly smile. 'You go to London and meet up with all the rich aunties who might leave you money. But don't think I'm going to take over your animals for ever. I'll want you back in plenty of time for the private view.'

He frowned. 'Sure, think of what happened last time. The critics might trash my work all over again.'

'No, they won't. You're the best, the most exciting artist I've seen for a long time. And Ben thinks you're special enough to make it worth me mortgaging my house to finance the gallery.'

'What do you mean? Jesus, you never did that, surely?'

Thea didn't want to deceive Rory and she had nothing but a faint instinct that anything was wrong, but she felt she must stress her conviction that his work was worth enormous sacrifices and that she was making them. The fact that she hadn't actually mortgaged her house was only a technical matter.

Rory was looking a little uncomfortable, although that could have been the hard kitchen chair he was sitting on. 'You're a wonderful woman and I'm truly grateful for everything you've done for me.'

To Thea, this sounded like she was being written off, but she produced a suitably modest smile. 'You're the artist.'

He nodded. 'You wouldn't have those slides you took, would you?'

Thea shook her head. 'I'm awfully sorry, Molly's sent them away to have postcards made. It takes ages, you see.' The lies tripped off her tongue like broken beads—they were only half-lies, anyway. They were going to have some postcards done.

'Oh. That's a bit of a blow.'

'Why? So you could show your work to your aunties? You should have asked me, I could have got you another set done.'

'How long would that take?'

Thea shrugged. 'Hard to say. How long will you be in London?'

'I was planning on staying a month.'

'A month? That's too long for a holiday, Rory. You can stay a fortnight, at the most, or'—she scooped up a sleeping bundle of black and white fluff—'the puppy gets it.'

He laughed. 'You're a hard woman, Thea. Did I ever tell you that?'

Thea got up very early the following morning and realised that when Rory had left he had not given her his address in London. She went downstairs to the kitchen and the puppies all bumbled around while she showed Lara the tiny garden, which was up a flight of rather narrow stone steps. Lara squatted and then made Thea send Rory messages of rage. How could he have left her with Lara and the pups when the dog did turds which wouldn't have shamed an elephant? Pursing her lips and trying not to breathe through her nose, Thea rummaged in the garden shed and found a shovel.

The pet shop opened early. She bought a book and realised she'd have to look after the pups herself, even if she had to take them backwards and forwards to the gallery with her in the car.

The book told her that pups of three weeks should be started on solid food. Well, it was too late for that. They should be fed in separate bowls, to make sure they all got an equal share, and they would need at least three meals a day.

'If I'd wanted to become a dog breeder,' she growled to the absent Rory, when she'd got the cornflakes (all the cereal she had in the cupboard) to the right temperature in the microwave, 'I wouldn't have chosen to do it while I was opening an art gallery. I'd have done it when I had absolutely nothing to do with my life except lie on my stomach and dabble my fingers in warm breakfast cereal.'

This sarcasm followed the many other curses she had sent to him over the ether. She cursed as she bought boxes of Weetabix and tins of puppy food, a proper water bowl and a set of new cereal bowls. Only at the last minute did she relent and let the lodgers have the new bowls, and use the old ones for the pups.

The lodgers were mostly delighted with Lara and the pups, even though it was only Thea who would clear up after her in the garden. Molly was very ambivalent. 'It's not that I don't love Lara'—she patted the huge head—'but an art gallery is no place for animals.'

'Tell me something I don't know,' Thea sighed. 'But what can I do? Besides, if I did ever feel like sleeping over at the gallery, Lara would be company. The lodgers are very good at taking Lara round the park,' she said. 'Pete in particular. Although of course I can't persuade them to clean up after her, so I have to walk her first.'

'Clean up after . . . ? Oh my God!'

'I shall leave them at home tomorrow, because I want to sand the floor and the noise will be dreadful, and Pete will be in to feed them.'

Molly swung into managerial mode: 'Thea, you cannot do that yourself. You must get someone to do it for you. It'll take you ages. I absolutely insist!'

'But I've booked the sander, now.'

'Then leave it to me. I'll get someone to do it. Thea, I've told you, I'm happy to finance the gallery. Derek's happy. We've allocated an amount and you haven't even spent a third of it yet. Save your energy and your talent for things that only you can do. I've chased the shippers, by the way. The paintings should arrive the day after tomorrow. You can think about where to store them.'

Thea heaved a larger sigh. Sometimes it was nice to be bullied. 'Most of them should fit in the bedroom at the gallery and the rest can go in the passage.'

'Good,' said Molly. 'Then you can't sleep there.'

The floor had been sanded and the pictures had arrived but the floor still had to be varnished and Thea wouldn't allow anyone else to do it.

She'd tracked down some quick-drying water-based varnish, which wouldn't poison her with fumes, and she planned to spend all evening and night putting on coat after coat until the floor would shrug off a diamond cutter, let alone hundreds of pairs of feet.

She had brought Lara and the pups with her, as there was no one at home to look after them. And a sleeping-bag and pillow in case she felt too tired to drive back. With Lara and the puppies for protection, a radio for company and a little stash of goodies for comfort, she felt equipped for a marathon of varnishing.

Molly had offered to do it with her, declaring that she didn't mind getting her hands dirty. But as Thea knew this wasn't true, and that the offer was made out of duty rather than a desire to get a repetitive strain injury, she refused. Molly was proving a boon and, so far, she and Thea hadn't fallen out. It was Molly who asked Thea what she intended to do or show 'after Rory'.

Up to now, Thea hadn't thought about 'after Rory'. But Molly was quite right. Rory was only the beginning.

'You need a theme, darling,' Molly had said, tentatively stroking Lara who had come upstairs into Thea's sitting room for some time away from her children. '"Seascapes and sunsets", something like that.'

Thea mentally reached for her sick bucket, but took the point.

'Then you put in a call for work and people send you slides. The girl at the magazine I was placing the advert in was awfully helpful when I explained I—er—we were opening a new gallery. Students are always desperate for somewhere to show their work, she said, but we must be careful about quality and make sure we don't have anything too weird or it won't sell.'

Thea picked a spot of white paint off her trousers. This was crunch time. This was when she had to explain to Molly that her vision of what the gallery should do was quite different from what Molly had in mind. 'Actually, Molly, I do want to show weird stuff, even if it doesn't sell.'

'But, Thea! How will we make any money if we can't sell the work?'

'We'll charge a fee for showing. Then we can show what we like—what I like. Otherwise we'll be just another art gallery selling Cotswold views. I don't want that.'

'But, Thea . . .!'

'Molly, you very kindly lent me the money to open. I'm hoping that Rory's stuff will sell so well that we'll get a huge amount in commission. If we do, I'll pay as much as possible back to you. If not, when I can arrange a mortgage I'll pay you back. You've been wonderful, Molly. But if we want different things for the gallery we'll have to part.'

Molly absorbed this. Before her marriage she had worked as a secretary to an important businessman when she really ought to have been in business herself. She left her job when she got married and since then her organisational skills had been confined to her husband and her committees. And her desire for adventure had been confined by the limits of Tiger Tours. Since she'd been involved in getting the gallery open, she had really felt fulfilled for the first time in her life.

'Very well,' she said at last. 'It's your gallery, after all. You can put what you want into it, but only if the people who exhibit *do* pay a proper amount *and* we charge commission. Otherwise you'll never make more than enough just to cover your overheads. I've done some costings.'

Thea laughed. 'I'm so glad I've got you, Molly. I'd be so hopeless on my own.'

It was impossibly hot. The first week in June had decided to live up to its name and be 'flaming'. Thea cursed herself for not getting the ventilators working. She had to be content with propping the street door open. At least the varnish was non-toxic.

When she'd given the pups and Lara a meal, and taken Lara to some waste ground, she stripped down to her bra, pants and old painting shirt and set to work with the roller.

She put Van Morrison on loudly and was well into the rhythm of both the music and her work when she straightened up to ease her back and noticed a section of ceiling which hadn't been painted.

She swore, deciding it would be better to paint it now than to depend on remembering to do it later. With Rory's work being so enormous, she couldn't rely on people not looking up that high. She set up the versatile ladder system Molly had been advised to buy, carefully working out which bit hooked over which other bit. It seemed to take for ever to assemble and she yearned for a straightforward pair of steps. Gingerly, she climbed up it, her pot of paint over her arm, her paintbrush stuck down her cleavage.

When she reached the top she realised that the wretched ladder wasn't quite near enough. She didn't like the fact that there was nothing to support her above her knees, and if she got down, moved the ladder and climbed up again, the whole grisly process would just go on longer. She knew it was silly, but she decided to get some paint on her brush, hang on for dear life and lean. With her painting arm outstretched, it might just reach.

Very carefully, holding on tight with one hand, she leaned over the front, aiming at the bit of ceiling with her brush, praying her arm would extend far enough. It did, just about, but she needed a dab more paint to finish the job. Her brush was just making a pleasing sucking sound as she dug it into the paint, when she heard a noise behind her. Startled, she jerked round and at the same moment that she saw Ben, she felt her ladder slip and begin to topple.

There wasn't time for her whole life to pass before her, but she did manage to wonder what on earth Ben was doing there and if she'd ever get the paint off the floor. One foot hit the floor first, sending a stab of pain to her ankle, then Ben caught her and she swayed downwards, unable to save herself. Her weight and the angle at which he caught her knocked him off balance and they landed on the floor together, breathless, she on one of his arms, the rest of him more or less on top of her.

'It's all right,' Ben said. 'Don't try to get up; just lie still and get your breath back. Thank God I managed to break your fall.'

Thea lay back. She felt strangely calm, considering that a moment ago she'd been confronting broken limbs or worse, and the pain in her ankle subsided to a dull throb. Then she became aware that her shirt was halfway up her back and that Ben's hand was on her bare waist.

Questions flitted irrelevantly through her mind: when did she last wax her legs? Was there paint all over the floor? What sort of knickers had she put on that morning? Praying it wasn't one of the older pairs, she wondered why Ben didn't get up. Was there some sort of medical reason why he should stay lying down too? Predominantly, she acknowledged, she didn't want him to get up. She liked lying under him, half naked, with this strange feeling of lassitude making it impossible to do anything except stay there.

'I must be squashing you to death,' he said, not moving.

Thea knew that if he got up she might never get this close to him again. On the other hand her ankle hurt and she should really find out if she'd broken anything before even considering following up on this opportunity. 'Not really. I wonder if you could just have a feel of my ankle. It hurt as I fell and I'd rather you checked if it was broken before I look. If I see it out of kilter I might be sick and this floor has suffered enough.' By now she could see paint, looking like yoghurt, splattered across the newly sanded wood.

His hand on her leg and ankle didn't recoil from broken bone. In fact, it appeared to be telling her there wasn't much wrong at all, as it glided smoothly up and down. The feel of his warm palm on her leg was comforting, extremely pleasant.

It obviously didn't have the same effect on him.

'I don't think anything's broken, you've probably wrenched it,' he said. 'I'll get up so I can help you up.'

A whimper escaped from her.

'What's the matter? Have I hurt you?'

'No,' she breathed, looking into his eyes, wondering if he would ever get the message and kiss her. He was aware of her lying under him, he must be, and he hadn't got up himself either, but why hadn't he done anything else?

He sighed deeply and the corner of his mouth lifted in the beginnings of a smile. Thea closed her eyes, waiting—hoping—to feel his lips on hers, knowing she'd die of embarrassment if she didn't. She'd practically asked him to kiss her.

His lips brushed hers so gently that it was almost a tease. Then he applied just enough pressure for it to qualify as a kiss but no more. It dawned on Thea that he was kissing her out of politeness, to save her the embarrassment of lying underneath him, offered but unwanted. He took his mouth away maddeningly soon.

He could have saved himself the trouble. She doubted if she could have felt more hurt and rejected if he'd just said 'thanks but no thanks'. She lay still, her eyes tight shut, hoping she wouldn't cry.

'I think we should get up. There's paint all over the floor. It's in your hair and everything.'

Just for that moment she didn't care about the paint, the floor or even the gallery. Because she realised that she'd fallen in love with Ben—at pretty much the same time that she'd discovered he didn't want her and had made it abundantly clear. She had had him in her arms and she hadn't been able to get him to do more than kiss her out of kindness. It was humiliating. How could she bring herself to look at him again?

She allowed him to help her up, not looking at him, with her eyes closed, but as she stood upright she was aware that her ankle really did hurt. She squeezed her eyes tighter shut. Pain was a perfect excuse for a few tears, but she couldn't let herself shed them. Gingerly she put her foot to the floor, still clinging on to Ben. She bit her lip and inhaled sharply. 'Ow!'

'Can you stand on it?'

She tried a little tentative weight-bearing. It was agony. 'Ow' no longer covered it.

'Do you think we should get you to casualty?'

'No!' Horror made it easy for her to look at him. 'I've got a floor to varnish, not to mention get the paint off from. I can't spend hours and hours in A and E reading old copies of the *Radio Times*. All it needs is a cold compress and a bit of a bandage.'

'Which you have in your first-aid kit?'

'There's no need to be sarcastic. We can make a bandage out of some rags or something. Haven't you got any initiative?' He accepted her anger with irritating calm as if he knew the real reason for it. 'There's a dust sheet next door.'

Ben nodded. Then he bent and picked her up.

She was reluctantly impressed. She was a healthy woman and was probably heavy to lift, but he not only got her up into his arms, he carried her through to the next room where there was a chair. Then he tore off the end of an old sheet Thea had been using to protect the floor and went to wet it.

He came back and lifted her foot. He was very gentle and she was reminded of the way he had handled the puppies when they were born.

'I wish I'd protected the floor next door,' she said, to give him a reason for her extravagant sigh, and to distract herself from the feel of his fingers on her foot and ankle. She had very sensitive feet and although her ankle hurt like mad, even the pain had a strangely erotic effect. It was no good having those sorts of feelings for a man who didn't want you. A tear got past her guard and trickled down her cheek.

She felt Ben stiffen, opened her eyes and saw that he too was angry now. 'How can you have been so stupid as to lean out from a ladder like that? It's incredibly dangerous. If I hadn't caught you, you could have been seriously injured.'

She wasn't prepared to be treated like a naughty child by a man who'd just hurt her far more than any number of sprained ankles could have done. 'It's easy to be wise after the event, isn't it, and you've no right to talk to me like that.'

'If I think you've been incredibly stupid and careless I'm not going to hold back. Have you no common sense? Don't you know that people die falling off ladders? And here you were, all on your own, risking your life. You could have lain there for hours, unable to get help.'

'Oh, bollocks!' she said, hoping the word would offend him. 'What an overreaction. I probably wouldn't have fallen off the bloody thing if you hadn't come in and startled me.'

'Don't go blaming me. That ladder had started to go before I came into the room—otherwise I'd have caught you before your ankle hit the floor. God! If only it hadn't taken me so long to find somewhere to park.'

Thea suddenly remembered the saying that you didn't get angry with people you didn't care about. And even if he didn't fancy her, he must be concerned for her welfare. She felt ashamed. But she was not ready to forgive him entirely—her pride and her feelings hurt more than her damn ankle did, which was saying something.

'Now,' he said, when he had finished binding her ankle, 'where are the rest of your clothes so I can drive you home? You won't be able to drive yourself for a bit.'

There was an anxious silence as Thea realised that she might not be able to drive. What with Lara and the puppies she'd never manage on public transport. 'I'm not planning to go home, not tonight,' she told him. 'I'm staying the night here, putting on coats of varnish whenever one dries, sleeping in between. I've got to get this floor done.'

'If you were varnishing the floor, what were you doing up a ladder with a pot of paint?'

'There was a bit of ceiling that got missed. I just thought I'd do it before I got to that bit of floor.' She summoned a carefree smile from somewhere. 'At least my hurt leg won't stop me varnishing.'

He opened his mouth to say all sorts of sensible things, but fortunately had the good sense not to. 'Then I'd better help you.'

She bit back a curt refusal. 'You don't have to. I expect you've got somewhere else to go.'

He shook his head. 'No. I came to see you. I wanted to see how things were going. I was in Bristol, having yet another interview, and I thought I'd catch up with you on the way home.'

Thea wasn't good at geography, but she was fairly sure that there were more direct ways back to London from Bristol than going via Cheltenham. He was probably planning to visit Molly, too. 'Where's Toby?'

'Staying with a friend. The friend he would usually have stayed with when I had to leave him with Molly.'

'Oh.'

'Thank you for looking after him that time. I heard all about you making pizzas and chocolate cake.'

'We had fun together. I really like Toby.'

A shadow of something, which might have been sadness or anger, flitted across his features.

Thea despaired. She couldn't even say she liked his son without some invisible code being violated. 'We'd better get on with this floor, then,' she said. 'I'll start cleaning up the paint. There are more rollers and things downstairs. Although you don't have to help if you don't want to. I'll manage.'

Before she could warn him, he had gone downstairs and she heard his exclamations as he met Lara and her puppies. He came up a few minutes later carrying a roller and a couple of brushes. 'What the hell is Lara doing there?'

'Rory left them with me. He's gone to London, to catch up on family, he said.' She frowned slightly, still worried about it.

Ben looked intently at her. 'Bloody inconsiderate.' He shrugged. 'Molly told me you're thinking about what to show after Rory. You should scour the colleges for promising talent. Have a graduate show.'

Thea's ankle was hurting, she was tired, Ben didn't want her and she might never get the bloody floor varnished. This whole art gallery thing was a crazy idea. 'Would I know promising young talent if it got up and bit me?' Her question sounded horribly plaintive.

'You recognised how good Rory's work was. I'll come with you. You pick who you like and I'll tell you if they've got talent or not.'

'You'd never have time to do that.'

'I would if I get this job in Bristol. I'll have far more autonomy.'

Thea allowed herself a sigh. It was still stinking hot.

'What's the matter?'

Thea bit her lip. 'I've just got a funny feeling about this trip of Rory's to London. I'm worried he might back out. I didn't let him have the slides or anything, so he's got nothing to show—only his charm to work with.' She sighed again. 'But that's not inconsiderable.'

There was the subtle change of expression again; something she'd said was wrong. 'I think you're wise not to trust him completely. Which is why it's important to have a plan B.'

'Oh, fuck it!' she said. 'I can't think about that now. Let's work. Put some music on and if you don't like my choice you can go home.'

At least the paint, being non-drip, hadn't spread too far, but the freshly sanded wood sucked it up. Thea had to scrub with sandpaper for ages to get the worst off.

She was very aware, as she sanded, that Ben could be looking at her bottom. She had debated putting her jeans back on, but the weather was so hot that bare legs gave her much more flexibility of movement. Besides, if she put on her jeans now, it would make some kind of statement, implying she wasn't decently dressed before. She hadn't been, of course, but it was too late to worry about that now.

She recalled his anger when he felt she'd been foolhardy. He had been very cross, far more cross than the situation warranted. The thought gave her a little breath of hope.

Chapter Six

THEA MANAGED TO WORK well enough with her bad ankle, and by keeping on the opposite side of the room from Ben, she stopped herself worrying about her rear end and his attitude to it. They finished the first coat quite quickly.

'You can still see where the paint was, though,' said Thea sadly. 'Should I get the sander back in, do you think?'

'No—a few more coats and that patch will disappear into the rest of it.'

'It was a silly thing to do. Now,' she went on brightly, because she didn't want Ben to start telling her off again, and hiding her fatigue and the sense of anticlimax, 'shall we get a takeaway or do you want to go? You've worked very hard. You deserve something to eat.' Too late she realised she was talking to Ben in the same way she talked to her lodgers: ever so slightly patronisingly.

His glanced flickered over her, not noticing her manner. 'I'll get the takeaway, seeing as you're not dressed. What would you like?'

'Whatever you can find, but you really don't have to stay. I can carry on on my own.'

'How will you get home? You're not really going to stay here all night?'

'I must. I've got to get that floor done and when I have, there are still two more rooms to prepare and that's not counting downstairs, where Lara is. I'm going to need every inch of space. I've got Rory's paintings but I'm still waiting for his drawings and sketches to come over from Ireland. The opening's less than six weeks away.'

She hadn't actually voiced her anxieties out loud before. She smiled, trying to pretend she had been joking. 'Actually, while you're here, you couldn't just take Lara out for me, could you? There's a bit of waste ground by the station.'

He stood looking down at her, where she sat on her chair, resting her ankle. She didn't look directly at him, but she was aware of his expression: exasperated, irritated and still a little angry. Eventually, he spoke. 'OK, fine. Have you got a lead?'

She nodded. 'And about a mile of kitchen towel in case she does anything.'

'Right. While I'm gone, think about what you want to eat, but don't get up. Or you won't be able to drive tomorrow either.'

While he was away, she limped to the loo and bravely looked in the mirror. Her hair was curling wildly all over the place, so she pulled at it with her fingers, washed her face in cold water, then had to put Molly's hand cream on it, because it felt so tight. She had no make-up with her, nor any scent, and she was wearing painting clothes. 'Give up, girlfriend,' she told her bedraggled reflection. 'He didn't want you when you were practically lying on a doily underneath him. He certainly won't want you now.'

This reality confronted, she limped downstairs to feed the puppies. Their little snuffling faces and scrabbling paws were incredibly endearing. It was nice to feel loved, even by things so small and young that didn't know any better.

After she had mashed their food and they had hoovered it up, she sat on the floor cuddling them. Who needed a man when she could have a puppy? She picked up Little Chap, the tiniest, and had a head-to-head conversation with him. After he had assured her that he was putting on weight, even if at a far slower rate than his chums, she lay down flat and let all the puppies clamber over her.

She was still lying there when Ben came back. 'How did you get down here? I thought I told you to rest?'

The puppy therapy had soothed her prickles and she felt much more relaxed. She smiled up at him. 'I am resting. I'm just not alone. Oh! Don't do that, little one.' Her ear, which had been gently nuzzled, suddenly received an investigative nip. 'I had to feed them,' she explained to Ben. 'Or they'd have eaten me.'

'I could have fed them for you.'

'Yes, but you wouldn't have brought them all upstairs for me to cuddle. Isn't Little Chap adorable?'

'I'm glad Toby didn't see them. Or he'd nag me about that, too.'

Thea decided not to follow this up, since it would be bound to get her into trouble. 'What takeaway did you decide you wanted? My bag's in the kitchen. Take some money before you go.'

'I think I can afford to buy some fish and chips without contributions from you.'

'Oh, come on! You've been working so hard for me all evening, it's only fair that I pay for supper. It's your wages, after all.'

Thea tried to get up. It wasn't easy. After she'd got herself free of puppies she struggled to her knees and had to accept a hand from Ben.

'I don't want wages.'

Thea didn't think she could offer him payment in kind in her present state of unloveliness so she gave up. 'Oh, well then, ask them if they do deep-fried Mars bars, will you? I'll have one of them as well.'

He brought fish and chips and cold lagers.

'Didn't they do Mars bars, then?' She'd never actually eaten a deep-fried Mars bar and thought they sounded disgusting, but she couldn't resist winding him up.

'They did, but I decided you shouldn't have one.'

She was indignant. 'How dare you make decisions for me! I'm not a child.'

'He who pays the piper calls the tune,' he said, and Thea realised she was being wound up in her turn. She cuddled a puppy, pretending to pout. 'We'll never get to eat these if we stay down here.' Gently, he removed a pup who had decided the smell of salt and vinegar was irresistible. 'Can you go back upstairs again, or do you want me to carry you?'

'I can crawl back up just fine, thank you.'

'Oh, good,' he said. 'Can I watch? I've got rather fond of the sight of your bottom.'

She found herself blushing. There was definite sexual innuendo in that remark. She contemplated telling him that if he were a gentleman he wouldn't look, but decided it might lead to all sorts of places she might not want to go. 'You take the fish and chips. I'll follow.'

'Are you sure? If I came behind, I could always give you a push if you needed one.'

'I'll give you a push if you're not careful,' she muttered.

She wished she'd put on her jeans, until she got upstairs and realised how hot it was. It had been blissfully cool in the basement, but now the full heat of the summer night hit her. 'God, it's hot up here,' she said, collapsing back into her chair.

'But it's a dry heat. The varnish should go off quickly. Now, what do you want? Cod or plaice?'

'Give me a cold can and whatever's nearest.' She opened the can and took a long cool draught. 'That is so good! I feel like an advertisement for the stuff.' She ate a piece of fish and suddenly found she was hungry.

'You were going to work all through the night?' he asked.

'I find it quite difficult to sleep in this heat,' she said with her mouth full, 'and what with lying on a hard floor with only a sleeping-bag, I didn't really think I'd do more than doze. I'd just listen to the World Service and lie there, picking my teeth. You're not eating. Was it something I said?'

He smiled and shook his head. 'Too hot.'

'What, the weather, or the chips?'

He ignored her question. 'You're very committed to this gallery, aren't you?'

She nodded. 'It's the first time in years I've really felt I'm doing the right thing. I mean, I loved doing the artistic side of the photography, but I was hopeless at the hard-nosed journalist bit. And even when I did it, it wasn't totally satisfying artistically. With this I feel I can really have fun.' She sighed. 'I just hope Rory doesn't pull out. At the moment I'm relying on him still hating the London art scene enough to stick with me.' She gave a little smile. 'Fingers crossed.'

'How would you feel if he did abscond, after all this work?'

'Terrible, but as it was me who wanted to do it, I can't really blame him. Which is why Molly and I've decided not to put all our eggs in

Rory's basket.' She took another thirst-quenching sip. 'At first, he was the reason I wanted to open a gallery, but now I've started doing all this I've realised what a waste it would be. Even if I could pay Molly back on what I earn from Rory, we can't just stop there.'

'So how is Molly involved?' He was frowning. Did he disapprove of his relation putting her money into a harebrained scheme?

'I couldn't get a mortgage in time to pay the deposit and things, so she's lent me the money. But she's also a sort of partner, because she's doing all sorts of admin. She's brilliant at it.'

'You don't find her too domineering?'

Thea shook her head. 'Derek told me—via her, actually—to channel her energies. It works a treat. She wanted Cotswold views and wild-flower watercolours. When she realised that I didn't and either she had to let me have artistic control or give up the gallery, she gave in.'

'It wouldn't have been a good idea to mortgage your house for some-thing so uncertain.'

'Well, thank you for your confidence! Actually, I might well sell it eventually, when I've got time to think about it.'

'But what about your lodgers? At least they're assured income.'

'You're such a pessimist. Property is cheaper here. I should be able to buy a nice little cottage with a garden and still have change from what I'd get for my present house. It probably won't happen until next year, although I should start doing it when the lodgers go home for the vac, only I've got the next show to sort out.'

'So how will you manage for money, when the lodgers go home?'

'You're very nosy.'

'Sorry. Of course, you don't have to tell me.'

She put down her fish-and-chip paper. 'Fortunately I'm not at all secretive and don't mind telling you, although if I started asking you such personal questions I expect you'd get very huffy.'

'I expect I would. So, how *will* you manage, without their money?'

'I used to have a job and I live cheaply. Not having them in the house saves a fortune in bills.'

'But you haven't got a job now.'

She smiled and made a sweeping gesture. 'I have my work.'

'But seriously—'

'Seriously, it's none of your business and you don't have to worry.'

'I worry about Rory letting you down. It would take ages for you to earn as much from anyone else.'

'I do wish you'd stop fussing. I am going to make a great success of this gallery. People will flock to it. They will buy paintings and they will pay a fortune to show their work in it. And if I think Rory's going to back out, I will go to Kilburn or wherever it is he's gone to in London and sort him out.'

'How will you do that?'

'On a train, I expect. Although I could take the coach.'

He humphed. 'I didn't mean that and you know it.'

Thea tried to look insouciant. 'I have my ways. Now, I must go to the loo. Lager always goes straight through me.'

Aware that this was a little more information than he wanted to hear, she hobbled past him. Alone, she felt despondency creep in. Ben had only been saying things and asking questions that she'd asked herself.

'What I need, of course,' she said a little later, getting into a corner with her varnish brush, 'is a rich husband.' The moment the words had left her mouth she regretted them. He would take them the wrong way whatever she said. 'I mean like Derek. He supports Molly in all sorts of mad projects. I might advertise. Anyone would do, as long as they were rich and indulgent.'

'It could be dull, being shackled to a man just because he was rich.'

'Then I'd take a lover, for entertainment.'

'Like Rory, for example?'

'Oh, yes. Perfect.' She paused for a few moments, wondering how she'd managed to talk herself into this situation. 'It's funny about fish and chips, but twenty minutes after I've eaten them, I always want them surgically removed. You wouldn't have a Rennie—or some sort of mint—about your person, would you?'

Later, Thea wanted to lie on her sleeping-bag and doze, but what would she do about Ben? 'Are you sure you don't want to go home?'

'I was going to be staying with Molly and it's too late to disturb her now. Why, do you want to get rid of me?'

'No, I just wanted to rest for a bit. We can't put on another coat for a couple of hours.'

'I'm tired myself.'

Thea exhaled in exasperation. 'OK, let's share the sleeping-bag. It's in the little room downstairs, but we'll have to tiptoe or we'll wake the puppies.'

Thea had opened out the sleeping-bag and had laid it in the corner of the room. She had brought a light blanket to put over her as she didn't want her limbs confined when it was so hot. Now, when she looked at it with Ben at her shoulder, she realised it looked like a love nest.

'I'm not sure I can share that space with you,' he said.

'Why not? It's a bit hard, but it'll do for a couple of hours.'

'I don't know how to put this . . .'

Thea wasn't going to help him out. She wanted him to say he wanted her, even if he didn't do anything about it.

'I don't have casual affairs.'

Thea was indignant. 'Neither do I!'

'You don't get it. I can't lie down there with you and not want to make love to you. Christ, Thea, you're half naked. You have been all night. I'm only human.'

'I'll put my jeans on. Would that help?'

'Only marginally.'

'This is silly. Surely we can lie down on the floor next to each other without'—how could she put it without sounding coarse?—'anything happening. Petal's lot often share beds platonically.'

She was suddenly too tired to go on arguing. She flung herself down on the sleeping-bag, in the space nearest the wall, and pulled the blanket over her. 'You can wander around all night watching the varnish dry, or lie down and rest, but I'm having a nap.'

He looked undecided.

'I don't know why you're making such a fuss about sharing a bed with me. Now either get in, or stay up, I don't care, but I'm going to sleep.' She turned on her side and pulled up the blanket, suddenly exhausted. Ben could take a running jump if he liked, as long as he didn't disturb her.

Later, she awoke and was aware of his dormant presence by her side. She lay still for a few moments, relishing his solidness and the sound of his breathing. It was a shame she needed the loo and would have to get out of bed, and somehow manage not to disturb him.

The easiest way would be to stand up and step over him, but although her ankle felt a lot better, she realised that if she tried to stand, she'd quite likely fall on top of him. She could crawl down to the bottom of the sleeping-bag and creep along by his feet. As long as they weren't sensitive this might work.

Her indecision must have disturbed him, because he suddenly turned over and put his arm round her waist.

She froze. It felt so good, so comforting, all she had to do was to shuffle backwards a bit and she'd be totally embraced . . .

He pulled her closer and nuzzled into the back of her neck.

It wouldn't do. She wanted him to make love to her while he was conscious, doing it on purpose. While he was asleep, thinking she was someone else, would not count. And his guilt would be unendurable.

Now his hands were on her rib cage, pushing upwards under the shirt. She cleared her throat. 'Ben. It's me, Thea. We're here varnishing the floor, remember?'

For a second or two he was bleary and confused. 'Thea? What? Oh my God, what did I do?'

'Nothing, it's all right. I'm just going to the loo.'

'Can you manage?'

'Of course.'

When she came back he said, 'I am so sorry. I thought you were someone else.'

'I know. Don't worry, it's a mistake anyone could make.' She smiled to hide her hurt. 'I'm going to put another coat on,' she went on. 'You stay here. If you're still sleepy you might as well sleep.'

'OK.'

Thea crawled back upstairs, wanting to cry. Rejected by Ben and now doing the floor by herself. It would take for ever and it would be no fun.

She'd just realised how like Petal she was sounding, when he joined her. 'I couldn't go back to sleep after all. Where's my roller?'

They didn't go back to bed again. They just worked through. They had four coats of varnish on by morning and Thea felt exhausted, more from the awkwardness between them than from the work and lack of sleep.

'So, shall we load up Lara and the puppies now?' Ben asked.

It was still early. Thea's ankle was hurting, although not as much, and she badly wanted to be at home. On the other hand, because she was tired, and despondent and irrational, she didn't want Ben driving her.

'Actually, Ben, I've got one or two things to do in town. I'll give Molly a ring later.' She glanced at her watch. It was still only seven o'clock. 'She'll come and give me a hand, if I find I can't drive.'

'I'm not happy about leaving you here like this.'

'You don't have to be happy about it. Just do it. I'll be fine. Really I will.' A whole lot more fine than if you stay looking down at me like that, as if I were a delinquent schoolgirl.

'Very well. But no more climbing on ladders if you're here alone. You could have been seriously injured.'

Thea put on an expression of mock contrition. 'Yes, Daddy.'

A spark lit the back of his eyes in a way she hadn't seen before. Too late she remembered that he was also tired and possibly frustrated.

'Daddy!' he said, in a dangerously quiet voice. 'Daddy, is it? I'll show you.'

His kiss was suitably punishing, hard, intense and intrusive. Thea closed her eyes. Even though it was anger that had motivated it, it was still extremely effective. At last he pulled away.

'Mm, that was nice,' said Thea foolishly. Then she stepped back, aware that she should have kept silent or at least been less flippant.

He glared down at her and Thea sensed that he wanted either to smack her or make violent love to her, or both. She also knew that he blamed her entirely for making him feel such primitive emotions.

He sent volts of silent fury at her and then flung himself out of the door. Thea watched him march down the road, half wishing she'd had the courage to push him beyond the limits of his civilised boundaries.

Two days later Thea received a phone call. It was Ben, as brisk and as 'nothing whatever happened between us' as possible: 'How's your ankle?'

'Fine.'

'Good. Now the reason I rang is I've got a couple of days winding up business with clients and I have to go to, or near, quite a lot of places which have art colleges. You'd better come and see the graduate shows that are on.'

Oh, to be a man and able to compartmentalise one's life so simply! What had nearly happened in the gallery was obviously filed under 'momentary aberrations'. Looking at graduate shows with Thea probably qualified as 'charity work'.

Thea put on her new assertive voice. 'I really haven't got time to go gadding about the country looking at art. I've still got to do something about the floor in the basement.'

He made a sound which could have been a chuckle. 'You haven't got time not to come. You need to be thinking about your next show.'

'Oh. OK. I suppose you're right. But it doesn't involve any overnight stays, does it? I've got no one to look after Lara and the pups.'

'Will Molly come in and see to them during the day?'

'I expect so.' She would if you asked her, Ben, she said silently, hoping he could hear. 'She's not really a dog person, though.'

'I'll have a word. If I explain how important it is for the gallery she won't mind.'

Yes! He might be an insensitive brute in some ways, but in others he was perfect.

Although, when Molly rang her later to confirm details, Thea wondered what on earth Ben had said. 'There's nothing funny going on between you and Ben, is there?'

Thea went hot and cold. 'What do you mean, "nothing funny"?'

'Nothing specific, it's just when he mentioned you he sounded a bit— well, brisk.'

'He always is, isn't he?' Brisk was OK. Molly couldn't read anything into brisk.

'Well, I don't know. But honestly, Thea, he's a very organised, controlled sort of person and you're—'

'Not his type?'

'Not really. When his wife was there their house made mine feel I had to rush out and get in an interior designer. And after the first girlfriend he had tried to mother Toby, he's never gone out with anyone who's remotely maternal. Or over a size eight,' she added.

Well, that's me put in my place, size fourteen if I'm a day and desperately maternal, even if I haven't got any children of my own. Aloud she said, 'Well, enough idle chatter. Do you mind coming in to see to Lara and the pups on the days I'm away all day?'

'No, that's fine. My cleaning lady's going to do it. She loves dogs and is very obliging, and she can do extra hours for me.'

Ben picked her up at ten o'clock two days later. It was pouring with rain. 'I've got a list of what degree shows are on. There's one in Winchester you ought to visit. I've got a couple of clients to see, so I'll drop you off at the art school and you can have a look around.'

'But, Ben, I don't know anything about art. You were going to help me choose. You said!'

'I seem to have said a lot of things I don't mean lately.'

Thea didn't have time to work this one out. 'You definitely said you'd help me choose work. You can't let me down. This is the gallery at stake here.'

'I don't want to let you down, but it has to be your taste.'

Thea realised, not for the first time, what an enormous undertaking she had made. 'But I might choose all the wrong people; we might never sell a thing. Oh God! Why did I have this stupid art gallery idea in the first place?'

'Something to do with Rory?' He glanced across at her, somehow implying that Rory had charmed her into it. 'But now you have had the idea you've got to persevere with it, if only to keep Molly happy.'

'I'm not doing it just for Rory and it's not just a whim. I really want this gallery to work and not only to keep Molly happy, either.' Her resentment at his implication that her gallery was some sort of distraction for idle women bubbled up. 'But if ever you find giving us advice and support too much trouble, just say. We can manage perfectly well without you.'

Ben frowned. 'I never meant to imply I objected to helping you. I just want you to be able to do this on your own, without being dependent on anybody. Tell you what, when you've chosen all the artists you're interested in—and you won't be able to get hold of some of them, and others will baulk at paying a fee, however small—I'll have a look at the postcards, or the slides, or whatever you've got with you.'

'I'm going to take pictures of anything I like, to make sure I don't only choose one type of work.'

He smiled the rare, wonderful smile that transformed his whole persona. 'You're not a complete idiot, are you?'

Thea decided not to comment. She'd only say something she'd regret.

Ben left her in a strange street in a strange town and told her that the art school was on the corner to the left. She reached it and eventually found herself in the middle of a huge, galleried space, full of works of art.

There were not many people about, and it was nice to be able to wander round on her own, though at first she thought she didn't like anything. Then, suddenly, she turned a corner and found an installation which made her laugh out loud.

It was a kitchen, cooker, fridge and microwave, only everything was made from tooth-rot-pink plastic, and covered with sequins and diamanté. Lace curtains served as the microwave's door, the cooker's hot plates were made from doilies, but on inspection it turned out that they were ceramic. The longer she looked, the more surprises she found—the black velvet washing-up gloves with fingers covered with rings, a lurex washing-up brush, plastic goldfish floating in the washing-up bottle, which was filled with glycerine soap, and cooker knobs made from icing. She was chuckling to herself when a tall, elegant, extremely pretty girl appeared.

'Is this your work?' asked Thea. 'I absolutely love it! I want to show it in my gallery.'

The tall, elegant, pretty girl threw herself into Thea's arms.

Cheered by this, Thea went round the rest of the show having decided that unless the work made her respond as strongly as the Barbie Kitchen had she wouldn't consider it. She had to feel passionate about everything in her gallery. Even if she didn't particularly like it, she had to admire it and feel it really was good.

She slept as Ben drove her home. She had a bag full of artists' post-cards, business cards and addresses, and three rolls of used film. She had picked far more than she would need from just one art school, but she wanted to have plenty to choose from the first time.

At the beginning of the day she'd wanted Ben to be with her and take responsibility. Now she didn't want him disparaging her selection. When she'd got all the work in, she might show him. Or she might not.

He commented on her reticence two days later, when he took her north to Leeds. 'At first you wanted me to come in with you to hold your hand. Now you won't even tell me about the work.'

'Once I'd realised you were right about me needing to decide on my own, I didn't want anyone else's opinion clouding my judgment.' She bit her lip and turned away so he wouldn't see her smile.

Their last trip was to Cornwall. Ben collected her very early in the morning. 'I wasn't expecting you to be ready,' he said, when Thea appeared, brushed, made-up and eager to go. 'I thought no woman could get dressed in under two hours.'

Thea gave him a disparaging look. 'You don't know many real women, do you, Ben?'

'Sorry—I apologise for my assumption.' He glanced at her. 'Two hours or ten minutes, the effect is . . . charming.'

Well, it was a compliment of sorts, but 'charming'! Couldn't he have said 'ravishing' or 'gorgeous'—or something sexier?

A couple of days after their last trip together, Thea was determined to have an early night. Her house was now a student-free zone, and she had just put an egg on to boil when the phone rang. She silently cursed. She would get whoever it was to ring back. It might well be Rory. Fine father of puppies he was! Not even a single tin of dog food had he sent for them.

It was Toby.

'Dad's out. I've got a baby sitter. We've been watching videos.' A pause. 'I just wanted a chat.'

'It's a bit late, isn't it?'

'Sorry.'

'Oh, well, I suppose it's Friday. But can I ring you back? I'm just boiling an egg and I hate them too hard.'

Thea mashed the egg onto toast and cut it into bits so she could eat it with one hand. She felt dreadfully clandestine dialling Ben's number, because she was quite sure Ben would be furious if he knew Toby had rung her. But on the other hand she and Toby had a relationship which was quite separate and a lot more satisfactory than hers with Ben.

Toby was quite a long time coming to the phone. The answering machine cut in and Thea was about to leave a quick message and ring off when Toby picked up. 'Oh, hi,' he said.

'It's me, Thea. Shouldn't you be in bed? I know I should be.'

'I always find it really hard to get to sleep when Dad's out. He's with a woman.'

It sounded awful, as if the woman were a prostitute or something. 'You shouldn't tell me things like that; he might not want me to know.' *And I don't want to know about the size ten models he's escorting round London, either.*

'Oh, but I must. We've just been watching this film where a little boy rings up a radio station, trying to find a wife for his dad.'

'I know the one.' If Ben found out about this, that baby sitter would never work again.

'Donna said I should ring you.'

'Well, you shouldn't. I mean, of course you can ring me for a chat, but you mustn't start matchmaking.'

'What's that?'

'Trying to get people together with other people. People want to find their own people. You probably wouldn't like it if someone said, "Go and play with Tommy, he's a really nice little boy and you've got lots in common."'

'Teachers do that all the time.'

'Oh. Well, isn't it irritating?'

'Yes, but this is important. I mean Dad goes out with these women that he chooses and they're crap!'

'Toby!' It was probably the baby sitter again. They had a lot to answer for . . .

'He doesn't choose anyone I like.'

'Why should he? He's a free agent.'

'What?'

'I mean, he can go out with who he likes. You don't have to like them.'

'But I do if they're going to be my stepmother.'

'Well, of course, that would be different—'

'And the women he chooses would be crap as mothers.'

Thea, not at all certain of the parentally approved way to proceed, cleared her throat. 'You have a mother, Toby, and she's special to you. No one your dad went out with, or married or anything, would ever be as good as her.' Thea was proud of herself. She sounded adult and sensible, like an agony aunt.

'But my mother's no good as a mother. I mean, she doesn't make cakes.'

Thea took a bite of toast and crunched it to give herself time to plan her reply. 'There's a whole lot more to being a mother than making cakes. Even I know that.'

'But we have cake sales at school. I want to bring a cake to one. And it's not just the cakes. It's the being there when I come home from school. My friend's mum is always there at home time. It's cool!'

'It probably is, but lots and lots of mothers work. They have to—'

'I want you to be my mother . . . stepmother. You're cool. I want to have a mum who *cooks*.'

'But I don't cook all the time,' she explained. 'Lots of times I just do boiled eggs.' She took another bite of hers. 'And lots of people would like to have a mother who was beautiful and had a glamorous job, who took you to nice places.' As she knew very little about Toby's mother it was hard for her to stress her good points, but she did her best.

'But I want a motherly mother as well.'

Exasperation was creeping in. 'That's greedy. And, lovey, even if you had me as a stepmother, it wouldn't all be cooking pizzas and chocolate cake. It would mostly be all "do your homework" and "have you brushed your teeth?". I may not know much about parenting, but I do watch *Neighbours*.' Trying to divert him a little, she added, 'What does it mean when they say "you're grounded"?'

'It means you can't go out.'

'Well, there you go. That's what sort of a stepmother I'd be, learning how to do it from Australian soap operas.'

'Why are they called "soap operas"?'

'It's a long story. Years and years ago, in America . . .'

But Toby had lost interest. Thea heard a muffled conversation going on in the background. The baby sitter doing her duty at last and putting him to bed. 'Donna says,' said Toby loudly, 'the important thing is, do you like my dad?'

Thea was tired. She'd done her best and, with half an ounce of luck, Toby wouldn't read anything into it. She sighed. 'Yes, Toby. I like your dad. He's a very nice kind man who's helped me a lot.' Hoping this sounded suitably platonic, she tried to end the call, but heard more whispering.

'Do you like him "like that"?'

'I really don't know what you mean, Toby. Now it's late and I do think you should go to bed.' Hoping she sounded a sufficiently cruel step-mother to make Toby feel glad she wasn't his, she added, 'Now, good night. Oh, and, Toby—'

'Yes?' He sounded a little hurt and Thea felt dreadful.

'Don't tell Ben about this conversation. I don't think he'd like it.'

He didn't like it. And it hadn't helped that it had been recorded on the answering machine. He was furious when he rang Thea the following night. 'What do you mean by encouraging Toby in this nonsense about a stepmother?'

'Excuse me! I made it very clear that although we'd had a very nice evening together, it wouldn't be like that all time.'

'Did it occur to you that you shouldn't have discussed it with him at all?'

'Yes—no—' Thea exhaled sharply. 'What was I to do? I tried to stop him—or explain. I did my best.'

'And does your "best" include telling my son to deceive me?'

'I never—'

'Oh yes you did! It's on the tape quite clearly. "Don't tell Ben about this, he wouldn't like it."'

'Well, I was right there, wasn't I?'

She slammed the handset down and indulged in a glass of wine, a few tears and a packet of chocolate biscuits. It didn't help at all.

Thea had got half of the downstairs carpet up, and was wondering if she'd ever fit it into her car to take to the tip, when Petal called down the stairs, 'Hi! Are you there? I've brought Dave over to have a look at the space. He's in the third year, so he'll want to be in your next year's graduate show.'

Oh, the confidence of youth! Thea wasn't certain of anything happening next year, except perhaps Christmas. 'How nice.'

'And the phone man's here. And I brought a letter for you from home. It's from Rory.'

Thea dropped the carpet and went upstairs. She snatched the letter from Petal as she passed and greeted the telephone man.

Only when he was happily muttering about junction boxes and extra lines, and Petal had made tea, did Thea take out the letter and open it. A cheque fell out of it.

'Shit! Shit! Shit! Shit! Shit! Shit!' she said loudly. 'Oh, sorry, everyone. But this is dreadful. Fucking—sorry, Petal—Rory!'

'What? What's happened?' Petal was worried. Thea rarely swore and hearing her do it now was alarming.

'I'll read it to you!

'*Dear Thea,*

I'm sorry if this is disappointing news for you, but I've decided that I really must show my work in London first. I've got a gallery really interested and they've advanced me some money! I enclose a cheque and I'd be grateful if you'd arrange to have my pictures sent to this address asap.

'And the address is just for someone's house, not a gallery, so I don't know where he's intending to show. He seems to have forgotten that he already owes me money for the framing! This is intolerable. And what I want to know is how he managed to get a gallery interested when he didn't have any slides.'

'But he did have slides,' said Petal, surprised. 'I sent them to him.'

'You *what*?'

'He rang one night and said you'd said you'd put them in the post, but as he hadn't had them, he thought you'd forgotten.'

'Forgotten on purpose. I didn't want him to have them!'

'Well, I didn't know that. I thought I was being helpful when I posted them to him. They were of his pictures, after all.'

'They were my slides! Thank God I can get copies. But anyway, why didn't you tell me you'd sent them?'

'I forgot.' Petal's mouth began to quiver. 'I didn't know I'd done wrong. I thought I'd done you a favour. He said you'd promised.'

Thea dimly remembered some conversation wherein she'd said she'd send slides when they were back from the printers, but she'd never meant to do it. Apart from Lara, whom she didn't think he cared about, they were her only bargaining chip. Now she'd lost it. 'It's all right, Petal. I should have told you I didn't want Rory to have the slides.'

'But why didn't you?' asked Dave.

'Because I want to show his work here first. If no one in London knows how great he is, I've got a better chance of keeping him.'

'So, is the show off, then?' asked Petal. 'Aren't you going to have a gallery now?'

Thea took a breath so she wouldn't take a swing at Petal. 'Yes, I *am* going to have a gallery now. I have not gone through all this time and effort, and Molly's expense, setting it up, not to have one now. And what is more, Rory's work is going to be on show on the appointed night. I've got his paintings. If he wants them, he's got to come and get them!'

'But he's sent you the money to send them. You can't just keep it!'

'Yes, I can.' Thea glanced down at the cheque. 'He owes me far more than this.'

'So, what are you going to do?' Petal's expression had become pained.

'I'm going to go to London to sort that Rory out!'

Chapter Seven

THEA WAS STARING into her wardrobe, trying to decide which of her clothes were the least shabby, when Molly phoned to tell her she'd found the perfect puppy solution. 'Well, almost perfect, anyway. It's two young men. Pet sitters. They come into your home and look after your pets, water your plants and things.' There was a tiny pause. 'I didn't dare ask if they were gay. It wouldn't have been politically correct.'

'No. And not really relevant, either, as it's out of the question. It would cost an arm, a leg and the whole damn torso besides.'

'Don't be disgusting. It's the only sensible solution and I'm paying. Who else could you get, for goodness' sake? The firm do stringent police checks and things, so they should be utterly reliable.'

Thea sighed. 'As long as they know what they're taking on.'

'Oh, yes. Apparently they're quite used to puppies and large dogs. In fact, they've just lost a Great Dane and will adore Lara. It's perfect.' Molly sounded more than usually pleased with herself.

'Not quite.'

'Well, what's wrong with it? Your dogs are going to be given first-class care. What's your problem?'

'It means I've got to tidy my house. If I had a student to do it for me, I could just pack up and go!'

Thea decided she'd clean for an hour and anything that wasn't cleaned in that time could just stay dirty.

She set the kitchen timer and swooped and swiped and banged the Hoover about, stuffed things under cushions and flung bedspreads and tablecloths over piles of boxes. The timer pinged just as she'd blocked the Hoover, trying to vacuum up a sock. 'Oh, well,' she said, switching off the offending appliance and kicking it into the cupboard under the stairs, 'if they need to use it, they'll have to sort it out first.'

Her packing was necessarily speedy. Although rushed, Thea had plenty of time to regret the clothes she'd given away before she'd left London. Those black jersey trousers, for instance, which gave her freedom of movement and relative smartness.

When she'd dealt with her packing as well as she could, she dithered over whether she should bring the file of material for the graduate show. It would be great to discuss it when she went to stay with Magenta. She had a good eye and a better idea of what was current, or 'hot'.

But it was of Ben she thought, as she flattened her carefully ironed clothes with the folder. What would he think of the video?

She'd fallen in love with it. It was of a patch of white willowherb, and the seeds had turned into silken fluff. Every so often a puff of wind would blow the seeds high up into the air, sending them up and around, catching the light as they flew.

Molly had been very sniffy about her having a video. 'But who will buy them?' she had asked when Thea had shown her.

'No one will buy them. But the artists might be asked to do an MA somewhere, or win a prize. This gallery isn't just about making money.'

'As if,' said Molly, sounding very like Petal.

The two young men were charming. They admired the original features in the house, didn't look sniffily at the traces of student, which were everywhere, and fell in love with Lara and the puppies.

Thea left them lying on the kitchen floor bonding with the puppies, happy that her charges were in such good hands.

Once on the train, after cursing herself for forgetting her mobile phone, Thea found herself feeling quite excited about her trip to London. Although she was furious with Rory for defecting, the thought of a little time away from the combined pressures of the gallery, the puppies and her confused emotions put her in a 'let out of school' mood.

Magenta was waiting for her at the end of the platform.

'Darling! You didn't need to meet me! I could have just got a cab. Or even the tube—'

Ignoring Thea's protests, and apologies, Magenta ushered her into a taxi. 'Now,' she said. 'Tell me, do you just want to concentrate on finding this Rory guy, or do you want to see some art as well? I mean, you didn't have much time to research this gallery idea. Perhaps you ought to see what other people are doing.'

Thea was tempted. She desperately needed to find Rory, but it would be silly to waste all her time in London's hottest art galleries looking for that ingrate. It would be nice to look at a few pictures as well.

'I tell you what,' said Magenta, 'I won't take you anywhere that will be of no use at all, but I will drag you to some of the more up and coming places that are really important.'

It seemed easier just to let Magenta take charge. What was it about her personality, Thea wondered, that made people want to organise her? Molly, Magenta, Petal, they were all at it. 'Fine.'

'I'm glad you decided to go with what I've got planned. It's a fabulous schedule that will blow you away. Have you got comfortable shoes on?'

Thea only needed a very short time to change into Petal's discarded trainers, brush her hair and demolish half a litre of fizzy water, so they were back in another cab less than half an hour later. When she protested about the expense, Magenta would have none of it.

'I'm working. I'll set the cab fares off against tax. Now, did you bring your portfolio?'

'If you mean that folder with a lot of postcards, Rory's slides, some brochures, and a dubious video, then yes. Although I left it in your flat.'

'Good. I've got a friend you can show it to tomorrow. If he approves, you'll know it's OK.'

Thea looked down at her feet and examined Petal's trainers. 'I thought I had a friend like that, too.'

'But you haven't now?'

Although Thea had deliberately made it impossible for Magenta to see her expression, she must have betrayed something in her voice. 'Well, I expect I've still got him as a friend. In fact, he's been great. Really helpful.'

'But you'd like something more than friendship, right?'

'Mm.'

'Tell me about him. We've got a while before we arrive at number five hundred and six. It's out near the Dome.'

'It won't take long. He thinks I'm a complete idiot.'

'Where did you meet him?'

Aware that she'd had no one to talk to about Ben, Thea relaxed into it. 'In my kitchen. I was standing in a rubbish bin at the time. I think it set the whole tone of our relationship.'

'So, when did you fall in love with him?'

'Well, I didn't know it at the time, but it must have been when I saw him deliver a litter of puppies.'

'Thea! I'll never leave you to your own devices again! What in hell have you been up to?'

'Not as much as I would have liked.'

'I hate to say this.' Thea pulled off her shoes and eased her hot feet on the cold marble. 'But I think I'm galleried out. How many have we seen?'

'Only half a dozen and I'm afraid I'm going to have to leave you to do the last one on your own. I've got a hair appointment.'

'Lucky you. Can't I come with you? I've seen so much art, so many galleries and not a sniff of Rory.' Thea was very tired and on the verge of becoming deeply depressed. 'It might be best just to forget about him and carry on with the degree show.'

'You can't give up now! I'm really into this guy now you've told me so much about him. And even though I've only had time to glance at his slides, they seem great.'

'Mm. Imagine them twenty times the size, or whatever.' Thea cast her mind back to when she had first dragged Rory's paintings out onto the Irish hillside and had seen them properly. The same prickles of excitement she had had then now stirred the hairs at the back of her neck once again. No, she had to be the one to bring his work to the eyes of the world. She'd earned the privilege.

'Let's go and find him,' she said.

Thea was quite relieved that Magenta had left for her hair appointment. She wanted to be an ordinary punter looking at art. She could ask questions later.

She found the last gallery quite easily, down a side street at the back of Harrods. From the outside she thought it looked far too small for Rory's work, but once inside the space was much larger than it had appeared, and wonderfully cool after the heat and dust outside. She heard voices and followed the sign to the exhibition upstairs. She could investigate the ground floor and find the owner later.

It was, she realised, the first gallery of the many they had seen that she actually envied. None of the other spaces, or the way the work had been arranged, had inspired her like this one. In some ways it was a relief. She had begun to think that she was too jealous of other galleries to judge them fairly. In this one, she knew she was looking at true class.

The work was an eclectic mix of paintings, ceramics and three-dimensional pieces. She didn't like all of it by any means, but she did respect it and felt that if art had been required always to please the eye it would never have progressed beyond tasteful paintings of children playing with puppies.

Some of the work she loved. There were wonderful paintings composed of the purest pigments, red so intense that from some angles it looked black, scored with a slash of a palette knife so the paper beneath was revealed. Others were blue-black, the night sky distilled and intensified into a three-foot square. This was the standard she was aiming for and she didn't want anything less good in her gallery.

The voices still murmured on, but she couldn't see the speakers because they were through in another section. Then she heard a familiar laugh and knew she'd found her quarry.

If this was the gallery Rory had found there was some sort of comfort in the fact that he had chosen such a wonderful one to abandon hers for. While she was still hurt, not to mention furious, at least she'd been left for a class act.

She had to think carefully how to approach him. After all, what could she say? Stamping her foot and telling the gallery owner that it wasn't fair, Rory had promised to show in her space first, wouldn't cut any ice.

It was her passion for Rory's work and the memory of her first sight of it that gave her the courage to pursue the matter. But what argument could she possibly offer Rory to make him change his mind?

Thea was about to go and confront him, hoping something halfway sensible would come to her, when another woman came in. She walked straight past her to where Rory and the owner were talking. Damn! Pratfalls were all very well, but Thea would have preferred to take hers without extra spectators.

The woman obviously knew Rory. Thea could hear the air kisses from where she was. Rory laughed again. It was, she had to acknowledge, a very sexy laugh and, judging by the laugh the woman gave in return, she thought so too.

Thea moved closer. She was well within sight, so it wasn't really eavesdropping.

'So, Rory, when are you going to let Edward have the paintings? He can't plan a show without them. Can you?' the woman said.

The man murmured something and everyone laughed again.

Thea wished she'd got a better look at the woman, or could see her now. But at least she knew that this was indeed the gallery in question, and it gave her some satisfaction that the pictures they wanted were in hers. Possession, after all, was nine-tenths of the law. In theory, anyway.

'I did explain.' Rory sounded apologetic. 'It is a little difficult. I promised this woman I'd show with her first.'

'You really don't need to worry about that,' the woman was soothing yet adamant. 'After all, she isn't anybody. No one would expect you to keep your word made in those circumstances. I mean, she may have got you to show your work to her, but that doesn't give her any rights to it whatsoever.'

'Well—'

'She didn't buy any of it, did she?' This time the voice was edged with irritation.

'She did pay to have the drawings and sketches framed.'

Well, thank you, Rory, for remembering, thought Thea.

'Then all you need to do is pay her back for the framing. A cheque will do it. You don't have to hide your work away as well.' Her voice became cooing and Thea was willing to bet she was now holding on to Rory in some way.

Thea began to shift uncomfortably. If she didn't reveal herself soon, it would get to the stage when she couldn't.

Just as she was plucking up the courage to say something ingenuous like 'Oh, hello, Rory, I didn't know you were here', to her enormous surprise she saw Toby and a young woman ascending the stairs from the gallery below. This was somehow a greater shock than coming across

119

Rory. In the nick of time she stepped behind an elevated circulating fridge and avoided being seen.

The couple reached the first floor, and Toby moved to the woman and said in a polite but strangely unenthusiastic voice, 'Hello, Veronica.'

Thea felt blood rush up through her body and sweat broke out at her hairline. Don't panic, she ordered herself. Veronica could be anyone; she doesn't have to be his mother. It's quite a common name—probably.

But 'Veronica' put out her arm and pulled Toby to her. 'Hello, darling. I see you're wearing that new shirt I bought you. It might look better tucked in.' There was no doubt. Only a mother or a teacher would tell a boy to tuck his shirt in.

This was the moment. She moved from behind the suspended fridge and cleared her throat. 'Hello,' she said, wishing she could think of something less banal.

'Thea!' said Toby and Rory at the same time.

It was Toby's presence that kept Thea calm. She couldn't shout and scream and throw things with him there. It wouldn't be fair.

'I'm sorry? Do I know you?' asked Veronica icily.

'This is Thea, the woman who made me get my work out of the shed,' said Rory. He seemed extremely put out.

Thea glanced at Toby. After his initial delighted greeting, he now seemed reluctant to look at her. Thea began to feel more and more certain that something very untoward was going on.

'Oh!' said Veronica. 'So you're the one.' She came forward, hand outstretched. 'I've heard such a lot about you.'

Thea took the hand, which was cool and hard, and at the same time took a good look at its owner. She was aggressively thin, attractive, though not pretty, and had that high-maintenance gloss which made it hard to tell her age.

'Sorry,' said Thea, 'I don't know your name.' *Even if I do know, perfectly well, who you are.*

'Veronica de Claudio. I discovered Rory.' Veronica smiled. She smelt strongly of some sophisticated perfume and her clothes were the sort Thea wouldn't know how to wear, even if she could fit into them. Layers of silk, trousers, a floor-length waistcoat and a sort of embroidered panel across her concave stomach which showed her hips were no more than six inches from point to point.

'Really?' Thea inclined her head graciously. 'I thought I did that.'

Veronica's eyes narrowed with pleasure. She gave Thea the sort of smile people give when delivering bad news that actually delights them. 'Oh, I was way ahead of you. I saw Rory's graduate show and his subsequent exhibition. In Cork Street.'

'Oh?' The implications of this announcement were many and Thea's stomach was beginning to churn alarmingly.

'It was stunning, absolutely stunning.'

'I thought the critics panned it,' said Thea.

'Oh, they did. And rightly so. Rory's work was far too immature and his behaviour at the show even more so. I told Maxim . . . you know? Maxim Applozzia? You must have heard of him—he's got three galleries in New York and is opening here next year?'

Thea nodded, hoping her ignorance wasn't as obvious to everyone else as it was to her.

'I told Maxim to take it all down, close the show. Rory just wasn't ready to exhibit.'

The nausea which had been threatening now seemed a real possibility. She didn't trust Veronica, but parts of her story were probably true—possibly all of it was. But why in God's name had Ben never said a word about his wife's part in Rory's downfall? 'Oh, really?' she said tightly. 'I'd heard Rory's story, of course, but he didn't mention your part in it.'

'Oh, he probably wasn't aware of my part in it.' She laughed gaily. 'The poor boy was in no state to be aware of anything—'

'Except that his show had been taken off and the critics had completely disparaged it.'

Veronica decided to take some time with this woman, who obviously was a little slow. 'Darling, Thea? Interesting name. I don't think you understand. The critics may have given Rory a very hard time, but that doesn't mean they didn't admire his work. They just thought it immature. I knew that in a few years he'd mature beautifully—'

'Which? Rory, or his paintings?'

'And of course, while we're terribly grateful that you found him for us in Ireland, you were only just a few steps ahead of us. Edward and I had put out a lot of feelers and were about to track him down.'

And the 'feeler's' name was Ben Jonson, without an 'h', like the poet. Thea began to shake, aware that she was suffering from shock.

Veronica went on, 'Of course, we will give you a credit in the catalogue, won't we, Edward? That would only be fair.'

Thea knew she had to get out of there and soon, or she'd vomit over Veronica's Manolo Blahniks. 'I think I need to talk to Rory about being fair. Would you give me a moment, Rory? Outside?' Her teeth were beginning to chatter.

Rory, looking shifty and embarrassed, was only too willing to follow Thea downstairs and into the street.

The sweet, dirty smell of a city when it's about to rain was refreshing after the powerful odour of Veronica's scent. Thea stood breathing deeply, trying to fight the physical symptoms of shock; she had been totally and utterly shafted by everyone. At that moment she could have suspected even Petal and Molly of being in on the act.

'Where would you like to go?' he asked.

'I don't want to go anywhere! I just want you to tell me why, when you never intended to show in my gallery, you let me go to all the trouble and expense of setting one up.'

He looked down at her and put his hand on her shoulder. 'Would you like to go to a pub or something? Somewhere we can talk.'

'No. I have to stay in the fresh air for a bit.'

'Let's find a park or something.'

'God, Rory! Can't you just tell me you've sold me down the river here and now? Or, being an artist, do you need some goddamn sylvan setting?' She set off down the street so fast that she could hardly avoid the oncoming pedestrians.

Rory hurried after her. 'OK, forget the park. Slow down, please.'

Thea couldn't slow down. She had to work off the adrenaline she could feel rushing through her veins, filling her with panic.

Rory took hold of her arm in an effort to calm her.

Thea ignored it but let it stay. 'So tell me. Did you ever mean to show with me?'

Just then a terrific clap of thunder deafened the world and rain, warm and hard, came down on them.

'Jesus, Thea, this is ridiculous! Come inside somewhere.'

'No! Why don't you just tell me the truth? I want to hear it from you, personally, the artist I've turned my life upside-down for!'

They were both drenched remarkably quickly. Thea was wearing only a long cotton skirt and a little vest top. In seconds even her underwear was soaking and she watched Rory's magnificent torso appear as the rain plastered his T-shirt to his body. 'Well?' She stopped on a street corner, ignoring rain and hurrying people alike.

'It wasn't like it seems! I'd—'

'*Thea!*'

She turned.

'Thea! You went so fast I could hardly keep up with you!'

'Toby! Darling!' He was drenched, his fine hair plastered to his head, and he was shivering violently. To crouch down and wrap him in her arms was entirely instinctive. 'What are you doing here?'

'I wanted to stop you running away.'

Thea, huddled on the pavement, still holding the shaking child, wanted to cry.

'I wasn't exactly running away, I wanted to talk to Rory, but it must have looked like that.' It had felt like that, too: escaping from Veronica's cloying scent, her glamour, the elegant gallery which had seemed to mock everything she'd done in the last two months.

'I'm so glad I've found you. Dad would have been so cross if you'd got lost or anything.'

Thea straightened up. She didn't think Ben would give a toss—if he could betray her as he had done, why would he care if she took a few wrong turnings and ended up miles from anywhere? 'Well, I haven't, so that's all right. Now, which way back to the gallery?'

Rory shrugged. The rain was still beating down.

'Which way, Toby?' Rory asked. 'You're the Londoner.'

'I don't live in Knightsbridge,' Toby said.

'I can't believe this!' Thea said. 'We can't have got so far away that we can't find our way back.'

'You were going at a hell of a lick, Thea.'

'So we are lost, after all?' asked Toby after they had all looked up and down the streets, searching for clues as to their whereabouts.

'It certainly seems that way.' She sighed. 'Well, never mind, we'll get a taxi and give the gallery's address. It's not really a problem. If we walk up to the crossroads, we've a better chance of getting one.'

'It's always hard to get a taxi when it's raining,' said Toby, after trying to spot an orange light on top of one of the many taxis that were speeding past them.

Thea had a belated thought. 'I suppose we should ring the gallery and tell them we've got Toby. His mother will be out of her mind. Have you got a mobile, Rory?'

'No. Haven't you?'

She bit her lip. 'No. I left it at home. I was in a hurry to get to London.'

'So, why did you come to London?'

'Why do you think?' she hissed, clutching Toby's hand like a lifeline. 'And I can't talk about it now!'

By the time they found their way back to the gallery, it was closed.

Thea rattled the door in frustrated disbelief. 'They can't just close it. They must have known we'd come back with Toby. Veronica must be beside herself with anxiety.'

'My nanny will be more worried, I expect.' Toby began to look nervous himself.

'It's all right, Toby,' Thea soothed. 'We'll sort it out. Where's Ben at the moment? Up here, or down in Bristol?'

'Here.'

'Were you going to go home with Veronica?'

Toby shook his head. 'No. She's too busy to see me this weekend, which is why we visited her at the gallery.'

'Then why didn't she stay there? Now we must think what's the best thing to do. Should we go back to your house, Toby? Or Veronica's?'

'Mine, but it's miles away.'

'Then why in God's na—I mean, then why did you visit Veronica at the gallery if it's miles away from where you live?'

Toby shrugged. 'I think she thought it would be fun for us, coming on the bus.'

'You don't remember which bus, Tobe?' asked Rory. 'We could get one back.'

'We had to change. It took ages.'

'Well, I've had enough. I'm going to lie down in the road outside Harrods until a taxi stops.'

'But, Thea,' protested Toby as he was pulled along behind her, 'they won't see you if you're lying down.'

Well,' said Rory a few moments later. 'I was a bit shocked by the way you pushed that old lady aside, Thea.'

'I didn't push her and she wasn't old. She was warm and dry, and had just indulged in a lot of retail therapy. Our need was the greater.'

'It'll cost an awful lot to go by taxi all the way to my house,' said Toby, who had given the address to the driver.

'Too late to think about that now, old man.'

'And even if it wasn't,' said Thea, 'I'd have still got in.'

Toby sighed. 'Do you think everyone will be dreadfully cross?'

'I expect so. People always are when they're worried. But it'll be all right. They'll be so overjoyed to see you. Veronica will probably buy you a mega present.'

'I don't expect she'll be there. She never comes to our house. She and Dad don't get on.'

'I expect that's why they got divorced,' said Rory.

Just as the taxi drew up outside Toby's house, a car drove up and tried to park in too small a space opposite the taxi. Thea was hunting for pound coins and didn't notice, but Toby said, 'Oh. It's Dad.'

Thea didn't want to see Toby's dad, unless she had a blunt and heavy instrument about her person with which to batter him to death.

The taxi pulled away at about the same time as Ben managed to park his car. He got out, slammed the door, his expression matching the weather, which was still thunderous.

'Dad!'

'Toby! Thank God you're all right. What in hell's name happened?'

'It's a long story,' said Thea defensively. 'It's not his fault.'

This time Ben's rage was not tempered by relief. He turned it on Thea at full force. 'Of course it's not his fault!'

Rory cleared his throat. 'Would it be a good idea if we went into the house? It's raining cats and dogs, and Toby is drenched. We all are.'

Ben thrust his hand into his pocket and gave his keys to Rory. 'Take him inside and get him a hot drink if his nanny's not there. You'—he took hold of Thea's shoulder in a vicious grip—'you, come with me and give me an explanation!'

It took all Thea's strength to rid herself of his hand.

'Now, what the hell do you mean by running off with my son?'

'What?' She was as angry as he was but also confused. 'What do you mean, "running off"? I haven't done anything of the kind. It's you who's totally and utterly betrayed me! God! I thought it was bad the first time it happened to me! But this . . . it's . . . worse.'

'Veronica told me Toby had been kidnapped.'

'Kidnap—' Thea shook her head to clear the rain from her eyes. 'You are mad. Stark, staring mad! Why on earth did you think I'd kidnapped Toby? And if I did, why did I spend a small fortune on a taxi taking him home?'

Ben shrugged dramatically. 'I don't know! Nothing you do ever seems logical.'

Thea's eyes flashed to rival the lightning. 'Well, let me explain! I took him home to you because that's where he said he wanted to go. Although it was bloody miles away and, as I said, cost me a fortune in fares. Don't you think you should be inside, comforting him, instead of shouting at me?'

'Don't tell me how to look after my own son!'

'I wouldn't dream of it! Though just one tip: tell your wife and your nanny that it's a good idea to stay where you last saw the child, rather than disappearing into Greater London!'

While Ben now realised that Thea had done nothing wrong, he was still upset. 'Don't stand there shouting. Tell me what happened.'

Thea was incredulous. 'I think you mean, "I am so sorry, Thea, I don't know how I could have been so stupid!" Only don't bother to apologise, because what you've done to me is so much worse than you just being a dickhead about Toby.'

The expression broke through his anger. 'Look, I'm sorry, I obviously got completely the wrong idea. Tell me what did happen.'

'I was talking to Rory—or trying to—in a pigging thunderstorm and Toby followed us. By the time he'd caught up with us we were all lost. It took us ages to get back to the gallery, and when we did, everyone had gone. I just cannot believe it! How could a mother just swan off when her son is missing in the middle of London?'

'She didn't swan off. She went back to her flat, in case Toby had gone there, then rang me at the office and said Toby had disappeared.'

'So naturally you all assumed I'd kidnapped him. And you accuse *me* of not being logical?'

Ben sighed. 'None of this is very logical. Let's go back to the house and get you warm and dry.'

'No! I'm not going into your house, Ben Jonson. I wouldn't if yours was the last house I could find sanctuary and a band of thugs were after me. Now I'm going to get a taxi.' Then she remembered she'd just spent almost all her money on the taxi they'd recently got out of.

Ben took hold of her shoulder again. It felt bruised from last time.

'Let me go, you ape!'

'Not until you tell me why you won't go into my house. Rory and Toby are there. You'll be quite safe from my lust.'

This unfortunate choice of word reminded Thea of when they'd been together varnishing the floor. She blushed hotly at the memory. 'I doubt if you know the meaning of the word,' she muttered, remembering her bitter humiliation.

His mouth hardened and his grip tightened. 'Then what is it?'

She put her chin up and her shoulders back, losing his hand as she did so. 'I'll spell it out for you. You let me go to all the trouble and expense, worry and hard work, of setting up an art gallery, when you knew bloody well your wife was going to make Rory an offer he couldn't refuse and I'd be left with a gallery but no star artist . . . and no chance of making any money.'

'What?' He frowned in puzzlement.

'Oh, come on, don't tell me you're deaf as well as stupid!'

'I'm not deaf and I'm not stupid, and because I'm not stupid we're going to carry on this conversation in the house.'

'No. I said I refuse—'

He didn't argue. He just picked her up in a fireman's lift and carried her up the steps to the house. Battering his back with her fists hurt her more than it seemed to hurt him. He pulled her down so she was on her feet when the nanny opened the door. 'Thank you,' he said to her. 'Now, you'—he turned to Thea—'upstairs and into the bath.'

Thea had been wet and cold too long not to yearn for the comfort of hot water. On the other hand she was damned if she'd take orders from Ben, even if it was more for her good than for his.

'I'm not listening to any arguments,' he went on. 'You can use my bathroom; you'll be quite private. But when you come out, you're going to tell me what the bloody hell you're talking about.'

Thea made a rapid plan. She would appear to comply, go upstairs, run the bath and, when he was out of the way, she'd tiptoe back downstairs and out, and run away. She was damned if she'd explain anything to him.

Thea's plan didn't allow for Ben actually running the bath for her, giving her a towel and a robe, and ordering her to get out of her clothes. Not that it was quite an order, more a suggestion it was hard not to comply with. 'If you give me your wet things I'll put them in the tumble drier.'

Thea bit her lip. 'Oh, all right.' She snatched the thick towelling robe. She might as well avail herself of the facilities, but she really didn't want a confrontation. She was too tired and angry to guarantee she wouldn't get emotional. Tears would just add to the many humiliations she had suffered recently.

The bath, she decided, was the nearest thing to heaven you could experience this side of the Pearly Gates. Forget sex, or chocolate—hot, deep water when one is really chilled has to be the best. She sank down so only her head was above it, abandoning her plans for escape.

Once the heat had penetrated every chilly cell and pore, she examined Ben's bathroom. It was a very male room, black and white tiled floor, shiny white suite, white tongue-and-groove panelling and a small mirror. It was also extremely tidy.

Mentally she doubled the size of the looking-glass, placed a large, spectacular shell in front of it and added some real sponges or large beach pebbles, something to provide a little cheer without making it feminine. Some big, square bottles would be nice, too.

She sighed. She was a cluttered sort of person and Ben wasn't. Even if he were the kind, sexy man she'd once thought him, they were totally wrong for each other.

Draped in towelling from head to foot in the form of Ben's bathrobe and the towel he'd given her, Thea went downstairs and found the kitchen. She'd already gone into Ben's spartan bedroom, telephoned Magenta and brought her up to speed.

Toby was sitting at a completely clear pine table, eating a plate of pasta. His nanny was leaning against the equally uncluttered work surface, drinking a glass of wine. There was no sign of Ben or Rory.

'Oh, hi,' said Thea.

Toby grinned. The nanny detached herself from the worktop and asked, 'Would you like a glass of wine? Ben will be back in a moment, but I've got to go home, now.'

'Are my clothes dry, do you know?' Thea accepted the glass of cold white wine.

'Nearly, I think. I'll just pop off. That's OK, isn't it, Tobe?'

'Fine,' said Toby.

Thea sipped the wine. It was not fine with her. If the nanny wasn't here she couldn't just get dressed and slink off, as she had planned. She'd have to stay with Toby. And it was a nuisance to have lost Rory again. Still, perhaps it was for the best. If she was going to have to seduce him into showing with her, she'd prefer to be dressed for the event. With Ben's robe gathered round her, she looked like the Michelin Man.

'Before you go, where's the tumble drier?'

'Oh, it's here, in the utility room. Just open the door and it'll stop and you can get them out,' said the girl casually. She put her hand in and felt the clothes as they stopped. 'Another ten minutes or so I'd say. Sit down and enjoy your wine. Ben'll be back in a minute. He's gone to get some things from the Eight till Late.'

Thea debated putting on her clothes as they were and making a run for it, while the nanny was still wiping the perfectly clean worktop with a perfectly clean cloth. But she badly needed to know if Rory had said anything before he'd gone. No, however unpleasant, some sort of confrontation with Ben was essential.

Toby had gone upstairs to play on his computer. Thea, dressed and made-up with the nanny's supply, planned what to say to Ben.

She tried to look surprised when he arrived in the kitchen, although she'd heard him come in, talk to Toby and come downstairs.

'Hello,' he said. 'I've bought some supper.'

'Nice for you.' *Don't be rude, Thea. If you're rude he'll guess how much you care. Keep it calm, polite and unemotional.*

'I hope it's nice for you, too.'

'Well, I think that's unlikely, don't you?' Good resolutions abandoned, Thea turned on him. 'Do you really think it's possible for me to sit opposite you and chat as if nothing had happened? As if your wife hadn't purloined Rory, just before he was going to show with me? Where is he, by the way?'

'Thea, I do wish you'd give me a chance to explain a few things, before you let your imagination go completely haywire.'

'What things would those be? Like why you watched me, *helped* me even, set up an art gallery when you knew from the beginning Rory wasn't going to show there?'

'Could we eat first? I'm starving and I'm sure you are too.'

'No, we couldn't. Tell me!'

He sighed, but switched the oven on before turning round to face Thea. 'I didn't know Veronica had any plans for Rory.'

'Right! You didn't come all the way to Ireland with Toby because Molly asked you to. You did it to track Rory down for Veronica, so she could put on the show he should have had first time round.'

'Veronica doesn't have a gallery. She's a patron, she collects artists, but she doesn't have space of her own.'

Thea made a dismissive gesture. 'Well, whatever, you knew Veronica was interested in him, which was why you went to Ireland. What I want to know is why you let me set up the gallery?'

'I tried to stop you. I pointed out the pitfalls. I didn't know Veronica

129

had plans for Rory and I don't believe she did until she heard about your gallery—and before you accuse me of telling her, she heard about it from Toby.'

'Hide behind your son, would you?'

His rage seemed to fill him like an implosion of explosive gas. Frightened, she prepared to run.

Seeing her hover, prepared for flight, enraged him more and his eyes glittered. He thumped his fist on the worktop and the glasses in the cupboard above clattered together.

'I am not hiding behind my son,' he said quietly. 'I am telling you the truth. If you don't choose to hear it and prefer to write your own little scenarios about what happened, don't let me stop you. But I'm not going to defend myself to you any more.'

'Fine.' Her voice was shaking. She didn't believe him, not because she didn't want to, but because it just didn't seem credible. Why on earth would Veronica have become interested in Rory again only when she heard about Thea's art gallery?

'I think we should eat,' said Ben.

His voice was shaking too and Thea wondered how near he had actually been to hitting her.

'Would you like a drink?'

'Yes, please.'

He got out two glasses and a bottle of whisky. He'd poured one huge measure when he stopped. 'I'd better not have anything if I've got to drive you home.'

'I can easily take a taxi.' Thea felt that half her life had been spent in taxis just recently.

'I'm sorry to mention this, but Toby said you spent all your money on the one from Knightsbridge.'

'When I wasn't kidnapping him, you mean?'

'I'm sorry about that, too. It was Veronica who suggested you'd kidnapped him.' A rueful grin disturbed his serious demeanour. 'Look at it from her point of view—you left her favourite gallery with her pet artist and her son. It did look quite like theft.'

Thea sighed. She could see that from Ben's point of view it had its funny side, but while in time she might see the incident as amusing, her life was nevertheless in tatters: she'd still lost her artist.

She sipped the drink he handed her. 'I think I'd like to go back now and not eat first.' She made a rather pathetic attempt at a smile.

'Thea—'

'I've got a lot of thinking to do.' She put down her glass. 'I'll go upstairs and get my bag.'

He was in the hall when she came down, holding his car keys.

'I'll just go and say goodbye to Toby,' said Thea.

Ben nodded. 'He's in the sitting room. I've asked my neighbour to pop over for a few moments.'

'Oh, I'm sorry. I didn't think. I'm not used to looking after children.'

'You don't do too badly.'

The moment was full of confused emotions, things unsaid. There was too much between them and too little. 'I'll say goodbye to Toby.'

He opened the door to the sitting room without speaking.

'Hi, Toby.'

Toby pressed something on his console and got up.

'I'm off now. Ben's taking me home. We've had quite a day, one way and another, haven't we?'

Toby came over to Thea. 'It wasn't Dad's fault, what happened.'

Thea put her arms round him. 'No, of course it wasn't. It was just a silly thing that happened. It wasn't anyone's fault.'

'So you will go on being friends with him?'

Thea was about to say that of course she would, when she realised he might well have heard them quarrelling. 'Relationships get very complicated when you're grown up, Toby. But whatever happens, we can still be friends.'

Toby shook his head. 'That might be quite difficult, actually.'

Thea nodded. 'We could try, though. Molly would help us.'

Toby suddenly smiled. 'Yes, she would, wouldn't she?'

Thea had to bite her lip very hard not to cry as she gave Toby a last hug. They both knew they probably wouldn't see much of each other in future and she felt she'd lost someone she loved very much.

In the morning, well rested and lured out of her pit by the smell of fresh coffee and the sound of Magenta's electric juicer, Thea was still heartbroken about Ben's defection, for however much she wanted to believe his story, logically she just couldn't. But, she told Magenta, she was going to fight for Rory tooth and nail. 'And as I don't care about my nails one-tenth as much as Veronica cares about hers, I'm bound to win.'

'Well, I'm glad you're feeling so upbeat about things this morning,' said Magenta. 'Have a multivitamin.'

'I don't feel upbeat. I feel as if I'm trying to sort out world peace single-handed, but I'm also too angry not to try my very hardest to succeed.' Thea took a sip of orange juice and swallowed the pill.

'But don't forget,' said Magenta. 'You have Rory's pictures and they don't.'

Taking vitamins and feeling angry was one thing. Actually fronting up at the gallery demanding to know Rory's home address required the loan of a beautiful linen skirt and a good squirt of some scent Magenta guaranteed would bring men to their knees.

Thea went in and approached the desk where Edward, the gallery owner, was sitting. He was in his early sixties, still very good-looking and immaculately dressed.

'Hi!' She gave him a warm, slightly apologetic smile. 'I sort of hope you don't remember me, but I was in yesterday.'

He smiled graciously back. 'Of course I remember you. How could I forget? Such turmoil you left behind you.'

'I'm so sorry. Was it very dreadful?'

'For a while. Veronica blamed the nanny and the nanny blamed Veronica. I had to calm them all down with nips of brandy.'

Thea laughed. 'Well, it wasn't really anyone's fault, expect Toby's, but he's under the age of criminal responsibility, so no one can pin anything on him.'

Edward laughed. 'Now, what can I do for you?'

'Well, I've hugely enjoyed this exhibition. And it's a lovely space . . .'

'Thank you. I selected the work and arranged it, and I also created the space. So what can I *really* do for you?'

Thea bit her lip. This was the hard part. 'I want to know where Rory's staying. I really do have to talk to him. Our conversation yesterday was cut short by Toby and a thunderstorm.'

'Now tell me, my dear, why should I give you the address of one of the most exciting young artists I've seen for years, when I know you're going to try to take him away from me?'

Thea took a deep breath. 'Because my chances of getting him to come to me instead of staying with you are so infinitesimal that it wouldn't be fair of you not to give me the opportunity to at least try.'

Edward nodded. 'True, but you're a very charming young woman. Your chances might be better than you think. Can I risk that?'

'I was a charming young woman when Rory abandoned me for you, so to speak. I've got to give it a last try because I've worked too hard and

committed too much of my partner's money to give up. But I will probably have to admit defeat.'

'What will you do? Abandon the idea of a gallery?'

'Good Lord, no! I'll have my graduate show and resign myself to
never making a penny. It is a fabulous space, you see. I think it could be
a really good gallery.'

Edward became thoughtful. 'Have you got any pictures?'

'Of the space? I've got all my slides and stuff for my graduate show at
my friend's flat and I think there are a couple of shots of the gallery as
well. I was a photographer in my past life.'

'Have them biked over.'

'What?'

'Get your friend to ring a courier and get them sent here. I'd like to
see what you've found in the graduate shows that really excites you.'

Still Thea hesitated.

'I'm not planning to steal all your young hopefuls,' said Edward,
laughing. 'I only want to get an idea of how good your eye is. I might
just need someone like you in my life.'

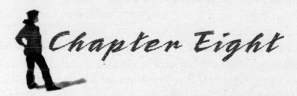

Chapter Eight

BY THE TIME THE WORK ARRIVED, one and a half hours later, there was only
one other person whose opinion Thea valued as much as Edward
Grampian's. And as she planned never to speak to Ben again it was what
Edward thought that made her anxious as she slit the parcel tape on the
package.

She couldn't bear to be present while he looked, so she prowled
around Harrods Food Halls for an hour, trying not to imagine what a
distinguished gallery owner might think of the Barbie Kitchen or the
video of willowherb seeds swirling up into the sunshine.

Eventually, she forced herself back to the gallery. Edward was sitting
at the desk, a very distinguished pair of gold spectacles on the end of his
nose. He looked over them at her.

'Well?' she demanded. 'Shall I give up my gallery and take up knitting instead?'

'Oh, no. I shouldn't think you'd be any good at knitting.'

'Edward!' By now she felt they were old friends. 'What do you think? Don't keep me in suspense. I'm on pins here!'

'I think you've got the makings of a very good show. I think you need to add something a little more mainstream, so you don't antagonise the more conventional members of the public, but you don't need to go too far. A half-decent painter would do the trick.'

'Not easy to find. I looked and looked, but it's just not in fashion at the moment.'

'It will be. When Rory's had his show.'

There was a silence between them. For a while they'd forgotten they were in competition for the same ground-breaking young artist. Edward had Rory and Thea had the paintings. Thea felt that having Rory put Edward ahead, because she knew she wouldn't be able to keep the paintings against everybody's will. But Edward might not know she had them, which gave her a smidgen of advantage.

'Edward, about Rory's show.'

'Yes, Thea?'

'If you told him he could show with you afterwards, at some time in the future, he might well do the decent thing and stick with me.'

'He might. And while I probably would always be happy to show Rory's work, I've no intention of telling him that. I saw Rory before he disappeared. I was an admirer long before you were. By the time you found him he was easy to appreciate. He'd refined his art, done years of concentrated work. I saw the talent behind the rawness.'

Thea sighed deeply and tried again. 'But you're an established gallery. People will come here and buy from you whatever you put in it. You don't need the recognition like I do.'

'I have a reputation to keep up. People buy from me because they trust me to know what's good, what will appreciate in value. You can afford to fail. You've only money to lose. I have my integrity—far more precious, I assure you.'

That's the trouble with being fair-minded, thought Thea despondently. I can see Edward's point of view perfectly.

Possibly sensing her surrender, Edward went on, 'But I will give you Rory's telephone number. If you can persuade him to show with you and not me, I won't hold it against him in future. Though I should warn you, Veronica has a lot of influence and she won't use it to your advantage if you take Rory.'

This was something of a blow. If Veronica had nearly ruined Rory the first time round, she could do it again and ruin her at the same time.

'Just as well I haven't got a towel about my person, then, isn't it? Or I might be tempted to throw it in.'

She met Rory at the pub he stipulated. It was not in a part of London she knew and Thea felt a little awkward going into a busy pub on her own, when she had no confidence in Rory's punctuality. But he was at the bar, entertaining a couple of young men with Irish jokes. 'Hey, Thea! Over here! What are you having?'

'If you're paying, a large one.'

'Of course I'm paying. Jimmy, a large Paddy for the lady.'

Thea almost changed her order to a mineral water, but then decided a bit of Dutch courage, or in this case, Irish courage, might not be a bad thing. 'Rory,' she said firmly, when she'd thanked him for her drink. 'I do need to talk to you. Can we go and sit down?'

'I suppose so, Thea, but I don't think you're going to like what I'm going to say when you've said your piece.'

'Probably not, but I've got to say it. I've got to try and make you do the decent thing.'

'Thea, Veronica would kill me if I changed my mind now, after she'd gone to so much trouble to introduce me to Edward and set up the show.'

'Oh! So you're not worried about *me* killing you? For pretty much the same thing? Only in my case it wouldn't be so much murder as justifiable homicide! I put my own money, Molly's money and the sweat of my brow into my gallery! Weeks of hard labour! Not to mention looking after your dog and your puppies so you could come to London and leave me stranded!'

'No,' he said baldly, unimpressed. 'Because you're not that sort of person. You wouldn't sabotage a vicar's tea party out of spite, let alone someone's career. Veronica wouldn't think twice about it.'

'I could learn to be that sort of person,' she muttered, wishing it were true.

Rory put out his hand and cupped her cheek in it. It was warm and comforting and trustworthy, quite unlike its owner. 'No, you couldn't. And that's why I love you.'

She looked at him, startled.

'I mean the word in its widest sense,' he added. 'I'm afraid I've come round to thinking that you and me are a beautiful relationship, destined not to happen. But I'm not completely brokenhearted.'

Thea suddenly felt tears spring to her eyes. She was tired and had gone through a lot in the past twenty-four hours. Despair, which she had kept at bay with every trick she knew, suddenly seemed very near. She took a large sip of whiskey. 'Oh God,' she murmured so quietly he couldn't hear her. 'I wish I could say the same.'

It was dispiriting to have to take the train back to Cheltenham to tell Molly that her mission had failed. The only good news was that Edward Grampian was seriously talking about giving Thea a job that she could do and still run her gallery. It would be hard, but she would scout around the country for work which wouldn't usually come his way. He might even offer exhibitions to artists who'd previously exhibited with her. This, she hoped, would be enough to stop Molly getting too downcast.

She decided not to tell Molly about Ben's part in it all. It wasn't her fault, but as his relation she'd feel bad about it. And worse, she'd probably feel obliged to stick up for him, to explain away his actions as being 'for the best'.

To her surprise, Molly was waiting on the platform with Petal as the train drew in.

'Hi, you two! How lovely of you to come and pick me up. Save me having to get a taxi.' She kissed Molly and was about to kiss Petal, when she saw the expressions on their faces. 'What's the matter? It's not the pups, is it? Oh, no, don't tell me. I couldn't bear it. Not Little Chap, the one I've been handfeeding?' That's why Petal's here, she thought distractedly. So I won't be alone in the house.

'The dogs are fine,' said Molly. 'Or they were when I picked up your keys half an hour ago.'

Thea's heart, which had begun to race, took a moment to realise all was not lost. 'Then it must be the gallery. A flood. Oh my God, not a fire! Not all Rory's pictures!'

'Thea!' said Molly. 'Why are you imagining all these disasters?'

'Because you two have got faces which could announce the outbreak of World War Three. What's happened?'

'Ben rang and told us everything,' announced Petal.

'What?' What 'everything' could Ben have possibly told them?

'We can't talk about it here,' said Molly. 'Let's get in the car. There's a lot to discuss. Though I must say it's very disappointing.'

'Can't argue with that,' Thea agreed.

Home was much tidier and cleaner than Thea had left it. The hall smelt of polish and air freshener, and the floor shone as it never had before. Even the kitchen was surprisingly orderly.

Thea picked up Little Chap and then the kettle. 'So, what did Ben say, to make you both look so miserable?'

'He told us that Rory definitely won't be showing with us,' announced Petal. 'Because Veronica has found a really wonderful exhibition space for him.'

'Well, I knew that.' Thea put down Little Chap so she could deal with mugs and tea bags.

'But this was our big chance to make a name for ourselves as a gallery,' protested Molly, as if Thea must have forgotten. 'We were going to get so much publicity and interest from the art world. Rory would have put us on the map.'

'I know. His paintings are wonderful, but I've got a really good degree show lined up. And we'll have a bit more time to get ready for that. We weren't ever going to be a one-show wonder, Molly. We'll just have to make our reputation a bit more slowly.'

'I still don't think . . .'

'Would you like tea, Molly?'

'Yes, please. But I don't see why you're not tearing your hair out over this. I mean, the whole reason for you dashing off to London was to convince Rory to change his mind, and you failed. We know you did, because Ben told us.'

'Ben doesn't know everything,' said Thea airily. 'Ben doesn't know that I showed my slides and stuff for the graduate show to the owner of the gallery where Rory's showing. He liked them a lot. He thinks I have a good eye and he wants me to be a scout for him. So there!'

'This proper gallery owner actually liked that ghastly pink kitchen and those weird videos?' Molly was appalled and disbelieving.

'Yup. You see, we don't need Rory. Have a cup of tea, both of you. And then, now I know that the gallery hasn't been burnt down, or been flooded, or anything, I would like to unpack and sort out my washing and stuff.'

They took the hint, drank their tea and left.

Thea spent the rest of the day at home. Somehow she couldn't face the gallery just yet. Although all her cheery statements about its future were true and she did believe them, she was more bruised by Rory's defection than she wanted Molly and Petal to know—probably because of Ben's part in it all. If only she hadn't fallen in love with him, or even if only she could fall out of love with him now she knew he was the root of all her troubles. It was a shame the heart didn't work like that.

She went to bed early and fell asleep immediately, aided by hot milk with whisky in it. She was in the middle of her deepest sleep when the phone finally penetrated her dreams enough to wake her.

It was Rory. He sounded drunk. 'Is that you, Thea? It's me, Rory. I'm ringing from a pub.'

'I guessed. What do you want?'

'I was just ringing to tell you that I've decided to show with you after all.'

'What?' Thea sat up in bed to make sure she wasn't still asleep.

'I said I'm going to show with you after all. I'll be down in a few days to tell you where to hang the pictures.'

'What? Why? What changed your mind?'

'I decided not to let my life be ruled by that bitch. I'll show where I want to show and let Veronica go hang. Let her try and ruin my career all over again!'

'Calm down, I'm sure she won't do that.'

'Yes, she will. She told me. But I don't care. And now I'm ringing off. Goodbye.'

Far too wide awake now to be able to go back to sleep, she lay in bed, mentally placing the pictures and wondering if it would be worth disturbing the puppies to make a cup of tea. It was half past five when she finally dozed off.

'I can't understand it! Ben definitely said that Rory couldn't show with you because Veronica would use all her influence to ruin him!'

Thea tucked the phone under her chin and picked up a puppy. 'Rory obviously felt differently. Perhaps he's not as frightened of Veronica as Ben is.'

The sarcasm floated past Molly. 'Oh, Ben's not frightened of her. But he has had to fight hard to keep on good terms with her for Toby's sake.'

Thea sighed. 'Well, anyway,' she said, 'Rory is showing with us, so we can get back on track and organise it all.'

'He can't change his mind again, can he?'

'No. I'm going to weld his pictures to the walls quickly, so there's no question of it.'

'But, Thea! You can't do that! You'll never get them off and we'd have to redecorate all over again.'

'Only joking, Molly.' Really, by this time she shouldn't have to explain all her jokes to Molly.

'Are you going to ring Ben and tell him the news?'

'Nope,' Thea said firmly. 'If you think he needs to know, you ring him. Personally I think he could just find out when he gets his invitation to the private view. Now, lovey, I've got a million things to do. I'll see you at the gallery in about an hour.'

The gallery seemed larger, whiter and brighter than it had done only a few days ago. The sun, shining through the massive windows, added to the impression of a huge light space. Thea enjoyed the sense of airy joy the place gave her.

She went downstairs to where Rory's pictures, shrouded in bubble-wrap, were stacked in the passage. She hadn't allowed herself to look at them when she thought they might be denied to her. Now she dragged one of them into the big gallery and undraped a landscape.

It took her straight back to Ireland. She could almost feel the cold air on her face, the bright sun in her eyes. She knew the feel of the sea against her ankles if she went down to the shore and took her shoes off.

She propped it against the wall and dragged out another. She wanted a really private view, just her and the paintings.

Her reverie was pitifully short. Molly arrived, the party for the private view her chief concern. She barely glanced at the paintings.

'I think we should serve things to eat, otherwise people will just lap up the free wine and get plastered.'

Well, she certainly didn't want Rory getting plastered—perhaps food was a good idea. 'OK, Molly, what sort of things do you think? Sandwiches, sausage rolls? Little quiches?'

Molly looked appalled; working with Thea could be very difficult. The poor girl had no idea what was what. 'I was thinking blinis with caviar, a little sushi, perhaps. That sort of thing?'

'That sort of thing won't stop anyone getting drunk and it'll cost a fortune. And who's going to make it?'

'We get a caterer! I know a lovely girl who'll do it all for us. She'll even provide waitresses.'

'But how much will it cost? Until we start earning, we can't afford unnecessary luxuries like that.'

Molly stuck out her chin. It was what she did when Derek said they couldn't afford something, and it always worked.

'It's too expensive,' said Thea.

'I'll pay,' said Molly.

Thea's own chin went out, rivalling Molly's.

'Oh, please let me! Just for this show.'

Molly's disappointment was more effective than her pouting. 'We should start as we mean to go on.'

'It's just that Ben has—'

'What?' Thea hadn't told Molly of her falling out with Ben, but Ben must have said something or Molly wouldn't have halted in mid-plea.

Molly started picking at a spot of paint on the light switch. 'He said he wanted to invite all sorts of people from London.' She turned to Thea. 'He really wants to help the gallery, Thea, whatever you think.'

'It's all right, Molly. If Ben wants to invite a few of his friends, he's welcome. If he thinks they'll come all the way out here.'

'That's my point!' declared Molly. 'If they do come, I don't want to look like a small-town gallery that doesn't know what's what.'

Thea didn't either. 'I'll compromise. No food, but I'll book a table at the Chinese for afterwards. At least that way we won't be buying food that won't get eaten.' She resolved to make sure Rory ate several large sandwiches before the opening, to line his stomach.

'The Chinese!' Molly couldn't have been more horrified if Thea had suggested going on to a strip joint.

'The Chinese Dragon is really elegant. I went there with friends when it first opened. It's fab. I'll book a table for ten or so and hope some of them pay for themselves.'

'OK, that sounds quite fun, but I want canapés!' The stamped foot was implicit.

Thea caved in. She had other, bigger battles to fight. 'Oh, all right, Molly, but only for Rory's show. When things are normal we'll just have wine, and charge them for the second glass.'

Molly hissed in horror.

'Well, you don't actually charge them, that's illegal, you just ask for contributions. It's what people do, honestly. I found out when I was in London.' This was a lie, but if Molly could stamp, then she could bend the truth.

'Very well, I'll let you know best on that one. But for our very first party—I mean show—I want to do things properly.'

Thea shrugged. 'She who pays the piper gets the sushi.'

Molly smiled, then became serious. 'Ben's worried, by the way.'

'Oh, dear. Poor Ben.'

'No, really—about Rory suddenly changing his mind. It did make me wonder if we really ought to let Rory show here. Veronica can be so spiteful and according to Ben she was spitting tacks when she heard.'

'I don't think anyone could ruin Rory's career now. Edward, the gallery owner in London, thought very highly of him. And although Veronica seemed to take the credit for getting the space, Edward would have shown him anyway. I really don't think she can hurt him.'

'I think Ben was more worried about what Veronica would do to this gallery than to Rory.'

'What could she do? Fire-bomb it?'

'Don't joke! She's a very influential woman! The wrong word from her and people will stay away in droves. She's never liked me and—'

'And what?'

'Ben says Veronica's livid with you. I think she's peeved because you got on so well with Edward Grampian, who Ben tells me is very impor- tant in the art world. And she doesn't like it if Ben gets interested in a woman. She doesn't want him herself, but she doesn't want anyone else to have him.'

'She needn't worry about that. Ben is not interested in me. Not in the slightest. Now, do you think we could stop gossiping and get on with some work?' Then, realising she shouldn't have shouted at Molly, Thea went on, 'Sorry. I am a bit stressed at the moment. And I do think Ben should have made it clear to Veronica that he and I aren't even good friends.'

'Aren't you?' Molly was so unaccustomed to seeing the easy-going Thea in this mood that she couldn't think of a better answer. 'He's rent- ing a house in Bristol, you know, to make it easier for house-hunting.'

'Oh? Well I hope Toby won't mind leaving all his London friends. Anyway, it's none of my business,' she said, trying to sound brisk. 'So, when is your pet man coming to fill in the windows? Or shall we tackle it ourselves?'

'Thea! I know it's good to be economical, but really, there are limits to DIY.' Molly shook her head. Sometimes she found Thea completely incomprehensible.

A lifetime later, at home, Thea sorted through the post, the puppies fighting with her ankles as she did so. Apart from junk mail there was one letter. She opened it. It was from Toby. He had typed it on his computer.

Dear Thea,
    I'm writing to say sorry for causing all that trouble. I heard Dad on the phone to Veronica and I know he doesn't think that you kidnapped me. I just hope you and Dad go on being friends. Please tell me you are.
    Love, Toby.

This rather formal communication was decorated with stars and space ships. Thea bit her lip. There was no point in her getting sentimental. Toby wanted her and Ben to get together, so he could have a proper mother. Now she'd met Veronica, Thea could see his point. At least she genuinely enjoyed Toby's company, which she doubted Veronica did.

She just hoped Ben didn't know how Toby felt. It would madden him. Relationships were difficult enough without having your son trying to influence your love life. Ben would never marry anyone Toby didn't like, she knew that instinctively. In the same way that she could now accept that if he said he didn't go looking for Rory for Veronica he probably hadn't; it was all a horrible coincidence.

Not that it would have made any difference. If she'd said, 'OK, I believe you,' it wouldn't have warmed Ben's tepid feelings into passion. The only passion he ever felt in connection with her was anger—not an emotion to build a relationship on. But still, if she got an opportunity, she would like to tell him that she no longer thought him capable of such a massive deception.

Which still left her with Toby's letter to reply to.

Later, she sat at the kitchen table with a lined pad, thinking what to write. She had a nice card she could copy it onto when she'd finally thought it out. So far, she hadn't got beyond 'Dear Toby'.

Eventually, after much crossing out, starting again and making balls of paper for the puppies to chase, she came up with,

Dear Toby,
    Adults don't always behave logically and, sadly, I don't think Ben and I can go on being friends, quite. [The 'quite' was because in spite of everything, she couldn't absolutely close her heart and mind to the idea.]

But that doesn't mean that we can't be friends separately. You can come and stay with me any time. Molly would arrange it. [She hoped this didn't sound furtive, or like custody arrangements.] She's told me that you are moving near to Bristol soon and I do hope you and Ben are happy there, and that you don't miss your London friends too much. The good thing is that Bristol is quite near me, so you can come and see the puppies, or make chocolate cake and pizza whenever you like.
   With much love,
   your friend, Thea.

She decorated her letter with drawings of Lara and the puppies, chasing each other round the page, leaving puddles behind them. By the time she'd done all this she realised it wouldn't fit on the card, especially if she wanted to re-create the drawings, so she just folded up the letter and sent it as it was.

The rhythm and pace of Thea's life became hard and fast. The main picture hanging, which Rory insisted on attending, took two days and included an over-indulgent evening at Thea's house, where Rory stayed.

It didn't take so long because he and Thea argued about what should go where—in fact, their ideas were surprisingly harmonious—but because there was such a lot of work to be fitted in and it was difficult to decide exactly where on the wall to hang each picture.

Arranging a lighting system took another two days and more money than Thea could bear to contemplate. But in the end they had one which was flexible, easy to change—provided you could cope with climbing ladders—and made the work look sensational.

Ben, who kept away from the gallery, occupied her thoughts only when he had a genuine reason to be there, like when she was wondering if she should have the prices discreetly stuck up next to the paintings, or on a sheet, to be handed to each person. In fact, she reckoned wryly, she only thought about him twenty or thirty times a day. That's practically over him, she told herself.

Molly began to do some serious PR, telephoning everyone she could think of to tell them about Rory and the exhibition. But the response was disappointing. Molly started to despair. 'If we're not careful it'll end up just being a social event for our friends.'

'Well, that's all right. Isn't it nicer to entertain your friends than a lot of London media types who'll just turn their noses up at the whole thing?' Thea was beginning to think that obscurity was better than success. If she was going to fail, she wanted to do it quietly, with no one looking.

'You don't think it's anything to do with Veronica, do you?' demanded Molly.

'That's paranoid. Why should she bother to sabotage us?'

Molly regarded Thea but, for once, didn't say anything.

Then, four days before the private view, when Thea was about to resort to ringing round her friends to make sure they at least came, things changed.

The first time the phone rang, and it was a London paper, Thea was thrilled. She called Molly immediately and told her about it. Molly, who'd planned a trip to the beauty therapist in preparation for the big day, cancelled her appointment. 'I'll be over!'

Thea had dealt with three more calls by the time she heard the gallery door open while she was scribbling down some details. 'Thank goodness you're here. The phone hasn't stopped all morning and I'm desperate to go to the loo. What kept you?' She looked up and saw not Molly, but Ben. 'Oh. You're not Molly.'

'No. Sorry.'

Thea's mouth was suddenly dry. She felt gauche and foolish, uncertain what to say. 'Well, come in, then,' she managed.

He came into the space and looked around. 'I wasn't sure how welcome I'd be.'

Thea smiled a little stiffly. 'Perfectly welcome.'

He looked very tired and formal, and more attractive than Thea had thought it possible for any man to look. She wanted to fling herself at him and hold on to him so tightly that he would never escape. She wanted to feel his touch again, even an angry touch.

'I came to make a confession.'

Oh, not now, thought Thea. Don't tell me anything dreadful now. 'Is it really necessary? I'm sure you'd never do anything really terrible.'

'Are you? Last time we met you seemed to doubt that.'

It was odd. A little while ago she'd have given much to have the opportunity to tell Ben that she knew he hadn't betrayed her. Now that it was presented to her she felt reluctant to do so. Was it spite? Did she want him to suffer a little of what she'd suffered? 'Well, I'm sure you can't blame me for doubting it. It was a little hard to accept that you really didn't know Veronica would snap up Rory the moment you found out where he was.'

'I do see that and I don't blame you for doubting me.'

'So what have you got to confess now?'

'I decided I had to do some damage limitation.'

Thea frowned. 'Oh?'

'Veronica was very bitter about Rory changing his mind. So that she didn't manage to convince everyone that your show wasn't worth crossing the street for, let alone visiting the wilds of Gloucestershire, I decided to take action.'

'What action? Oh, excuse me, there's the phone again.'

It rang again, twice, before she had a chance to carry on her conversation with Ben, by which time Molly had arrived. 'What is going on?' she asked. 'And what are you doing here, Ben?'

'I came to warn you both. I asked a friend of mine to do a press release and ring up a few of her contacts. She knows everybody.'

'Oh.' Thea felt ambivalent about this piece of information. She should be thrilled to have so much publicity and interest in her gallery. But she also felt she should have been consulted. 'Shouldn't I have written the press release?'

'I'm sorry. I would have consulted you, but writing press releases is a fairly skilled art.'

'Oh. Well, could you at least show us a copy of the press release?' asked Thea. 'So we have some idea what the story is?'

'Sure.' He put his briefcase on the desk and took out a sheaf of papers. He handed one each to Molly and Thea. It read:

There are pots of gold at the bottom of rainbows in Ireland, but something even more exciting has been discovered in the far west of County Mayo. A young man, whose work hasn't been seen since just after his graduate show, has been working in private on a series of landscapes that is creating enormous excitement in the art world. Offered a show in London by the Edward Grampian Gallery, he decided instead to exhibit at a brand-new provincial gallery, opened by one-time girlfriend Thea Orville, who created the gallery just to show his work. Why he should make his debut in a completely unknown location instead of in a well-established London gallery is a mystery, but the art world will be flocking to see. The fact that he happens to be 'a ride' is just a bonus.

A photograph of Rory staring out over Clew Bay, which Thea remembered taking herself, shared the page. She had to admit that he looked as beautiful and romantic as possible.

'Well,' she said, feeling very ambivalent, handing back the page. 'It's obviously done the trick. The phone hasn't stopped—oops, there it goes again.' After she had dealt with the call, she turned back to Ben. 'But I'm not at all sure it's ethical. I've never been Rory's girlfriend and it's his work they should be talking about, not what he looks like and whether or not he happens to be "a ride".'

'What does that mean, anyway?' demanded Molly.

'I think it's what Petal would describe as "well-fit", in Irish,' said Thea. 'And I haven't time to keep answering the telephone to journalists who are more keen to know whether or not Rory and I were an item than about his work.'

'Well, are you? An item, that is?' asked Ben.

'What has that got to do with the price of fish?' demanded Thea, furious with him for asking, especially in front of Molly, so they couldn't have a proper row.

'Possibly nothing. It's just helpful to know the facts. From a PR point of view.'

'Oh, really? Going on what I've just read, you just make it up. Facts have nothing to do with it.'

'Oh, stop bickering, you two,' Molly snapped. 'How are we going to cope with the phone when we've got so much to do?'

Ben's eyebrows flicked upwards. 'Get Petal back to do it for you. Tell her exactly what to say about your romantic status, and when the private view is.'

'Molly's insisting on canapés, so we have to know how many people are likely to come.'

'Many more than you've invited, that's for sure.'

'I'd better get onto the caterer,' said Molly. 'I hope they can manage the extra numbers.'

'But first, can you ring Petal and ask if her father can bring her over? I can't keep racing back up the stairs every time the phone rings and I've got things to see to down there,' Thea pleaded as the phone rang again.

'I'll use my mobile,' said Molly, as Thea picked it up.

'I'll have a look round,' said Ben. 'If you don't mind.'

Thea was on the phone, so she couldn't tell him that, actually, she minded very much. She wanted to show him round herself.

The next time the phone rang Thea made Molly answer it and went down to see what Ben was up to. She felt terribly cheated that she hadn't been there to show it to him, to see his face when he saw the paintings properly hung for the first time.

He was downstairs in the large gallery and turned when he heard her come in. 'It's fabulous. You've done a brilliant job.'

'I only got the pictures up on the walls. It's Rory who's brilliant.'

He shook his head. 'The setting is important.'

Thea bit her lip. She'd so yearned for his praise, but now that she'd had it she didn't know what to say.

'Thank you for writing to Toby,' Ben said. 'He was thrilled.'

'Oh, good. You know he wrote to me? I felt I had to answer.' What she really wanted to know was whether Ben had read her letter.

'It was kind of you to think of a small boy when you've got so much else on your plate.'

Thea smiled. 'It wasn't a small boy, it was Toby! That's quite different. He and I are friends.'

'But you and I can't be?'

Oh. So he had read the letter. 'Well, what do you think?'

He sighed. 'No. I've got plenty of friends, but none of them are like you.'

'But I hope it won't mean Toby and I can't see each other. I'd be really sorry not to. I love him.' The words came out on a sigh. It was true, she did love Toby, but she also loved the man she was talking to. It was like blowing a kiss in the wrong direction.

Ben nodded.

'Thea!' Molly called downstairs. 'Petal's father's driving her over now. You'll have to come and mind the phone. I've got to see the caterers. Oh, and Rory rang to say he's coming.'

Ben gave a wry smile. 'Well, I'll go now. I've got a house I really want to have another look at.'

'In Bristol?'

'No. Near here. So you and Toby can carry on your relationship.'

Thea spent a few seconds trying to find an appropriate response.

'It's in Goldenley,' Ben went on when she failed.

'Oh. Lovely views up there.'

'I know. It's why I bought it.'

'I look forward to seeing it some time.'

'I'm sure you will. Molly will make me have a housewarming party.'

If Thea hadn't been so ferociously busy she'd have wept.

Rory was wonderfully uncomplicated, and when he appeared in the gallery doorway Thea went to embrace him. His strong arms were comforting and she clung on to him, wishing they belonged to someone else—someone not comforting at all.

'Hey, Thea! Put me down!'

'I'm just so pleased to see you.'

'Well, I'm not staying long. Now, what's happened? You're not usually so keen to put your arms round me.'

Thea laughed, feeling better. 'Nothing's happened, exactly. It's just the phone is ringing constantly and until Petal arrives to answer it I've got to. And Molly is stressing about your statements. She says if we're to get them typed, copied and laminated, she has to have them now. Or yesterday, for preference.'

'I'm not writing any statements.'

'Not even one? Molly wants one for each picture.'

'Well, she can't have them. They're a load of shite.' He grinned. 'Or, at least, mine would be. Why is it that artists, who communicate visually, are expected to become writers? It's like asking novelists to illustrate their work, or paint pictures for their covers.'

Thea laughed. 'That sounds like a well-rehearsed argument. You'd better polish it up for when Molly gets back from the printer's.'

'I'm back now,' said Molly from behind some boxes. 'What argument?'

'No statements, Molly,' said Rory firmly. 'They're shite and they interfere with the work on the wall.'

'People like to know what they're looking at.'

'They can see what they're looking at,' Rory told her. 'They're landscapes. What more can they possibly need than a bloody great picture, eight foot high?'

'I've visited a lot of galleries just lately to find out what they do, and I like to have something to read.'

Rory laughed. 'Shite galleries, if you'll forgive the expression.'

'Oh, don't apologise now,' snapped Molly. 'You've already used that word several times.'

Thea put her hand on Molly's arm. 'Rory's right, Molly. His work doesn't need any explanation and I like things simple. People should be able just to wander around and enjoy themselves without having to carry a huge book to refer to.'

Rory was getting bored. 'So, when you've got the rest of the prints up it'll be finished, with a whole day to spare. You've worked miracles, Thea.'

'We have,' Thea agreed. 'But we haven't got a day to spare. Have you seen the state of the lavatory?'

'I suppose I must have done. I've certainly used it.'

'Then you'll realise it needs decorating. You wouldn't like to do it for us? I can lend you a boiler suit.'

'Sure, I'd love to help you. But I've got to see a woman about—'

'*Please* say it's about a dog, or even a whole pack of them. I'd let you off painting the john for that.' Thea, who was still going home to soggy newspaper and piles of poo, had given up hope of Rory ever taking responsibility for Lara and her pups again.

'Thea, I promise you I'll sort out Lara and find homes for all the pups very soon.' He grinned. 'But actually it's about a television programme she wants me to make. Talking about art through the ages. They saw my picture and thought I'd be perfect for it. Something to do with my cheekbones.'

Thea and Molly exchanged glances but didn't comment. 'Well, as long as you're back here tomorrow by five thirty at the latest—sober! I've got all my photography friends coming to take pictures. I'll need you—or at least your fabulous cheekbones.'

'Bitch,' he said fondly, 'of course I'll be back. I might even beg a bed for the night tonight.'

After he had gone, Molly and Thea smiled at one another. 'Well, I hope he's better at art through the ages than he was on Cézanne,' said Molly.

'He was so crap!'

Molly frowned. 'I know you've been spending a lot of time with Petal, but do you have to raid her limited vocabulary?'

Thea shrugged. 'Crap or not, as he's not going to paint the loo I'd better do it while you're here to man the phones.' She yawned. She'd been keeping very late hours recently.

'Did I tell you I've got my cleaning lady to come in tomorrow and give things a final polish? It's so important that everything is gleaming.'

'Molly, love, I despair of you. We're supposed to be running this gallery on a shoestring. I'll let you get away with it this time, for Rory's show, but after this we're going to have to clean the place ourselves.'

Molly made a face. 'What are you going to wear for the opening?' she asked Thea nervously, as she watched her climb into the boiler suit she had offered Rory. 'Not that, I hope.'

'Oh, I thought I would. I thought it would be cool and funky, a sort of urban statement.'

'Thea, really, I don't know . . .'

'It's all right, I'm joking again. You should know me by now.'

'So, what *are* you going to wear? I'm willing to bet you've nothing suitable in your wardrobe.'

'And nothing suitable in my bank balance, either, so it doesn't matter that I haven't time to buy anything new.' Thea chewed her lip. This problem had crossed her mind a few times, but as she couldn't think of a solution to it she just let it pass right on through.

'Thea.'

Molly was so stern that Thea put down the paint she had just picked up. 'What?'

'I am begging you, please, please, please let me take you shopping to buy something. You are the human manifestation of this gallery. It is essential that you look absolutely beautiful.' She held up her hand before Thea could even draw breath, let alone speak. 'Yes, the work will speak for itself, but when half the art world think you and Rory are having an affair, you don't want them wondering why.'

'Oh my God! They don't, do they?'

'What? Think you and Rory are having an affair? Of course they do! I know you're not, of course.' Molly gave Thea a sidelong glance to check she was right about this. 'But I'm willing to bet all those arty London types will assume it. Why else would he show here? So it's essential that you look so drop-dead gorgeous that it seems perfectly logical.'

Thea tried to protest. 'But I want the gallery—'

'No. You're not having them come through the door, take one look at you and think, my God, those rumours can't be true. Apart from anyone else, there's Ben!'

'What about Ben?'

'The women he's been toting around like Lulu Guinness handbags! There was a family party last week and he brought this . . . woman.' Molly obviously couldn't think of a word bad enough for her. 'She looked about nineteen, but it turned out she was twenty-five—hardly any better for a man Ben's age—and she smoked continuously.'

'What has this got to do with me and what I wear for the opening?' Thea asked, trying to match her expression to the casualness of her words.

Molly looked discomfited. 'Oh, nothing really. I just think Ben has no sense when it comes to women.'

'Really.'

'But none of this is to the point. We need to get you a dress. I'll give you two hours to paint the loo, then I'm taking you away. I know a lovely shop in Cheltenham.'

Reluctantly, two hours later to the minute, Thea climbed out of the boiler suit. In fact, she'd rather have finished painting the lavatory. There was something very soothing about white paint.

The shop was terrifyingly tiny—the sort you could never go into on spec, because you'd be too embarrassed to leave without buying anything. The owner, an extremely attractive woman who was fifty if she was a day, was a huge relief. Thea might not feel she was nearly as good-looking as this elegant person, but knowing she was fifteen years younger did give her some advantage.

Molly and the owner kissed each other fondly. 'Caroline, this is Thea. I've brought her to see you because she needs something absolutely stunning. We're . . . she's opening an art gallery tomorrow.'

'Oh! Is that the one I heard about on local radio this morning? With the new Irish artist? It sounds so exciting.'

'I hope it will be,' said Thea somewhat glumly. The enormity of what she'd taken on suddenly seemed a terrible mistake.

'Of course it will be! With Molly on your side it'll be smashing. Now, what do you feel comfortable wearing?'

Caroline asked a lot of questions and then said, 'Right. You two sit down and have a glass of wine, while I find a few for you to try on.'

'She didn't ask me what size I was,' whispered Thea anxiously.

'No need. She can tell at a glance. Most of the women who come in here have got personal trainers,' Molly went on.

'Personal trainers?' Thea was awestruck. 'Does that mean no one else can wear them? How lovely!'

Molly opened her mouth, and then closed it again. 'Oh, you're joking. Sorry.'

Thea wondered if it was the wine on an empty stomach, or whether she really looked as good as the mirror in front of her told her she did. The dress was black, strapless, short and close-fitting. Thea felt like a minor film star on Oscar night.

'That's the one,' said Caroline.

'It's fabulous!' said Molly.

'I bet that it costs a fortune,' said Thea glumly, 'and I'm not going to

151

have many opportunities to wear it. The cost per wear is going to be horrendous.'

'Usually'—Caroline poured more wine into Thea's glass—'I'd agree with you totally about the cost per wear. But some occasions are worth more than others. After all, a wedding dress, which could cost thousands, is only worn once. But for that occasion it's worth it.'

'And this isn't thousands, after all,' Molly argued.

'And I'm not getting married, nor likely to be. So this could be the equivalent dress. Expensive but exquisite. How much is it?'

'Don't tell her!' Molly put up a silencing hand. 'Darling, this is a present from me and Derek—I've had such fun and he's had such peace and quiet. Buying you a dress is the least we can do.'

'But it's not the least you have done! You've already . . .'

'That was all boring stuff; this is fun.' Molly dismissed the matter of cost with an airy wave. 'Now, Caro, what have you got for me?'

The two photographer friends who, unlike Magenta, hadn't had a hand in her present existence, arrived halfway through Saturday afternoon. Fortunately, when they saw Rory, the work and the space, Thea didn't have to spend too long convincing them she'd made the right decision about her life at last.

'Magenta told us the work was fantastic. She didn't say anything about Rory,' said Elizabeth.

'She only saw the slides of his work, not him,' Thea explained. 'I didn't come across him until after she'd gone to the beauty parlour.'

'Foolish Magenta! I think this is a great gallery and much better for you than being a landlady. I bet those students walked over you.'

Petal, who was running a cloth over the skirting boards—her gesture to manual work—looked up indignantly.

'Well, some of them did. Not you, Petal, of course.'

Petal made a face. Unlike her aunt, she knew when Thea was being sarcastic or making a joke.

The photographers set up their equipment and snapped happily. They took roll after roll of film of Rory, Petal and Thea doing things.

'Did I tell you that a journalist pal is arriving soon? She wants to do an article about you for one of the gossip mags,' said Zelda.

'Oh my God! All I need now is for someone to tell me that the *Sunday Sport* are coming to photograph me and Rory topless. I think everyone else has already been in touch.'

'That would be fine by me,' said Rory. 'I like the idea of Thea topless in front of one of my daubs.'

'Well, there are going to be pictures of your pecs all over the press,' said Thea. 'Satisfy yourself with that thought.'

'Seriously,' Magenta put in. 'You should be really grateful for all this publicity. It's not easy to get and it's very hard to get started without it.'

'It was Ben,' said Molly proudly. 'He arranged it all.'

'Who's Ben?' asked Elizabeth.

'He's connected to one of the London galleries,' Magenta said, protecting Thea from probing questions. 'Bloody useful, too.'

'He's also my cousin,' Molly added. 'Now, Thea, when are you going to get changed? You have to leave enough time to go home, change and get back.'

'Oh, I'm not going home.' Thea laughed. 'I'm going to change . . .'

'In my hotel room.' Magenta was firm. 'It's just across the road. I'm going to do her hair and make-up.'

Thea started on the 'Oh no you're not' but saw she was outnumbered and closed her mouth again.

At five to six Molly, Petal and her crowd, Rory and Thea were ready. They were all nervous, although Rory refused to acknowledge it. He was impossibly good-looking in his casual suit, clean shirt and new shoes. Thea was aware that every woman who saw him would metaphorically fall at his feet.

'Well, we're all here,' said Rory, 'and the champagne and smoked salmon are here. Let's forget about the punters and just have a lovely party!'

Too late Thea remembered she'd resolved to fill him up with stodge. 'Rory, can I have a word with you?' She drew him away and gathered a plateful of canapés. 'Before you drink anything you're to eat these. I'm not having you jeopardising your second chance because you got drunk again. Apart from anything else, it would do for my gallery before it's even had a chance.'

'It's all right. No need to panic. I drank a tablespoon of olive oil before I came, which is what the Russians do to line their stomachs. I forced down a pint of water, so I'm too full to drink much.' Rory paused. 'You know you look sensational, Thea. You knock those other women right out of the frame.'

'Really?' She didn't believe him for a minute, but his flattery was lovely.

Chapter Nine

ALTHOUGH DESPERATE FOR A DRINK to relieve her nerves, Thea had decided not to have anything alcoholic until it was all over. She couldn't risk even the tiniest lapse of concentration. Petal, who had a stream of beautiful girlfriends as well as copious male friends, had turned two of each into waiters and waitresses.

Now Rory said, 'Right, let's open a bottle and have a stiffener before the hordes arrive.'

'I'll have an orange juice,' Thea said. 'And I hope they do arrive.' She opened the door and looked anxiously up and down the street.

'They're not due until six thirty,' said Molly.

'Oh my God! A massive black car has just drawn up.' Thea ducked back into the gallery. 'I don't want anyone to come now!'

Rory put a glass of champagne into Thea's hand. 'Here, one drink won't knock you over and it'll help keep the smile on your face.'

Thea was still clutching her glass, as yet untouched, when the contents of the huge car entered and she found herself wrapped in a cloud of Eau Savage. 'Thea, my dear, this looks fabulous!'

'Edward! You came!' Thea returned his embrace heartily. 'Come in and have a drink. Let Rory show you the work.'

'Oh, Rory's here, is he? How did you manage to keep him in line when so many of us have failed?'

Thea laughed and asked quietly, 'Will Veronica come?'

'Darling, I don't think she could keep away.'

To her relief, there were a few serious art journalists among the gossip columnists and photographers. They fought their way to Thea who discovered she was mistress of the sound bite. She decided to put Veronica to the back of her mind.

But even while talking to genuinely interested people, she found her eye flicking towards the door, looking for Ben and Toby.

Her expensive dress, which was causing a minor sensation among her friends, had been for Ben's benefit. In her heart she knew that. As was the make-up and the hair styling. If she hadn't been hoping to prove to him that she too could be attractive and glamorous, she would never have let Molly talk her into any of it. She wanted Ben to see her at her shining best and wonder why on earth he had let her get away. It was petty, childish and about as unfeminist as it was possible to be, but it was human and she couldn't help herself.

It seemed several lifetimes had passed before at last she saw Ben's tall figure appear in the doorway.

Toby wasn't with him, but two thin, glamorous women were. One was Veronica, wearing a twist of fuchsia-coloured silk and a diamond choker; the other was a much younger woman. Ben was holding the younger woman's elbow in a very protective way.

Thea suddenly felt in need of a bit of protection herself. She looked wildly around and spotted Rory. 'Hold my hand, Rory, quickly, please,' she whispered urgently.

Without asking for an explanation, Rory obligingly put his arm round her and rested his hand on her bottom. 'Will this do?'

'Perfect. Veronica's just come in, with Ben.'

'Veronica! Oh my God!'

'We'll both be very cool and very polite. Use your charm, but subtly. For God's sake, Rory, if you can't charm the pants off a woman like Veronica you're not the man I thought you were!'

'I never managed to charm the pants off you!'

Ben spoke first. 'Hello, Thea. You're looking very . . . thin.'

She decided against kissing him. She had kissed everyone else in the room, man and woman, but she couldn't kiss Ben like that.

'Oh, Ben, hi,' she said, 'and Veronica! How kind of you to come. I've been hearing how influential you are and I'm so grateful you've slogged all the way out here to see the show.' She squeezed Rory's hand to make him say something.

'Veronica!' He released Thea and embraced Veronica. 'Will you ever forgive me?' He looked down into her eyes in a way that Thea recognised. If Veronica had a speck of oestrogen in her body she'd have to respond. 'Come with me to find some champagne. I want to drink it from your slipper.'

'Silly boy!' Veronica allowed herself to be led away, aware of the envious glances of several other women. 'I'm wearing sandals.'

Now Veronica was out of the way, Thea felt free to ask Ben a question.

'Where's Toby? He promised to come to my show.'

'He wanted to, but private views aren't really the place for children, are they?' said Ben's companion. 'He'd be dreadfully bored.'

Thea was hurt on Toby's behalf. He'd want to be here for her sake.

'He can always come and see it another time,' said Ben. 'Oh, sorry, I haven't introduced you. This is Poppy Jacks. Thea Orville, the director and creator of the gallery.'

Thea waited in vain to be told that Poppy Jacks was terribly important in the art world, which would also tell her that Ben had only brought her to be useful, not because he had anything to do with her.

Poppy Jacks extended her hand. 'Hi! I think it's terribly brave what you're doing. Opening an art gallery against all the odds. Ben told me how much effort he's put into it himself, just so it wasn't a complete flop before it even opened.'

For the first time that evening, Thea found herself without anything to say. Eventually she managed, 'I've got a hundred people I must talk to. Ben, why don't you show Poppy round?'

Who's Ben with?' demanded Molly. 'I saw Rory working on Veronica. I must admit, when he chooses to use it, that man has the charm of the devil.'

'And the cheekbones of an angel,' said Magenta, scooping a glass of champagne off a passing tray. 'See you later!'

'So?' Molly hadn't had her answer yet.

'You could ask him yourself, but she's called Poppy.'

'So is she the one who did all the PR?'

'You're the one who knows all about Ben's private life. Why don't you go and get an update?' Thea smiled to soften her crispness. 'Now I must find Edward Grampian.'

Molly found Thea a little later. 'It's not the PR woman. Poppy's just a popsy. Oh! I've made a pun. I think.'

We're going now. It's a wonderful show.' Ben kissed Thea's cheek.

'Yes,' Poppy added. 'It's been such fun. Now we're going to eat. Edward has taken Veronica on somewhere, so we're off the leash.'

'That's nice,' said Thea. 'We're all going to the Chinese Dragon, if you'd like to join us.' Watching Ben flirting with Poppy all night would be torture. The thought that she might never see him again if she let him escape was even worse.

Poppy laughed. 'Oh, no. Ben's promised me something a little more sophisticated than we can get here.'

Thea's jaw clamped. If she wasn't careful she'd burst into tears.

'Poppy doesn't like Chinese food,' said Ben.

Thea forced her mouth open. 'So, what are you going to do?'

'Ben knows a little place near Chipping Norton.' Poppy almost clapped her hands in anticipation. 'Sounds wonderful!'

'Sounds a long way away,' said Thea.

'So what are you going to do again?' Ben asked.

Why was Ben still there when, if he'd had an iota of tact, he would have left Thea to allow herself a short, violent display of emotion? 'The Chinese Dragon. Rory and I are going to get rat-arsed. I think we deserve it, don't you?'

There was a flicker of something in Ben's expression, but it was probably just shock that she'd used such a vulgar expression. He steered his woman out of the gallery into the warm summer night.

There were nearly twenty of them in all at the Chinese Dragon, although they had only booked for ten. The staff were courteous and welcoming, and moved tables about, found chairs and chopsticks.

Thea didn't sit next to Rory. He was very excited, high on his success. The art-buying public had, in Thea's opinion, lost their heads completely. Once the first red sticker went on, everyone was desperate to get a piece of this exciting new talent, notwithstanding the enormous prices Thea and Rory had decided on. Not one of them objected when Thea told them that the paintings were possibly to be shown in London, and that they might not be able to get their hands on their prize for months. This was after Edward had told her he still wanted Rory to exhibit and would she not let any of the work be taken away before he'd had a chance to decide what he wanted.

Thea had no appetite. When people ordered, she just agreed to share a set menu someone else had decided was good.

Rory was the young lion, the centre of attention, charming the socks off everyone present. Thea was glad she wasn't at his side. She didn't want them to be seen as a couple. It wasn't fair to him when he probably wanted a woman to end the evening with. There were several other young women in the party, all hungry for his smile or anything else he might be giving away.

She sipped her mineral water. All she wanted to do was to drive home, on her own, and go to bed. She was so tired she could have slept where she sat and was just slipping into a state not far removed from sleep when she became aware of someone calling her name.

She looked up and saw Ben. 'Thea, can I have a word? In private?'

He spoke urgently and Thea wondered what on earth could have happened. She got up immediately. 'What's the matter? Is it Toby?'

He shook his head slightly, but lost nothing of his urgency. 'Bring your bag and coat.'

Thea looked at Molly, who seemed not to have noticed Ben's appearance. Rory was Blarney-stoning one of Thea's photographer friends and hadn't noticed either. Thea picked up her jacket from the back of her chair.

Once in the street, he took her by the shoulders and looked intently down at her. 'I have to know. Are you really going to sit with that lot all night and get "rat-arsed" as you so elegantly put it?'

'And why shouldn't I?'

'There's something I want to show you.' He didn't release his grip.

'What is it? I can't just walk out on everybody.'

'Most of them are drunk and Molly will see to anyone who isn't.'

'But I don't want to walk out on them!'

He stared down into her face intently. 'Don't you really?'

Honesty fought with pride and won. She shrugged.

'Then come with me. I promise you, you won't regret it.'

'But where's your friend? Popsy—Poppy?'

'I put her in a taxi. Now, will you come with me or not?' He didn't wait for her answer. He just took her wrist and pulled her along the road to where his car was parked across a double yellow line.

He drove up and out of the town to a valley Thea didn't know. She stared out of the window at the beauty of the summer darkness. The moon had risen, bathing everything with light, casting strange shadows. The trees stood out against the sky. The hills took on the shapes of enormous mythic beasts and honeysuckle-scented hedges were dotted with bindweed flowers, strangely white. She didn't let herself think about where she was going or why, she just hoped the drive would go on for ever. At the moment it was perfect: she didn't have to speak and she was with Ben. The minute they had to talk they'd start fighting with each other again.

He took his car down a drive to where a house sat silhouetted in the twilight. Roses, in dire need of pruning, grew almost across a leaning wooden porch. A FOR SALE sign, with a SOLD SUBJECT TO CONTRACT band stuck across it, stood by the front gate.

Ben stopped the car and got out. Then he walked round and opened her door. 'Come on.'

Reluctant as she was to spoil it all by opening her mouth, she had to protest. 'Ben, we can't call on people at this time of night!'

He didn't answer; he just manoeuvred her up the path to the front door. They were standing very close together and she was intensely aware of his physical presence. She yearned for him to catch her mood and take her in his arms. He didn't. He held back the roses, so she wouldn't get scratched, then produced some keys and unlocked the door. 'There.'

She stepped past him, away from his disturbing nearness, and looked about her.

The house was obviously empty and had been for some time, because there was dust everywhere. Thea stood in the entrance, trying to make out the details in the moonlight.

The door opened directly into the front room, which had probably been two rooms at one time, judging by the beam that ran across it. She could make out a massive fireplace at one end and a staircase at the other. There was a window almost opposite the front door, through which Thea could see a garden and tree-covered hills beyond. The house was enchanting.

'It's amazing,' said Thea. 'But I don't understand. You kidnap me—and you really did kidnap me—take me away from all my friends and important contacts to show me a house you could have shown me at any other time.'

'I couldn't wait any longer. I couldn't risk it. If I hadn't taken you away when I did, you'd have gone to bed with Rory.'

'Oh. Why did you want to stop me? You've got Poppy, after all. You've never shown any interest in me, so it can't be jealousy.'

'Jealousy! If you knew what I've gone through. What do you mean, I've never shown any interest in you? You must know by now how I feel about you.'

'How was I supposed to do that? You've only ever kissed me when you've been angry and couldn't hit me.' Suddenly she found herself smiling. 'You're angry now, aren't you? You want to hit me again.'

She heard him laugh softly as he walked towards her. 'Well, yes, but not quite as much as I want to kiss you.'

He swept her into his arms, crushing her expensive dress and her with the same ruthlessness. His mouth came down on hers and his fingers pushed up into her hair. She couldn't move, could hardly breathe, and wanted to stay there for ever. It felt as if all the kisses he'd never given her were concentrated in that one kiss.

Eventually, breathless, he released her mouth, but kept hold of her body. It was as well he did, otherwise she'd have fallen over. 'So,' he said, breathing hard. 'Now can I ask you to marry me? And don't say it's all so sudden, because it isn't and you know it isn't. I've been in love with you since I first helped you step out of a rubbish bin. We may fight like cat and dog, but we're destined for each other and you know it as well as I do.'

Thea swallowed. While she wanted nothing better than to go on kissing Ben for the rest of her life, she had to get a few things straight first. 'What about those other women? Like handbags?'

'What are you talking about?'

'Always another pretty girl dangling off your arm. Molly told me about them. You took one to a family party. She wasn't Poppy, I assume, or Molly would have recognised her.'

He laughed again. For possibly the first time since she'd known him, he seemed carefree. 'Cilla was just to stop the family gossip and Poppy was a smoke screen so Veronica wouldn't guess I cared about you.'

'You used her!'

'She's used plenty of people in her time. It'll do her good to be useful for once.'

'You are a bastard!'

'Thea, have you any idea how utterly terrifying it is to realise that the woman you love could be seriously harmed by the woman you once loved? And if I'd gone to a family party without a woman, they'd have pestered me with questions about this woman that Toby likes so much. Word would have got back to Veronica and she'd have had her knives into your gallery so deep you'd never get them out. Now, can we please stop arguing?'

'I'm not arguing. You're doing it all on your own. And if you liked me so much, why didn't you ask me out, like a normal human being?'

'I've told you. Because of Veronica.'

'Well, Veronica's still alive, isn't she? Why is it all right to bring me here now?'

'Because now your gallery will be a success whatever she does. And no judge would give her custody of Toby, if she tried that one, when they hear Toby tell them how much he wants to live with us.'

A horrible thought struck her. 'Ben, you're not doing all this because of Toby, are you? I mean, I really do love him, but I'm not going to marry you just to make him happy.'

'What about making me happy?' he whispered. 'Or you? Would marrying me make you happy? Because that's the most important thing.'

She couldn't speak. If she tried, she'd burst into tears.

'Listen, why don't you come and sit down? Your feet must be killing you in those ridiculous heels.'

Glad that he was back to criticising her, she said, 'They're not ridiculous, they're essential to go with this dress.' She turned to him. 'Don't you like it? It was very expensive.'

'It's wonderful, but I can't stop thinking about what you'd look like without it on.'

'Oh.'

'I'll give you two seconds to get to the door, but if you don't run I'm very much afraid that I'm going to have to make love to you.'

She gave a petulant little sigh. 'These heels are all very well, but they're hell to walk in.'

He growled and came towards her, picking her up with terrifying ease. She started to giggle. 'This is terribly romantic, Ben, but where are you going to take me?'

He carried her up the dusty staircase, along a moonlit corridor to a bedroom. He kicked open the door and revealed a double sleeping-bag, some pillows and some carrier bags.

He lowered her to her feet and Thea turned to him, pushing her arms round his body under his jacket, feeling the heat of his skin through the fine cotton.

'Oh God, Thea,' he breathed and seconds later her dress had rustled to her feet, leaving her in her high heels and her briefs. 'You are so beautiful. I could look at you for ever.'

She tutted and kicked her dress out of the way. 'Not if I have anything to do with it, you couldn't.'

At first they were so urgent and hungry for each other that there was no time for tender caresses. It was only after they fell apart, sweating and panting, that they had time really to enjoy each other.

'I didn't realise sex could be like that,' said Thea, still out of breath.

'I'm a bit surprised myself. Would you like a glass of champagne? I may not be able to offer you a goose-feather duvet, but I did get in a few essential supplies.'

He sat up, his muscled torso highlighted by moonlight, and reached for one of the carrier bags. 'Two bottles of champagne, originally ready-chilled, but possibly warmer now. A tin of foie gras, some Bath Oliver biscuits, a few tomatoes and some cheese. Oh, and some chocolate truffles for pudding.'

He rolled off the sleeping-bag and crossed the room to where his trousers lay in a heap. From the pocket he produced a Swiss army knife.

Watching him move, Thea longed to have a camera with her, to capture for ever the sight of his beautiful masculine body as he moved about in the moonlight. Then she remembered she didn't need a photograph of it after all. It was hers to look at whenever the moon was full. 'I think I'm going to like being married to you, Ben,' she said when he handed her a biscuit loaded with pâté.

'I'm going to make absolutely sure you do.'

His kiss tasted of champagne.

KATIE FFORDE

As a writer, Katie Fforde draws extensively upon her own experiences in life and never more so than in her latest novel, *Artistic Licence*, which is set in and around her home town of Stroud, Gloucestershire. In the book, Katie's heroine, Thea, opens an art gallery which is based on the real Stroud House Gallery where the author herself often helps out. 'I adore art but don't paint myself, although I yearn to be a watercolour artist. A friend runs the gallery and I help her with the cleaning if she's having an exhibition. Occasionally I gallery-sit too, which is great fun.' But Katie is the first to admit that her knowledge of the art world has increased enormously in the course of researching *Artistic Licence*. 'Before I started writing, I'd look at a piece of contemporary art and think: "I don't understand it". But now I'm seeing much more in it, which is very exciting. I have even started buying a few paintings.'

When I met Katie Fforde she was accompanied by another close friend, Gilli Allan. It was with Gilli that Katie recently embarked on her own 'Tiger Tours' art appreciation course in Aix-en-Provence, 'although it was very different to the tour described in the novel. And Gilli is nothing like Molly,' Katie adds with a laugh, reassuring her friend with a pat on the hand. 'For a start she is not at all bossy and she doesn't snore! But she does have a rigorous beauty regime, which I gave to Molly.'

Having left school at fifteen, without much formal education, Katie initially trained as a ballet dancer before embarking on a cookery course and marriage. With her sailor husband, Desmond, she ran a floating hotel on two narrow boats on the canals of England—a setting she later used in her novel, *Life Skills*—before settling in Gloucestershire. But the Ffordes' love of boats has never waned and they have recently bought a Dutch barge, which is moored in London, for one of their sons to live on while he is at university. 'It's also a place for us to stay when we are in town and it gives me a wonderful chance to rid my house of all the pictures of boats that we have dotted about the place! Then there will finally be room for my new contemporary art collection.'

Katie did not begin her writing career until she was thirty-two, and it took ten years for her first novel to be published. Her advice to writers is 'to have perseverance and dogged determination. There are lots of very talented people out there but they give up far too easily.'

Always busy, Katie has just finished her next novel, *Highland Fling*, which explores the latest fad of having a virtual assistant. 'It's like having a secretary that you never see. Everything is done via email or the phone. It must be a brilliant job if you live in a remote location.'

Katie's enthusiasm for life and writing spills over as we talk and Gilli listens quietly. 'I love being a writer,' Katie tells me. 'I think I'm quite realistic about what I do, though. It's great fun and quite light-hearted, isn't it? It's not rocket science, after all. Just entertainment.'

Jane Eastgate

Summer Island

Kristin Hannah

'Hello and welcome. You're on the air with
Nora Bridge.'

These are the words that every night unleash a
wealth of suffering and regret as Nora listens to
the problems of her radio audience and tries to
help them with her straightforward, moral
advice. Her listeners adore her, but to her own
family she is a stranger. For, many years ago,
Nora walked out on her marriage and left her
daughters behind, with no word of explanation.
Now the tabloids have unearthed a scandalous
secret from Nora's past, and the time has come
for her to tell her story for a change.

Chapter One

An early evening rain had fallen. In the encroaching darkness the streets of Seattle lay like mirrored strips between the glittering grey high-rises.

The dot-com revolution had changed this once quiet city, and even after the sun had set, the clattering, hammering sounds of construction beat a constant rhythm. Buildings sprouted overnight, it seemed, reaching higher and higher into the soggy sky. Purple-haired kids with nose rings and ragged clothes zipped through downtown in brand-new, bright red Ferraris.

On a corner lot in the newly fashionable neighbourhood of Belltown, there was a squat wooden structure that had been built almost one hundred years earlier, when few people had wanted to live so far from the heart of the city. The owners of radio station KJZZ didn't care that they no longer fitted into this trendy area. For fifty years they had broadcast from this lot. They had grown from a scrappy local station to Washington's largest. Part of the reason for their current success was Nora Bridge, the newest sensation in talk radio.

Although her show, *Spiritual Healing with Nora*, had been in syndication for less than a year, it was already a bona fide hit. And her weekly newspaper advice column, 'Nora Knows Best', appeared in more than 2,600 papers nationwide.

Nora had started her career as a household hints adviser for a small-town newspaper, but hard work and a vision had moved her up the food chain. The women of Seattle had been the first to discover her unique blend of passion and morality; the rest of the country had soon followed. Reviewers claimed that she could see a way through any emotional conflict; more often than not, they mentioned the purity of her heart.

But they were wrong. It was the *impurity* in her heart that made her successful. She was an ordinary woman who'd made extraordinary mistakes. She understood every nuance of need and loss.

There was never a time in her life, barely even a moment, when she didn't remember what she'd lost. What she'd thrown away. Each night, she brought her own regrets to the microphone, and from that wellspring of sorrow, she found compassion.

She had managed her career with laserlike focus, carefully feeding the press a palatable past. Even the previous week when *People* magazine had featured her on the cover, there had been no investigative story on her life. She had covered her tracks well. Her fans knew she'd been divorced and that she had grown-up daughters. The hows and whys of her family's destruction remained—thankfully—private.

Tonight Nora was on the air. She scooted her wheeled chair closer to the microphone and adjusted her headphones. A computer screen showed her the list of callers on hold. She pushed line two, which read MARGE/MOTHER–DAUGHTER PROBS.

'Hello, Marge. You're on the air with Nora Bridge.'

'Hello . . . Nora?' The caller sounded hesitant.

Nora smiled. Her fans, she'd learned, were often anxious. 'How can I help you, my friend?' she asked gently.

'I'm having a little trouble with my daughter, Suki.'

'How old is Suki, Marge?'

'Sixty-seven this November.'

Nora laughed. 'I guess some things never change, eh?'

'Not between mothers and daughters. Suki gave me my first grey hair when I was thirty years old. Now I look like Colonel Sanders.'

Nora's laugh was quieter this time. At forty-nine, she no longer found grey hair a laughing matter. 'So, Marge, what's the problem with Suki?'

'Well'—Marge made a snorting sound—'last week she went on a singles cruise, and today she told me she's getting married again, to a man she met on the boat. At *her* age.' She snorted again. 'I know she wanted me to be happy for her, but how could I?'

Nora asked, 'Do you love your daughter?'

'I've always loved her.' Marge's voice caught on a sob. 'You can't know what it's like, Nora, to love your daughter so much and watch her stop needing you. What if she marries this man and forgets all about me?'

Nora closed her eyes and cleared her mind. She'd learned long ago that callers were constantly saying things that struck at the heart of her own pain. 'Every mother is afraid of that, Marge. The only way to really hold on to our children is to let them go. Let Suki take your love with her, let it be like a light that's always on in the house where she grew up. If she has that for strength, she'll never be far away.'

Marge wept softly. 'Maybe I could call her, ask her to bring her boyfriend around for supper.'

'That would be a wonderful start. Good luck to you, Marge.' Nora cleared her throat and disconnected the call. 'Come on, everybody,' she said into the microphone. 'I know there are plenty of you who have mended families. Call in. Marge and I want to be reminded that love isn't as fragile as it sometimes feels.'

She leaned back in the chair, watching as the phone lines lit up. Parenting issues were always a popular topic—especially mother–daughter problems. On the monitor she saw the words: LINE FOUR/TROUBLE WITH STEPDAUGHTER/GINNY.

She picked up line four. 'Hello and welcome, Ginny. You're on the air with Nora Bridge.'

For the next two hours Nora gave her heart and soul to her listeners. She never pretended to have all the answers or to be a substitute for doctors or family therapy. Instead she tried to give her friendship to these troubled, ordinary people she'd never met.

When the show was finally over, she returned to her office. There she took the time to write personal thank-you notes to those callers who'd been willing to leave an address with the show's producer. Anyone who'd been courageous enough to publicly ask for advice from Nora deserved a private thank-you.

By the time she finished, she was running late. She grabbed her briefcase and hurried to her car. Fortunately, it was only a few miles to the hospital. She parked in the underground lot and emerged into the lobby's artificial brightness.

It was past visiting hours, but this was a small, privately run hospital, and Nora had become a regular visitor—every Saturday and Tuesday for the past month—and she smiled and waved to the nurses' familiar faces as she walked down the corridor towards Eric's room. Outside his closed door, she paused, collecting herself.

Although she saw him often, it was never easy. Eric Sloan was as close

169

to a son as she would have, and watching him battle cancer was unbearable. But she was all he had. His mother and father had written Eric off long ago, unable to accept his life's choices, and his beloved younger brother, Dean, rarely made time to visit.

Nora pushed open the door to his room and saw that he lay in bed sleeping. With his hair almost gone, his cheeks hollow, and his mouth open, he looked as old and beaten as a man could be. And he hadn't yet celebrated his thirty-first birthday.

She went to him, gently caressed the bare top of his head. The few thin strands of his hair, delicate as spiderwebs, brushed across her knuckles.

He blinked up at her sleepily, trying for a boyish grin and almost succeeding. 'I have good news and bad news,' he said.

She touched his shoulder and felt how fragile he was. There was a tiny catch in her voice as she said, 'What's the good news?'

'No more treatments.'

She clutched his shoulder too hard. 'And the bad news?'

'No more treatments.' He paused. 'It was Dr Calomel's idea.'

She nodded dully. In the eleven months since his diagnosis, they'd spent dozens of nights talking about this moment. She'd even thought she was ready for it, but now she saw her naiveté. There was no 'ready' for death, especially not when it came for a young man you loved.

And yet, she understood. She'd seen lately that the cancer was taking him away.

Eric closed his eyes, and she wondered if he was remembering the healthy, vibrant man he'd once been, the boy with the booming laugh . . . the teacher so beloved by his students . . . or if he was recalling the time, a few years before, when his partner, Charlie, had been in a hospital bed like this one, fighting a losing battle with AIDS.

Finally Eric looked up at her. His attempt at a smile brought tears to her eyes. In that second she saw pieces from the whole of his life. She pictured him at eight, sitting at her kitchen table, eating Lucky Charms—a shaggy-haired, freckle-faced boy with banged-up knees and soup-ladle ears.

'I'm going home,' he said quietly.

'That's great,' she said, smiling too brightly, trying to pretend they were talking about where he was going to live, instead of where he'd chosen to die. 'I'll visit you during the day. I'll still have to work the show at night, but—'

'I mean the island. I'm going *home*.'

'Are you finally going to call your family?' She hated his decision to handle his cancer privately, but he'd been adamant. He'd forbidden Nora to tell anyone, and as much as she'd disagreed, she'd had no choice but to honour his wishes.

'Oh, yeah. They've been so supportive in the past.'

'This is different than coming out of the closet, and you know it. It's time to call Dean. And your parents.'

The look he gave her was so hopeless that she wanted to turn away. 'What if I told my mother I was dying and she still wouldn't come to see me?'

Nora understood. Even a thin blade of that hope could cut him to pieces now. 'At least call your brother.' She forced a smile. 'If you can wait until Tuesday, I'll drive you—'

'I haven't got much time. I've arranged to be flown up. Lottie's already at the house, getting it ready.'

Haven't got much time. It was infinitely worse, somehow, to hear the words spoken aloud. She swallowed hard. 'I don't think you should be alone.'

'Enough.' His voice was soft, but she heard the barest echo of his former strength. He was reminding her that he was an adult, a grown man. 'Now,' he said, clapping his hands together, 'let's talk about something else. I listened to your show tonight. Mothers and daughters. That's always tough on you.'

Just like that, he put them back on solid ground. As always, she was amazed by his resilience. When life seemed too big to swallow, she knew he made it through by cutting it into bites . . . ordinary conversations were his salvation.

She pulled up a chair and sat down. 'I never really know what to say, and I feel like the biggest hypocrite on the planet. How would Marge feel if she knew I hadn't spoken to my own daughter in eleven years?'

Eric didn't answer the rhetorical question. It was one of the things she loved best about him. He never tried to comfort her with lies. But it helped Nora that Eric recognised how painful it was to think about her younger daughter.

'I wonder what she's doing now.'

It was a common question between them, one they speculated about endlessly.

Eric managed a laugh. 'With Ruby it could be anything, from having lunch with Steven Spielberg to piercing her tongue.'

171

'The last time I spoke to Caroline, she said that Ruby had dyed her hair blue.' Nora laughed, then fell abruptly silent.

Eric leaned forward. There was a sudden earnestness in his eyes. 'She's not dead, Nora.'

'I know. I try to squeeze hope from that thought all the time.'

He grinned. 'Now get out the backgammon board. I feel like whopping your ass.'

It was only the second week of June, and already the temperature hovered at one hundred degrees. A freak heatwave they called it on the local news, the kind of weather that usually came to southern California later in the year.

No one could sleep in this heat, and Ruby Bridge was no exception. She lay sprawled in her bed, the sheets shoved down to the floor, a cold pack pressed across her forehead.

The minutes ticked by, each one a moaning sound caught in the window air-conditioning unit, a *whoosh-ping* that did little but stir the hot air around.

She was lonely. Only a few days earlier her boyfriend, Max, had left her. After five years of living together, he'd simply walked out of her life, like a plumber who'd finished an unpleasant job. All he'd left behind were a few pieces of furniture and a note.

Dear Ruby,
  I never meant to fall out of love with you (or into love with Angie) but shit happens. You know how it is. I need to be free.
  Max.

The funny thing was, she hardly missed him. In fact, she didn't miss *him* at all. She missed the idea of him. She missed a second plate at the dinner table, another body in bed. Mostly she missed the pretence that she was in love. Max had been a physical embodiment of the belief that she could love, and be loved in return.

At 7.00am, the alarm clock sounded. Ruby slid out of bed on a slug-like trail of perspiration and went to the bathroom, where she took a lukewarm shower. She was sweating again before she was finished drying off. Grabbing the grease-stained black polyester trousers and white cotton blouse that lay tangled on the floor, she got dressed and went out into the stifling heat.

She walked downstairs to her battered 1970 Volkswagen Bug.

After a few tries the engine turned over, and Ruby drove towards Irma's Hash House, the trendy Venice Beach diner where she'd worked for almost three years.

She'd never meant to *stay* a waitress. The job was supposed to be temporary, something to pay the bills until she got on her feet, caused a sensation at one of the local comedy clubs, did a guest spot on *Leno,* and—finally—was offered her own sitcom. But at twenty-seven, after almost a decade spent trying to break into comedy, Ruby was brushing up against 'too old'. Everyone knew that if you didn't make it by thirty, you were toast.

She parked in the crowded parking lot and headed for the diner. When she opened the front door, the bell tinkled overhead.

Irma, her three-storey beehive hairdo leading the way, bustled towards Ruby, then came to an abrupt halt in front of her. Irma's heavily mascaraed eyes narrowed. 'You were scheduled for last night.'

Ruby winced. 'Oh, shit.'

'I'm letting you go,' Irma said. 'We can't count on you. Debbie had to work a double shift last night. Your final pay cheque is at the register. I'll expect the uniform back tomorrow. Cleaned.'

Ruby's lips trembled mutinously. The thought of pleading for this shitty job made her sick. 'Come on, Irma. I *need* this job.'

'I'm sorry, Ruby. Really.' She turned and walked away.

Ruby stood there a minute, breathing in the familiar mixture of maple syrup and grease. Then she snagged her pay cheque from the counter and walked out of the restaurant.

She got into her car and drove away aimlessly, up one street and down the other. Finally, when it felt as if her face were melting off her skull, she parked in front of a high-rise building on Wilshire Boulevard. Before she had time to talk herself out of it, she went to the elevator and rode it up to the top floor. The doors opened, and she walked briskly down the corridor towards her agent's office and pushed through the frosted-glass double doors.

The receptionist, Maudeen Wachsmith, had her nose buried in a romance novel. Barely looking up, she said, 'Hi, Ruby. He's busy today. You'll have to make an appointment.'

Ruby rushed past Maudeen and yanked the door open.

Her agent, Valentine Lightner, was seated behind the glassy expanse of his desk. When he saw Ruby, his smile faded into a frown. 'Ruby, I wasn't expecting you . . . was I?'

Maudeen rushed in behind Ruby. 'I'm sorry, Mr Lightner.'

He raised a slim hand. 'Don't worry about it, Maudeen.' He leaned back in his chair. 'So, Ruby, what's going on?'

She waited for Maudeen to leave. 'Is that cruise-ship job still available?' She'd laughed about it three months before—cruise ships were floating morgues for talent—but now it didn't seem beneath her. It seemed above her.

'I've *tried* for you, Ruby. You write funny stuff, but the truth is, your delivery sucks. And that's no ordinary chip on your shoulder, it's a section of the Hoover Dam. You've burned too many bridges in this business. No one wants to hire you.'

'Someone—'

'No one. Remember the job I got you on that sitcom? You slowed down the first week's production and made everyone insane with rewrites.'

'My character was an idiot. She didn't have one funny line.'

Val looked at her, his eyes narrowing. 'Shall I remind you that another—less talented—comedian is now making thirty thousand dollars an episode saying what she's told to say?'

Ruby collapsed into the plush leather chair in front of his desk. 'I'm broke. Irma fired me from the diner.'

'Why don't you call your mother?'

'Don't go there, Val,' she said quietly.

'I know, I know, she's the bitch from hell. But come on, Ruby, I saw that article in *People*. She's rich and famous. Maybe she could help you.'

'You're rich and famous and you can't help me. Besides, she's *helped* me enough. Any more motherly attention and I could end up strapped to a table in Ward B singing "I Gotta Be Me".' Ruby got to her feet. 'Well, thanks for nothing, Val.'

'It's that sparkling personality that makes helping you so damned easy.' He sighed. 'I'll try Asia. They love US comedians overseas. Maybe you can do the nightclub circuit.'

She winced, imagining herself in one of those men's bars with naked women writhing up and down silver poles behind her.

Val had always been her champion, her biggest fan. She'd been with him a long time—since her first days at the Comedy Store. But in the past few years she'd disappointed him. She didn't know what was wrong with her, except that she seemed to be angry all the time. 'I appreciate everything you've done for me, Val. I know it's hard to get work for a prima donna with no talent.'

He said, 'You have as much raw talent as anyone. You light up a room with your smile, and your wit is as sharp as a blade. Let me ask you a question. When did you stop smiling, Ruby?'

She knew the answer, of course. It had happened in her junior year of high school, but she wouldn't think about that time—not even to give Val an answer.

'I don't know.' She wished she could let Val see how frightened she was, how alone she felt. But she couldn't do it. No matter how hard she tried, Ruby couldn't let down her guard. Her emotions were packed tightly inside her, hermetically sealed so that every wound and memory stayed fresh.

'Well,' she said at last, straightening her shoulders, puffing out her unimpressive chest. She had the fleeting sense that she looked absurd— a wounded sparrow trying to impress a peregrine falcon. 'I guess I'd better go home and learn to speak Japanese.'

'That's my girl.' Val smiled wanly. 'I'll make the calls about Asia.'

'I'm grateful. Sayonara.' She wiggled her fingers in an oh-so-California-darling wave and did her best to sashay out of the office. It was tough to pull off in a sweat-stained waitress uniform, and the minute she was out of his office, she let go of her fake smile.

Outside, she headed for her car. There was a parking ticket on her windscreen. She yanked the paper from beneath the rusted windscreen wiper and wadded it into a ball. To her mind, ticketing this rattrap and expecting to get paid was like leaving a bill on the pillow at a homeless shelter. She felt the hot sting of tears.

Absurdly, she thought, If only it would rain.

June was a hard month in Seattle. It was in this season, when the peonies and delphiniums bloomed, that the locals began to complain that they'd been cheated. The rains had started in October. By the last week in May, even the meteorologically challenged denizens of Seattle had had enough. They'd put up with nearly nine months of dismal weather, and it was past time for the sun to deliver.

So it was hardly surprising that it rained on the day Nora Bridge celebrated her fiftieth birthday. She didn't take the weather as an omen or a portent of bad luck. In retrospect she should have.

She stood at the window in her office sipping her favourite drink— Mumm champagne with a slice of fresh peach. On her windowsill were dozens of birthday cards. The most treasured card had come from her elder daughter, Caroline. Of course, the joy of that card was tempered by the fact that, again this year, there had been no card from Ruby.

Nora gave herself a little time to wallow in regret, and then she rallied. Fifteen years of therapy had granted her this skill; she could compartmentalise. She turned away from the window and glanced at the crystal clock on her desk. It was four thirty-eight.

They were down in the conference room now, setting out food, bottles of champagne, plates filled with peach slices. Assistants, publicists, staff writers, producers—they were all putting together a 'surprise' party for the newest star of talk radio.

Nora set her champagne flute down on her desk and opened one of her drawers, pulling out a small black Chanel make-up case. She touched up her face, then headed out of the office.

The corridors were unusually quiet. Probably everyone was helping out with the party. At precisely four forty-five, Nora walked into the conference room.

It was empty. The long table was bare; no food was spread out. A HAPPY BIRTHDAY banner hung from the overhead lights. It looked as if someone had started to decorate for a party and then suddenly stopped.

It was a moment before Nora noticed the two men standing to her left: Bob Wharton, the station's owner and manager, and Jason Close, the in-house attorney.

Nora smiled warmly. 'Hello, Bob. Jason,' she said, moving towards them. 'It's good to see you.'

The men exchanged a quick glance.

She felt a prickling of unease. 'Bob?'

Bob's fleshy face creased into a frown. 'We have some bad news.'

'Bad news?'

Jason eased past Bob and came up to Nora. 'Earlier today Bob took a call from a man named Vince Corell.'

Nora felt as if she'd been smacked in the face. The air rushed out of her lungs.

'He claimed he'd had an affair with you while you were married. He wanted us to pay him to keep quiet.'

'An *affair*, Nora,' Bob sputtered angrily. 'While your kids were at home. You should have told us.'

She'd told her readers and listeners a thousand times to be strong. *Never let them see you're afraid. Believe in yourself and people will believe in you.* But now that she needed that strength, it was gone. 'I could say he was lying,' she said, wincing when she heard the breathy, desperate tone of her voice.

Jason opened his briefcase, took out a manila envelope, and handed it to her. Her hands were shaking as she opened it.

There were black and white photographs inside. She pulled the top one halfway out. 'Oh God,' she whispered. She crammed it back into the envelope. 'There must be a way to stop this. An injunction. Those are private photographs.'

'Yes, they are,' Jason said. 'His. It's obvious that you . . . knew the camera was there. You're posing. He's probably been waiting all this time for you to become famous. That piece in *People* must have done it.'

She looked at them. 'How much does he want?'

There was a pregnant pause. 'A half-million dollars,' Jason said.

'I can get that amount—'

'Money never kills this kind of thing, Nora. You know that.'

She understood immediately. 'You told him no,' she said woodenly. 'And now he's going to go to the tabloids.'

Jason nodded. 'I'm sorry, Nora.'

'I can explain this to my fans,' she said. 'They'll underst—'

'You give *moral* advice, Nora.' Bob shook his head. 'This is going to be a hell of a scandal. When these photos hit the air, we'll lose advertisers instantly. We've been promoting you as a modern version of Mother Teresa. Now it turns out you're Debbie Does Dallas.'

Nora flinched but tried to appear calm. 'What do we do?'

'We want you to take some time off.' Jason touched her shoulder gently. 'You've spent the better part of the past decade telling people to honour their commitments and put their families first. How long do you think it will take the press to uncover that you haven't spoken to your own daughter since the divorce? Your advice is going to ring a little hollow after that.'

Bob nodded. 'The press is going to rip you limb from limb, Nora. Not because you deserve it, but because they can. The tabloids love a celebrity in trouble . . . and with sexy pictures.'

And just like that, Nora's life slipped beyond her grasp. 'It'll blow over,' she whispered, knowing in her heart that it wasn't true. 'I'll take a few weeks off. See what happens.'

'For the record,' Jason said, 'this is a scheduled vacation. We won't admit that it has anything to do with the scandal.'

'Thank you.'

'I hope you make it through this,' Jason said. 'We all do.'

There was an awkward silence. Then Jason and Bob walked past Nora. The door clicked shut behind them.

She stood there, alone now, her gaze blurred by tears. After eleven years of working seventy-hour weeks, it was over, blown apart by a few naked photographs taken a lifetime ago. The world would see her hypocrisy, and so too—oh God—would her daughters.

They would know at last that their mother had had an affair and that she'd lied to all of them when she walked out of her marriage.

Ruby had a pounding headache. She'd slept on and off all day. Finally she stumbled into the living room, leaned against the wall, and slid down to a sit, her legs stretched out. She should walk down to Chang's Mini-Mart and pick up a newspaper, but the thought of turning to the want ads was more than she could bear.

The phone rang. Ruby didn't want to answer. It could hardly be good news. At best it would be Caroline, her yuppie sister, who had two perfect kids and a hunk of a husband.

It was *possible* that Dad had finally remembered her, but Ruby doubted it. Since he'd remarried and started a second family, her father was more interested in midnight baby feedings than in the goings-on of his adult daughter's life. The ringing went on and on.

Finally she crawled across the carpet and answered on the fourth ring. 'Hello?' She heard the snarl in her voice.

'It's me, darlin', your favourite agent.'

She frowned. 'Val? You sound pretty happy, considering that my career is circling the hole in the toilet bowl.'

Val laughed. It was a great, booming sound. 'I *am* happy. You won't believe who called me today.' There was a palpable pause. 'Joe Cochran. He had a cancellation and wants to book you for tomorrow's show.'

How could a world spin around so quickly? Yesterday Ruby had been pond scum; today the host of *Uproar,* the hottest, hippest, raciest talk show in the country, wanted her. It was a young comedian's dream gig.

'He's giving you two minutes to do stand-up. So, kiddo, this is it. I'll send a car around to pick you up at eleven tomorrow morning.'

'Thanks, Val.' Before she hung up, Ruby remembered to ask, 'Hey, what's the topic of the show?'

'It's called "Crime and Punishment: Are Mommy and Daddy to Blame for Everything?"'

Ruby should have known. 'They want me because I'm *her* daughter.'

'Do you care why?'

'No.' It was true. This was her shot. Finally, after years of play dates in smoke-infested bars in towns whose names she couldn't remember, she was getting national exposure.

She thanked Val again, then hung up the phone. Her heart was racing so hard, she felt dizzy. She ran to her bedroom and flung open the doors of her closet. She couldn't afford anything new.

Then she remembered the black cashmere sweater. It had come from her mother two Christmases earlier, disguised in a box from Caroline. Although Ruby routinely sent back her mother's guilty gifts unopened, this one had seduced her. Once she'd touched that beautiful fabric, she couldn't mail it back. She grabbed the black V-neck sweater off its hanger and tossed it on the bed. Tomorrow she'd jazz it up with necklaces and wear it over a black leather miniskirt with black tights.

When Ruby had picked out her clothes, she kicked the bedroom door shut. A mirror on the back of the door caught her image. Her short black hair had been moulded by last night's sweatfest into a perfect imitation of Johnny Rotten. 'I'm Ruby Bridge,' she said, grabbing a hairbrush off the dressing table to use as a mike. 'And yes, you're right if you recognise the last name. I'm *her* daughter, Nora Bridge's, spiritual guru to Middle America.' She flung her hip out, picturing herself as she would look tomorrow. 'Look at me. Should that woman be telling you how to raise kids? It's like—'

The phone rang.

'Damn.' Ruby raced into the living room and yanked the cord out of the wall. She couldn't be bothered for the next twenty-four hours. Nothing mattered except getting ready for the show.

Like all big cities, San Francisco looked beautiful at night. Multicoloured lights glittered throughout downtown, creating a neon sculpture garden tucked along the black bay.

Dean Sloan glanced longingly at the wall of windows that framed the panoramic view. Unfortunately, he couldn't leave his seat. He was, as always, trapped by the flypaper of good manners.

Scattered through the ornately gilded ballroom of this Russian Hill mansion were a dozen or so tables, each of which seated four or five couples. The women were expensively, beautifully gowned, and the men wore tuxedos. The party's hostess, a local socialite, had hand-chosen the guest list from among the wealthiest of San Francisco's families. Tonight's charity was the opera, and it would benefit mightily, although Dean wondered how many of the guests actually cared about music. What they really cared about was being seen, and even more important, being seen doing the *right* thing.

Dean's date was a pale, exquisite woman named Sarah. 'That was a lovely sentiment, don't you think?' she said softly.

Dean had no idea what she was talking about, but a quick look around the room enlightened him. An elderly, well-preserved woman was standing alongside the ebony Steinway. No doubt she'd been waxing poetic about the opera and thanking her guests in advance for their unselfish contributions. There was a smattering of quiet applause, then the sound of chairs being pushed back.

Dean took hold of Sarah's hand, and they slipped into the whispering crowd. The band was playing something soft and romantic. On the dance floor he pulled Sarah close, slid his hand down the bare expanse of her back, felt her shiver at his touch. If he cared to, he could lead her out of this crush and take her to his bed. After that he would call her, and they would probably sleep together a few times. Then, he would forget her. Last year a local magazine had named him San Francisco's most *ineligible* bachelor because of his reputation for nanosecond affairs.

But what the reporter hadn't known, hadn't even imagined, was how tired Dean was of it all. He wasn't even twenty-nine years old, and already he felt aged. Money. Power. Disposable women who seemed to hear his family name and become as malleable as wet clay. For more than a year now, he had felt that something was wrong with his life. Missing. At first he'd assumed it was a business problem, and he'd rededicated himself to work, logging upward of eighty hours a week at Harcourt and Sons. But all he'd managed to do was make more money, and the ache in his gut had steadily sharpened.

He'd spoken to his parents about it, but that had proved pointless. Edward Sloan was now—and always had been—a charming playboy who jumped at his wife's every command. It was Mother who held the ambition, and she'd never been one to care about things like fulfilment or satisfaction. Her comment had been as he'd expected: 'I ran this company for thirty years; now it's your turn. No whining allowed.' He supposed she'd earned that right. Under his mother's iron fist the family business, begun by her grandfather and expanded by her father, had become a $100-million dollar enterprise. That had always been enough for her, but that same success felt hollow to Dean.

He'd tried to talk to his friends about it, and though they'd wanted to help, none of them understood his feelings. It wasn't so surprising. Dean had grown up in a slightly different world than they.

Lopez Island. Summer Island.

He'd spent ten perfect years in the San Juan Islands. There, he and his brother, Eric, had been—for a short time—ordinary boys. Those remote islands had formed and defined Dean, provided a place he felt whole.

Of course, Ruby had been there. And before she went crazy and ruined everything, she'd taught him how love felt.

Then she'd shown him how easily it was broken.

Dean sighed, wishing he hadn't thought about Ruby now, when he had a beautiful, willing woman in his arms. Suddenly he was tired. He simply didn't have the energy to spend tonight with another woman he didn't care about. 'I'm not feeling well, and I've got a crack-of-dawn conference call from Tokyo,' he said. 'I think I'll take you home, if you don't mind.'

Once he'd made his decision, Dean couldn't get out of the room fast enough. He manoeuvred through the crowd like a Tour de France cyclist, saying good night to the few people who really mattered, then hurried out with Sarah to his car. They made idle chitchat on the way to her father's hilltop mansion.

Less than fifteen minutes after Dean had dropped Sarah off, he was standing in his living room, staring out at the night-clad city. On the walls all around him were framed photographs—his hobby. Once, the sight of them had pleased him. Now all he saw when he looked at his photographs was how wrong his life had gone.

Behind him the phone rang. He strode to the suede sofa, collapsed onto the down-filled cushion, and answered it.

'Dino? Is that you?'

'Uh . . . Eric? How in the world are you?' Dean was stunned. He hadn't heard from his brother in what? Eighteen months?

'Are you sitting down?'

'That doesn't sound good.'

'It isn't. I'm dying.'

Dean felt as if he'd been punched in the gut. A cold chill moved through him. 'AIDS?' he whispered.

Eric laughed. 'We *do* get other diseases, you know. My personal favourite is cancer.'

'We'll get you the best treatment. I—'

'I've *had* the best treatments. I've seen the best specialists, and they,' Eric said softly, 'have seen me.' He took a deep breath. 'I don't have much time left.'

Dean couldn't seem to draw a decent breath. 'You're thirty years old,' he said helplessly, as if age were relevant.

'I should've told you when I was first diagnosed, but I kept thinking I'd tell you when it was over, and we'd laugh about it.'

'Is there *any* chance we'll someday laugh about it?'

It took Eric a moment to answer. 'No.'

'What can I do?'

'I'm going back to the island. Lottie's already there.'

'The island,' Dean repeated slowly. A strange sense of inevitability drifted into the room. It was as if Dean had always known that someday they'd end up back there, where everything had begun. Where everything had gone so wrong. Maybe a part of him had even been waiting for it.

'Will you come up?'

'Of course.'

'I want us to be brothers again.'

'We've always been brothers,' Dean answered uncomfortably.

'No,' Eric said softly. 'We've been members of the same family. We haven't been brothers in years.'

Chapter Two

THE SCANDAL BROKE with gale force. Those humiliating photographs were everywhere, and the newspapers and television stations that didn't own them described them in excruciating detail.

Nora sat huddled in her living room, refusing to go anywhere. The thought of being seen terrified her.

Her assistant, Dee Langhor, had shown up bright and early in the morning—*I came as soon as I heard*—and Nora had felt pathetically grateful. Now Dee was in Nora's home office, fielding calls.

With everything on Nora's mind, one thing kept rising to the surface—she should have called Caroline the day before to warn her about the coming media storm. But how did you tell your child something like this? In the end, Nora had chosen to handle the impending disaster as she handled all difficult things: she'd taken two sleeping pills and turned off her phone. Now, with the story on every morning show, she had no choice. She had to call. She reached for the phone, accessed the second line, and pushed number one on the speed-dial list.

'Hello?'

It took Nora a moment to respond. 'Caro? It's me—Mom.'

There was a pause that seemed to strip away a layer of Nora's tender flesh. 'Well, I hope you're going to tell me you were kidnapped yesterday and the FBI just freed you from your prison in the back of some psycho fan's trunk.'

'I wasn't kidnapped.'

'I found out this morning when I dropped Jenny off at preschool.' Caroline laughed sharply. 'Mona Carlson asked me how it felt to see pictures of my mother like that. How it *felt.*'

Nora didn't know how to respond. Defending herself was pointless. 'I'm sorry. I couldn't . . . call.'

'Of course you couldn't.' Caroline was quiet for a moment. 'I can't believe I let it hurt my feelings. I should have known better. It's just that I thought—'

'I know. We've been getting closer.'

'No. Apparently *I've* been getting closer. You've been like some Stepford mom, pretending, saying the right things but never really feeling connected to me at all. I don't know when I got stupid enough to expect honesty from you.'

'I know I screwed up. Don't shut me out of your life again.'

'You really don't get it, do you? I'm not the one who shuts people out, not in this family. Maybe Ruby was the smart one—she hasn't let you hurt her in years. Now, I've got to go.'

'I love you, Caroline,' Nora said in a rush, desperate to say the words before it was too late.

'You know what's sad about that?' Caroline's voice broke. A little sob sounded in her throat. 'I believe you.' She hung up.

The dial tone buzzed in Nora's ears.

Dee rushed into the living room, her eyes wide. 'Mr Adams is on the phone. I told him you weren't here, but he said to tell you to pick up the phone, or he was going to call his lawyers.'

Nora sighed. Of course. Tom Adams hadn't become a newspaper mogul by playing nice. 'Put him through.'

'Thanks,' Dee said, hurrying back into Nora's office.

Nora answered the phone. 'Hello, Tom.'

'Nora, what in heaven's name were you thinking? I heard about this godawful mess when I was eating breakfast. If I hadn't had the television on, I don't know when I'da found out.'

'Sorry, Tom. I was caught off guard by the whole thing myself.'

'Well, you're on guard now, little lady. You haven't gotten any letters yet, but you will.'

'You've got two months' worth of columns from me on file. That'll give me some time to figure out how I want to handle this.'

He made a barking sound. 'I pay you a wagonload of money to answer readers' letters, and now that they finally got something interesting to ask about, you aren't going to play possum. Scandals sell newspapers, and I mean to cash in on your heartache. Sorry, Nora. I've always liked you, but business is business.'

Nora felt sick. 'The radio station is giving me some time off—'

'Don't you confuse me with those tie-wearin' pantywaists. I haven't backed down from a fight in my life, and my people aren't going to, either.'

'OK, Tom,' Nora said softly. She'd say anything to end this conversation. 'Give me a few days. Use what you have for now, and then I'll start to answer the hate mail.'

He chuckled. 'I knew you'd see the light, Nora. Bye now.'

She hung up. Tom actually expected her to read angry, disappointed letters from the very people who used to love her.

Impossible.

Ruby stood in her steam-clouded bathroom staring through the mist at her watery reflection. The lines beneath her puffy eyes looked like they'd been stitched in place by a sewing machine. It wouldn't do to look this old, not in Hollywood. She'd use make-up to take off the years. Enough 'heroin-chic' black eyeliner, and people would assume she was young and stupid.

Ruby dressed carefully—cashmere sweater, black leather mini-skirt, and black tights. A lot of gel made her hair poke out everywhere. She layered fourteen cheap necklaces round her neck, then she grabbed her handbag and headed outside.

The sleek black limousine was already parked at the kerb. A uniformed driver stood beside the car. 'Miss Bridge?'

She grinned. No one ever called her that. 'That's me.'

The driver opened the door for her. Ruby peered into the interior and saw a dozen white roses lying on the back seat. She slid into the seat, heard the satisfying thud of the closing door, and plucked the card from the flowers: *People as talented as you don't need luck. They need a chance, and this is yours. Love, Val.*

God, it felt good, as if those tarnished dreams of hers were finally coming true.

She had never meant to need it all so much. But after her mother abandoned them, everything had changed. *Ruby* had changed. From that moment, nothing and no one had been quite enough for her. She'd come to need the unconditional acceptance that only fame could provide.

She scooted closer to the window, grinning as the limo pulled up to the security booth at the entrance to Paramount. The twin white arches announced to the world that through these gates was a special world, open only to a lucky few. The guard waved them through.

The driver proceeded to soundstage nine, a hulking flesh-coloured building. He stopped the car, then came round, opening Ruby's door.

She took a deep breath and headed towards the entrance. A neon sign read UPROAR! A NEW KIND OF TALK SHOW WITH JOE COCHRAN. Inside was a kaleidoscope of lights, darkened seating, and people scurrying around like ants with clipboards, checking and rechecking.

'You're Ruby Bridge?'

Ruby jumped. She hadn't noticed the small platinum blonde who now stood beside her. 'I'm Ruby.'

'Good.' The woman led her into a small waiting room. On the table beside a brown sofa were a bowl of fruit and a bottle of Perrier on ice. 'Do you need make-up?'

'No. My make-up's fine, thanks.'

'Good. Sit here. I'll come and get you when it's time to go on.' The woman consulted her papers. 'You get two minutes up front. Be fast and be funny.' She was gone.

Ruby collapsed on the couch. Suddenly she was more than nervous. She was terrified. *Be funny.*

What had she been thinking? She wasn't funny. Her material might be funny, but *she* wasn't. 'Calm down, Ruby,' she said. She focused on her breathing: in and out, in and out.

There was a knock at the door. The same lady with platinum blonde hair stood there. 'They're ready for you, Miss Bridge.'

'Oh my God.' Ruby shot to her feet. She'd been hyperventilating for thirty minutes, and now she couldn't remember one line of material. She exhaled slowly. 'I'm ready,' she said. She *was* ready—she'd been ready all her life.

She followed the woman towards the stage. Ruby was sweating like a geyser. Mascara was probably running down her cheeks. She'd look like something out of *Alien* by the time—

'Ruby Bridge!' Her name roared through the sound system.

Ruby pushed through the curtains. She forced herself not to squint, although the lights were so bright, she couldn't see anything. She just hoped she didn't walk off the end of the stage.

She went to the microphone. 'Well,' she said, 'it's nice to know I'm not the only person who can come to a talk show in the middle of the day. Of course, it's easy for me. I was fired yesterday from a trendy restaurant I won't name, but it sounds like Irma's Hash House. I won't even tell you what I thought we'd be selling—'

A smattering of laughter. It gave her confidence. She grinned, then launched into the rest of her routine, saving the best jokes—about her mother—for last.

At the end of her routine Ruby stepped back from the mike. Amid the sound of applause Joe Cochran crossed the stage towards her. He was smiling. He placed a hand warmly on her shoulder and turned to face the crowd. 'You've all met the very funny Ruby Bridge. Now let's meet our other guest—family therapist Elsa Pine, author of the best-selling book *Poisonous Parents*.'

Elsa walked onstage. She and Ruby followed Joe to the artfully arranged leather chairs. Joe sat down and looked up at the audience. 'I don't know about you, but I'm sick of the way our judicial system handles criminals. Every time I open the paper, I read about some jerk who killed a little girl and got off because the jury felt sorry for him. I mean, who's looking out for the victims here?'

'Now, Joe,' Elsa said, 'criminals aren't born. They're made. Some people have been so abused by their parents that they no longer know right from wrong.'

Joe looked at Ruby. 'You know something about toxic parents, Ruby.

Is everything wrong in your life your mother's fault?'

Elsa nodded. 'Yes, Ruby. You of all people should understand how deeply a parent can wound a child. I mean, your mother is a huge proponent of marriage. She positively waxes poetic about the sanctity of the vows. You were probably the only person in America who wasn't surprised by the *Tattler* today.'

'I don't read the tabloids,' Ruby answered.

A whisper moved through the audience. Joe's enthusiastic smile dimmed. 'You haven't read today's *Tattler*?'

Ruby's frown deepened. 'Is that a crime now?'

Joe reached down, and for the first time, Ruby noticed the newspaper folded beneath his chair. He picked it up, handed it to her. 'I'm sorry. You were supposed to have known.'

Ruby felt a sudden tension in the room. She took the newspaper from him. At first all she noticed was the headline: RAISING MORE THAN SPIRITS. Then she saw the photo. It was a blurry, grainy shot of two naked people entwined. The editors had carefully placed black privacy strips across the pertinent body parts, but there was no denying what was going on. Or who the woman was.

Ruby looked helplessly at the faces around her, then tossed the newspaper down in disgust. 'There's a lesson to women everywhere in this. When your lover says, "One little photo, honey, just for us," you better cover yourself and run.'

Elsa leaned forward. 'How does it make you feel to see—'

Joe raised his hands. 'We're getting off the topic here. The question is, how much of our screwups are our fault? Does a bad parent give someone a free ride to commit crime?'

Ruby sat perfectly still. There was no reason for her to speak. She knew she'd given *Uproar* what it had wanted—a reaction. By tomorrow her blank-eyed, dimwitted response to the scandal would lead every report. She should have known it would be like this—her big break. What a joke. How could she have been so naive?

Finally she heard Joe wrapping up. The APPLAUSE sign lit up, and the audience responded immediately, clapping thunderously.

Ruby rose from her chair and moved blindly across the stage. People were talking to her, but she couldn't hear anything they were saying.

Someone touched her shoulder. She jumped and spun round.

'Ruby?' Joe was standing beside her, his handsome face drawn into a frown. 'I'm sorry about ambushing you. The story broke yesterday. It never occurred to us that you'd miss it. And since so much of your material is about your relationship with your mother . . .'

'I turned off my phone and television,' she answered, then added, 'I was getting ready for the show.'

'You thought this was your big break. And it turned out—'

'Not to be.' She cut him off. The pity in his eyes was more than she could bear. 'I have to go now.' Without glancing at anyone, she raced out of the studio.

In her apartment, Ruby closed all the blinds and turned off the lights. She slumped onto her worn sofa. *Mommy Dearest had an affair, after all.*

It didn't surprise her. Any woman who would leave her children to go in search of fame and fortune wouldn't think twice about having an affair. What surprised Ruby was how much it still hurt.

Her fingers shook as she reached for the phone and dialled her sister's number. Caroline answered on the second ring. 'Hello?'

'Hey, sis,' Ruby said, feeling a sudden tide of loneliness.

'So you finally plugged your phone in. I've been going crazy trying to reach you.'

'Sorry,' Ruby said softly. Her throat felt embarrassingly tight. 'I saw the pictures. Did you know about the affair?'

'I suspected.'

'Why didn't you ever tell me?'

'Come on, Rube. You've never mentioned her name to me all these years. You didn't want to know anything about her.'

'I suppose you've already forgiven her, Caroline the Saint.'

'No,' Caro said softly. 'I'm having a hard time with this one. Yesterday I said some really nasty things to her. I couldn't seem to help myself. I'm going to call her back when I calm down. Maybe we can finally talk about some of the stuff that matters.'

'Nothing she has to say matters, Caro.'

'You're wrong about that, Rube. Someday you'll see that.'

Before Ruby could respond, the doorbell rang. 'I gotta run, Caroline. There's someone here to see me.'

She hung up, then padded across the carpet and peered through the peephole. It was Val, standing beside a woman so thin she looked like a windscreen wiper.

Ruby wrenched the door open. Val grinned at her. He leaned forward and kissed her cheek. 'How's my newest star?'

'Up yours,' she whispered. 'I never saw it coming.'

Val drew back, frowning. 'I tried to call you.'

Ruby would have said more, but the way the lady was watching them made her uncomfortable. She turned to her, noticing the woman's severe haircut and expensive black dress. 'I'm Ruby Bridge,' she said, extending her hand.

The woman shook it. Firm grip. Clammy skin. 'Joan Pinon.'

'Come on in.' Ruby backed away from the door. She tried not to see the apartment through their eyes, but it was impossible—tacky furniture, dusty carpet, garage-sale decor.

Val sat down on the old velour armchair. Joan perched on the end of the sofa. Ruby flopped down on the sofa's other cushion.

Val leaned forward. 'Joan is an editor for *Caché* magazine in New York. She's here because of your mother.'

Ruby turned to Joan. 'What do you want?'

'We'd like you to write an exposé on your mother.' Joan smiled. 'Val tells me you're a first-rate writer.'

A compliment. That felt good. Ruby settled back in her seat, eyeing Joan. 'You want a daughter's betrayal.'

'Who betrayed whom?' Joan said. 'Your mother has been telling America to honour commitments and put their children first. These photographs prove that she's a liar and a hypocrite.'

'It's just an article, Ruby,' Val said. 'No more than fifteen thousand words. And it could make you famous.'

'*Rich* and famous,' Joan added.

Ruby looked at Joan. 'How rich?'

'Fifty thousand dollars. I'm prepared to pay you half right now and the other half when you deliver the article.'

'Fifty thousand *dollars?*' For a few measly words. And all she had to do was serve up her mother's life for public consumption. 'I don't know my mother that well,' Ruby said slowly, trying to think through it. 'The last time I saw her was at my sister's wedding nine years ago. We didn't speak.'

'We don't want cold facts. We want your opinions and thoughts on what kind of a person she is, what kind of a mother she was.'

'That's easy. She'd step on your grandmother's throat to get ahead. Nothing—and no one—matters to her except herself.'

'You see?' Joan said, eyes shining. 'That's exactly the perspective we want. I brought the contract with me and a cheque for twenty-five thousand dollars.' She reached into her black briefcase and pulled out a stack of papers with the cheque on top.

Ruby stared at all those zeros and swallowed hard. She'd never had that much money at one time.

Joan smiled, a shark's grin. 'Let me ask you this, Ruby. Would your mother turn down this offer if you were the subject of the article?'

The answer to that question came easily. Her mother had once had to make a choice like this. She could have chosen her husband and her daughters . . . or her career. Without a backward glance, Nora Bridge had chosen herself.

'This is your chance, Ruby,' Val said. 'Think of the exposure. The networks will be fighting over you.'

She felt flushed. She heard herself say, 'I'm a good writer.'

Joan was smiling. 'We've tentatively booked you on *The Sarah Purcell Show* for a week from now to promote the article.'

Ruby wanted it so much. She'd clawed through life for so long, been a nobody. She thought of all the reasons she should say no—the moral, ethical reasons—but none of them found a place to stick. Slowly she reached for the cheque. 'OK,' she said. 'I'll do it.'

Ruby cranked the Volkswagen's radio to full blast. A raucous Metallica song blared through the small black speakers.

Fifty thousand dollars. She wanted so badly to share this day with someone. If only she had Max's new number—she'd call him and tell him what he'd missed out on.

She drove into Beverly Hills. Usually she didn't even drive past this area, but today she was flying high. She felt invincible.

When she saw an open spot on Rodeo Drive, she pulled over and parked. Grabbing her bag—with the deposit slip for $25,000 inside—she got out of the car.

She strolled around for a while, then looked into a store window and saw a sheer, beaded, silvery blue dress with a plunging V neckline and a split in the side that came up to mid-thigh. It was the most perfect dress she'd ever seen, the kind of thing she'd never imagined she could own. She pushed through the doors.

A saleswoman came over. 'May I help you?'

'I saw a blue dress in the window,' Ruby said.

'You have excellent taste.' The woman led Ruby to a changing room bigger than the average bedroom. 'Would you like a glass of champagne?'

Ruby laughed. Now, *this* was shopping. 'I'd love some.'

Within a minute a man in a black tuxedo was handing Ruby a sparkling glass of Champagne.

'Thanks,' she said, collapsing onto the cushy seat in the dressing room. For the first time in years, she felt like somebody.

The saleslady peeked in. 'Here you go. Holler if you need me.'

Ruby trailed her fingers down the beaded, sheer-as-tissue fabric, then quickly undressed and slipped into the dress. Self-consciously she stepped out of the dressing room and walked over to the wall-size mirrors in the corner. Her breath caught. Even with her hair too short and her make-up too heavy, she looked beautiful. The plunging neckline accentuated her small breasts. Her waist appeared tiny, and the slit slimmed her fleshy thighs.

'Oh, my,' the saleswoman said wistfully. 'It's perfect.'

'I'll take it,' Ruby said in a thick voice.

She wrote a cheque—almost $3,500—and hung the dress carefully in the back seat of the Volkswagen.

Then, cranking the music up again, she sped towards the freeway. She was almost home when she passed the Porsche dealer. Ruby laughed and slammed on the brakes.

Nora lay curled on the elegant sofa in her darkened living room. Hours ago she'd sent Dee home and disconnected the phone. Then she'd watched the news.

Every station had the story. They showed the lurid blacked-out photographs again and again, usually followed with sound bites of Nora expounding on the sanctity of the marriage vows. What hurt the most were the man-in-the-street interviews. Her fans had turned on her; some women even cried at the betrayal they felt. 'I trusted her' was the most common refrain.

She knew, too, what was happening in the lobby downstairs. The press was outside, cameras at the ready. One sighting of Nora Bridge, and they would spring on her like wild dogs. Her doorman claimed that the garage was safe, but she was afraid to chance it.

She sat up, then walked to the makeshift bar in the kitchen that she kept for guests. Nora hadn't drunk spirits in years. But now she needed *something* to help her out of this hole. She poured herself a tumbler full of gin. It tasted awful at first, but after a few gulps the booze slid down easily, pooling firelike in her cold stomach.

On her way back into the living room, she paused at the grand piano, her attention arrested by the framed photographs on the gleaming ebony surface. She almost never looked at them, not closely. It was like closing her hand around a shard of broken glass.

Still, one caught her eye. It was a picture of her and her ex-husband, Rand, and their two daughters. They'd been standing in front of the family beach house, their smiles honest and bright.

Nora finished the drink, then went back for another. By the time she finished that one, she could barely walk straight. That was fine. She didn't want to think too clearly right now.

She swayed drunkenly and plugged the phone into the wall. Bleary-eyed, she dialled her psychiatrist.

A moment later a woman answered. 'Dr Allbright's office.'

'Hi, Midge. It's Nora Bridge.' She hoped she wasn't slurring her words. 'Is the doctor in?'

A sniff. 'He's not in, Ms Bridge. Shall I take a message?'

Ms Bridge. Only days ago it had been Nora.

'Is he at home?'

'No, but I can put you through to his service. Or he left Dr Hornby's number for emergencies.'

'Thanks, Midge. There's no need for that.' Nora hung up. Then she ripped the cord out of the wall again.

In some distant part of her mind, she knew that she was sinking into a pool of self-pity, and that she could drown in it, but she didn't know how to crawl out.

Eric. He would be on the island by now. If she hurried, maybe she could still make the last ferry.

She grabbed her car keys and staggered into her bedroom. After cramming a blonde wig over her cropped auburn hair she put on a pair of sunglasses. On the bedside table she found her sleeping pills. Of course it would be bad—wrong—to take one now in her drunken state. But she wanted to. She tossed the brown plastic bottle into her bag and left the apartment, tottering towards the elevator.

Once inside, she prayed there wouldn't be a stop in the lobby. She got lucky; the elevator went all the way down to the garage, where it stopped with a clang and the doors opened.

She peered out; the garage was empty. She careened unsteadily towards her car, collapsing against the jet-black side of her Mercedes. It took her several tries to get the key into the lock, but she finally managed. She slid awkwardly into the soft leather seat. The engine started easily—a roar of sound in the darkness.

Nora caught sight of herself in the rearview mirror. Her face was pale, her cheeks tear-streaked.

'What are you doing?' she asked the woman in the sunglasses. She heard the slurring, drunken sound of her voice, and it made her cry. Hot tears blurred her vision.

'Please,' she whispered, 'let Eric still be there.'

She slammed the car into reverse and backed out of the spot. Then she headed forward and hit the accelerator. Tyres squealed as she rounded the corner and hurtled up the ramp. She didn't even glance left for traffic as she sped out onto 2nd Avenue.

Dean stood on the slatted wooden pier. The seaplane taxied across the choppy blue waves and lifted skyward, its engine chattering as it banked left and headed back to Seattle.

He'd forgotten how beautiful this place was, how peaceful.

The tide was out now, and the beach smelt of sand that had baked in the hot sun, of seaweed that was slowly curling into leathery strips. It was a smell that pulled him back in time. Here he and Eric had built their forts and had buried treasures made of foil-wrapped poker chips; they'd gone from rock to rock, searching for the tiny crabs that lived beneath the stones. They had been the best of friends.

Of the two of them, Eric had been the strong one, the golden boy who did everything well and fought for his heart's desires. At seven Eric had demanded to be taken to Granddad's island house on Lopez, the one they'd seen pictures of. And it was Eric who'd first convinced Mother to let them stay and go to the island school. The truth was, she was so busy running Harcourt and Sons that she didn't care where her children were.

Dean closed his eyes. He hated what had brought him home, hated that it had taken a disease to bring him back to his brother. Even more, he hated the way he felt about Eric now; they'd grown so far apart. And it was all Dean's fault. He saw that, knew it, hated it, and couldn't seem to change it.

It had happened on a seemingly ordinary Sunday. Dean had moved off the island by then, gone to prep school; Eric had been at Princeton. They were still brothers then, separated only by miles, and they'd spoken on the phone every Sunday. One phone call had changed everything.

193

I've fallen in love, little bro. Get ready for a shock. His name is Charlie, and he's . . .

Dean had never been able to remember more than that. Somehow, in that weird, disorientating moment, he'd felt suddenly betrayed, as if the brother he'd known and loved was a stranger.

After that they had drifted apart. By the time Dean graduated from Stanford and went to work for the family business, too much time had passed. Eric had moved to Seattle and begun teaching high-school English. He'd lived with Charlie for a long time; only a few years before, Dean had received a note from Eric about Charlie's lost battle with AIDS.

Dean had sent flowers and a nice card. He'd meant to pick up the phone, but every time he reached for it, he wondered what in the world he could say.

He turned away from the water, picked up his bag and walked down the pier, then climbed the split-log steps to the top of the bluff.

The sprawling Victorian house was exactly as he remembered it—salmony pink siding, steeply pitched roof, elegant white trim. The lawn was still as flat and green as a patch of Christmas felt.

As Dean headed towards the house, a glint of silver caught his eye. He turned and saw the swing set, rusted now and forgotten. A whispery breeze tapped one of the red seats, made the chains jangle. The sight of it dragged out an unwelcome memory . . .

Ruby. She'd been right there, leaning against the slanted metal support pole, with her arms crossed.

It was the moment—the exact second—he'd realised that his best friend was a *girl* and that he loved her. He'd wanted to say the words to her, but he'd been afraid, and so he'd kissed her instead. It had been the first kiss for both of them, and to this day, when Dean kissed a woman, he longed for the smell of the sea.

He spun away from the swing set and strode purposefully towards the house. At the front door, he paused, gathering courage, then knocked.

The door burst open, and Lottie was there. His old nanny flung open her pudgy arms. 'Dean!'

He walked into the arms that had held him in his youth, and breathed in her familiar scent—ivory soap and lemons.

He drew back, smiling. 'It's good to see you, Lottie.'

She gave him the look—one thick grey eyebrow arched upwards. 'I'm surprised you could still find your way here.'

Though he hadn't seen her in more than a decade, she had barely aged. Her ruddy skin was still wrinkle free, and her bright green eyes were those of a woman who'd enjoyed her life. He realised suddenly how much he'd missed her. Lottie had never had any children, and Eric and Dean had become her surrogate sons. She'd raised them for the ten years they'd lived on Lopez.

'I wish I were here for an ordinary visit,' Dean said.

She blinked up at him. 'It seems like only yesterday I was wiping chocolate off his little-boy face. I can't believe it.'

Dean followed her into the living room, where a fire crackled in the huge hearth. Cream-coloured sofas on carved wooden legs faced each other. A large, oval, rosewood coffee table stood between them.

Dean glanced towards the stairway. 'How is he?'

Lottie's green eyes filled with sadness. 'Not so good, I'm sorry to say. The trip up here was hard on him.'

'Did Eric call our parents, tell them about the cancer?'

'He did. They're in Greece—Athens.'

'I know. Did he speak to Mother?'

Lottie glanced down at her hands. 'Your mother's assistant spoke to him. It seems your mother was shopping when he called.'

Dean's voice was purposely soft. He was afraid that if he raised it, he'd be yelling. 'Did Eric tell her about the cancer?'

'Of course. He wanted to tell your mother himself, but . . . he decided he'd better just leave a message.'

'And has she returned his call?'

'No.'

Dean released his breath in a tired sigh.

'Go on up.' Lottie smiled gently. 'He's a bit the worse for wear, but he's still our boy.'

Dean nodded stiffly, settled the bag over his shoulder, and headed upstairs. He passed his old bedroom and came to Eric's door. He paused, then walked into his brother's room. The first thing he noticed was the hospital bed. It had replaced the bunk bed that once had hugged the wall. The new bed—big, metal-railed, and tilted up like a lounging chair—dominated the room. Lottie had positioned it to look out of the window.

Eric was asleep. Dean seemed to see everything at once—the way Eric's black hair had thinned to show patches of skin, the yellowed pallor of his sunken cheeks, the smudged black circles beneath his eyes. Only the palest shadow of his brother lay here.

Dean grabbed the bedrail for support; the metal rattled beneath his grasp. Eric's eyes slowly opened.

And there he was—the boy Dean had known and loved. 'Eric,' he said, wishing his voice weren't so thick.

Eric looked up at Dean, his eyes filled with a terrible, harrowing honesty. 'I didn't think you'd come.'

'Of course I came. You should have told me . . . before.'

'Like when I told you I was gay? Believe me, I learned a long time ago that my family didn't handle bad news well.'

Dean fought to hold back tears and then gave up. They were the kind of tears that hurt deep in your heart. He felt a stinging sense of shame that he'd been a bad person, that he'd hurt his brother deeply and known it and never bothered to make it right.

Eric smiled weakly. 'You're here now. That's enough.'

Dean wanted to smooth the thin strands of hair from Eric's damp forehead, but his hands were trembling, and he drew back. He would give anything to erase the past, to be able to go back to that Sunday afternoon, listen to that same confession of love from his brother, and simply be happy. But how did two people move backwards through time?

'Just talk to me,' Eric said sleepily, smiling again. 'Just talk, little brother. Like we used to.'

Chapter Three

THE PHONE RANG in the middle of the night. Ruby groaned and glanced bleary-eyed at the bedside clock: one fifteen. It had to be one of those idiot reporters. She reached across the bed, yanked the phone off the hook, and brought it to her ear. 'Bite me.'

'I gave that up in kindergarten.'

Ruby laughed sleepily. 'Caro? Oh, sorry. I thought you were one of those bottom-feeders from the *Tattler*.' Through the phone lines Ruby could hear a baby crying—a high-pitched wailing only dogs should be able to hear. 'Does the baby always wail like that?'

'Mom's been in a car accident.'

Ruby gasped. 'What happened?'

'I don't know. All I know is that she's at Bayview. Apparently she'd been drinking.'

'She never drinks heavily. I mean, she never used to. How bad is it?'

'I don't know. I'm going to go to the hospital first thing in the morning. But I don't want to do this alone. Will you come?'

'I don't know, Car—'

'She could be dying,' Caroline said sharply.

Ruby sighed heavily. 'OK. I'll come.'

'I'll call Alaska Airlines and put a ticket on my card. There's a flight at five forty-five. You can pick it up at the counter.'

'Uh . . . you don't have to do that. I have money now.'

'*You?* Well, that's great.'

'I'll be there by noon.' Ruby hung up.

She had been angry at her mother forever. She couldn't really remember *not* hating her. But now . . . an accident. Horrible images slammed through her mind: paralysis, brain damage, death.

Ruby closed her eyes. It took her a moment to realise she was praying. 'Take care of her,' she whispered. 'Please?'

When Nora woke up the next morning, she had a moment of pure, heart-pumping fear. She was in a strange bed, in an austere room she didn't recognise. Then she remembered she'd been in a car accident. She recalled the ambulance ride, the flashing red lights, and the doctors. The orthopaedic surgeon who'd spoken to her just before and after the X-rays: *a severe break above the ankle, another small fracture below the knee, a sprained wrist.* He'd said she was lucky.

Now her leg was in a cast. She couldn't see it beneath the blankets, but she could feel it. The skin tingled and the bones ached. She sighed, feeling sorry for herself and deeply ashamed. Drinking and driving. As if the *Tattler's* photographs weren't enough to ruin her career, she'd added a crime to the list.

There was a knock at the door, short and sharp, and then Caroline swept into the room. Her back was ramrod straight, her pale hands clasped at her waist. She wore a pair of camel-coloured trousers and a matching twin-set. Her silvery blonde hair was cut in a perfect bob, one side tucked discreetly behind her ear. 'Hello, Mother.'

'Hi, honey. It's nice of you to come.' Nora recognised instantly how distant she sounded, and it shamed her. She and Caroline had worked hard in the past few years, trying to come back together in an honest way. Nora had treated her elder daughter with infinite care, always letting Caro make the first move. Now, all that progress had been blown to hell as she saw a coldness in Caroline's eyes that she hadn't seen in years.

Caroline glanced at Nora. She looked vulnerable suddenly.

Nora couldn't stand the awkward silence that fell between them. She said the first thing that popped into her mind. 'The doctors say I'll need to be in a wheelchair for a few days, just until my wrist gets strong enough to make crutches possible.'

'Who is going to take care of you?'.

'I guess I'll hire someone. The big question is, where will I go? I can't go back to my condo. The press has it staked out.'

Caroline took a step towards the bed. 'You could use the summer house. Jere and I never find time to make it up there, and Ruby won't step foot on the island. The old house is just sitting there.'

The house on Summer Island. A stone's throw from Eric. It would be perfect. Nora looked up at her daughter. 'You'd do that for me?'

Caroline gave her a look of infinite sadness. 'I wish you knew me.'

Nora sagged back into the pillows. She had said the wrong thing again. 'I'm sorry.'

'God, I've heard that from you so often. Quit saying you're sorry and start acting like it. Start acting like my mother.' Caroline reached into her bag and fished out a set of keys. Pulling a single key from the ring, she set it down on the bedside table, then stepped back, putting distance between them. 'I have to go now.'

Nora nodded stiffly. 'Of course. Thanks for coming.' She wanted to reach out for Caroline, hold her daughter's hand and never let go.

'Goodbye, Mom.' And she was gone.

Ruby stepped out of the main terminal at SeaTac International Airport. Rain thumped on the skybridge and studded the tarmac. The early morning air smelt of evergreen trees and fertile black earth. Like a dash of spice in a complex recipe, there was the barest tang of the sea, a scent only a local would recognise.

As she stood beneath the bloated grey sky, smelling the moist, pine-scented air, she realised that memories were more than misty recollections. They stayed rooted in the soil in which they'd grown. There were places up north, in the San Juan Island archipelago, where bits and pieces of Ruby's life had been left scattered about like seashells on the shore. Somewhere up there sat the shadow of a thin, bold-eyed girl tearing the petals off a daisy, chanting, 'He loves me, he loves me not'.

Ruby hailed a cab and climbed in, tossing her bag beside her. 'Bayview,' she said, thumping back into the seat.

When they arrived, she handed the driver the fare and a tip. Then she grabbed her bag and headed towards the hospital's double glass doors, where a few people stood milling about.

Ruby was almost in their midst when she realised they were reporters.

'It's her daughter!'

The reporters turned to her, yelling and elbowing for position.

'Was your mother drunk at the time of—'

'What did you think of the photographs?'

Ruby heard every shutter click, every picture frame advance. She pushed through the crowd, holding her head up, looking straight ahead. Their questions followed her as she strode through the pneumatic doors. They whooshed shut behind her.

Inside, the lobby was quiet. The air smelt of disinfectant.

'Ruby!' Caroline rushed forward. Her hug almost knocked Ruby off her feet. As she held her sister, Ruby could feel how thin Caro had become, could feel the tremble in her sister's body.

At last they drew back.

'So how is Nora?' Ruby asked.

Caroline gave her a sharp look. 'She still hates it when we call her Nora.'

'Really? I'd forgotten that.'

'I'll bet you did. Anyway, she drove her car into a tree. Her leg is broken, her wrist sprained. She'll be in a wheelchair for a few days. That makes it pretty tough to do the ordinary bits and pieces of life. She'll need help.'

'I pity the poor nurse who takes *that* job.'

'Would *you* want to be cared for by a stranger?'

It took Ruby a minute to get her sister's drift. When she did, she burst out laughing. 'You're delusional.'

'Ruby,' Caroline said. 'A stranger could sell her out to the tabloids. She needs someone she can trust.'

'Then you'd better do it. She can't trust me.'

'I have kids. A husband.'

A life. The implication was clear, and the truth of it stung. 'Doesn't she have any friends?'

'It should be you, Ruby.' Caroline looked disgusted. 'You're going to be thirty in a few years. Mom's fifty. When are you going to get to know her?'

'Who says I'm *ever* going to?'

Caro moved closer. 'Tell me you didn't think about it last night.'

Ruby couldn't swallow. 'About what?'

'Losing her.'

The words hit dangerously near their mark. There was no doubt in Ruby's mind what she should do—go out through those front doors and fly home. But it wasn't quite so easy this time, especially with the *Caché* article out there to write. A little time with Nora Bridge would certainly make the piece better. A *lot* better.

Ruby took a deep breath. 'One week,' she said evenly. 'I'll stay with her for one week.'

Caroline pulled Ruby into a fierce hug. 'I knew you'd do the right thing. Go tell her. She's in six-twelve west. I'll wait for you here.'

'Coward.' Ruby flashed her a nervous smile, then headed for her mother's room on the sixth floor.

The door was ajar, and Ruby stepped inside.

Nora was asleep. Ruby stared down at her mother's pale, beautiful face and felt an unexpected tug of longing. She had to remind herself that this lovely red-haired woman who looked like Susan Sarandon wasn't really her mother. Ruby's mother—the woman who'd played Scrabble and made chocolate-chip pancakes every Sunday morning— had died eleven years ago. This was the woman who'd killed her.

Nora opened her eyes, gasped, and pushed up to a sitting position. 'You came,' she said softly, a note of wonder in her voice.

'How are you?' Ruby felt off-balance.

'I'm fine.' Nora smiled, but it was an odd, uncertain smile.

'So I guess you've lost your good-driver discount.'

'That's my Ruby—quick with a joke.'

'I wouldn't say *your* Ruby.'

'I'm sure you wouldn't.' Nora exhaled softly. 'I see you still think you know everything and you still don't take any prisoners.'

'I don't know everything,' Ruby said evenly. 'I don't think I ever knew my mother.'

Nora laughed—a tired sound. 'That makes two of us.'

They stared at each other. Ruby felt a mounting urge to escape; it was a survival instinct. Already she knew she couldn't spend a week with this woman and feel nothing. The anger was so sharp right now, it overwhelmed her. But she had no choice.

'I thought I'd stay with you, help you get settled.'

Nora's surprise was almost comical. 'Why?'

Ruby shrugged. There were so many answers to that question.'You could have died. Maybe I thought of what it would be like to lose you. Or maybe this is your darkest hour, the loss of everything you left your family for, and I don't want to miss a minute of your misery. Or maybe I got a contract to write a magazine article about you, and I need to get the inside scoop. Or maybe I—'

'I get it. Who cares why. I need help and you obviously have nothing better to do.'

'How do you do it—slam me in the middle of a thank-you? You just thought you'd point out that I have no life. It wouldn't occur to you that I've rearranged my life to spend some time with you, would it?'

'Let's not start, OK?' Nora's fingers slid close to touch Ruby. She looked up. 'You know I'm going to the summer house, right?'

Ruby couldn't have heard correctly. *'What?'*

'Reporters are camped outside my condo. I can't face them.' Nora's gaze lowered. 'Your sister offered me use of the summer house. If you want to change your mind, I'll understand.'

It had seemed doable a few moments ago—go to this woman's glasswalled high-rise that success had purchased, make a few meals, look through a few old photo albums, ask a few questions. But at the summer house—it was where so many of the memories were buried, both good and bad.

Fifty thousand dollars. That's what she had to think about. She could handle the summer house. 'I guess it doesn't matter where we are.'

'You mean it?' There was a disturbing wistfulness in her mother's voice. 'You'll need to hire me a wheelchair, and I'll need a few things from my apartment.'

'I can do that.'

'I'll talk to my doctor and get checked out of here. We'll have to leave quietly, through the back way maybe.'

'I'll rent a car and pick you up in—what? Three hours?'

'OK. My bag is in the closet. Use the platinum Visa for anything you need. And, Ruby, get a nice car, OK?'

Ruby tried to smile. This was going to be bad. Her mother was already making demands—and judgments. 'Only the best for you, Nora.' She went to the closet, saw the expensive black handbag, and grabbed it. Without a backward glance she headed out.

Her mother's voice stopped her. 'Ruby? Thank you.'

Ruby shut the door behind her.

Ruby walked into her mother's penthouse condominium and closed the door behind her. She dropped her jacket onto the gleaming marble floor, then turned the corner and literally had to catch her breath. It was the most incredible room she'd ever seen.

A wall of floor-to-ceiling windows wrapped around the whole living room, showcasing a panoramic view of Elliott Bay. Brocade-covered furniture sat in a cluster around a beautiful gold-and-glass coffee table. In one corner stood an ebony Steinway, its lacquered top cluttered with framed photographs.

A dimly lit hallway led to the master bedroom. Here the windows were dressed in steel-grey silk curtains that matched the woven cashmere bedspread. There were two huge walk-in closets. Ruby opened the first one and a light came on automatically, revealing two rows of clothes—designer silks, cashmeres, expensive woollens—organised by colour. The thought *This is what she left us for* winged through Ruby's mind, hurting more than she would have expected.

She backed out, closing the closet door. At the rosewood gilt-trimmed chest of drawers, she opened the top drawer. Little piles of perfectly folded lingerie lay there. She picked out a few pieces, then gathered up some shorts and cap-sleeved tops from the second drawer. She set the pile on the bed and moved to the other closet.

The clothes here looked as if they belonged to another woman—worn grey sweatpants; baggy, stained sweatshirts; old jeans; a few brightly coloured sundresses.

Her mother had expensive designer clothes, and lie-around-the-house clothes, but nothing in between. No clothes for going out to lunch with a friend or stopping by to catch a matinée.

No clothes for a real life.

As she reached for a sundress, Ruby saw that the hem was caught on the upraised flap of a cardboard box. On the side of the box, written in red ink, was the word RUBY. Her heart skipped a beat. She fell to her knees, dragging the box towards her. Her fingers were trembling as she opened it.

Inside, there were dozens of wrapped packages, some in the reds and greens of Christmas, some in bright silvery paper with balloons and candles. Birthdays and Christmases.

She counted the packages: twenty-one—two each year for the eleven Nora had been gone from them, less the black cashmere sweater that Caroline had sneaked past Ruby's guard. These were the gifts that Nora had bought every year and sent to Ruby, the same ones Ruby had ruthlessly returned unopened.

'Oh, man.' She let out her breath in a sigh and reached for a small box wrapped in birthday paper. Carefully she peeled the paper away and lifted the lid. Inside, on a bed of opalescent tissue, lay a silver charm. It was a birthday cake, complete with candles. Inscribed on the back was *Happy 21st. Love, Mom.*

The silver charm blurred.

Ruby could imagine her mother, dressed perfectly, going from store to store for the ideal gift, saying to the salespeople, 'My daughter is going to be twenty-one. I need something extra special.' Pretending that everything was normal, that she hadn't abandoned her children when they needed her most.

At that, Ruby felt a rush of cold anger. What mattered was not what Nora had tried to give Ruby, but rather what she'd taken away. A few nicely wrapped gifts found stuffed in a cardboard box in a closet couldn't change that.

Ruby wouldn't let it.

As Ruby neared her mother's hospital room, she slowed. A man was standing by the door and as she approached, he looked up. Narrowed, penetrating black eyes fixed on her. 'Are you Ruby Bridge?'

She came to a stop. 'Who wants to know?'

Smiling—as if that was precisely what he would have expected Ruby Bridge to say—he extended his hand. 'I'm Leonard Allbright, your mother's doctor.'

'Where's your white coat?'

'I'm her psychiatrist.'

That surprised Ruby. She couldn't imagine her mother spilling her guts to anyone. 'Really?'

'I've just spoken to her, and she told me all about your . . . arrangement.' He said the final word as if it tasted bitter. 'I'm aware of your past history, so I thought I'd ask why you have offered to care for her.'

'Look, Doc, when it's all over, you can ask Nora all the questions you want. She'll pay you a huge fee to listen to her moan about the bitch daughter who betrayed her. But *I'm* not going to talk to you.'

'"Betrayed" is an interesting word choice.'

Ruby flinched. 'If that's all . . . '

He reached into his pocket and handed her an expensive business card. 'I don't know if it is a good idea for you to take care of Nora. Especially not in her current state of mind.'

Ruby took the card. 'Yeah? Why not?'

He studied her, and she could see by the deepening frown that he wasn't pleased. 'You haven't seen or spoken to your mother in years, and you're obviously very angry at her. Considering what happened to her, it could be a bad mix. Maybe even dangerous.'

'Dangerous how?'

'You don't know her. She's fragile right now—'

'I lived with her for sixteen years, Doc. You've talked to her once a week for . . . what, a year or two?'

'Fifteen years.'

Ruby's chin snapped up. '*Fifteen* years? But everything was fine then.'

'Was it?'

His question threw her into confusion. Fifteen years ago, Ruby had been barely out of braces, singing along to Madonna and imagining that her future would follow the course of her childhood, that her family would always be together.

'Your mother keeps a lot to herself,' Dr Allbright went on, 'and as I said, she's fragile. I believe she always has been.' He took a step towards her. 'Ruby, your mother was doing almost seventy miles per hour when she hit that tree. And on the same day as she lost her career. Pretty coincidental.'

Ruby couldn't believe she hadn't made that connection. A chill moved through her. 'Are you telling me she tried to kill herself?'

'I'm saying it's coincidental. Dangerously so.'

Ruby released a heavy breath. Suddenly, it didn't seem like a good idea to be responsible for her mother. No one emotionally unstable should be entrusted to Ruby—hell, *goldfish* couldn't survive her care.

'You don't know your mother. Remember that.'

That observation put Ruby back on solid ground. 'And whose fault is that? I'm not the one who walked out.'

He stared down at her. 'No, you're not,' he said evenly, 'and you're not sixteen any more, either.'

Ruby should have rented a Winnebago. This minivan was too small for her and Nora. They were trapped in side-by-side front seats. With the windows rolled up, there seemed to be no air left to breathe and nothing to do but talk. Ruby cranked up the radio. Celine Dion's voice filled the car, something about love coming to those who believed.

'Could you turn it down?' Nora said. 'I'm getting a headache.'

Ruby's gaze flicked sideways. Nora's skin appeared to have the translucence of bone china. Tiny blue veins webbed the sunken flesh at her temples. She turned to Ruby and attempted a smile, but, in truth, her mouth barely trembled before she closed her eyes. *Fragile.*

Ruby couldn't wrap her arms round that thought. It was too alien from her experience. Her mother had always been made of steel. Even as a young girl, Ruby had known her mother's strength. The other kids in her class were afraid of their fathers when report cards came out. Not the Bridge girls. They lived in fear of disappointing their mother.

Not that she ever punished them particularly, or yelled or screamed. No, it was worse than that.

I'm disappointed in you, Ruby Elizabeth. Life isn't kind to women who take the easy road.

'Ruby? The music?'

Ruby snapped the radio off. The metronomic whoosh-thump, whoosh-thump of the windscreen wipers filled the sudden silence.

A few miles from downtown Seattle, the city gave way to a sprawling collection of shopping malls. A few miles more, and they were in farming land. Rolling tree-shrouded hills and green pastures fanned out on either side of the freeway.

At Anacortes, the tiny seaside town perched at the water's edge, Ruby bought a one-way ferry ticket and pulled into line. An orange-vested attendant directed her car to the bow of the ferry, where she parked and set the emergency brake.

The Sound was rainy-day flat. Watery grey skies melted into the sea. Puppy-faced seals crawled over one another to find a comfortable perch on the swaying red harbour buoy.

Ruby glanced sideways and saw that Nora was asleep. She got out of the car and went upstairs onto the deck. The rain had diminished to little more than a heavy mist. Lush green islands dotted the tinfoil sea, their carved granite coastlines a stark contrast to the flat silver water. Houses were scattered here and there, but for the most part the islands looked empty.

Ruby closed her eyes, breathing in the salty, familiar sea air. In eighth grade she had started taking the ferry to school at Friday Harbor on San Juan Island. She and Dean had always stood together at just this spot, right at the bow, even when it was raining.

Dean. It had been more than a decade since she'd seen him, and still it hurt to remember him. Sometimes, when she woke in the middle of a hot, lonely night and found that her cheeks were slicked and wet, she knew she'd been dreaming of him. She knew from Caroline (who knew from Nora) that he'd followed in his mother's footsteps, that he was running the empire now. Ruby had always known that he would.

At last the ferry turned towards Summer Island. The captain came on the loudspeaker, urging passengers to return to their vehicles.

Ruby raced downstairs and jumped into the minivan. The captain cut the engine and the boat drifted towards the rickety black pier. Once the deckhands had secured the ropes, Ruby drove off the ferry, past the post office and general store. What struck her first was the total lack of meaningful change. Here, on Summer Island, with only one hundred year-round residents, it was still 1985.

To her left the land was a Monet painting, all golden grass and green trees and washed-out silvery skies. To her right lay Bottleneck Bay, and beyond that was the forested green hump of Shaw Island. Weathered grey fishing boats sat keeled on the pebbly beach.

As Nora blinked awake, Ruby approached the beach road and turned. The narrow one-lane road wound snakelike through the towering trees, their drooping branches heavy with rain. At last they came to the driveway. The knee-high grass that grew in a wild strip down the centre of the road thumped and scraped the undercarriage. At the end of the tree-lined road Ruby hit the brakes.

And stared through the windscreen at her childhood.

The farmhouse was layered in thick white clapboards, with red trim around the casement windows. A porch wrapped around three sides of the house. It sat in the midst of a pie-shaped clearing that jutted towards the sea. A white picket fence created a nicely squared yard. Inside it, the garden was in full, riotous bloom.

Obviously, Caroline had paid a gardener to keep the place up. It looked as if the Bridge family had been gone a season instead of more than a decade.

With a tired sigh Ruby got out of the car.

The tide made a low, snoring sound. Birds chattered overhead.

Ruby went round to the back of the van and pulled out the wheel-chair, then helped Nora into the seat. Taking hold of the rubber-coated grips, she pushed her mother down the path. At the gate Ruby stopped and unlatched it. She cautiously guided the wheelchair in front of her. They had just reached the edge of the porch when her mother suddenly said, 'Let me sit here for a minute, will you? Go on in.' Nora handed the key to Ruby. 'You can come back and tell me how it looks.'

'You'd rather sit in the rain than go into the house?'

'That pretty much sums up my feelings right now.'

Ruby walked onto the porch. The wide-planked floor wobbled beneath her feet like piano keys, releasing a melody of creaks and groans. At the front door she slipped the key into the lock.

'Wait!' her mother cried out.

Ruby turned. Nora was smiling, but it was grim, that smile. 'I . . . think we should go in together.'

'Let's not make an opera out of it. We're going into an old house. That's all.' Ruby shoved the door open, then went back for Nora. She manoeuvred the wheelchair up onto the porch, bumped it over the threshold, and wheeled her mother inside.

The furniture, draped in old sheets, huddled ghostlike in the middle of the room. Ruby could remember spreading those sheets every autumn, snapping them in the air above the furniture. It had been a family ritual, closing up the place for winter.

The house may not have been lived in for a while, but it had been well cared for. There couldn't have been more than a few weeks' dust on those white sheets.

'Caroline has taken good care of the place. I'm surprised she left everything exactly as it was.' There was a note of wonder in Nora's voice, and maybe a touch of regret. As if, like Ruby, she'd hoped that Caroline had painted over the past.

'You know Caro,' Ruby said. 'She likes to keep everything pretty on the surface.'

'That's not fair. Caro—'

Ruby spun round. '*Tell* me you aren't going to explain my sister to me.'

Nora's mouth snapped shut. Then she sneezed. And again. Her eyes were watering as she said, 'I'm allergic to dust. I know there's not much, but I'm really sensitive. You'll need to dust right away.'

Ruby looked at her. 'Your leg's broken, not your hand.'

'I can't handle it. Allergies.'

It was the best reason for not cleaning Ruby had ever heard. 'Fine. I'll dust.'

'I guess I'll have to sleep in your old room. There's no way we can get me upstairs.'

Ruby dutifully wheeled Nora into the downstairs bedroom, where two twin beds lay beneath a layer of sheeting.

'I think I'll lie down,' Nora said. 'I'm still fighting a headache.'

Ruby nodded. 'Can you get out of the chair by yourself?'

'I guess I'd better learn.'

'I guess so.' Ruby turned for the door.

She was almost there when her mother's voice hooked her back. 'Thanks. I really appreciate this.'

Ruby knew she should say something nice, but she couldn't think of anything. The memories in this room were like gnats, buzzing around her head. She slammed the door shut behind her.

Chapter Four

DEAN TOSSED HIS BAG on the floor of his old bedroom and sat down on the end of the bed. Everything was exactly as he'd left it. Dusty baseball and soccer trophies cluttered the bureau's top. Posters covered the cream-coloured walls, their edges yellow and curled.

Dean hadn't taken anything with him when he left here, not even a photograph of Ruby. *Especially* not a picture of her. He got to his feet and crossed the room. At the bureau he bent down and pulled at the bottom drawer; it screeched and slid open.

And there they were, reminders of Ruby. There were pictures, shells they'd collected together on the beach, and a couple of dried button-holes. He reached randomly inside, drawing out a small strip of black and white pictures—a series that had been taken in one of those booths at the Island County Fair. In them she was sitting on Dean's lap, smiling, then frowning, then sticking her tongue out at the unseen camera. In the last frame they were kissing.

He dropped the photos back into the drawer and kicked it shut. Someone knocked at the door, and Dean opened it.

Lottie stood there, clutching a large bag. 'I'm off to the store.' She thrust a champagne glass at him. Inside was a thick pink liquid. 'This is your brother's medicine. He needs it now. Bye.'

Dean walked slowly to Eric's bedroom and went in. The room felt stuffy and too warm. The curtains were drawn. Eric was asleep. Dean moved quietly towards the bedside table and set down the glass.

'I *hope* that's my Viagra,' Eric said sleepily. In a second, the bed whirred to life, eased him to a near sitting position.

'Actually, it's a double shot of Cuervo Gold. I added the Pepto-Bismol to save you time.'

Eric laughed, and Dean opened the windows and flung back the curtains. The windows boxed a grey and rainy day and let a little watery light into the room.

'Thanks. Bless Lottie, but she thinks I need peace and quiet. I haven't the nerve to tell her I'm getting a little scared of the dark. Too coffinlike for me.' He grinned. 'I'll be there soon enough.'

Dean turned to him. 'Don't talk about that.'

Eric gave Dean a gentle look. 'What am I supposed to talk about? The Mariners' next season? The next Olympic Games? Or maybe we could discuss the long-term effects of global warming?' He sighed. 'We used to be so close,' he said quietly.

'I know.' Dean saw Eric move, trying to look up at him; he saw, too, when the sudden pain sucked the colour from his cheeks. 'Here,' Dean said quickly.

Eric's hands were shaking as he brought the glass to his colourless lips. Wincing, he swallowed the whole amount.

Eric tried to smile. 'I'd kill for a margarita from Ray's Boathouse right now and a platter of Penn Cove mussels . . .'

'Tequila and shellfish—with your tolerance for booze? Sorry, pal, but I'll have to pass on that little fantasy.'

'I'm not seventeen any more,' Eric said. 'I don't slam alcohol until I puke.'

There it was, the sharpened reminder of how they'd drifted apart. They'd known each other as boys; the men were strangers to each other.

'Will that medication help?' Dean asked.

'Sure. In ten minutes I'll be able to leap tall buildings in a single bound.' Eric laughed.

209

KRISTIN HANNAH

Dean relaxed a little. 'It's good to hear you laugh. It's been a long time.' He moved idly to a chest of drawers where a collection of pictures sat clustered together. Most of them were photographs of Dean and Eric as boys. There was one shot of the brothers and another boy standing with their arms around each other, grinning. It looked ordinary enough, but when Dean turned back to Eric, he couldn't help wondering, Had it been there all along, the difference between him and his brother? Had Dean simply missed the obvious?

'I wish I'd never told you I was gay,' Eric said. It was as if he had read Dean's mind. 'I knew our folks wouldn't accept it. But you . . .' His voice cracked a little. 'You, I didn't expect. You broke my heart.'

'I never meant to.'

'You stopped calling me.'

Dean sighed. 'You were away at college, so you didn't know what it was like back here. The technicolour meltdown of the Bridge family. And then Ruby and I broke up.'

'I always wondered what happened between you two. I—'

'It was awful,' Dean said quickly, unwilling to delve into that heartache. 'I called Mother and demanded to be transferred to Choate. I hated it there. I couldn't seem to make friends. But every Sunday night my brother called, and that one hour made the rest of the week bearable. Then one Sunday you forgot to call.' Dean remembered how he'd waited by the phone that day, and the next Sunday and the next. 'When you finally did call again, you told me about Charlie. I was seventeen and nursing a broken heart. I didn't want to hear about your love life. And yeah, the fact that it was with another man was hard for me to handle.'

Eric leaned deeper into the pillows. 'When you stopped returning my calls, I assumed it was because you hated me. I never thought about what it was like for you. I'm sorry.'

'Yeah. I'm sorry, too.'

'Where do these apologies take us?'

'Who the hell knows? I'm here. Isn't that enough?'

'No.'

Suddenly Dean understood what Eric wanted. 'You want me to remember who we used to be, to remember *you*, and then . . . watch you die.'

'I want *someone* in my family to love me while I'm alive. Is that so much to ask?' Eric closed his eyes, as if the conversation had exhausted him. 'Just stay here until I fall asleep. Can you do that for me?'

210

Dean's throat felt tight. 'Sure.'

He stayed at his brother's bedside until long after Eric's breathing had become regular and his mouth had slipped open.

He would have given his fortune—hell, he'd have given everything he had or owned or could borrow—in exchange for the one thing he'd always taken for granted, the one thing Eric needed. Time.

Nora shifted against the bed and leaned back against the wobbly wooden headboard. She knew she needed to handle Ruby with kid gloves, to treat her daughter's pain (which Nora never forgot that *she* had caused) respectfully, to let Ruby make all the first moves towards a reconciliation. No matter how much it hurt, how deeply the ache went, Nora didn't want to bulldoze the situation.

If they'd gone somewhere else, maybe this would have been easier, but nothing new could grow here, not in this soil contaminated by the past. It was in this house that Nora had made her biggest mistake. This was where she'd come when she had left Rand. She had meant for it to be temporary. At the time she'd simply thought, If I don't get some space, I'll start screaming and never stop. She remembered that summer and the bad years that had preceded it, how it had felt—that slowly descending depression, like a thick glass jar that closed around you, sucking away the air you needed to breathe.

She picked up the bedside phone and dialled her psychiatrist's number. Dr Allbright answered on the second ring. 'Hello?'

'Hi, Leo. It's me—Nora.'

'How are you?'

'I'm fine,' she said.

'You don't sound fine.'

'Well, Ruby and I are crowded in with a lot of old ghosts.'

'I don't think you should be there. With all that's happening, you should be in the city.'

'And let the vultures pick at me?' She smiled ruefully. 'It appears to be open season on Nora Bridge wherever I go.'

'Ruby.'

'I knew it wouldn't be easy.' That much was true, at least. She'd known how much it would hurt to see her daughter's bitterness in such sharp, close detail; and it did.

'If Ruby hates you, it's because she was too young to understand.'

'I don't understand it all either.'

'You owe it to yourself and to Ruby to tell her the truth.'

She sighed wearily. 'You ask too much of me, Leo.'

'And you ask too little, Nora. You're so afraid of your past. Talk to her. Try this: tell her one personal thing about you every day, and try to find out one thing about her. That would be a start.'

Nora considered it. Yes, she could do that. It wasn't much, and it wouldn't change everything, but it felt possible. For now, that was all she could hope for.

Ruby strode through the house, yanking the gingham cotton curtains open, letting what little light was possible into every room. By now it was nearly three o'clock; soon there would be no daylight through the clouds at all. She wanted to catch what she could. At last she found herself in the kitchen/dining room.

Nothing had changed.

A round maple table sat beneath the window, its four ladder-back chairs pulled in close. A centrepiece of dirty pink plastic dahlias was flanked by a set of porcelain salt-and-pepper shakers shaped like tiny lighthouses. A cookbook was in its rack on the kitchen counter.

Ruby passed into the living room, where an overstuffed sofa and two leather chairs faced a stone fireplace. On the back wall were bookcases. There was an RCA stereo, and a red plastic milk box held all of the family's favourite albums. The photos on the mantel caught her eye. They were in different frames from the ones she remembered. Frowning, she walked towards the fireplace.

All the pictures were of Caroline's children. There was not a single shot of Ruby. Not even one of Ruby and Caroline.

'Nice, Caro,' she said, turning away and heading up the creaking narrow steps to the first floor. She felt forgotten.

She pushed the door open to her parents' old bedroom and flicked a light switch. A big brass bed filled the room, flanked by two French provincial end tables. The bedside lamps were yellow.

Ruby remembered her grandmother, sitting in that corner rocker, her veiny hands making knitting needles work like pistons. *You can never have too many afghan blankets,* she'd said every time she started a new one. It had been a long time since Ruby had had so clear a memory of her nana. Maybe all she'd needed to remember the good times was to see this place again. It was exactly as Nana had made it. Nora had never bothered to redecorate. When Nana and Pop had died, they had willed the house to Ruby and Caroline. Dad had then moved their family into the bigger house on Lopez Island, and left this house for summer use.

Ruby crossed the room and went to the French doors, opening them wide. Sweet, rain-scented air made the lacy curtains tremble and dance. She stepped out onto the tiny, first-floor balcony. A pair of white deck chairs sat on either side of her, their slatted backs beaded with rain. For a split second she couldn't imagine that she'd ever lived in a valley so hot and airless that boiling water sometimes squirted out of ordinary green garden hoses.

Ruby backed off the balcony and turned into the room. Out of the corner of her eye she noticed the new photographs on the bedside table. They were all pictures of Caroline's new life.

Frowning, Ruby marched back downstairs and went outside. She grabbed the suitcases from the car and carried them inside, dropping her mother's in front of the closed bedroom door.

Upstairs, she opened the closet's louvered doors, then yanked down on the light chain. A lightbulb came on in the empty closet and shone on a cardboard box with 'Before' written across the top in marker pen.

Ruby opened the box . . . and found herself.

Photographs. Dozens of them. These were the pictures that used to sit on every flat surface in this house—pictures of two little girls in matching pink dresses, of Dean and Eric in Little League uniforms, of Dad waving from the stern of the *Captain Hook*. And one of Nora.

She slowly withdrew that one.

This was the mother she'd forgotten, the woman she'd grieved for. A tall, thin woman, with auburn hair cut in the layered Farrah Fawcett style, wearing crisp white walking shorts and a celery-green T-shirt.

And Ruby understood what Caroline had done. Caro, who couldn't stand conflict, who just wanted everything to be *normal*. It had hurt her sister to look back on these years. Better to start over, pretend there had never been happy summers spent in these rooms.

Ruby released her breath in a heavy sigh and boxed the photographs up. She'd already lost her equilibrium in this house, and it had only been a day. She had to get back on track.

The magazine article—*that* would keep her focused.

She unzipped her suitcase and withdrew a yellow legal pad and a blue pen. Then she crawled up onto the bed, drew her knees in, and wrote the first thing that came to mind.

In the interest of full disclosure I must tell you that I was paid to write this article. Paid handsomely, as they say in the kind of restaurants where a person like me can't afford to order a dinner salad. Enough so that I could trade in my beat-up Volkswagen Bug for a slightly less beat-up Porsche.

I should also tell you that I dislike my mother. No, that's not true. I dislike the snotty salesclerk who works the night shift at my local video store. I hate my mother.

The story of us starts eleven years ago in the San Juan Islands up in Washington State. My dad was—is—a commercial fisherman who repairs boat engines in the winter months to make ends meet. He was born and raised on Lopez Island. Although my mother was born off-island, she was a local by the time I came along. She volunteered for every town charity event and was a fixture around school. In other words, we were a perfect family in a quiet little town where nothing ever happened. In all my growing-up years I never heard my parents argue.

Then, in the summer before my seventeenth birthday, everything changed. My mother left us. Walked out the door, got into her car, and drove away.

I can't remember now how long I waited for her to return, but I know that somewhere along the way, in the pool of a thousand tears, she became my mother and then, finally, Nora. My mom was gone. I accepted the fact that whatever she wanted out of life, it wasn't me.

The worst of it was my father. For my last two years of high school I watched him disintegrate. He drank; he sat in his darkened bedroom; he wept.

And so when Caché came to me, asking for my story, I said yes. I figured it was time that America knew who they were listening to, who was giving them moral advice—a woman who walked out on her marriage and abandoned her children and—

'Ruby!'

She tossed down the pen and paper and went to the doorway, poking her head out. 'Yeah?'

'Can you breathe OK with all this dust?'

Ruby rolled her eyes. As always, her mother was as subtle as an exclamation mark. 'I see you found enough air in your lungs to scream at me,' she muttered, hurrying downstairs.

As she passed her mother's bedroom, she heard a sneeze.

In the kitchen, she knelt in front of the cabinet beneath the sink and opened the doors. Everything she needed stood in four straight rows. When she realised that the supplies were organised in alphabetical order, she burst out laughing. 'Poor Caro,' she whispered. 'You were *definitely* born into the wrong family.'

Then, as tired as she was, she started to clean.

Nora tried not to watch her daughter clean the house. It was simply too irritating. Ruby dusted without moving anything, and she clearly thought a dry rag would do the job. When she started mopping the floor with soapless water, Nora couldn't help herself. 'Aren't you going to sweep first?' she asked from her wheelchair.

Ruby slowly turned around. 'Excuse me?'

Nora wished she'd kept silent, but now there was nowhere to go except forward. 'You need to sweep the floor before you mop, and soap in the water is a big help.'

Ruby let go of the mop. The wooden handle clattered to the floor. 'You're criticising my cleaning technique?'

'I wouldn't call it a technique. It's just common sense to—'

'So I have no common sense either.'

Nora sighed. 'Come on, Ruby. You know better than that. I taught you—'

Ruby was in front of Nora before she could finish the sentence. '*You* do not want to bring up the things you taught me. Because if I do as I've been taught, I'll walk out that door, climb into the minivan, and drive away. I won't even bother to wave goodbye.'

Nora's irritation vanished; regret swooped to take its place. 'I'm sorry.'

Ruby took a step back. 'According to Caro, those are your favourite words.' She stomped into the kitchen, grabbed some liquid soap, and squirted a stream into the bucket. Then she began mopping again; her strokes were vicious.

Nora tried a different approach. 'Maybe I could help?'

Ruby didn't look at her. 'I stripped the bed upstairs. You could take care of your bed and start a load of laundry.'

Nora nodded. It took her almost an hour to strip the sheets off her bed, manoeuvre her wheelchair into the cubicle-size laundry room, and start the first load. By the time she rolled back into the kitchen, she found the room sparkling clean. Ruby had even replaced the horrid plastic flowers on the table with a fragrant bouquet of roses.

'Oh,' Nora said, taking her first decent breath since coming into the house. 'It looks beautiful.' She looked at her daughter. 'I thought I'd help you make dinner.'

Ruby turned to her. 'I don't know how to cook.'

'I could teach you.'

'Lucky me.'

Nora refused to be hurt by that comment. She wheeled into the kitchen and scavenged through the cupboards, finding several tins of tomatoes, a bag of angel-hair pasta, a bottle of olive oil, jars of marinated artichoke hearts and capers, and a container of dried Parmesan cheese.

Ruby walked over to the stove. 'OK, what do you want me to do?'

'See that big frying pan hanging on the rack? Take that and put it on the front burner.'

The pan hit with a clang.

Nora winced. 'Now put about a tablespoon of olive oil in it and turn on the gas.'

Ruby opened the oil and poured in at least a half cup.

Nora bit back a comment as she reached for the tin opener. She was proud of herself for saying simply, 'The measuring spoons are in the top drawer, to your left.' Then she opened the tinned tomatoes. 'Here, add these and turn the flame to low.'

When Ruby had done that, Nora went on. 'Cut up the artichoke hearts and add them.'

Ruby went to the counter and began chopping. 'Ow!'

Nora spun the wheelchair towards her daughter. 'Are you OK?'

Ruby stepped back. Blood was dripping in a steady stream from her index finger.

Nora yanked a clean towel off the oven door. 'Come here, honey.' She gently took hold of her daughter's hand. Seeing that blood—her child's—made Nora's own hand throb. She coiled the towel round the wound and, without thinking, wrapped her own hands round Ruby's. When she looked up, Nora saw the emotion in Ruby's eyes and knew that her daughter remembered this simple routine. The only thing missing was a kiss to make it all better.

Ruby yanked her hand back. 'It's just a cut, for God's sake.'

That gap yawned between them again, and Nora wondered if she'd imagined the longing in her daughter's eyes. Her voice was shaking when she said, 'Put a big pot of water on to boil, won't you?'

For the next thirty minutes Ruby did as she was told. Finally the meal was ready, and they were seated across from each other at the round wooden kitchen table. Ruby picked up her fork and rammed it into the pasta, twirling it. Nora tried to eat, but the silence tore at her nerves. Leo's advice came back to her: *one personal thing.*

She was still trolling for an icebreaker when Ruby got up from the table and started filling the sink with water.

Nora hadn't realised that eating was a timed event. She cleared the table, stacked the dishes on the counter at Ruby's elbow. In an unnerving silence Ruby washed and Nora dried. When they were finished, Nora wheeled herself into the living room. Ruby swept past her, practically running, and headed for the stairs.

Nora had to think fast. 'Why don't you make us a fire? June nights are always chilly.'

Without answering, Ruby went to the hearth, knelt down, and built a fire exactly as she'd been taught by Grandpa Bridge.

'I guess some things you never forget,' Nora said.

Ruby sat back on her heels and held her hands out towards the fire. 'Except how it feels to have a mother.'

'That's not fair. You and Caroline were my whole world.'

Ruby laughed drily. 'We weren't your whole world the summer I was sixteen. That was the year you walked into the living room, dropped your suitcase on the floor, and announced that you were leaving, wasn't it? And what was it you said to us? "Who wants to come with me?" As if Caroline and I would move away from our dad and our home just because you decided you didn't want to be here.'

'I didn't decide. I left because—'

'I don't care *why* you left. That's what you care about.'

Nora longed to make Ruby understand. 'You don't know everything about me.' She thought she saw a war going on inside her daughter, as if Ruby wanted both to keep fighting and to stop.

'Tell me something about you, then,' Ruby said at last.

This was Nora's chance. She knew she needed to tread carefully. 'OK. Let's go sit on the porch, like we used to. We'll each share one piece of information about ourselves.'

'I asked you to tell me about *you*. I didn't offer to reciprocate.'

Nora stood her ground. 'I need to know about you, too.'

Ruby studied her. 'This should be interesting. I'm twenty-seven. You were fifty . . . When? The day before yesterday? I guess it's time we talked. Come on.'

Nora finally allowed herself to smile—Ruby had remembered her birthday. She followed Ruby onto the porch, thankful to see that the rain had finally stopped. The cool night air breezed across her cheeks. Sunset tinted the sky purple and pink.

Ruby looked young and vulnerable, with her black hair so poorly cut and her clothes all tattered and torn. The urge to reach out, to brush the hair off Ruby's face and say softly—

'Don't say it, Nora.'

Nora frowned. 'Say what?'

'"Ah, Ruby, you could be so beautiful if you'd just try a little."'

It startled Nora—that bit of mind reading. Sure, she'd said that often to Ruby, had thought in fact to say it a second ago, but it meant nothing. To Nora the comment had simply been grains of sand in the desert of a mother's advice. Obviously, Ruby had felt otherwise, and she'd carried the words into womanhood with her.

Nora was ashamed. 'I'm sorry, Ruby. What I should have said is, "You're beautiful just the way you are."'

Silence settled between them, broken only by the sounds of the sea and the occasional caw of a lone crow hidden in the trees.

'OK, Nora,' Ruby said, leaning with feigned nonchalance against the porch rail. 'Tell me something I don't know.'

'You think I don't understand you,' Nora began softly, 'but I know how it feels to turn your back on a parent. On the day I graduated from high school, I left home and never went back again.'

'Did you run away?'

'From my father, yes. I loved my mother.'

'And you never saw him again?'

'Never again.' Nora wished those two words didn't hurt so much. 'I didn't even attend his funeral, and all my life I've had to live with that decision. It's not regret I feel so much, but I wish he had been a different man. Most of all, I wish I could have loved him.'

'Did you *ever* love him?'

'Perhaps . . . when I was young. If so, I don't remember it.'

Ruby turned and stared out to sea. Without turning, she said, 'I read the *People* magazine article about you. It said—and I quote: "The cornerstones of Nora Bridge's message are forgiveness and commitment."' Ruby turned round at last. 'Did you ever try to forgive him?'

Nora wanted to lie. It was easy to see that Ruby was asking as much about *their* relationship as she was about Nora and her father's. But there was little enough chance for Nora and Ruby; with deception there would be none at all. 'After I'd had my own children—and lost their love—I regretted how I'd treated him. As a young woman, I didn't understand how hard life can be. Of course, that understanding came too late. He was already gone.'

'So I should forgive you now, while I still have the time?'

Nora looked at Ruby sharply. 'Not everything is about you. I told you something painful about me tonight. I expect you to handle my life with respect if you can't manage care.'

Ruby looked abashed. 'I'm sorry.'

'Apology accepted. Now tell me something about you.'

Ruby stared at Nora. 'One night, the summer after you left, I just . . . snapped. I drove to Seattle and went to a dance club. I picked up some kid. I went back to his apartment and let him have sex with me.' She paused for effect. 'It was my first time. I did it to hurt you. I thought you'd come home eventually, and then I'd tell you. I used to imagine the look on your face when I described it.'

'You wanted to see me cry.'

'At the very least.'

'I would have, if that makes you feel better.'

'It's too late for any of us to be feeling better.' Ruby sighed. 'Dean didn't take it very well either.'

That was all it took—the simple mentioning of Dean's name—and Nora was lost. That's how the grief hit her lately. Sometimes she went whole hours without thinking about Eric, and then she would suddenly be reminded. She knew she should say something—the pain in Ruby's eyes when she said Dean's name was unmistakable—but Nora's throat was blocked too tightly to speak.

'That's enough quid pro quo for one night,' Ruby said sharply. 'I'm going to go upstairs and take a bath.'

Nora watched her daughter leave. Then said quietly, 'Good night, Ruby.'

Wheeling back into her bedroom, Nora elbowed the door shut behind her and crawled up onto the bed. Then she reached for the phone and dialled Eric's number.

He answered on the third ring, and she could tell that he was heavily medicated. 'Hello?'

'Hey, Eric,' she said. 'Are you OK?'

'Sshure. Jesst a little doped up. New meds . . .'

Nora had seen him go through this before. It was always hell to get the pain prescription just right. She knew this wasn't a good time for them to speak. 'I'll let you sleep now, OK? I'll call back tomorrow.'

'Ssleep,' he murmured. 'Yeah. Morrow.'

'Good night, Eric.'

'Goo' night.'

Ruby went upstairs, where she grabbed her yellow legal pad and crawled up onto the bed.

> *My mother and I have battles to fight. But I'm afraid to ask the questions, and she, I can tell, is afraid to answer them.*
>
> *My secret for one of yours—this is the game we have begun to play. I will learn things about my mother that I don't want to know. I know, for instance, that she ran away from home after high school and never spoke to her father again.*
>
> *Even yesterday I wouldn't have been surprised by that. I would have said, 'Of course. Running away is what Nora Bridge does best.' But I watched her eyes as she spoke of her father. I saw the pain. Part of me wishes I hadn't seen that, because as I stood there, listening to my mother's heartache, I wondered for the first time if it hurt her to leave her children.*

Chapter Five

DEAN SAT CROSSLEGGED on the end of the pier watching the sun rise. The Sound was rough now at the changing of the tides. He heard the sound of motors in the distance, and he smiled.

The fishing boats were going out. How many times had he and Ruby stood on the pier watching Rand's boat chug out to sea? She'd always squeezed Dean's hand when the *Captain Hook* rounded the point and disappeared. He had known, without her telling him, that she lived with the fear that one day her father wouldn't return.

Tiredly, he got to his feet and turned round. To his right the old family sailboat bobbed wearily in the tide. The mast—once a bright white—had been discoloured by the endless rain and pitted by the wind. The deck around the steering wheel was hidden beneath a layer of slimy leaves and green-grey mould.

He heard her voice. *Let's take out the* Wind Lass, *Dino. Come on!*

He closed his eyes, remembering Ruby. In the beginning, he'd flinched at every memory and waited for the images to pass, but then he'd gone in search of them, reaching out like a blind man.

He grabbed the line, pulled the boat closer to the jetty, and stepped aboard. He had always felt free on this boat. The flapping sound of sails catching the wind had buoyed his spirits like nothing else, and yet he'd walked away from it, let sailing be part of the life he'd left behind. Suddenly he knew what he needed to do. He would restore the *Wind Lass*—scrape the old paint away, strip the wood and re-oil it. If he could get Eric out here for just a single afternoon, maybe the wind and the sea could take them back in time.

Ruby woke to the smell of frying bacon and brewing coffee. Picking yesterday's leggings off the floor, she pulled them on underneath her long nightshirt and padded downstairs.

Nora was in the kitchen, manoeuvring the wheelchair like General Patton along the front. There were two cast-iron skillets on the stove, one with steam climbing out. Nora smiled up at Ruby. 'Good morning. Did you sleep well?'

'Fine.' Ruby poured herself a cup of coffee. After a sip she felt more human. She saw that her mother had made bacon and pancakes. 'I haven't eaten breakfast like this since you left us.'

It was an effort for her mother to keep smiling. 'Do you want me to put an M&M face on your pancakes like I used to?'

'No, thanks. I try to avoid carbohydrates layered with chocolate.' Ruby set the table, then dished up two plates and sat down.

Nora sat across from her. 'Did you sleep well?' she asked.

'You already asked me that.'

Nora's fork clanged on the plate edge. 'Tomorrow I'll remember to wear a bulletproof vest under my nightgown.'

'What am I supposed to do? Be like Caroline—pretend everything is fine between us?'

'My relationship with Caroline is not for you to judge,' Nora said sharply. 'You've always thought you knew everything, but there's a dark

221

side to all that certainty, Ruby. You . . . hurt people.' Ruby saw her mother swell up with anger and then as quickly fade into a tired thinness. 'But I suppose it's not entirely your fault.'

'Not *entirely?* How about not at all my fault?'

'I left Caroline, too. It didn't make her cold and hard and unable to love people.'

'Who said I can't love people? I lived with Max for five years.'

'And where is he now?'

Ruby pushed back from the table and stood up.

Nora looked up. There was a gentle understanding in her gaze. 'Ruby Elizabeth, sit down and eat your breakfast. We won't talk about anything that matters.'

Her mother spoke in one of those voices that immediately turned a grown woman into a child. Ruby did as she was told.

Nora took a bite of bacon. 'We need to go grocery shopping.'

'Fine. We'll leave in about thirty minutes?'

'Make it an hour. I have to figure out how to bathe.'

'I could lasso your leg and lower you into the tub.'

Nora laughed. 'No, thanks. I don't want to drown naked with my leg stuck up in the air.'

The remark took a moment to sink in. When it did, Ruby said, 'I wouldn't let you drown.'

'I know. But would you rescue me?' Without waiting for an answer, Nora spun round and rolled into her bedroom.

Later that afternoon, when they had returned from the town's only grocery store, Ruby sat on the bed in her parents' old bedroom with her yellow pad in her lap. She had surreptitiously bought a copy of *USA Today* when they were shopping and hidden it until she got up to her room.

The headline in the upper right-hand corner read WHERE IS NORA BRIDGE HIDING? A grainy photograph of her mother stared up at her from the page.

> My mother is being destroyed in the press. It's only fitting, I suppose. She ruined her family in pursuit of a career, and now that career is detonating.
> It's what I wanted to happen, if not for vengeance, then for fairness. And yet something about it doesn't sit well with me.

'Ruby! Come and help me make dinner.'

Ruby yanked open the top drawer in her mother's nightstand. Pens and junk clattered forward. As she started to put her pad away, she saw a brown prescription bottle: VALIUM. NORA BRIDGE. 1985. The doctor listed was Allbright.

Ruby frowned. Her mother was on Valium in 1985? In 1985 everything had been fine. Or so Ruby had thought.

She went downstairs and found Nora already in the kitchen.

'We're going to make chicken divan. How does that sound?'

Ruby groaned. 'Cooking together.'

For the next half hour they worked side by side. Ruby chopped broccoli and cut up the chicken, while Nora did everything else. Finally the casserole was in the oven.

'I have a surprise for you,' Nora said. 'There's a big cardboard box in my closet. Will you get it?'

Ruby went into the bedroom and found the box. She took it into the living room and set it down on the coffee table.

Nora had followed her into the living room. 'Open it.'

Ruby pulled the flaps apart and peered inside the box. It was their sixteen-millimetre movie projector and a reel of film.

'Home movies,' Nora said with a forced smile.

'Don't tell me you want us to bond over old times?'

'I want to watch them, that's all. You can join me . . . or you can set it up and leave me.'

Ruby was trapped. Whether she watched the movies or not, she'd know that the film was here, waiting like a monster beneath a child's bed. She reached deeper into the box and found a folded white sheet and a set of thumbtacks—their old 'screen'. She set up the projector on a table in the living room, tacked the sheet onto the wall, and turned off the lights. With a dull, clacking sound, the film started. Ruby lowered herself to the sofa. There was a buzz of people talking, then her mother's voice: 'Rand, she's coming.'

Ruby couldn't have been more than five years old—a scrawny, puffy-cheeked kindergartener dressed in a ragged pink tutu. She twirled and swirled drunkenly across the stage.

'Oh, Rand, she's perfect.'

'Hush. I'm trying to concentrate.'

The picture went dark, then stuttered back to life. This time they were down at the beach. Caroline, in a skirted one-piece bathing suit, was splashing in the ankle-deep water, laughing. Ruby was wearing a bikini. Her mother was looking through a plastic bucket full of shells and rocks. Ruby ran over to her. Mom leaned over and fixed a strap on her sandal, then pulled a wriggly, laughing Ruby into her arms for a kiss. Mom . . .

How was it Ruby had forgotten how much they'd laughed or how regularly her mother had hugged and kissed her?

There was Dad, twirling Ruby round and round in a circle; Mom, teaching Ruby how to tie her shoe; a rainy Halloween with two princesses skipping hand in hand, carrying pumpkin-headed flashlights; Mom and Dad, dancing in the living room.

By the time the final bit of film flapped out of the reel and the screen went black, Ruby felt as if she'd run a ten-mile race. She was unsteady as she turned off the camera and hit the lights.

Her mother (*Nora,* she reminded herself) sat hunched in her wheel-chair. Tears glistened on her cheeks and lashes.

At the sight of her mother's tears Ruby felt something inside of her break away. 'You and Dad looked so happy together.'

Nora smiled unevenly. 'We were happy for a lot of years. And then . . . we weren't.'

'You mean *you* weren't. I saw what it did to him when you walked out. Believe me, he loved you.'

'Ah, Ruby, there's so much you don't know. No child can judge her parents' marriage.'

'You mean you won't tell me why you left him?'

'Beyond saying that we were unhappy? No, I won't.'

Ruby wanted to be angry, but the movies had hurt so much, she couldn't think straight. For the first time in years, she'd seen *Mom.* 'I had forgotten you,' Ruby said softly. 'I've never dreamed of you or had a single childhood memory with you in it. But tonight I remembered the locket you gave me on my eleventh birthday.'

Nora wiped her eyes and nodded. 'Do you still have it?'

Ruby got up. She'd been sixteen the last day she'd worn it.

That summer, the Bridge family had stayed huddled in their too quiet house. Dad had started drinking and smoking when Nora left in June. By August he never came out of his room. The *Captain Hook* sat idle, and by the fall Dad had had to sell off another chunk of land to pay their bills. Finally, on the first day of school, Ruby had taken the locket off and thrown it to the ground.

She turned and looked at her mother. 'I threw it away.'

'I see.'

'No, you don't. I didn't throw it away because I hated you. I threw it out because it hurt too much to remember you.'

'Oh, Ruby . . .'

In the kitchen the oven's timer went off.

Ruby lurched to her feet. 'Thank God. Let's eat.'

Nora wrestled through a long and sleepless night. Around dawn she gave up and went out onto the porch to watch the sunrise. *I had forgotten you.* Nora had known that Ruby blamed her, hated her. But to have *forgotten* her? Nora didn't know how to combat that. She needed to attack the problem with Ruby aggressively. But how?

'OK,' she sighed. 'Pretend this is a reader letter.'

> *Dear Nora,*
>
> *Years ago I walked out on my marriage and left my children. My daughter has never forgiven me. Now she tells me that she's forgotten all memories of me. How do I make amends?*

She took a deep breath, thinking it through. If Nora had received a letter like this, she would have taken the woman to task for her unpardonable behaviour. Then, after moralising for a few sentences, she would have said, *Force her to remember you.*

The answer came easily when offered to a stranger.

Behind her, the screen door squeaked open. 'Nora?'

Nora wheeled round, smiling brightly. 'Hi, honey.'

Ruby frowned. 'You're awfully chipper for eight in the morning. Do you want a cup of coffee?'

'I've got some. Why don't you get a cup and join me?'

Wordlessly Ruby went back inside, then came out a few minutes later and sat down in the rocker.

Nora took a sip of her coffee. 'Remember the Fourth of July barbecues we used to have out here? Your dad was always gone fishing, and the three of us girls would load up on firecrackers.'

Ruby smiled. 'Sparklers were my favourite. I couldn't wait for it to get dark.'

'We wrote things in the light, remember? I always wrote, "I love my girls." You only wrote Dean's name. Year after year.'

'Yeah. He and Eric always showed up right when you put the salmon on the barbecue.' Ruby sighed. 'Caroline tells me you've stayed in touch with Eric. How is he?'

Nora had known this moment was coming. She'd thought she was prepared for it, but she wasn't. How did you tell your daughter that one of her best childhood friends was dying? Nora wiped her eyes and met her daughter's expectant gaze. 'Eric has cancer.'

Ruby paled. 'Oh my God. How bad is it?'

'Bad.'

'Is he going to die?'

It hurt to answer. 'Yes, honey, he is.'

Ruby buried her head in her hands. 'I should have stayed in contact with him.' She fell silent, shaking her head, and Nora knew she was crying. 'It seems like yesterday we were all together. I can't imagine him sick. Can we visit him?'

'Of course. He's staying at the house on Lopez. I know he'd love to see you.' Nora leaned back and stared out at the Sound. 'Sometimes, when I close my eyes, I can picture all of us. You, me, Caroline . . . Eric and Dean. What I remember most are days out on the *Wind Lass*. Dino and Eric loved that boat . . .'

'I know what you're doing,' Ruby said after a long pause; her voice was thick and low. 'You want me to remember.'

'Yes.'

'Remembering stuff like that hurts.'

'I know, honey. But—'

Inside the house, the phone rang. Ruby got slowly to her feet and went inside. 'Nora!' she yelled. 'It's your assistant—Dee.'

Nora wheeled into the kitchen and took the phone. 'Dee?'

'Oh, Nora, a box of letters just landed on your desk. There was nothing I could do about it. Tom Adams called. He threatened to get me fired if I didn't forward them to you.'

'Did you read the letters? How bad are they?'

'It's ugly, Nora. A lady in Iowa went on TV last night and said she was going to file a lawsuit against you. Fraudulent advice.'

'OK, Dee. Send me the letters.'

'I thought I'd send your "Best Of" file, too. In case you wanted to sneak some old letters in. Tom wouldn't know.'

'Good thinking. Thanks for everything, Dee. Really. Goodbye.' Nora leaned forward and hung up the phone.

Ruby stood by the refrigerator. 'What was that all about?'

'My boss at the newspaper expects me to answer some rather unflattering letters from my readers.'

'Well, it *is* your job.'

Nora didn't bother answering. Ruby didn't know how it felt to *need* acceptance and how, without it, you felt invisible. She closed her eyes. For two days, she'd been able to forget that her life was unravelling, that she was a national scandal. No more.

She heard Ruby run upstairs. In a minute she was back, holding a section of newspaper. 'I bought this yesterday at the store. Maybe you should read what they're writing about you.'

Nora took the paper and glanced through the article. 'It's over,' she said dully, letting the newspaper fall to the floor.

Ruby frowned. 'You'll get through this. Look at Monica Lewinsky. She's selling expensive handbags now.'

'Thank you for that comforting comparison, Ruby. My career is over. I have no intention of answering a single letter. I'm going to hide out until this is over. Another story will come along, and they'll forget about me. Then I'll just fade away.'

'But with the right spin, you can—'

'You don't understand my career, Ruby. Everything I think and feel and believe is found in my words to strangers. That's why they believed in me—they sensed my honesty.'

Ruby's eyebrow arched upwards. 'According to the press, your columns said you believed in marriage. Is that the kind of honesty they got from you?'

'I *do* believe in marriage. And love and family and commitments. I just . . . failed at it.'

Ruby looked surprised by that answer. 'I would have thought you'd see leaving us as a success. You did it so well. Like leaving a job you hate. You might miss the income, but you're proud of yourself for finding the guts to quit.'

'I wasn't proud of myself.'

'Why?' Ruby asked the question in a whispered voice. 'Why did you do it? Couldn't you have a career *and* raise children?'

Nora sighed. 'What happened to us isn't some event, like the sinking of the *Titanic*. It's little things, strung together over decades. To really understand it all, you'd have to see the way things really were in our family, but you don't want to do that. You want to forget I ever existed, forget *we* ever existed.'

'It's easier that way,' Ruby said quietly.

'Yes. And it's easier for me to walk away from my career. I can't fight these charges, not with the choices I've made in my life.'

'I never saw you as a quitter.'

Nora gave her a sad, knowing smile. 'Ah, Ruby . . . you, of all people, you should have.'

The package arrived in the late afternoon while her mother was taking a nap. Ruby knew what it was. She debated with herself for a few moments—after all, she'd never chosen to read her mother's newspaper columns—but the *Caché* article changed things. Now Ruby needed to know what 'Nora Knows Best' had been about.

She opened the box and pulled out a manila envelope marked BEST OF. She withdrew a pile of clippings. The one on top was dated December 1989.

> *Dear Nora,*
> *Do you have any tips for getting red wine out of white silk? At my sister's wedding I got a little drunk and spilled a glassful on her gown. Now she's not talking to me, and I feel awful.*
> *Wedding Dress Blues.*

Nora's answer was short and sweet.

> *Dear Wedding Dress Blues,*
> *Only your dry cleaner can get the stain out. If it can't be done, you must offer to replace the gown. This is more than an ordinary accident, and your sister deserves a perfect reminder of her special day. It may take you a while to save the money, but in the end, you'll feel better. It's so easy to do the wrong thing in life, don't you think? When we see a clear road to being a better person, we ought to take it.*

Reading the columns, Ruby noticed that her mother's mail changed gradually from household-hint questions to earnest, heartfelt questions about life. Ruby had to admit that her mother was good at this. Her answers were concise, wise, and compassionate.

As she read a column from a sixteen-year-old who was having a problem with drugs, Ruby remembered the time in her own life when she'd been fourteen, and Lopez Island—and her own family—had seemed hopelessly small and uncool. For a time, skipping school and smoking pot had offered Ruby a better way.

Dad had gone ballistic when Ruby got suspended, but not Nora. Her mother had picked Ruby up from the principal's office and driven her to the tip of the island. She'd dragged Ruby down to the secluded patch of beach that overlooked the distant glitter of downtown Victoria and plopped down crosslegged on the sand. Then she had reached into her pocket and pulled out the joint that had been found in Ruby's locker. Amazingly, she had put it in her mouth and lit up. Then she had held it out to Ruby.

Stunned, Ruby had sat down by her mother. They'd smoked the whole thing together, and all the while, neither of them had spoken.

Gradually night had fallen, and Nora said, 'Do you notice anything different about Victoria?'

Ruby had found it difficult to focus. 'It looks farther away,' she had said, giggling.

'It is farther away. That's the thing about drugs. When you use them, everything you want in life is farther away.' Nora had turned to her. 'How cool is it to do something that anyone with a match can do? Cool is becoming an astronaut or a comedian or a scientist who cures cancer. Don't throw your chances away. We don't get as many of them as we need.' She stood up. 'It's your choice. Your life. I'm your mother, not your warden.'

Ruby remembered that she'd been shaking as she'd stood up. That's how deeply her mother's words had reached. Very softly she'd said, 'I love you, Mom.' That was Ruby's last specific memory of saying those words to her mother.

She turned her attention back to the columns now. The item on top was a handwritten letter.

Dear Nora,

My daughter—my precious baby girl—was killed by a drunk driver this year. I find that I can't talk to people any more, not even my wife. I see her sitting on the end of the bed, her hair unwashed, her eyes rimmed in red, and I can't reach out to her, can't offer comfort.

I want to gather my belongings, put them in a shopping cart, and disappear into the faceless crowd of vagrants in Pioneer Square. But I haven't the strength even for that. So I sit in my house, seeing the endless reminders of what I once had, and I ask myself why I bother to breathe at all.

Lost and Lonely.

Across the top of that letter someone had written: *FedEx the attached letter to this man's return address immediately.* Paper-clipped to the letter was a photocopy of a handwritten note.

Dear Lost and Lonely,
    I will not waste time with the pretty words we wrap around grief. You are in danger; you are not so far gone that you don't know this. I am going to do what I have never done before. You will come and talk to me. I will not take no for an answer.
    My secretary will be expecting your call tomorrow, and she will set up an appointment. Please, please, do not disappoint me. I know how much life can wound even the strongest heart, and sometimes all it takes to save us is the touch of a single stranger's hand. Reach out for me. I'll be there.
    Nora.

Ruby's hands were trembling. No wonder these readers loved her mother. She carefully put the columns and letters back in the manila envelope and left the package on the kitchen table for her mother to find. Then she went upstairs.

She hadn't realised that she was going to call Caroline until she'd picked up the phone. But it made sense. Ruby felt unsteady, and Caroline had always been her solid ground.

Caro answered on the third ring. 'Hello?'

Ruby couldn't help noticing how tired her sister sounded when she answered. 'Hey, sis. You sound like you need a nap.'

Caroline laughed. 'I always need a nap. Of course, what I do that makes me so darned tired is a complete mystery.'

'What *do* you do all day?'

'Only a single woman would ask that question of a mother. So what's going on up there? How are you and Mom doing?'

'She's not who I thought she was,' Ruby admitted softly. 'Like, did you know she was seeing a shrink when she was married to Dad or that she took Valium in 1985?'

'Wow. I wonder if her doctor told her to leave Dad.'

'Why would he do that?'

Caroline laughed softly. 'That's what they do, Ruby. They tell unhappy women to find happiness. I wish I had a buck for every time my therapist told me to leave Jere.'

'You see a shrink, too?'

'Come on, Ruby. It's like getting a manicure. Good grooming for the mind.'

'But I thought you and Mr Quarterback had a perfect life.'

'We have our problems, just like anyone else, but I'd rather talk about— Aah! Darn it, Jenny! I gotta run, Ruby. Your niece just poured a cup of grape juice on her brother's head.'

Before Ruby could answer, Caroline hung up.

Everything was ready, Dean knocked on Eric's door and went inside.

Eric was sitting up in bed, reading. When he saw Dean, he smiled. 'Hey, bro. It's almost dinner time. Where have you been?'

'I've been working on something,' Dean said. Slowly he lowered the metal bedrail. 'Are you up to a little trip?'

'Are you kidding? I'm so sick of this bed, I could cry.'

Dean leaned forward and lifted his brother up from the bed. *God, he weighed nothing at all.* It was like holding a fragile child. Dean carried him downstairs, through the house, across the lawn and down the bank to the beach. On the slanted wooden jetty, he'd already set up an over-sized chair and piled pillows onto it.

'The *Wind Lass*,' Eric said softly.

Dean carefully placed his brother in the chair, then tucked a cashmere blanket tightly round his thin body.

It was nearing sunset. The sky was low enough to touch. The last rays of the setting sun turned everything pink—the waves, the clouds, the pebbled beach. The sailboat was still in bad shape, but at least she was clean.

Dean sat down beside Eric. 'I still have some work to do on her. The sail should be done tomorrow. The cushions are being cleaned. I thought maybe if we could take her out . . .' Dean let the sentence trail off. He didn't know how to sculpt his hope into something as ordinary as words.

'We could remember how it used to be,' Eric said. 'How *we* used to be.'

Of course Eric had understood. 'Yeah.'

Eric drew the blanket tighter against his chin. 'So what's it like being the favoured son?'

'Lonely.'

Eric sighed. 'Remember when she loved me? When I was a star athlete with awesome grades and a promising future.'

Dean remembered. Their mother had adored Eric. The only time

Mom and Dad came on the island was football season. Every homecoming game, Mom had dressed in her best 'casual' clothes and gone to the game, where she cheered on her quarterback son. When the season ended, they were gone again.

Eric had lived in the warm glow of his parents' affection for so long, he'd mistaken pride for love, but when he'd told them about Charles, he'd learned the depth of his naiveté. Mother hadn't spoken to him since.

So it had been Dean, the younger, less perfect son, who'd taken over the family business. It had never been something he wanted to do, but family expectations—especially in a wealthy family—were a sticky web.

'I heard the phone ring last night about eleven o'clock,' Eric said. 'It was her, wasn't it?'

Dean looked away. Eye contact was impossible. 'Yeah.'

'Are they coming to see me?'

There was no point in lying. 'No.'

Eric released a thready sigh. 'What good is an agonising death by cancer if your own family won't weep by your bedside?'

'I'm here,' Dean said softly. 'You're not alone.'

Tears came to Eric's eyes. 'I know, baby brother. I know.'

Dean swallowed hard. 'You can't let her get to you.'

Eric closed his eyes. 'Someday she'll be sorry. It'll be too late, though.' His eyes blinked open again, and he smiled. 'Tell me about your life.'

'There's not much to tell. I work.'

'Very funny. I get the San Francisco newspapers just to read about you and the folks. You seem to be quite the bachelor-about-town. If I didn't know better, I'd say you had everything.'

Dean wanted to laugh and say, 'I do. I do have everything a man could want,' but it was a lie, and he'd never been able to lie to his brother. And more than that, Dean wanted to talk to Eric the way he once had. Brother to brother, from the heart. 'There's something . . . missing in my life. I don't know what it is.'

'Do you like your job?'

Dean was surprised by the question. No one had ever asked him that, and he'd never bothered to ask himself. The answer came quickly. 'No.'

'Are you in love with anyone?'

'No. It's been a long time since I was in love.'

'And you can't figure out what's *missing* in your life? Come on, Dino. The question isn't what's missing. The question is, what the hell *is* your life?' Eric yawned and closed his eyes again. Already he was tiring. He

232

fell asleep for a second, then blinked awake. 'Remember Camp Orkila?' he said suddenly. 'I was thinking about that yesterday, about the first time we went up there.'

'When we met Ruby,' Dean said softly. 'She climbed up into that big tree by the beach, remember? She said arts and crafts were for babies and she was a big girl.'

'She wouldn't come down until you asked her to.'

'Yeah. That was the beginning, wasn't it? We'd never seen a real family before. . . .' Dean let the words string out, find one other, and connect. Like threads, he wove them together, sewed a quilt from the strands of their life, and tucked it round his brother's thin body.

Chapter Six

NORA WOKE UP groggy from her nap. She lay in bed for a minute, listening to the gentle whooshing sound of the sea through her open window. It was almost nighttime. *Eric.*

She pulled the phone onto her lap and dialled the number.

Eric came on the line. 'Nora? Well, it's about time.'

She laughed. 'I've had an . . . interesting last few days. I'm on Summer Island. Caroline is letting me relax here for a while.'

'Ah, the lifestyles of the rich and famous. I suppose it's tough to make time for a friend who is facing the grim reaper.' Eric laughed at his own joke, but the laughter dwindled into a cough.

Nora made an instant decision: she wouldn't tell him about the scandal. He didn't need to worry about her. But she had to tell him *something*—she couldn't just show up at his house in a wheelchair. 'I had an accident and wound up in Bayview.'

'Oh my God. Are you OK?'

'For a fifty-year-old woman who drove into a tree, I'm great. I came out of it with a broken leg and a sprained wrist. Nothing to worry about. But that's why I haven't been to see you.'

'There's something you're not telling me.'

She forced a laugh. 'Your intuition is wrong this time.'

'Nora?' He said her name with infinite tenderness, and in it, she heard the gentle, chiding reminder of all they'd been through together. For the first time since this mess had begun, she felt truly cared for. 'No, really, I—' She started to cry.

'Nora, you know you can talk to me about anything.'

'You don't need to hear about my troubles.'

'Who sat by me in the hospital while Charlie was dying? Who held my hand at the grave? Who was there when I began chemotherapy?'

Nora swallowed hard. 'Me.'

'So talk.'

All the emotions she'd bottled up in the past few days came spilling out. She didn't cry. She was almost preternaturally calm, in fact. But as she spoke, it felt as if the very fabric of her soul was ripping. 'The *Tattler* just published pictures of me naked and in bed with a man.'

'Oh, God.' His voice was a whisper.

'That's not even the worst of it. The photos were dated, proving that I was married to Rand at the time they were taken. The press is crucifying me. My career is over.'

'Come on, this is *America*. Celebrities screw up all the time. So you flashed your ass. Big deal. Hold your head up, cry when you admit your mistake, and beg for a second chance. Your fans will love you more for being like them—human.'

'That's why I love you, Eric. The glass is always half full.' Nora sighed. 'How about if I come to see you tomorrow? Between the wheelchair and the hospital bed, we'll look like a scene from *Cuckoo's Nest*.'

'That'd be great. And you won't believe who's here.'

Nora laughed. 'Believe me, you won't believe who is *here* either.'

'Dean—'

'Ruby—'

They spoke at the same time.

Nora was the first to recover. 'Dean is on the island? How is it between you two?'

'Awkward. A little unsure. And Ruby?'

'Angry. Truthfully, she hates me.'

'But she's there. That means something. Hey, do you know what happened between Dean and Ruby? He won't talk about it.'

'She won't either.'

'It must've been bad. Dean went all the way to boarding school to get away from her. But it's interesting neither ever married.'

'Are you thinking what I'm thinking?'

'How do we get them together?'

Nora grinned. It felt great to talk about something besides Eric's illness or her own scandal. And this made her feel like a mother for the first time in years. 'Carefully, my boy. Very carefully.'

After Nora hung up, she wheeled herself out of the room and was halfway into the kitchen when she saw the package on the table. She stopped dead. Slowly she wheeled closer. It had been opened.

She pulled the slim box onto her lap and went into the living room. Her fingers were shaking as she pulled out the stack of mail marked NEW LETTERS. On top was an envelope postmarked GREAT FALLS, MONTANA. She opened it and began to read.

> Nora,
>
> I can't bring myself to write 'Dear' any more. I've written to you a dozen times over the last few years. Twice you have published my letters, and once you wrote me a private letter, saying that you hoped things were getting better.
>
> Can you imagine how it now feels to know the kind of person I've been taking advice from?
>
> Don't bother answering this letter. I don't care about your opinion, and I certainly won't be reading your columns any more. If I want to read fiction, I'll go to the library.
>
> May God forgive you, Nora Bridge. Your fans will not.

Nora folded the letter and slid it back into the envelope.

After reading a few more, she couldn't seem to move. A tremor was spreading through her, chilling her from the inside out.

'Nora?' Ruby came into the room and sat down on the leather chair across from Nora. 'Did you sleep well?'

Nora stared down at her own hands and thought, Oh, please, just go away, don't talk to me now. 'Yes,' she managed.

'I take it you read a few of your new letters,' Ruby said.

Nora wanted to say something casual and flip, but she couldn't. 'They hate me now.'

'They're strangers. They don't even know you.' Ruby flashed a smile. 'Leave the big, ugly emotions to your family.'

Who also hated her.

That only made it worse. 'What family?' Nora moaned quietly. 'Really, Ruby, what family have I left myself?'

Ruby looked at her for a long minute, then said, 'Do you remember when I was twelve and my class elected me to run the dance where the girls asked the boys?'

Nora sniffled. 'Yeah, I remember that.'

'I wanted the local newspaper to cover the event. You were the only one who didn't laugh at me.' Ruby smiled. 'I watched you charm that fat old editor from the *Island Times*.'

Nora remembered that day. 'The minute I walked into that office, I loved it. For the first time in my life I felt as if I *belonged* somewhere. I'd always known I had words banging around in my chest, but I'd never known what to do with them.'

Ruby's gaze was solemn. 'I realised later that I'd shown you the way out of our lives.'

Nora took a deep breath. 'I didn't leave my family for a career, Ruby. That had nothing to do with it. For me, leaving your dad started before I met him.'

'I don't understand.'

Nora stared out the window. 'My dad was an alcoholic. When he was sober, he was almost human, but when he was drunk—which was most of the time—he was pit-bull mean. It was a secret I learned to keep from everyone. Hell, it took me fifteen years of therapy to even say the word alcoholic.'

Ruby's mouth fell open. 'You never told us that.'

'On our farm the neighbours couldn't hear a woman's scream. Or a girl's. And you learn fast that it doesn't help to cry out. Instead you try to get smaller and smaller, hoping that if you can become tiny enough and still enough, he'll pass you by.'

'He abused you?'

'He didn't do the worst thing that a father can do to his daughter, but he . . . moulded me. I grew up trying to be invisible, flinching all the time.' Nora made direct eye contact with her daughter. 'For years I thought that if I didn't talk about my dad, I could forget him.'

Ruby drew in a sharp breath. 'Did it work?'

Nora knew her daughter was making the connection. *I'd forgotten you.* 'No. All it did was give him more power and turn me into a woman who couldn't imagine being loved.'

'Because your own father didn't love you.'

'Not unlike how a girl would feel if her own mother abandoned her.' Nora wouldn't let herself look away. 'Did you ever fall in love . . . after Dean?'

'I lived with Max for almost five years. Then I came home from work one day and he'd moved out.'

'Did you ever tell him you loved him?'

'Almost. Practically.'

'Did he say he loved you?'

'Yeah, but Max was like that. He told the checkout girl at Safeway he loved her.'

Nora could see she'd have to be more direct. 'My point is this. You lived with a man for almost five years and never told him you loved him, even after he'd said those precious words to you. The question isn't why he left. It's why he stayed so long.'

Ruby looked helplessly at Nora. 'I never thought of it like that.'

'I told your father I loved him the first time we made love. I'd never said the words before to anyone. It wasn't the sort of thing my family did. And do you know when Rand told me he loved me?'

'When?'

'Never. I waited for it like a child waits for Christmas. Every time I said it, I waited, and every second of his silence was a little death.'

Ruby shook her head. 'No more. Please.'

'I wanted to raise you to be strong and sure of yourself, and instead I turned you into me. I made you afraid to love. I was a bad mother. I'm so, so sorry for that.'

'You weren't a bad mother,' Ruby said, 'until you left.'

Nora was pathetically grateful for that. 'Thank you.' She knew she was following a dangerous path, falling in love with her daughter all over again, but she couldn't help herself. 'I still remember the little girl who cried every time a baby bird fell out of its nest.'

Ruby got to her feet. 'That girl is long gone.'

'You'll find her again,' Nora said softly. 'Probably about the same time you fall in love. And when it's real, Ruby, you'll know it, and you'll stop being afraid.'

Before dinner, Ruby stayed in the bath until the water turned cold.

The world—her world—had changed, but she couldn't put her finger on precisely how.

She climbed out of the clawfoot tub and stood on the fuzzy pink bath mat, dripping. By the time she had dried off and slipped into a pair of sweats and an oversized sweatshirt, she could smell dinner cooking.

She finger-combed her hair and lay down on the bed with her yellow pad open in front of her.

Today I talked to my mother. This is a remarkably ordinary sentence for a truly revolutionary act.

I talked to her. She talked to me. What I don't know is where we go from here. How can I walk downstairs and pretend that nothing has changed? And yet, it was simply a conversation, words passed back and forth between women who are strangers to each other even though they share a past.

Why then did I cry? Why did I look at her and feel like a child again and think—even for a moment—'What if?'

Dean carried the breakfast tray up to his brother's bedroom. He found him already awake, sitting up in bed.

'Heya, Dino,' Eric said.

Dean carefully placed the tray across Eric's lap. He noticed how wan his brother looked this morning. 'Bad night?'

Eric nodded. 'I can't seem to sleep any more, which is pretty ironic, since it's all I do. The pain cocktail knocks me out, but it's not the same as a good night's sleep.' He smiled tiredly.

Dean pulled a chair up, sat down and held his brother's hand.

Eric turned to him. 'I always thought we'd come back to this house as old men. I pictured us watching your kids running up and down the jetty, looking for shrimp.' Eric's eyes fluttered shut. 'You and Ruby used to play down on that jetty for hours.'

Dean swallowed hard. He thought about changing the subject, but suddenly he wanted to remember her, to reminisce with someone who'd known her. 'Sometimes when I close my eyes at night, I hear her laughing, yelling at me to hurry up. She was always running off ahead.'

'I thought I'd be the best man at your wedding. You and Ruby were sixteen years old, but I thought it was true love.'

'I thought so, too.'

Eric looked at him. 'And now?'

'Now I know it was.'

'She's on Summer Island.'

Dean frowned. It took a moment for the full impact of those words to hit him. 'Ruby's at the summer house?'

Eric grinned. 'Yep.'

Dean leaned back. 'What . . . With her husband and kids?'

'She's never been married. I wonder why that is?'

Dean's heart was beating so fast, he felt faint. *Ruby is here.*

'Go see her,' Eric said softly.

Dean grabbed his ten-speed from its resting place beneath the eaves. The sun was shining brightly as he pedalled down the winding hill to the Lopez Island pier. A ferry was loading. He got right on and stood with his bike at the bow of the boat, barely noticing the cars streaming into lines behind him.

On Summer Island, he cycled off the boat onto the pier. By the time he swooped onto the Bridges' driveway, he was sweating and out of breath. He jumped off the bike and let it clatter to the ground.

Then Dean stopped. For the first time he wondered what he was doing, running towards his first love as if eleven years hadn't passed. Their last day together came at him in a rush of images.

The sky had been robin's-egg blue. Strangely, he remembered looking up, seeing the white trail from a passing jet. When he'd turned to point it out to Ruby, he saw what he should have seen before: she'd been crying.

'I had sex with a boy last night.' She'd said it without preamble, as if she'd wanted to wound him with her confession.

He had pulled the whole sordid story out of her, one painful syllable at a time, and when she was finished, he knew all the facts, but they hadn't added up to a whole truth he could understand. If he'd been older, more sexually experienced, he would have known the question to ask, the only one that mattered. Why? But he'd been seventeen and a virgin himself. All he'd cared about was the promise he and Ruby had made—to wait for each other until marriage.

Anger and hurt had overwhelmed him. She'd lied to him, and she hadn't loved him as much as he'd loved her. He'd felt foolish and used. He waited for her to beg for forgiveness, but she just stood there, close enough to touch and yet so far away, he couldn't see her clearly. Or maybe it was his tears that were blurring the world, turning her into a girl he'd never seen before.

'Go ahead,' she'd said, staring dully up at him. 'Go. It's over.'

He'd had to leave fast, before she could see that he was crying. He'd turned away from her and run back to his bike. He'd pedalled hard, trying to outdistance the pain, but it had raged inside him.

Now Dean released his breath in an even stream. There was no turning back. He walked down the path, stepped onto the porch, and knocked.

And she answered.

The minute he saw her, he understood what had been missing from his life. What he'd been longing for, without even realising it, had been that elusive, magical mixture of friendship and passion that he'd only ever found with her.

'Ruby,' he whispered. It actually hurt to say her name. She was so beautiful that for a second he couldn't breathe.

'Dean,' she said, her eyes widening.

The moment felt spun from sugar, so fragile that a soft breeze could shatter it. 'I . . . uh . . . I came home to see Eric.'

'How is he?' Her voice was barely audible.

'Not good.'

She closed her eyes for a second, then looked up at him again. 'I'm here with my mother. She had a car accident, and I'm taking care of her.'

'*You?*' It slipped out. An intimate observation from a man who'd once known the girl. He was instantly afraid he'd offended her. 'So you've forgiven her, then?'

Sadness darkened her eyes. 'Forgiveness doesn't matter, does it? When a thing is done, it's done. You can't unring a bell.' She smiled, but it wasn't the smile he remembered, the one that crinkled her whole face and sparkled in her eyes. She seemed to be waiting for him to say something, but he couldn't think fast enough, and as usual she didn't wait long. 'Well, it was good seeing you again. Say hello to Nora before you leave. She'd hate to miss you.'

And with that, she walked past him, heading for the beach.

Ruby thought she was going to be sick. That was why she'd left Dean so quickly. She couldn't stand there, making polite conversation, not when it felt as if carbonated water had replaced her blood.

She ran down the path towards the beach and sat down on her favourite moss-covered rock, just as she'd done so often in her life.

'Ruby?'

She heard her name, spoken softly in the voice that had filled her dreams since adolescence, and she froze. Her heart picked up a wild beat. She hadn't heard his footsteps.

'Can I sit with you?'

She tried not to remember all the hours they'd spent here, huddled out on this rock, staring first out to sea, then gradually at each other. She sidled to the right—it had always been her side. Dean sat down beside her. She felt his thigh along hers, and she ached to lay her hand on his the way she'd done so many times before. But she'd lost that right. In her angry, confused youth, she'd thrown it away.

'This brings back memories,' he said softly.

She didn't mean to turn to him, but she couldn't help herself. When she gazed into his blue eyes, she was sixteen again. Except he had become a man. If it were possible, he was even more handsome now. She felt a rush of shame. If only she'd worn better clothes today than torn shorts and a ragged T-shirt. He was probably disgusted that she'd let herself get so ugly. She reached deep inside for a casual voice. 'I hear from Caro that you're a corporate bigwig now.'

'It doesn't mean much.'

'Spoken like a rich man.' She tried to smile.

'I saw your act once. At the Comedy Store. I thought you were really funny.'

Her smile softened into the real thing. 'Really?'

'I wanted to talk to you after the show, but there was a man—'

'Max.' She felt the sting of that missed opportunity. 'We broke up a while ago. And what about you? Are you married?'

'No. Never.'

She felt euphoria. Then it fell away, left her even more confused. She'd loved him so much, and yet she'd broken his heart. She barely knew why. 'That summer . . . I found out from Lottie that you'd moved away,' she said, her voice unsteady.

'I couldn't face you,' he answered, looking at her. 'You didn't just hurt me, Ruby. You ruined me.'

'I know.' She lurched to her feet, terrified that she would burst into tears. 'I have to get back to Nora.'

Slowly he got to his feet and reached for her. She stumbled back so fast, she almost fell. His hand dropped back to his side, and she could see the disappointment in his eyes. 'Time is precious,' he said. 'If I didn't know that before this week, I know it now. So I'm just going to say it: I missed you.'

She couldn't imagine what to say next, how to answer. She had missed him, too. A more trusting person could have changed the future in this very moment, but Ruby couldn't imagine that kind of strength.

He waited, and the silence stretched out between them. Then, slowly, he turned and walked away.

Nora sat on the porch. She could see Dean and Ruby sitting out on that old rock of theirs. Ruby was the first to stand. Dean followed. They stood frozen, close enough to kiss. Then Dean turned and headed back towards the house, leaving Ruby behind.

He saw Nora on the porch and came up to her. At the railing he stopped, hung his arms over the wisteria-covered edge, and smiled tiredly. 'Hey, Miz Bridge.'

She smiled. 'Call me Nora. It's good to see you again, Dean. I'm glad you finally made it back to the island.'

'It's good to see you, too.' In his eyes she saw pain. 'Thank you, Nora,' he said softly. 'You're everything to him.'

She nodded, knowing she didn't need to say anything. Everything that mattered had passed between them in silence.

Dean turned back, stared down at the beach. Nora knew that they both wanted to talk about Ruby, but neither of them knew what to say. Finally Dean pulled away from the porch. 'Will you guys come over on Saturday? I've got the *Wind Lass* working. I'm going to take Eric sailing.'

'That would be great.'

Dean shot a last, lingering look at Ruby, then walked away.

A few minutes later Ruby headed up the path. When she saw Nora on the porch, she paused.

Nora noticed that her daughter's eyes were red. Her heart went out to her. 'Come,' she said, 'sit with me.'

Ruby walked onto the porch and sat on the railing.

Nora longed to touch her daughter. But such intimacy was still impossible between them. 'You know what I was remembering just now? The winter I was pregnant with you. The snow came earlier that year than anyone could remember. Just after Thanksgiving. For almost a month after that, things on the island went a little crazy. Roses bloomed on prickly bushes that had been dead for weeks. Rain fell from cloudless skies. We believed it was magic. But what I remember most of all were the sunsets. From then until the new year came, the night sky was always red. We called it the ruby season.'

Ruby said softly, 'Is that where my name came from?'

'We never talked about naming you after it, but when you came, we knew. You'd be our Ruby. Our own bit of magic.' Nora paused and looked at her. 'Dean invited us to go sailing on Saturday.'

'What will I say to Eric?'

'Oh, Ruby,' Nora said gently, 'you start with hello.'

Ruby barely slept that night. She knew that she had hurt people, and she didn't want to hurt Dean again. He deserved a woman who could return his love as fully and freely as he gave it. That was the one thing she'd known even as a teenager.

Finally, at about three thirty, she went out onto the balcony and sat. *Write. That'll get your mind off everything.* Then for the first time she considered the impact of her article. She'd agreed to write it because she'd *wanted* to hurt her mother, to strike back for all the pain she'd suffered as a young girl. But she wasn't a child any more.

Before, she hadn't wanted to know why Nora left them. But marriages broke up for *reasons*; women like her mother didn't just up and leave their husbands on a sunny summer's day.

And Ruby had glimpsed images in the past days that didn't fit with the picture she'd drawn of her mother.

She closed her eyes and remembered a cold, crisp October day a few months after her mother had left home.

Dad had been in the living room, sitting in that leather chair of his, drinking and smoking cigarettes. Caroline had been gone on a field trip to Seattle. Ruby had been in the bedroom, reading *Misery* by Stephen King. There was a knock at the front door. Ruby heard her dad's footsteps, then heard him say 'Nora' in a voice that was too loud, belligerent.

Ruby froze. Then she crept to the door of her room.

Dad was in his chair. Mom was kneeling in front of him.

'Rand,' Mom said quietly, 'we need to talk.'

He stared down at her; his hair was too long, and dirty. 'It's too late for talking.'

Ruby couldn't stand it another minute, seeing her father's pain in such sharp relief. 'Get out,' she yelled.

Mom got to her feet, turned round. 'Oh, Ruby,' she said, holding her arms out.

As Mom came towards her, Ruby saw the changes in her mother—the grey pallor in her cheeks, the weight she'd lost, the way her hands, always so strong and sure, were blue-veined and trembling.

Ruby sprang back. 'G-go away. We don't want you any more.'

Mom stopped, her hands falling to her sides. 'Don't say that, honey. There are things you don't understand. You're so young.'

'I understand how it feels to be left behind, as if you were . . . nothing.' Ruby's traitorous voice broke, and the sudden rawness of her pain made it difficult to breathe. 'Go away, Mother. No one here loves you any more.'

Mom glanced back at Dad, who'd slumped into his chair again. He was holding his head in his hands.

Ruby wanted to put her arms round him and tell him she loved him, but it was all she could do to keep from wailing. She stepped back into her bedroom and slammed the door shut.

She didn't know how long she stood there. After a while she heard footsteps crossing the living room, then the quiet opening and closing of the front door. Outside, a car engine started; tyres crunched through gravel. And quiet fell once again, broken only by the sound of a grown man crying.

Even then her mother had had a story to tell, but no one had wanted to hear it. Now Ruby was ready. She wanted to learn what had happened more than a decade earlier within her own family.

And if her mother wouldn't answer those questions, there was always an alternative.

She would ask her father.

Chapter Seven

IT HAD BEEN EASY to get out of the house. Ruby had simply left a note— *Gone to Dad's*—on the kitchen table. Now she was driving up the tree-lined road that led away from the Lopez Island ferry pier.

Ruby was a fourth-generation islander, and at this moment, seeing all the new houses and bed-and-breakfasts that had sprouted on Lopez, the full impact of that heritage hit her. She had roots here, a past that grew deep into the rich black island soil.

Her great-great-grandfather had come to this remote part of the world from a dreary, industrialised section of England. He'd brought his beautiful, black-eyed Irish wife and seventeen dollars, and together they'd homesteaded 200 acres on Lopez. His brother had staked his own claim on Summer Island. Both had become successful apple and sheep farmers. Now, more than 100 years later, there were only ten acres on Lopez that belonged to her father.

Randall Bridge was an island man through and through. He'd grown up on this tiny, floating world, and he'd raised his children here. He lived on a financial shoestring, from one fishing season to the next, making it through the lean months doing boat repairs.

Ruby turned off the main road. A gravel road wound through acres of apple trees. At last she was home. She parked alongside her dad's battered Ford truck and got out of the car. The yellow clapboard house sat wedged between two huge willow trees.

It was exactly as she remembered. She walked towards the back porch. The yard was still a riot of weeds and untended flowers. A tattered screen door hung slanted, a set of screws missing.

She paused on the porch, steeling herself for the sight of her dad's new family. She knew she'd be entering another woman's house—a woman she barely knew—seeing a baby brother for the first time. Taking a deep breath, she knocked on the door and waited. When there was no answer, she eased the screen door open and stepped into the kitchen. 'Dad?' Her voice was weak. She stepped past the table into the living room.

He was there, kneeling in front of the small black woodstove, loading logs into the fire. When he looked up and saw her, his eyes widened in surprise; then a great smile swept across his lined face. 'I don't believe it. You're here.' He clanged the stove's door shut, got to his feet, and pulled her into an awkward hug. 'Caroline told me you were home. I wondered if you'd come see me.'

She clung to him, fighting an urge to cry. 'Of course I'd come,' she said shakily, drawing back, although both of them knew it was a half-truth, a wished-for belief. She hadn't even called him, and the realisation of her own selfishness tasted black and bitter.

He touched her cheek. 'I missed you,' he said.

'I missed you, too.' It was true. She had missed him every day and all the time. She glanced uneasily up the stairs, wondering where Marilyn was. 'I don't want to intrude—'

'Mari took Ethan off-island for a doctor's appointment.' He grinned.

'And don't even pretend you aren't happy about that.'

Ruby smiled sheepishly. 'Well, I wanted to see the kid. My brother,' she added when she saw the way he was looking at her. She winced, wishing she'd said it right the first time.

'Don't worry about it.' But she knew she'd hurt his feelings. He sat down on the threadbare floral sofa, cocked one leg over his knee. 'How's it going between you and your mom?'

She flopped down onto the big overstuffed chair near the fire. 'Picture Laverne and Shirley on crack.'

'I don't see any visible bruising. I have to admit, I was shocked when Caro told me you'd volunteered to take care of Nora. Shocked and proud.'

'She isn't quite what I expected.' Ruby experienced a momentary lapse in courage. She drew a deep breath. 'What happened between you two?'

He got to his feet and walked past her to the window. 'Are you in for the long haul this time, Ruby?'

'What do you mean?'

'Ah, Rube.' He sighed. 'You have a way of moving on. You went off to California and started a new life without us. But after a while it was *our* fault—Caroline's and mine. We didn't call enough or not on the right days, or we didn't say the right things when we did call. You didn't come to my wedding or call when your brother was born or come to see Caroline when she suffered through that terrible labour. Now you want to stir up an old pot. Will you be here tomorrow or next month to see what comes of it?'

Ruby wanted to say he was *wrong*. But she couldn't. 'I don't know, Dad.' It was all she could manage now; a quiet, simple honesty.

He stared down at her for a long time, then headed into the kitchen. Ruby followed him through the doorway. Her father was standing at the table with a bottle of tequila. He thumped it down hard, then yanked out a chair and sat down.

The sight of her father holding a bottle of booze shook Ruby to the core. 'I thought you'd quit drinking.'

'I did.'

'You're scaring me.'

'Honey, I haven't begun to scare you. Sit down.'

Ruby pulled a chair out and perched nervously on its edge.

Her dad seemed different. This man, hunched over, staring at a full bottle of Cuervo Gold, looked as if he hadn't smiled in years. He looked up suddenly. 'I love you. I want you to remember that.'

She saw the emotion in his eyes. 'I could never forget that.'

'I don't know. You're good at forgetting the people who love you. The story starts in 1967, just a few years before the whole damn world exploded. I was at the University of Washington, finishing my senior year, and I was certain I'd get drafted into the National Football League. So certain, I never bothered to get a degree.

'And then I met Nora. She was scrawny and scared. Still, she was the most beautiful girl I'd ever seen. She believed absolutely that I'd play pro football.' Her dad slumped forward a little. 'But it didn't happen. No one called. Then my draft number came up. I could have got out of it— said they needed me to run the farm—but I hated this island, and I wanted someone to wait for me, to write me letters. So I asked Nora to marry me.'

Ruby frowned. She'd heard this story a thousand times in her childhood, and this was not the way it went. 'You didn't love her?'

'Not when I married her. No, that's not true. I'd just loved other women more. Anyway, we got married, spent a wonderful honeymoon at Lake Quinalt Lodge, and I shipped out.

'Your mom's letters kept me alive over there. It's funny. I fell in love with your mother when she wasn't even on the same continent. I meant to *stay* in love with her, but I didn't come home the same cocky, confident kid who'd left. Vietnam, war—it did something to us.' He smiled sadly. 'Anyway, I turned cynical and hard. Your mom tried to put me back together, and for a few years we were happy. Caroline was born, then you.'

Ruby had this bizarre sensation that her whole existence had turned into sand and was streaming through her fingers.

'When I came home, your mom and I moved into the house on Summer. I went to work at the feedstore. Everyone thought I was a failure. I hated my life. I didn't mean for it to happen.'

Ruby swallowed convulsively. 'Don't say—'

'I slept with other women.'

'*No.*'

'Your mom didn't know at first. I was drinking a lot by then—God knows *that* didn't help—and I knew when she started to suspect. But she always gave me the benefit of the doubt. Finally that summer someone told her the truth. She confronted me. Unfortunately, I was drunk at the time. I said . . . things. It was ugly. The next day she left.'

Ruby felt as if she were drowning or falling.

'We've all been carrying this baggage for too long. Some of us have tried to go on.' He looked at her. 'And some of us have refused to. But all of us are hurting. She's your mother. Whatever she's done or hasn't done, or said or hasn't said, she's a part of you and you're a part of her. Don't you see that you can't be whole without her?'

Ruby's past seemed to be crumbling around her. There was nothing solid to hold on to. 'I'm leaving.'

He smiled sadly. 'Of course you are.'

'Call Nora. Tell her I'm going to Caroline's.'

'I love you, Ruby,' he said. 'Please don't forget that.'

She knew he was waiting for her to say the words back to him, but she couldn't do it.

Ruby had never been to her sister's house, but the address was imprinted on her brain. Caroline was the only person on earth who regularly received a Christmas card from Ruby.

The traffic was stop-and-go as she crept towards the sprawling suburb of Redmond. Not so many years earlier this had been the sticks. Now it was Microsoftland. Ruby checked the handy rental-car map and turned down Emerald Lane. One big brick-faced house followed another, each built to the edge of its lot. At last she found it: 12712 Emerald Lane.

She drove up the blue concrete driveway and parked next to a silver Mercedes station wagon, then headed up the path to a pair of oak doors trimmed in beaded brass.

She knocked. From inside came a muffled 'Just a minute'.

Suddenly the door sprang open, and Caroline stood there smiling, looking flawless at one o'clock in the afternoon. 'Ruby!' She took Ruby into her arms, holding her tightly. Finally Caro drew back. 'I'm so glad you came.' She pulled Ruby into the house.

Of course, it was perfect—uncluttered and flawlessly decorated. Not a thing was out of place. Caro led her through the pristine kitchen, then through the formal dining room and into the living room, where two wing chairs, upholstered in a brandy-coloured silk, flanked a gold-and-bronze tapestried sofa.

'Where are the kids?'

Caroline brought a finger to her lips and said, 'Shh. We don't want to wake them up. Trust me.'

Ruby got a glimpse of something behind Caro's perfect face, but it was gone so fast, it left no imprint. She felt a prickle of unease. 'Something's going on with you,' Ruby said. 'What is it?'

Caro sat on one of the chairs. Her perfectly manicured hands were clasped so tightly together, the skin had gone pale. A smile flashed across her face. 'It's nothing, really. Just a bad week.'

Ruby couldn't put her finger on it exactly, but *something* was wrong here. Suddenly she knew. 'You're having an affair!'

There was no mistaking the genuineness of Caro's smile. It showed how false the others had been. 'Since Fred was born, I'd rather hit myself in the head with a jackhammer than have sex.'

'Maybe that's your problem. I try to have sex at least twice a week, sometimes even with someone else.'

Caro laughed. 'Oh, Ruby, I missed you.' She sounded normal now. 'So what brought you racing to my door? You left Mom strapped to the wheelchair and ran screaming out of the house?' Caro grinned at her own black humour.

Ruby couldn't even smile. 'I went to Dad's house today.' She didn't know how to put a pretty spin on such ugliness, so she just said it. 'When Nora left, Dad was having an affair.'

Caroline sat back. 'Oh, *that*.'

'You *knew*?'

'Everyone on the island knew.'

'Not me. She's not who I thought she was, Caro. We're trapped in that house together, and I'm getting to know her. We talk.'

'*You're* getting to know her?' Something passed through Caroline's eyes. If Ruby hadn't known better, she'd have called it envy. Suddenly Caro walked out of the room. A few minutes later she returned with a packet of cigarettes.

Ruby laughed. 'Smoking? You're kidding, right?'

'No jokes, Ruby. Please.' She opened the French doors and led Ruby to a seat at an umbrellaed table. A golf course stretched beside the garden.

Caroline pulled a cigarette from the packet and lit up. 'I've been talking to Mom for years, meeting her now and then for lunch, calling her on Sunday mornings, being the daughter she expects, and we're polite strangers. And *you*'—she shot Ruby a narrowed gaze—'you, who treats her like Typhoid Mary, she talks to.'

'Have you forgiven her?' Ruby asked. 'I mean *really*?'

'I tried to forget it, you know? Most of the time I do, too. It's like it happened to another family, not mine.'

A scream blared through the open window behind them.

Ruby jumped. 'Good God. Has someone been shot?'

Caroline deflated. Her shoulders caved downwards, and the colour seemed to seep out of her cheeks. 'The princess is up.'

Ruby moved closer to her sister. 'Are you OK?'

The smile was too fleeting to be real. 'I'll be fine,' Caro said. She got up and walked woodenly back into the house.

Ruby followed her. This time there were two screams.

'Go,' Caro said with a tired smile. 'Save yourself.'

The screams were getting louder. Ruby fought the urge to cover her ears. 'Let's go upstairs. I want to see my niece and nephew.'

'Not when Jenny's in this mood.' Caroline turned to her. 'You'd better get going. The ferry lines are hell this time of day.'

Ruby checked her watch. 'You're right.'

Caroline looped an arm round Ruby and guided her towards the door. 'I'm sorry you had to find out about Dad, but maybe it'll help. We're human, Ruby. All of us. Just human.'

Ruby hugged her sister. She had the strange thought that if she said anything except goodbye, Caro would simply shatter.

So goodbye was all she said.

Nora sat at the kitchen table staring down at the package of letters. Idly she rubbed her throbbing wrist. She'd spent an hour in the morning practising with her crutches. By the end of the week she hoped to be out of the damned chair completely.

She'd tried giving herself a little pep talk. The letters were just words from strangers, she told herself. Certainly she could find the strength to pick up a pen and fashion some kind of response. Not true. Every response she'd attempted began, 'I'm more sorry than you can know' or 'How can I begin to say what's in my heart?'

But there was never a second sentence. And if all that wasn't bad enough, she was worried about Ruby. Her gaze landed on the note she'd found on the kitchen table: *Gone to Dad's.*

It looked innocuous enough, but appearances were often deceiving. Ruby wasn't coming back. It was Nora's own fault. She'd pushed her younger daughter too hard in the past few days, and her daughter had had enough.

Nora heard a car drive up, footsteps on the porch. The door opened, and Rand stepped into the kitchen.

Nora understood instantly: Ruby had sent her father to deliver the bad news. 'Hey, Randall,' she said. 'Have a seat.'

He glanced around. 'I've got a better idea.' He crossed the room, scooped her into his arms, and carried her outside. He walked across the shaggy lawn to the edge of the bank and gingerly set her down beneath a huge madrona tree, then sat down beside her.

'Still can't stand to be inside on a sunny day?' she said.

'Some things never change.' His face was solemn. 'I'm sorry, Nora.'

'About what?'

He stared at a point just beyond her left shoulder. 'I should have said it a long time ago.'

She drew in a breath. Time seemed to hang suspended between them. She smelt the familiar fragrance of the sea at low tide.

He looked at her finally, and in his dark eyes she saw the sad reflection of their life together. 'I'm sorry,' he said again, knowing that this time she understood. He touched her face. 'It was *my* fault. All mine. I was young and stupid and cocky. I didn't know how special we were.'

Nora was surprised by how easy it was to smile. Maybe that was all she'd needed all these years. Just those few, simple words. She finally felt at peace. 'We were both at fault, Rand.'

He leaned closer. She thought for a breathless moment that he was going to kiss her. But at the last second he drew back, gave her a smile so tender that it was better than a kiss. 'That day you came back, I should have dropped to my knees and begged you to stay. In my heart I knew it was what I wanted, but I'd heard about you and that guy, and all I could think of was *me*. How would it look if I took you back after that?' He laughed—a bitter, harsh sound. '*Me*, worrying about that after the way I'd treated you. It makes me sick.'

Nora reached out, brushed the hair from his eyes. 'You've gone on now. Married. I'm happy for that.' She realised how true it was. Those few small words—*I'm sorry*—had released her, turned Rand into what he truly was: her first love. She smiled and arched one eyebrow. 'And are you being a good boy, Randall?'

He laughed. 'Even a stupid dog doesn't get hit by the same bus twice.' He gazed at her. 'I told Ruby the truth about us.'

Nora felt sick. 'That was a foolish thing to do.'

'It's something I should have done a long time ago.'

'Perhaps, but when you didn't—when I didn't—we buried that little piece of family history. You shouldn't have dug it up. It won't make a difference now.'

'After all these years you deserved it, Nora,' he said.

'Oh, Rand, she believed in you. This will break her heart.'

'You know what I learned from us, Nora?' He touched her face. 'Love doesn't die. And that's what Ruby's going to discover. She's always loved you. I just gave her a reason to admit it.'

After two hours of waiting in line for the ferry, with two hundred eager tourists and a few beleaguered locals, Ruby remembered why she'd been so eager to move off-island. Timing your life around a state-operated transportation system was miserable.

Finally she drove aboard, and as the ferry left the quay, she adjusted her seat to a more comfortable position and closed her eyes. She still felt shaky, as if the foundation of her life had turned to warm jelly and was letting her sink.

I slept with other women.

One thing she knew: Her novelisation of the past, with Dad cast as hero and her mother as villain, wouldn't work any more.

She reached under the seat and pulled out the pen and legal pad she'd packed in the morning. She started to write.

I was sixteen years old when my mother left us. It was an ordinary June day; the sun rode high in a robin's-egg blue sky. It's funny the things you remember.

We were an average family. My father, Rand, was an islander through and through, a commercial fisherman who repaired boats in the off-season. It never occurred to any of us, or to me anyway, that he was anything less than the perfect father.

There was no yelling in our family, no raging arguments. I often look back on those quiet years, searching for an inciting incident, a moment where I could say, 'Aha! There it is, the beginning of the end.' But I never found one. Until now.

Today my parents pulled back the curtain, and my dad was revealed to be an ordinary man.

I didn't know that then, of course. All I knew was that on a beautiful day my mother dragged a suitcase into the living room. 'I'm leaving. Is anyone coming with me?'

That's what she said to my sister and me.

That was the day I learned the concept of before and after. Her leaving sliced through our family with the precision of a scalpel. I saw what her absence did to my father. He drank; he smoked; he spent the day in his pyjamas. He ate only when Caroline or I cooked for him. He let his business go to hell.

I formed an image of my mother that summer. From the hard stone of everything that happened, I carved the image of a woman and called it Mother. The statue was a collection of hard edges—selfishness, lies, and abandonment.

But now I know the truth. My father was unfaithful to my mother. He wore a wedding ring and had sex with women other than the one he'd sworn to love, honour and protect.

My mother didn't leave him—and us—for fame and fortune, but simply because the man she loved had broken her heart.

Before she could finish, the ferry honked its horn. They were docking on Lopez. As soon as the ferry had unloaded a few cars, the boat would turn to Orcas Island. Summer Island was the last stop before the boat turned back to the mainland.

Ruby made a snap decision. She started the car, pulled out of line, bumped over the ramp and drove off.

The Sloan house was only a few blocks from the ferry terminal. She pulled the minivan into the driveway. It was twilight now; a purple haze fell across the garden. Ruby walked up the pathway to the front door. She gathered her courage and knocked.

Lottie opened the door. She looked just as Ruby remembered her. 'Ruby Elizabeth!' Lottie said, pulling her into a hug.

Ruby drew back, trying to maintain a smile. 'Hello, Lottie. It's been a long time. I came to see Eric.'

'He's upstairs. Dean had to fly to Seattle on business.'

Ruby was relieved. 'Can I go up?'

'Why, I'd beat you with a stick if you didn't.'

Ruby took a deep breath and released it, then slowly mounted the stairs. She turned towards Eric's room. The door was closed. She gave it the tiniest push to open it. 'Eric?'

'Ruby? Is that you?'

'It's me, buddy.' She walked into his room.

Only sheer willpower kept her from gasping. His beautiful black hair was practically gone. Bruise-dark shadows circled his eyes. His cheek-bones stood out above the pale, sunken flesh.

He gave her a smile that broke her heart. 'I must be dead if Ruby Bridge is back on the island.'

'I'm home,' she said, looking away quickly.

'It's OK, Ruby,' he said softly. 'I know how I look.'

Suddenly, she couldn't pretend, couldn't make small talk. 'I missed you, Eric. I should have stayed in better touch with you. What happened between Dean and me—I shouldn't have let that extend to you.'

'You broke his heart,' Eric said softly.

'All of our hearts got broken that year, I guess, and the king's horsemen couldn't put us back together.'

'What your mother did—it was really bad. But you're not sixteen any more. You ought to be able to see things more clearly.'

'Like what?'

'Come on, Ruby. The whole island knew your dad was screwing other women. Don't you think that makes a difference?'

So it was true: everyone did know. 'Caroline and I didn't do anything, and she left us, too.'

There it was, the thing she still couldn't get past.

'You know who got me through those tough times when I first realised I was gay and my parents disowned me?'

'Dean?'

'Your mother. I wrote to her column, anonymously at first. She wrote back praising my bravery, telling me to keep my chin up, that my mom was sure to come round. It gave me hope. But after a few more years I knew she was wrong.' He grabbed his wallet from the bedside table. Opening it, he withdrew a piece of paper and carefully unfolded it. 'Here. Read this.'

Ruby took the piece of paper from him. It was yellowed from age and veined with tiny fold lines.

Dear Eric,
   I can't express the depth of my sympathy for your pain. That you would choose to share it with me is an honour I do not take lightly.
   For me you will always be Eric, the rope-swing king. When I close my eyes, I see you hanging monkeylike from that old rope at Anderson Lake, yelling 'Banzai!' as you let go. I remember a sixth-grade boy, his face reddened by new pimples, his voice sliding down the scale, who

was never afraid to hold Mrs Bridge's hand as they walked down the school corridor.

This is who you are, Eric. Whom you choose to love is a part of you, but not the biggest part. I hope and pray that someday your mother will wake up and remember the very special boy she gave birth to, and smile at the man he has become. But if she does not, please don't let it tear your heart apart. You must go on. Life is full of people who are different, broken, hurting, who simply put one foot in front of the other and keep moving.

It is your mother I fear for. If she continues on this path, it will eat her up inside. She will find that certain pains are endless. So forgive her and go on. It is the only way to lighten this ache in your heart.

I love you, Eric Sloan. You and your brother are the sons I never had, and I am proud of who you've become.

Nora

Ruby folded the letter back into the small triangle that fitted in his wallet. 'That's a beautiful letter.'

'It saved me. Literally. It took lots of work, but I forgave my mom, and when I did that, my chest stopped hurting all the time.' He smiled. 'Forgive your mother, Ruby.'

She looked down at him. 'How do you forgive someone?'

'You just . . . let go. Unclench.' He kissed the tips of his own fingers, then pressed the kiss to her cheek. 'I love you, Ruby. Don't forget that.'

'Never,' she whispered. 'Never.'

The next morning Ruby woke late. A shower made her feel almost human, and she stayed in it until the water turned lukewarm. Then she stepped out and through the mist saw herself in the mirror.

She experienced one of those rare moments when, for a split second, you see yourself through a stranger's eyes. Her hair was too short and raggedly cut. And what had made her choose to dye it Elvira Mistress of the Dark black? Ruby realised she'd been *trying* to make herself unattractive. All that mascara, the black eyeliner, the haircut and colour—all of it was a camouflage.

She dropped her make-up bag in the metal trash can. It hit with a satisfying clang. No more heroin-chic make-up or refugee clothing. She'd even quit dyeing her hair and find out what colour it really was. Her last memory was of a nice, ordinary chestnut brown.

The decision made her feel better. She dressed in jeans and a jade-green V-neck T-shirt, then hurried downstairs.

Nora was standing by the counter, leaning on her crutches. The plop-drip-plop of the coffeemaker filled the kitchen with steady sound. She looked up as Ruby entered the room. An almost comical look of surprise crossed her face. 'You look . . . beautiful.' She flushed. 'I'm sorry. I shouldn't have sounded surprised.'

'It's OK.' Ruby laughed, and it felt good. 'I guess I didn't look so great with all that make-up on. I need a haircut badly. Is there still a beauty salon in Friday Harbor?'

'I used to cut your hair.'

Ruby hadn't remembered until that moment, but suddenly it came rushing back: Sunday evenings in the kitchen, a dishcloth pinned round her neck with a clothespeg, the soothing clip-clip-clip of the scissors. 'Could you cut it again?'

'Of course. Get the stool from the laundry room and take it outside. It's such a pretty morning.'

Ruby gathered up the necessary supplies and carried everything outside. She set the stool on a nice flat patch of grass overlooking the bay and sat down on it. She heard Nora coming towards her: Thump, step. Thump, step. Her mother moved around behind Ruby, wrapped a towel around Ruby's neck, and pinned it in place. 'I'm just going to give it some shape.'

The steady snip-snip-snip of the scissors seemed to hypnotise Ruby—that and the comforting familiarity of her mother's touch.

A few minutes later Nora said, 'Ah, there we are.' She stepped aside and handed Ruby a mirror.

Ruby looked at her reflection. She looked young again—a woman with most of her life ahead of her, instead of a bitter, struggling comic who'd left her youth sitting on a barstool. 'It looks great,' she said, turning to her mother.

Their eyes met, locked. Understanding passed between them.

'I went to see Dad yesterday.'

'I know. He came to see me.'

Ruby should have guessed. 'We have to talk about it.'

Nora sighed. 'Yes.' She bent down and retrieved her crutches. 'I don't know about you, but I'll *definitely* need to sit down.' Without waiting, she hobbled towards the porch.

Ruby followed. Nora sat on the love seat; Ruby chose the rocker.

'Dad told me he'd been unfaithful to you,' Ruby said in a rush.

'What else?'

'Well, he sort of blamed it on Vietnam, but I got the feeling he thought he would have fooled around anyway.'

'Don't judge him too harshly, Ruby. His infidelity was only part of what broke us up. I needed so much reassurance and love, I sucked him dry. No man can fill up all the dark places in a woman's soul. I knew he'd be unfaithful sooner or later.'

Ruby didn't understand. 'You *knew* he'd be unfaithful?'

'You lived with a man. Did you expect him to be faithful?'

'Of course.' Ruby said it quickly. Too quickly. Then she sighed and sat back. 'No. I didn't expect him to want only me.'

'Of course not. If a girl's mother doesn't love her enough to stick around, why should a man?' The smile Nora gave Ruby was sad. 'That's the gift my father gave me, the one I passed on to you.'

Ruby walked towards the railing and stared out at the Sound. 'I remember the day you came back.' She heard her mother's sharp intake of breath and turned round.

Nora was sitting there, hunched over, as if waiting for a blow. 'I don't like thinking about that day.'

'I'm sorry . . . Mom,' Ruby said quietly. 'I said some awful things.'

Tears filled her mother's eyes. 'You called me *Mom.*' She stood up, hobbled towards Ruby. 'Don't you dare feel guilty over what you said to me. You were a child, and I'd broken your heart.'

'Why did you come home that day?'

'I missed you girls so much. But when I saw what I'd done to you, I was ashamed. You looked at me the way I'd once looked at my father. It . . . broke my heart.'

Ruby couldn't avoid the question any longer. 'OK. I know why you left Dad, but why did you stay away?'

Nora gazed at her steadily. 'The leaving, the staying away—to you these were the beginning of the story. To me it was deep into the middle.' She took a deep breath. 'Everyone thought Rand and I were the perfect couple. I was young then, and I cared about appearances more than substance. Living with an alcoholic will do that to you.

'It hurt me to suspect your dad of having affairs, but that wasn't the worst of it. The worst was his drinking. He started drinking after dinner, and by ten o'clock he was wobbly, and by eleven he was stumbling drunk. And he got mean. Every time he yelled at me, I heard my dad's voice, and though Rand never hit me, I started expecting it, flinching away from him, and that only made him madder.' She went on, 'So, you see, I was half of the problem. I couldn't separate my past from my present. But I was handling everything OK until Emmaline Fergusson told me about Shirley Comstock.'

Ruby gasped. 'My soccer coach?'

'It's a small island,' Nora said ruefully. 'There weren't a lot of women to choose from. He started drinking more and coming home less, and I fell apart. It started with insomnia. I simply stopped sleeping. Then the panic attacks hit. I got a prescription for Valium, but it didn't help. I would lie awake at night with my heart pounding and sweat pouring off me. Every time I picked you up from soccer, I went home and threw up. Finally I started to black out. I'd wake up lying on the kitchen floor, and I couldn't remember huge chunks of my day.'

'Did you tell Dad?' Ruby asked softly.

Nora gave a shaky smile. 'Of course not. I thought I was losing my mind. All I had to hold on to was the pretence of a marriage. You and Caro were the centre of a world that kept shrinking around me.'

Nora looked up, wondering if it was possible to make a single twenty-seven-year-old woman understand how stifling marriage and motherhood could sometimes be. 'I couldn't handle it all—your dad's drinking, his screwing around, my insomnia, my sense of being overwhelmed and trapped. It was a combustible mix. And then . . . '

Nora closed her eyes. The early summer day she'd worked so hard to keep at bay welled up inside her. She'd gone to the soccer field early to drop off cookies, and she'd seen them—Rand and Shirley kissing right out in the open, as if they had every right. 'I took too many sleeping pills. I don't remember if I meant to or if it was an accident, but when I woke up in the hospital, I knew that if I didn't do something quickly, I was going to die. So I packed my bag and ran. I only meant to stay away for a few days. I thought I'd come here, get some rest, and be healthy.'

'And?'

Nora stared down at her hands. 'And I met Vince Corell.'

'The guy who sold the pictures to the *Tattler*.'

'He was a photographer, taking pictures of the islands for a calendar. He told me I was the most beautiful woman in the world. By then your father and I hadn't been intimate in a long time, and I *wasn't* beautiful. I was rail-thin, and I trembled all the time. When Vince touched me, I let him. We had a wonderful week together. For the first time I found someone I could talk to about my dreams, and once I'd said them aloud, I couldn't go back to the way I'd been living. And then he was gone.

'I was devastated. I knew your father would have heard about Vince. When the affair was over and I realised I'd thrown my marriage away and lost my girls, I took too many sleeping pills again. This time I ended up in a mental institution in Everett.'

'How long were you there?' Ruby's voice was whisper-soft.

'Three months. It was Dr Allbright who saved me. He came every day and talked to me. I worked so hard to get better so I could come home. But when I did—'

'Oh God,' Ruby said softly. 'That was the day.'

Nora felt tears sting her eyes. 'It's not your fault,' she said.

'But Dad should have let you come home.'

'I didn't ask Rand to take me back,' Nora answered. 'I didn't want my marriage back. I wanted . . . me. It's a horrible thing to say. But it's the only truth I can give you. The world is full of regrets and times where you think "If only . . ." We have to move on. Your dad was angry and arrogant. I was frightened and fragile. You were heartbroken. And on that one day we came together, and we hurt each other.' She longed to take her daughter into her arms. 'But I want you to know this, Ruby. I never stopped loving you or thinking about you. I never stopped missing you.'

Ruby stared at her. Then softly she said, 'I believe you.'

And Nora knew the healing had finally begun.

Chapter Eight

RUBY RETREATED TO her bedroom, opened the drawer of the bedside cabinet and pulled out her legal pad. She'd learned that it calmed her to write down her thoughts. She sat on the bed and drew her knees up, angling the pad against her thighs.

I'd always believed that the truth was easily spotted, a dark line on white paper. Now I wonder.

My mother was in a mental institution. This is her newest revelation. Today Mom painted a portrait of our family I'd never imagined—a drunken, unfaithful husband and a depressed, overwhelmingly unhappy wife. She was right to hide this truth from me. Even now I wish I didn't know it.

The phone rang. Ruby was startled by the sound. Tossing the pad aside, she leaned over and answered, 'Hello?'

'Ruby?'

It was Caroline's voice, soft and thready. Ruby immediately felt the hairs on the back of her neck stand up. 'What's wrong?'

'Wrong? Nothing. Can't a girl just call her little sister?'

'Of course. You just sounded . . . tired.'

Caro laughed. 'I have two small children. I'm *always* tired.'

'Is motherhood really like that, Caro?'

Caroline was quiet for a minute. 'I used to dream of going to Paris. Now I just want privacy when I use the toilet.'

'How come we never talk about things like that?'

'There's nothing to say.'

'Are you happy, Caro?'

'Happy? Of course I'm—' Caro started to cry.

The soft, heartbreaking sound tore at Ruby's heart. 'Caro?'

'Sorry. Bad day in suburbia.'

'Just one?'

'I can't talk about this now.'

'What's wrong with our family that we can't talk about anything that matters?'

'Talking doesn't change things. Believe me. It's better to just go on.'

'I used to think that, but I'm learning so much up here—'

'Ruby!' It was Mom's voice. She must be at the bottom of the stairs.

Ruby held the phone to her chest. 'I'll be right down. Hey, Caro,' she said, coming back on the line. 'Why don't you come here for the night?'

'Oh, I can't. The kids—'

'Leave them with the stud muffin. It's not like you're stapled to the house.'

Caroline's laughter was sharp. 'That's exactly what it's like.'

'Ruby! Can you hear me?' It was Mom's voice again.

Ruby accepted defeat. 'I gotta go. I love you, big sis.'

She hung up, then hurried downstairs. 'Good God, is there a fire in the—' She skidded to a stop in the kitchen.

Dean was there, holding a bouquet of Shasta daisies.

'Oh,' Ruby said, feeling heat climb into her face.

Mom stood beside the table grinning. 'You have a visitor.'

Dean handed Ruby the flowers. 'We need to talk.' His voice matched the soft pleading in his eyes. 'Please.'

The way he said it made her shiver. 'OK.'

They stood there, staring at each other. Finally Mom thumped towards them and gently tugged the flowers out of Ruby's hand. 'I'll put them in water,' she said.

'Thanks, Mom.'

Ruby turned to Dean. He gave her a quick smile; then they headed out of the door.

Outside, there were two bicycles. Ruby stopped. 'You've obviously confused me with a woman who likes to sweat.'

He smiled. 'Too old to ride a bike, Rube? Or too out of shape?'

He *knew* she couldn't refuse a challenge. She grabbed the handlebars and yanked the bike around. 'Lead on.'

Dean jumped on his bike and pedalled on ahead of her out of the gravel driveway. Ruby sped up to him. Soon they were flying, racing side by side down the long, two-lane road. Golden pastures studded with apple trees rushed past them. The road wound into a long, even S curve and into the entrance of Trout Lake State Park.

Ruby should have known he'd bring her here. 'Not fair, Dino,' she said softly, wondering if he even heard her.

He did. 'What's that they say about love and war?'

'Which one is this?'

'That's up to you.'

Ruby jumped off her bike and set it against a wooden bike rack, then walked towards the lake. She had forgotten how beautiful it was here. The heart-shaped sapphire-blue lake was surrounded by lush green trees and rimmed in granite. A ribbon of water cascaded over the 'giant's lip'—a flat, jutting rock at the top of the cliffs—and splashed onto the placid surface of the lake.

Dean came up beside her. 'Are you up for a climb?'

'Lead on.'

Side by side, they walked round to the western side of the lake, through the hoard of picnickers, Frisbee-catching dogs and screaming children. When they reached the trees, they left the people behind. The gurgling, splashing sound of falling water grew louder and louder.

The trail was rocky and narrow, corkscrewing straight up through the trees. Finally they reached the top—the giant's lip. It was a slab of grey granite as big as a swimming pool and as flat as a quarter. Thick green moss furred the stone.

Ruby stepped onto the rock and saw the picnic basket. It was sitting on a familiar plaid blanket, which Dean had carefully spread out on a spot where the moss was several inches thick.

They sat down, and Ruby leaned back on her elbows. 'We used to come up here all the time.'

'This is where you first told me you were going to be a comedian. You said you wanted to be famous.'

'I still do. And you wanted to be a prizewinning photographer.' She didn't look at him. It was better to stay separate and talk about the past, as if they were just two old high-school friends.

'I still wish for it. If I could, I'd throw everything away and start over. Money sure doesn't make you happy.'

It bothered her to think of him as unhappy. 'Spoken like a man whose family business is on the Fortune Five Hundred index.'

He laughed softly. 'Yeah, I guess.'

A quiet settled between them, and she was vaguely afraid of what he would say, so she said, 'I saw Eric yesterday.'

'He told me. It really meant a lot to him.'

'I wish I'd stayed in better touch with him.'

'You? I'm his brother, and I hadn't seen him in years.'

That surprised Ruby. She rolled onto her side. 'You guys were always so close.'

'Things change, don't they?'

'What happened?'

He stared up at the sky. 'I seem to have a problem with really knowing the people I love. I get sidetracked.'

'You're talking about his being gay?'

He looked at her. 'That's part of what I'm talking about.'

She understood and knew it was time. For more than ten years she'd sworn to herself that if she ever got the chance with Dean, she would say the thing that mattered. 'I'm sorry, Dean,' she said. 'I didn't want to hurt you.'

He rolled onto his side, facing her. 'You didn't want to hurt me? Ruby, you were my whole world.'

'I knew that. I just . . . couldn't be someone's world then.'

'I tried to take care of you after your mom left, but it was hard. You were constantly picking a fight with me. But I kept loving you.'

Ruby didn't know how to explain it to him. 'You believed in something I didn't. Every time I closed my eyes at night, I dreamed about you leaving me.'

'What made you so sure I would leave you?'

'Come on, Dean, we were kids. I knew you'd go off to some college I couldn't afford and forget about me.'

Their faces were close, and if she'd let herself, she could have lost her way in the blue sea of his eyes.

'So you dumped me before I had a chance to dump you.'

She smiled sadly. 'Pretty much. Now let's change the subject. This is old news, and we both know it doesn't matter any more. Tell me about your life. How is it to be a jet-setting bachelor?'

'What if I said I still love you?'

Ruby gasped. 'Don't say that . . . please.'

He took her face in his hands, gently forced her to look up at him. 'Did you stop loving me, Ruby?'

She wanted to say 'Of course; we were just kids', but when she opened her mouth, the sound she made was a quiet sigh of surrender. His lips brushed against hers, and she melted against him, moaning his name as his hand curled round the back of her neck. It was the kind of kiss they'd never shared before, the kind of achingly lonely kiss a pair of teenagers couldn't imagine.

When he drew back, he said, 'I've waited a long time for a second chance with you, Ruby.'

She closed her eyes, battling a wave of helplessness. She wished desperately to have grown up, to have been profoundly changed by all that she'd seen and learned in the past days. But it wasn't that easy. Her fear of abandonment was so deep, she couldn't get past it. She'd discovered a long time ago why the poets called it falling in love. It was a plunging, eye-watering descent, and she'd lost her ability to believe that anyone would catch her. She pushed him away. 'I can't do this. It's too much too fast. You've always wanted too much from me.'

'Damn it, Ruby,' he said, and she heard the disappointment in his voice. 'Have you grown up at all?'

'I won't hurt you again,' she said.

He touched her face. 'Ah, Rube, just looking at you hurts me.'

She had never felt so alone. When he'd kissed her, she'd glimpsed a world she'd never imagined. A world where passion was part of love, but not the biggest part. Where a kiss from the right man, at the right time, could make a grown woman weep. 'I can't give you what you want. It's not in me.'

He brushed the hair from her eyes, his fingertips lingering at her temple. 'You ran me off when I was a boy. I'm not seventeen any more, and we both know this thing between us isn't over. I don't think it ever was.'

Dean followed Ruby back down the trail. Though they didn't talk, the forest was alive with sounds. Birds squawked and chirped in the trees overhead, squirrels chattered, water splashed.

At the car park, he tossed the picnic basket—still filled with a lunch unpacked and uneaten—in the trash can. Curling the heavy blanket round his shoulders, he climbed tiredly onto his bike.

When they reached the summer house, he pulled off to the side of the road and got off his bike.

Ruby stopped and turned to him. 'I guess this is goodbye.'

The crack in her voice gave him hope. 'For now,' he said.

'It was just a kiss. Don't turn it into *Gone With the Wind*.'

He took a step towards her. 'You must have confused me with one of your Hollywood idiot boys.'

She wanted to move backwards. 'Wh-what do you mean?'

Now he was close enough to touch her, but he stood still. 'I know you, Ruby. You can pretend all you want, but that kiss meant something. Tonight we'll both lie in bed and think about it.'

Ruby flushed. 'You knew a teenager a decade ago. That doesn't mean you know *me*.'

He smiled. 'You might have built a wall round your heart, but somewhere, deep inside, you're still the girl I fell in love with.' At last he touched her cheek—a fleeting caress.

He wanted to do more, to pull her into his arms, hold her close and whisper, *I love you*, but he knew he couldn't push her that far. Not yet.

Her mouth trembled. 'I'm afraid.'

'The girl I knew wasn't afraid of anything.'

'That girl's been gone for years.'

'Isn't there some part of her left?'

She stood there a long time, staring up at him.

He knew she wasn't going to answer. 'OK,' he said, 'I'll concede this round.' He climbed onto his bike and started to go.

'Wait.'

He stumbled off his bike so fast, he almost fell. It clattered to the ground as he spun back to face her.

She took a step closer. 'You sound so sure.'

He smiled. 'You taught me love, Ruby. Every time you held my hand when I was scared, or came to one of my ball games or left a note in my locker, I learned a little more about it. Maybe when we were kids, I took that for granted, but I'm not a kid any more. I've spent a lot of years alone, and every date I went on only proved again how special we were.'

'My parents were special,' she said slowly. 'You and Eric were special.'

'So your point is, love dies.'

'An ugly, painful death.'

It saddened him, knowing how her heart, once so open and pure, had been trampled by the people who should have protected it. 'OK, love hurts. I can't deny that. But what about loneliness?'

'I'm not lonely.'

'Liar.'

She stepped away from him. Without a backward look she jumped on her bike and rode away.

'Go ahead,' he called after her. 'Run away. You can only go so far.'

Ruby walked into the kitchen and found her mother at the stove stirring something in an old iron pot.

'Ruby,' Nora said, looking up in surprise, 'I didn't expect you back so soon.' She glanced at the door. 'Where's Dino?'

The kitchen smelt of pot roast, slow-cooking all day with carrots and oven-browned potatoes. Homemade biscuits were rising on the counter. And unless Ruby missed her guess, that was vanilla custard Mom was stirring. She'd made Ruby's all-time favourite dinner.

Ruby didn't know which hurt more—the effort her mother had made to please her or the fact that Dean wasn't here to share it.

'Dean went home,' she said.

A frown darted across her mother's face. She turned off the burner. 'What happened?'

'I don't know. I guess we started something we couldn't finish. Or maybe we finished something we'd started a long time ago.'

'This won't be like Max,' her mother said.

'I love Dean,' Ruby admitted. 'But that's not enough. It wouldn't last.'

'Love is nothing without faith.'

'I lost that faith a long time ago.'

'Of course you did. And you're right to blame your dad and me for it, but that doesn't matter any more—whose fault it is. What matters is *you*. Can you let yourself jump without a net? Because that's what love is, what faith is. You're looking for a guarantee, and those come with auto parts. Not love.'

'Yeah, right. Love put you in a mental institution.'

Mom laughed. 'I think it makes lunatics of us all.'

It felt good to talk to her mother this way—as friends. It was something Ruby had never imagined.

It was true; love made everybody crazy. All those years Ruby had spent angry with her mother, sending back presents unopened, and refusing all contact—it wasn't because she'd felt betrayed. Those years, those feelings and actions, had been about . . . longing. Simple longing.

She'd *missed* her mother so much that the only way she'd been able to go on in the world was to pretend she was alone.

I'm not alone any more. That one sentence, once thought, formed a road that led Ruby to herself. *I can't write the article.*

'I've got to go upstairs,' she said suddenly, seeing the surprise on her mother's face. Ruby didn't care. She ran upstairs, went to the phone, and dialled Val's number.

Maudeen answered on the second ring.

'Hi, Maudeen. It's Ruby Bridge. Is the Great Oz in?'

Maudeen laughed. 'No. He's in New York, but he's calling in.'

'OK. Tell him I won't be delivering my article.'

'Oh, my. You'd better give me your address and phone number again. He'll want to talk to you.'

Ruby gave out the information, then hung up. She reached for her writing pad and slowly began to write.

> *I have just called my agent. When he calls back, I will tell him that I can't turn in this article. I never thought about what it meant to write an exposé on my own mother.*
>
> *Can you believe I was so blind? I took the money that was given to me—my thirty pieces of silver—and I spent it like a teenager would, on a fast car and expensive clothes.*
>
> *But I didn't think.*
>
> *I dreamed. I imagined. I saw myself on Leno—a witty, charming guest plugging her own skyrocketing career. I never noticed that I'd be*

standing on my mother's broken back to reach the microphone. But my dreams were all about me, and now I know what the price of my selfish actions will be.

As I write, I am reminded of that passage from the Bible—the one that is read at every wedding: 'When I was a child, I spake as a child, I understood as a child, I thought as a child.'

Now I understand as an adult. Maybe for the first time in my life. This article would break my mother's heart. That didn't matter to me a week ago; in fact, I wanted to hurt her then.

I can't do it any more—not to her and not to me. For the first time I have drawn back the dark curtain of anger and seen the bright day beyond. I can be my mother's daughter again. She is the keeper of my past. She knows the secret moments that have formed me, and even with all that I have done to her, she still loves me. Will anyone else ever love me so unconditionally?

At Friday Harbor on San Juan Island, the marina was a hive of activity, with boats coming in and going out, kids racing along the quays. The downtown area was an eclectic mix of art galleries, souvenir shops, gift emporiums and restaurants.

Dean walked aimlessly up and down the streets. Today had depressed him, and it shouldn't have. Nothing had ever been easy with Ruby. Love would be the most difficult of all.

He heard the ferry's horn and knew it was time to get down to the pier. He jumped on his bike, raced downhill, and followed the last car onto the boat.

On Lopez, he stopped by the grocery store and bought a few things. Then he pedalled home as fast as he could. When he reached the house, he hurried up the stairs to Eric's room.

'Hey, bro,' Eric said. 'How was your bike ride?'

Dean went to him. 'Guess what I bought?' He opened a small blue insulated bag and withdrew a melting Popsicle.

Eric's eyes widened. 'A Rainbow Rocket. I didn't think they still made them.'

Dean unwrapped the soggy white wrapper and handed his brother the dripping multicoloured Popsicle. Eric made groaning sounds of pleasure as he licked it. When he finished, he set the gooey stick on the bedside tray. 'That was great,' he said. 'I'd forgotten how much I loved those things.'

'I remembered. I've been remembering a lot of things lately.' Dean leaned over the bedrail. 'I went to see Ruby today.'

'And?'

'Let's just say the door hit me in the ass on the way out.'

Eric laughed. 'That's our Ruby. Never gives an inch. So when is round two?'

Dean sighed. 'I don't know. I'll need to stock up on defensive weapons. Maybe something will happen tomorrow when we all go sailing.'

'Well, I hope it works out fast. I wanted to be the best man at your wedding.'

'You will be.' Dean struggled to keep his voice even. Their eyes met, and in his brother's gaze he saw the sad truth. They both knew Eric would not be putting on a tuxedo and standing in shiny shoes beside Dean at the altar.

'I'm glad you came home, Dino. I couldn't have done this without you.'

Home. The simple, complex word found purchase in his heart. He'd known it would be hard to stand by and watch his brother die, but until this moment, he hadn't realised that it would end. This goodbye, strung out as it was over the briefest of time spans, was all that was left to them. There were so many things left to say between him and Eric, but how— where—did you begin? What if Dean ended up moving through a colourless, Eric-less world in which he couldn't think of anything except what should have been said?

'Don't,' Eric said.

Dean blinked, realising he'd been silent too long. Tears stung his eyes. 'Don't what?'

'You're imagining the world without me.'

'I don't know how to get through this.'

Eric reached out. His pale, blue-veined hand covered Dean's. 'When I start feeling overwhelmed, I go back in time instead of ahead. I remember how we used to play at Camp Orkila. Or how you used to sit cross-legged in your room, trying to levitate your toys when Lottie made you clean your room.' He smiled and closed his eyes, and Dean could see that he was losing his brother to sleep once again. 'I remember the first time I saw Charlie. He was making a sandwich at the college lunch hangout. Mostly, I just remember what I've had and not what I'm leaving behind.'

Dean's throat was so tight he couldn't answer.

'The best part is you.' Eric's voice was barely above a whisper. 'Since you're back, I dream again. It's nice.'

'Dream,' Dean said softly, placing his brother's hand on top of the blanket. 'Dream of who you would have been and who you were—the bravest, smartest, best brother a kid ever had.'

After dinner, Nora went out to the porch and sat in her favourite rocking chair. In this magical hour, poised between day and night, the sky was the soft hue of a girl's ballet slipper.

The screen door squeaked open and banged shut. 'I brought you some tea,' Ruby said, stepping into the porch light's glow.

'Thanks,' Nora said. 'Join me.'

Ruby sat down. Leaning back, she crossed her legs at the ankle and rested her feet on the small, frosted glass table beside the loveseat. 'I've been thinking.'

'There's aspirin in the bathroom cabinet.'

'Very funny. It didn't give me a headache. It gave me . . . heartache.' She leaned forward and studied Nora. 'All those years, when you sent letters and gifts, I knew you cared about me. I knew you were sorry, and I was *proud* of hurting you. So, don't disagree with me when I say that I have been the architect of some of my own pain.'

Nora smiled. 'We all are. Growing up is when we finally understand that. You've built a hard shell to protect your soft heart. Only it doesn't work. I know I made you that way, but it's a half-life. Maybe you see that now. Without love, the loneliness just goes on and on.'

Before Ruby could reply, she heard the sound of a car driving up. It parked, and a door slammed shut. She glanced towards the garden. 'Are we expecting someone?'

'No.'

Footsteps rattled on gravel. A rusty gate creaked open. Someone thumped up the porch steps and walked into the light.

Nora stared up at her elder daughter in shock, wondering what had brought her here. It was unlike her daughter to do anything spontaneously. 'Caroline?' she whispered.

'I don't *believe* it!' Ruby pulled her sister into a fierce hug.

Nora got awkwardly to her feet and limped forwards. 'Hey, Caro. It's good to see you.'

Caroline drew back from Ruby's embrace. 'Hello, Mother.' Her smile seemed forced. It wasn't surprising—even as a child, she'd been able to smile when her heart was breaking.

Nora studied Caroline. She was dressed in a pair of white linen

269

trousers and a rose-coloured silk blouse. Not a strand of silvery blonde hair was out of place. And yet in all that perfection there was a strange undercurrent of fragility. As if she were hiding some tiny, hairline crack.

Ruby peered round her sister's shoulder. 'Where are the kids?'

'I left them with Jere's mom for the night.' She glanced nervously at Nora. 'It's just me. I hope that's OK.'

'Are you *kidding*? I begged you to come,' Ruby said.

She looped an arm round her sister's narrow shoulders. The two women moved into the house, their heads tilted together. Nora limped along behind them.

In the living room, Caro turned towards Nora. She offered a smile that didn't reach her eyes. 'Would you like to see the newest photos of your grandchildren?'

'We could start there,' Nora said. 'But if we really want to get to know each other, it will take more than pictures.'

Caroline paled, then went on seamlessly. 'Good.' She unzipped her overnight bag and took out a flat photo album. She went to the sofa and sat down. Ruby rushed over and sat beside her, and Nora sat down on the other side of Caroline.

Slowly Caroline opened the book. The first photograph was an eight-by-ten colour shot of her wedding. In it Caroline stood tall, sheathed in an elegant beaded-silk off-the-shoulder gown. Jere was beside her, breathtakingly handsome in a black Prada tuxedo.

'Sorry,' Caro said quickly. 'The new photos are in the back.' She started to turn the page.

Nora boldly laid her hand on top of Caroline's. 'Wait.'

Who gives this woman to be married to this man? When the priest had asked that question, it had been Rand alone who'd answered, 'I do.' Nora had been in the back of the church, doing her best not to weep. It should have been *We do—her mother and I.*

Nora had been there for Caroline's wedding, but she hadn't *been* there. Caroline had invited her, placed her at a table reserved for special guests, but not family. Nora had known that she was a detail to her daughter on that day, no more or less important than the floral arrangements. And Nora, lost in her own guilt, had thanked God for even that.

Who had acted as Caroline's mother on that day? Who had sewn the last-minute beads on Caro's dress or taken her shopping for ridiculously expensive lingerie? Who had held her one last time as an unmarried young woman and whispered, 'I love you?'

Nora drew her hand back, and Caroline quickly turned another page. 'This is our honeymoon. We went to Kauai.'

Nora noticed that Caroline's fingers were trembling. 'You look so happy,' she said gently.

'We were.'

Nora saw the sadness stamped on her daughter's face. And she knew. 'Oh, Caro . . .'

'Enough honeymoon shots,' Ruby said. 'Where are the kids?'

Caroline turned to a photograph of a hospital room. She was in bed, and for once, her hair was a mess. She held a tiny baby in her arms. Here at last was a genuine smile.

Nora should have seen that smile in person, but she hadn't. Oh, she'd visited Caroline in the hospital, of course. She had come bearing an armload of expensive gifts. She'd commented to her daughter on how pretty the baby was . . . and then she'd left.

Nora hadn't been there when Caroline realised how terrifying motherhood was. Who had said to her, 'It's OK, Caro—God made you for this.'

No one.

Nora clamped a hand over her mouth, but it was too late. A small noise escaped. She felt the tears streak down her cheeks. She tried to hold her breath, but it broke into little gasps.

'Mom?' Caroline said, looking at her.

Nora couldn't meet her daughter's gaze. 'I'm sorry.'

Caroline was quiet. Nora didn't realise that her daughter was crying until a tear splashed onto the album.

'That was the day I missed you most,' Caroline said. Another tear fell. 'I remember the first night. Jenny was in a bed beside me. I kept reaching out for her, touching her little fingers. I dreamed you were standing beside my bed, telling me it would be OK, not to be afraid. But I always woke up alone.'

Nora swallowed hard. 'Oh, Caro, there aren't enough words in this galaxy to say how sorry I am for what I did to you and Ruby.'

Caroline let Nora take her in her arms.

Nora's heart cracked open like an egg. She was crying so hard, she started to hiccup. When Nora drew back, she saw Ruby, her face pale. Only her eyes revealed emotion; they were shimmering with unshed tears.

Ruby stood up. 'We need to drink.'

Caroline wiped her eyes self-consciously. 'I don't drink.'

'Since when? At the junior prom you—'

'It's a dozen lovely memories like that one that keep me sober. In college Jere used to call me E.D., for easy drunk.'

'E.D.? *E.D.?* Oh, this is too good. I'm twenty-seven years old, and I haven't got drunk with my sister since before it was legal. Tonight we're changing all that.'

Nora laughed. 'The last time I drank, I drove into a tree.'

'Don't worry. I won't let you drive,' Ruby promised.

Caroline laughed. 'OK. One drink. *One.*'

Ruby did a cha-cha-cha towards the kitchen, threw back her head, and said, 'Margaritas!' Before Nora had been able to figure out how to start another conversation with Caroline, Ruby was back, in the living room with glasses that could have doubled as Easter baskets.

Nora took her drink, then laughed out loud when Ruby went to the record player, picked an album, and put it on.

'*We will, we will, rock you . . .* ' blared through the old speakers. Ruby had the volume so high, the windows rattled.

She took a laughing gulp of her drink, slammed it down on the coffee table, then snapped a hand towards Caroline. 'Come on, dance with Hollywood's worst comic.'

Caroline frowned. 'That's not true.'

'Dance with me.'

Shaking her head, Caroline grabbed Ruby's hand and let herself be pulled into a twirl. Nora cautiously sipped her cocktail and leaned forward, mesmerised by the interplay between her daughters. They looked so happy and carefree, it actually hurt Nora's heart.

The girls danced and drank and laughed together until Caroline held up her hands. 'No more, Ruby. I'm getting dizzy.'

'Ha! You're not dizzy enough. That's your problem.' She handed her sister her margarita. 'Bottoms up.'

Caroline wiped the damp hair off her face. 'Oh, what the hell.' She drank the rest of her margarita without stopping, then held out the empty glass. 'Another one, please.'

'Yee ha!' Ruby danced into the kitchen.

On the stereo the next album dropped down—an album by the Eurythmics. '*Sweet dreams are made of this . . .*' pulsed through the speakers.

Caroline stumbled unsteadily to one side and held her hand out. 'Dance with me, Mom.'

'If I step on your foot, I'll break every bone.'

Caroline laughed. 'Don't worry. I'm anaesthetised.' The last word came out hopelessly mangled, and Caroline laughed again. 'Drunk,' she said sternly. *'Drunk.'*

Nora grabbed a crutch and limped over to Caroline. She slipped one arm round her daughter's tiny waist and used the crutch for support. Slowly they began to sway from side to side.

'This is the song I had them play at my wedding, remember?'

Nora nodded. She was going to say something impersonal, but then she noticed the way Caroline was looking at her. 'Do you want to talk about it?' Nora asked gently.

'Talk about what?'

Nora stopped dancing. 'Your marriage.'

Caroline's beautiful face crumpled. Her mouth quavered. 'Oh, Mom, I wouldn't know where to start.'

Ruby spun into the room, singing, 'Margaritas for the señoras.' She saw Nora and Caro standing there and stopped in her tracks. 'I leave you two for five minutes, and the waterworks start again.'

Nora shot her a pleading look. 'Ruby, please.'

Ruby frowned. 'Caro? What is it?'

Caroline took an unsteady step backwards. She looked from Nora to Ruby and back to Nora. She was weeping silently, and it was a heart-wrenching sight. It was the way a woman wept in the middle of a dark night with her husband beside her in bed.

'I wasn't going to tell you,' Caro said in a broken voice.

Ruby stepped towards her, hand outstretched.

'Don't touch me!' Caro said. 'I'll fall apart if you touch me, and I'm so damn sick of falling apart I could scream.'

Caroline sank slowly to her knees on the floor. Ruby sat down beside her, and Nora followed awkwardly.

Caroline's eyes were dry now, but somehow that only made her look more wounded. A little girl looking out through a woman's disillusioned eyes, wondering how she'd stumbled into such heartache.

'Are you sleeping?' Nora asked.

Caroline looked shocked. 'No.'

'Eating?'

'No.'

'Medications?'

'No.'

Nora nodded. 'Well, that's a good thing.' She held Caroline's hand. 'Have you and Jere talked about this?'

Caroline shook her head. 'I can't tell him. We're always going in different directions. I feel like a single parent most of the time. And I'm lonely. I'm so lonely sometimes, I can't stand it.'

'I know what you're going through, believe me,' Nora said. 'You're at that place where your own life overwhelms you and you can't see a way to break free. And you're suffocating.'

Caroline drew in a gulping, hiccuping breath. Her eyes rounded. 'How did you know that?'

Nora touched her cheek. 'I know,' was all she said for now. There would be more to come, she knew, but now they had to lay all the cards on the table. 'Is Jere seeing another woman?'

Caroline made a desperate moaning sound. 'Everyone always said he was just like Daddy.' She wiped her eyes. 'I'm going to leave him.'

'Do you love him?' Nora asked gently.

Caroline went pale. Her lower lip trembled. 'So much . . .'

Nora's heart felt as if it were breaking. Here was another legacy of her motherhood: she'd taught her children that marriages were disposable. 'Let me tell you what it's like, this decision you think you've made,' she said to Caroline. 'When you leave a man you love, you feel like your heart is splitting in half. You lie in your lonely bed, and you miss him. You drink your coffee in the morning, and you miss him. You get a haircut, and all you can think is that no one will notice but you. But that's not the worst of it. The worst is what you do to your children. You tell yourself it's OK—divorces happen all the time, and your children will get over it. Maybe that's true if the love is really gone from your marriage. But if you still love him and you leave him without trying to save your family, you will . . . break. You don't just cry in the middle of the night. You cry for ever, all the time, until your insides are so dry, there are no tears left, and then you learn what real pain is.'

Nora knew that what she was saying wasn't true for all marriages, all divorces. But she was certain that Caroline hadn't tried hard enough, not yet, not if she loved Jere. She closed her eyes, trying to think of Caroline . . . but then she was thinking about her own life, her own mistakes, and before she knew it, she was talking again. 'You walk around, and get dressed, and maybe you even find a career that makes you rich and famous. But you find out it doesn't matter. You don't know how to feel any more. Somewhere your daughters are growing up without you . . . You know that somewhere they're out there, holding someone else's hand, crying on someone else's shoulder. And every single day, you live with what you did to them. Don't make my mistake,' Nora said fiercely. '*Fight*. Fight for your love and your family. In the end, it's all there is, Caroline. All there is.'

Caroline whispered, 'What if I lose him anyway?'

'Ah, Caro,' Nora said, 'what if you find him again?'

Chapter Nine

RUBY FELT AS IF someone was pounding a drum inside her head. Though she was exhausted, she couldn't sleep.

After their evening of margaritas and tears, she and Caro had finally stumbled to bed. They'd lain in the darkness for hours, talking, laughing, crying. They'd said all the things they'd gathered up in the years between then and now, but finally, Caroline had fallen asleep.

Ruby closed her eyes and pictured Mom as she'd been a few hours earlier, talking quietly to Caroline.

They'd held hands, Mom and Caro, and whispered about marriage, about how it wasn't what you expected. Their two voices had blended into a music that Ruby couldn't comprehend. At first, she'd felt left out. She'd been right there, sitting beside them, and yet she'd felt isolated and alone. Unconnected. Never in her life had Ruby felt such an intense sense of her own shortcomings.

She'd been unable to join in the conversation because she'd never made a commitment to another human being; she'd never tried to love someone through good times and bad.

Mom had looked at Caroline and said softly, 'I let the bad times overwhelm me, and I ran. It wasn't until I'd gone too far to turn back that I remembered how much I loved your father, and by then it was too late. For all these years, I've been left wondering, "What if?"'

Ruby closed her eyes. *I've waited a long time for a second chance with you.* Dean's words came back to her, filled her with longing.

But did she believe in second chances? 'I do,' she said out loud, hoping that tomorrow when they went sailing, she would find the courage to say the same words to Dean.

Before tonight, it would have seemed impossible to expose her heart so openly, so boldly. To admit she wanted to love and be loved. But tonight, life seemed different.

As if anything were possible.

The next morning, Nora woke feeling refreshed and rejuvenated. She thanked God that she'd sipped a single margarita all night.

In the living room, she saw the relics of last night's blowout. For the first time this summer, the house looked lived in. This was a mess made by Nora and her daughters, and she'd waited a lifetime to see it.

She put a pot of coffee on, then limped upstairs. The bedroom door was closed, and she pushed it open. Caroline and Ruby were still sleeping. They looked young and vulnerable, sleeping together in the bed that had once held their parents.

Nora walked towards them. Slowly she reached down and caressed Ruby's pink, sleep-lined cheek. 'Wake up, sleepyheads.'

Ruby blinked awake, smacking her lips together as if she could still taste the last margarita. 'Hi, Mom.'

Caro woke beside her, stretching her arms. She saw Nora and tried to sit up. Halfway there, she groaned and flopped backwards. 'Oh my God, my head is swollen.'

Nora clapped her hands. 'Get a move on, girls. We're going sailing today with Dean and Eric. Remember, Ruby?"

Caroline turned green. 'Sailing?' She rolled out of bed and dropped onto the floor, landing on all fours. Then she crawled towards the bathroom. At the door she hauled herself upright and gave Ruby a pained smile. 'First in the shower!'

Ruby sagged forward. 'Don't use all the hot water.'

Nora smiled. 'It's like old times. I'm going to start breakfast and pack us a light lunch. Dean's supposed to bring the boat around eleven.'

She turned and headed downstairs, thumping down each step. She was halfway down when she heard a car drive up. She made it into the kitchen just as a rattling knock struck the door. She opened it.

Standing on her porch was one of the best-looking young men she'd ever seen. Though she hadn't seen him since the wedding, she'd recognise her son-in-law anywhere. 'Hi, Jeremy,' she said, smiling.

He looked surprised. 'Nora?'

'I guess it's a shock to realise you have a mother-in-law.' She took a step backwards, motioning for him to come inside.

He smiled tiredly. 'Given my other shocks in the past twenty-four hours, that's nothing.'

Nora nodded. 'Caroline is upstairs. She's not feeling real well.'

He looked concerned. 'Is something wrong? Is that why she left?'

'Tequila. That's what's wrong. Can I get you a cup of coffee?'

'That would be great. I missed the final ferry last night, so I slept in my car on the pier. My body feels like it's been canned.'

Nora went into the kitchen and poured him a cup of coffee. She returned and handed the cup to Jere.

'Thanks.' He glanced towards the stairs. 'Is she awake?'

The look he gave Nora was so utterly helpless that she said, 'I'll get her. You wait here.'

'I'm here.'

Nora and Jere both spun round. Caroline stood there, wearing the same silk and linen clothes from last night, only now they were wrinkled beyond recognition. 'Hi, Jere,' she said softly. 'I heard your voice.'

Ruby came stumbling down the stairs and rammed into her sister. 'Sorry, Caro, I—' She saw Jeremy and stopped.

Jere walked over to Caroline. 'Caro?'

The tenderness in his voice told Nora all she needed to know. There might be trouble between Caro and Jere, but underneath all that there was love, and with love they had a chance.

'You shouldn't have come,' Caro said, crossing her arms.

'No,' he said softly. '*You* shouldn't have left. Not without talking to me first. Can you imagine how I felt when I got your letter? All these years and you leave me a *letter* that says you'll be back when you feel like it?' His voice cracked.

Caro looked up at him. 'I thought you'd be glad I left, and I couldn't stand to see that.'

'You thought.' He sighed, ran his hand through his hair. 'Come home,' he whispered. 'Mom's watching the kids for the rest of the weekend.'

Caroline smiled. 'She'll be bleeding from her ears before tomorrow morning.'

'That's *her* problem. We need some time alone.'

'OK.' Caroline went upstairs. She came down a minute later with her overnight bag. She enfolded Ruby in a fierce hug, then walked across the kitchen to Nora. 'Thanks,' she said quietly. 'I won't miss you any more.'

'No way. You can't get rid of me now. I love you, Caro.'

'And I love you, Mom.' Nora pulled her daughter into her arms and held her tightly, then slowly released her.

Jeremy took the overnight bag from his wife, then held on to her hand. Together they left the house.

Ruby and Nora watched as the grey Mercedes followed the white Range Rover out of the driveway.

Ruby sidled up to Nora. 'I'm sorry, Mom.'

Nora turned to face her daughter. 'For what?'

'For all the presents I sent back and all the years I stayed away. But mostly I'm sorry for being so unforgiving.'

Nora wasn't sure how it happened, but suddenly they were clinging to each other, laughing and crying at the same time.

At exactly eleven a boat horn blared—a loud a*h-oo-gah, ah-oo-gah*. The *Wind Lass* pulled up to the pier.

Ruby glanced towards the water, watching Dean tie the boat down. 'They're here.' There was a strand of worry in her voice.

Nora understood. 'Are you afraid to see Dean?'

Ruby nodded.

'You could travel the world, and you wouldn't find a better man than Dean Sloan. Just let go. Have fun. Let yourself remember the good times, not only the bad.'

Ruby looked at her. 'I want that so much.'

The sailboat honked its horn again.

'Grab the picnic basket,' Nora said.

Within minutes they were headed down the path to the beach. Dean was on the bow of the boat. 'Welcome aboard.'

Nora stepped carefully onto the boat. She took her crutches and tossed them below decks. Then, limping awkwardly, she sidled round the giant silver wheel and sat down beside Eric. A pillow rested behind his head, and a blanket covered his body. Although he was smiling, he looked terribly pale and weak. Nora curled an arm round him gently and drew him close.

He rested his head against her shoulder, shivering a little. 'You feel good,' he murmured.

Dean started the engine. Ruby untied the boat and jumped aboard. They motored out of the bay, and when they passed the tip of the island,

Dean rigged up the mainsail. The boat immediately heeled starboard, caught a gust of wind and sliced through the water.

Eric pressed his face into the wind, smiling brightly. Nora tilted her head against his and stared out at the lush green islands. Ruby was standing on the bow. Nora didn't have to see her daughter's face to know that she was grinning.

Eric looked at Ruby, then at Dean. They were the full boat length apart, each trying not to get caught staring at the other. He said to Nora, 'You think they'll figure it out?'

'I hope so. They need each other.'

'Take care of him for me,' Eric said in a throaty voice, wiping his eyes with the edge of the blanket. 'I thought I'd always be there for him.'

'You will be.'

A swift breeze rose suddenly, filling the canvas sail with a *tharumping* noise. The boat keeled over and cut through the sunlit, glistening water.

Dean looked at Eric. 'Do you want to take the wheel?'

Eric's face lit up. 'Oh, yeah.'

Dean slipped an arm round his brother's frail body and helped him hobble towards the wheel. Eric took hold. Dean stood behind and beside him, keeping him steady.

Wind-tears streaked across Eric's temples, and his thinning hair flapped against the sides of his face. 'I'm the queen of the world!' he yelled, flinging his arms out. He laughed, and for the first time in weeks it was *his* laughter, not the weak, watered-down version that cancer had left him with.

Nora knew that when she looked back on Eric's life, she would picture him now—standing tall, squinting into the sun, laughing.

When they got back to the house, Lottie served them a delicious dinner of Dungeness crabs, Caesar salad and French bread. They'd descended on dinner like *Survivor* contestants. Eric had even managed to eat a few tender, buttery bites.

While 'the girls' washed and dried the dishes, Dean carried Eric up to bed. Finally, Nora and Ruby went upstairs, and they all stood round Eric's bed talking softly until he fell asleep.

Now the three of them were back on the *Wind Lass,* headed for Summer Island. The trip, being undertaken at night, took twice the usual amount of time. And still Ruby hadn't found the courage to hand Dean her heart. All day she'd waited for The Moment. The one when she could turn to him and say she wasn't afraid any more. She was still waiting when the *Wind Lass* glided up to the Bridges' jetty.

'Get the lines, Ruby,' Dean yelled.

She grabbed the lines and jumped onto the jetty. She was tying the boat down when her mother stepped onto the jetty. 'Thanks, Dean,' she heard her mother say. 'Ruby? Honey, I'll need some help up to the house. The bank is slippery.'

Ruby shot a glance at the boat; it was all shadows. She couldn't see Dean. What if he left before she could get back?

'Ruby?'

She dropped the excess line and headed towards her mother. And there he was, beside the wheel. She could make out his golden hair and yellow sweater. 'Bye,' he said in a subdued voice.

'Uh, if you need help leaving—you know, untying or something—I could come right back down,' Ruby said.

There was a pause before he answered, 'I can always use help.'

Ruby felt a rush of relief. She took hold of her mother's shoulders, and together they walked up the bank and across the lawn.

At the front door, Mom smiled. 'Go ahead. And, Ruby?'

Ruby reached down for the afghan blanket on the rocker and slung it round her shoulders. It was getting chilly out here. 'Yeah?'

'He loves you. Try not to be your usual obnoxious self.'

Ruby couldn't help laughing. 'Thanks, Mom.'

She hurried across the yard. At the edge of the bank she paused. Dean was standing at the end of the jetty with his back to her. She moved soundlessly down the bank towards him. 'I remember when we used to jump off of this jetty at high tide,' she said softly.

He spun round.

She was afraid to speak. She wanted to simply put her arms round him and kiss him. But she couldn't do it. For once, she had to do the right thing. She owed Dean a few words—small, simple words—and she couldn't be too cowardly to speak. 'I remember the first time you kissed me. I got so dizzy, I couldn't breathe. I was glad we were sitting down, because I would have fallen. But I fell anyway, didn't I? I fell in love with my best friend. When we were seven, you promised that someday we'd own a boat as big as a ferry, with a bathtub in the master stateroom, and that Elvis would sing at our wedding.' She gave him a smile. 'The dreams of children playing at adulthood. We should have known we were in trouble when Elvis died.'

Dean closed his eyes, and she wondered if it hurt Dean to hear the old dreams. 'Yeah,' he said woodenly. 'We were young.'

'I tried to forget how it felt when you kissed me,' she said. 'I kept telling myself it was a crush, that I'd grow up and go on and feel that way again. But I didn't.' She was exposed now, vulnerable.

'You never fell in love again?'

'How could I . . . when I never fell out of love the first time?'

'Say it.'

She tilted her face up to his. 'I love you, Dean Sloan.'

He didn't respond for a heartbeat, just stared down at her. Then he pulled her into his arms and kissed her the way she'd always dreamed of being kissed. And suddenly she wanted more. More . . .

She fumbled with his T-shirt, shoved it over his head, and let her fingers explore the hair on his chest. She moved her hands across the hardness of his shoulders, down the small of his back.

He yanked the afghan down, letting it puddle around their feet. With a groan he slipped his hands beneath her shirt, scooped it off her, and tossed it away.

Kissing and groping, they knelt on the blanket, then collapsed on top of it, laughing at their awkward movements. And then he was kissing her again, and she couldn't think. Her body was on fire. His hands were everywhere. His mouth followed the path of his magical fingers and Ruby gave in to sex in a way she never had before. She relinquished control over her body and let him bring her to the throbbing, desperate edge of pain. Finally, she couldn't stand it any more; her whole body was aching, needing . . .

'Please,' she moaned beneath his touch.

He flipped onto his back and pulled her on top of him, entering her with a thrust. His hands were on her bottom, holding her against his grinding hips, teaching her to match his movements.

Her release was so intense it felt as if she were breaking apart. 'Oh God,' she said, breathing heavily, feeling his own climax inside her.

She collapsed on top of him, buried her face in his sweaty chest.

He held on to her tightly, as if he expected her to pull away, and stroked her damp back.

'Oh my God,' she whispered, finally rolling off him. She remained tucked against him, one leg thrown across his thighs.

'We should have done that a long time ago.'

'Believe me, it wouldn't have been as good.'

So simple. It had always been like this between them. Just a touch, a gentle brushing of his skin against hers, and she'd known a kind of peace that could be found nowhere else. She rolled onto her side and stared down at him. 'Let's live together.'

He gave her a strange look. 'In Hollyweird?'

'God, no.' It was an instinctive answer. She hadn't even thought about it, but she knew she didn't want to live there any more. 'I could live in San Francisco.'

He laughed. 'No, thanks.' He reached up, touched her hair. 'We've had those lives, Ruby. I don't know about you, but I don't want to go back to anything that came before. I want to start over. And I'm *not* going to live with you.'

'Oh.' She tried to sound casual, as if he hadn't just stomped on her heart.

'We're getting married, Ruby Elizabeth. No more excuses or running away or lost time. My vote is that we move back here and try like hell to find out what we want to do with the rest of our lives. I'm going to give photography a try. It's what I've always wanted to do. Most importantly, we're going to grow old together.'

'We'll have children,' she said, dreaming of it for the very first time.

'At least two, so they'll each have a best friend.'

'And our son—we'll name him Eric.'

Ruby would have slept on the jetty all night, wrapped in Dean's arms and that old blanket, but he wanted to get back to Eric, and so they kissed—and kissed and kissed—goodbye.

Then she helped him untie the boat and walked up to the top of the bank to watch him leave. Moonlight shimmered on all the white surfaces of the boat, turned everything to silvery blue. He started the engine and the boat pulled away from the jetty.

Ruby stood there until the boat disappeared into the choppy silver-tipped sea, then she turned and went to the house. The kitchen light was on, and Mom's bedroom door was closed. She was just about to knock when the phone rang. She ran for the kitchen and answered it on the second ring. 'Hello?'

'Ruby, where have you been? I've been calling all night.'

'Val?' She glanced at the clock. It was one in the morning.

'What is this about you not turning in the article?'

'Oh, that. I'm not going to deliver, that's all.'

'That's *all*? Look, comedy princess, *Caché* magazine has reserved the space in the issue. They've printed the cover—with *your* picture on it, I might add—and leaked the story.' He paused. 'And I've got some interest in you from the networks—NBC wants to talk to you about writing a pilot.'

'A . . . pilot? My own sitcom?' Ruby felt sick.

'Yeah, your own sitcom. So no dicking around. You're supposed to deliver the article tomorrow. I FedExed your plane tickets yesterday. They're probably at your front door now. You're scheduled for *Sarah Purcell* on Monday morning.'

'I can't do it, Val.' Panic rushed through her.

Val drew in a deep breath, then exhaled. 'I gave them my word, Ruby. You can't just break your contract. Is the piece written?'

She hated the weakness that made her answer. 'Yes.'

'And the problem is . . .'

'I like her.' Ruby felt like crying. 'No. I love her.'

Val was quiet for a moment. Then he said, 'I'm sorry, Ruby.'

'I am, too,' she answered dully.

'You'll be on the plane, right? I'll have Bertram pick you up.'

Ruby hung up the phone in a daze. She wandered out onto the porch, found the FedEx envelope. Inside, there was a first-class ticket and a short itinerary. They were taking her to Spago to celebrate after the taping of *Sarah Purcell*. With a sigh she turned and went upstairs. She flopped onto the bed and reached for her pad of paper.

> *I just got off the phone with my agent. The joke is on me, it seems. I can't get out of this deal. I have to deliver the article as promised. Monday I will appear on* The Sarah Purcell Show.
>
> *And I will lose my mother—this woman whom I've waited and longed for all of my life. Whatever we could have become will be gone. And this time it will be all my fault.*
>
> *But I want to say this for the record, although I'm aware it comes too late and at too great a price: I love my mother.*

Nora sat at the kitchen table sipping a cup of coffee. She was waiting for Ruby to come downstairs. She had tried to wait up for her daughter the previous night, but at about twelve thirty she'd given up. It had to be a good sign that Ruby hadn't come home early. At least that's what Nora told herself.

The phone rang. Ignoring the crutches leaning against the wall, she hobbled to the counter and answered, 'Hello?'

'It's me—Dee.'

'Hi, Dee. What excellent news do you have today?'

'You're not going to like it. I just got off the phone with Tom Adams. He called me to tell me to tell you that if you didn't get those blankety-blank columns on his desk by Wednesday morning, he was going to slap a ten-million-dollar lawsuit on you.'

'He can't do that,' Nora said, though, of course, she had no idea whether or not he could. 'What else is going on there?'

'The *Tattler* reported that the guy in the pictures wasn't your first . . . affair. They're saying that you and your husband had an "open" marriage and you both slept with other people. And sometimes'—Dee's voice dropped to a conspiratorial whisper—'you did it in groups. Like in that movie *Eyes Wide Shut*.'

Nora's head was spinning. For the first time since this whole mess began, she started to get mad. *Group sex?* She'd made mistakes—big ones, bad ones—but this she didn't deserve. They were trying to make her out to be some kind of whore. 'Is that it? Or am I carrying some space alien's mutant child, too?'

Dee laughed nervously. 'That's mostly it. Except there was a thing in Liz Smith's column that made it sound as if someone close to you was writing an ugly tell-all story about you.'

'I see.' Nora had expected this, and yet still it hurt. 'Goodbye, Dee.' She hung up and wrenched the cupboard doors open.

There they were—the cheap yellow crockery plates she'd bought at a garage sale a lifetime ago. She picked one up, felt the heft of it in her hand. And hesitated. There was no point in making a mess.

Like Eyes Wide Shut . . . *group sex.*

She wound her arm back and threw the plate. It went flying through the air and smacked the wall by the arch, shattering.

Open marriage.

She threw another. It hit with a satisfying smack. She should have tried this years ago. It actually helped. She reached for another plate.

Just then, Ruby came running downstairs. 'What in the—' She ducked. The plate brushed past her head and hit the wall. 'Jeez, Mom, if you don't like the plates, buy a new set.'

Nora sank to her knees on the hard, cold floor. She laughed until tears leaked out of her eyes, and then she was crying.

'Mom?' Ruby knelt in front of her. 'What happened?'

'Someone close to me—apparently a friend—is writing an ugly tell-all about my life. Oh, and don't be surprised when you hear that your dad and I engaged in group sex.' She tried to smile. 'But don't you worry. I can get through this. I've been through worse. The only thing that matters is how much I love you.'

Ruby jerked back. 'Oh, man,' she whispered.

Nora got awkwardly to her feet, hobbled to the kitchen table, and slumped onto a chair. It occurred to her then, as she watched her daughter, who still knelt on the floor with her head bowed, that there was no silence more cruel and empty than the one that followed 'I love you'. She'd spent a childhood waiting to hear those words from her father, then an eternity waiting to hear them from her husband. Now, it seemed, she was destined to wait again.

'Would you like some coffee?' she asked, her voice calm and even.

Ruby looked up at her, and Nora saw that her daughter was crying. 'Don't pretend you didn't say it. Please.'

Nora had no idea how to respond. Ruby got up, turned, and went upstairs. Nora heard each footfall on the steps. She couldn't seem to draw a steady breath. *What in the world just happened?*

Then she heard the steps again—Ruby was coming back downstairs. She walked into the kitchen carrying a suitcase in one hand and a tablet of yellow paper in the other.

Nora's hand flew to her mouth. 'I'm sorry. I thought we'd got to the point where I could say that to you.'

Ruby dropped the suitcase. It landed with a thunk. Tears welled in her dark eyes, bled down her cheeks. 'I love you.'

Ruby's voice was so soft, Nora thought at first she'd imagined the words. 'You love me?' she dared to whisper.

Ruby stood there, a little unsteady. 'Just try to remember that, OK?' She slapped the yellow pad of paper on the table. 'I spent all of last night making you a copy of this. Read it.'

Nora peered down at the paper, squinting.

> In the interest of full disclosure I must tell you that I was paid to write this article. Paid handsomely, as they say in the kind of restaurants where a person like me can't afford to order a dinner salad. Enough so that I could trade in my beat-up Volkswagen Bug for a slightly less beat-up Porsche.

I should also tell you that I dislike my mother. No, that's not true. I dislike the snotty salesclerk who works the night shift at my local video store. I hate my mother.

Nora looked up sharply.

Ruby was crying now, so hard her shoulders were trembling. 'It's an article for *C-Caché* magazine.'

Nora knew it was all in her eyes—the stinging betrayal, the aching sadness . . . and yes, the anger. 'How could you?'

Ruby grabbed the suitcase and ran out of the house. Nora heard the car start up and speed away. She tried not to look at the yellow pages, but she couldn't help herself: *I hate my mother.*

Her hands were shaking as she lifted the pad and began to read. It was only a few sentences later that Nora began to cry.

Ruby made it all the way to the end of the driveway. Then she slammed on the brakes. She was running away again, but there was nowhere to hide on this one. She'd done a terrible, selfish thing, and she owed more to her mother than an empty house.

She put the minivan in reverse and backed down the driveway. She parked, then walked out to the edge of the bank, sat down on the grass and closed her eyes. When Mom finished the article, she would undoubtedly head for the porch—it was her favourite place. Then she would see her daughter sitting out on the edge of the property.

Ruby knew she would remember this day for the rest of her life and at the oddest times—when she was elbow-deep in sudsy water, washing the dinner dishes; in the shower, with the sweet, citrusy scent of shampoo all around her; or holding the babies she prayed someday to have. In a very real way this would be the beginning of her adult life. Everything that grew afterwards would be planted in the soil of what she and her mother said to each other right here.

'Hey, Rube.'

Ruby opened her eyes and saw her mother standing beside her. She was leaning awkwardly forward on her crutches.

Ruby jackknifed up. 'Mom,' she whispered.

'I'm glad you came back. You can't get away from me so easily on an island, I guess.' Nora tossed her crutches aside and sat on the grass. 'I read every word you wrote, and I have to admit, it broke my heart.'

'I knew those words would hurt you. In the beginning that's what I wanted to do, and now I'd give anything to take them back.'

Nora smiled sadly. 'The truth always hurts, Ruby.' She glanced out at the Sound. 'When I read your article, I saw myself. That doesn't seem like much, but I've spent a lifetime running away from who I am and where I came from. When I started my advice column, I knew people wouldn't like me, so I made up Nora Bridge, a woman they could trust and admire, and then I tried to live up to that creation. But how could I? The mistakes I'd made kept me on the outside all the time, looking in at my own life.' She looked at Ruby. 'But I trusted you.'

Ruby squeezed her eyes shut. 'I know.'

'I was right to trust you, Ruby. I knew it when I finished reading. You listened, and you wrote, and you revealed *me*. From the girl who hid under the stairs, to the woman who hid behind the metal bars of a mental institution, to the woman who hid behind a microphone.' She smiled. 'To this woman, who isn't hiding now.'

'I'm not going to publish the article. I won't do that to you.'

'Oh, yes, you are.' Nora took Ruby's hands. 'I *want* you to publish this article. It's a beautiful, powerful portrait of who we are, and it shows who we can be. It shows how love can go wrong and how it can find its way back if you believe in it.'

Ruby swallowed hard. 'I do love you, Mom. And I'm sor—'

'Shh. No more of that. We're family. We're going to trample all over each other's feelings now and again.' Her eyes were bright with unshed tears. 'And now we're going to go call your agent. I'm appearing on *Sarah Purcell* with you.'

'No way. They'll eat you alive.'

'Let 'em. I'll be holding my daughter's hand for strength.'

Ruby stared at her mother in awe. 'You're amazing.'

Nora laughed. 'It took you long enough to notice.'

I had my fifteen minutes of fame, and amazingly, when the clock struck the quarter hour, I was still famous. My mother and I had become, it seems, symbols that the world wasn't on such a fast and ugly track after all.

What Mom and I discovered was that people want good news as well as bad, and they loved the story of my redemption. They loved it. They loved me. But most of all, they loved my mother. They heard the story of her whole life laid out before them like a novel, and they cheered at what she had overcome.

I listen to her on the radio now. Every now and then she gets an angry caller who labels her a hypocrite and a loser. The old Nora Bridge, I think, would have fallen apart at such a personal attack. Now, she listens and agrees, and then goes on, talking about the gift of mistakes and the miracle of family. By the end of the show her listeners are reaching for tissues and thinking about how to find their way back to their own families. The smart ones are reaching for the telephone.

There's no substitute for talking to the people you love. But someone has to make the first move. I guess that's one of the things I learned this summer. As mothers and daughters, we are connected with one another. My mother is in the bones of my spine, keeping me straight and true. She is in my blood, making sure it runs rich and strong. I cannot now imagine a life without her. A daughter without her mother is a woman broken.

I left Los Angeles as a bitter, cynical woman. On Summer Island, I became complete. And it was all so easy. I see that now.

I went in search of my mother's life and found my own.

'Do you think they'll be coming home soon?'

Dean didn't need to ask who Eric was talking about. In the three days since Nora and Ruby had left, he and Eric had speculated endlessly about their return. Dean knew that Eric often forgot their conversations on the subject. Sometimes they would end one discussion, and moments later Eric would ask the question again: 'Do you think they'll be coming home soon?'

'They'll be here any day,' Dean answered. Although he always answered similarly, he wasn't so sure, and the uncertainty was killing him. It was Nora who called every night to talk to Eric. Ruby was always off somewhere, doing publicity or 'taking a meeting'. She'd talked to them only once, and although she'd said all the right words to Dean, he'd felt a distance between them.

'Can we go outside?' Eric asked. 'I can see what a beautiful day it is.'

'Sure.' Dean ran outside and set up a wooden lounge chair so that his brother could see all the way to the beach. Then he bundled Eric in heavy blankets, carried him outside, placing him in the chair.

Eric settled back into the mound of pillows. 'Man, that sun feels good on my face.'

Dean looked at his brother. What he saw wasn't a thin, balding young man huddled in a multicoloured blanket. What he saw was courage, distilled to its purest essence. He lay down in the grass beside Eric.

'Do you think they'll be home soon?'

'Any day now.' Dean rolled onto his side. 'Ruby's famous. Remember we saw her on *Entertainment Tonight* yesterday?'

'You think *fame* is what she wanted?'

'It can be a pretty wild thing, everybody loving you.'

'That's not love. I know what love is, pal. She'll come back to you, and if she doesn't, she's too stupid to live.'

Dean came up to a sit. This was the one subject they'd steered clear of, the thing Dean had never been able to ask and Eric had been too cautious to mention. But it had always been between them, waiting to be released. 'What was it like between you and Charlie?'

Eric made a little sound of surprise. 'You sure you want to go there?'

'Yeah.'

A slow, heartbreakingly earnest smile transformed Eric's face. 'I looked at Charlie and saw my future.' He grinned. 'Not that this seemed like a good thing at the time, mind you. I mean, I knew I was supposed to see my future on a body that held a uterus. I didn't want to be gay. I knew how hard it would be . . . that it would mean giving up the American Dreamkids, a house in the suburbs, my own family. It tore me up inside.'

Dean had never thought about that, about what it really meant to be gay. To have to choose between who you were and who the world thought you should be. 'I'm sorry.'

'I wanted to talk to you about it, but you were sixteen years old. And I was afraid you'd hate me. So I kept silent. Finally, what I felt for Charlie was more important than anything else. I loved him so much. When he died, a huge part of me went with him. I wouldn't have made it without Nora. She was always with me.' He closed his eyes. His breathing made a fluttering sound. Then suddenly he woke up. 'Where did I leave my eraser?'

Dean touched his brother's forearm. 'It's on the kitchen table.'

He stroked Eric's forehead. When he heard his brother's breathing even out into sleep, he lay back in the grass and closed his own eyes.

He woke when a car drove up. 'Hey, Lottie,' he called out, waving sleepily.

'Is that any way to greet your newly famous fiancée?'

Dean's eyes snapped open. Ruby was standing beside him. He scrambled to his feet and swept her into his arms, giving her the kisses he'd been counting since she left.

She drew back, laughing. 'I'm going to make a point to leave *lots* of times in our marriage. Coming home is great.' She bent down to Eric, who was still sleeping. 'Hey, Eric,' she said softly.

Eric blinked up at her. 'Hi, Sally.'

She frowned at Dean.

'He's getting pretty bad,' he whispered. 'Keeps forgetting where he is.'

Ruby sagged against him. Dean anchored her in place with an arm around her waist. 'We watched you and Nora on *The Sarah Purcell Show*. You were great.'

Ruby grinned. 'It was fun. In a "reporters following you into the bathroom stall" sort of way. Being famous is harsh. I turned down the sitcom offers and took a book deal. A novel this time. I figured it was something I could do up here.'

'Hey, guys!' Nora shouted, waving. She limped up beside them.

Eric's eyes opened again, focused. 'Nora? Is that you?'

She bent down to him. 'I'm here, Eric.'

'I knew you'd be here any minute. Have you seen my eraser?'

'No, honey, I haven't seen it.' Her voice was throaty. 'But do you know what day it is? It's the Fourth of July.'

'Are we gonna have our party? With sparklers?' He smiled sleepily.

'Of course. You go ahead and sleep for a minute. I'll get your brother to start the barbecue.'

Nora leaned forward and kissed Eric's cheek. When she turned round, Dean saw the moisture in her eyes. He reached for her hand, held it. The three of them stood there, holding hands in the middle of the garden for a long, long time. No one spoke.

Finally, Ruby said, 'Let's get this party rolling.' June hadn't yet turned into July, but this party was exactly what Eric needed.

While Nora and Ruby set the groceries and supplies out on the picnic table, Dean went upstairs and turned on the stereo. He stuck the old-fashioned black speakers in the open window, pointing them towards the garden. By the time he got back outside, Nora and Ruby had everything ready. The corn on the cob had been wrapped in tinfoil, and the salmon was seasoned and layered in slices of sweet onions and lemons.

They spent the rest of the day laughing, it seemed. They reminisced about the old days. They ate dinner off paper plates balanced on their laps. Eric even managed a few bites of salmon. And when darkness finally came, they lit up the sparklers.

Ruby stood at the bank with her back to the Sound and wrote RUBY LOVES DEAN in glittering white bursts of light. Beside her, Nora wrote I LOVE MY GIRLS and SUMMER ISLAND FOREVER. They were both grinning as they waved at Dean and Eric.

Eric turned his head. When their gazes met, Dean felt fear. His brother looked hopelessly old and tired. 'I love you, baby brother.'

'I love you, too, Eric.'

'No funeral. I want you guys to have a party, something like this. Then throw my ashes off the *Wind Lass*.'

Dean couldn't imagine that—standing on the boat, watching grey ashes float on the surface of the choppy green sea.

Eric's breathing grew laboured. He closed his eyes. 'Get Mom, would you? I need to talk to her. She's here, isn't she?'

Dean nodded, wiping the tears from his eyes. 'Of course she's here. I'll go get her.' It seemed to take him an hour to cross the patch of lawn.

'Come on, Dino,' Ruby laughed, reaching for him. 'You haven't written my name yet.'

Dean couldn't hold out his hand. He felt as if he were unravelling and the slightest movement could ruin him. 'He's asking for Mom.'

Nora covered her mouth with her hand. A small gasp escaped anyway. Ruby dropped her sparkler. It shot sparks up from the grass, and she carefully stomped it out with her foot.

In utter silence the three of them walked towards Eric. Ruby was the first to kneel beside him. Dean could see the tears in her eyes.

Eric smiled up at her. 'You're unclenched . . .'

Dean frowned at the garbled words. Amazingly, Ruby seemed to understand. 'I am,' she said softly, then kissed his cheek.

'You take care of my brother.'

'I will.'

Eric fell asleep for a few minutes, then opened his eyes. 'Mom?' There was an edge of panic to his voice. 'Mom?'

Dean clung to Ruby's hand. The feel of her was a lifeline, the only thing that kept him steady. Nora lowered herself to the chair, sitting on the edge beside Eric. 'I'm here, honey. I'm right here.'

Eric stared up at her, his eyes glassy. 'Dino came home to me. I knew you would, too. I knew you wouldn't stay away.'

Nora stroked his forehead. 'Of course I came home.'

Eric smiled, and for a split second his eyes were clear. 'Take care of Dino for me. He's going to need you now.'

Nora swallowed hard. 'Your dad and I will watch over him.'

'Thanks . . . Nora. You were always my mom.' Eric smiled and closed his eyes. A moment later he whispered, 'Charlie, is that you?' And he was gone.

KRISTIN HANNAH

Epilogue

THE CHAPEL ON SUMMER ISLAND was a narrow, pitch-roofed clapboard building set on the crest of a small rise. Even now, in December, the building was cloaked in glossy green ivy.

'I can't believe you wouldn't let me fill the church with flowers.'

Ruby laughed at her mother. They were standing in the tiny parking lot adjacent to the church, waiting for the ferry to dock.

'This is exactly how we wanted it. There's only one decoration that matters to me.'

'It's the dead of winter. You know there's no heat in the chapel.' Nora crossed her arms. Her elegant green knitted suit set off the flawless ivory of her skin. Unfortunately, it was about thirty degrees—unusually cold for Christmas week. She tried to smile. 'I wanted to plan this day for you. Make it perfect in every way.'

Ruby's smile was soft and understanding. 'No, Mom. You wanted to plan it for you.'

'And that's my right, damn it.' Nora moved closer. 'I love you, Ruby. Oh, I'm crying already.'

Ruby started to say something, but the ferry honked its horn. Within minutes three cars drove up, parked side by side. The doors opened, and the rest of the gang appeared.

Caroline, looking as cool and elegant as a water flower, was in pale ice-blue silk. Beside her, Jere brought up the kids.

Caroline's eyes were full of tears as she smiled. 'My baby sister in—' She frowned. 'What are you wearing?'

Ruby posed. What had once been her dress of shame had become her wedding gown. 'Isn't it great? It's Versace.'

Caroline grinned, noticing the plunging neckline and the slit up the side. 'It certainly is. You look gorgeous.'

Then Rand was there, wearing an elegant black tuxedo. Marilyn was beside him, holding their son. Lottie was there, too.

Rand kissed Ruby, whispering, 'Heya, Hollywood, you look like a princess,' before he drew back.

'Hey, Dad.' Ruby looked at Marilyn, who stood back from the crowd. Ruby gave her a bright smile. 'Hi, Marilyn. It's good to have you here. How's my beautiful baby brother?'

Marilyn broke into a smile. 'He's great. You look fabulous.'

After that they all started talking at once. Then another car roared into the parking lot, and Dean stepped out. In his Armani tux he was so handsome that for a moment Ruby couldn't breathe. He gave her a slow, seductive smile. Gently he took her hands. 'Are we ready to do this thing?'

Her heart was so full, she could only nod.

Together they went into the church. Inside, an aisle separated two short rows of benches. The altar was a plain wooden trestle table that held two thick white candles. In the corner stood a small fir that sparkled with white Christmas lights.

The family found their seats and crowded in. Dean walked down the aisle alone and took his place at the altar.

'Are you ready?'

Ruby heard her father's voice and turned slightly. She slipped her arm through his and let him guide her down the aisle.

At the altar he leaned down and kissed her cheek. 'I love you, Hollywood,' he whispered, leaving her standing beside Dean.

In front of them, on the altar, was a big photograph framed in ornate gilded wood. The only decoration that mattered: Eric.

In it he was fifteen years old, standing on the bow of the *Wind Lass,* half turned to face the camera. His smile was pure Eric.

Dean stared at the picture, and she knew he was remembering. She slipped her hand in his and whispered, 'He's here.'

'I know,' he answered, holding her hand tightly. 'I know.'

'Dearly beloved, we are gathered here to celebrate the union of this man and this woman in holy matrimony.' The priest's rich, melodious voice filled the small chapel.

Finally he came to, 'Who gives this woman to be wed?'

It was the only thing Ruby had requested of this service—that question—and when she turned around and saw her mom and dad standing together, she knew she'd done the right thing.

Rand looked at Nora, who was weeping openly. He slipped his arm round her. 'We do,' he said proudly. 'Her mother and I.'

Caroline was crying now, too, and Ruby saw the way Jere moved closer to her, sliding his arm round her waist. Then Ruby gazed up at Dean and forgot everyone else. The service kept going, words thrown into a silence broken only by the soft organ music.

'You may kiss the bride.'

Dean stared down at her, his eyes moist. 'I've waited a lifetime for this,' he said softly. 'I'll always love you, Ruby.'

'That's good,' she said, grinning up at him, tasting the salty moisture of her own tears. She knew she was ruining the makeover her mother had paid for, but she didn't care.

He leaned down and kissed her.

Behind them the family clapped and cheered and laughed.

Suddenly Elvis—in a full beaded white jumpsuit—pushed through the doors. The King ran a hand through his pompadour, gave a sneering little half-smile, and burst into song.

He was all shook up.

KRISTIN HANNAH

Kristin Hannah lives very much in the midst of the glamorous world of show business as her husband is 'in the movie business', and the couple count several actors and celebrities among their friends. Yet the competitive world of Hollywood is about as far as you can get from the remote tranquillity of the San Juan Islands off the coast of Washington State, where Kristin Hannah set *Summer Island*. But Kristin knows these islands as well as Hollywood, for her great-grandfather homesteaded 500 acres there, and her family still keep a house on one of the islands.

Kristin Hannah first began to write when she was at law school and her mother was in hospital. Together they passed the time writing the first chapter of a historical novel. 'And that first chapter was pretty bad,' Kristin recalls, 'though my mother was sure I had a writing career ahead of me. And when she eventually turned out to be right—well, I know she sees it all, and reads everything I write, even though she's not here.'

After her mother's death from breast cancer in 1985, the grieving Hannah went on with her planned law career. 'I put one foot ahead of the other, did my work, studied for the bar exam, even though every time I got into the car, I'd cry.' She did pass the bar exam, however and joined a prestigious law firm.

But Kristin Hannah's career was to take an unexpected turn. Married and pregnant, she went into premature labour five months early, and spent the remaining months in bed. It was during this inactive period that she started to write seriously, thinking that if the book didn't work out she could always go back to the law. She eventually sold her first book when her son was two; he's now thirteen, and Kristin Hannah has published a book a year ever since.

'For me a book really begins with a theme,' says the author. 'In *Summer Island*, I wanted to explore the issue of forgiveness: is there an unforgivable act? If so, what is the price to a woman's soul if she can't forgive someone who has hurt her? Once I know what I want to explore, I begin to figure out how to craft a story around it.'

Kristin Hannah's mother has also been much on her mind of late, with the writing of *Summer Island*. 'Alongside the theme of forgiveness, I also wanted to explore a contemporary mother–daughter relationship, where both are adults,' Kristin says, 'and the daughter sees the mother as a woman. I wish I could have that kind of relationship with my mother now that I am a mother, too. I imagined what we might have said, how we might have felt, and those thoughts were an integral part of *Summer Island*. I hope Mom likes it.'

Jane Eastgate

HAVING IT AND EATING IT

Sabine Durrant

⚘

At school, Claire Masterson was the girl who Maggie Owen wanted to be: so cool, so beautiful, the girl who stole boyfriends. Twenty years on, it seems to Maggie that nothing has changed. Claire has a glittering career and a glamorous lifestyle—Maggie is a dull housewife and mother of two, with a perpetually absent partner.

But as Claire and Maggie take up their friendship again, Maggie begins to suspect that Claire is up to her old boyfriend-stealing tricks—this time with Maggie's partner, Jake, in her sights. Well, two can play at that game . . .

⚘

June
ants
chapter one

IT IS NOT OFTEN you really want someone else's life. You might say you do: wouldn't mind being her or him with her or his looks, or wealth, or fame. But you don't really mean it. It would involve far too much upheaval for one thing.

But Claire Masterson. I'd have given anything to be her. I'd have sacrificed friends and relations, not to mention my Donny Osmond posters, for one week in her shoes—the patent leather pumps with shiny buckles, for example, or the pink ballet slippers with real blocks in the toes or those big red clogs she wore when clogs were it.

There were lots of Clares in my class, but only one of them had an 'i'. Claire Masterson had other extras too. She had long, tawny legs under her gym-slip and marble-blue eyes, flecked with green, and hair the same colour and texture as the straw in our regulation summer boaters. And her parents were actors: God, that was exciting. Her mother spent long nights in the West End, whole days in bed. Her father, handsome, famous from some ad—Schweppes was it?—pretended to pull our mothers at the school gates and gave us all rides in his car with the roof down. Their house was tattier than you generally found along the green streets of our London suburb, where even the trees were pollarded as if to avoid any verdant vulgarity, but it was bigger, grander, too. There were piles of washing up in the sink and furniture that didn't *match* like ours. 'Family money,' said my mother coolly, dropping me at the mossy stone lions at their gates.

And Claire was amazing. Claire lunched with 'Olivier' and holidayed in New York ('NY' she called it). She was the first at everything, too: the first to know the facts of life, the first to hoick the waist of her grey serge skirt up under her money-belt, the first to Sun-In her hair, the first to go all the way. She was certainly the first, and probably the last, to go all the way behind Pizza Hut in Morton High Street.

And then she left. She was the first to do that, too. At sixteen, sweet 'n' sour sixteen, she went. As we padded about our all-girls sixth-form common room, we dreamed of the life she was leading in her progressive mixed boarding school, experimenting with cider and Rizlas and English teachers, far from our secure, stultifying teenage existence. She said she'd write, but she never did. Instead, you'd hear the odd piece of news picked up from someone who'd met her mother's secretary in a queue at the bank: the parties, the dorm fire, the time she 'got caught'. Later, there was other news too: the *Vogue* talent competition, the shiny, glossy job at the shiny, glossy magazine, the journalistic assignments abroad. She was everything we, I, wanted to be. And wasn't.

So it was quite a surprise to bump into her in the High Street that day. I'd got the double buggy caught on a slightly raised kerb—you have to angle it right and really yank it up; mistime it, as I had, and you're lost—so, what with reassembling Fergus's electric Thomas the Tank Engine, which had lost a battery in the manoeuvre, and repositioning Dan's Postman Pat dummy, which had fallen out, I didn't see her until she was standing right in front of me.

'Maggie?' she said. 'Maggie Owen?'

The moment I heard her voice, creamy with catches in it, like chocolate chip ice cream, I knew it was her. She looked the same too. She hardly seemed to have aged at all. It's funny how close friends can suddenly put on ten years in a week, how the whole texture of their face can shift in an evening, so that you can hardly bear to look in their eyes for pity and fear of what you might see back, and yet people you haven't seen for aeons quite often confound you by looking just how you remember them. Teachers who looked fifty then still look fifty, years later. Claire Masterson, sixteen plus twenty, was a sophisticated version of her younger self, not a line out of place.

'Maggie?' she said. She was smiling at me, slightly quizzically. Her hair was longer and she was thinner than she had been, her body brown and lean in a dazzlingly orange cotton dress with velvet straps and purple ribbon round the neckline. On her feet were a pair of embroidered slingbacks with kitten heels and in her hand a hard, candy-pink hand-bag, clashing with everything else in a manner that only models in a magazine, or Claire, could carry off with style. I felt suddenly sick. I wished I hadn't seen her. More to the point, I wished she hadn't seen me. My unwashed hair. My sleep-deprived make-up-free face. The Weetabix on the sleeve of my left-over-from-pregnancy white/beige/whatever T-shirt. The mud Fergus's shoes had left on the thighs of my jeans the last time he'd demanded to be carried halfway through a stomp in the park. I thought, Fuck, fuck, fuck. And then I pulled myself together. Never mind, I thought, never mind: a quick wave, a smile, a waft of contented motherhood and into Woolworth's. Come on, get wafting.

'Juice. I WANT MY JUICE!' Claire was still smiling at me, peering now. Fergus wasn't. Fergus was scowling. He'd twisted his lean, wiry body round in his seat and was pushing against the footrests to stand up, straining against the leashes. His arms were flailing in the direction of Dan's dark head. He was beginning to tip the buggy backwards. Dan, struck, spat out Postman Pat and started screeching. A motorbike screamed past. I lunged. The buggy tipped. The Sainsbury's bag dangling on the back of the buggy split. There were jars of Organix baby food in the gutter, fish fingers under foot. Claire was still standing there, patience on a monument, smiling at *my* grief. I burst into tears.

There was a hand on my shoulder. 'How about a coffee?' Claire said.

We made our way, me wiping my eyes, saying sorry I'm stupid, to Pollyanna's, Morton High Street's contribution to the coffee revolution. My arms were full of broken plastic bag, so Claire took control of the buggy, pushing it gingerly at arm's length, pausing only to produce half a KitKat from her matchbox bag to appease Fergus and to coo charmingly to Dan until, astounded by the attention, he stopped crying. When we got there we ordered two cappuccinos; I was busy sorting out the children at the table so she got them from the counter. Just before she reached me, bearing the two cups, she turned sideways to negotiate the buggy, which was blocking the way. Somehow she became entangled with someone else who had just got up from their seat, someone in a beige polyester mac, shoulders heaving with annoyance, elbows jerking at cross angles at the inconvenience. Someone whose tutting followed me like the ticking clock in Captain Cook's crocodile. It was my neighbour, Mrs Allardyce, who had, I had long since learned, very little time for 'ridiculous modern contraptions' or 'today's mothers'.

'Mrs Allardyce,' I said, jumping to my feet. 'Sorry . . . Just let me . . .'

Mrs Allardyce glared at me, her chin folded down onto her neck like a cross toad. 'Sorry,' I said, yanking my ridiculous modern contraption out of her way with my knees. She shook her head and said, 'Tt'ahhh,' which I didn't take as a form of thanks, and departed.

'Who was that?' said Claire after she'd gone.

'Mrs Allardyce,' I said. 'She's a neighbour. She hates me.'

'Ooh, that's grown up.'

'What, being hated?'

'No, having neighbours. Having neighbours who have an opinion about you, at least.'

'It goes with the territory,' I said, gesturing at Fergus and Dan. 'People do have opinions about you when you have children. You become sort of public property somehow.'

'I wouldn't know,' she said, putting the cups down on the table.

The vinyl tablecloth was damp from a recent mopping and she sat at an angle to it so as not to get her knees wet. This wasn't an option for me: Dan was making powerful splashing movements in my lap, and Fergus was trying to get the salt and pepper, squirming in his chair, every inch of him twitching with the shock of constraint like a salmon on the end of a line.

'Ants in your pants?' said Claire, which made him laugh.

'Pants!' he giggled. 'Pants!'

She reached across to take Dan on her knee. 'Can I?' she said.

I had forgotten how charming she was. In fact, for the first five minutes, as we conducted that 'catch-up dance', in which you move from subject to subject, leaping great chasms of time, plunging into giant life-altering moments, while so rigid with the social trauma of unexpected encounter that you don't actually listen or follow up a word the other person says, she did such a good job of blowing raspberries for Fergus and kisses for Dan that I tried not to mind when she pulled an ashtray over from a neighbouring table and continued to blow Silk Cut over them.

'So, hey,' she said, exhaling. 'So who do you still see from the old days? Do you ever see Serena? Serena La-Di-Da Mills?'

I told her I thought Serena Mills was in hairdressing, which made Claire hoot. 'Natch,' she said, grinning. 'Patricia Wells?'

'Someone told me she was an airline pilot.'

She laughed even more. She said, 'That figures.' And I laughed too. That was the thing about Claire. She made you feel in collusion with her against the rest of the world, blissfully superior, until in a quiet moment you would wonder what she might say about you.

'And what about the boys' school? Do you ever see any of the old gang from there?'

'Well, actually,' I began.

'What about whatsisname? That hunk with the floppy, dark hair we all pretended to be in love with. God, what was his name? Jock . . .?'

'Oh—well . . .'

She was laughing. 'What did we see in him? He was in that crap band, wasn't he? What were they called? The Nasal Passage, was it? I almost got off with him once, glad I didn't. Handsome, but dull.' She opened her eyes wide to make a face for Dan, then said with exaggerated mouth movements, more to entertain him than me, 'Dullsville.'

'No. Yes,' I said. 'I do. See him, I mean. Actually, um.' I tried to laugh. 'Actually I *did* get off with him. These, I'm afraid—' I shrugged hopelessly to show no hard feelings—'are his kids. Er, and . . . the Snot Goblins. The band was called the Snot Goblins.'

'Oh shit. I'm sorry.' Claire flushed. There was a moment of silence. Then she gave a loud, exaggerated gulp, which sounded like a coin landing in the bottom of an empty charity tin, and raised her eyes to the ceiling. She could always self-dramatise herself out of trouble, could Claire. 'My big mouth,' she said, opening her eyes wide and clasping her hand to her forehead. 'It has a life of its own. I don't know why I said it. I never even really knew him. And twenty years is a long time. He's probably changed. I mean, not that there was anything wrong with him before. Oh God, I'm digging myself deeper into a hole, aren't I?'

I laughed. 'It's all right. Dull's good. Dull's fine.' I watched Dan, who was trying to wriggle out of her arms, grab the sugar bowl and begin to chew on the end of a pink saccharine sachet. 'Anyway, what about you? Last I heard you were with *Vanity Fair* in New York.' I pulled the sugar bowl back to the other side of the table. 'NY,' I added.

'Yes, I was,' she said. 'But I was running away . . . You can be away too long, do you know what I mean?' I didn't, but I nodded. Her voice had shifted gears now, her sentences beginning to go up at the end as if turning into questions despite themselves, statements of fact in search of approval. 'It was fine when I was working for the *Sunday Times*. You know me, Maggie, I was never very dilligent, not like you. All I had to do was write a weekly diary column, make a few jokes about Woody Allen or satirise Starbucks' bid for global domination, and then interview the odd film star for the mag. And it was great. It suited me fine. But then

Vanity Fair offered me a contract and I was flattered, so I took it.'

'That's good though, isn't it?' I said. 'They must have been impressed.'

'No, It was awful. They never ran any of my pieces and I was having to travel all over the US all the time, doing proper stories, investigations, and it was all crap. I was crap. And I was in this relationship with this English bloke. And he was over here and I was over there and I was beginning to think it was make-or-break time . . . And then luckily my grandmother died, no, I don't mean luckily, of course, I mean unluckily, but *coincidentally*—she was old anyway—and I thought I've got to get out. And Granny's flat was just sitting there. And I'd come into a bit of money from . . . oh, just from this little screenplay I'd sold—'

'Screenplay?' I had to try very hard not to yell it.

'It was nothing much. I was just lucky. I wrote this little thing about an Englishwoman in New York and I suppose I just tapped into something a bit Zeitgeisty? Anyway, Disney wanted it and—'

'DISNEY?'

'Well, one of their offshoots. Anyway, look, Maggie. None of that matters. It was just time to come home. I had a lot of issues. I saw a therapist for a bit out there—God, can of worms or what?' She raised her eyes to the ceiling. 'Anyway, what with one thing and another, I thought it was time to stop running away.'

Fergus had got down from his chair and was pretending to be Scoop under the table. Scoop with his scoop of sugar. 'Mind your head,' I said.

'Anyway,' Claire was saying, 'it's time to shift priorities. I've been running away from decisions, you know? And letting time run away from me. And as for men . . .' She stopped as Dan began making irritated thrusting gestures with his legs and waving his arms about, and for a moment I was distracted, so I missed what she said next. Something in a quiet voice about clocks ticking and a birthday coming up.

Fergus reared up like a digger and knocked my coffee over. Only some of it splattered on Claire's frock. 'Don't worry,' she said with a fixed smile. 'It will dry-clean.

'Anyway,' she said brightly, as I mopped the brown liquid off the table. 'I'm having a party on Saturday and I'd love it if you came. Catch up properly. And bring Jock. I'd love to see him too. Honestly.' She made a silly-me eyes-to-the-ceiling face and scrawled her address on the back of a napkin.

I studied the napkin. I knew the road—elegant Georgian houses overlooking the common. 'We'd love to come. I'll see if we can get a baby sitter. It's quite short notice, but . . . And I don't know whether Jake has anything planned. But . . . yes.'

Claire had started smiling politely and I could see she wanted to get going. 'See you then, then,' I said.

She kissed me on both cheeks. 'Great to see you, Maggie. You look . . . fulfilled. Really you do.' And she walked off down the road, young and tall and free and lovely.

'So what's she doing now?' asked Jake that evening.

'What isn't she doing?' I said. 'Film scripts, columns here, assignments there . . .'

'Is she married? Does she have children?'

'I don't know. I don't think so. No, I think she would have said.'

'You didn't get much out of her then.'

He put down his tray and went through to the kitchen. I heard the fridge door open, the clatter of unidentified objects falling onto the floor.

'Well, you know what it's like. I had both children with me,' I called. 'Fergus spilt some coffee . . .'

Jake came back into the room holding two yoghurts. He chucked one of them and a spoon onto the sofa next to me.

'Still as selfish as ever, is she?' he said.

'She's not selfish,' I said.

'Oh go on, of course she is. I know she was good fun, but always on the lookout for herself, wasn't she?'

I felt a sudden dark twist of pleasure—fault found with perfection—which was immediately overwhelmed by irritation. It was unlike Jake to be like this. What right did he have to criticise my friend, my past? He'd always seemed to like her enough when we were teenagers. He'd tried to get off with her, she'd said. 'Well, she always thought you were . . .' I stopped.

'Thought I was what?' he said.

I tore the strip of lid off my yoghurt and licked it. It was gooseberry and stung my tongue. Could I tell him he was dull?

'Handsome,' I said, deflating. 'She thought you were handsome.'

During the period that these events took place, Jake and I and our two children were living in a terraced house in a nice street near a common on the in-skirts of London. Morton, or Morton Park as our particular patch was called, was ideal for children—green spaces, fresher air, Pizza

Express—and only ten minutes on the train, if you wanted it, from the centre of town. Not that I ever went there. I'd found family life to be a gradual process of zoning down, like old age: any trip involving more than a packet of breadsticks or one flight of steps or too many lavatorial unknowns was out of the question. So we tended to stick within a crutch's length of home, plumb in the middle of what the property supplements called 'Cape Cot': it was said to have the highest concentration of under-fives in Europe. And, as Jake used to say, most of them seemed to live in our house.

Jake and I had met at school. We would do our homework together sometimes, and on the nights when a gang of us would trawl south London in search of a party, it had always been Jake who'd lend me his jacket and find us a night bus home. But I had never thought I was his type back then. I was too mousy. Jake, stocky and dark like a walk-on in *The Godfather*, was famous for his gap-toothed blondes. They'd drape themselves over his shoulder in the pub on Fridays and stand shivering on the side of the pitch during his Saturday-morning football commitment. He went off to Oxford and had a wild old time, juggling work and women and his Saturday-morning football commitment.

I was far more sober. I didn't juggle anything. I balanced. Through school and at Bristol, where I wandered aimlessly through university, and in my early working life, I was always 'married' to someone. My friend Mel used to say I was the queen of the long-term monogamous relationship. Two years here, four years there, five . . .

I was going out with David the summer Jake and I got together again. We were at a wedding, a posh do with a marquee on the lawn and strawberries bobbing in the Spumante, when Jake came up behind me in the queue for coffee. "Ello, 'ello,' he said in the mock cockney he used to bring out when he was nervous. 'Fancy a turn?' 'A turn at what?' I said crisply. 'A turn round the dance floor, you pillock,' he answered. David was talking to a woman further up the queue about his new job in chambers. He'd just got his coffee—I saw the blue glint of his Hermesetas tin as he whipped it out of his top pocket. Jake was giving me a wolfish grin. 'OK,' I said.

We danced and at midnight, by which time there were rings of wet on his white dress shirt and his bow tie was hanging loose round his neck . . . and my dress was torn at the hem and my face flushed, and after I'd given up searching for David, who appeared to have left with his Hermesetas in a huff, he walked me to the taxi rank, and kissed me.

HAVING IT AND EATING IT

That time it felt grown up, as if now I was playing it for real, no more rehearsals or trial runs. David said I was a heartless hussy, or similarly unoriginal words to that effect—but I was too much in love to care. Jake, this newly discovered adult Jake, interested me. It wasn't just sex, though there was a lot of that. It was more that he touched me in other places too. He was sexy and funny and kind, but he also had a different take on life from the men or boys I'd known before. Beneath the jokes and the fooling about were unmined seams of seriousness and self-confidence. He didn't, when it came down to it, care very much what other people thought. Oh, I know he wasn't perfect: he could be moody and distracted, and sometimes he could be quite tactless, but he also had an ability to rise above the pettier aspects of life. He didn't get cross or insanely irritated, like most of the other men I'd known, with silly things like parking tickets, or mistimed video recorders, or the time I spilt a ten-litre can of paint (eggshell) on the back seat of his car (new). Most of all, he made me feel really cared for. Not just in a mimsy, doing-the-bills, filling-out-the-census-form kind of way, but because I knew he wanted me. Though I'd have to add, for the sake of balance, that he was good at the census forms too.

So we moved in together, and we moved back to Morton Park because it seemed like the natural thing to do. A homing instinct. And there we were, eight years and two children down the line: Mr and Mrs Convention. Minus the Mr and Mrs, though. This, as they say in advertising circles, was the nitty-gritty of the situation: Jake did not want to get married. He must be the only offspring known to man to have been put off not by his parents' divorce but the occasion of their silver wedding. This took place in the banqueting suite of the Horse and Groom in Norwich, where they now live. Jake's mother wore her wedding dress. 'Can you believe it still bloody well fitted?' Jake said when he told me. (Jake has a complicated relationship with his mother. She still keeps the cards from boxes of PG Tips for him. It was only after we got together that he stopped putting them in a scrapbook.)

That was his excuse. 'Who needs a piece of paper?' he'd say, as people always do, but it wasn't the piece of paper I cared about, it was the ring-less left hand and the awkwardness I'd feel fifty-eight times a week, or maybe it was only five but even so, when I'd refer, pregnant or small child in hand, to 'my boyfriend'. Sometimes I'd lie and say 'my husband' and that would feel worse. Anyway, the long and the short of it was: no Wedding. At first I had minded a lot—I liked things to be clear—but I

307

had got used to it. Sometimes I even forgot I was still waiting for something to happen.

Jake worked for TMT&T (Titcher, Maloney, Titcher and Titcher), a medium-sized advertising agency in the centre of London. He was a planner—a Board Planning Director, to use his correct title. Planners are 'the brains' of an agency, who think about strategies and consumer profiles and brand definition and . . . well, that sort of stuff. Whatever he did, it took up a lot of his time. He often worked late, usually missed bathtime. And if he wasn't working, he was socialising. There was a lot of socialising in his line of work. He'd sigh and say he'd much rather be at home with us, kicking a ball about with Fergus in the garden, as he would on the summer evenings when he did get back before dark, elbows neatly at his side, head wobbling, just a subtle gentleness in the lower half of his body to indicate his opponent was only two. Or in winter, sitting back on the sofa, his tie undone, a small child tucked under each arm, three heads in three shades of brown, watching *Fireman Sam* with expressions of pure concentration on their faces.

But that didn't happen often. And his long hours was one reason why I gave up my job. I had always wanted children, always wanted to create the perfect family life I had never quite had myself. And it was all right when we just had one child, but once we had two, both of us working didn't seem fair any more. And of course it was me who gave up. That's the way things were in our circle. People talk about 'having it all', but you can't. You can have some of one thing and some of the other, but you can't have all of everything. You might be able to have the company car and the nativity play; you might be lucky and may even get home in time to see your baby's first step. But what you wouldn't see is the six wobbly attempts that went before your baby's first step. To some women that might not matter. But I minded enough that I decided, after Dan was born, that I was going to be around.

Actually, I wasn't very good at my job anyway. I was several escalators down from the glass ceiling. I wouldn't have recognised it if it had shattered about my ears. I, like Claire, was a journalist, but I'd never made it like her. I just burbled around on the sidelines. I'd worked in newspapers for a bit, and then in publishing, and before I gave up I was working for a literary journal, owned and edited from the basement of his flat in Bloomsbury by an eccentric elderly Czech called Gregor. I'd proofread and harry his contributors and sort through the piles of correspondence that provided comfortable sleeping quarters for his cats, and, sometimes long into the evening, listen to Gregor's reminiscences of his life in Paris in the fifties, of drinking with Beckett and lunch with Cocteau. It was nothing. Dispensable, poorly paid, easily surrendered.

I missed it like hell.

But I had the children. And really I couldn't complain. Oh, I know there were days when I was subsumed by the *task* of it, by the things none of the manuals tell you: the mess and the noise and the chaos and the clobber and the palaver, and the squeezing of the person you used to be into this dull, one-tracked, *loaded down* creature with opinions on the introduction of solids and an encyclopedic knowledge of nappy absorbency. But things would change. The children would get bigger. They'd go to school. I'd read a grown-up book again. And it seemed important not to become entirely a member of the Bleat Generation. Because there were moments even then, 'trapped at home with the children', when I would feel my soul soar with the freedom of it all. And it might just be the sense, waiting at the station on platform two for a train to take you to the seaside or the swimming pool or a distant park, when everyone else was on platform one, briefcases at their ankles, pinched, impatient faces scanning the empty tracks behind, that you were going against the tide, that you were your own boss, the big cheese in a corporation of one—and two halves.

I know, of course, that if I had bundled onto their train with my slow-wobbling toddler and my pushchair and my wailing baby, I would have seen pity or contempt in their faces. But I didn't care. Because I thought what I was doing was what really counted—just keeping them alive, keeping them off the road, getting nourishment into them, keeping illness out. So you could keep your spreadsheets and your projected figures for 2005. I made life-and-death decisions every day.

Not that Jake's sister, Fran, believed it. She called us 'Them Indoors' because we were so boring, still to be living round the corner from where we grew up. But I found familiarity comforting. I liked hanging out with my takeaway polystyrene coffee in the same playgrounds (safer now, of course, with their flexi-firm floor coverings) that I used to hang out in as a child. I liked knowing that Blockbusters used to be a shop called Cuff's selling school labels, that the man I lived with, Mr Advertising Exec with a bag of clubs in his boot, used to bleach his hair and play drums for a band called The Snot Goblins.

I was a creature of habit, I suppose. And I could have sworn, until the day I met Claire again, that Jake was the same.

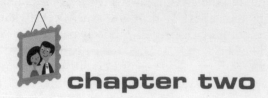

chapter two

THE NEXT DAY was Thursday, when Fergus went to playgroup—Little Badgers (or Little Buggers, as Jake called it)—so I took the baby round to see my mother.

'Darling, how nice. Have a sherry,' she said.

'Mum, it's eleven in the morning.'

'Is it? Just a little one then. Oh, Daniel. Why's he crying? Does he want a little something?' For a moment I thought she was going to pour him a sherry. 'How about a biccy? Oh, Daniel, don't you want to come to your grandmother? What's this on his head?'

'Cradle cap,' I said. 'And his name is Dan. Just Dan.'

'I just can't understand it. I suppose I'll get used to it. But all these short names. I'm sure he won't like it when he grows up.'

She was very well meaning, my mother, and devoted to her grand-children. She'd do anything for them, except on a Wednesday when she had tennis, or a Friday when there was art class, or Monday or Tuesday or Saturday or Sunday when there were music groups and upholstery sessions and trips to the National and she and her new husband had just a few friends round for a bite to eat.

I put Dan down and he crawled gratefully out of the room.

'I met Claire Masterson yesterday,' I told her. 'You know, from school.'

'Which one was she?' she said absent-mindedly, riffling through her bag and pulling out a packet of photos of her trip to Bruges.

'Claire Masterson,' I said, looking at the photos. 'You remember. Parents were actors. Ran away on the French exchange.'

'Oh, Claire Masterson,' said my mother, 'Clive Masterson's daughter.' She paused to remember something, while a small smile played about her lips, then she added sharply, 'Claire with the painted fingernails. The girl you all wanted to be.'

There was a silence while I registered this uncharacteristic moment of insight. I picked up a carriage clock on the side table next to me and fiddled with its brass handle. 'Yeah, I suppose so.'

'Still looking out for herself, is she?' she said.

'Not you too,' I said, turning it upside-down to see what happened.

'What do you mean, "not you too"?'

'Oh, nothing,' I said. I put it back down with a clatter. There was a silence. 'What do you mean?'

'I don't know, dear. I know you all thought she was terrific fun, but I just remember that party she took you to and she got offered a lift home and you rang from Virginia Water on your own in tears.'

'That was a long time ago, Mum. Anyway, I just . . . you know . . . seeing her, it's just made me feel a bit funny somehow. I love my life, of course I do, but since I bumped into her I keep thinking of all the things she's done and all the things I haven't. You know she's been living abroad. New York. She's written a screenplay . . .'

My mother took a sip of her sherry. 'But she's back now, then?'

'Well . . .'

'Married?'

'Well . . .'

'Children?'

I didn't say anything.

'Well, there you are, dear.' Problem solved. Anguish over. 'I had the most terrible night,' she said, moving on to more important matters. 'I didn't sleep a wink. Frank'—that was her latest husband—'had to go and sleep in the other room. I had to take two of my pills in the end.' My mother was of a generation for whom ongoing supplies of prescription-only pills and lunchtime sherry were as normal as vitamin C supplements and bottled water to mine. She reached into her bag and brought out a matted sliver of tissue. For a moment I thought she was going to use it to clean my mouth—you never know with mothers—but she pulled it into a usable shape and blew her nose as if stifling some enormous grief.

'Margot rang yesterday. In floods. Her Burmese had run out into the road and a horrible, horrible van driver ran over him and didn't stop—I mean, people are awful—and poor Petrushka . . . Well, she rushed her round to the vet and that lovely Mr Pelt did what he could. Cost her two hundred and forty pounds—well, I told her she should have had Petplan but too late now, of course.'

She had begun to gulp with tragedy recollected in tranquillity. My mother's response to misfortune never failed to astound me: she skirted over the horrors of life, but was thrown by small things. Take the time she was burgled. The thieves threw her underwear all over the bedroom, smashed the glass in the family photographs she laid out like chess pieces on the mantelpiece, and defecated in the bath. I found my mother with a bottle of Dab-It-Off on the stairs. 'You'd think they could have wiped their feet,' she said. She also never talked about my father, the Gentleman Bolter, though she had plenty to say about the unscheduled departure of her last cleaner—'And did she bring back the key? No she didn't. And it wasn't for want of asking.'

I propped Dan into a nest of cushions on the sofa, where he sat fiddling with his own fingers, bringing them up to his eyes and examining them as if he'd only just discovered them, and went through to the kitchen to put the kettle on. My mother still lived in the house I grew up in, and it never changed, just accrued. She only ever seemed to add things: utensils, ornaments, husbands. Frank, number four, was always tinkering about with his tool box trying to make shelf space.

I filled the kettle, pulling a couple of thick Italian mugs (lugged back from their last holiday in Puglia) down from their place next to the decorated pasta bowls (free with 180 petrol tokens from the local garage). The kettle, I noticed, was new, rounded white plastic: an ocean-going liner compared to the old aluminium tanker.

'New kettle?' I said, when I went back into the sitting room with two cups of coffee.

'Ah yes. I didn't tell you, did I?' she said, fully recovered now. 'I bought it in Peter Jones the other day when we went to buy the new dishwasher. Now, that was an adventure. In the end . . .' Her voice slowed down and hushed in preparation for some momentous news. 'We went German. There was this lovely girl assistant. And she just persuaded us it was worth the difference. And it really is a super machine. I couldn't be more pleased with it. Very quiet.'

'That's good,' I said, and I drank my coffee.

'Well, lovely to see you, darling,' she said into Dan's face as I carried him to the door. 'Give my love to "Jake".' She always said his name in inverted commas as if I'd made him up. 'How is he?'

'Fine,' I said.

'And do bring both the children round soon. I'd love to have them. We could go for a lovely walk, couldn't we, Daniel?' Dan didn't respond.

'Well, actually,' I said, 'you're not free on Saturday, are you? You couldn't baby-sit, if you are? We've been invited to a party and . . .'

She thought quickly. 'Saturday? This Saturday? Oh, what a bore,' she said. 'It's Morton Park Music Society at the church. They're doing Flanders and Swann. I'd give it a miss but . . . I do love them, don't you? "I'm a Gnu"—do you remember?'

'No, I don't,' I said, gnu-like. And left.

I was first in the queue of parents at Little Badgers, so Fergus was very cheerful when I picked him up. Second's good, third's fine, fourth was a disaster with tears all the way home. Today, though, he was chipper and really quite forthcoming. Apparently, he bumped his head on his chair. 'I was very brave and I went to the moon in my helicopter.'

He was so busy telling me about his adventures in space, he didn't notice me take a detour to drive slowly down the road where Claire lives. I stopped when we had just passed number 38. 'What are you doing, Mummy?' he said then, jolted from his mental moonscape.

'Just checking something,' I said, craning over my shoulder. It had been bothering me, the house. Property envy can be a terrible thing. When anyone I knew bought a new house, I wanted to know three things. One, how much—exactly—did it cost? Two, how big was the garden? And three, however big it was, was there a Tube line at the end of it? Claire's writing said 38b: b for basement or b for beautiful view? I couldn't see any numbers, but there were steps up and steps down. Four floors of windows. Not a maisonette, surely? Not *two* whole floors of beautiful view?

The door of the raised ground floor opened then and suddenly there she was on the doorstep. In a dressing gown the colour of pigeon. One o'clock in the afternoon—in the week—and wrapped in something soft and textured. She was talking to someone back in the recesses of the hallway. And as she turned to look into the street, a man came up behind her and pulled her round to face him. They kissed. Lingeringly. One of his hands slid down her back and clenched her bottom through the fabric of her gown; the other was tangled in her hair. They wouldn't have noticed me staring at them, but through some sort of modesty I turned and watched them in the mirror anyway.

'Baa, baa, black sheep, have you any tractors?' bellowed Fergus.

'Ssh,' I said. 'Don't wake Dan.' The man was coming down the steps. He turned and said something. Claire laughed and shut the door. Quickly I grabbed an A–Z and studied it intently until he'd passed by the car. Then I looked up again. He was wearing a suit and carried a pigskin briefcase. He was walking quickly, flicking shoulder-length hair away from his face. Just after he passed me, he paused, retrieved something from his pocket, brought it to his nose and sniffed deeply. He walked to the end of the street and turned the corner.

'I want my lunch,' shouted Fergus.

'OK, OK,' I said, turning the key in the ignition and pulling out. There was a screech of brakes, the scrunch of metal and a jolt. 'Oh fuck,' I said, opening my door and getting out, braced, as you are in London, for aggression. The other car was a red transit van, and was now at a funny angle to the road. I could see that the rear passenger side of my car was bashed in. The front of the red van was a bit of a mess.

A man in combat trousers was coming round towards me.

'I'm sorry. I'm really sorry,' I said. 'Are you all right? I'll give you my details. It was all my fault. I wasn't looking. I'm sorry. The children . . .' I gestured to the inside of the car. Dan was still asleep. Fergus was pushing his bottom out of his seat in excitement, gesticulating like Peter Snow on election night. 'Crash,' he said, laughing. 'Crash, crash, crash.'

'Calm down,' said the man, smiling. I realised he was Australian when he opened his mouth—'Ca'm de-yeown,' he'd said—but you could have guessed from his stance: legs apart, arms out at an angle, a body not closed like English bodies against the elements, but open to the warmth. He had blond curly hair with darker roots, scrunched up as if he'd been through a hedge backwards, and coppery freckles on his forehead. His hands were broad, the fingernails ingrained with dirt. He said, lazily, 'Look, I was probably as much to blame myself. I wasn't looking where I was going. Are the kids all right?' He opened the back door. 'Fuck, fuck, fuck,' continued Fergus.

'Oh shit,' I said, and shut it again.

The man laughed. He was younger than me, nice-looking. 'Hey, let's look at the damage.' He went to the back of my car and poked about. 'It's not too bad. New bumper probably, new headlight. I expect they can beat the panel out. And as for mine . . . Well, it was about time I had a new one anyway.' He gave a half smile, half grimace. His eyes were ginger. There was a fan of white lines on the outside corner of each as if he'd been squinting into the sun.

'You're being so nice,' I said. 'People are usually so horrible about these sorts of things. What shall we do? Shall we swap details anyway?'

His T-shirt was creased oddly. He tweaked it at the shoulders. 'Yeah, perhaps that wouldn't be a bad idea.'

I found an old pay-and-display ticket on the dashboard and wrote my name and number on it. He handed me a card. 'Peat and Dug', it read beneath a pen-drawn spade. 'Garden services. No job too small.' Then there was a name, 'Pete Russ', and two phone numbers. So he *had* been through a hedge backwards.

'Oh, you're a gardener,' I said. 'No wonder you're nice.'

He smiled, looked at the used ticket and then, I could have sworn, at my ringless left hand. 'And you're a meter maid.'

I felt myself go pink. 'Not really a maid,' I said. He looked at me for a bit, but didn't say anything.

After a moment or two, I said, 'So is there a Doug?'

'Come again?'

'Peat and Dug. Is there a Doug?'

'Oh no. No, there's no Doug. There's a Lloyd. Will you be all right?'

'Yup, yup, of course,' I said, getting into the car. The baby was stirring, screwing up his face in his sleep in preparation for Armageddon. 'Thanks,' I said through the window. Pete was bending down and trying to wedge something back onto his car. 'And sorry again.'

'No worries,' he said, not looking up.

And I drove, or rather clanked, off down the road—back to microwave baked beans and put a wash on and feed the baby, screaming at full throttle now, and persuade Fergus to have a rest, and do the ironing and remember to ring the garage and if I was lucky later and the sun was out maybe collect some stale bread and go and feed the ducks. It was my life. I loved it. It was just . . .

What was Claire doing all this time? Had she watched me from the window? Had she seen me, a boring thirtysomething mother, flirting stupidly with a kind, indifferent man? Or had she, after kissing her lover, returned, sleepy-headed, to her warm, crumpled sheets? Percolated herself a tiny *tasse* of strong espresso and curled up in an armchair with the latest copy of *Vogue*? Slipped into a long, deep bath, fragrant with amber or mimosa or *fleurs d'oranger*? I wondered about that intently all the way home.

That night Jake rang to say he'd be late. He had an important 'strategic development meeting' to prepare for. All his meetings were called things like that. Sometimes he had brand definition meetings; other times he had status meetings. But it all came down to bread in the end. Bread (Wheato), spot cream (Zap-it), Pot Noodles (Ecram Foods) and cars (Kyushi, the Japanese multinational). Those were his accounts, his bits of business. Today it was the zit cream. He had the results of some focus group to go through. To spot-check.

'Ha, ha. Go on,' he said at this. 'Squeeze it for all it's worth.'

'I'm squeezing,' I said. 'I just wish it would pop.'

Then I told him about the car and he said as long as we were all OK and I said we were and he said, 'OK then, sweetie. Laters.'

'Laters,' I said.

After I'd put the phone down, I sat quite still for a few seconds and then I got on with putting the children to bed on my own. Later, when they were asleep, I rang round some baby sitters to try to find someone—unsuccessfully—for Saturday night, spoke briefly to Jake's mother, who wanted to know how his nasty cold was (I didn't have the heart to tell her I didn't know he had one) and then, after I'd tidied the sitting room and swept the kitchen floor, I settled on the sofa and rang Mel.

I'd known Mel since my second year at university. Our paths shouldn't have crossed—she was a medic and I did languages—but Adam, the boy she went out with in her second year, was a friend of Tom, the boy I was going out with, and we were hurtled together in a series of double dates in the days when double dates were easier than having to talk to each other on your own. Our romances both fizzled out before the end of the year but our friendship didn't, and it was Mel and I who ended up moving in together at the beginning of the third year. She was different from me. She was a scientist, I was an arty-farty nothing. She came from a big family in the centre of Manchester, and had a resilience and a toughness that I envied and admired. And she also made me laugh. Nowadays, she lived with her three-year-old daughter in a two-up, two-down terrace near our local hospital, where she used to work. She was going to be a surgeon but, as for many women, ambition became impractical once she'd had Milly. She was a GP now. A doctor and a single mother: every inch of her life was a reproach to mine—as she rarely let me forget. She was my dearest soul mate and my harshest critic.

I said, 'I have sooooo much to tell you.'

She said, 'Well, be quick. I'm on another call.'

I said, 'I met your future husband today.'

She said, 'I'll phone you straight back.'

Mel's daughter was the result of a brief relationship with a consultant in Obstetrics and Gynaecology who left her, when she was pregnant, for a drugs rep. Mel was slim and dark and compact, Milly had unruly blonde hair and big blue eyes. Mel used to say Milly needed a proper

father, that she herself needed a proper man in her life, not just a signa-
ture on the end of a monthly cheque, but I was never so sure she meant
it. For the moment she was seeing a very nice anaesthetist called Piers,
who would have done anything for her. But Mel asked for nothing.
Secretly, I suspected she liked her life just the way it was. Which is not
to say I didn't still try.

The phone rang. 'God,' she said, as soon as I picked it up. 'Middle-
class mothers! Non-working middle-class mothers—no offence—they
are the worst. I've just had one on the phone. Whinge, whinge, whinge.
Why won't I give her daughter antibiotics? She's sure it's not viral. Blah,
blah, blah. She came into the surgery earlier today and her kids were
running riot and I told her then that she didn't need them, but she
thinks she knows best and that, just because I know her a bit from
Milly's nursery, I'm going to give in. Well, I'm not.'

'Are you going to let this non-working middle-class mother cheer you
up, then?' I said.

She sighed. 'Yes. Go on. Who's this bloke?'

So I told her about bumping into Claire and the party invitation and
the pigeon-coloured dressing gown, and then I told her about bumping
into the red van. 'And this man comes out', I said, 'and starts walking
towards me and he's smiling. You know, he's being nice. And he was
sweet with the children, and he didn't get nasty or start talking about
insurance details. He was Australian—does that matter?—and—'

'Handsome?' she interrupted.

'Yes,' I said. 'He was. Very handsome. Very blond-ish and . . . an
amazing body. Great muscles. You could see them under his T-shirt,
they sort of rippled sweatily.'

'Go on,' said Mel. 'What does he do?'

'Oh. He's a gardener.' I started laughing.

Mel did too. 'A gardener?' she said.

'Yes. Isn't that great? We never meet gardeners, do we? It's always
solicitors or managing directors or advertising executives; men who
spend their whole time indoors, worrying about money and accounts
and all that, not out in the open air, in touch with the elements, up to
their arms in soil. I mean, how sexy is that? Anyway . . . the best thing is
I've got his number.'

'He'll do,' she said, after I'd rabbited on for a bit longer, 'though I
don't know how you're going to get us together.'

'Leave it to me,' I said.

I was reading in bed when Jake finally got home that night. I'd had my nightly flick through my stash of pornography. Mini Boden, with its sun-kissed six-year-olds in their stonewashed sweatshirts, dipping for crabs on a Cornish beach; Toast, full of willowy women with enough time on their hands to lie languidly in the shade in their Cambodian hand-woven shot-silk sarongs and duck-egg-blue thong sandals. I knew I had to kick my mail-order catalogue habit because I always felt guilty afterwards. Wistful too. In my most downtrodden moments, I used to think it was a pity it was only the clothes they were offering and you couldn't send off for the life. Mind you, you probably wouldn't want to hang around for too long in those thong sandals: they looked like they'd be murder between the toes.

I was deep into a Georgette Heyer—comfort-reading, the literary equivalent of a treacle sponge—when the front door slammed. 'Hello,' Jake said, poking his head round the bedroom door. He came in with a sheepish air about him, kissed me and sat on the edge of the bed to take off his shoes. There were dark shadows across his cheeks and his green eyes looked bright—with tiredness perhaps. He smelt of cigarettes and taxis and something else almost floral—the summer night air, or the scent of another woman.

'What's that smell?' I said, pulling a corner of his shirt to my nose.

'What smell?' he said, bending his face too. 'Oh that. I popped my head round the door of Charlotte's leaving do on the way home. I wasn't going to but Ed persuaded me. He said we needed cheering up. It was at La Renne and they spray you in the Gents there. Like aftershave. Or air freshener. You know what they're like in these posh restaurants.'

'Actually, I don't,' I said. I tried to keep the tone out of my voice. Because there certainly was a tone to be ushered in if I'd let it. Recently there seemed to be a leaving party every week at his office. And I was beginning to feel fed up with Jake's colleague, Ed: he always seemed to be leading Jake astray, or turning him back from the tube at the last minute, anyway.

Jake had got up and was rattling about in the bathroom. When he came back, he said, 'Sorry. I tried to ring but you were engaged.'

'It doesn't matter,' I said.

Jake threw his clothes—his button-down blue shirt, his chinos—on the back of the chair and clambered into bed, pulling the duvet off my legs as he did so. 'Oi,' I said playfully, yanking it back.

Jake wasn't in a playful mood. He switched on his light and, reaching

318

down for *Campaign* on the floor, said, 'It's getting worse and worse. I had to see the MD today. Those bastards Kyushi want a European realignment. I've got a nightmare month ahead of me. We're going to have to get a pitch together to blow all the other European agencies away. One thing is, I think that means we won't be able to go on holiday this year. Not until it's sorted, at least. We're going to have to do it well. We can't afford to lose them.'

'Oh,' I said. 'Oh well.'

He looked at me. 'Sorry.'

'It's OK.'

He turned back to his magazine. After a bit, I turned on my side and pressed against him. I rested my cheek on his shoulder. 'But this week-end: will you have to work then? Or can we go to this party?'

'What party?'

'You know, Claire's.'

'Oh, Maggie.' He still had his eyes on his page. 'Do we have to? I really, really don't want too. Anything but that. Claire Masterson's? Do we need that? I wouldn't feel comfortable.'

'Why not?'

'I don't know. Who would we know? It'll just be her Disney crowd.'

'I'd like to,' I said. 'It'll be fun, won't it?'

'OK, then.' His expression was blank. 'If you want to.'

'I do,' I said. I was moving my chin further up his shoulder, in little jerky movements, trying to get him to look at me. He didn't. After a bit, I lifted my chin, shifted away, over to my side of the bed and went back to my book. 'Who shall we get to baby-sit?' I said.

'I don't know,' he answered shortly, turning a page. I felt a flare of unexpected anger. Of course he didn't know. It was something I always dealt with, just as I always got the dry-cleaning. And cleaned the kitchen floor. And did all the mundane things that kept our life together. I didn't mind the chores but I did mind any inkling of his contempt for them.

I put my book down and closed my eyes. Other things had changed between us recently too. Jake used to go to the gym, played five-a-side on Saturdays. But over the last year there seemed to have been a gradual accretion of middle-aged things around him: predictable clothes, corporate entertaining, golf. It was all very well growing old together, but did it really have to happen this quickly? 'Night,' I said, thinking all this, thinking of Claire, Claire and her screenplay. Disney. Had I told Jake about that, then? I didn't remember.

'Night,' he said, not looking up.

I turned onto my stomach and thought about cotillions and Corinthians for a while. There was a crackle of pages next to me. I opened my eyes, and half turned. Up close, Jake smelt of wine and smoke and a day in the office. The duvet smelt stale too: the old-sheet smell of marriage. It had been a month or so, now I came to think of it, since we'd last had sex. That was another thing that had seized up. It was fine when it was still the topic of jokes between us, but less fine now it had passed into silence. I wondered if I should make another approach, not so obvious as to make rejection, if it came, feel too awkward, but obvious *enough*. I stroked my hand low across Jake's stomach. His skin felt soft and fuzzy.

He said, not moving except to turn another page, 'So, as a result, I'm going to have to go to the agency office in Amsterdam next week.'

I said, 'Oh right, fine,' and took my hand back.

'Night,' I said, curling away from him. Claire had said I looked fulfilled. Was I fulfilled? She'd said Jake was dull. Was he?

'Night,' he said.

chapter three

'I'M GOING TO START with Delia's baby summer vegetables with lemon vinaigrette. Followed by the River Café's pan-roasted pigeon stuffed with cotechino with wood-roasted whole organic carrots. And then for pudding—well, I'm not quite sure. Have you ever done Nigella's almond and orange-blossom cake?'

It was Friday afternoon and, after taking the car to the garage across the common, I was sitting on a warm, damp bench in the playground talking, or rather listening, to Rachel, another playground mother. There had been a quick burst of rain, but the sun had come out again. Dan was in the sandpit, seeing how much of it he could fit into his mouth, and Fergus and Rachel's son, Harry, were trying to climb up the slide. A smaller child in a white sundress and pink Teletubby wellies, which she was banging crossly on the metal at the top, was waiting to slide down. One of us needed to intervene but I couldn't be bothered.

'Nigella?' I said. I wasn't really listening. Rachel was a good cook—it's where she put the energy she used to expend as a conference organiser—and always assumed I was too. She didn't hear me.

'It does seem to take an awful lot of eggs,' she was saying. 'Do you think it might be a bit rich after the cotechino?'

'Maybe,' I said.

'Really? Even with the loganberry and mascarpone coulis?'

'Maybe not, then,' I said. She darted me a look, but then luckily noticed the situation building on the slide.

'Fergus!' she yelled. 'Harry! Get off the little girl! We go *down* slides, not up them.' She pursed the corners of her mouth and held her hands out apologetically in the direction of the pink girl's mother, who inclined her head stiffly. 'Now go and play on the climbing frame, you two. And, Fergus, stop pushing Harry, please.' Rachel, who approached motherhood like a military exercise, was convinced that my son was out to get hers. It was a sort of persecution complex by proxy. Personally, I thought Harry should learn to fight back. Little whiner.

Rachel came and sat down next to me again. She had fresh, young skin, but there were firm lines edging their way down from her mouth and across her forehead. She was one of my new friends, one of the 'playground mums' as Jake called them. The personal criteria for friendship change when you have kids. You don't need to get on too well, or to have that much in common—in some respects, that can get in the way: better to withstand the constant interruptions that children bring to a conversation about recipes than one that really interests you about, oh, I don't know, what did interest me these days? Playground friends take the same role as work friends: someone to gossip with at the photocopier, when half your mind's on something else; someone, anyway, to gang up with against the strain.

I said, 'Oh look, it's Maria.'

Rachel said, 'Oh yes, so it is.'

That's the kind of conversation our sleep-deprived brains stretched to. It wouldn't, now I come to think of it, have lasted two minutes at the photocopier.

'Maria!' I called her over.

'Oh, hiya!' she said. Maria, slim and toned and usually in Lycra from hours in the gym, was several years younger than us and married to a banker. She had two small children and a house the size of a hotel down the road in Wandsworth. 'Ohmigod,' she said, wiping the seat with a muslin that had been hanging off the back of her three-wheel all-terrain mountain buggy, and sitting herself down next to us. 'Another riotous night at Casa Jennings. I'm so hung over. I couldn't tell you how much I drank. God knows what the neighbours think of us. It was supposed to be just a quiet kitchen supper—we had Flossie's godfather and his new girlfriend over. But it ended up with Patrick out in the middle of the road at midnight on Flossie's Micro Scooter. It was hilarious. I was laughing so much I'm sure I woke the whole street.'

'Thursday night,' remarked Rachel. 'I don't know how you do it.'

We both knew how she did it. I said, 'You don't think Merika might be free on Saturday night, do you?' Merika was her au pair, a devastatingly attractive and capable twenty-five-year-old, whom Maria called 'My Slovakian'. Merika was a paediatrician before she came to England, one of many Slovaks putting their qualifications at the mercy of the British middle class.

'Oh,' said Maria, sounding dubious. 'The thing is, I've got people coming over, just a small party, and I was rather hoping that she might help out, passing round the nibbles.'

'What sort of nibbles?' asked Rachel, with genuine interest.

'Oh, I haven't asked . . . we've got this sweet girl coming in to cook—a friend of a friend . . .'

Rachel turned to me. 'I served this delicious hors d'oeuvre last week,' she said. '*Crostini di fegatini di pollo e acciughe*. River Café Two—I do think it's better than River Café One, don't you?'

'Artemis! Octavia! Heel.' A loud voice pealed across the green sward.

'Shit,' I said, under my breath. Rachel elbowed me in the ribs.

It was Lucinda, an investment banker, who, on the rare occasion that she was spotted in the week, did her upmost to undermine the rest of us. More polished, more efficient, more organised, morally, intellectually and financially superior in every way (or so she believed), she was Public Enemy Number One in the battle between mothers-who-work and mothers-who-don't. She towered over us physically too—with the body of a tennis player and the thick, long, springy hair of Medusa. Only Lucinda's hair was never wild—she would never let her hair down—so if she was Medusa, she was Medusa after a visit to Michaeljohn.

'Hiya,' we chorused, as she tied her brace of Highland terriers to the railings and bustled her brood through the gate. Lucinda's children were called Cecily, Gwendolen, Ned and Sid in accordance with a peculiar Morton Park fashion for naming girls after Noël Coward and boys after New York pickle salesmen. All four were delivered by elective Caesarean because she was, as they say, too posh to push.

'Off you go, children—swings. WHAT A DAY!' she said, marching over to the bench. She adjusted the grip of her padded hairband which, on 'family days', replaced the tight chignon she wore to work. 'The Audi wouldn't start. And Cecily was late for ballet and Miss Trisha gets so cross if they're not there for their *barre* exercises. And Ned and Sid had Toddler Massage the other side of Morton and I've been lugging Gwendolen around with me when really she should be at home practising for her violin grade five. Her teacher suggested she skip two to four as she is really very advanced,' she added as an aside. '*And I* should be at work. But Hilda, our nanny, bless her, is in hospital. Honestly, you lot don't know how lucky you are. It's not the work that's so backbreaking, or the childcare, but the *juggling*.'

'Nothing serious, I hope,' I said.

'What?'

'Hilda.'

'Only a perforated appendix, but the fuss she's making. Two months off? Quite absurd. And guess who's paying? Well, anyway, enough of that. I expect she needs the rest. Who doesn't?' She fixed Maria in her sights. 'I haven't got nearly enough help. Your Croatian is super, isn't she?'

Maria began to look helpful and then frowned.

'No poaching,' said Rachel.

'Slovakian,' I added.

'And the house is still in a state after the builders,' said Lucinda, bending down and rubbing a chink of mud from the buckle of her court shoe. 'I don't know what Matty, my cleaner, does all day. Well, that's out-of-work actresses for you. Maybe I should go back to the agency and get someone a bit more committed.'

'To a long-term future in lavatory bowls,' I said.

Lucinda's mobile phone started ringing. As she listened, red blotches of anger appeared beneath her foundation. 'Oh no,' she screamed into her Nokia. 'Gregory, I told you . . . All right, I'll deal with it. OK, OK. Yes, I know. OK. OK.' Pause. 'OK. OK. See you later. OK.' She slipped the phone back into her stiff olive-green Mulberry shoulder bag. 'Ach,' she said. 'This sort of thing never happened when we were in Fulham.'

'What *has* happened?' asked Rachel.

Lucinda closed her eyes, as if the light was hurting, but kept on talking. 'Flower Power were due to come today,', she explained with exaggerated calm, 'to prune the cherry and plant out a few pots for the terrace so that it looks halfway decent for Sunday when Gregory's boss is coming for lunch. And the main woman has rung Gregory to say she can't come today, will Monday do? Well, no, it won't do.'

'What's her excuse?' asked Rachel. 'Stung by a nettle?'

Lucinda ignored her.

'I know a gardener.' Everyone looked taken aback, including me.

Lucinda looked at me directly for the first time.

I pulled the card out of the wallet that the man from the crash had given me. 'Here,' I said.

She looked at it. '"Peat and Dug,"' she read. 'Any good?'

'Someone I bumped into. Seemed very nice. Ask for Pete.'

'Should I mention you?'

'You could do. But he probably wouldn't remember.'

Lucinda jotted down the number and I went off to find Fergus.

It took me a while. He'd broken out of the playground through a vandalised gap in the fence and was poking about in the roots of a tree with a long stick.

'Bang,' he said when he saw me. 'You're dead.'

'I know,' I said. 'But it's also time to go home.'

'NO!' he shouted. 'I DON'T WANT TO GO HOME!' He went rigid and dug his heels in.

'Yes,' I said patiently, trying to undig them with my fingers. Rachel, Maria and Lucinda were looking over at me with pained sympathy. 'Pleeze,' I whispered. He slackened. Sometimes even under-threes respond to desperation. In gratitude, I let him walk all the way home.

When we finally got there, Fran, Jake's sister, was sitting on the doorstep.

'Oh God, I'm so sorry,' I said. 'I had to take the car to be mended and then we walked back by the playground and I completely forgot you were coming.'

She heaved herself up. She was twenty-two weeks pregnant and already into the self-righteous, martyred stage.

'It's all right,' she said in the tone of one for whom it wasn't. 'You're here now.' She fondled her tiny bump, which was on proud display between a crop-top purple vest and a pair of shocking-pink drawstring trousers. 'As soon as I've had a drink I'll feel better.' She sighed and rubbed both hands up and down her lower back.

Fran, who was an interactive artist, had never been one for strict timekeeping, for such conventional notions as appointments and routines—unless you were the one keeping her waiting, in which case punctuality suddenly seemed to rise on her list of priorities. She was twenty-nine, seven years younger than Jake, a much-longed-for second child, a girl at that, and had the kind of looks—a large, vulnerable mouth, deer-like brown eyes, tumbling curls and pale white skin that bruised easily—which made you want to look after her. I loved her and was infuriated by her in equal measure. Her parents just gazed at her most of the time with open mouths. It was as if Fran had gathered up every unconventional gene the Pritons had ever had, and run off with them, carefree in the knowledge that she could do her own thing and no one could stop her. Her own thing had included psychotherapy, aromatherapy, and finally moving in with a fellow artist called Rain. He may not always have been called Rain—his parents lived in Croydon—but Fran accused us of being bourgeois when we asked. They lived in West Kensington in the mansion flat the Pritons once bought for her and Jake to share, but which appeared since to have become wholly hers. She made virtual art on the Internet. Rain . . . well, I'm not quite sure what Rain did. Rain, who was so handsome you wanted to weep, didn't say much.

'How are you feeling, sweetie?' I said. 'And how's Rain?'

'Rain, rain, go away,' said Fergus.

Fran ignored him. 'Just so, so well,' she said, slipping out of her shoes at the door. 'I feel as if the world has just begun to make sense, you know? As if it's been black and white and now it's in colour.'

'Jolly good,' I said, steering her through the house and into the garden. She plonked herself down into a deck chair. Fergus ran off to find his fire engine. I put Dan on a rug on the grass. He immediately made for the borders. I had a few minutes before he found a snail and started eating it. 'Tea or coffee?' I said. 'Or fizzy water?'

'Have you any raspberry leaf?' she asked.

'No.'

'Dandelion? Ginger? Blackcurrant?'

'No, no and no.'

'What about camomile? Surely you've got camomile.'

'I think we're out.'

'Sod it, I'll have coffee,' she said and lit a cigarette. 'Low tar,' she said defensively. 'Nothing in them. Anyway, they're organic.' She took a few deep drags and then twisted it out on the grass and chucked the dead end into the busy Lizzies.

'Fran!' I said.

'Sorry,' she said and rubbed her eyes.

I grabbed Dan by the legs and pulled him away from a daffodil bulb, which he was on the verge of sinking his two rabbity teeth into. I could tell Fergus was all right because I could hear him shout 'Emergency, emergency, fire on the sofa, fire on the sofa,' in the sitting room. I put my arm round her shoulder. 'Are you OK, Fran? You seem a bit down.'

'Sorry,' she said a bit tearfully. 'I've just convinced myself I've had a missed abortion. It's just that it's been a while since I felt the baby move. And I was reading last night about detached placentas. And I'm sure I felt a sharp pain when I was waiting on your step. So it could be that. I just don't feel that things are right.'

I laughed. That may sound like an unsympathetic response, but one of Fran's more touching characteristics was incorrigible hypochondria. I'd had four months of this, of early pre-eclampsia, of threatened toxoplasmosis, of blighted ova. She looked at me through watery eyes. 'Why are you laughing?' she said in a little voice.

'Fran, there's nothing wrong with you. Or the baby. You've had your scan. When did you last feel a movement?'

'At breakfast?'

'Well then, the little mite's obviously having a kip. I'll get you some orange juice and we'll wake him or her up. How about that?'

I put my finger under her chin, but her eyes had filled again. 'Fran?'

'Oh God, I know you don't get any sleep either, but I'm just so tired, you know? And . . . and . . .'

'What?' I said.

'I've got piles,' she whispered.

'Poor you,' I said with genuine sympathy. 'I know. It's all awful. It's an awful business. But it's worth it in the end.'

'Is it?' She looked at me keenly. 'Oh God, I don't know. I suddenly feel really scared. I feel like I've been invaded. And I feel so fat. And I'm desperate to smoke all the time. Typical, the one time when you really need a fag it's the worst thing for you. And I don't know if I'm going to be able to cope. And . . . I mean, Maggie, do you ever look around yourself and think how have I got here? Where has my life gone?'

'Oh God,' I said, straightening up. 'Don't go down there.'

Luckily Fergus came into the garden then, clutching a packet of frozen dinosaur nuggets. I could hear the deep-freeze alarm beeping. Fergus said, 'There's a fire in the freezer, but I got the animals out.'

'Well done, you,' I said, taking them back off him Dan had crawled off to the steps and was about to plunge down head first. 'Actually,' I said, going after him and then returning the ice-age pterodactyls to the kitchen, 'it's not the big things I miss so much, the freedom and the independence . . . as being able to finish a sentence without interruption, have a proper conversation now and again.'

'Sorry?' said Fran. She'd been too busy wresting her packet of cigarettes from Fergus to hear me.

'Doesn't matter,' I said. 'Now, guess who I saw yesterday? Claire Masterson. Do you remember, my year at school?'

'God, yes. Wasn't she always going off with everyone's boyfriends?'

'Ye-es,' I said doubtfully. 'Anyway, she's invited us to a party. Tomorrow night.' I paused.

'And?'

'And I don't suppose you could baby-sit? All my regulars have gone AWOL. Good practice . . .'

She cast her eyes at Fergus and Dan. Fergus was on top of Dan, trying to chew his ear off. 'All right,' she said. I almost fainted.

'Good,' I said. 'Good,' I said again, before she could change her mind. 'Thanks.'

Before she went, Fran came upstairs to find me something to wear. I left Fergus in front of *Thomas the Tank Engine*, and Fran held Dan while I flicked self-consciously along the hangers in my rickety pine wardrobe. She said: 'You can't wear that!' and 'What the hell is that?' and 'Doubt you'll get into that,' and 'Hm. Thought not.'

'It's all too black and middle-aged in here,' she said. 'You need something with colour. Haven't you got an old nightie and a little cardie?'

'I've got an old nightie,' I said, producing it.

'Not that old,' she said grimacing.

'This is hopeless.' She put Dan onto the floor and picked up my dog-eared FCUK Buy Mail catalogue. 'Oh, what about this?' She held up the page with the White Sprinkle Sequin Dress. I loved that dress. It had tiny straps beneath the model's tumbling auburn locks and was about four inches long. It probably would have fitted me—three years earlier.

I wrinkled up my nose. 'Dry-clean only,' I said.

Fran looked bored. 'Oh, right.'

I turned back to my cupboard. Dan had started pulling out the shoes from the shoe rack: one of Jake's old loafers; several pairs of grey-white plimsolls; a red suede stiletto!

'What about this?' I said, holding it aloft like Cinderella's prince, spinning it round on the top of my finger. 'Would this jazz something up?'

Fran laughed. '"Jazz"?' she said. 'Oh, Maggie. This is what I'm worried about. Am I going to start talking about "jazzing things up"? Am I going to have a wardrobe full of yesterday's clothes? It's fine for you, you're Maggie. But does motherhood automatically mean letting yourself go?'

I was smiling at her, but I could feel the blood draining from my face and then flood back into all the wrong places. It was throbbing under my eyes. My throat suddenly felt tight. I had to keep smiling or I would cry.

'I don't know,' I said, still smiling. 'I suppose it, well, I mean it . . . it depends on . . .' I couldn't seem to get the words out.

'Oh God. Have I upset you?' She got up and put her hands on my shoulders. 'Oh sorry. I didn't mean to. Was it very tactless? I didn't think you minded about things like that. It's the inside that counts. And you're so relaxed with things and people love you for it. Jake, I know, loves you for it.'

I turned away and picked up Dan, who had emptied the shoe rack now and had started on Jake's ties. When I stood up, I was standing by the mirror and I turned to give myself a long look. It was like catching my face in a Tube window. I knew I was going through a dowdy phase—it's a *time* thing as much as anything—but I saw my face properly for the first time in ages. There it was: distorted and flattened, with hard angles for cheeks and dark rings where the eyes should be, as if all the old bad points were accentuated, all the good ones dissolved. This wasn't a phase. This was how I looked, middle-aged. I said, quietly, 'Yes, well, I wouldn't know, because he's hardly ever here.'

Fran had diverted her attention back to the clothes on the bed. She was holding a pair of black leggings against her bump. She said, 'Oh, that reminds me. Tell him I saw him last night. I yelled at him from the car, but he didn't see me. He was too busy yakking. Can I borrow these? They look blissfully comfy.'

I turned. 'Who was he yakking with?'

'Oh, just some girl.' She chucked the leggings back on the bed, stretched and whirled her hands around above her head—a pregnant ballerina. 'So can I have them?' She looked at her watch. 'Oh shit.

Better go. I've got prenatal yoga. Bugger, I meant to buy some almond oil to massage my perineum.'

'The little touch that means so much,' I said.

'What?'

'Nothing,' I said. 'Of course you can borrow them. They're probably too tight for me anyway.'

At the door, she said, 'Sorry if . . .' and I said, 'Doesn't matter. Thanks for baby-sitting tomorrow.' And she said, 'Give my love to Jake,' and I said, 'I will if I see him.' And we both laughed. So everything was all right then.

I was bathing the children when Jake got home. He came straight upstairs, hollering, 'Where's my family!' like a hungry monster, and made Fergus laugh so much he went under the water. While I was fishing him up, Jake came up behind me and kissed me on the neck.

'You're early,' I said, putting my arms back to keep him there.

'I bunked off,' he said. For a moment, he buried his nose in my hair, but then he was tickling Fergus and hauling him out of the bath and chasing him, squawking and shrieking and wet, up the stairs and round our bedroom and over our bed and got him so overexcited I couldn't get him to sleep for hours.

chapter four

SATURDAY STARTED EARLY. It was 5.30am when Fergus began hollering for his breakfast in the other room and then, a few minutes later, in my ear.

'Whose turn is it?' Jake muttered.

'Yours,' I said, but he didn't move. I got up with big exaggerated getting-up noises and left the door open on the way out, which was code for 'I'm happy for you to carry on sleeping if you can bear to do so through the guilt'. Nobody ever warns you about the guilt quota in family relationships.

'Shut the door!' yelled Jake after me, which was code for 'Shut the door'.

I took Fergus down to the kitchen, where he played on the floor, driving his Matchbox cars along the ridges between the tiles while I emptied the dishwasher. I loved my house in the early morning. It felt cool and clean and monastic without the toys out and papers everywhere. The kitchen was small—I'd never wanted to waste garden by filling in the side return like all the other newcomers in our street—so it had windows on two sides and on June mornings like this the sun slipped in, past the pots on the sill, still sleepy, not bright enough yet to glare accusingly at the egg-stains on the table or the crayon on the walls, but strong enough to throw the creamy whiteness of the walls into relief and send geranium shadows dancing up the cabinets.

It was almost nine when Jake stumbled down the stairs with Dan in his arms. Fergus and I were watching Saturday-morning telly by then, curled up around each other on the sofa, and while half my mind had been actively following Buzz Lightyear's conflict with Evil Zurg, the other half had been worrying away at 'things', picking at them like fingers on a spot. The previous evening Jake and I had had what we called a QNI (a Quiet Night In), but this one had been even quieter than usual. Jake had seemed preoccupied once the children were asleep, and we had eaten and cleared up in silence. He'd gone to bed early, leaving me in front of *Frasier*, so I hadn't told him about Fran seeing him with 'a girl'. I hadn't asked him who she was. I hadn't made a joke of it, got to the bottom of it, as I would have done a few months before. A few months before I would never have believed it for an instant. But now? I didn't know what I thought. I just felt uneasy and distant. I hadn't, now I came to think of it, even told him that Fran had agreed to baby-sit tonight.

'Oh hello,' I said when he came in. 'By the way, the good news is Fran says she'll baby-sit tonight.'

He looked bemused. He frowned. He handed me Dan, who snuggled into my neck. 'Why?' he said.

'So we can go to Claire's party.'

He groaned. 'Oh God. We're not really going, are we?'

'We have to,' I said firmly. Then more weakly, 'I said we would.'

Jake was walking round the room with Fergus standing on his feet, like human stilts. He sighed heavily, and put Fergus back on the sofa. 'I'd better go and have a shower now then.'

It was only an excuse, of course. Like, 'Just popping out to get the papers', or 'I've just got to get this off in the post'; 'having to have' a shower is one of the few times you ever get to have any time to yourself when you have small children.

So Jake had his shower—a long shower; you could have cleaned the Statue of Liberty with a toothbrush in the time it took him to wash—and Fergus and Dan and I sat on the kitchen floor and studied the ants. Children are the gods of small things. When I was little, I was always finding dying fledglings in the garden. I'd make a bed for them in an old plastic breadbin and bring them milk and worms. And then I'd rush home from school, and up the stairs and into my bedroom to see them . . . and, well, usually my mother had discreetly cleared them away by then. Or I'd find money on the pavement, or stag beetles in the gutter, or powder-blue blackbirds' eggs cracked open on the grass: objects you never find when you're grown up. You have to be a mother for your nose to be brought back to the ground.

The ants in our kitchen knew they were on to a winner. No Nippon in this house. Far too toxic. Over previous days, Fergus and I had studied their advance on the kitchen cupboard: one, two, three, up the cabinet, into the jam. At the moment, they were marching in a line from the back door across the tiles to a hole in the skirting.

'Is that their house?' Fergus asked.

'Maybe,' I said. 'Or maybe they live in the garden and they just come here to shop.'

'They're busy,' said Fergus. 'Aren't they?'

'Busy doing nothing,' I said. 'They are amazing things ants. The industry, the organisation. Did you know that when—'

'OH, MUMMY!' Fergus cried. 'Dan's eating them!'

The phone rang just then—in time to divert a crisis. It was Angela, Jake's mother. I told her Jake was in the shower, but she was quite happy to talk to me—as long as the subject was Jake. Like many women I knew, I had taken on the role of mediator between my cohabitee and his parents, a domestic hostage negotiator. I was the one who remembered birthdays and anniversaries, who made interested enquiries about the garden and the Nile cruise. I was the one who cooked Sunday lunch and kept them up to date with their son's career advancements. Angela babied her only son and we all colluded in it. Only sometimes did I let it irritate me. After I'd put the phone down, promising he'd ring her when he was dry, I rang Mel.

'What are you doing?' I said. 'Why don't you bring Milly round to play?'

'I would, but I've got a half-leg, an underarm and a bikini at eleven.'

'Well, come after. Isn't the bikini ag?'

'Absolute ag but not as ag as the underarm which is major ag. I'll ask

Milly. MILLY! Do you want to go and play with Fergus?'

Fergus was jumping up and down next to me trying to grab the receiver. 'What do you want?' I said.

'Can she bring her guns?' he hissed into my ear.

Mel came back on the line. She said they'd come for lunch. I told her to come armed.

Jake clumped down the stairs then, looking spruce. 'Hello, gorgeous,' he said happily, and unstringing the belt of my dressing gown.

'Hey,' I said. We kissed—a brief moment of happy families: parents united, baby frolicking on the carpet, toddler busy with a box of matches, before Fergus jumped on Dan and the usual mayhem broke out, everybody shouting and yelling and trying to kill each other. Jake didn't look so happy after that. I was still feeling disgruntled.

'Ring your mother,' I said. 'You never ring your mother.'

Mel and Milly arrived at midday. Milly and Fergus threw themselves into each other's arms, and ran upstairs giggling. Mel said, patting Jake's stomach through his shirt, 'What's this?'

'Oh no,' he said, anguished.

'It's all right,' she teased. 'It's nice. Makes you look cuddly.'

'I don't want to look cuddly,' he said.

'All right then: *commanding*.'

'That's better,' he said. 'How's Piers?'

'Don't.'

'Poor Piers,' I called from the kitchen where I was making coffee.

'Poor Piers nothing,' called out Jake. 'He can always get out if he wants to. He doesn't have to stay with her.'

'I know,' I said, coming back in with the cafetiere and a packet of chocolate digestives. 'It's just . . . '

'Excuse me,' said Mel from the sofa where she had put her legs up. 'It's my love life you're discussing, if you don't mind. I am in the room.'

'Well?' said Jake. 'How is it?'

Mel sighed. 'Uninspiring. He's sweet, but . . . there's no spark.'

I handed her a coffee. 'Sex?'

'Yes, please, but no sugar.'

'Ha-ha.'

'Darling,' she camped. 'He's an anaesthetist. It passes in a blur. I count to ten and when I wake up it's all over. Completely painless.'

Jake said, anguished, 'Oh no, I can't bear it. The thought of anyone talking about me like this . . .' He got up from his chair. 'I've got to go and do some work anyway.' He mussed Mel's hair. 'Staying for lunch?' She nodded. 'Good. See you in a bit.'

After he'd gone, Mel and I went into the kitchen. She took Dan on her knee while I defrosted a quiche, and told me about this man who'd come into the surgery the day before, particularly requesting her, and how he'd stood shyly in the doorway, hands in his pockets, a bit greasy looking but otherwise harmless, and told her how he had a problem 'down there'. 'So I said I'd do an examination and a funny look came over his face and he dropped his trousers and shrieked, "It goes all hard, it goes all hard," and started cackling with laughter. I had to push him out of my room. Apparently he's done it to all the women doctors, just no one had warned me!' I laughed with her at this, but maybe I stopped too soon, because she said, 'Are you all right?'

I said, turning away from her and looking out of the window, 'What would you say if someone told you they'd seen Jake with a girl?'

Mel said, 'What?'

I turned back. 'A girl.'

'Doing what?'

'I don't know. Yakking.'

'Who told you this?' She was looking at me as if I was mad.

'Fran. She said she saw him. He told me he was with Ed.'

'Well, I'd say you or Fran needed your head examining. Why would Jake see a girl? He's got you. Or if he did, it was probably someone from work. Why don't you ask him?'

'I can't bear to.' I sat down next to her. 'In case it's true.'

'Oh, Maggie. How could it be? He loves you. You're the best couple I know.' She looked into my face. 'You've got no reason to—'

'I don't know, Mel.' I cleared the papers on the table into a pile, sorted Jake's post from mine. 'Things aren't great at the moment. He's distant, disengaged. I thought relationships were supposed to get easier. But they don't. Everything speeds up and intensifies. Things that used to take weeks now happen in a day. One minute we seem to love each other, and the next we seem to hate each other. Honestly, I really do hate him sometimes. It's frightening. And then I love him again and it happens so fast. It's so changeable.' I stood up. 'Like the English weather.'

Mel said, 'Well, in my experience, these feelings are easily solved.'

'How?' I'd opened the fridge and was spooning puréed carrots into a bowl of leftover rice for Dan.

'A good shag's what you need. Clears the air like a thunderstorm.'

I gave her a rueful look. 'Yes, well, easier said than done.'

'Oh dear.' She grimaced.

I took Dan off her knee and, plonking him in his highchair, began coaxing purée into his mouth. I looked at the door and back again and hissed, 'And it's not like him.'

'Oh dear.'

'So something's up,' I whispered.

'Maybe it's just a phase?' she suggested.

'Yes, or maybe it's me.' I gave up on Dan, who didn't seem hungry or certainly not hungry for puréed carrots. 'Maybe he just doesn't fancy me any more.' I wiped Dan's mouth and hands with his bib. 'Or maybe this is always what happens after a bit. Maybe it takes two years or five or ten, but finally you can't summon it up any more. I mean'—I got up to find Dan a hunk of bread—'do you think you can ever go back to the days when every pore seems to tingle and you can't wait to tear their clothes off? When sex really is preferable to a good book? Do you think it's a choice between that and settling down? Can you ever have both?'

'I haven't got either,' said Mel, laughing.

'I know but—'

'Maggie. It'll be fine. You're just stuck in a rut. My sister Siobhan felt just the same when her children were this little. You just need something to get you out of it. What about this party tonight? Why don't you dress up? Make yourself feel like a proper woman again.'

'I do feel like a proper woman.'

'Exactly,' she said darkly. 'Too proper.'

I wanted to ask her more, seek more reassurance, but instead I got up and handed her the cutlery. 'I wonder what you'd think of Claire,' I said.

'Would I like her?' Mel started to lay the table.

I reached up to get the plates from the cupboard. 'I don't know.' I put them down and then leaned for a moment against a chair. 'She's quite high maintenance and she doesn't let you get a word in edgeways. But she's . . . remarkable really. She has this glamorous life and she's funny and successful and she's got nice clothes.'

'Oh well, if she's got nice clothes.'

'She's definitely got nice clothes.'

'Are you a teensy bit jealous?'

The microwave pinged. 'LUNCH!' I yelled up the stairs. 'Of course not,' I said. 'With a life as glamorous as mine? Of course not.'

After we'd eaten, Mel and I and the children went over the common to laugh at the weekend dads. It was one of our regular pleasures. There was a whole different scene in the park at weekends. There were two types of weekend dad. Type one: the lawyers and City men, shiny black shoes poking under their razor-sharp jeans, crisp work collars folded like envelope flaps over 'fun' holiday jumpers, white-lipped and dazed by the limitless potential for wildness and disagreeableness of children they had only seen flush-cheeked against a pillow all week. Then there was type two. Maybe they worked in the music business or film; either way, they were at home in their weekend Timberlands (laces undone), their plaid shirts and Ralph Laurens. They were *so* busy showing you how they could squeeze a week's worth of 'quality time' into forty-eight hours, chasing their children around the playground—crazy people, crazy guys—they almost forgot to keep an eye on their Micro Scooters or their expensive mountain bikes. There were a couple at it today, playing crocodile tag for, oh, at least five minutes before two of their children clonked their heads and another crashed into a brown labrador and everybody left in tears.

'It's enough to put you off family life for good,' said Mel, as we sat together on the metal fence round the swings, legs dangling.

I didn't answer. I was too busy watching two people further away under the trees, lying on their stomachs on a rug, with the papers spread out around them and a bottle of wine on the grass. Their ankles were entwined.

'All right?' said Mel.

'Yup, fine,' I said. 'Let's go.'

When we got home we had tea and cake. *Homemade* cake. Banana and walnut, to be accurate. I could hardly be trusted with a stew, but I was fine with a sponge. You have to be if you don't work, otherwise people don't understand what you do all day. When Working Mothers talk about their guilt, it's always bringing Mr Kipling to the school fête they mention first. The humiliation of that, or the misery of being up at midnight creaming eggs. As if it really mattered. It must be a conspiracy between the PTA and husbands whose mothers were always baking. You could write a thesis on the subject. Cake: its Role in Family Politics.

'Hm,' said Mel. 'Very moist.'

'I want a chocolate cake,' said Fergus. 'One of those shiny purple ones.' You see, children prefer Mr Kipling's mini-rolls anyway.

I had just cut a slice for myself when Jake came in, yawning, leaned over me and picked it up clumsily for himself. Half of it fell on the floor before he got it to his mouth.

'Jake,' I admonished. 'That was mine. Anyway, what happened to the packet of chocolate biscuits? They've all gone.'

'Funny you should say that,' said Jake, putting his hand to his forehead and waving his head around woozily. 'I was just making myself a cup of coffee earlier and suddenly—brwwwwww, I woke up and I was on the floor and there were crumbs all over my face.'

Mel laughed. She hadn't heard it as many times as I had. She picked the slice off the floor, put it on a plate and handed it to him. 'Bit of cake won't hurt anyone,' she said.

chapter five

JAKE BECAME QUIET after Mel and Milly left. It was as if they took all his energy with them, as if they switched the light off when they went.

'Do we have to go to this party?' said Jake behind me, as I pushed Alpha-bites around in the frying pan for the children's supper. 'We won't know anyone. And anyway, what about our curry?' Saturday was, traditionally, takeaway night in our house.

'OK.' I turned abruptly, fish slice dripping fat onto the floor tiles. 'Let's stay in like we always do and wallow in biryani instead.'

Jake held out his hands and turned. 'Fine, fine, fine. We're going. Forget I said anything.'

Which is how it was left until there we were at 9.15pm, scrubbed and stilettoed (well, I was stilettoed), on the steps of Claire's house. 'Let's not go,' I said suddenly. 'Let's go and have a meal instead.'

'WHAT?' mouthed Jake in a silent shout.

'I'm nervous,' I said. 'We won't know anyone.'

'Oh behave,' he said. 'We're here now and we're going in.'

The buzzer went, Jake pushed the door open and we passed through to another open door. And there was Claire. She was dressed in an aquamarine curve-clinging frock, with a thick band of darker green velvet round the hem and tiny, sequinned straps over her shoulders. 'Beautiful dress, Claire,' I gasped.

She wrinkled up her nose. 'I bought it in America,' she said. Her blonde hair was piled up high, tendrils tumbling around her ears, and she was either wearing a very clever bra or her breasts had magical floating properties. Most of them were bobbing above her dress. They looked new to me. I wondered if she'd bought them in America too.

'Gosh, hello,' mumbled Jake. 'Long time no see.'

'Jake!' she said. 'How lovely that you've come. Maggie too. And how nice that some of my married friends have made it. All the others have cancelled.'

'Children?' I said.

'No: wives,' she said, winking at me over her shoulder as she threaded her arm through Jake's. 'Now, come in, you handsome man, and meet some people.'

She took us, or him—me tripping along behind, feeling clumsy in my heels—into a wide, empty drawing room where a waiter handed us a glass of kir. You could see the sun floating low over the common through the floor-to-ceiling windows, throwing pinkish-gold light across the bare floor and up faded green walls.

'Everyone's in the garden,' said Claire, and led us through some French windows to the top of a wrought-iron spiral staircase below which, in a dusky grotto of urns and figurines and sculpted box trees, a small throng milled and swayed, cigarette ends glowing. 'I hope you're not going to find it all horribly media,' she said, waving to a chap with a bald head behind a bay. 'Political editor of the *Indy*,' she said, 'married to Sue Batsby on the *Mail*. Darling.' She broke off to kiss a young man with sideburns the shape and size of New Zealand. 'How's life on "Culture"? Oh, I know, they're all absolute philistines . . .' She was still gripping Jake tightly by the arm. He was smiling inanely. She said, 'Remind me what you do again, Jake.'

'I'm in advertising,' he said patiently.

'Ah, you must meet Omar,' she said. 'He writes "Back in five" in *G2*.'

She pulled Jake away behind a mossy angel but, before I'd quite finished sinking to the ground in horror, was back. 'Now, Maggers,' she said. 'Who shall I get for you? Now . . . there's Pooley who edits my copy at *The Times*, but looks a bit tied up at the moment . . . Ah—' She put out her hand and grabbed a woman with plastic pansies in her hair. 'Katya, Katters, quick, meet my oldest, oldest friend in the world. Katya does "Talk of the Town" for the *New Yorker*. She's also studying at Columbia for her doctorate in comparative literature. And Maggie . . .' she broke off and then resumed an octave higher, 'isamum!'

Katya, who looked about twenty-five, stared at me wonderingly, and then at the departing back of Claire reproachfully. 'Hi,' she said kindly.

'Hello,' I said. And then, 'Sorry, you don't have to talk to me if you don't want to,' which was the worst thing I could have said because of course it meant after that she did. She was very nice. She made a good fist of it. She asked me lots of questions about my children's ages (one probably would have sufficed) and was sweetly generous in the information she was happy to impart about life in the Big Apple (I must remember to try Cello at 53 E 77th Street next time I'm there). But I knew she was desperate to get off, so after a while I said, 'Oh, your glass is empty,' and she caved in with relief and disappeared.

After she'd gone, I scanned the crowd for Jake and could just about make out his top half through a clash of bodies. He appeared to have taken off his jacket. He was bending down to hear someone over the hubbub and was laughing. I was just about to go over to him when someone next to me said, 'Any chance of another kir?'

'Sorry?'

'A KIR,' the man said, as if I was deaf or mad. 'Are you serving or not?'

'Not,' I said.

'Oo, I'm sorry.' He turned and giggled with the woman next to him.

I sat down on the step. My toes had begun to hurt. I was wearing a short-sleeved white linen shirt, which looked like the kind of jacket worn by milkmen and which I only ever wore because it had been expensive, a short, black chiffon skirt which I'd thought made me look quite sexy but which I now realised was an inch too short, and black tights because I hadn't had a chance in the end to shave. Twenty denier. None of the other women here had sullied their brown legs with anything as tacky as nylon. Or as dull as black. Nobody else had dressed like a waitress. Not even the waitresses.

Jake was nowhere to be seen now. Nor was Claire. I looked idly for Rowena, her actress sister, but I didn't see her either. I felt beached. It had been so long, I'd forgotten how parties could make you feel like that—sometimes they pick you up and roar and crash about your ears and carry you along with them, but most often they just leave you stranded.

'Angel on horseback?' said a voice above me. It was a waitress, a waitress in hot-pink chiffon, bearing a tray.

'No, thanks.'

'What about a devil then?'

'Do you have something in between?' I said, but she didn't smile.

I stood up. I ought to find Jake and check he wasn't having too awful a time. I should never have made him come. It was mean of me to have insisted. We should leave, find some quiet restaurant, our local Indian maybe, in which to sit and be ourselves, to sort things out between us. I manipulated my way through the scrum, thicker now, louder now the band—salsa—had struck up in the drawing room, until I reached the place where I thought I'd spotted him before. He wasn't there. I grabbed a glass of Perrier from a passing tray and navigated a path through some more jostling bodies ('Soho House,' they were all saying, 'Oh yes, The Ivy, Babington') until I got to the bottom of the garden. He wasn't there either. I sat on a wall, took off my shoes and fiddled with the feet of my tights, unpicking the net at the toes. After a while, I thought I might as well go to the loo, the last resort of the socially desperate.

I had made my way halfway back when I realised there were a few people in the drawing room now. It was dark and the room stood out like a magic lantern. Two or three couples were dancing to the music, holding hands and coming together and apart again, rubbing hips and rocking shoulders. Up close they probably looked self-conscious, but from a distance, up there in the candlelight in that big empty room, they looked enchanted, like inhabitants of some suburban *Grand Meaulnes*. I was almost at the steps when I realised that one of the men, the one holding his partner's hand above his head and spinning her round in an enclosed circle of his own making, his mouth open, laughing, was Jake. And then I realised that the girl was Claire.

My first thought was surprised pleasure. Jake danced so rarely in these days, so rarely let himself go. And he looked young and free and handsome, twirling Claire and her green dress around. For a moment I reflected on how cool, how together he looked. He had always been a good dancer. And then I felt dizzy with something less charitable, with the sense that I was lost and alone and socially inept, and he was up there, part of it all, part of the party. And even though I recognised it as self-pity it didn't make it any easier when I thought: When was the last time he danced with me?

I had stopped on the spiral staircase, one foot on the first step. In the next moment I would, I think, have continued up—gone to join him, make a joke to Claire and cut in—but in that moment a small middle-aged man with straggly grey hair and a pregnant paunch under his camel V-neck started coming down, feet tumbling after each other in an erratic manner, so I had to jump quickly back down into the garden to get out of his way. I backed into a tub of marguerites to let him pass. But he didn't. He lurched towards me, using his girth to block my escape. I said brightly, 'I'm just on my way up.' He swayed precariously, and grabbed my arm to steady himself.

'D' I know you?'

'No,' I said, manoeuvring halfway round him. 'You don't.'

'S' what's a pretty girl like you doing on their own?'

'I'm not on my own,' I said, trying to sound upbeat and relaxed with his drunkenness, and trying not to sound censorious, which was how I was really feeling. 'I'm on my way up to see my husband.'

'Waste of time: marriage,' he said, suddenly vicious, kicking a private wound. He let go of my arm then and the loss of security sent him reeling. He grabbed the wrought-iron banister. Red wine spilled from his glass onto my stilettos. That would jazz them up.

I said, caught now, 'Have we perhaps had a drop too many?'

'You mean, am I drunk? Yes I am.' He bent his head towards me. His face was all twisted. I could see the hairs lurking in his nostrils. I thought for a moment that he was going to kiss me, so I put my hands out and was about to push him off when a man came up behind me and propelled the drunk gently down onto the step.

The drunk looked up at the newcomer and said, 'Fuck off.'

'Hey. No need to be like that. Maybe you should be going? Shall I get you a cab?'

'I' sfine. Got the car.'

'Okey-dokey. I'll just go and find our hostess, shall I?' The man straightened up and for the first time he looked at me and with a shock of recognition I saw who it was. It was the gardener from the crash. My gardener. *Mel's* gardener. 'Hello,' he said, squinting as if he couldn't quite place me.

'Maggie,' I said. 'The meter maid. From the crash,' I added.

His face relaxed. 'Oh yeah.' He put out his hand. 'Pete. Pete Russ.' He had had a haircut since I'd last seen him and his head now looked like a recently sheared sheep, and he was smartly dressed in an ash-grey linen suit, but he still looked out of place in this company, a footballer in his interview-best, a cat among the pigeons, a fox among the hens.

'I remember,' I said, taking his hand. 'But what are you doing here?'

'I live here,' he said flatly.

'Oh, with Claire,' I said, suddenly understanding. Bad luck for Mel: he was taken.

'Claire, Claire, the moment I met you I swear,' droned my friend on the steps, his chin now sagging onto his chest.

'No, downstairs. The basement.' He gestured to a dingy barred window abutting the ground. 'With my partner. Look, I'd just better go and call matey here a cab. I'll be back in a sec.'

He jumped over the man, leapt up the steps two at a time, and disappeared into Claire's drawing room. I waited, crocheting my fingers in and out of the cast-iron railings, not sure whether to leave, wondering if I was supposed to be standing guard over the now almost comatose drunk at my feet. A minute or two later, though, Pete was back, this time with Claire. She said, 'Ooh dear. What have we here? Oh shit, Cyril. Why do you always do this?' She turned to me and added, 'I knew I shouldn't have invited him. He always gets pissed.'

'Has he got far to get home?' I said.

'No, since his divorce the poor sod lives in Tooting.'

'A fate indeed,' I said.

She and Pete heaved him to the top of the steps, where they stood in conference for a while, and then Claire took Cyril off into the house.

Pete came back down the stairs. 'Hello again,' he said, smiling.

'Hello.'

'Are you all right? I mean, after the . . . You know. I almost thought I should ring and check you were OK. You looked a bit shaken up.'

'I'm fine,' I said. 'And God, I'm so sorry. It was so totally my fault and your van and—'

He made a noise with his teeth. 'Aw, it's nothing. The garage could bang it out in a jiffy. No worries.' He bent to study the pot of marguerites next to him. Cyril had squashed some of the flowers, and now Pete snapped the damaged stems off with his fingers.

'You look like you know what you're doing,' I said.

He patted down the compost at the base of the daisies and straightened up. 'Oh yes. Gentle but firm. That's how you treat women and plants.' He gave me a teasing look.

'I wouldn't know about that.' I looked away and scanned the party. 'So, anyway, which one's your partner. The lucky lady who likes it gentle but firm.'

'Partner?'

'You said you lived with your partner.'

'Oh, partner. No, no, not that kind of partner. Lloyd. My partner's called Lloyd.'

'Oh I *see*,' I said.

'No, not like that.' Pete looked amused. 'My business partner. Lloyd.'

'Oh, I see,' I said again. 'As in Doug?'

'What?'

'Nothing.'

'Look . . . er . . .'

'Maggie.'

'Yes, of course. Look, Maggie. I'm parched. Want to find a drink?'

I looked around me. I looked up into the sitting room. There was no sign of Jake or Claire now. I hesitated, then I said, 'Yes, all right.'

We worked our way back through the throng. Pete walked ahead of me, moving with his arms at an angle to his body, as if his muscles got in the way of smart clothes. He stopped at a table at the far end of the garden with an abandoned tray of drinks on it. 'There you go,' he said, handing me a glass. It was half full of red wine, but had a smudge of lip-stick on the side. 'Get that inside you. You look as if you need it.'

'I do,' I said, taking a sip.

'Are you not having a good time?' There was concern in his voice.

'Well, there was someone who thought I was a waitress, and then I thought that man was going to be sick on me, but apart from that—'

'A waitress?' he laughed. There was a scar under one of his eyes and little dimples above each side of his mouth, as if someone had prodded him with a Biro. 'You mean you're the hired help?'

'Like you,' I said.

'Like me,' he said, and grinned as if I'd said something very funny.

'Do you do Claire's garden? It's very nice.'

'I looked after it for her grandmother, yeah. Not recently. She was a nice lady. That was very sad.' He looked down at his hands.

'Her dying you mean?'

'Yeah.'

'Yes, it was,' I said. There was a silence as we both contemplated the passing of Claire's elderly relative. 'Though, um . . .' I felt a giggle rise in my throat. 'Actually, I never met her.'

'Oh.' He started laughing too. Then he nudged me with his elbow, then he nudged me again so that I spilt a tiny bit of my drink.

'Hey!' I said.

'Sorry.' He was grinning. Then he said, 'It's nice to hear you laugh. You don't mind me saying this but you look a bit . . . tense?'

'That's just life with small children,' I said. 'And I'm having a bad week. Crashed into someone's car the other day . . .'

He raised his eyes to the sky and then back to me. 'How old are they, your kids?' Unlike Katya, Pete looked genuinely interested.

'Fergus is two and a half, Dan's seven months.'

He puffed out his cheeks. 'That's close. My sister's got kids. And she can hardly get out of the house. It can be rough, can't it?'

'Yes, it can,' I said. 'I mean, I love them and everything—'

'My sister's kids are great, but, you know, they're pretty full on. But she does a smashing job and, um, well, I'm sure you do too.'

'I don't know about that,' I said.

'Hey. You shouldn't beat yourself up.'

'I know, I know.' I wanted to change the subject. For some reason, I suddenly felt like crying. I pulled myself together. 'Anyway, hey, here I am: at a party! Who's complaining?'

He was still looking at me with a concerned expression. Then I remembered Lucinda and I told him about giving his number out and he said she'd already been in touch and had a lot of work for him. 'Which,' he said, 'I really appreciate. Thanks.' I told him it was the least I could do after our little prang. He laughed and, raising one eyebrow, he said, 'And what would be the most?'

'What would be the most what?' I said.

The corners of his mouth were twitching. He was giving me a look. 'What would be the most you could do?'

Was he flirting? Or was he one of those men who was so aware of the effect of his looks that he was always like this? Either way, my cheeks tingled. It had been a long time since anyone had talked to me like that. Or had looked at me in that way. It was not how things were supposed to be conducted, but I felt a flicker of something inside. Afterwards, I imagined myself saying enigmatically: 'Less is more.' But, of course, at the time I didn't say that. I said dumbly, 'I don't know.'

And then he said, 'Do you want to dance?'

I thought about it for a moment, but then I thought about Jake so I shook my head. 'Actually, I'd better go,' I said. I put down my glass. 'Got to find someone.' I rubbed my hands together and then did a sort of half clap. 'So, um, bye. Maybe we'll bump into each other again.'

'Not if I see you indicating,' he said very cheerily.

343

I turned my back on him and went up the spiral staircase and into the drawing room. I stood there for a bit, getting my breath back, stopping my head from spinning. That's a kir on an empty stomach for you. I should have had an angel or a devil—one or the other.

There were lots of people dancing now. Jake wasn't one of them. He was leaning against a wall with a group of people having a whale of a time. Spouting with laughter.

'Sorry to interrupt,' I said, 'but I think we ought to be leaving. Baby sitter . . .' I added. The people he was with smiled at me politely. 'Righty-ho,' he said, though, as I stood there like a teacher waiting for home-work, it took a good ten minutes to extricate himself from what had clearly been a fascinating and side-splittingly amusing conversation about ABCs, and it was a further twenty minutes before he'd said good-bye to all the people who needed saying goodbye to and we were out on the street.

'That wasn't so bad after all,' he said, balancing, one foot in front of the other, on the edge of the kerb, arms bent from the elbow on each side, surfing an imaginary wave. He toppled and jumped across the pavement. 'I actually quite enjoyed myself.'

'So I can see,' I said, turning for a moment to look back at the house.

July
wasps
chapter six

YOU SEE A LOT OF PEOPLE you recognise in the street when you walk about, pushing small children in a buggy. I stared through most of them as if I'd never seen them before, or as if they'd never seen me. There were some familiar faces that I knew and said hello to, but there were others that for some unfathomable reason I blanked. I did it at school too. There was my clan, the Claire Masterson clan, and we'd fall on each other in the morning as if we hadn't been on the phone until 9.00pm the night before, but there were other girls who wouldn't even merit a smile. Perhaps it's a tribal thing, a class thing, or a city thing; certainly none of those people ever smiled back, or perhaps it was particular to me. My life was just fine, thanks. I had just what I needed. And I didn't need anything, or anybody, to muck it up.

But that all changed after Claire's party. It rained all day Sunday and Monday and it was so cold in the house I almost put the heating on. But on Tuesday the sun came out. It felt hot on my face when I opened the back door, and before long the shine had been taken off the roofs opposite and the puddles on the pavement began to slip away.

'Right, we're going out,' I told my offspring, gathering them up before they had time to protest. We set off down the street, the buggy back-heavy with its usual package of nappies, wipes, juice, biscuits, jumpers, waterproofs. But there was a new lightness to my step. There were people out there you could meet. There were other lives to cross.

Some of the private schools had broken up. In a couple of weeks the skateboarders would be ruling the streets; there would be teenage girls loitering at the corner. But for now the public school children had the place to themselves. Two little girls in pink fairy tiaras were trotting along ahead of me behind their mother, who had a Little Red Riding Hood wicker basket in one hand and a rolled-up rug in the other. I turned and smiled gaily as I passed.

At the chemist, Mrs Allardyce, my nemesis in a beige mac, was sitting on a chair waiting for her tablets. I braced myself in preparation for the tutting. She had once told me at the bus stop that I didn't know I was born. Like many older people who, in their own time, managed without disposable nappies or washing machines, she did not suffer the Bleat Generation gladly. I suppose there was less pressure on women of her age to be anything else. Or perhaps if you've lived through a war or directly in the aftermath of one, you have a different perspective.

Still, I usually tried to steer clear of Mrs Allardyce. Not that day, though. That day I went up and said, 'Hello, Mrs Allardyce,' and before long found myself offering to drive her to the hospital for her lung X-ray.

'You're a good girl,' she said, as I left. 'But you can't control your kids.'

When we got home later, I felt quite pleased with myself, as if I had begun a programme to open up my own life. And then I decided to open up Mel's for her by phoning the gardener. I put Dan to bed and Fergus in front of the telly and then I dialled the number.

'Hello,' I said. 'Is that Peat and Dug? Is that . . . Pete?'

The line was crackly as if the person on the other end was entangled in the branches of a tree.

'Sorry?' shouted a voice at the other end. 'Can't hear you. Hold on.'

There was more crackling, crashing. And then, 'Sorry, I was entangled in the branches of a tree. What can I do for you?'

I said, 'Oh, sorry, sorry to have got you down. Er . . . it's Maggie. Maggie Owen. You know, the . . . um.'

'Yes, I know,' he said. 'Of course I know. How are you?'

'Fine, thanks.'

'Good. Did you enjoy the party the other night?'

'Yes,' I lied. 'Very much.'

There was a pause. I realised I was gripping the bridge of my nose between my thumb and forefinger. My toes were curled. My eyes were closed. My mouth was twisted in something between a rictus and a grin.

'And?' he said. 'What can I do for you?' I could hear voices in the background, a loud noise started up, sending zigzags down the line. 'HOLD IT A MINUTE,' he yelled. It stopped.

I bit my lip. 'Just wondered,' I said, 'I mean, I don't know how busy you are, or whether you've got time or whether this isn't the sort of thing you do, but um . . .'

'Yeah?'

'Well, I just wondered whether you'd come and look at my garden.' I'd taken the phone to the back door and was looking out at my little beloved patchwork of cherished plants and rampant weed. 'It needs a bit of work and although I love doing it I just don't have time at the moment, what with one thing and, um . . .'

'Another?' he said.

'Exactly,' I said gratefully.

He sounded businesslike. 'Fine,' he said. 'Let me think. It's a very busy time of year, but . . . Where do you live? . . . Right. Um, tell you what. I'll pop round on my way to a job tomorrow afternoon. Between two and three: is that OK with you?'

There, I thought, when I put the phone down, don't say I'm not a good friend, Mel. See what lengths I'm prepared to go to for you. Then I rang Mel to tell her as much and she agreed to slip round between surgeries. 'I think I'll have a sickie tomorrow anyway,' she added. 'I haven't had one for a bit.' Mel was always having sickies, and she didn't seem to suffer from the guilt that the rest of us feel. I think meeting so many sick or malingering people must distort your impression of how much time off the average person takes. 'Oh, all doctors have sickies,' she said when I raised this. 'It's because we work so hard we need them.'

I was halfway to the front door to put the rubbish out after this, when the phone rang. I ran back in, snagging the bin-bag on the children's pegs in the hall, dripping burst tea bag and eggshell on the carpet.

'Maggie!' gusted the voice on the other end. 'I'm so glad I've caught you. I just wanted to say how glad I was that you both managed to come on Saturday. But I've been feeling dreadful that I didn't get a chance to talk to you. Did you have an awful time? Was it the worst, worst party you've ever been to?'

'Hello, Claire,' I said, taken aback. 'Not at all. It was very nice. I should have rung you to thank you. I had a great time. And Jake did too. In fact, I haven't seen him enjoy himself so much in . . . well, for years.' Why is she ringing me? I was thinking. It was so out of character. The old Claire never rung me. I was always the one who rang her. Now she wanted me. The thought pleased me, flattered me.

'God, you are an angel to say so,' she was saying. 'Listen, when are we going to meet up? I'm longing to see you properly and really, really catch up. It was fantastically frustrating not to talk to you properly at the bash. I wanted to just wrench everybody else aside to find you, but you know what it's like.'

'Of course,' I said.

'And . . .' Her voice shifted a gear. 'I wanted to ask if you were all right. You were looking quite tired and . . .'

'Children,' I said.

'. . . and run down.'

Oh great. 'Probably goes with the territory,' I said.

'. . . and what's happened to your hair? Didn't it use to be curly?' Her voice was overburdened with sympathy.

'Yes,' I said. 'No, it has changed. I think that's pregnancy. Tragedy really.' I meant it facetiously. I didn't really care if my hair was straight or wavy. All that mattered was that it was out of my eyes.

'Oh, Maggie,' she said. 'We do need to sort you out, don't we?'

'Yes,' I laughed jollily, hollowly.

'So listen, get your diary, girl. Right now.'

I went and got my diary. I used to be rather fussy about diaries. I'd had a Filofax stage, in both big and small format. I'd had a dinky little Mulberry stage, and when I was at the journal, a big cloth-bound desk-job stage, which also kept me abreast of the birthdays of various dead literary figures. But since the children, and since giving up work, there wasn't much call for any form of diary really. I could keep most of my appointments (a dental appointment here, a swimming-pool meet there) in my head. At that stage in my life, I was scrawling the odd thing in a freebie off the front of *Cosmo* the woman in the newsagent's had given Fergus (she was always saving things off magazines to give Fergus, sometimes he hit pay dirt with a Rosie and Jim fridge magnet; other times he'd leave the shop with a baffled expression and a plastic artist's modelling scalpel).

Open in front of me now was my *Cosmo* freebie. Blank.

'You must be busy, busy, busy,' said Claire. 'What with the children and everything. And I'm quite tight this week. Tomorrow, let's think . . . I've got a meeting with my agent in the morning. I'm seeing a publisher to discuss turning my *Times* column into a book in the afternoon. And then on Thursday—'

'Busy, busy, busy,' I interrupted.

'No, actually Thursday is quite clear. I've got to write my col some time, but . . . I don't know, Thursday morning? Coffee?'

I was staring at my blank diary. I panicked. I grabbed the nearest other thing to hand. The Yellow Pages (south London) was on the kitchen counter. I opened it at random. 'No good, er, electrolysis,' I said.

She didn't miss a beat. 'Lunchtime?'

'Engine tuning. Got to take the car engine to be tuned.'

'Thursday evening?'

'Escort agencies. Sorry, no.' Frantically I turned the page. 'Exercise equipment. I mean exercise class.'

'OK, then. Friday morning?'

I'd reached explosives engineers. 'That's great,' I said, closing the book. 'I can make that. Here?'

'Fantastic. Can't wait.'

I was about to put the phone down when she added, 'Oh, and just one other thing. Jake said . . . he was being very interesting about "pester power" the other night, about how advertisers target purchasers through their children, and it struck me it would make a very good piece and I just wondered . . . Could you ask him to give me a ring?'

'He's working very hard at the moment,' I said. 'You might be better off trying him at the office.'

'Actually I have. I just thought if I left a message here too . . .'

'Of course,' I said. 'Right. Bye then. See you.'

And then Claire said, '*Ciao.*'

When I put the phone down I said '*ciao*' crisply to myself in the mirror. And then I said it again, with a provocative curl to my lip: '*ciao*'.

And then I twisted my body away, so I was looking at myself over my shoulder, and I pushed my nose up with my finger and, with my top teeth digging into my tongue, I said, with comic exaggeration, 'Ci-ao. Ci-ao. Ci-ao.' And then I felt much better.

Jake hadn't got back before midnight all week, creeping into bed long after I'd gone to sleep, but that night he'd promised to be home in time to see Fran and Rain, who were coming round for supper.

Fran had left her birth plan behind on Saturday. In the meantime, Jake had defaced it. He'd replaced 'Mozart, Elderflower, Birthing Pool' with 'Pethidine, Epidural, Emergency Caesarean'.

'You. Are. Such. A. Child,' she said, chasing him round the kitchen with the birth plan curled up in her hand like a rolling pin.

'Help me. Help me,' he squawked, trying to hide behind me while I was cooking. 'Mad, pregnant hippie on the loose.'

Later, when they were laying the table, he pretended to be intensely interested in something above her waistband. 'What? What?' she said, craning her neck and panicking.

He peered closer. 'Fran,' he whispered. 'Maggie, Rain, quickly come and see. It's . . . a . . . yes . . . it's . . . a . . . STRETCH MARK!'

She screamed and hit him on the head with the paper.

I said, 'Fran, ignore him. He wouldn't know a stretch mark if it bounced off and twanged him in the eye.'

I suppose I was asking for it because Jake just laughed and said, 'Oh yeah?'

'Charming.' I said it jokingly, and normally it wouldn't have bothered me, but a bit later, after dinner, when the others were settled in the sitting room listening to Rain's CD of whale sounds set to a garage backing track, I went upstairs into the bathroom. I undid the top button of my jeans and pushed them down over my hips so I could inspect the marks left behind by my children: white ridges across the outer reaches of my stomach like bad embroidery. I pulled my jeans back and rummaged around in the bathroom cabinet until I found the 'Maternity Lotion' that I'd once bought and never used and went back downstairs.

'Here,' I said to Fran, handing her the lotion. 'This might have worked if I'd bothered to use it.'

'Maggie, you're an angel,' she said. She closed her eyes and rolled her shoulders round.

After they'd gone, I said to Jake, 'You have to be nicer to Fran. You can be very sensitive about your body when you're pregnant.'

He was standing up, but still flicking through the channels. He wasn't looking at me. He said, 'Don't be silly. She can take it. Tough as old boots, my sister. One thing you don't have to be is touchy on her behalf.' He stopped flicking, seemed suddenly engrossed in a man swinging a club on a piece of green sward somewhere where the sun was out. 'She can look after herself,' he added.

I said, 'Well, maybe I'm being touchy on my behalf.'

But he wasn't listening. He said, 'Oh yesss.' And I don't think it was directed at me.

I was halfway out of the room when I remembered the message. I said, 'Oh, can you ring Claire. She rang for you earlier. About some conversation you'd had . . .'

That certainly got his attention. 'She rang here?' he said.

'Yup. The number's in the kitchen.'

He looked uneasy. 'I'll ring her tomorrow,' he said. 'I'm sure it's not urgent.'

 **chapter seven**

THE NEXT DAY, Jake got up early, packed a suitcase and left. Bound for Amsterdam. A taxi arrived, containing Ed Brady: colleague, best friend and chief lead-astrayer. Ed Brady was an account director at TMT&T, and his job involved dealing with the client. He was charming and smooth and whenever I overheard him talking about work to Jake, he'd be saying things like, 'We had a very, very positive meeting with the client yesterday; they thought the presentation was fantastic. Terrific. They just have a teensy-weensy concern with the central concept. If they could just have a couple more options, to put it in context?'

Jake: 'So you mean they think it's shit?'

Ed: 'Er . . . yeah, well . . . maybe . . . yes.'

That day, I heard the taxi purr throatily outside the window first and then I heard the door knocker clatter and then I heard Ed calling, 'Get your sorry arse out here, my son,' through the letterbox.

'Bye, sweetie,' Jake said, bending down with his elbows buried in the pillow on either side of my head. He kissed me. 'Will you miss me?'

'You'll only be gone one night,' I said.

'It might be two—or three.'

'Oh?'

'I'll ring.' He kissed me again. There was more banging from downstairs. 'I'm coming. I'm coming.' He jumped up, grabbed his bag and charged from the room. Jake always said he hated work trips, but it was hard not to detect, when he was poised for departure, a lightness in his step. The father of young children leaving on a business trip: the definition of the great escape. He slammed the front door behind him. The baby upstairs started crying.

But it was another beautiful morning, and I couldn't feel put out for long. There was a hazy softness in the air, light slanting already through the apple tree at the bottom of the garden. Fat grey wood pigeons were waddling across the lawn like elderly women whose thighs were rubbing. There were motes dancing in the bathroom. I changed Dan's nappy and took him downstairs to give him his bottle. It was peaceful with just the one child for a bit. There were moments when I thought we made a mistake having two. When we had Fergus we still felt like a couple who just happened to have a child. Now we were a family, and you can get lost in families. Or if you don't get lost you get sat on. Or shouted at and sent up to your room. And that's just the parents.

The phone kept going that morning. First it was Rachel. She wanted to know if I'd have Harry while she 'whizzed round' Sainsbury's. 'Of course,' I said, 'Fergus would love it. He gets bored playing with himself.' Fergus was sitting dreamily on the stairs, still in his pyjamas, proving me wrong. 'The more the merrier,' I added.

I still hadn't got dressed when Lucinda, in super-efficient mode, rang from her City office to inform me that, due to complications arising from nanny Hilda's appendicitis (peritonitis), invitations to Cecily's third birthday party had been late getting in the post. She told me the party was 'Bring a Barbie'. I told her, in rather dubious tones, that we didn't have one, and she said, 'Well, improvise,' which panicked me a bit. How could one improvise a Barbie? Do something imaginative with an egg box and a teddy?

I was trying to fill the washing machine while holding a struggling Dan with one arm and preventing Fergus from opening the remaining

Persil tablet sachets with all the patience I could muster when there was a banging on the door. It must be Rachel.

'Coming,' I called. 'Now, Fergus, put that one in the drawstring bag. Ye-es. And the other. No. That's enough. Put that one down. Coming.'

She had started banging again, more insistently. 'COMING,' I shouted. I thrust the machine shut with my knee, yanked Fergus's fingers away from the controls and made for the front door.

'All right,' I said, opening it. 'You don't have to break the door down.'

I looked out. It wasn't Rachel. It was Pete. What the hell was he doing here? He was due that afternoon. To coincide with Mel. This was a disaster. My beautiful plan. 'What are you doing?' I said. 'You're early. I wasn't expecting you until this afternoon.'

'I can see that,' he said. He was wearing big, dusty boots, a faded T-shirt and a wide grin on his face that made his dimples tighten. He made a big play of looking me up and down. 'Just got up, have you?' There was a slit in the knee of his combats.

I was still in my dressing gown.

'I've been up since six,' I said. 'I haven't had a minute to get dressed.'

It was not a glamorous dressing gown. I think it might once have belonged to Jake's father. I pulled it round myself.

Pete said, 'It's just that one of my jobs was cancelled. So I thought I'd see if I could come now instead of later. I can come back if . . .'

For a moment, I wavered. 'Well, actually . . .' I began. I was staring at his knee. There were light golden hairs on it. I gave up. 'Now's fine,' I said. I steered Fergus, who had come to stand meekly by me, back against the hall wall. 'Come in. The garden's this way. Out the back.'

'It usually is,' he said.

We went through to the kitchen. I had to reach up to turn the keys at the top of the back door. Pete was right behind me. I could feel his breath on my neck. 'You have to give it a shove,' I said.

He put his arm past me and shoved. 'There you go,' he said. I moved to one side so he could get by, but the cupboard was in the way and there was a moment of awkwardness as he squeezed past me. 'You're going to have to lose some weight there,' he said once he'd got through, and grinned. I laughed and pulled my dressing-gown belt tighter round my waist. Fergus, awed by his presence, had followed him. The two of them, the big man and the small boy, wandered around the garden for a bit, in and out of the sunshine like pieces on a chessboard. At one point, he bent to coax something onto the palm of his hand with his finger to show Fergus and the two of them studied it for a while before Pete gently placed whatever it was back on a leaf. Finally Pete came back to the house, followed by Fergus. 'It's a nice little garden,' he said. 'You've done well. Was there anything major you had in mind?'

Fergus said, 'Mummy. Come and look. We found a caterpillar.'

'Um . . . I'm not sure.' Fergus was pulling me up the garden. 'Maybe some new trellis?'

'But you've got perfectly decent trellis.'

'But at the back?'

'What? Over there?' He walked back up the garden to the scrubby end under an apple tree by the shed. He stood looking around for a minute, sizing something up, while Fergus and I tried to find the caterpillar, and then he came back.

'Not much point,' he said. 'What were you thinking of growing up it?'

'Wisteria?'

'Too dark,' he countered. 'You'd do better growing that up the back wall of the house. You could train it in with the ivy.'

'Well, what about that, then?' I said.

He laughed. He said, 'You don't really know what you want, do you?' I said, 'No.'

He said, 'I tell you what I think. I think it's just general maintenance you need. The basics are all here, but it could do with a bit of love and attention, couldn't it?' He put his hand out and cradled the head of a hydrangea. It was blue. I thought it might change to pink any minute.

'I think general maintenance might be a good idea,' I said.

I looked at him straight on for the first time. I had tidied up his face in my mind, ironed out its irregularities. His eyes were closer together than I'd remembered but he was still more handsome than anyone else who'd ever been in my garden. I could still imagine how you might want to put your hands in his tufty, wavy hair, run your fingers along the knotty veins in his forearms.

I cleared my throat. 'I'd better get dressed,' I said.

'You don't have to on my account.' He smiled. He was tapping his hands on his trousers, his fingers wide apart from each other.

'Do you want a coffee?' I said.

He looked undecided. 'Ooooh,' he said in a 'go on then' tone of voice. And then the door went again. 'Actually, no,' he said. 'Don't worry. You're busy. I'd better be off.'

'No, stay,' I said.

I went to the door. Pete came with me and sidled out as I opened it. 'Hello,' he said to Rachel and Harry, who were standing there. 'I'm off. Cheers,' he said to me. 'Give me a buzz if you think you need me.' And then he was gone.

Rachel raised an eyebrow and said, 'Not dressed?'

That day it got hotter and hotter. For the rest of the morning Harry and Fergus, slicked with sun cream, splashed about in the paddling pool, raiding the kitchen cupboards for utensils with which to empty the water onto the flowerbeds and then demanding the hose for refills. Harry was fine until Rachel came to pick him up, when he developed a passion for Fergus's spatula and threw himself onto the grass in despair when the passion turned out, at Fergus's insistence, to be unrequited.

'Oh, *honestly*.' Rachel sighed heavily. 'I just don't know why these children don't get on. Fergus, please share.'

It was quite an innocuous comment, but was just weighted enough in her son's favour to ignite something in me, to set me stamping off across the minefield that is competitive motherhood. I said, sympathetically, 'Oh dear, is Harry a bit tired? Is he still waking up every night?'

She said, 'Yes, but you can't have everything. At least he's a good eater' (a veiled reference to Fergus who, as Jake said, lived on snot and air). I surrendered then, arms up.

This is how we measure out our children's days.

She had a quick cup of coffee before going. She told me she'd seen Lucinda out for a jog with the dogs across the common; that even in the throes of physical exertion, she still looked immaculate.

'Alice band?'

'Absolutely,' she answered. 'I think she sleeps in it. Probably more comfortable than all those pins you need for a bun.'

I told her Jake was away again. Rachel's husband, Clive, who was a physicist, didn't get out much, let alone abroad. There was still some tension zinging in the air so there was a little too much sympathy in her response. She said, 'Oh, poor you. It's a bit much again, isn't it? Does he have to go away so much or does he choose to?'

I mumbled something or other. And then she said, 'Do you think it would be different if you were married?'

Smiling broadly, I said, 'Not a jot!'

She stirred her coffee absent-mindedly. 'Why *aren't* you married?' she said. I'm sure she'd asked before. Most people asked at least twice.

'I don't know,' I said. 'It just always seemed too late.'

'It would be nice, though, wouldn't it?' she said. 'For the children.'

After she left, I felt miserable, but it wasn't long before Mel arrived with Milly. Arms outstretched in an attitude of despair, I greeted Mel with the news that the Pete plan was in tatters, that he'd come that morning and left. She didn't seem too concerned. 'Oh well,' she said. 'Nice idea. Never mind. Got anything to eat? I'm starving.'

Later I told her what Rachel had said about Jake and me not being married. Mel laughed and said I was being stupid and that it didn't make any difference and that a blind man could see Jake loved me. 'How is he, by the way?' she said.

'Away,' I said.

She laughed. 'Oh, well, he clearly doesn't love you that much then.'

'Still no sex,' I said.

'Give him a chance, Maggie, he's *away*. Wait till he gets back . . .'

We were lying on a rug on the grass, cups of tea making scalded patches on either side of us. The children were filling the paddling pool with earth from the flowerbeds. 'Shall I . . .?' asked Mel.

'Don't bother,' I said. 'Leave them.'

It was too hot to move. The air was heavy, like a rich pudding, silent except for the distant roar of traffic. I was about to ask whether she really did think he still loved me, when she plucked a blade of grass and, putting it in her mouth to chew, said, 'Actually, I went on a blind date last night. And it was such a disaster, I didn't really feel up to meeting someone new today anyway.' She spat the grass out, tucked the bottom of her shirt into her bra to sun her midriff and lay back down again. I sat up.

'A blind date?' I felt rather outraged as if suddenly my gardener wasn't good enough for her.

'Tara our receptionist's brother. Called Leo. Works for some bank. In the City. Divorced.'

'And? Kids?'

She turned over. 'Two. Nine and seven. It was fine. He was perfectly nice. Talked a *tiny* bit too much about his ex-wife. And didn't quite pick up the signals that I wasn't *that* interested in paint-balling.'

'What sort of signals?'

'Oh, you know, the usual. Putting my finger down my throat and pretending to be sick. That sort of thing. Funny really, because Tara's such fun. Anyway, never again.'

'Did he try and kiss you?'

'Did he try and kiss me? They always try and kiss you, Maggie. You've been out of the game too long. But I turned just in time and he got my ear. Millie! Not in his mouth. He's only a baby.'

'Gave you an earful, then?' I got up to comfort Dan, who had his mouth full of flowerbed.

From behind me, Mel said, 'What I don't understand is, why you didn't nip to a phone and ring me. About the gardener being here, I mean. I could have been here in five minutes.'

She said it wonderingly, but not so enquiringly that I felt I had to answer. I was busying myself with Dan, finding a jammy dodger in my pocket to cheer him up. But then she said, all singsong, her voice a stick to poke me with, 'I know. You fancy him yourself, don't you? Maggie? Am I right? Are you blushing?' I was about to turn round, about to say something, when there was a yowl from Fergus.

'Nyowooooooooo,' he cried, clutching the side of his neck. 'Mummmmmmmyyyyy. Nyoowooowowwo.'

'What, darling? What?'

He was sobbing. There was a bright spot on his neck, with a surrounding weal getting wider by the minute.

'Oh dear. Has he been stung?' said Mel coming to look.

'Poor Fergus,' I soothed. 'It must have been a wasp. Is it better now?'

'Nerrrrrrrrrrrr. Nerrrrrrr,' he said, which I took to mean no.

You always think you've got Bite-Eze; you can visualise it at the back of the bathroom cabinet, underneath all the free samples of Zap-it Jake brought home from work, but when you go to find it when you really need it, it turns out to be haemorrhoid cream or Jungle Formula. I couldn't remember either if it was bicarbonate of soda or vinegar you're supposed to apply, but Mel, the doctor, said, 'Oh, don't bother. All that matters is that he hasn't gone into anaphylactic shock,' while Milly went to get her Tweenie doll to cheer him up. 'You can lend it if you like,' she said. After about ten minutes, Fergus stopped gulping, reached out for the Tweenie and put his head on my shoulder.

'Poor Fergus,' Mel cooed. 'Wasp stings really hurt, don't they?'

He lifted his head. 'Where's the wasp now?' he said.

'In the garden,' I said.

Mel and Milly left soon after that. They wanted to get to the shoe shop before it closed. If they'd stayed a little longer I'd have answered her question. It wasn't like I had anything to hide.

chapter eight

JAKE DIDN'T RING ON Wednesday evening—which was unusual. Normally he tried to talk to Fergus before bedtime. And he didn't ring on Thursday morning either, which was doubly odd. No playgroup because of the holidays so we met my mother for an early lunch at the café attached to the local garden centre.

When we got home Jake had rung and left a message. I couldn't make out most of what he said because of the background noise—hollering and laughing as if he was in a bar. He broke off halfway through the message to say something to somebody else—'Mine's a Pilsner,' I think. I tried to ring him on his mobile, but it was switched off.

'What's your father doing in a bar on a lovely day like this?' I said to Fergus.

'Hunting,' he replied sagely.

'He'd better not be,' I said.

I opened the back door.

'WASPS,' shrieked Fergus, fleeing back into the bowels of the house.

'It's all right; they're not here now. There's nothing to hurt you in the garden. I promise.'

He went out reluctantly and hovered on the steps. I took Dan, who'd fallen asleep in his car seat, up to his cot, lowered him gently in, then tiptoed gingerly across to the door. The last board creaked. It always does. I stood in the doorway listening to him stir, and then whimper and then cry. He was standing up and shaking his bars when I went back in so I picked him up and took him downstairs again. 'My life,' I muttered. 'Where has it gone?'

The phone was sitting by the back door. I picked it up and dialled. Just like that. He picked it up straight away. His voice sounded drowsy.

'Were you asleep?' I asked.

'No, no,' he said sleepily. No one, child or adult, ever likes to admit to having been dozing.

'It's Maggie. From Chestnut Drive.'

357

'Hello, Maggie from Chestnut Drive.'

'Hello. Sorry. I just—'

'Mummeeeeee.' Fergus was calling from the garden. He sounded desperate. Maybe it was another wasp.

I speeded up. 'Look, just to say, I'd be really keen if you could fit me, fit my garden, into your schedule. I really do think it needs it. So whenever suits you really.'

'Mummeeeeeeeeee.'

'Hang on, let me just look in the diary.' There was a rustle and I wondered what his diary looked like. A big, brown folder with bits of paper falling to the ground like leaves, perhaps.

'OK,' he said, 'Psion at the ready. Just wait for it to boot up. A-ha. I've had a cancellation tomorrow afternoon. Would that do you?'

'Mummeeeeeeeeeeeeeeeeeeeeee.'

'Tomorrow afternoon would do me fine,' I said.

When I got out to Fergus he was sitting on a deck chair. 'There you are!' he said with that disconcerting shift of tone that children have. 'I needed you, but now I don't.'

I was half expecting Jake home that night, but only half, so it wasn't that much of a surprise when he rang instead.

'Hi, hon,' he said, all soft and conciliatory. 'How are things?'

'Fine. Where are you?'

'In my hotel room,' he said, as if it was obvious.

'When are you coming home?'

'Tomorrow,' he said, as if it had always been the case.

'Oh, right. You've missed Fergus. He's in bed. He was whacked.'

'Oh well. Kiss him for me. Has it been all right?'

'Yes, it's been fine. I told you. How's it going there?'

'Tortuous. Crap hotel in the middle of nowhere. Horrible sandwiches for lunch. And we've just been stuck in this room, going round and round in circles. We're just fighting our corner really.'

'What corner is that?' I said.

'You know, the new Kyushi Pondura. Hatchback. Second car. Kyushi want to target women twenty-five to forty. They want the same advertising campaign throughout Europe and we want it to be ours. So I've got to get them to accept my brief.'

'You'll be fine, won't you?' I said reassuringly.

Jake snapped, 'I don't know.'

'All right, you don't have to snap.'

'I'm not snapping. I'm just saying I don't know. I hope so.' He took an intake of breath, a suspiciously sharp intake.

I said, 'Are you smoking?'

'No,' he said, breathing out loudly. 'No. Hang on, got to go, that's Ed at the door. We're meeting the others down in the bar at nine.'

'OK then, bye,' I said. Hard work, obviously, but someone had to do it. 'Love you,' I added. But he'd already hung up.

It is an unpleasant but unavoidable truth that women who don't work soon become resentful of the fact that their husbands do. The office can very quickly become the Other Woman. Jake's Other Woman was young and glamorous and hung out in bars and spoke with a sexy cigarette-laced foreign accent. She drove a Kyushi hatchback. And she ate sliced bread. And she had spots.

I began to feel better.

chapter nine

I'D FORGOTTEN CLAIRE WAS COMING. I was cooking when she came to the door on Friday morning. Smiley Carrot and Lamb Faces from *Bigger Helpings!*, Anjelica Knurgle's latest guide to feeding children. Rachel had lent me the book a few weeks previously after witnessing me remove a packet of Mr Men sausages from the freezer. 'Have you seen what's in these?' she'd said, appalled.

'Lips and arseholes?' I'd countered.

'No, much worse,' and she'd reeled off a list of Es.

'What about fish fingers?' I said.

'Well, OK,' she said. 'But take the breadcrumbs off Harry's. The sulphur dioxide in them, which is only E220 by another name, turns him into a raving lunatic.'

'The "E" generation, then?' I'd said. She hadn't looked amused.

So there I was, resentfully poking shepherd's pie by any other name into the compartments of an ice-cube tray, when there was Claire, immaculate in velvet-trimmed denim pedal-pushers and a T-shirt, the whiteness of which hadn't been seen in our house since Fergus discovered you could pick up the coals in the real-effect coal gas-fire.

She said, standing on the doorstep, head tilted to look up at the roof, 'What an angelic house. *Sweet.*'

I said, 'Come in. It's a bit messy, I'm afraid.'

She squeezed past the buggy into the hall. '*Adorable.*'

We went into the kitchen and she sidled into a chair at the table. The back door was open and a fresh breeze was toying with the corners of the tablecloth. Fergus had retreated, doglike, to the garden. Dan was asleep, catlike, in the hall. A couple of hover flies were bumping their heads against the skylight in the ceiling. Claire seemed on edge. 'God, I'm gasping for a coffee,' she said.

I should have gone to the shops. 'Is Gold Blend all right?' I asked.

She made a polite wincing face. 'Do you have any real?'

I checked in the tin, though I knew what I would, or rather wouldn't, find. 'Sorry.'

'I'll have tea,' she said bravely.

There were no clean mugs either, so I fished a couple out of the dishwasher to run under the tap.

She said, 'How are things?'

I said, 'Fine. Great. Terrific. You?'

She said, 'Don't ask.'

She took a packet of Silk Cut out of her basket and lit up. Her hands shook a bit. There was a clot of lipstick on one of her teeth.

I said, 'I love your bag.'

She said again, closing her eyes this time, 'Just don't ask.'

I started to say something else. 'How's your—?' I began.

'I mean. Christ,' she said. 'Just. Do. Not. Ask.'

I smiled. 'What?'

She looked around for an ashtray and then, as if forgetting what she was looking for, dropped her cigarette to the floor and rubbed it into the tiles with the toe of her plimsoll. 'Do you really want to know?'

'Of course. Tell me.'

'Oh, Maggie, I'm in such a mess. My love life is just . . . I mean, how do you keep things together? How have you got this far? I'm just all over the sodding place.'

'No, you're not,' I said. 'You're amazing. You've got everything: job, success, Disney contracts! Looks—'

'Yeah, but no kids. No husband. Look at me, Maggie. I'm thirty-six.' She rocked her head from side to side, making a rhythmic clicking sound with her tongue. 'Clock ticking—all that.'

'Thirty-six is nothing,' I said. 'Especially these days.'

'Is it? I don't know. I just would so love to have a baby. You know, I see you and other friends and it's like being locked out of a club, and if I knew that one day I would have a child I would feel all right about it, but it's the fear that I might never and I couldn't bear it.'

'Oh, Claire.' I felt really sorry for her suddenly. I put my arm round her shoulders. 'There's bags of time.'

'Yes, but without a man on the scene.'

'And isn't there a man on the scene . . .?'

'Well . . .'

'Go on,' I said slowly. I turned and busied myself with the kettle and the tea bags.

'I'm seeing someone at the moment but . . .' She broke off, paused as if to consider something, and then began again. 'There was this other bloke, the bloke I left England to get away from, really. We were mad about each other and I really thought he was the one, but . . .'

'But what?' I said, squeezing out the tea bag.

'Unavailable. Temporarily off the shelf. Out of stock.' She started talking faster. 'We had this fantastic time together, great sex and fantastic weekends away—we managed to get to Venice once. It was just heaven—and he gave me lovely presents . . .' She waved her wrist in my direction and I had time to make a quick appreciative 'nice watch' face, before she was off again. 'He was the love of my life, but it was all just a waste of time. He didn't have the guts.' She was staring into my face beadily as if looking for something there.

'What stopped him?' I said, wondering why anyone would not leave his wife for her?

'He thought he'd miss his child,' she said.

I had been looking back at her sympathetically. But at this I looked out into the garden. Fergus had managed to get into the shed where there was a hose-winding contraption that fascinated him. There was also a lawnmower with open blades and shears and damp boxes of weedkiller trailing their lethal powders onto the floor.

'Honestly,' she was saying. 'It just wasn't fair on me.' She pulled her hair together and tied it in a casual knot. 'It completely battered my self-esteem and I had to get out, which is why I moved to New York . . .'

I got up and went into the garden to extricate Fergus from the den of knife and poison. He didn't want to come so I brought him out under my arm like a piece of rolled-up carpet. His back half flapped uselessly. His front half hollered. When I had calmed him down with the help of a trowel and an empty polystyrene plant tray, I went back into the kitchen.

She carried on talking as if nothing had happened. 'And it was in New York,' she said, 'that I met Marcus. He's English, but he was there on business. I was in the Plaza to interview Lou Reed and he was there with clients and we started talking in the lobby. And one thing led to another and . . . business trip led to business trip. He's also married—did I mention that? But he stopped sleeping with his wife months ago. Anyway, I thought it was only the distance that was keeping us apart, but now I'm back he's behaving all oddly and I don't know what to think. And being back's confused me too. I keep thinking about the other guy but he won't answer my calls and . . . I'm just fed up with it all. Anyway, I've given Marcus an ultimatum. He's got until next week to make up his mind: the wife or the mistress. His choice. And this time I'm not going to be fobbed off. I'm worth more than that.'

I put her mug of tea down on the table. 'How do you know they've stopped sleeping together?' I said.

After that I thought she'd never go. She wanted to talk about it. She really, *really* wanted to talk about it. She wanted my angle (the wife's angle), which would have been flattering if it hadn't made me feel so uneasy. So what with one thing (Married Man number one) and another (Married Man number two), she was still sitting at the table smoking when Pete arrived. I could see his shape, his height, his shoulders, through the glass in the door. Bugger, I thought.

'Oh,' I said to Claire, as if it was all totally normal. 'It's your downstairs neighbour. He's come to do my garden.'

'Really?' she said, intrigued.

'It's a long story.'

She followed me to the door. 'Pete?' she said, coming up behind me as I got there. 'Why, hello,' she said over my shoulder, as I opened it. 'Sweetie,' pushing past me—'fancy meeting you here!'

'Hi, Claire,' he said, surprised. 'Hello, Maggie,' he said to me.

And then Claire had thrown an arm round his shoulder and was taking his bag of garden tools off him, making a big, lopsided show of how heavy they were, and propelling him into the house as if she owned the place. 'Goodness,' she said, 'now I get to see you at work. Muscles and everything. Maggie, are you going to get Pete a cup of tea?'

'Of course,' I said. 'Milk and sugar?'

'No sugar,' he said, winking at Claire. 'I'm sweet enough already.'

'Don't you think Maggie's house is lovely?' said Claire as I busied myself about the kettle.

'Great,' he said. 'Probably worth a bit, too.'

I raised my eyes to the ceiling. 'Maybe,' I said. 'The property prices round here . . .'

Claire was poking him in the side. 'Got to get on the property ladder, Pete.' She was slipping off her shoes. God, it was infuriating: she always became someone else when men were around.

'Oh, I'm not one for owning property,' Pete said. 'I don't like the responsibility. I prefer not to be pinned down.'

Claire gave him a nudge with her bare foot. 'Well, maybe sometimes,' he said. They both laughed.

'Right,' I said crisply.

They looked at me.

Claire said, 'Good thing I'm here, what with Maggie's husband being away. Wouldn't trust you on your own with anyone.'

'Away, is he?' said Pete to me.

'He's always away,' I said lightly. How did she know he was away? I must have told her on the phone.

Pete was giving me a funny look. 'I don't know if I'd go away if I had this . . . house.'

'He'll be back later.'

'With a big bunch of flowers and big present from wherever he's been, I should think.'

'I should think,' I said. 'Not.'

He grinned at me.

Claire was stretching her arms above her head so that her breasts were straining against her T-shirt. 'Right,' she said crisply.

'Right,' said Pete, standing up. 'All play and no work . . .'

'Anyway, we're not married,' I added, to no one in particular.

It became quite clear, shortly after this, that there was no getting rid of Claire. Now Pete had turned up, she was in for the duration.

'How well do you know Pete?' I asked at one point.

'Oh, we're great friends,' she said. 'Don't you think he's gorgeous? I think he's one of the most fantastically gorgeous people I've ever met. Very uncomplicated,' she added.

'Nice body, too,' I said.

At teatime, I went out and said, 'Can I get you anything?' and he said, 'What are you suggesting?' and I said, 'A sandwich or something,' and he laughed and said, 'Never turn down a free feed.' And pretty soon, after he'd eaten a pile of bread and cheese, he said he'd better be going, and did I want him to come again to tackle the bindweed?

I glanced back at the house. 'Yes, yes, I do want you to come again to tackle the bindweed.'

'I'll drop by when I'm passing,' he said, as he went out through the kitchen. To Claire, he said, 'Seeya.' And she said, in a singsong, 'Darling, I'll be waiting.' And he left. Halfway out of the door, he said, 'Don't mind Claire, will you? She's quite a one,' and then he tousled Fergus's mop of hair and said, 'Great kid,' which brought a lump to my throat, and then he was off across the road with a cheery wave. When I went out the back, the garden looked as tidy as if it had had a haircut, though there was a pile of plastic dinosaurs on the steps which he must have found scattered in the beds.

Jake got back from Amsterdam shortly after 6.00pm. He gave me a bear hug at the door and twirled the children round until they almost brought up their carrot-and-lamb smiley faces. And he said to Fergus, 'Guess what I've got you!' and made him rummage around in his suit bag, until he'd found the miniature Pan Am 727.

'Anything in there for me?' I asked.

'Oh. I was going to get you some perfume in duty-free but I couldn't remember whether it was Diorella or Diorissima you liked.'

'Ma Griffe,' I said.

He didn't get the joke. He was too busy trying to look into the kitchen. 'Who's here?' he mouthed.

I said loudly, 'Come and see Claire! She's spent the day here. She's waited all this time to say hello.'

Claire was standing in the doorway. 'Hello.'

It was quite rude of Jake not to look up at that point. 'Hello,' he said, rebuckling his suit bag. He straightened up. 'How are you?'

'Fine,' she said. 'You?'

'Fine.'

It was rather awkward for a moment. Maybe Jake was tired because of the journey. Maybe finding someone in the house when he got home was the last thing he needed.

I said, 'So who wants a drink?'

Jake said, 'Sorry I haven't rung you. I've been away.'

'Forget it,' said Claire. 'Actually, I'd better be going.'

'Don't feel you have to rush off,' I said. Jake didn't say anything. She paused to search for something in her bag. I nudged Jake.

'Yes, do stay for a drink,' he said, stilted.

'No, no. I must be going. I've been here hours. Maggie must be longing to get rid of me.'

I said, lying, 'No. Of course not.'

Claire wavered. God, either go or stay, I thought. Preferably go.

'Daddy, Daddy, Daddy.' Fergus was jumping up and down, trying to get Jake's attention. He had Milly's Tweenie in his hand, the one she'd lent him after the wasp incident, and was waving it in front of him.

'No definitely. I'm off,' she said, suddenly galvanised. 'Fantastic day, Maggie. Just the most gorgeous children. What on earth is that?'

'Fizz,' said Fergus, waving the doll.

She looked bewildered. 'Anyway, I've had a heavenly time. Good thing I was here to keep Pete away. He's a bit of a devil with the women.'

'Pete?' said Jake.

'I'll explain later,' I said quickly.

Claire darted us both a look. She kissed me and then she went to kiss Jake. She went for his cheek at the same time as he made a small movement away from her so that her mouth hit his. She laughed uncomfortably. Jake didn't do anything.

'Daddy, Daddy, Daddy.' Fergus was pounding Jake's knees with his fists, desperate to be picked up. I was holding Dan but he was stretching out his arms to clasp Jake too, pushing away from me like someone casting off in a boat.

'Look, you two,' Claire said, as something occurred to her. 'Are you free on Tuesday? Come to supper. I've got some friends coming over. I'd love it if you came.'

Jake frowned. 'Errr . . .' he said.

I said, 'That would be lovely, Claire.'

'Fantastic. Right then, I'm off.' She was halfway to the door when she turned suddenly and said, 'How was Kyushi?'

'Tricky,' said Jake.

I was thinking, Kyushi? Did I tell her that too?

Later, after supper, Jake said, 'Odd to find Claire here when I got back. Why is she inviting us to supper?'

'What do you mean "odd"?'

'Nothing,' he said, picking up the newspaper and studying the headlines as if he hadn't already had a two-hour flight in which to do so. 'I just mean I'm surprised you've seen her again. I can't imagine you've got much in common any more.'

'Oh yes?'

'Well, she's nothing like your usual chums.'

'My usual chums?' I said.

'The other playground mums you hang out with.'

'The other playground mums?' I repeated acidly. 'In what way? You mean she's more glamorous?' I scraped some mashed potato remains into the sink and clattered the cutlery into the cutlery holder.

'No, not glamorous.' He flicked the paper back on the table and sifted through his post. 'She's just different. You know . . .'

'No, I don't,' I said, clicking the dishwasher shut and turning to face him. 'You're just saying you fancy her.'

'I do not fancy Claire Masterson. She's not my type.'

'Why not?'

He sagged his head towards the table as if it had suddenly got too heavy. 'All I said was I was surprised to see her here.' Then he put the mail down and looked at me directly for the first time. 'But I suppose it is unusual, not pleasant, just unusual, to meet someone here who doesn't recognise a Tweenie.'

If the babies hadn't been upstairs, I would have slammed the door then. As it was I closed it very quietly and went through into the sitting room. I knew I was overreacting but that knowledge never makes you feel better, it makes you feel worse: more impotent somehow. I felt twisted inside as if someone was pulling and tugging me in different directions. I stood in the middle of the floor for a bit. Everything around me was mine. The faded green sofa I'd picked up at a local junk shop, the rugs I'd lugged back from holiday in Morocco, the cushions I'd sewn. Then on the table by the television, I spotted the scrapbook Jake kept his precious childhood collection of PG Tips cards in, still there from a few days before when he'd shown them to Fergus. For a moment I considered taking it outside and stuffing it into the dustbin. Then I relented. Instead, I picked it up and dropped it behind the toy cupboard. And then I felt a little bit better.

chapter ten

THAT WEEKEND, we had a brunch date. Who has brunch in England? Well, Ed Brady, Jake's much maligned (by me) colleague, that's who. The first time he invited us, Jake had rung up to double-check what time we were due. 'One for one thirty,' Ed had said. Most people would call this lunchtime. 'Yeah, all right,' Jake said, when I pointed this out. 'Don't blame me.' But of course I did blame him. For being Ed's friend in the first place.

Ed Brady was everything I dreaded Jake being. He was Jake on a bad day. He was Jake played by Jim Carrey, only he was much thinner under his loose designer suits, etiolated like a daffodil bulb that has been kept too long in the cupboard under the stairs. He had so much nervous energy you kept expecting him to fizz across the room like a released balloon. He was married to Pea, or Pee (short for Penelope), who was 'in film', which is to say she worked for the BBC. They had one of those baffling marriages in which one side of the equation had so much more power than the other, that you couldn't see how they stayed upright, why they didn't topple over. Jake and I were always convinced Pea was on the verge of leaving Ed. She seemed perpetually irritated by him, wincing when he spoke as if he set her teeth on edge, and so obviously contemptuous of his job (trashy, empty, ephemeral compared to the real, nitty-gritty work of addressing the world's injustices on . . . er, tele- vision), you wondered what they had ever had in common.

'Come in, come in, come in,' Ed said at the door that brunchtime. 'Maggie: You. Look. Fantastic. Give us a kiss. And another. And is this the baby? Gosh, isn't she big now?'

'He,' I said.

'And Fergus, my man!' He clapped Fergus on the shoulder, sending him sprawling. 'Oopla,' said Ed, bending to pick him up. (Fergus was too stunned to complain.) 'Jaaaaaaake.' They shared an ironic high five. This was part of the charade played out by Ed, with Jake's assistance, that they were, contrary to appearances, in fact eighteen. And black.

Finally, in his own voice, he said, 'What a fucking week, eh?' Jake raised his eyes to the ceiling and pretended to mop his brow.

Ed turned to me again. 'Come in, come in, Maggie. Pea is longing to see you. She's just been saying it's been too long.'

'Hi,' said Pea, coming out of the sitting room, switching a smile on and off, and then disappearing upstairs.

Ed cleared his throat and widened his mouth into a mouth-organ grimace. 'PMT,' he joked to Jake, then tipped his head back. 'Dah-ling,' he yodelled. 'Can I bring you something? Teensy-weensy glass of bubbly?' There was no answer. 'Terrible headache,' he said to me. 'Poor love.'

We went through to the sitting room, where their five-year-old daughter, Clarice, was kicking some marbles about on the seagrass. Clarice had been squeezed into a miniature version of her mother. She took the world very seriously, so seriously that she seemed to have lost the ability to do what children do better than anyone else, which is play with nothing—or at the very most a piece of flex and a bare plug—very happily, and very *unseriously*, for hours on end.

'Clara, mind the coffee table,' trilled Ed, hurrying over to return the marbles to the decorative soapstone solitaire board on the coffee table. 'Clara darling, take Fergus upstairs and show him your new lap-dancing . . .' nudge to Jake, 'I mean, Caribbean Holiday Barbie.'

Fergus looked as though he was up for it, but Clarice rearranged her hair in its sparkly heart-shaped kirby grips and said in a clear, bell-like voice, 'No. I don't want to. I don't like Fergus. I want him to go home.'

Fergus looked nonplussed. Ed mouthed, 'Sorry, she's overtired.'

'Perhaps she's got a headache,' I said. Dan was wriggling to get out of my arms, so I put him down on the floor, as far away as I could from the jagged-edged glass and steel coffee table. Not far enough. He shuffled over to it and, before I got there too, had scattered neatly stacked copies of *Interiors* and *Wallpaper* in all directions. Fergus, delighted, scampered over and started yanking at his hair and shouting, 'No, Dan. Naughty.' Fergus was reprimanded. Dan cried. Jake hid in an armchair. Ed wheeled his arms around, suggesting other activities Clarice might enjoy sharing with Fergus. Clarice went to find her mother. Fergus started crying. Welcome to the Brady brunch.

I had just managed to distract Fergus with a page in *Elle Décor* about kitchen appliances—the subject he would choose if ever invited on *Mastermind*—when another couple arrived: he with pewter hair and thick, leather-clad thighs; she with eyebrows plucked to within an inch of their life. He, it was explained to me, was Ed's equivalent at Blue Fish, another agency. She was a 'conference organiser'. Pea must have approved of them because she launched herself down the stairs to greet them, bubbling over with effusive greetings, which reached almost hysteria at the realisation that they were all going to be on holiday in Majorca for the same two weeks of August.

'What bit? What bit?' squawked the eyebrowless one.

'The north,' squealed Pea. 'You?'

'Oh, the same. We always go to the north. The rest is rubbish.'

'Absolutely! We must meet up. Jake, Maggie, what about you? What are your holiday plans this year?'

Jake said, 'Er. Well, actually . . .' His eyes darted across to Ed. 'Well, because of this Kyushi stuff, I doubt I'll be able to get away.'

Ed looked as if he was about to sink behind the sofa. Pea said, 'But Ed's working on the same account. Surely this . . . Ed?'

Ed said, 'Er, yeah.' And then he gave a little laugh and wrinkled up his nose. 'Let's . . . er . . . let's talk about it later.'

Hefty Thighs said, 'Oh yeah, I heard about this Kyushi pitch. What's happening?'

Pea, her blue eyes like drills, ignored him. She said, still looking at Ed, 'But—'

I said quickly, 'So we're just going to enjoy Morton Park this summer.'

Ed said soothingly, 'It'll all be over by September. And that's a much better time to go away.'

Pea said, 'But we always go to Pollensa in August.'

Ed said, his voice a pointed reminder of social obligation, 'Darling . . . Shall I go and get the blinis?'

He escaped into the kitchen, leaving the conversation to flounder a bit before Hefty Thighs threw it a lifeline in the form of House Prices. It had moved via Commuting Complaints on to Kitchen Extensions by the time Ed came back in with a plate of smoked salmon morsels, and from there it was just a hop and a skip to Child Care and the impossibility of finding a good nanny. In the course of this conversation, I noticed Pea refer to the intervals she herself spent with Clarice as Child Care, as in, 'I was late getting to the shoot because of Child Care,' like it was a double maths lesson or an evening class.

'What do you mean by "Child Care"?' I said. 'Didn't that used to be called being a family?' I knew I was being twitchy but I couldn't let it lie somehow. Pea looked daggers at me and then, while Ed passed round plates of lasagne, gave me a long lecture about the difficulties faced by working mothers in contemporary society. She would probably describe me afterwards as being part of an army of non-working mothers determined to undermine her. I didn't care. I just smiled weakly.

The others, meanwhile, had turned away and were busy talking about something else. Jake was telling them about a sticky meeting he'd had with the men from Wheato, about how they'd invented a loaf that tasted like toast and how they wanted to target kids and he'd told them that it was pointless, that it was mums who bought bread. And in the course of this anecdote, he mentioned the name of the MD at TMT&T and Hefty Thighs suddenly said, 'Oh, Philip . . . Oh, we all know about Philip.' He opened his eyes wide and pushed his chin into his neck, like Les Dawson in the post office ad.

'What?' asked his wife.

'Yes, what?' said Pea, frowning.

'Philip's women,' he said. He was slapping his knees open and closed with excitement.

Ed was looking embarrassed.

Pea said, 'What women?'

Hefty Thighs said, 'He's a terrible womaniser. Can't keep it zipped up, if you know what I mean.'

Pea said frostily, 'Yes, I know quite what you mean.'

Ed said, 'Anyone been watching the tennis?'

Hefty Thighs was nudging his wife, chortling to himself. 'At the moment he's seeing a chartered accountant in Barnes. He even slips out for a shag in the middle of the evening sometimes. He says he's nipping out to buy some fags. Once he even said he had to move the car!'

'She must know, then,' said Eyebrows. 'Must have guessed.'

'Knows which side her bread is buttered,' said HT. 'Nice five-double-bedroom house in Holland Park. Place in Wiltshire. Harvey Nichols charge account. Why rock the boat?'

'Ab-so-bloody-lutely,' joshed Ed.

'Excuse me?' said Pea.

There was an awkward silence as Ed registered that he had said the wrong thing. I concentrated on Delaney, their Burmese, who had come and sat next to me on the sofa. I stroked him and he yawned, exposing the inside of his mouth, which looked like a fillet of Dover sole.

Pea said, 'It's not a joke, Ed.'

'No, no, no, I know,' he said.

'No, I'm serious,' she said. 'It really isn't funny. I know you blokes think it's all a laugh and good for Philip and I'm not interested in that. But it's just not acceptable to think it's funny that his wife turns a blind eye. It's a fundamental betrayal of women's rights. Don't you think? Don't you think, Maggie? Polly?' I murmured something, desperately tried to drag up an opinion. Where did people find opinions like this? Were they just born with them? Pea was saying, 'I mean, we each have a responsibility to other women, not to put up with things like that.'

Polly was nodding in agreement. Pea said, 'God, advertising! Sometimes it just makes me—'

Ed looked green. 'Ab-so-bloody-lutely,' he said weakly.

I looked at Jake. He was staring out of the window with an odd expression on his face.

We left shortly after this. Ed said goodbye to us at the door. 'Catch ya later,' he said, in an irritating fake voice to Jake. I must have given him a look because I heard him say, 'Oops, hope you're not in the doghouse too,' which irritated me even more.

While we were walking home, I said, 'Why on earth do you like Ed? He's so false.' And Jake said, 'He's different when he's on his own.'

'Aren't we all,' I said.

chapter eleven

ON SUNDAY MORNING, Jake went to the office, going straight on in the afternoon to the MD's 'country' (if Hemel Hempstead counts as country) club for a round of golf. He didn't get back until late. And on Monday, Pete came to the house. I hadn't expected him to come that soon. I would have washed my hair if I'd known. I'd certainly have washed my hair if I'd known this time he'd be wearing shorts.

It was just after one when he arrived. Dan was building a tower out of bricks on the kitchen floor. Fergus and I were making chocolate corn-flake cakes, as a distractionary measure.

At the door, Pete said, 'Thought I'd crack on with the job now I've started,' he said. 'That bindweed gets into everything. You only need to leave a tiny piece of root in the earth and it spreads.'

'Is it the worst thing you can have?' I said, wiping Fergus's chocolatey fingers with the corner of my apron.

'No, Japanese knotweed's worse. Get that in your foundations and you can start getting cracks.'

'I'd better be thankful for small mercies, then.' I smiled, trying not to look down at his ginger-brown muscular calves. The shorts looked ancient, tatty, army surplus; one of the pockets, combat-style, was half hanging off. There was a scab on one of his knees but an old one, an etching of New South Wales.

'Yes, you had,' he said, his eyes crinkling up as he smiled back.

He worked in the garden all afternoon, mowing the lawn and digging sharp trenches between the grass and the beds, banging in some netting for the climbers along the fence, tangling himself up in the shrubs. Fergus was out there most of the time, too, watching him, jumping up and down with excitement every time Pete brought through a new implement from his van. I watched most of the time, too, but from the upstairs window. I watched him bend and hoick and stretch. I watched his T-shirt wrinkle up across his back. I watched the circles of sweat widen under his arms. Occasionally, he'd stand and squint in my direction. But I don't think he could see me through the sun on the glass.

This time, when he'd finished work, he stayed for tea. And a chocolate cornflake cake.

'God, these take me back,' he said between mouthfuls. He was sitting opposite me with his feet up on the rungs of the chair next to him, and one elbow on the table. His forearms were richly sunburnt and freckly like the top of crème brûlée. He stretched suddenly, pushing his arms up in two Vs above his head, and I got a glimpse of the hollow beneath his arm, the whiter skin and the darker damp hairs, like a secret place. 'Reminds me of my mum,' he said.

'Where is your mum?' I said. 'Is she still alive?'

'No. She cocked it in '97.'

'Cocked it?' I tried not to laugh.

'Died.' He smiled ruefully. 'She died.'

'I'm sorry. And what about your father?'

'Oh, Dad's alive and kicking. He's back in Sydney. He was as weak as a kitten for a bit but he's got used to life on his own now.'

'Does he miss you?'

'I guess so. But he's got Mo, my big sister, and her brood to keep him busy. You got any brothers and sisters?'

'No. I'm an only child.'

'Spoilt?' He smiled.

'No, thank you very much.' I played mock-hurt. 'I think if anything it's made me more vulnerable; it's made it hard for me to read people.'

'Uh-huh?'

I laughed. 'Oh all right, spoilt.'

He said, 'You don't seem spoilt to me. Quite the opposite. I'd say maybe you could do with a bit more spoiling. It's just a hunch, but—'

I laughed nervously. I said, 'And is Sydney where you grew up?'

He leaned back in his chair. 'Yeah. Sydney. It's a great place. You should come visit some time.'

'I'd love that, but . . .' I shrugged. 'In another life.'

He leaned forward. 'You'd love it. The space and the beaches and . . . You really should come one day. I'll show you round.'

I laughed as if, even in another life, this wasn't worth considering.

'And there's so much to do for kids. They'd have a great time.'

'So are you planning on going back soon?' I said. It seemed important, for whatever reason, to know more about him.

'I dunno.' He shrugged. 'Your guess is as good as mine. I like it here. I like London. I like the people.'

'So how long have you lived under Claire?'

'If only.' Pete raised an eyebrow. I laughed, a ha-ha-not-very-funny laugh. 'Not that long,' he said. 'It's Lloyd's place. I'm subletting my room off someone who's travelling round the world.'

'When are they back?'

'You're asking a lot of questions.' He wiggled his eyebrows.

'The Spanish Inquisition,' I replied.

'The Spanish what?' he said. He picked up Dan, who was crawling under the table, and dandled him on his knee. His bare, brown knees.

I said, 'It doesn't matter.'

There was a pause. Pete was making Donald Duck noises for Dan out of the corner of his cheek. I smiled. 'Have you always been a gardener?'

'No,' Pete said, still as Donald Duck. 'Have you always been a mother?'

'Now you're evading. Do you like it?'

'What, evading?'

'No. Being a gardener?'

Dan was wriggling so Pete put him back on the floor. In his own voice, he said, 'In summer I do. I'm outdoors. I like being outdoors. Winters get a bit long. I do decorating and a bit of construction work if I need it. This year I've got some saved up so I might go snowboarding.'

'Aren't you a bit old for that?' I said.

'You're as old as the woman you feel.'

'And how old is she?' I said lightly.

Pete said, 'Now that would be telling.'

There was a pause. And then Fergus came in carrying a fork. Pete jumped up and said, 'Hey, big fella, want to give that to me before you do some damage?' Fergus handed it over without a whimper and went back into the garden. Pete said seriously, 'You have, you know, you've got great kids.'

I had started clearing the table, with Dan clinging on to my knees. 'They're a handful,' I said.

'Spirited. Not a handful: *spirited*.'

'Maybe.'

'And good-looking.'

I grinned. 'I'm biased, but—'

'They take after their mum.' He was studying me.

I tried not to look flustered, turned to busy myself frantically with the washing-up. 'Flattery will get you everywhere,' I said.

'But will it get me another chocolate cornflake thing?'

I wiped my hands on a tea towel. 'It will certainly get you one of those.'

I passed him the plate, and he spent a long time with his head bent choosing. He held the plate with his hand so I wouldn't move it away. There were some tiny, dark green leaves in his hair. Ceanothus probably. Finally, he took one.

'Hey,' I said. 'That's the biggest.'

'I'm terrible that way,' he said, still holding his side of the plate so I couldn't get away, while looking me straight in the eye. 'I always take what I want.'

They're tricky, moments like that. You think you know what's going on, but you don't know for sure. You can't say, 'Well here I am, take me,' or 'Well, you can't have me: I'm not available,' because there is always the chance that it's totally innocent banter, no double entendre intended, or at least intended but only to be taken so far.

And let's face it. It had been a long time since I'd embarked upon anything even remotely flirt-related. I had, as Mel had so recently reminded me, been out of the game for aeons. Not only did I not know the rules—Jake and I were practically pre-AIDS, certainly pre-AIDS-as-a-serious-consideration—but I didn't even know the game any more. At least, I didn't know what I was playing at.

So what did I do? I panicked. I defused. I put the emotional jigsaw back in its box. I tidied up the sexual skittles. I stepped back. I said, 'I bet you do. You young things are all the same. Now get those grass-stained boots off my kitchen floor. And how much do I owe you?'

He looked a bit uncomfortable, but his smile didn't shift. He said, without even glancing down, 'I'll clear up the mess, no worries. And as for payment, I'll bill you. Do you want me to come again in a week or two? Just to get you back on track?'

I wavered and told him I'd let him know. I felt breathless and sick, churned up like the grass in the back garden. I knew what I had to say, though. I had to say it before he left. I took a deep breath, leaned back against the kitchen counter and said, 'This may sound a little odd, but there was something I wanted to ask you. I'm all embarrassed now, but: are you seeing anyone at the moment?'

He was knocking the grass off his soles on the back doorstep. He turned round with a lopsided smile. He said, 'No. And?'

I had to say it. It was now or never. I said, through a forced laugh, 'It's just that I've got a friend. She's really great and I think you'd really like her. And I just wondered . . .'

He said, still grinning, 'A "*friend*"?'

I said, 'No, honestly, I mean it. A friend. My friend Mel. She's great. She's a GP and she's feisty and funny and . . .'

Pete's smile evened out. He said, not that nicely, 'Little Miss Matchmaker, are you? *Mrs* Matchmaker, I should say.'

'Oh, well, if you're not,' I said quickly.

'I don't think so,' he said, coming alongside me to wash his hands at the kitchen tap. 'If that's all right with you.'

It was a bit frosty for a moment or two. Then, picking up his bag, he said, 'Do you think I look desperate or something?'

'I didn't mean that. It was nothing. It's just that you don't often meet nice single men.'

'I see. Well, I'll think about it, OK? Maybe when I come next time I'll take her number.'

'OK,' I said.

After he left, I finished off the cornflake cakes. All eight of them.

I saw Mel that night. I asked Jake to make sure he was home early, which he did with much puffing and lugging of heavy papers onto the kitchen table and important phone calls over bathtime. 'They will go to sleep, won't they?' he said, finally coming up to take over the towelling. 'Only I've got to work on this pitch.'

'Of course they will,' I lied. Of course Fergus won't get out of his bed five minutes after you've put him there. Of course he won't want another story. Of course he won't want a drink of water. Of course Dan will let you put his pyjamas on without wriggling. Of course he'll go down without a murmur. 'They're angels,' I called, skipping out of the door.

Mel and I met at the Drunken Stoat, the brasserie-cum-Mexican-cum-tapas-bar round the corner. That night it was busy with a post-work crowd. Lads in suits with their ties undone. Girls in Dorothy Perkins' Whistles range. Lots of loud laughter and sitting on knees and piles of nachos with cheese. Could have been us fifteen years ago, only no one was blowing smoke rings.

'That's because no one smokes any more,' said Mel, as we sat down in the corner. 'Haven't you noticed the link between the decline in smoking and the rise of tapas bars. Young people have to do something with their hands. People don't smoke any more; they snack.'

'Except for doctors,' she added, lighting up.

'And advertising execs,' I said. I was sure Jake had started again. I could smell something musty on his jacket.

'Wouldn't he have told you if he was?' Mel said.

'I don't know. I'm not so sure about him these days. He's still behaving a *bit strangely*.' I said these last two words in a Vincent Price voice. I might have expanded but the waiter came along then.

'Hi, guys,' he said, perching on the edge of our table.

'Hi, guy,' said Mel.

I ordered the deep-fried Camembert, with gooseberry sauce, starter-size. 'I mustn't eat too much,' I told Mel. 'I've been eating cake all day.'

I was about to tell her then about my encounter with Pete. I was longing to have someone to dissect our conversation with, but her mind was still on Jake. She said in a sympathetic voice, 'In what way is he still behaving strangely?'

'I don't know. He's at the office all the time. Still no sex. Something's up with him. It's almost as if he's seeing someone else.' I snorted, as if I realised this was ridiculous.

Mel looked serious. She said, 'Oh, Maggie. You've always been like this. Whenever someone's really in love with you, you always think they're going to leave you. Just because your father left your mother doesn't mean every man leaves every woman. Jake is a good bloke. Talk to him if you're worried. Don't be too hard on him. He was looking really tired the other weekend. Is he under strain from work?'

'Er . . .' I said, chastened, 'I think so.'

She gave me a sharp look.

'Yes, yes, no, he is. He's got a big pitch coming up.'

'What pitch?'

'Kyushi want one agency across Europe or something. TMT and T have got to rebid for the business from scratch, fighting off all the opposition, and then they might lose the account altogether.'

'What implications would that have?'

'I don't know. I haven't felt like asking.'

Mel shook her head. 'Well, maybe you should. You're lucky not having to work, you know. I know you can get fed up at home with the children all day, but it's your choice and Jake has made it possible for you.'

'I know,' I said.

Mel said, 'You don't have to stay at home. You've got a degree. You could go back to magazines or publishing. It's been your decision.'

'Yes, I know, but it's not that simple.' I was about to talk about the invisible tug between mother and child, the fear of what they'd be without you . . . my own crapness in every job I'd ever done. But then she said softly, glancing away, 'Some of us don't have a choice.'

'Point taken,' I said, putting my hand on her arm.

The food arrived then and, while I picked at crispy Camembert and Mel tucked into a plate of fettucini with salmon, we moved on to Mel's day and the problems she'd been having with one of the other partners, a woman of her age who Mel didn't think was pulling her weight, and we discussed tactics and the redistribution of nights on call. And then she told me about one of her patients, an elderly woman who'd been in to the surgery a lot over the last couple of years with heart problems and blood pressure issues, and how she'd seen Mel a few weeks back because she'd been coughing for a bit and maybe even seen a bit of blood. Mel had sent her off for an X-ray, and, 'You just knew,' Mel said, putting down her fork, 'what the results were going to be. She's smoked for years and . . . Anyway, she came in yesterday saying she felt a bit better and I had to tell her and it's just awful. *Awful.*'

'Oh God,' I said, stricken. 'I have to take my neighbour for a chest X-ray soon. Oh God, I hope that's not cancer. I've only just got to know her.'

'Might not be. Anyway, I had to go straight from her to two "emergency patients" who, it turned out, were a young couple who'd forgotten to have their jabs. They were going on holiday to Kenya in three days' time. Well, I just hit the roof. I mean, there are people who really are emergencies and here they were . . . Anyway, I had a real argument with them, but I ended up giving in, but I was so grumpy.'

I laughed in sympathy.

'But,' Mel lowered her voice, 'after they'd gone I realised that I'd given the woman the polio and the yellow fever and the Hep A, but I hadn't given her the typhoid.'

'Oh my God!'

'I know, isn't it awful? I didn't know what to do. And because we'd had such a barney I couldn't ring her, so I've just left it.'

'Oh my God!'

'Is that just awful, do you think? It is, isn't it? I think they were just going to a resort on the coast, but even so. It's just that I've had two nights on call, and then the cancer woman and . . . Oh.' She pushed her plate to the other side of the table and pulled over an ashtray. 'I wish I could give it up and do something else. I don't know . . . marry a rich banker or something.'

Which took us to Piers, her anaesthetist. She raised her eyes to the ceiling when he was mentioned, lit another cigarette and poured herself another glass of wine. I told her I didn't understand why she didn't just finish it, that it wasn't fair on him to keep him dangling. 'I know,' she said guiltlessly. 'I keep trying. I'm so horrible to him. But he just doesn't get the message. What I need is to fall madly in love with someone else. What happened, by the way, about the gardener chap?'

'Oh,' I said. Even to my ears I sounded hesitant. 'I think maybe we'd better forget it. It turns out he's seeing someone.'

Mel looked unconcerned. 'Oh drat,' she said. 'Oh well, I wasn't that sure about the dirty fingernails anyway. Piers's, at least, are always so clean.' She looked around the room. A girl was shrieking with laughter at the next table. Probably because the man next to her—a colleague? her boss?—had his hand up her skirt. 'Too clean,' she added gloomily.

We left soonish after that and Mel said she'd come back to my house for a nightcap. 'It would be nice to see Jake,' she said. 'See how mysterious he is with my own eyes.'

When we got in, he was at the kitchen table, surrounded by papers.

'Mel's here,' I said.

He stood up and stretched and gave her a long hug. 'How nice,' he said, still with his arms around her.

We sat on the steps up to the garden with a bottle of wine between us. Mel told him about the difficult partner at work and Jake, who as the head of a department knew about these things, told her what to say and how to approach her. ('The thing is to be nice, always nice, but firm. Explain how things seem to you, and see what she has to say. Then, if there's still a problem, go to the head of practice.')

'And how are the spots?' she said. He proffered his chin for her to inspect. She ran a medical hand over it. 'Hmm. Have you tried . . .? Might I suggest . . .?' She pretended to delve into her bag and bring something out, holding it like a dart in front of her eyes, 'ZAP-IT?'

'STOP-IT!' he said, pretending to grab it off her.

She only stayed for half an hour, but it was a nice half-hour, almost like old times. I felt warm and comfortable with my two favourite people around me. I said, 'Let's go away somewhere August bank holiday, us and Mel and Milly and maybe even Piers.' Mel winced. 'All right. Not Piers then. We could get a cottage, by the sea or something.'

Mel looked enthusiastic, but Jake gave a weary grimace. 'Oh, Maggie. Have you forgotten? You know . . . Ed and Pea?' I frowned. I didn't remember. 'We said we'd go and stay with them in Suffolk?'

'Did we?'

'To make up for Majorca?'

'Were you going to go to Majorca?' asked Mel.

'No,' I said shortly.

'Never mind,' Mel said. 'Another time.'

When Mel's minicab came, I walked her to the kerb. 'Try and be a bit more understanding with Jake,' she said. 'Otherwise, I'll have him.'

When I got back inside, Jake was back at the kitchen table. 'Sorry about Suffolk,' he said, not looking up from his papers. 'I think I'm guilty on that one. I was just waiting for an opportunity to slip it in.'

'You slipped it,' I said.

He still didn't look up.

'Are you all right?' I came up behind him and rested my chin on the top of his head. There were lines of grey in among the dark brown.

'Knackered actually.' He kept his eyes on his paperwork. But he reached behind to put an arm round my legs. 'Perhaps you could go and check on your children. I think I might have heard Dan.'

'They're my children now, are they? Only yours when they're quiet?'

'Absolutely,' he said, smiling. 'Oh, and Fran rang earlier. Can you ring her? Something about a tennis machine?'

'A TENS machine,' I said. 'You know, the thing you strap on your back when you're in labour. Nothing to do with tennis. You pillock.'

I was about to give him a playful slap, but he'd already bowed his head again and was back to his figures, so I went upstairs to check on the children instead. Dan's hair was all sweaty on one side from where he must have been lying; Fergus's mouth was squashed open against the pillow and he was breathing through it: thick, wet, rasping snores that pulled at my heart. Still clasped in his hand was the 747 Jake had bought him at Amsterdam airport. My children. Our children. What had I been thinking of? We were a family. Nothing could come between us. It was just a rough patch, that was all.

I rearranged their blankets and went back downstairs to make Jake some tea.

The next morning, I took the children to the urban zoo: held Dan up to stare blankly at the penned-in sheep and let Fergus sit for our entire visit in the rusty old tractor, fighting off the other children with his feet.

On the way home I drove up to the common, and parked in a bus stop and scribbled a note:

Dear Pete,
    On further reflection, I think it's best if we call it a day on the garden front. I'm thrilled with the work you've done so far, but on further reflection [I scratched those last three words out] it's probably getting a bit too expensive in the long term. Thanks for untangling the bindweed and [I thought for a while before adding] your care and attention. It was much needed! Let me know how much I owe you for services so far rendered. [I regretted that last bit, but felt I couldn't cross anything else out without having to find another piece of paper. I wondered hard how to finish. In the end I wrote—]
    Best wishes,
    Maggie (Owen)

Then I opened the car door, ran down the steps of the house he shared with Claire and posted the note through the basement door.

I didn't feel sad as I drove home. I didn't really feel anything. There was nothing to feel anything about.

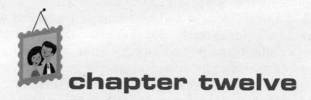

chapter twelve

'I'M GOING TO HAVE TO MEET YOU THERE,' said Jake on the phone that afternoon. 'I'm sorry. I can't get away early tonight. I've got people breathing down my neck left, right and centre. Not just Kyushi; the people at Zap-it want a whole new cradle-to-grave strategy by the end of the week.'

'Cradle to grave?'

'It's not just teenagers who get spots, they say. They want the new, improved cream to be really big.'

'You mean, in your face?'

Jake didn't laugh. He sounded impatient. He said, 'So, what with everything, Maggie . . .'

I said, 'Well, just don't be rudely late.'

'I'll try and be there by nine thirty pm . . .'

'Jake!' I said.

'Look, I've got to go. Bye.'

I found it much easier finding something to wear than I had a few weeks before. It might have been because I was browner after a few days on the common. Or it might have been because my self-esteem had been lifted out of my shoes on the fork of a flirtatious gardener. Either way, I got out a spotty tea-dress I'd once found in a jumble sale, and decided, looking at myself sideways in the mirror, that it was just fine. I put on some earrings and some make-up, and felt, in the bathroom light at least, almost glamorous.

Merika, Maria's Slovakian au pair, cycled over from Wandsworth to baby-sit. She was bang on time so I got to Claire's a bit early. I sat in the car for a bit, watching the house as I'd watched it before. There was no sign of life in the bottom flat. I wondered what Pete was doing. Who he was with.

At 8.45pm I rang Claire's bell.

'Magsarama,' she cried. She was wearing cropped jeans, bare feet and no make-up. Immediately, I felt overdressed. She steered me in. '*Entrez.*'

I was not the first. Her sister, Rowena, the television presenter, was reclining on the sofa in the sitting room. She exclaimed, 'Maggie Owen, the French-skipping Queen of the Lower Fourth! Remember me after all these years? Claire's little sister!' I said of course, not adding the fact that I'd caught her elfin figure bottle-feeding a lamb on *Animal SOS* only a few weeks before. Celebrity always made me awkward. She pointed across the room to her boyfriend, Johnny Something—whom I also recognised from the telly or the pages of the *Mail* or *Hello!*—who was slipping a CD into the machine. He furrowed his handsome forehead into one long eyebrow as he straightened up and, white man's overbite at the ready, pointed his finger at me in a faux familiar 'my man' gesture. I pointed my finger back at him and then put it in my pocket.

I said, 'What's this?' meaning the music.

Johnny said, 'M&M.'

'Like the sweets?' I said.

He looked pained. 'No. E.M.I.N.E.M.'

From then on, Johnny Something clearly thought I was an imbecile. Every time anybody said anything about anybody, he turned to me and, sideburns standing to attention, gave me a quick Ladybird explanation. He'd just said, 'That's Guy Richie, the film director, they're talking about. He directed *Lock, Stock and Two Smoking Barrels* and *Snatch*. He's married to Madonna,' when the buzzer went and almost immediately there were shrieks in the hall. I could hear a high voice and a deeper one—for a gut-wrenching moment I thought this was Pete's—but when the couple entered, the deep voice belonged to a balding, burly-looking bloke who turned out to be a cookery writer on one of the Sundays.

'Maggie er . . . cooks too,' said Claire.

'No, I don't,' I parried. 'I microwave. Though I can make cakes.'

The man, who was called Tom, laughed and introduced me to his wife, Lily, a book editor with pouting lips and Louise Brooks hair. They smiled so broadly I liked them both at once. When Claire was in the kitchen, and Rowena and Johnny were busy flicking through a book of 'promos', Tom mouthed conspiratorially, 'Any news on Claire's man?' as if we'd known each other all our lives.

I whispered, 'Not sure. Do you think he's coming?'

Lily hissed, 'I think he's had his chips. I asked Claire on the phone earlier this week and she said, "Curtains".'

'Oh really, "curtains"?' I repeated, interested.

'What do you mean curtains?' said Claire, coming up behind me with a bowl of marinaded olives.

'Nothing,' I said, trying to keep a straight face. 'Just discussing cur- tains v. blinds.'

'God, you marrieds,' she said. 'You've got to get out more.'

Lily and I exchanged glances.

Soon after that, the buzzer went again and I thought with relief, That'll be Jake: he's not embarrassingly late after all. But Claire was gone quite some time—you could hear muffled discussions from the hallway. When she came back she looked pink and there was a triumphant bounce to her gait and in her wake, holding her hand like a reluctant teenager dragged onto the dance floor by a tipsy aunt, was a tall man in his forties with shoulder-length grey-brown hair. Claire said, after a deep breath, 'Everybody. Meet Marcus.'

Marcus, who was, I was almost sure, the man I'd seen leaving Claire's flat, looked dazed but gave a sheepish smile. He was wearing a pin-stripe suit but the stripes were exaggerated as if to announce his distance from conventionality and proximity to youth. There were deep notches in his cheeks and furrows across his forehead, and a burnt-orange hue to his face, which didn't look entirely natural. He waved slightly to Rowena to acknowledge having met her before and then rummaged in his jacket pocket to retrieve a nasal spray, which he applied noisily to his nose. Ah! So he *was* the man I'd seen leaving Claire's flat.

'Sorry to interrupt,' he said, after he'd cleared his throat. Then he looked down blankly at the pigskin briefcase in his hand as if he didn't know what to do with it.

'You're not interrupting,' said Claire slowly as if explaining etiquette to a child. 'You're invited. Remember?'

He made a high-pitched sound, somewhere between a sob and a laugh and took his briefcase into another room—possibly the bedroom.

'Have a drink,' called Claire after him. 'He's had a hard day,' she said *sotto voce* to the rest of us. 'Sony v. Visconti,' she added, wrinkling her nose. She was smiling, but there was something vulnerable in the set of her mouth. Johnny was whispering to me, 'Breach of contract. Visconti, the sixties crooner recently revived through the Ibiza club scene, is—'

'Sorry? What?' I said. I was trying to catch Claire's eye. 'Yeah, I know,' I said, though actually I didn't.

Thinking back to the conversation with Claire in my kitchen, I did some mental calculations. It was, technically, next week. Did this mean Marcus had left his wife? And did this mean Claire had decided to forget the other man, the one she said she *really* loved? Was she happy with this? I managed to catch her eye when she was pouring herself a glass of wine, and opened mine wide enquiringly. She gave me a halfhearted thumbs up. So he had . . . and apparently she had too.

Marcus sat dazed in an armchair, jacket off, tie undone, nursing his drink, while the rest of us chattered around him. Johnny and Rowena had just been on holiday in Madagascar and were full of lemurs. ('Nocturnal,' Johnny assured me in an aside. 'Similar to monkeys.') Tom and Lily were thinking of downsizing. They'd seen a house in Suffolk. Tom wanted pigs. 'For the bacon,' said Lily, raising her eyebrows. Rowena and Claire did a funny double act about their parents, who had moved to an old rectory just north of Oxford. 'Handy for Stratford for Mummy,' said Rowena. 'And a handy supply of female students for Daddy,' said Claire. And all the while I surprised myself by my sociability. It was like being single again: I could be who I wanted. So I did impressions of some of the more awful 'playground mums' and discussed books with Lily and told tales on Claire that made her squirm with pretend-embarrassment and the others howl.

It was almost 10.30pm when Jake finally turned up. The olives had long been eaten and too much wine had been consumed on top of too many empty stomachs. He was definitely rudely late. 'Sorry, sorry, sorry, sorry,' he was still saying, as Claire brought him into the sitting room. He looked windswept, full of energy. 'Hello,' he said to the others. 'Sorry,' he said again to Claire.

'It's all right,' Claire said gaily. 'I'm too pissed to care. And it's only risotto. Burnt to a cinder. You can have the charred bits from the bottom. Now, Maggie you know. Rowena, you remember. This is Johnny, her boyfriend. Lily and Tom: did you meet them at the party? Oh good. And this—' she put her arm round Marcus as if presenting a soufflé that might collapse at any moment—'is Marcus.'

Jake had been smiling and shaking hands, but he turned the charm off for a fleeting moment then. No one but me would have noticed, but it was almost as if he'd met Marcus before, or as if he had something against him. 'Hi,' he said smoothly, a muscle twitching in his cheek. Then, quickly, he turned to me. 'Hello, sweetie.' He gave me a single peck. Then mouthed, silently, 'Sorry, I couldn't get away.' I shook my head as if to say, it doesn't matter.

We had finally started eating when the phone went. We were in the kitchen, which was the most dead-grannyish of the rooms in the flat. It had spice racks on the walls, though the jars had gone, the lino on the floor had white swirls in it like the trail left at the back of a cross-Channel ferry. Jake was sitting next to Rowena, who was laughing at whatever he was saying, her head cocked at an angle, so that she could look out at him from behind her hair. Sometimes I forgot how sexy Jake was, what an effect he could have on other women. Johnny was looking handsomely pensive at the end of the table, rigid with the effort of not minding about Jake, occasionally frowning winsomely as he caught his own eye in the darkened window. And Lily and I were trying to cheer up Marcus. We were doing party-style good cop, bad cop. I asked the questions, she administered the flattery.

Me: 'So what does a show-biz lawyer actually do?'

Marcus: 'I'm principally involved with the drawing up of contracts, with protecting my clients' reputation and trademark and any disputes that might arise as a result of damage to that reputation or trademark.'

Lily: 'It must be so demanding dealing with all those egos. You must need to be such a patient, strong person.'

Marcus, preening: 'Well, I don't know about that.'

After a while, under the influence of Lily, and with a little help from the bottle of Australian Shiraz by his side, he stopped looking nervously at his watch every few minutes. He even looked up from his glass to blow a kiss in Claire's direction. 'Lovely girl,' he said to me.

And then the phone rang. It was about 11.00pm. Claire had a tray of hot pears in her hand and went to put them down. Jake and Rowena were still giggling. Johnny was examining the back of a spoon. Tom, who had been helping her whip some cream, was standing by the phone. Claire made a gesture at him to pick it up.

'Hello,' he said. 'Hello? Hello?'

He put the phone back on the counter. 'No one there,' he said.

Almost immediately it rang again. This time Tom handed it to Claire. 'Hello.' Pause. 'It's Claire speaking.' Longer pause. 'Yes, I have . . . Yes, he is. I'm not prepared to discuss that with you.' She had gone very red but the blood was now draining away, except for two spots high on her cheeks. Her lips were pale. We'd all stopped talking now. Marcus had stood up. He had his hand out for the phone. Claire said, magisterial, the actor's daughter, 'I repeat, I am not prepared to discuss that with you. It is my personal business. If you wish to talk to Marcus he is here and you may do so. Right . . . I'm sorry to hear that but you must understand it is not my concern. Marcus is an adult. I am an adult.' Long pause. 'I'm sorry, I'm not prepared to listen to this, and I'm going to—'

She looked as if she was about to hang up, but Marcus grabbed her arm before she could do so, took the phone from her and left the room.

Claire sat down abruptly in the empty seat next to Jake and burst into tears. She buried her head on Jake's shoulder. He patted her hair.

'Hey, hey,' he said softly.

Tom took over then. 'Right,' he said. 'What was all that about?'

Claire took her head out from under Jake's hand and said, through her tears, 'She was so horrible. How dare she? She has no right to ring me during a dinner party and say those things. If Marcus wants to leave her for me, it's not my fault, is it? What she's going through shouldn't be any of my business. It's his, not mine.'

Her emotion slunk across the room like dry ice. Most of us shifted in our seats, suddenly awkward and embarrassed.

Rowena said, 'Come off it, Claire. He's a married man. Married men tend to have wives. And quite a few of them—including this one—have kids. So I have to say it is your business.'

Claire looked daggers at her sister and said, 'But it's not my fault that I fell in love with him. I didn't have a choice.'

'I don't think you're in love with him,' said Rowena. 'Not really. And anyway, there's always a choice. You knew he had a wife and kids when you met him. You could have walked away.'

Claire said unconvincingly, 'I didn't know, actually. He didn't tell me about the meat and two veg until our second date.'

'"Meat and two veg?"' echoed Rowena.

Claire looked flustered. 'Wife and two kids. You know what I mean.' She glanced round the room, 'Look, all I'm saying is, we don't choose who we fall in love with and when Cupid steps in—'

'Come off it.' Rowena was looking more and more irritated. 'Cupid? Which planet are you on? Look, Claire, think about it. Is Marcus the one? Isn't he just the result of panic? What about—?'

Claire said, 'But, Rowena.' She slumped. She looked suddenly tired.

Tom said quickly, 'Those pears look delicious. Let's eat them before they get cold.'

Claire was about to dole them out when Marcus came back into the kitchen, looking, despite the exaggerated stripes, like an old man. He said to Claire, 'I'm sorry. I'm going to have to go.'

'You can't,' she said wearily. 'You've only just come.'

'Look, look,' he said, trying to draw her into some privacy in the shelter of the fridge. 'Look, I've got to go,' he whispered intensely. 'She's in a state. She's got the letter. She knows. But Alfie has got a temperature. It's thirty-nine point nine. She's rung the doctor, but they don't know what time they'll be able to come. I've got to go. I've got to be there.' There were a couple of loud sniffs as the inhaler came back into use. 'I'll ring you,' he said, backing out of the door. 'Tomorrow. I promise.'

'Fucking hell,' she said quietly after the front door had closed. 'Sorry, everyone, but . . . Fuck.'

Jake, who had been silent through all this, said, 'I didn't much like him anyway.'

For a moment, I thought Claire was about to laugh. It could have gone either way. But she didn't laugh. She stood up. She said, enunciating every word very clearly, 'Fuck you, too,' and threw the whole plate of pears on the floor. Luckily they'd cooled down, so no one was hurt.

Why did you say that?' I asked Jake in the car. 'I can't believe you said it. It was so tactless. Do you know him or something? You were very odd. And,' I thought I might as well throw it in for good measure, 'what was all that flirting with Rowena?'

Jake looked pensive. I was driving. He was slumped against the passenger window. He said, 'It's just that it all seemed such a charade.'

'You didn't help. If you hadn't been so late getting there, we'd have eaten earlier and people wouldn't have got so drunk.'

'I didn't help?' He was laughing. 'What about *Claire* didn't help? Or Martin or Marcus, or whatever he's called, didn't help?'

'Marcus. His name is Marcus.'

Oblivious to my mood, Jake put his feet up on the dashboard and said, chuckling, 'Meat and two veg. I've not heard that one before.'

'It's not funny,' I said.

The next night, Claire rang to apologise. Jake was still out. He hadn't rung but I assumed he was at work. I was about to settle down in front of the television with a bowl of pasta when the phone rang. I thought it might be Mel—I hadn't heard from her for a few days—or Fran with some new life-threatening symptom, but it was Claire. Again.

'Hello. How are you?' I said, trying to suppress the surprise in my voice, wanting to say, Why do you keep ringing? Don't you have any other friends? Deep down, though, I was flattered. Maggie the schoolgirl, sunbathing in her attention.

She said in a small voice, 'Are you in?'

'Er, yes.'

'It's just that I need someone to talk to. I'm so sorry about last night. I really lost it. I just wondered if I could ask your advice?'

'Is this about Marcus?' I said. 'I don't know if there's anything more I can say to help.'

'Marcus and . . . you know. I'm so confused. Please, Maggie? You were always there for me. In the past.'

'Sure,' I said doubtfully, trying to remember an occasion when I'd 'been there for her' before. I did find her crying once in the school loos. I think I copied out my wordsheet of 'Bohemian Rhapsody' for her to cheer her up. I didn't know if I could do anything similar now. 'Come round. Jake's out, so I'm on my own. Come and have a drink.'

She said, 'Oh. Where is he . . . Jake?' She sounded puzzled. It was past nine, but that was nothing these days.

'Late meeting,' I said. 'But he'll probably be back quite soon.'

'Oh, right,' she said.

I set the video up to tape *ER* and waited. Forty-five minutes went by before I caught the small thump and clatter that means someone is about to knock at the door. Except they didn't. There was a louder clatter that means someone is letting themselves in with a key.

'Hi,' said Jake, coming into the sitting room.

I was about to warn him about Claire when at that moment there *was* a knock at the door.

'That'll be Claire,' I said.

He stood stock-still, his nose wrinkled in disbelief.

It was an extreme reaction, but I didn't think too much of it at the time. I went to let her in. She was looking fetchingly tearful, though I noticed her mascara hadn't run. Jake was still standing where I'd left him when we came into the sitting room.

She hurled her bag onto the sofa. 'Marcus *has* gone back to his wife.'

Jake shrugged unfeelingly. 'That was obvious.'

I said, 'Oh, Claire, I'm so sorry. What Jake means is—'

She said dramatically, 'I really believed him. He said we'd buy a place in Epsom so he could be near the kids. He said we'd get married when the divorce came through. He said we could start a family. I thought I'd finally found a man I could trust.'

Jake snorted. 'So he wasn't so trustworthy, after all.'

'Well, at least he *almost* left his wife,' said Claire. 'Unlike . . . many men.'

'But he didn't, did he?' said Jake coolly.

'Well, he might still.'

'What? When his son's temperature goes down? What happens next time he gets a cold?'

'Jake,' I said with a laugh, trying to brush over his insensitivity. 'You can take your bad day out on me, but not on Claire. She's upset. Leave her alone. Claire, ignore him.'

Claire sat down on the sofa; the cushions whooshed as they deflated beneath her. She said quietly, 'Oh, it's all a mess. Rowena's right: I don't even know if my heart was in it. But then that makes it all the more awful that he's left me. I can't even keep the second division interested.' She looked at the back of her hands, and then she looked at Jake. 'Of course, Maggie said it first: I'm still in love with . . . with someone else.'

'Maggie said what?' Jake sounded perturbed.

I explained. 'Her ex. Also married.' I tried not to sound censorious.

Claire said, still looking at Jake, 'I can't get him out of my head. Even when I was with Marcus, he was the first thing I thought of in the morning, the last thing I thought of at night.'

Jake was staring at her. I said, 'I know what we need: tea.' And when Jake didn't get the hint, I went into the kitchen and put the kettle on. When I came back into the room, they were both sitting down on the sofa. Jake had his arm along the back of it. Claire was leaning forward, with her head down. They were talking softly. Claire looked up at me when I came into the room. She seemed more cheerful.

When I put the tray down, she said, 'Shall I be mother?'

'You'd better not be,' Jake said, which made Claire smile.

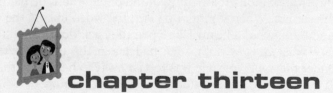

chapter thirteen

WE HAD A BAD NIGHT that night. Dan was cutting a molar and started crying shortly after Jake and I went to sleep. He was hot, so I gave him some Calpol and then a bottle to soothe him. I was stroking his head through the bars of his cot when Fergus stirred and got out of bed. He was half asleep, still in the middle of a dream, and he went rigid when I tried to pick him up, pulling his head away from me as if I was a night-fright monster, and it took a while for me to calm him down. By the time he had woken up enough to snuggle into me, Dan had dropped off and I didn't want to risk waking him again by trying to settle Fergus, so I took Fergus into our room. Jake grunted when he realised what was going on, and went off to sleep in the spare room.

I lay there, curled round my son, feeling the bones in his back through his pyjamas, one arm encircling his head, sensing the warmth of him, filling my nostrils with the smell of crayons and Matey, until he pushed me closer and closer to the edge of the bed. And then I lay there, gripping the sheet, uncomfy, uneasy, as Jake's side grew cold, wondering why I felt so distant from him, and whether we'd ever make love again.

In the morning, after Jake had left, Mrs Allardyce—minus mac in honour of July—came to the door to check I could still take her to the hospital the following day. She came into the kitchen and had some tea and a comforting moan about the litter from Pizza Express. When Dan came and clung to her support stockings, she called him 'Lamb' and she did 'Two Little Dickeybirds' for Fergus, using two bits of tissue on her knobbly fingers, until he left the doorjamb which he'd been swinging round warily and came and stood by her side.

'You can get people so wrong,' I told Jake later when he came in.

'Hm?' he said, looking at his bank statement.

'Mrs Allardyce. She's really quite nice and—'

'Good,' he said absent-mindedly. 'Good.'

I left him to it, found a beer in the fridge and went into the sitting room to watch my tape of the previous night's *ER*.

I wouldn't have thought anything of the phone call if he hadn't taken it into the garden. When it rang, I paused the video in case the call was for me and then, when I heard Jake open the back door, I went into the hall to see what he was doing. He had taken the phone over to the bench under the apple tree. He was too far away to hear from the hall so I slipped into the kitchen and stood by the open window.

He didn't say much at first; he just seemed to be listening. Then he said, 'Yes,' and, 'I know, I know.' And then there was another long silence at the end of which he gave a sequence of sighs and then he sort of groaned, and said, 'You're very persuasive. Did anyone ever tell you that?' And finally, as if conceding, he said, 'OK. OK. Lunch tomorrow. Ring me at work in the morning just to check. No, she won't . . . No . . . All right . . . No, fine. One-ish. OK, Claire. Bye.'

I hadn't moved. I was standing in the same place. In the same kitchen, gripping the sill as if a wind was ripping through my house. There was a delay between hearing the information and feeling it, as when you stub your toe and there's a moment of nothing when you think you've got away with it before the pain hits you. And then it hit me. Claire. Claire Masterson, who always had to have everything I had. *Jake* was the married man she was in love with. The love of her life. At some point, they had had an affair. And now she wanted him back.

Everything suddenly fell into place. The way they danced at her party, as if they knew each other better than they should. His attitude at finding her in our house the day he got back from Amsterdam. The fact that *she* knew about Kyushi. That *he* knew about Disney. The smell of smoke on his clothes. His oddly detached attitude at dinner the other night and in our house the evening after. His behaviour towards Marcus. And his complete lack of interest in sex. With me, at least. This sense I'd had recently that he was slipping away from me, that his life was elsewhere. And her new friendship with me? Ringing me up all the time, coming round whenever she could, inviting us to everything, wheedling herself into my, our, *his*, life. I'd thought, foolish me, that she'd wanted to be my friend. But she hadn't, had she? She'd come back from America, determined to get him again, and he must have said no, so, while stringing poor old Marcus along, she'd just used me to get close to him, to thrust herself under his nose, to insinuate herself back into his heart.

I was back on the sofa in front of *ER* when Jake came in from the garden and started clanking about in the kitchen cupboards. After a short while, he came into the sitting room with a pot of coffee on a tray. 'Who rang?' I said, without moving my eyes from the screen. I waited what seemed like a million years for him to answer.

'Work,' he said. 'Just someone from work.'

That night I lay awake for hours, listening to Jake breathe. I had been on the verge of confronting him all evening. But I'd open my mouth, and then the words, which were jumbled up in my head, the anger, the tears, the how-could-yous, would disappear, and I'd sit there silent.

In bed I went over and over in my mind when their affair must have started. Before she went to America and she'd been there—what, two years? So, before we had Fergus? No, it must have been after that because she'd said, that day in my kitchen, that 'the love of her life'—of *her* life—couldn't leave his child. Child singular. So after Fergus, but before Dan. It was a horrific thought. I'd believed we were happy then, him and me and our little boy. But all that time . . . As I thought about it, the past moments of contentment went off like sour milk. Those nights when I'd been working and came back to find Jake at the kitchen table, and he'd made me tea and massaged my shoulders, had she been there with him until minutes before I got home? The weekend he'd spent at St Andrews with Ed when I was pregnant, cheering poor Ed up, he'd said, one last fling, one last swing, before Dan was born, had that been an alibi? Had Ed been an accomplice? Had he been off on some little holiday with *her*. And then his behaviour over the last year, withdrawn, self-contained, guilty almost—was that bitterness against me, unhappiness at what he'd given up? I often wondered what my mother had felt like when my father left her. Had she felt like this? As if someone had taken their life together, all the things they'd shared, and thrown a bucket of dirty water over it.

But some things still didn't add up. Why did she refer so dismissively to him the day we bumped into each other? Dullsville, she had called him. Why would she say that? A smoke screen?

And what was happening now? She wanted him back. That was obvious. Now Marcus had dumped her. But would he go? What would he choose? Claire Masterson, the glamorous girl about town, with her Disney contract and her faultless skin and her flat stomach. Or me, plain, mousy Maggie who had none of those things? There was a murmur then from the room next door, a moan with a kick at the end of it, not a cry exactly, not quite a word. Fergus fighting dragons in his sleep. Maybe, I realised, I didn't even come into it. Maybe Jake's choice was between Claire Masterson and his children.

As I lay there, sleeplessness coiled in my stomach like hunger, I realised how impotent I was. Part of me wanted to hurl his clothes out of the window, bundle the kids in blankets and roar off down the street. That's what they did on the telly, in the two-part Sunday/Monday ITV dramas Jake and I watched—used to watch—together. But when you have children, life isn't simple any more. I knew that if I confronted him, I might force him to make a decision that he might otherwise turn away from.

I'd intended to take Fergus and Dan with me the following day to the Marsden for Mrs Allardyce's lung X-ray. But at the last minute I rang Maria to see if I could borrow Merika for the morning. Maria didn't exactly sound thrilled—one of the rules concerning other people's au pairs is that you don't nab them in the day—but I said, darkly, that it was an emergency, and reluctantly she agreed.

It was a quarter past eleven when I knocked at Mrs Allardyce's door. I felt dazed with exhaustion, but I smiled chirpily when I saw her. She had traces of talc on her tortoise cheek, pink lipstick across her lips and a turquoise silk scarf, with proper rolled edges, round her neck.

'Come in, dear,' she said. 'I won't be a minute. I'm just out the back feeding the neighbours' cats.'

She left me in her front room. There were thick net curtains at the window, and a swirly, red-and-black carpet on the floor. On the mantel-piece and on the sixties sideboard in the alcove, there were photo-graphs. I was bending to look at one of the smallest, black and white, of a young man in uniform, when Mrs Allardyce came in behind me.

She said, 'That was Arthur, just after we got married.' She paused before gesturing to another. 'And this is us on our silver wedding.'

The picture was old, in faded blues and greens. It showed a plump, middle-aged couple under a rose swag in a suburban garden. I asked her when it was taken and she said thirty-five years ago, in 1965, and while I was inwardly wondering how anyone's marriage could last that long, she told me that they'd lived in that house since 1950 and seen a lot of changes, but that life hadn't been the same since Arthur had passed on, cancer it was, that not a day went by that she didn't miss him, that he was a good man. I asked how long she'd been a widow and she said twenty-five years, which I said was a long time.

'Yes, dear.' She seemed impatient suddenly with my sympathy. 'But I've got my boys.' She pointed to another photograph. 'That's Philip. He's a teacher, but he's retired now and they live in Newcastle, near her parents. Those are his kids, all grown themselves. I've got four grand-children, and six great-grandchildren. They're always saying I should come and visit but, well, it's too far for me now. And this is Nicholas. He went to work for Boeing.'

I asked her where he lived and she said Seattle and I said that struck me as quite a long way.

She looked at me beadily. 'They grow up, dear. You think it's going to go on for ever, but it doesn't. They fly off and you hear from them at Christmas and they always remember my birthday. And Flora, my grand-daughter, she lives in Streatham and she pops in whenever she's passing. But I hope you'll make the most of it while you can. I've seen you around, with your heart in your heels, and I know it's hard, but—'

'But it's not nearly as hard as it was for you,' I finished for her.

'Well.' She looked oddly satisfied. 'Everything's different now.'

We had to hurry a bit after that to lock up the house, and get her into the car and to the hospital on time. I parked on a meter and took her arm to guide her through the long cream-walled corridors and up the cranky lift to the right department. The nurse at the desk said Mrs Allardyce would have to see the doctor after the X-ray and then hang around for the results to take back to her GP. It would be a couple of hours, she said. Mrs Allardyce heaved herself down into a chair with a copy of January's *Good Housekeeping* on her knee and said she didn't mind if I went off for a bit. 'You go and do some shopping, dear. I'm fine here.'

So at 12.30pm I was on the steps outside the hospital. For a moment I wondered whether I *should* do some shopping. We were out of a few things. There had to be somewhere in South Ken you could buy soap powder and ketchup. But I'd made up my mind earlier. Jake's phone conversation with Claire played in my head. One-ish, he had said. Lunch. I didn't know exactly what I expected to see, but if I witnessed them with my own eyes, I'd be sure then. I would have proof.

I half walked, half ran to the tube, where I waited '4 mins' for a train, then wandered in a crush of people along endless stygian corridors to change trains at Victoria, only to endure two crowded stops to Oxford Circus. When I finally reached the open air, the sky was deep blue. There were people everywhere, getting off and on the buses as they idled at the lights, or crossing between cars, or selling the *Big Issue*, or weaving through the crowd with Styrofoam cups of coffee balanced in each hand. There seemed to be a businessman with his arm out for a taxi on every corner. No pushchairs. No three-wheel all-terrain mountain buggies. No babies in slings. No young mums in Boden. No sense of time lingering like you get in the suburbs, but time divided into holiday diaries, and production diaries and rotas, a world of work. Oh, of course I knew central London was *there*, but it still always came as a shock.

Jake's office was in a side street between Oxford Street and Soho. It was a big, glass-fronted building with rotating doors and leather retro arm-chairs, in bright colours and bulbous shapes, in reception. Appearances matter in advertising in a way they don't in other businesses. It's how you perceive the product, after all, not the product itself, that counts. Jake's building said, 'cutting edge, out there, classic with a twist'. There were other buildings adjacent saying other things, but I made for a small old-style caff on the opposite side of the road, with sandwich fillings lined up like different types of sick in the window and hot water gushing into stainless-steel teapots from a network of metal pipes.

I sat at the Formica table closest to the door with a can of Coke as cover and waited. Over the next fifteen minutes, people drifted out of the TMT&T office in dribs and drabs, but there was no sign of Jake. I was beginning to think he wasn't coming, that maybe, perhaps, he'd decided not to meet Claire after all, my stomach tightening in hope, when at ten past one, the swing doors swung and there he was. There was Jake. He stood for a split second in the street to slip on his sunglasses, and then he began to walk briskly down the road towards Soho. I jumped up and was halfway out of the door when someone else came out of the building behind him and called him to stop. It was Ed. I hid in the doorway, suddenly fascinated by the sandwich fillings, as Jake turned and waited for him to catch up. Then they both walked off together.

It isn't difficult following somebody if they're not expecting it. I stayed on that side of the road, twenty yards or so behind them, until they reached a small restaurant in a nondescript street. I knew this restaurant. Jake and I had met there a few times, before we had children, before I'd retired to the warm-milk world of the suburbs, and I had loved it. It felt dark and Dickensian inside, with its cigarette-stained walls and the candles making fairy-tale palaces of wax out of the bottles on the tables. It was full of people you knew, but it still felt like a secret. Our secret. And now he'd gone there to meet Claire.

The two men were, for the moment, still standing outside. Maybe Jake was trying to get rid of Ed. They seemed to be talking with some heat—Ed was waving his arms about and Jake at one point rubbed his eyes slowly—but finally Ed walked on up the road and Jake stood watching him for a bit and then went inside.

I stood across the street, wondering what to do. There was no café to hide in here. But there was a hat shop, which I spent some time in, one eye on the mirror, one on the glass, pretending to be in need of something for a wedding. 'Not my own,' I jested with the bored young man who was serving. After a while, I ran out of hats and had to leave, so I walked up and down the road a couple of times, bought a paper from a newsagent's and hovered as inconspicuously as I could manage. I even walked directly in front of the restaurant, peering quickly past the menus in the window to see if I could spot them, but it was too dark and too busy. In the end I sat in a patch of sun on some office steps a few doors down and pretended to read the paper. After a while, the sky began to fill up with clouds and the sun went in. Was this the lowest point of my life? Almost.

I was about to give up—there was only half an hour before I had to pick up Mrs Allardyce—when the door of the restaurant opened and Jake came out. He was with Claire. She was wearing the same orange shift-dress she had been wearing the day I first bumped into her in Morton High Street. She looked very blonde, very fragile, next to Jake. I ducked into the doorway of the hat shop. I watched as he ran his hands through his hair, and then took both her hands in his. He talked earnestly, looking into her eyes, and then hugged her close.

I turned and ran to the end of the road where a taxi was just pulling off. I threw out my arm, yelled at it to stop and then hurled myself into the back seat. My limbs felt numb. By the time we reached the Marsden it had begun to rain and the streets had emptied of people.

That night, Jake rang to say he'd be staying late at the office again, and to warn me that he'd have to work all weekend. 'Kyushi?' I said. He said yes, putting on a tired, tense tone. 'Or sushi,' I said, after I'd put down the phone.

I ranged around the house for a while, feeling lost and impotent. I sorted through the fridge and put three tins of half-eaten pickles and unopened jars of Gentleman's Relish, past their sell-by date, into the bin. In the bedroom, I went through the pockets of Jake's clothes, smelling the collars and then chucking restaurant receipts and loose change onto the bed, sorting through them as if they'd bear up a secret. There were enough receipts to be deeply incriminating. But then Jake was in advertising, so they were nothing of the sort.

And then I did something I'd been putting off all day. I rang Mel.

'Maggie,' she said. 'I was just about to ring you. I'm off to Shrewsbury tomorrow to meet Piers's parents . . . I know, I know. You're right, blah blah. But I'm doing it . . . And at some point, I must collect Milly's Fizz. We had tears about that yesterday. I told her Fergus was looking after her, but I must get her some time. And . . . Maggie, are you all right?'

I said, 'Yes.'

'You're not, are you?'

'No.'

'Are you crying?'

It took me a while to say anything. Finally, I managed to say, 'Yes.'

'Maggie, what's the matter? Do you want me to come round? Milly's asleep but I can get a neighbour to sit in.'

I blew my nose. 'No, don't,' I said. 'I'm fine. It's just . . .' I started crying again but while I was doing so I told her what had happened.

She said, 'I'm coming round. Give me ten minutes.'

When she got there, I'd pulled myself together and we sat in the sitting room and I went through everything again. Mel kept shaking her head and saying she didn't believe it. She said Jake just wouldn't. I was very calm. I said it explained everything, that I knew it was true. She said I should talk to him. I said I thought it was important that I didn't, that all that mattered for now was keeping our marriage—huh, I corrected with a self-pitying laugh, our *relationship* going for the sake of the children. 'And maybe for the sake of me, too.'

She said, 'But if it's true, how can you put up with it? And if it isn't, you need to find out.'

I was silent for a long time and then I said, 'I just don't want to lose him.' She put her arms round me and said should she cancel her week away? 'No, of course not,' I said. 'But you're meeting the parents?' Even under the circumstances, I started laughing at this.

She laughed back. She said, 'I know, I know. I'm up to my neck here. It's just he's so . . . nice.' She stroked my hair with her voice. 'I'm so sorry,' she kept saying. 'Maggie, I really am. I'm so, so sorry.'

I was pretending to be asleep when Jake came home and again when he went off on Saturday morning. He left me a note. It said, 'Maggie. XXX.' Either he was kissing me or crossing me out.

chapter fourteen

WHEN YOU'RE A GROWN-UP who has recently discovered the father of your children in the arms of another woman, there are few things as unimportant as a child's birthday party. But when you are two and a half, there are few things that matter more. I was pushing the buggy past Monkey Business, after a hot, sticky picnic on the common, my mind full of single parenthood, when I remembered. There, in the window of the toy shop, was a Barbie hair salon, complete with working hair dryer.

'FUCK!' I said.

'What?' said Fergus.

Over the last week or so our life had shrunk to essentials. I had steered past the playground, seen and spoken to no one. I could just about get through, pretending everything was unchanged, if I avoided social contact. I had hardly even seen Jake. He had been at the office (or with her) and when he had touched down at home, I had managed to behave as normally as I could. But I wasn't normal. I was close to losing it.

'We've forgotten Cecily Alberge's fucking birthday party,' I said. The invitation was on the mantelpiece. I thought I could just about visualise '3–5pm', under a pink cavalcade of dancing dolls. It was just past three now. It was the last thing I felt like doing, but Fergus was looking up at me, his face pinched with anxiety and suspended excitement.

'But if we leg it . . .' I said.

We legged it. I nipped into the shop. Bought a Barbie hair salon—nothing like emergency for engendering generosity—wheedled a gift wrap, and ran straight across the common, past the pond, past the bowling green, over the main road, down some side streets, to the Alberges' double-fronted Victorian residence.

It was twenty past three when we got there.

'Oh, you're early,' simpered Lucinda at the door, looking down at me in my dismal T-shirt with its sweat rings under the arms. She was the definition of cool in shades of grey. Her silky trousers skimmed the heels of her camel slingbacks. Her luscious, dark hair was tamed back behind her head in her office chignon, I noticed: a children's party obviously being as close to real work as 'home life' gets. My hair was a mess. I wasn't wearing make-up. I was wearing shorts. And flip-flops. I'd cried a bit earlier and I was sure there were dirt streaks down my face. 'Never mind,' she said, smiling, 'everyone else will be here in ten minutes.'

Cecily came to the door, in a frou-frou party dress with smocking on the front. Her white socks had frills on the top of them like teenage tennis players'. 'Is that my present?' she said. 'Where's your Barbie?'

Fergus, who had strings of Ribena trailing from his faded, blue T-shirt, across his shorts, which were a bit too big about the waist and hung, builder-like, across his hips, to his dusty plimsolls, held on to the present tightly and said sweetly, 'I hate Barbies. So does Mummy. And no, it's mine. Where's the party?'

'Sweetheart!' said Lucinda. 'Come . . . in.'

We trooped in. I realised to my horror that Dan's nappy needed changing. He was only wearing a vest and it was sagging at the crotch, bulging horribly to one side. Lucinda, whose nostrils, permanently flared, had clearly already identified the smell, was looking pointedly at the bottom of Fergus's shoes.

'I'd better just use the bathroom,' I said.

I fled upstairs, where I tried to pinion Dan to the fluffy white bath mat while I struggled with his poppers. He was wailing and banging his head against the marble floor. I got the nappy off, but not before I'd got poo on his vest and poo on the bath mat and poo on his feet and poo on my hands. I wrestled the new nappy on, poppered him up wrongly and released him while I set about mopping up the floor. All the towels were white. I had to make do with loo roll and a scrap of J-cloth I found on the U-bend of the loo. I dabbed frantically while trying to keep Dan from pulling the Floris off the shelf by the bath.

'Maggie? Are you all right?' Lucinda was outside the door. 'Fergus wants you. Can you let him in?'

'Yes, yes,' I said, in a panic turning the bath mat upside down.

I opened the door and there was Fergus with wet shorts. 'Why didn't you tell someone you needed the loo?' I said, despairing.

'I don't know,' he said in a small voice.

I gave him a cuddle. It was too late to do anything else, and the three of us trooped back downstairs. The bad news was now we had wee and poo to add to our sweat and Ribena. The good news was at least the party was in medium swing.

'Hi!' said a friendly voice. It was Rachel with a plate of smoked salmon sandwiches in her hand. 'I haven't seen you for days. You look as if you've been in the wars!'

'No wipes!' I hissed.

'I've got a spare packet in the back of the buggy you can have,' she said over her shoulder as she proffered her plate to a passing mother. 'Salmon, anyone. It's Loch Fyne.'

'Too late,' I said.

Fergus was ran off to play with Lucinda's twins, Ned and Sid, in a plastic sandpit on the patio. Lucinda seemed to be busy altercating with Mr Twistletoes, a sinister fellow with a beard, about rearranging the furniture in the sitting room. With Dan on one hip, I followed Rachel's raised plate into the kitchen where bottles of champagne and platters of food—sausage rolls and slices of cake and more sandwiches—were laid out on the side (for the adults, it seemed; the children's tea was in individual Barbie boxes on tiny trestle tables outside). Lucinda's husband, Gregory, was laid out on the sofa, his eyes closed.

'Dead?' I asked Rachel.

'Ssssh,' she said. 'I think the pressure has got to him. Hello, Jill.' She kissed an arriving mother. 'Pâté? It's wild boar.'

Gregory came to as if on cue. 'Party. Gosh. Cost a fortune,' he said to no one in particular. I was closest so I felt I had to respond.

'I know, awful,' I said. 'It really adds up.'

'Ten pounds a head,' he said, searching under the sofa for his champagne flute. 'Twenty kids. Two hundred pounds. Plus a hundred and eighty for the entertainer. Little darling, though, Cecily. Worth it. Wants a pink marquee next year. Anyway, better mingle.'

With that, he swayed off into the garden. I took Dan into the playroom where Cecily was fighting over the Brio with two small boys. A couple of women were deep in conversation. They stopped when I entered, paused while they registered the state of my clothes, and continued. I sat on the floor and built Dan a tower of bricks.

'So I'm so thrilled he's got into Bolton Prep,' the one with goldstrapped loafers was saying. 'It's so much nicer than Howarth Hall. Of course, I was disappointed that he failed his interview at Howarth. Apparently it was just the fridge question that did it. He said, "For keeping food in," which is right on the button, but the answer they wanted was, "For keeping food cold." Well, I mean, honestly. He's only three. And a May birthday. It's hardly surprising.'

'Hm, hm,' said the other woman, tucking a stray bit of hair back into a baseball cap with a Chanel logo on the front.

'And we just really, really liked the atmosphere at Bolton,' continued Gold Buckles. 'Lovely children. Lovely garden. And I do think it's fairer that they screen the parents and not the children. The headmistress couldn't have been nicer at our interview. And the other parents seem so jolly. What about you? Where's Dylan going?'

'He got in to Howarth Hall actually.'

'When's his birthday?' said Gold Buckles quickly.

'March.'

'Ah.'

I said, to help out as much as anything, 'Aren't all the private schools much of a muchness?' Which got me a withering look from both mothers.

Luckily, games were starting up in the garden, so I gathered Dan and went to find Fergus.

A game of 'Pass the Parcel' had just begun when we got there. Gwendolen, Lucinda's eldest, was operating the tape recorder with an officiousness only a seven-year-old can muster, while a smart elderly couple, whom I took—from the height of the man and the thickness of the woman's hair—to be Lucinda's parents, looked on. Harry, the first unwrapper, refused to give the parcel up when the music restarted. Cecily, who was sitting next to him, began to tug and scream. Some of the other children, meanwhile, were lying back on the ground, pretending to be crocodiles. 'Come on, children, back into a circle. Stop biting, Matilda. Maud, sit up. Come on. You—little boy, the little boy in shorts, what are you doing?' Lucinda's mother appeared to be addressing Fergus. I turned away slightly. I didn't have the strength. Perhaps she wouldn't know he was mine. But then Gwendolen chipped in, giving the game away, 'Fergus Priton. Sit down. It's not your turn.' I felt a tide of panic in my throat. I could hear the dogs barking manically, locked up somewhere in the house. Mr Twistletoes was standing in the doorway, idly folding a long, thin balloon into the shape of a dachshund. Rachel was at my elbow, circling like a bottletop with a tray of food. Her voice came in and out. 'Wild boar, Loch Fyne, more tea.' I knew I should move forward to investigate Fergus, but my knees felt weak. 'The Wheels on the Bus' was starting up. Pass the Parcel had been abandoned for Musical Statues. Lucinda's father was holding Fergus's hand. Children. Husbands. Grandparents. Family life. All this. What was Jake doing now? Was he really working or was he with her?

'Excuse me,' I said and I turned my back on the party and made for the bottom of the garden, for the bit round the corner, where I could have a quick cry in peace.

And there was Pete.

He was crouched down on his haunches, filling a tarpaulin bag with weeds, his hands in and out of the soil. There were wet patches across the shoulders of his T-shirt. The surprise of seeing him stopped my breath. I should have turned and scurried back across the lawn, but I was so taken aback, I didn't move. I said, 'Hello.'

He looked up, squinted to see me against the sun.

'We must stop meeting like this,' I said, laughing merrily to disguise my embarrassment.

He said, 'Hey . . . How are you?' He stood up, wiping his hands on his shorts. 'I got your note. Er . . .' He peered closely at me. 'Are you OK? Is everything all right?'

I rubbed my eyes. 'Yes, I'm fine.'

'Are you sure?' he said kindly. 'It's just that you look . . .'

I swallowed. 'I'm fine,' I said again, but I started crying anyway.

'Hey,' he said again. He put one hand on my shoulder, guided me over to a patch of low wall. 'Sit down,' he said. 'Take a minute.'

He sat down next to me and put his arm round me. 'Is there anything I can do? If you want a shoulder, I'm a good listener.'

I shook my head. 'Just stuff at home.' I sniffed. 'It's been a bit of a week. I'm sorry, I'm being silly.' I sniffed again, rummaging for a tissue.

'Well, don't worry about me. Cry away.'

Some time went by. 'I've stopped now,' I said. 'Can't get any more out.'

He smiled, he still had his arm round my shoulder, then he said, 'I wondered if you might be here. I know you—not one to miss a party.'

'Hm,' I said, making a noise at the back of my throat, which was almost a laugh.

'That's better,' he said, putting his finger under my chin. We looked at each other. In the silence between us, you could hear Mr Twistletoes calling the children into the house for the puppet show.

When we spoke, we spoke together. I said, 'I mustn't keep you,' and he said, 'You've got something in your hair.' He disentangled a small twig and handed it to me. He smiled. 'There you go.'

I said, speaking quickly, 'I'm a state. I thought we were late so I ran all the way.' I half brushed, half mussed my hair with my fingers as if to remove the print of his hand. 'I probably stink to high heaven.'

'Let me tell you.' He took his arm away and swept the small area of brick between us with his hand. 'You don't.'

He looked up and was about to say something else, when there was a flash of red T-shirt on the other side of the azalea. Pete stood up abruptly. 'Ah, that's, er . . . Have you met Lloyd?'

I stood up too. 'No.'

'I'll introduce you.'

'No,' I said quickly. 'No, it's fine. I'd better get back to the baby.'

I started moving off when he put his hand on my arm to stop me. 'Are you sure there's nothing I can do? Can I at least give you and the kids a lift home? It's quite a way and as you're a bit under the weather . . .'

I shifted my weight onto a different foot which meant I moved away from him a fraction. 'Look, I don't know.'

'I'm leaving in a little while; I can wait for you round the corner if you don't want to be seen hanging out with the staff. It's not a problem.'

'No, honestly . . .'

He winked at me. 'Go on. Live dangerously.'

I didn't hesitate then. 'All right,' I said.

I returned to the party and stood at the back of Mr Twistletoes, watching giant magic wands crumble. Then it was tea and I helped Fergus to the table and opened his Barbie box, and then I helped pass round the Barbie cake and cleared all the uneaten sandwiches and uneaten Baby Bels and empty crisp packets into the bin. And then I took my two grubby children to say goodbye-nicely and collect their party bags (one model aeroplane, one bubble mixture, one packet of Smarties, one pencil sharpener in the shape of a baboon: times twenty, about the value of the gross national product), and we left the house.

Maria was on the doorstep, talking to a woman I didn't recognise. She said, 'Oh, Maggie: is everything OK?'

'Yes,' I said quickly.

'I mean last week. The emergency—Merika coming over.'

'Oh that,' I said, hurrying by. 'Oh, it's fine. It was nothing in the end.'

Pete's van was tucked out of sight round the corner behind Lucinda's Mitsubishi Shogun. He was standing by it, waiting. The van still had a battered front bumper and missing headlight. 'Oops,' I said. 'Y-es,' he said pointedly. He took the buggy off me and put it in the boot. I clambered after Fergus, with Dan in my arms, into the front seat.

It didn't take long to round the common to our house. Fergus, strapped in between us, chattered about the petrol dial and the windscreen wipers the whole way. Pete and I didn't say anything much. But when we got there, as I undid Fergus's belt, Pete said, 'Maybe I could pop round in the next couple of days? Check you're OK?'

'Do you like a damsel in distress?' I said.

He didn't smile. 'No. It's just that I don't like to see you like this.'

I wiped the dust off the clock face on the fascia in front of me. 'All right, then,' I said. Come for a cup of tea or something.'

'When?'

'I don't know.'

'Monday,' he said. 'Monday morning?'

Maybe it was the solemnity of the expression on his face, or the sincerity of his tone, but I couldn't help myself. I leaned across and kissed him quickly on the lips. Then I pulled away. 'OK,' I said.

On Monday, I was up at dawn to have a shower, shave my legs, wash and blow-dry my hair before the children woke. 'What's up with you?' said Jake when he stumbled down to breakfast. 'Nits again?'

'No,' I said, 'not nits. I just couldn't get back to sleep. Look,' I waved something in front of his eyes as a distraction. 'I've found your PG Tips scrapbook. It was under the toy cupboard. Fergus must have—'

'Thank God,' said Jake, putting down his coffee cup. 'I'd looked everywhere for it. I was wondering where I might have left it.'

'What were the options?' I said. He didn't pick up on it. He was slotting his dirty cereal bowl into the dishwasher.

'I'll be late again tonight. If I even make it home. I'm going to have to go to Amsterdam again this week. We've got to present our pitch to the Central European Office. And on top of that I've got to find time for the Zap-it brief.'

'It's amazing what you can find time for when you try,' I said. He didn't pick up on that either.

It was eleven days since I'd seen him with Claire. Sunday was the first day he'd spent any time at home. It was surprising how normal things had seemed. There was no confrontation. There was tension but it made itself felt in such small things, such tiny absences—a missing kiss here, a door closed with no goodbye—that an untutored observer would have noticed nothing wrong.

After Jake had left, I took Dan and Fergus to my mother's. 'Long time no see,' she said when I dropped them off. I'd rung her to say I was going to the dentist. 'Can you make sure you're back by one? I've got aqua-aerobics this afternoon,' she said.

It wasn't that I was excited at the prospect of Pete's social visit. I was too emotionally exhausted for that. It was more that I felt I wanted to meet him looking my best, not tearful and sweaty, but languid and relaxed. So when I got back from dropping off the kids, I put on my best accidental-chic linen trousers and a vest top with the bra strap showing. I took a long time over shoes. Nothing I had really worked. In the end, I painted my toenails and went barefoot. I sat in the kitchen and waited. I made myself some coffee, flicked through the papers and got them tangled. Spilt the coffee. Mopped it up and made some more. Remembered I hadn't brushed my teeth, ran upstairs. Dropped some toothpaste on my top. Attempted to lick it off. Finally took it off and tried to hold just the toothpasty bit under the tap. Got the whole lot wet. Tried to dry it under the hair dryer. Put it back on damp.

This was ridiculous. What was wrong with me? I went down to the sitting room and looked out into the street and saw Mrs Allardyce walking past. I banged on the window to get her attention and went to the door. 'So?' I said. 'Have you had the results yet?'

'Oh dear . . .' she began. 'I haven't. I rang the hospital and they said to ring the GP so I rang him and he said he hadn't heard from them yet.'

It was then, of course, behind her, coming down the street towards me, that I saw Pete. He was wearing clean jeans and a button-down shirt, and proper lace-up shoes. He stopped when he saw me talking to Mrs Allardyce, but then carried on coming. 'And who's this lovely lady?' he said as he got to us.

'Mrs Allardyce,' I said. 'This is Pete Russ. He's a gardener.'

Mrs Allardyce looked flustered and patted her hair. 'Marjorie,' she said.

He took her hand and kissed it. 'Delighted to make your acquaintance,' he said, like something out of Jane Austen (except with an Australian accent).

When we'd said goodbye to Mrs Allardyce, got into the house and closed the door, I felt suddenly embarrassed and flustered. I said, 'You and the ladies, you don't let a chance go by, do you?'

'Aw. She's a sweetie,' he said, leaning up against the hall radiator.

I stood there, barring his entrance into the kitchen. 'But you are, aren't you? You're a charmer, a womaniser. You're shameless.'

'No, I'm not,' he said. 'I just like women, that's all. I understand them.'

'Well, that's good,' I said briskly, turning to go into the kitchen. 'I'm glad someone does. It would be awful to think we were going un-understood.' I was talking in short sergeant major sentences, trying to make a joke out of it. 'Of course you're not a womaniser, you're a woman-*liker*. Altogether different.'

I had my back to him, filling the kettle with water, but I could tell he was standing in the doorway. He was silent. Then he said in a very different sort of voice, 'Hey. If you don't want me here, just tell me to go.'

I turned round to face him. 'I don't want you to go,' I said, still holding the kettle. I looked at him hard for a bit, then I smiled.

He smiled too. He put the holdall he was carrying down on the floor. 'Well, at least you got dressed this time, but I can still see your bra.'

'That's a style issue,' I said, from under my eyelashes. 'It's supposed to be part of the effect.'

He leaned against the door frame. 'Where are the kids?' he said.

'At my mother's.'

'Where's your husband?'

'At work. Though, um . . . we're not actually married.'

'Where are your shoes?'

I smiled again. The tension broke a bit. He said, 'How are you feeling? Are things any better with . . . it's Jake, isn't it?'

'Up and down. Mainly down. But . . .' I turned to plug the kettle in. 'But that's all boring. I'm sure your life is much more interesting.' I took some cups out. 'Is it? I don't know anything about you really.'

When I turned back, he was still looking at me with an odd expression. And he said, 'What do you need to know?' And he came close to me then and slipped his hand under my bra strap, which had fallen over my shoulder, and fitted it back under the strap of my top. And then, with his other hand, he slowly and deliberately pulled the strap on the other side down. He smelt of aftershave and Polo mints.

I said, drawing a little bit back, 'Watch out. I'm a married woman.'

'Except,' he said, 'you keep saying you're not.'

And then, his ginger-flecked eyes still looking into mine, very softly he ran the tip of his finger from my nose, over my mouth and down to the hollow under my neck, circled it there for a moment and then gently trailed it into the crack between my breasts. I was leaning against the kitchen counter and gripping it behind my back with both hands. I wasn't breathing. I didn't move. I was thinking about pulling away, but I couldn't. He left his finger where it was for a moment, coarse against my skin. And then he coaxed it under the fabric and ran it over my nipple. I leaned towards him finally, lifting my face. And then, with one hand in my bra and the other firm against my lower back, he pulled me to him and brought his mouth down to mine. And then I closed my eyes and kissed him back, and in the course of that kiss he had pushed me up onto the work surface, knocking over a jar of coffee, which clattered into the sink, and he had pulled my top over my head and unhooked my bra and then his tongue was on my nipples, and his hands, which were rough and sandpapery, were round my waist and his fingers were down under my linen trousers, pushing against my skin until he'd got the trousers over my hips and down to my ankles, and he moved out of the way for a second, until I had kicked them off and I was naked next to him still in all his clothes. I pulled him back to me, tugging at his shirt, and then we were kissing and licking and sliding to the floor and his clothes came off too and his breaths were coming faster and deeper and louder and I was seconds from infidelity.

Afterwards, we lay side by side in silence, getting our breath back. The tiles felt cold behind my back. I could feel the ridges digging into my vertebrae. Pete had his eyes closed. I moved onto my side so I could see the air widening and narrowing his nostrils. There were tight coils of blond hair on his chest, a line of fuzz leading from his tummy button down to his groin. The muscles on his torso were ridged like a piece of armour. You saw stomachs like that in adverts for perfume, and now there was one on my kitchen floor.

'You're so muscly,' I said. 'I suppose that's working outdoors.'

He sighed and opened his eyes, making a 'mmm' sort of noise, which seemed to express self-satisfaction as much as satisfaction.

What have I done? I thought. What am I doing? Not with any crashing sense of shame, but almost wonderingly, amazed. I began to see how easy adultery could be if you surrendered yourself to the moment. Was that how it was for Jake and Claire? Or had they moved beyond that into something more permanent? Pete put his hand out and, twisting round, tangled his fingers in my hair. Leaning on his elbow, he kissed me on the forehead and the chin and the nose, and said, 'You are one very desirable lady.'

I emitted a sort of horrified laugh.

'What's the matter?' he said.

'Nothing,' I said. 'Nothing at all.'

After he'd gone, I stood in the bath and ran the shower over myself. Then I put on some old jeans and an old shirt and threw my underwear in the basket. And then I went downstairs again and scrubbed the kitchen floor. Not to wash away all signs of what had happened, but because I'd noticed some dried-on yoghurt under the table while I was down there. Clean house, as they say, clean mind.

Loose woman, light woman, light o' love, wanton, hot stuff, woman of easy virtue, demirep, flirt, piece, wench, jade, hussy, minx, nymphet, baggage, trollop, drab, slut, mantrap, temptress, seductress, scarlet woman, Jezebel, adulteress, nymphomaniac, Messalina.

You can look up the words in the thesaurus, but none of them sounded like me. It was astounding to me how completely the same I felt. I suppose I felt cheered up—even gently thrilled by the memory of it. Most of all, I felt amused. I wanted to run around the house laughing at what I, Maggie Owen, stretch-marked mother of two, had just done. It was so incongruous, so out of character, so *funny*. And so gloriously clichéd. I'd had sex with the gardener. It wasn't quite a gamekeeper, but still: how Lady Chatterley was that?

I found I could justify it fairly easily, too. In the light of what Jake had done. In the light of what Jake was *doing*. I was simply redressing the balance. And if it made me feel better about myself, which up to a point I thought it did, then wasn't it time something, or somebody, did that?

These moments of rational clear-sightedness would be offset periodically by waves of withering guilt and dizzying anxiety.

I wasn't late picking up the children from my mother's. I was there at 12.30pm and would have been gone by 12.35pm if there hadn't been a new chip-fryer to inspect. I was a lovely daughter. I raved about the chip-fryer. Exalted over the new cushion covers. Drew tears of admiration for the new all-in-one TV remote control. And, for the rest of the afternoon, I was a wonderful mother too. I took Dan and Fergus to the park and played the sort of energetic games with Fergus normally reserved for weekend dads. He laughed and squealed and threw his arms round my knees in delighted exhaustion. Dan crawled around under the trees and I let him play with the Tennant's cans to his heart's content.

That day, I didn't think about the future. I didn't know, or even care, if I would ever see Pete again. Of course it was a one-off. A weird but rather fabulous single occurrence. I was a woman of thirty-six, at her sexual peak. What a shame to let that go to waste—as it had been, night after night, over the last few months. And it didn't mean the end of Jake and me. Just as Claire and Jake didn't mean the end of us either. Don't they say that a little infidelity can bump-start a stale marriage? Maybe this would sort things out between us once and for all.

When we got home, there was a message from Mel on the answering machine. She was back from Shrewsbury. Was I OK? Could she come round? I felt the guilt again. How do you tell a friend who, only days before, has been the concerned recipient of your anguish, that actually . . . things have moved on a bit since then? You don't, do you? So I didn't ring back. Instead, Fergus and I made fairy cakes. With icing. And those little silver balls on top that are supposed to look like metal and taste like sugar—only, they don't: they taste like metal too.

Smokers who are trying to give up say it is not the first errant cigarette that represents the downhill slope, but the second. It was hard to say, after my one lapse with Pete, whether full-blown infidelity in the form of An Affair was already inevitable, or whether it was the second

encounter that led to this. I got through Tuesday and Wednesday, pretending everything was normal. I spent the days looking after my children, and my evenings as distant with Jake as two people could be while
still sharing a bed and a joint bank account. I also rang Mel when I
knew she'd still be at the surgery and left a message saying that everything was fine this end, that I'd speak to her soon.

But then it got to Thursday. On Thursday, several events conspired
against me, or maybe *for* me, I didn't know. In the morning, Jake left for
another 'big meeting' in Amsterdam. All his meetings were now big;
they were never small or medium-sized. This one was so big it was
going to last four days. He didn't kiss me as he left. He kissed Fergus
and Dan and he said 'bye' to us all in a general kind of way, blowing a
vague kiss in my direction at the door. Naturally I found this suspicious:
I didn't doubt the existence of this meeting, but I did wonder whether
he was flying alone. After he left, I felt empty.

And then in the middle of the morning, Rachel brought Harry round
and Maria dropped in with her two on the way to the bank, and I served
coffee and biscuits and juice and listened to tales of Maria's Mark
Warner holiday in Turkey (drunk every night etc.) and talked about the
rumours that Vodaphone wanted to erect a cancer-inducing aerial on
the church roof and all the time I was trying to quell the waves of claus-
trophobia that had started breaking over me.

And the final straw was the Percy yoghurt. It was lunchtime. Dan was
smearing mashed-up Marks & Spencer tuna fishcakes into his highchair. Fergus was fretting over his pudding. I said, 'There's Toy Story
chocolate mousses or yoghurts.'

'What yoghurts?' Fergus said.

I went to the fridge. I said, 'Thomas the Tank Engine, though there's
only one left of those, Noddy, or Pokémon fromage frais.'

He said, 'Noddy.'

'Please,' I said.

'Please,' he said.

I brought Noddy to the table and peeled the lid off.

'Noooooooooo,' panicked Fergus. 'I want the lid ON.'

I quickly tried to stick it back, using the yoghurt round the edge as
glue. Fergus took it and eyed it suspiciously. He was momentarily
thrown. Then inspiration struck. 'I said I wanted Thomas. I don't want
Noddy.' He threw his spoon on the floor. His face crumpled.

It's quite clear in the manuals that at moments like this you should not give in. If you give in, a cycle of bad behaviour is established. What the manuals never say is, anything for an easy life. I went to the fridge and found one last remaining Right Reverend rip-off. I brought it back to him, my emperor in his booster chair.

'That's not Thomas. That's Gordon,' he yelled, his voice rising.

I snapped. 'No, it's not. It's Percy.' And I took it off him and threw it in the sink where its sides dented and splattered against the aluminium.

Fergus started crying, and because he was crying Dan started crying and I would have cried too if I hadn't been so busy comforting them. And my life suddenly seemed so small and so hopeless and a solution seemed so easily come by that I couldn't help myself. I rang Pete.

He came straight round that afternoon. Fergus and I were playing sea monsters in the garden when he knocked.

'As I was passing,' he said at the door.

'Well, if you're passing.' I laughed back. I said, 'You can come in, but we're playing sea monsters.'

He said 'Er-aghhhh', which made Fergus, who had wandered up behind me, scream and run back into the garden.

Pete came out with me and I said, 'You probably can't stay. It's probably not a good time.' But I could feel my mouth stretching into a smile.

He said, 'I left my secateurs. I've only come to pick them up.'

'And you've done without them since Monday?'

'I've got a spare pair,' he said, looking into my face and laughing.

'Er-aghhhh,' he said again to Fergus, who had come up behind him with a stick. He turned and chased him. Fergus squealed in delight. They fell on the ground and Pete pinioned Fergus between his feet and held him high, horizontal in the air.

'Again, again!' my son shouted.

I felt uncomfortable. It seemed important to keep the children away from Pete, to keep them pure and untainted, even if I wasn't. I said, 'Stop now, Fergus, you're overexcited. Come here and find some worms.' Pete made a face at him, which made him giggle some more.

'Where do you think you left your secateurs, then?' I asked Pete.

He gave me a hot look. 'In one of the beds?'

'Well, let's search for them,' I said, looking back. 'Fergus, Pete the Gardener has lost his secateurs in the flowerbeds. They're like big scissors. Are you going to help us find them?'

Dan was having his nap upstairs. Fergus was head down in the bushes. Pete said, 'They might be in the shed. Come see.' And he pulled me by the arm to the back of the garden. The door, which was half off its hinges, was kept shut with a big stone. He kicked it out of the way with his foot and pushed me into the shed in front of him. We kissed hungrily, almost violently. There were old cobwebs in our hair, dead spiders down our neck. We were pulling each other down, dented cans of antifreeze were toppling over on the wobbly shelf above us. A rake slid to one side, scattering rust. Pete was tugging at my clothes. I had my hands in his thick hair, yanking it, my nails in his scalp.

'We've got to stop,' I said, not stopping.

'Quickly,' he said. 'No. Quickly, come on.'

It was then I caught a glimpse of Fergus through the dusty window, through the cobwebs. He was pottering happily across the lawn. He had a stick in one hand and in the other . . . the kitchen scissors. Open. Facing up. I said, 'No, no, stop.' And I pulled away, disentangled myself and ran out into the light, towards my son.

Pete came out, after a short while, looking amused. 'Is that it, then?'

I looked at him carefully. 'No,' I said, sealing my fate. 'It's not.'

Later that day, Mel dropped round between surgeries. 'A house call!' I said brightly. 'How nice!' She frowned. She was worried about me. She wanted to know if I was really all right. I almost told her how things were, but something— guilt? Fear that she'd stop me doing what I wanted to do?—held me back. Instead I hugged her and said I didn't feel up to talking about it. And, even though she gave me a funny look, she took me at my word. Big mistake.

August
dead flies
chapter fifteen

AND SO IT BEGAN. In the week in which Jake was away, and when the children were safely asleep, Pete came to the house on three separate occasions. He'd leave the van round the corner. We'd have sex against the radiator in the hall or on the stairs, quick and urgent, half our clothes still on. I wouldn't let him upstairs in case the children woke up,

411

or in case our reflection was branded for ever in the bedroom mirror. And he didn't hang around afterwards—just left me with a carpet burn or a radiator ridge and went. Maybe he took a beer from the fridge. Or a slice of cake. And again I would wonder what the hell I was up to.

'What do you see in me?' I asked him once.

'You're wild,' he said, through the crumbs. 'You seem all English and prissy but inside you're wild.'

'Wild?' I said, checking the lights on the baby monitor.

'OK, then.' He grinned. 'Sex.'

If he saw sex in me, I don't exactly know what I saw in him. I saw a handsome man, certainly, with the kind of looks I would once have considered way out of my league; a handsome man who was, of all things, attracted to me. So handsome, and so apparently attracted (fixated, you might almost say), it would have seemed churlish to turn the opportunity down. This sounds flippant, I know, and I have no ready defence for it now. In fact, quite the opposite. My flippancy was a guard: I used it to hide behind, to protect myself from thinking about my actions too deeply, or too carefully. Infidelity brought out the worst in me. I may, in moments of pious self-justification, have told myself that I was equalising things with Jake, that he started it, that I had been forced into an impossible position by his own digressions, by his absence, by the late nights that continued after his return from Amsterdam. But it was much more than that. Something in me, I confess, liked the way Pete was proof that I hadn't completely hunkered down into a cocoon populated by children and playground mums, that there was a side to me that nobody else had seen—including me up to that point. And yet, of course, the whole situation was ridiculous. Impossible. Miserable. I was full of guilt. But I can't pretend it didn't thrill me.

Of course I was always meaning to stop it. We had two close shaves. There was one time, when the children were with my mother and Jake was 'busy with Kyushi', that Pete and I 'went for a drive'. That was one of his euphemisms. Pete seemed to prefer making love in his van to anywhere else. The risk, maybe even the grubbiness of it, gave him an extra thrill. We had driven to a road just off the common and parked up. On the way back he needed some petrol so he drove into the forecourt of the nearest Shell garage. He went into the kiosk to pay and I was just sitting there in the passenger seat, feeling stunned at myself, when I turned and right next to me, so close I could reach down and stroke his hair, was Jake. He was bending over, negotiating the petrol cap on our car, so he had his back to me, but I dived onto the floor by the seat nonetheless.

'What you dropped?' said Pete when he climbed back in.

'Nothing,' I said. 'Just drive. Now.'

And after that, I did feel awful, though the experience seemed to have turned Pete on. I tried not to think too much about why.

And then there was the day that Pete came round at 7.00pm. That summer my children went to bed earlier and earlier. I'd pull their curtains tight shut, blocking out the sun, still hitting its head on the window like it was midday. Jake had rung to say he had the results of a focus group to go through, and was it all right if he and Ed went for a drink afterwards? I said that was fine. It would give me at least two safe hours.

I was wearing my old jumble-sale tea-dress when Pete got there. We took a couple of beers into the garden to drink on the bench under the tree. Pete put his bottle down on the lawn where it wobbled and fell over, glugging into the grass. I bent and made as if to pick it up, but he pulled me onto his lap and, slipping the dress over my head, started kissing me instead.

The bench was concealed from the neighbouring gardens by the jasmine on one side and the overgrown honeysuckle on the other, the branches of the tree hiding the upstairs windows. I closed my eyes for a moment as Pete threw off his shirt, breathing in the slightly contradictory scents of midsummer flowers and Australian male. Pete was kissing me and taking off his shorts at the same time. I was drifting. I was almost lost. And then suddenly the atmosphere was split open like a coconut, by a voice, not that close yet, but enquiring, echoing through an empty house. 'Where are you?'

'FUCK!' I yelped. 'It's Jake. Quick into the shed!'

I jumped up and, yanking my dress back on, herded Pete, still confused, behind the tree and the recently pruned shrubs, into the safety of the shed. I ran back out to the bench, gathered up his clothes, threw them into a bush, called in a high, artificial voice, 'I'm here! Coming!' and charged back into the house, where I found Jake bent down, peering into the fridge.

'Oh, there you are,' he said coolly. 'I could have sworn there were a couple of beers left. Ed and I thought we'd head out of the office and go through our stuff here. We both feel like we've been living there recently. Are Fergus and Dan in bed? I thought I'd catch them.'

'Oh, I think, we . . . Yes they are . . . I thought you . . .'

'Did we drink them?'

413

'Yes, we must have.'

Ed was in the sitting room, standing with his back to the door, looking out of the window. He seemed subdued. 'Hi, Maggie,' he said. 'Sorry to, er . . .'

I was curling and uncurling my fists. But my voice managed to sound casual. 'Hello. I'm surprised you could get away. It's only . . .' I looked at the clock on the video. 'Half past seven. Gosh, that is early. You've both been working such long hours.' I was studying him carefully.

He said, rather too quickly, 'Yes, we have, we have.'

'No beers.' Jake came in behind me. 'So how about wine? Or coffee?'

'. . . or the pub,' I said quickly. 'You could go to the pub.' I was looking from one to the other. Please say yes. Please say yes. Jake raised his eyebrows. Ed raised his to match. 'Go on,' I said. 'I'm all right here. I've got some things to . . . finish off in the garden.'

After they'd gone, I ran back to the shed, my toes fizzy with leftover panic. Pete was sitting on the old chest of drawers, looking sullen. 'Jesus Christ,' he said. The sight of him, disconsolate and naked, caused me to roar with laughter. 'I'm sorry,' I kept saying, 'I'm sorry,' and I'd straighten my face in line with his but then I'd think about it again and the crosser he looked, the funnier it seemed. 'Look, look, please,' I burbled finally, 'you'd better go, but don't be angry. I'm sorry. It's just seeing you . . . it's just tension, that's all it is.'

'Has he gone then?' he said irritably. 'Is the coast clear?'

'Yes, yes,' I said, calming. 'It is. And you'd better go.'

I smoothed him down and got him to the door, but as he left, he said, 'Don't laugh at me, Maggie. I don't like being laughed at.'

And then there were other, more localised, difficulties. Fran and Rain came round one evening in the middle of the month to sort through some baby things and collect the TENS machine. It was a Saturday and I'd slipped off for an hour earlier in the day, under the pretence of buying light bulbs (as good an excuse as I could think of: sometimes the more mundane, the more convincing), and had met Pete in the car park of Homebase.

We'd had a sticky time. I hadn't really wanted to meet: Dan was fretful that day and Fergus clingy and Pete, for an instant, seemed one more demand on my time. But he'd rung several times and in the end I'd gone because it seemed easier to do so than not. When I'd got there, hot and my back sweaty from the plastic seats of the car, I hadn't even wanted to make love, though Pete had been insistent. 'Be a sport, Mags,' he'd said. He was fed up: Lloyd was away and he was kicking his heels, a bored, single man stuck on his own on a fuggy weekend.

'Oh all right,' I'd said.

'I'm hoping to do without medical intervention altogether,' Fran was saying now. She was sitting on the bed in the spare room as I searched the cupboards. She took a pillow and squashed it on her lap. 'And I'm not sure if it works in the birthing pool.'

Jake, who had wandered in with a bottle of beer in his hand, said she'd probably get electrocuted.

I told her I'd found it a waste of time. 'It just set my nerve ends on edge,' I said, finally finding the box tucked behind Jake's Hornby railway set, which he'd put away until the boys were older (until they'd left home, I suspected, and he could play with it without them getting in the way). I reached for it and handed it to her. 'But take it because it works for some people and you won't know until you need it.'

Jake said, sitting on the bed, 'Actually, it did really help you. It really helped her in stage one.'

'No, it didn't,' I said. 'I hated it.'

'You liked it,' he said. 'She liked it. She said it helped. It was only after transition that she didn't want it.'

'Don't talk about me as if I'm not here. Don't talk about my labour as if you know more about it than me,' I said.

'Oooooh. Sorry,' he said, getting up and backing away.

'And don't say oooooh sorry like that,' I said.

'Oooooh. Sorry.'

Fran flicked at him with a muslin, which he grabbed off her and put on his head, folding his hands together and bowing his head like a mullah. Then he went downstairs to the kitchen. I carried on folding romper suits—so tiny, volelike—thinking with one half of my brain how quickly my children had grown, and with the other how quickly my relationship with their father had changed. It was like reciting a poem you know off by heart: everything goes well until you let your concentration lapse, or think too hard about it, and then the words tumble about your ears, unformed and chaotic. When Jake was the unfaithful one, at least I could still take refuge in hating him. Now I just hated myself. I put the rompers in a plastic bag and closed the cupboard door. There were dead flies in the bottom of it but I didn't sweep them up. I'd do it later. I'd do everything later.

Fran said, 'We've been thinking Lakshmi for a girl. She's the Hindu goddess of wealth. Bede for a boy. What do you think?'

'Heavenly,' I said.

Downstairs, Jake and Rain had got the menu out and were about to get a takeaway. Jake ordered chicken biriani.

'Why don't you order something different for once?' I said.

'Like what?' he said, in mock outrage.

I picked up the menu. 'What about fish tandoori? Or egg korma or . . . go on, have egg korma. I've never seen anyone have that.'

Jake looked as if I'd suggested he fry up some nappies. 'Give over,' he said. 'I want chicken biriani. I always have chicken biriani.'

'So you do,' I said.

Fran looked from one of us to the other. 'All right, you two?' she said.

I said, 'Jake always has the same thing. He's never adventurous. I have something different every time. Jake never takes risks.'

'I take risks all the time,' he said quietly. 'But when it comes to ordering an Indian takeaway, I like chicken biriani. It is not a crime, as far as I know. Unless I'm suddenly living under a new political administration.'

'Oh yes, risks. I forgot about the risks,' I said.

'Just order!' said Fran.

They went soon after we'd eaten. Fran hugged me. I hugged her back. 'Take care,' I said. 'Ring me if you need anything else.'

'I will,' she said. 'And, Maggie? Have you ever thought about Pilates? There's a very good course at the House of Eternal Peace, though it's quite booked up. Or how about You Too Can Heal at the Inner Potential Centre? You look as if you need something to take you out of yourself.'

'I think at the moment I've got enough things with which to take myself out of myself,' I said, closing the door.

A few minutes later I was in the bathroom washing my face, when Jake came in. 'Are you all right?' he said, reaching past me for the toothpaste.

'Fine,' I said as he started brushing. 'Absolutely fine.'

He spat. I moved my hand. 'Are you sure?' He sounded solicitous. He was looking at me carefully in the mirror. He said, 'This thing with Kyushi, it's almost over. It's not going to go on for ever.'

I nodded. I turned to go but he grabbed me by the hand and, still looking at me in the mirror, started nibbling my neck. Then he let me go. 'How about coming to bed?' he said.

My heart sank. I said, 'You go ahead. I'll be a few minutes.' And I went downstairs and tidied up the kitchen until I knew he'd be asleep.

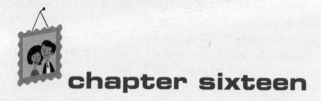

chapter sixteen

I HAD MANAGED TO AVOID MEL quite successfully over this period. She had a course in Bournemouth (Complementary Medicine in General Practice), which took her away for one week. And she left several messages on the answering machine, which I didn't return. You can tell you're in trouble if you start steering clear of your closest friends. I didn't want to see Mel because I knew how shocked she would be, and in witnessing her shock, I'd have to confront all the stuff I'd been so busy burying. But I couldn't hide from her for ever.

'So what's going on?' she asked. 'I can understand the eyebrows, but why the bikini wax? I thought you never had your bikini done?'

It was Saturday afternoon, a week after Homebase, and we were lying on our backs, on green cushioned sun loungers, naked but for towels discreetly arranged, large mango-and-banana smoothies at our sides, gazing up at a magnolia network of exposed heating pipes.

'This is the life,' she said, as a dab of condensation dropped from above onto her forehead. 'Ugh,' she added, shaking her head like a dog.

It was an annual event. Every year, before our holidays (although this year only Mel was going away—two weeks in the Lot with her brother and his family), we'd get day passes to Paddle, an all-women's health club in the centre of London. So far, we'd had a steam and a sauna and we'd frolicked for a while in the pool, where you could dangle above the water on a rope swing and pretend you were Brooke Shields in *Blue Lagoon*. And now we were relaxing from the business of relaxing.

'I'm just bucking my self-image,' I said. 'After all, a bit of pampering never went amiss,' and took a sip from my fruit shake.

She said, 'Maggie. What is going on? I know you're avoiding me. I haven't seen you on your own for weeks. I know you don't want to talk, but I think you should. What is happening with Jake?'

I closed my eyes. 'Ummmm . . .' I began.

She said, sitting up, 'I'm putting my clothes on and walking straight out unless you talk to me. I know something's up. Please, Maggie. I hate

417

it when you shut down like this. What's going on? Is he or isn't he?'

I said, deadpan, 'Yes, he is.'

She lay back down, banging her head against her cushion. She said, 'Bastard.' She sat up again. 'You talked to him, then? What did he say?'

A woman on the next lounger who had been reading *Marie Claire* had looked up during this. I glared at her until she looked back down. I said, 'If I tell you something, do you promise you won't hate me?'

'Of course not.'

I put my hands over my eyes. 'I'm seeing someone too.'

Mel swung her legs over her lounger and bent over me. 'What?'

I took my hands away. 'I'm seeing someone. I'm having an affair too,' I said. 'Now do you hate me?'

'Of course I don't.' She was frowning.

'So only I hate me, then.'

She said, 'Who? Who? How? When?' and I told her about Pete coming on to me and how eventually, after finding out about Claire, I'd given in and she said, 'What: my Pete?' and I said yes, even though she'd never actually met him. I told her how at first it had made me feel better about myself, physically better as much as anything, but that now I felt awful and angry all the time. And she said gently, shaking her head, 'What were you thinking?' And I said, 'I didn't think. I just did.' And she said, 'Maybe it wasn't an affair you needed, but an exercise class.' And I saw the girl on the next lounger smile.

I was called for my stack of treatments then—an eyelash tint, and an underarm, a half-leg, a bikini and an eyebrow shape, the full knick-knack Paddle wax. As I lay there, the beautician said, 'Any particular occasion?' and I wanted to say, 'Yes: I'm sleeping with someone I'm not married to; actually I'm sleeping with two people I'm not married to, but that's another story.' Instead, I simpered and said, 'Oh, just August.'

When she'd finished tidying me up, the beautician studied my face. 'There,' she said, rubbing an excess streak of blue-black dye off my cheekbone. 'You'll feel more human now.'

Mel was already dressed when I came out. She had to pick Milly up from her next-door neighbour and then she had to rush home to cook Piers a goodbye dinner. She hugged me and said she'd ring and not to worry, but that we needed to talk some more soon. 'It'll all come out in the wash,' she said, and there was something comforting in the triteness of that, as if none of it was any more important than a good spin cycle.

I left Paddle on my own and wandered around Covent Garden for a while looking for salvation of a more transient nature, putting off going home. In one of the shops in the plaza I found a dress that reminded me of the frock Claire was wearing the day I'd bumped into her in the high street. This one had tiny straps and ribbon along the hem, and was, according to the assistant, cut on the bias, which she concluded was flattering 'to the curvier figure'. It did look nice, even with my plimsolls, but the assistant said it would look better with some kitten heels. 'Have you tried our shop next door? And what about a little cardigan?' she added. 'Cerise would look nice. For evening.'

I was laden down with bags when I finally got home. I'd bought everything guiltily on the joint account so it was a relief to find an empty house. I bashed the bags into the back of the cupboard, poured myself a drink and went into the garden to read the papers. There was a small ribbon of sun left at the bottom of the lawn and I sat my deck chair on it, with the shade creeping up my legs. I hadn't got much further than the travel section, when Jake arrived back with the children.

'Hello,' he said, as Fergus hurled himself on top of me. 'Nice day?'

'Lovely. Thanks,' I said politely. The deck chair lurched to one side under the force of Fergus's hug. 'You?'

'We've had a great time, haven't we, boys?' said Jake, straining to keep hold of Dan, who was reaching his arms out to me. 'Such nice weather.'

'Isn't it just?' I said, taking Dan from him. How nice we were. How civilised. I said, 'Thank you for looking after the kids,' thinking, Why do mothers always thank fathers? Good thing they don't thank us or there'd be no room for any other conversation. I was about to repeat this thought, make a joke about it, but it seemed too intimate, too engaged with the daily ebb and flow of our relationship. So I didn't.

Jake peered round the children at me. 'Let's see,' he said. 'You look different.'

'I know,' I said. I stood up and put Fergus and Dan down on the grass. The spot of sun had gone now. I started folding up the deck chair. 'Fergus—mind your fingers. I am different. It's a whole new me.'

Rachel was on to me too. On the following Monday, in the changing rooms at the swimming pool, she wanted to know what the new undies were for. 'Classy,' she said, as I slipped off my new 'second skin' knickers from Lycra'n'Lace, a lingerie shop in the Southgate Centre that thinks it's in Beverly Hills, and stuffed them in a Sainsbury's carrier bag. 'Matching bra, hmm. Very nice. Very underrated, purple.'

I was a bit too busy trying to prevent Fergus from scattering his clothes all over the damp floor to answer immediately. I grunted as I finally got the straps of my Speedo over my shoulders. 'Crushed grape,' I said noncommittally, whirling Dan round to sit on one hip. 'Yup. Just got myself remeasured—after all that breastfeeding, you know. It's amazing how your shape changes.'

'Isn't it?' she agreed, still eyeing me up.

The swimming pool, Splashdown! as they'd recently renamed it, had changed since my day. Less of a 'rec' (or wreck), more of a whole wrap-around swimming experience. We used to come on Wednesday after-noons with school. In those days, the most exciting thing on offer was the illustrated notice banning 'heavy petting'. Wasted on me: I didn't know what heavy petting was then, but suspected it was something to do with gerbils. Now it was all elephant slides and wave machines and huge inflatable monsters. You used to get crisps and a can of drink from the machines in the foyer, then devour your booty on the steps with your ears still humming and an itchy wetness under your clothes. Now there was a whole café space, specialising in whale-shaped fish morsels and crocodile-mouthed chicken pieces.

I jammed the plastic bag into a locker, which was as crap as they always had been, and slipped the rubber band round my wrist. Fergus and Harry, miniature Michelin men in their striped floaties, ran ahead of us to splash in the ankle-deep beach-style shallow end. Rachel's preg-nant friend Martha was waiting for us there already, sitting on her bum in the water, legs splayed like a Beanie Baby plonked on a nursery shelf. Her two-year-old daughter, Phoebe, frolicked with a piece of yellow foam at her ankles. Martha smiled weakly when she saw us. We shiv-ered down next to her. It was not the water that was the problem, heated as it was to Caribbean germ-breeding balmitude, it was the air above it.

'How are you?' asked Rachel.

Martha sighed. 'Exhausted,' she said. 'I'm just—'

I missed what she said next because the attendant blew his whistle loudly and started gesticulating crossly just to the right of us. I turned to see what the nasty big boys were doing, but all I could see was Fergus and Harry climbing on one of the crocodiles, and then hurling them-selves off with enviable fearlessness.

'Tooooooooooooot,' the whistle went again. The attendant was head-ing for Fergus and Harry, waving his track-suited arms.

'No jumping off the animals,' he said to them. 'Or you're out.'

I busied myself with Dan—'Whoosh,' I said, twirling him round, 'Whoosh'—to show they weren't mine, but Rachel stood up and strode over. 'Can't you two behave for one minute?' she said. For once she didn't seem to be blaming Fergus. 'Fergus,' she added. 'Off!'

After that, Martha said she'd mind Dan, while Rachel and I waded the boys over to the deeper end. It's still only about three foot, but we slouched across, alternating between our bottoms and knees, keeping as much of our upper torsos as we could in the warmth.

When we reached the ropes separating kiddy chaos from the lengths lane, Rachel said, 'God, Martha doesn't know she's born. For one thing Phoebe is very well behaved, and for another she has so much help it's untrue. She's got an au pair and Phoebe goes to nursery one morning a week and her mother comes and helps out all the time.'

'Gosh,' I said, trying to stop Fergus from putting both his feet on the rope, 'that is a lot.' Non-working mothers are all obsessed with other people's help, as if our children's preoccupation with fairness has rubbed off on us. Fergus was swinging on the rope now, his hands in mine, his feet pushing it back and forth. Rachel was saying, 'And her husband's an angel. He gives her a lie-in every Saturday and is home two nights a week for bathtime. And,' she lowered her voice, 'she's getting a maternity nurse when the baby's born. So really, I don't know how she can say she's exhausted.'

'Not like we're exhausted,' I said.

'Exactly.'

'ERRRR. Excuse me!' There was a cross, spluttering voice suddenly in my ear. I'd let my attention lapse and Fergus had swung a little too forcefully and pushed the rope, complete with his feet, right into the smooth path of an oncoming swimmer. A wet face was staring at me, her hair dark and wet, two ringed fingers flicking droplets of water from under her eyes. She was wearing a black halter-neck bikini, her slim, tanned body flickering brown and white under the water.

'Oh,' I said, speechless. Oh. God. Her. Here. Together in the same water as me. Almost naked. How unspeakably awful. 'Claire,' I said.

'OH. Oh, Maggie!' Her annoyance dropped immediately, plunged into embarrassment instead. She started rabbiting inanely. '*Fancy* meeting you here. Actually, do you know, I was just thinking about you. There were all these small children in the changing room and I thought, Oh, I wonder if Maggie brings her boys here.'

421

Her duplicitousness was quite dizzying. 'Sorry Fergus kicked you,' I said, wishing he'd done it a bit harder.

'Oh, don't worry. High spirits etc. It just gave me a shock, that's all. But, Maggie, I haven't seen you for *ages*.' She was burbling, launched into hyperspace with the awkwardness of seeing me. It was quite gratifying to watch. 'You must think I'm *terrible*,' she gushed. 'I've just been so—well, it's been eventful, let me tell you. Just—oh God.' She was shaking her head. 'But we must get together again soon.'

Rachel was smiling hopefully, looking from one to the other of us, waiting for an introduction. I was silent. Claire gave a wide smile and said, 'I'm Claire. Maggie and I are old, old friends from school.'

'Er, yes,' I said, pulling myself together. I'd have to do introductions, but I didn't want to. 'This is Rachel.' She'd probably steal her too.

Fergus and Harry were whooping and splashing. Claire gave a gay laugh and said, 'Oops, there goes my waterproof mascara!' as quite a lot of water ricocheted off their bodies into her face. 'Where's your other little one?' she added.

I waited, hoping she'd lose interest. I didn't want her even to look at my baby. Finally I said, '*Dan's* over there,' pointing vaguely in the direction of Martha. Claire gave a twee wave, one hand flapping invisible castanets open and shut, in his direction. He didn't wave back.

Rachel was looking at Claire with fascination, clearly intrigued as to how someone as dull as me could have such a glamorous friend. 'It is brilliant,' she said. 'It hasn't run at all. Is it Dior?'

'No, Clinique,' said Claire conspiratorially. 'Worth its weight in gold.'

'I must get some,' said Rachel. 'Now. I want some now. This minute.' They both laughed.

'And how do you two know each other?' said Claire.

Rachel told her about the postnatal support group run by the surgery, and I could see Claire's interest wander, but I wasn't going to interrupt. I wanted to slouch away, low down, so she wouldn't see my body out of the water, but I also couldn't stop looking at her. I wanted to see what Jake saw. Suddenly I was imagining them and . . . I said, 'Oh, Rachel, Claire's not interested in all that.'

Rachel said, 'Oh sorry. You forget how boring children are to people who haven't got them.'

Claire smiled. She darted me a look. She said, 'No, it's not true at all. I'd love to have children, only the man I'm seeing—'

I interrupted. I said, 'Claire's boyfriend's married.'

I pulled Fergus onto one hip and Harry onto the other, and, with a child in each arm, splashed up and down in the water until they squealed and screamed with delight.

I still couldn't drown out the answer, couldn't hide from the nervous look Claire threw in my direction.

'They always are,' she said.

I started asking Pete what he did when he wasn't seeing me. He said, 'Hang out.' But I wanted to know where. 'Bars,' he said. 'You know.'

'Which bars?'

'I dunno. Fiction. Oblivion. Anonymous. Meltdown. The usual.'

'Sounds like my life,' I said. 'Who with?'

'Mates.'

'But who are your mates?'

'Lloyd. Some blokes I used to live with when I lived in Catford. People from about.'

'Women?'

'There are girls there, Maggie, yes.'

We were lying in the back of his van by the river at Putney, down the end by the towpath. It was midweek and quiet, though you could still hear muffled squeals from the playground across the road. Fergus was having lunch at Lucinda's. I'd left Dan with Fran on the pretext of a Big Sainsbury's Shop.

Pete was pulling on his clothes. He had looked at his watch and said he'd better be getting on. I lay there, with my arms behind my head.

I said, watching him burrow into his T-shirt, 'I know, let's do something different for once.'

'Different from what?' His head emerged.

'From *this*.' I sat up, pulled my knees into my chest. 'We could go on a date. Go somewhere normal. Do something.'

He winced, turned away from me towards the door. 'Bit tricky.'

'I could manage it. I could work it. It would be good. It's important.'

'Whatever,' said Pete sunnily. He chucked my clothes at me. 'Get your kit on. I haven't got all day.'

I wriggled into my clothes and Pete crouched down to undo the back doors. He clambered out and then bent to fiddle with the number plate at the back of the van. It was held on with string and was hanging off on one side. I followed him out and went to stand against the railings, looking down into the sludge below. It was low tide. There was a Dulux paint bucket among the driftwood, sticking out of the mud.

I said, 'I should bring Fergus here. He'd love it down there.'

Pete, still with his head under the bumper, said, in a half-grunt, 'Huh?'

'He could dig around with sticks,' I said. 'In the mud.'

I turned, but Pete wasn't listening.

The relationship, once the initial charge had left, wasn't following the kind of pattern I was used to. I was not, in these hot August days, at my most clear-headed, but I thought I knew two things. 1: that I didn't want it to carry on the way it was, and 2: that I didn't want it to end. Or did I? Did I want to try to make something more of it? Did I want to think about a future with this man?

I stood staring at the strip of river, sparkling in the sun. 'What now?' I said, turning again. 'Where do we go from here?'

'Well.' Pete was jangling his car keys. 'I've got to pick up some bedding plants, then I've got an appointment at Lucinda's at three.'

I think we both knew that wasn't what I meant.

Then he said he wasn't going my way, so could he drop me at the station? 'Be a sport,' he said. 'It's only one change.'

chapter seventeen

'I CAN'T BELIEVE WE'RE DOING THIS,' I said. 'We must be mad. Criminally insane. How did I let this happen?'

'It's too late,' he said. 'We've gone too far.'

'I can't bear it,' I said. 'I'm leaving behind my house, my garden, my life.'

'Tough,' he said. 'There's no turning back now.'

We were in the car, Jake and I, on our way to Suffolk, the guests of Ed and Pea, who had invited us, along with Mark, another of Ed and Jake's colleagues at TMT&T, and his wife, Louisa, to a cottage booked through Barn D'Or. Barn D'Or was the Rolls-Royce of holiday cottage companies: exposed beams and properly lagged hot-water tanks, yours for two nights, for the cost of a small Lear jet.

The weekend had been in the diary for ages, but I'd filed it away in the region of my mind labelled 'Get Out Of That Nearer The Time'. What with one thing and another—small children, unfaithful husbands, rampant sex with near strangers—I hadn't got round to it and suddenly there we were, on our way, hardly speaking, Mr and Mrs Dysfunctional, having to put on a brave face for a Bank Holiday Weekend With Other People.

I was in a terrible mood. I hadn't managed to see Pete all week, but I'd managed to pin him down for our date which was to take place the following Tuesday. In the meantime, if I'd had my choice, I would have spent the weekend on my own with my kids, thinking about things if I was feeling brave, burying them if I wasn't; but at any rate not forced into artificial merriment.

'I don't even understand why they've invited us,' I said to Jake crossly. 'She hates me as much as I hate her.'

'No, she doesn't,' he said back, calmly, infuriatingly. 'She's probably just a bit confused by your attitude. She's probably just waiting to like you, if you'd let her.'

'What about Ed?' I said.

He was staring ahead at the bumpers in front of him. 'You may not like him, but he is my friend and my colleague. And I don't see why we shouldn't socialise with them once in a while.' He darted me a look and then glanced away again. 'It's embarrassing not to.'

We lapsed into silence. Fergus and Dan had been asleep since the Elephant and Castle. Two months ago a traffic jam with comatose children could have been classified as 'quality time', a chance to catch up, listen to music together, chat idly. As it was, it felt like purgatory. Over the last month, things had, if it were possible, become even more strained. Jake had become withdrawn to the point where even the routine politeness between us had seized up.

I said, after a while, 'Well at least I like Mark and Louisa.'

Jake grunted. It's true, I did. They lived in north London, and in the way in which friendship as you get older is increasingly dictated by geography, we never saw as much of them as we'd have liked. Mark, a copywriter at Jake's agency, was one of those energetic people who is always said to be 'brilliant' with children. He was the one who'd run the barbecue and untangle the lines for tickling the crabs. He was the one his children, or anyone's children, ran to when they scraped their knees. Louisa, on the other hand, would emerge death-white at 10.00am, grope for a cigarette and a mug of black coffee and wail what a terrible mother she was, while wishing she was somewhere else. We always had a nice time with them. Or we used to.

I looked across at Jake and noticed how grey around the gills he was looking. There were bags under his eyes and a nick on his chin, where he must have cut himself shaving. I said, suddenly disarmed by his vulnerability, 'Are you knackered? Would you like me to drive?'

'I'm fine,' he said coolly.

We had reached the fast bit of the A12. When the traffic had cleared after a roundabout, Jake had put his foot down sharply on the accelerator and we had swerved to the left so aggressively I had gripped both sides of my seat. I gripped on, right foot on an imaginary brake, just a little bit longer than was necessary—to make a point. When the point wasn't picked up, I said, 'So what's happening with Kyushi?'

There was a pause. Then he said, as if it didn't matter, 'They liked our pitch best. So, er, yup, they're sticking with us.'

'Really?'

'Yes.'

'Really? Jake? When? When did you find out?'

'Yesterday. It's what I was celebrating last night. I thought you realised.'

'But I didn't . . . When you said you were having a few beers, I thought . . . You might have said.'

'I didn't think you were interested,' he said. 'As long as I bring in the money.'

'I cannot believe you said that,' I said. 'It's unfair.'

'Is it?' he said, turning to look at me. 'Is it?'

'Yes, of course. Anyway, I wish I'd known.'

'Too late now,' he said briskly. 'And, Maggie, do me a favour. At least pretend to enjoy yourself, OK?'

It was dark when we arrived at the Old School House, Cotley. Ed and Pea's Kyushi Adventurer (four-wheel drive; profile: would-be urban warrior, or adman keen to make impression with client) had already rammed a path through the shingle up to the front door. A Renault Espace was squeezed in behind it.

'Last here, then,' I said, as we parked in the lane outside.

I got out and breathed in the sharp, fresh country air, a cocktail of leaves and salt, mown grass and manure. Jake heaved our bags out of the boot and together, in silence, we eased our way up the drive, past the kangaroo bars, to the front door.

'Hello, allcomers!' hailed Ed, coming to greet us at the door. 'Find it OK? Great. Come in. Welcome. Welcome. Lovely to see you, Maggie. How are you?' He put on his teensy-weensy little girl's voice for this last question, as if addressing a flower fairy. 'I'm fine,' I said, heartily, but he had already turned to Jake and was gripping his forearm. 'Kyushi, Kyushi, Kyushi,' he said in his ear. 'Fucking brilliant.'

Jake said, 'Yup. Isn't it?'

'What an evening,' Ed continued. 'I hear you made it into the office today. I was going to but . . .' He flicked his finger across his brow.

Jake suddenly felt the pocket of his jacket. 'Shit. I left my mobile at home. I forgot to cancel something next week.' He looked at his watch. 'Is there a phone here? I might just catch Judy in the office.'

Ed was steering us into the house. 'There isn't,' he said. 'But you can use mine. It's in my jacket. In there.' He moved his head to indicate a door behind him, then turned to me. 'Maggie. I'll show you round.'

The house was nice, all so tastefully *Elle Décor* that you fully expected to find a list of stockists taped to the back of a door. The woodwork was painted powder-blue, the floorboards were sanded and the sofas loosely covered in various neutral shades of linen. A fire was lit in the main sitting room. What else could you want? All mod cons and a candle sconce in the shape of an antelope. A tumble drier and the stars at night.

'Where are the others?' I said.

'Oh, right.' Ed's voice lowered. 'Pea, I'm afraid, has gone to bed. Migraine, poor love. She's had a terribly stressful week at work. She had a very important film to finish. It was about battered women, phwoo.' He shook his head in admiration. 'Mark and Louisa have gone for a quick drink in the pub. I'm holding the fort. Clarice went out like a light, but the other two . . .' He gave a small shudder. 'Bit *wild*, I think.'

It occurred to me that Mark and Louisa's children, who seemed no wilder on the few times I had met them than any other six- and eight-year-olds, attended a state school. It may perhaps have disconcerted Ed to meet children who didn't speak more poshly than their parents.

'We'd better get ours in,' I said.

'Yes, come up, come up, and I'll show you where you are first,' said Ed, bounding up the stairs. 'We're in here. Clarice is in—here. Mark and Louisa have got this room so they can be next to the room with the bunk beds and you're in . . . um . . . in here.' He opened the door to a perfectly adequate room at the end of the corridor, its only immediate drawbacks being the extra mattress on the floor and the cot in the corner. 'Thought you'd want to have the children close to you,' he said.

'Can Fergus not share with Clarice?' I said, not even going in.

'Do you mind terribly if he doesn't? Only she's such a light sleeper . . .'

I stomped out to the car, muttering under my breath. Jake came up behind me, and when I told him about the sleeping arrangements, pulled me by the arm. 'Grow up,' he said. 'It doesn't matter.'

'Oh right, you don't care if you don't get any sleeep, then?'

'Of course I care, but come on . . . it's only a weekend. Anyway,' he added half under his breath, 'it's not as if the children are going to interrupt us having sex.'

It was the first time either of us had referred to the situation between us, and his words hung in the air as we disembarked the children. Then we heard giggles coming up the lane behind us and Mark and Louisa appeared round the corner. I was always taken aback at how handsome they both were. He looked like a male model with a chiselled jaw and rangily muscular body. She was tall and willowy with a large nose and hanks of gingery hair, which she tidied up in a collection of kirby grips. She was holding Mark's hand inside one of his pockets. That was the other thing about them: thirteen years of marriage and two children and you could tell they were still at it like rabbits—a suspicion that tended to make the rest of us rather grumpy.

'Oh great, you made it!' called Louisa, crunching onto the drive. 'Reinforcements!'

'I expect you need them,' I said, bending to kiss her over Dan's sleeping head. 'After a few hours of Pea.'

She looked enquiringly.

'I hear she's had a "terrible week" saving the world.' I mocked Ed's tone of uxorious concern.

Louisa laughed dubiously.

Jake said, 'For Christ's sake, Maggie. Behave.' He clapped his hand round Mark's back. He looked visibly relieved to see them. Perhaps because they had rescued him from me.

After I'd settled the children, I combed my hair and went downstairs to join the others for 'a nightcap'.

Mark was leaning back on one of the sofas. Louisa was reclining on a kilim on the floor, resting against his legs. Jake was at a table in the window reading out extracts from the visitors' book: '"Disappointing weather for June. Recommend the scampi-in-the-basket at the Pig and

Gristle in Appleton"; "Wonderfully hot water. And exceptionally soft towels".' I thought he'd look up when I came in, raise an eyebrow at me, particularly when he got to the bit about 'exceptionally soft towels', but he kept his eyes on the page.

'Maggie,' said Ed, coming in from the kitchen behind me. 'A glass of wine? And what about some boeuf bourguignon?'

'Goodness, where did that come from?' I said.

'I made it at home and brought it with us in a Tupperware,' Ed said. 'I thought people might be hungry.'

Louisa stretched her legs out. 'God, you are brilliant, Ed,' she said. 'I wish Mark could cook.' She gave him a backward jab with her head. 'What a lucky woman Pea is.'

Ed went pink. 'I don't know about that,' he said.

'I should be so lucky,' I sang, going over to an armchair by the fire and throwing myself into it. 'I should be so lucky in love.' The others, with the exception of Jake, looked at me oddly. 'Sorry,' I said. 'Country air.'

There was a lot of talk about the Kyushi pitch then. Ed said, 'I knew, I just knew, when they started talking about Claudia Schiffer, that we'd got them.' Mark said, 'Not to mention when they said we'd hit the nail on the head strategically,' and I realised then, for the first time, what this weekend was all about. It had been planned as a celebration or a commiseration. One I'd let go over my head.

I stood up then and said I was going to get a glass of water. Nobody seemed to notice me leave. I went into the kitchen and filled a glass from the tap. I drank it with my back against the sink. I felt a pang for Pete. I longed for him suddenly, for the feel of his rough hands. Just to hear his voice would be to take me away from all this. He was my escape from the rat race, my escape from the middle classes. I wished I'd managed to ring him before we left. I wished I could hear his voice *now*. Then I saw Ed's jacket flung on the back of a chair, with the pocket hanging down as if it had excess weight inside it. Without moving, I put my foot out and felt it. It was his phone. I could hear the others laughing in the sitting room. 'Bang on brief!' I heard Ed yell. I reached across and drew the phone out quickly. Ericsson. I pressed a little red button at the bottom left. The screen flickered and emitted a series of beeps that seemed to echo round the kitchen, so I quickly unlatched the back door and slipped into the garden. The screen had dimmed. Maybe it needed reactivating. I pressed another button, green this time, which read 'OK' and a number flashed up, followed by 'Call?' It was a moment before it registered. It was the last number the phone had rung. The phone Jake had used only minutes before. The phone was giving me the option to call it. I quickly looked over my shoulder and then pressed OK again and heard the number dial. It rang three times and then an answering machine picked it up. No matter how hardened I thought I'd become, I still felt winded when I heard her voice. 'Hi,' she began, 'you've reached Claire Masterson . . .'

I heard a noise behind me. Louisa was poking her head into the garden. 'Maggie,' she cried. 'What are you doing out here?'

Panicked, I dropped the phone under some rosemary. 'Just getting some air,' I said. 'Clearing my head.'

I had to go down later when everyone was asleep to retrieve it. Pete's Vodaphone was switched off. Ed's Ericsson smelt of lamb chops.

chapter eighteen

SATURDAY. THE OLD SCHOOL HOUSE, Cotley. Raining.

The day did not start well. Dan and Fergus were up with the lark. Didn't hear the lark. Just heard the rain pounding against the window and Fergus saying, 'Is it MORNING?' and waking Dan up.

I took them down the stairs of the otherwise silent house into the kitchen, where I tried to entertain them with a plastic colander, some metal measuring spoons and a pack of playing cards I found in a drawer. I tried to make card houses, but every time I had more than two floors balanced, Dan gave them a swipe like a kitten irritated by a fly and they'd fall down and scatter over the flagstones. Fergus would put as many screeched syllables as he could manage without giving himself a sore throat into his disappointment, and then swipe Dan back, a puppy irritated by a kitten.

Ed's phone was in his jacket on the kitchen chair where I'd left it. Several times I thought about using it, but I couldn't see how without Fergus making a scene when I didn't let him talk too. It was also painfully early to ring a childless man, not least a childless man who may have been out half the night at Oblivion. I wondered who he'd been with and the thought made me feel jagged with a kind of jealousy that was new to me. I may have looked like a slightly under-slept mother playing nicely with her children. But actually I was a witch.

It seemed like five days later when the others began to emerge. First Mark with Penny and Joe, all in their pyjamas. And later Pea with Clarice. Pea and Clarice were already dressed. Pea was wearing a pair of linen trousers and a mushroom-coloured shirt. Clarice looked like a summer bridesmaid in a fitted linen frock, the colour of puy lentils.

'Hello, Pea,' I said, getting up off the floor. 'Lovely linen thing.'

'Agnès B,' she said.

'I meant Clarice's.'

'That's right. Agnès B.' There was a pause. 'Did you sleep well?'

'Yes, thank you,' I lied. 'You?'

She sighed. 'Bearably.'

I wanted to say, 'Well, I didn't either, then,' but Mark nudged me out of the way to get at the cereal bowls.

'Come on, everyone,' he said. 'Breakfast.'

He looked up when he'd got the kids sorted. 'It's raining, then,' he said. 'Must be August Bank Holiday.'

'Nothing wrong with a bit of rain,' clipped Pea.

'Except we'll need a plan,' I said. 'Mine need to get out of the house.'

'We could still go to the sea,' said Mark. 'Wrap everyone up.'

'Or there's the zoo,' I said. I'd had plenty of time that morning to study the leather folder in the kitchen labelled 'Information'.

'The world's our oyster,' said Mark.

'The sea, the sea, the sea,' shouted the children. Fergus had already got down from the table. Clarice, who was picking the raisins out of her muesli, one by one, said, 'I don't like the sea. It makes me wet.'

'As if you weren't wet enough already,' I muttered over by the kettle.

I didn't think anyway had heard me, but Mark came over to pour himself some coffee and said, 'Oooh, back in the drawer, Ms Sharp.' I giggled, but then I noticed Pea studying me and I felt a bit bad so I hauled the children upstairs and got us all dressed. I didn't bother to keep them quiet any more and when Jake got up he looked stormy.

I said, 'No need to look at me like that. It's nine o'clock.'

Louisa was coming out of the bathroom. 'Everybody happy?' she said. And then Ed appeared wearing a paisley dressing gown. His blond hair was mussed up at the back like a piece of candy floss.

'Morning,' I said. 'Almost ready to go out?'

'No, he's not,' said Jake. 'None of us are.'

'Well, I am,' I said. But Ed had already scurried into the bathroom like a guinea pig darting for cover.

Louisa looked at me. 'You're very smart,' she said. 'For the country.'

'This old thing?' I said, damping down the dress I'd bought after my day at Paddle (my 'Claire dress').

'You're going to be cold,' she said.

Jake was stony-faced by the time we got to the small seaside town nearby. We'd taken two cars but Louisa came with us, which gave us an opportunity to bitch about Pea (well, I bitched with all the twisted humour of my bad blood, and she laughed) until Jake, who was driving, said, 'Lay off, Maggie,' and I had to make stupid faces at her instead. Then we couldn't park and had to drive round and round until, finally, we found a Pay and Display in a housing estate miles from the beach.

'Oh,' I said, pointedly not undoing my seat belt. 'It's just stupid. I'm sure there's a better place to park.'

'We can't drive around any more,' said Jake. 'Maybe you should have worn something more sensible. It's only spitting.'

Louisa had disembarked and was putting her mac on. Dan was grizzling in the back. Fergus had twigged my mood and was moaning too. 'It's raining. I don't want to walk. I want to be carried. Carry, carry, carry.'

'Now look what you've started,' said Jake.

Louisa yanked open the passenger door. She handed me my Puffa jacket from the boot. 'Come on, you lot,' she said. 'Stop being horrid. It's the Bank Holiday weekend. Everybody has to be nice.'

'That's put us in our place,' I said. Jake didn't say anything. He got out of the car and walked off ahead. I got out and joined Louisa. We followed with Fergus and the buggy.

Louisa was chatting away about this and that, pointing out interesting cottages, telling me about the holiday they'd just had in California, when suddenly the monster that was screaming in my head started hammering to get out. I said, without realising I was going to, 'I've met someone else. I'm seeing someone else. A man. Pete.' It was a thrill to say his name out loud.

'You what?' said Louisa. She had stopped walking.

'A man,' I said. 'I've met a man.'

'What kind of man? What are you talking about?'

I walked on. She followed. She was still trying to look into my face.

'Watch where you're going,' I said. 'I've met a man. I'm having an affair. Or trying to.' I giggled, but she was looking horrified.

'I can't believe it,' she said. 'This is awful.'

I paused to pull Fergus away from some dog shit.

'Are you coming?' yelled Jake, from the top of the road.

I called, 'Yes, we are,' and to Louisa, I said, 'It's nothing. I'm not really. Forget it. I shouldn't have told you.'

It's true: I really shouldn't have told her. It was just, shameful as it was, I wanted to smash something up for a moment. I wanted to see shock on her face. Even though it belonged to a person I liked. And after I'd said it, even though I knew I'd opened myself up to danger, I felt relieved. As if I was beginning to make it more real.

Jake had seen the others on the street opposite. They were crossing over to meet us. Clarice and Pea were looking sulky. When they got to us, Pea said, 'I'm just going to look round the antique shops. We haven't got anything waterproof for Clarice and, anyway, she doesn't want to get sand in her shoes. So we'll meet you later.'

Ed's feet were shifting to and fro in their Church's brogues. 'Meet you back at the car in an hour, then?' he said in a high, nervous voice as they walked away. Clarice turned her head and stuck out her tongue.

When we got to the beach, the children galumphed down to the water and were soon hooting with laughter, playing Russian roulette with the North Sea. Mark and Jake joined them, picking them up one by one, turning them horizontal and pretending to throw them in, like life belts being hurled overboard. I carried the buggy over the pebbles to join Ed, who was sitting glumly on an upturned boat.

'Budge up,' I said, putting Dan down so he could watch the waves, and pulling my jacket down to protect my bottom from the damp wood. 'Good news about Kyushi, then.'

'Yes,' he said.

'Tight competition, too.'

'Yup.'

We were staring ahead. Louisa had walked down to join Mark and put her arms round him from behind. We both watched them for a bit. I said, 'They're the perfect couple, Mark and Louisa, aren't they?'

Ed shrugged. The dance seemed to have gone out of him. His face looked pouchy and pale. An actor waiting outside make-up.

I said, 'Put the rest of us to shame.'

He made an indeterminate noise in his throat.

Louisa had taken off her shoes and was trying to splash Mark with her feet. Jake was showing Fergus how to skim stones.

Ed and I seemed to have nothing to say to each other, which was disconcerting. He was not usually one to let a silence grow beneath his feet. He was playing with some pebbles, shifting them between his fingers and throwing the odd one as if it were a cricket ball onto the sand further along the slope.

I bent down to rearrange Dan's blanket. 'Your daddy and I don't behave like that, do we?' I said chirpily.

Suddenly, Ed spoke very quickly. 'Look, I'm probably speaking out of line here, but I know that you and Jake are going through a bad patch. I know it's none of my business, but . . .' He swallowed hard. 'But I just wanted to tell you that I think he's a great bloke and that he really cares for you and . . . that's all really.'

'Ed!' I said, straightening up. 'What do you mean?'

'None of us is perfect.'

'I know, but what do you mean?'

Ed began to take in a deep breath as if he was about to say something, but then stopped as if he'd changed his mind. He dropped the stones he was playing with and stood up abruptly, pulling himself physically together. 'No,' he said. 'No, no, no. Just forget it.'

'Go on,' I said. 'What do you mean? Who's not perfect?'

'I was just making conversation,' he said. 'I didn't mean anything.' He'd started moving away and down the beach. He began to run, careering downhill into his usual self. He put his arms out like an aeroplane. 'Ngwooooow,' he said, charging into Penny and Joe. 'OK, campers!' he hollered. 'How about a bite of lunch?' Even from where I was sitting I could see him pretending to take a chunk out of Louisa's shoulder.

We should, in retrospect, have gone back to the cottage for warmed-up stew. As it was, we went to one of those cosy-looking seafood cafés, which pretends it's cheap and cheerful but is full of people eating seriously, and expensively, off gingham tablecloths, heads ducked so as not to bang against the plastic lobsters hanging from the ceiling.

Ed darted off when we got to the main square and returned with Pea and Clarice. Clarice had been bought a jigsaw puzzle from a souvenir shop and she started unwrapping it while we were still waiting for a table, dropping pieces left, right and centre, and squealing whenever somebody trod on a piece of Little Mermaid. We were all squashed against the door, out of the wind, and Dan was writhing in my arms, trying to poke his fingers through the fishing net that was slung across the window, and everyone else was milling and tripping over chair legs. People at the tables kept looking round to see what the commotion was, and I was about to suggest we beat a retreat when Pea said from the floor where she was picking up pieces of puzzle, 'I don't know why we're doing this. There's lots of delicious bourguignon left back at the house.'

Suddenly, I was eating out's biggest fan. 'Yes, but no hot crab ramekin. I can't wait for my hot crab ramekin.'

When we finally squeezed onto a table, settling each child in proximity to at least one parent, matters disintegrated even further. Fergus was overexcited. He was bouncing up and down in his chair. He was banging the table, chanting, 'Er, er, er,' in a moment of regression. The older children joined in too, turning it into a game. Joe got hold of the salt and pepper pots and started banging those too and made Clarice cry by spilling her Coke. 'Grow up, all of you,' shrieked Pea. 'Enough, I say. Enough.' We all turn into our parents in the end.

I was at the opposite end of the table from Jake with a small mountain range of children's heads between us. Ed was next to me on my right. Ignoring the chaos, he had his face in the wine menu. 'White all right for everyone?' he said, as if he was offering us a choice, then, without pausing, to the waiter, 'Pouilly-Fumé, please.' He sniffed it when it came, swirled it in his glass and brought it to his nose. He nodded at the waiter without looking up.

'Aren't you supposed to taste it?' I said.

'Actually, no. A sniff's all that's needed. All you're looking for is whether it's corked or not and you can tell that from the slightest of signs.'

'Like many things in life,' I said, taking a large glug from mine. 'The smallest of clues . . .'

He looked at me and then looked away very quickly.

I waited until the food arrived to ask him what he had meant on the beach. I was sure he had been about to say something about Jake's affair. Could he be an unexpected ally? But, before I could, Clarice wanted him to hear her count her scallops in French.

'Un. Deux. Trois . . .'

'So what's the name of your French teacher?' I interrupted.

'Madame Charbonnel,' she said.

Unfortunately, this caught Pea's attention across the table. She looked up from her squid. 'Not for long. Madame Charbonnel is leaving at half-term to have a baby. So *she's* in no one's good books at the moment.'

Ed had caught Jake's eye. 'Madame Charbonnel,' he said, with his hand on his heart, pretending to swoon.

Pea said, 'Except clearly in Ed's. Madame Charbonnel can't do a thing wrong as far as you're concerned, can she? But leaving in the middle of a school year couldn't be more disruptive for the children.'

A flinch of irritation contracted Ed's forehead. 'I'm only messing about,' he said.

'Yes, well, not in front of . . .' Pea inclined her head towards Clarice.

Ed's jaw stiffened almost imperceptibly. I waited until it got noisy again, until there was a rising tumult around us, blurred voices and children's cries, like the sea heard through a shell.

Ed was picking at his Easter-bonnet garnish of twirled carrot and parsley. When no one was listening, I said softly, 'What did you mean, "no one's perfect"? What were you referring to? I wish you'd tell me.'

He looked frightened. You could almost see the cogs in his brain trying to think of a joke to get him out of it; urgently needed, an ejector seat of wit. 'I don't know,' he said. 'Look, this is a madhouse. Let's eat up and go.'

Pea heard this and said. 'Aren't we going to have coffee?'

'I thought . . .'

She looked irritated with him, and turned to the others as if she had decided no longer to register his presence. 'Who wants coffee?' she said.

I had been busying myself with Dan. I said, 'Ed and I thought we'd take the children for a run around. You lot have coffee. Jake, will you take Dan? We'll take the others.'

Jake said, 'Er, sure.' He looked a bit nonplussed, though not as nonplussed as Ed, who looked as if he wanted to curl up like the carrot on his plate. I felt defiant, though. I wanted to know what Ed knew.

We bundled up the children and walked without talking back to the beach. As the children ran off back down to the sand I stopped to take my shoes off and perched on the edge of a breakwater. 'Listen. You started to say something earlier and then you bottled out.'

He looked flustered. 'Did I?'

'Yup. I know we don't really get on, but I liked you for it. I appreciated the fact that you wanted to talk to me about it.'

'Really?' He flushed. He started picking at some dried-up seaweed, which had stuck to the breakwater. 'I don't know what to say, really.'

'Well, you don't have to say anything else, because I know about her. About Claire, I mean.'

'Do you?' He sat down on the stump next to me. It was wet but he didn't seem to notice. The red had drained away, leaving his face white. 'Did Jake tell you?'

'I worked it out. I'm not stupid.'

'Oh, Maggie.' He picked at a bobbly string of seaweed attached to the breakwater next to him.

The children were huddled together further across the beach. Penny was kneeling on the sand and was poking at something with a piece of driftwood. The others were watching her.

'So?' I tried to make my voice sound light. 'How serious do you think it is?'

Ed rubbed his eyes with his seaweedy hands, pushed them back through his hair. 'I think it's very serious. I wish it wasn't. I wish I could tell you it wasn't . . .'

I didn't know what I was expecting, but I don't think that it was this. Part of me had assumed that Jake's relationship with Claire was just about sex. The fabric of my dress suddenly seemed very thin. I said, shivering, 'Oh fuck.'

Ed was looking paler than usual. 'It's a terrible mess,' he said in a tight voice.

'You can say that again.'

He had turned his head to stare at the olive sea. There were some sailing boats out there now, white envelopes cutting through the waves. I pulled on his shoulder. 'So what are you saying, Ed? Time to leave?'

There was a pause before he turned his head back to me. 'Maybe. I know Pea wouldn't stand for things if she knew. What do you think, Maggie? It's a hard thing to ask, but maybe you could talk to Claire. See what's going through her mind. That's one thing I don't know.'

'The last thing I want to do is talk to Claire,' I said.

The children had moved apart from each other now. Penny was taking something on the end of her wood down to the water. The smaller ones were following her, but Clarice had started back up the beach towards her father, her face screwed up. I said quickly, before she got to us, 'So is it just about sex, Ed? Or is it love?'

He paused before answering. 'Are they different?'

Clarice, sobbing, was a few steps from us. 'Fergus . . .' she began.

'I wish I knew,' I said.

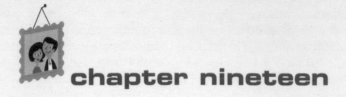

chapter nineteen

THAT EVENING, after I'd put the children to bed, I told everyone I needed some air and walked down to the pub in the village. It was your typical country affair: video games built into low tables, wide-screen TV and local lads discussing crack cocaine in a gaggle in the corner. I ordered a gin and tonic and sat nursing it on a stool. I didn't know how long I could be away from the house without drawing attention, but I had to speak to Pete. Ever since my conversation on the beach with Ed, I'd been feeling desperate. It would do me good to hear Pete's voice: to hear him be nice to me, to check he was still all right for Tuesday. All this would quell my confusion. Jake didn't want me any more, but Pete did. Didn't he? Obviously Pete and I didn't know each other very well, but that was soon to change. Wasn't it? We were proceeding in the right direction. Or were we? Oh hell.

There was a payphone on the bar. I pushed twenty pence into it and called Pete. He picked up straight away. 'Oh, Maggie. Hi,' he answered.

'I just needed to hear your voice,' I said. 'It's awful here. I'm longing to see you. It feels like ages.'

'I'm sorry, Mags. I've been busy as shit.'

'It's all right, I understand. But you're still on for Tuesday?'

'You bet. Can't wait. A whole evening of . . .'

'Yes, but we're going to go out, aren't we? Do something?'

'Oh yeah. Of course. How are you?'

'Oh God. You wouldn't believe . . .' I began to tell him about the weekend, but he cut me off. 'Look, my little pumpkin'—he said this ironically—'I'm sorry. But I'd better go. There're some people waiting for me upstairs—'

'Oh, OK,' I said. 'Do you miss me?'

'Of course. Mmmmmm.' He paused. 'See ya, all right?'

'See you.'

I didn't feel much better after this conversation, but I could at least take comfort in having spoken to him.

There was an atmosphere when I got back to the house. Pea was clattering about in the kitchen, making a meal out of cooking a chicken. Louisa and I had wanted to get a takeaway from the Thai in the village, but Pea had insisted. When I asked if there was anything I could do to help, she told me it was all under control *now*, thanks. She had been cool with me ever since Ed and I had taken the children for a walk.

When the meal had been cleared away, Louisa, clearly keen to emulate a weekend in the country with jollier companions, suggested we play a game. I said I was tired and that goodness knew what time Fergus would get up in the morning, but she told me to pull myself together. Pea, sitting stiff-backed on the edge of a hard chair with a bottle of wine on the side table next to her, wanted to know what kind of game.

'Mr and Mrs,' Louisa said. 'We played it in Cornwall at New Year. It was hilarious. One half of a couple leaves the room and you ask questions about them to the other. Then they come back in and answer the questions themselves. Their partner gets a point for each correct answer. I got everything wrong about Mark. I even got his A levels wrong.'

'You know nothing about me,' her husband said, pretending to sob.

'Yeah, well, I know more now than I did. It was quite an eye-opener. Stag weekend indeed . . .'

'All right,' said Pea. There were two bright spots on her cheeks. The bottle by her side seemed to be going down suspiciously fast.

The rest of us agreed too, largely, I suspect, through fear of being considered dull.

Louisa left the room first and Mark answered questions on 1) her favourite film ('Easy. *The Silence of the Lambs*.'), 2) her favourite food ('Toad-in-the-hole. My mother taught me how to make it and she *loves* it.'), and 3) her favourite flowers ('Tough one . . . er . . . carnations, I think.'), all of which he got wrong. Her answers, when she came back in, were, 1) *An American in Paris*. ('How can you say *Silence of the Lambs*?' 'We saw it on our first date.' 'Yes, well just because I remember it fondly doesn't mean I *liked* it.') 2) Scallops with bacon. ('But you love my toad-in-the-hole!' 'Oh sorry, of course, scrap scallops, put greasy sausage in artery-thickening batter. My mistake.') And 3) Night-scented stock. When informed that Mark had guessed carnations, she sighed and shook her head pityingly. 'All men think women like carnations. It's one of the great tragedies of life.'

Their score so far in the game then was nil. 'Which just goes to show,'

Louisa said, snuggling up to her husband on the sofa, 'that knowing things about each other, just like "having things in common", is a greatly overrated quality in a marriage.'

Pea was the next woman out, which meant that this time Mark and Louisa had a hand in the questions. Ed floundered as to whether Pea 'scrunched or folded' her loo paper. 'Shit,' he said. 'She's quite anal so I'd say folded, but then if you are literally anal I suppose you scrunch. I'll have to guess on this one. I'll say scrunch.' Her desert-island luxury caused him equal trouble.

'What about a vibrator?' suggested Louisa.

'Phh.' He made a sound like a horse snorting through its mouth. 'No. Perfume? No . . . There's some face cream she's always going on about, but . . . Um, I know: her contacts book.' And as for whether she had any recurring nightmares, he tapped his fingers on the side of his head in thought, then finally, he said, 'I don't think she likes heights much.'

Pea smiled brittlely when she came back in. She'd taken her drink with her and I noticed she was swaying a little bit. 'So,' she said. 'What revelations?'

She looked a mite offended at the scrunch/fold question but admitted to scrunching, awarding her marriage one point. For her desert-island luxury, she said quickly, 'My photo album; I'd like to have my loved ones with me,' which made Ed pretend to slink under the table in shame. And for her recurring nightmare, she said, staring at me, 'Discovering my husband has been unfaithful.' I felt myself go red. Did she think I'd been flirting with Ed? Or did she know about Jake and Claire and was being cruel? Or was I being paranoid? I opened my mouth to say something, but Louisa had got up and was bustling me out of the room so that Jake could be questioned. I stood in the corridor taking deep breaths.

When I came back in, they were all staring at me. Jake was looking embarrassed. Louisa said, in the honeyed singsong tone of a travel-show host, 'From the table, to the bathroom, to the bedroom . . .' Then in her own voice, 'Tough luck, Maggie. We're braving sex now. The first question: With whom did you lose your virginity?'

'Easy,' I said, smiling, but not looking at Jake. 'Patrick Unwin. Lower sixth. His bedroom. "Is She Really Going Out With Him?" on the stereo.'

Jake looked relieved. 'Well done,' said Louisa. 'One point to the Priton/Owens. Next question: Have you ever had a one-night stand?'

'No,' I said. 'Unless two-nights count?'

440

'They don't. Sorry.' Louisa marked a cross on her piece of paper.

'So who do you think I had a one-night stand with?' I asked Jake.

'I don't know,' he said. 'I just thought you must have done.'

'Well, I haven't.'

Louisa cleared her throat, and then said in a rush, 'And finally, not my question this, Mags, blame Pea . . . Have you ever been unfaithful?'

'Sorry?' I said. My heart was thudding in my rib cage. My mouth was dry, my face hot.

Pea said, 'Have you ever been unfaithful?'

'What?' I tried to laugh.

Louisa and Mark had started horsing around on the sofa, busy with a private joke on their own. Ed was looking anxious. Jake was studying his fingernails as if he wasn't even listening. But Pea was glaring at me. 'Come on,' she said. 'Answer the question.'

'No,' I said. I tried to breathe normally. 'No. Never.'

Jake looked up. 'Liar,' he said.

I stared at him. I felt the colour drain from my face.

'What about with me?' he said.

'What about with you?' My voice sounded choked.

Everyone was looking at us now.

'And David.'

It was a moment before I understood what he was getting at and then relief flooded through me. I took an enormous breath. 'Oh yes,' I said. 'I'd forgotten. There was, shall we say, a slight matter of overlap between David the lawyer and Jake.' I put my hands up in an act of surrender.

'Thank you,' said Jake.

'Which,' said Louisa, back in official mode, 'puts the Priton/Owens in the lead with two points.'

The next round passed without incident—until it was Jake's turn to leave the room. I failed completely to come up with a figure for his golf handicap. I didn't even know what kind of a figure to be playing with. Finally, racking my memories of P. G. Wodehouse, I said, 'Fourteen under five,' which made Mark fall off his chair laughing. I also didn't know what the first account in his first job was. 'Oh dear,' I said. 'I should know, shouldn't I? Can I have a clue?'

Mark said, 'Who's a pretty bird, then?'

I said, 'Something to do with animal feed, um . . .'

'Pretty Polly,' he hissed.

'Oh yes,' I said, 'I knew that . . .'

But it was the next question, asked by Pea, that really got me. 'Does Jake have any secrets from you?' she said. Did he have any secrets from me? Oddly, my first instinct was to laugh. I thought of saying yes—I mean everyone has some secrets, don't they?—but her eyes were boring into me, and I suppose it was dignity or pride that made me say, 'No.'

When Jake came back in he didn't seem very amused by my ignorance on questions one and two, but he smiled when he came to this one, or it might have been a grimace. Ed said, 'Unfair question. Don't make him answer it,' but Jake replied with remarkable cool. 'Yes,' he said. 'I do. Doesn't everybody have some secret or other?'

Pea was looking triumphant. I couldn't let her. I said, suddenly feeling sober, 'No, you haven't. You think you have. But you don't.'

I got up and went to the door. 'Anyway, we're disqualified,' I said. 'We're not married.'

The following day, Jake and I had arranged to take the children to visit his parents who lived across the border in Norfolk, a short drive away.

'I'm not coming,' I told Jake when we woke up, after a short night (it had been past two by the time we finally made it to bed). My head throbbed with hangover and misery. It felt like a child's toy, my brain clonking against my skull like the sound box in a mooing cow. 'You can take Fergus and Dan on your own. They're your parents after all.'

'But you're the one they'll want to see,' he said. 'Please come.' He bent over Fergus, who had got into bed with us in the night, and said quietly, 'Let's be friends. It's awful being like this.'

'I know,' I said. We looked at each other, but I was the first to look away. 'I just don't feel like coming, that's all.'

'About last night, Maggie. The secret—'

'Look,' I said. My head pounded. 'I don't want to talk about it. I don't want to know.'

I got up and went to the bathroom where I could hear splashing and squeals of 'get off' and then a sort of lapping sound. Mark and Louisa were clearly having sex in the bath. Depressed, I went back to the bedroom where Jake was mucking about on the bed with Fergus and Dan.

'Fine,' he said, without rancour. 'We'll go without you then.'

The expression on his face made me want to kiss him. But I couldn't. It had been too long.

They set off quite soon after that. Pea and Ed took Clarice off to a museum in a local market town so she could do some work on her

442

ancient Roman, project. Penny and Joe made a camp in the garden. Louisa wanted to know if I was all right.

I told her everything was hunky-dory.

'So who's this bloke?' she said. 'Are you going to tell me about him?'

I told her he was nobody really and that it had not been going on for long. That he was a gardener. That he had hands like sandpaper. That he had earth under his nails. That he was younger than me. That maybe it would be better if I didn't talk about it.

'Whatever,' she said.

We went for a walk down the lane to a little bridge over a stream.

'You're bound to have up and down patches, you know,' she said. 'We all do. You met him young. It's so difficult with small children. Ninety per cent of all divorces take place in the first year of the second child's life. Or something.'

'Another two months to get through then,' I said.

We stood, looking down into the water, a trickle at this time of year, with a few crisp packets entangled in the weeds. Louisa bent to fiddle with her flip-flops. 'I quite like Pea, actually,' she said.

'You like everybody,' I said. 'It doesn't count.'

When we got back to the house, Ed, Pea and Clarice had been back, packed and left. Mark was eating a sandwich in the kitchen.

'They said they wanted to beat the Sunday-evening traffic,' he said. He took another bite, dropping lettuce on the floor. 'And Clarice had her Sanskrit homework to do. Or something.'

Penny and Joe trailed in, covered in mud. 'We're starving,' said Penny.

'Shoes!' yelled Louisa.

Mark started cutting more bread, and made big doorsteps with cheese spilling out of the edges. My stomach turned. I went upstairs and lay down on the bed. The noises of the house drifted up. Mark was playing some energetic game in the garden. 'Da-ad. Da-ad. Over here.' Their voices got fainter and fainter. I felt a deep sense of unease. Something was nagging at the back of my mind. Something not right. Images came into my head. I could see box hedges, clipped into the shape of birds and animals. I walked along a row of them towards a man in the distance. He had secateurs in his hand and was bending over. His back was broad and he was wearing combats. When I got closer, he straightened up and turned towards me and I saw then that it was Jake.

I must have slept for a long time because when I woke up the room was getting dark and the pillow beneath my cheek was wet.

September
spiders
chapter twenty

IT HAD BEEN STORMY in London that weekend too. When we got back there were leaves all over the common; green leaves, but harbingers of autumn nonetheless.

A change seemed to come over Jake and myself, something less zingy and more subdued. When he said he was really sorry but he did have to go into the office on the Bank Holiday Monday to 'tie up a few loose ends', I didn't tell him to 'tie away' in reference to what I knew he was really off to do. I smiled and said, 'Whatever.'

'As long as you don't mind,' he said, looking sad.

Fran had left a couple of messages over the weekend. She was planning a trip to Peter Jones' nursery department. 'So I could really do with the Definitive Maggie List: I mean, what do you think of the three-in-one car seat/carry-cot/pushchair option? Worth five hundred pounds?' I could tell when I rang her back that she wanted me to go with her. Any item I mentioned, she made a sort of strangulated wheedling sound, as if it was all too much for her to cope with. 'N'eghgh. What on earth are muslins anyway?' she said. 'Don't you use them for making jam?'

I told her she should ask an assistant. 'When are you going?' I said.

'Wednesday?' she said in a small voice.

'Good luck, then,' I said heartily. When I put the phone down, I felt lost for a moment, but I couldn't have gone with her, played the jolly sister-in-law. Not under the circumstances.

I had a strange sensation in the pit of my stomach all day Tuesday, the day of my date with Pete. I didn't know if it was excitement or anxiety or dread, but I felt breathless and jumpy. I'd waxed my legs and re-varnished my toenails when Fergus was napping. Scarlet Lady, the polish was called. And I set to with body lotion before getting dressed. I wore my Claire dress and my new kitten heels. Jake was baby-sitting. I'd told him in the morning that I was having a girly night out with the playground mums and that I'd get Merika, but he'd frowned and said he could do it, which felt a bit odd. I was surprised he could get away from

444

work. 'You look nice,' he said, standing in the hallway as I left.

I got the tube. Pete and I had arranged to meet down the line, in a district composed of street upon street of identical thirties housing. Safe houses. A long way from anyone we knew. Pete was waiting outside the station in his van. When he saw me he leaned across to open the passenger door. I hadn't seen him for more than a week. I'd expected him to look different. He was still in his work clothes. He had more dirt than usual in his fingernails. He kissed me.

'Look at you, all done up,' he said.

'Yes, and look at you!' I said. 'You haven't exactly made an effort!' I laughed, but I felt foolish suddenly in my new frock, my new heels, my cerise cardie slung over my newly Clarinsed shoulders.

Pete had taken his arm from my shoulder and had turned the ignition. 'Where are we going then, Mags?' he said.

'Shall we just drive until we find somewhere?'

'You're the boss,' he said, pulling out.

We roved around, getting lost for a while in an industrial estate, negotiating the same one-way system several times, rejecting this theme bar and that steak restaurant, until we came to a pub, the Three Bells, on a nondescript roundabout. Pete drove into the car park to check the A–Z. 'What about here?' he said. 'It looks OK, doesn't it?'

It had filthy net curtains at the windows and a garish banner advertising some television event 'Live'. It wasn't quite what I'd imagined, some little local bistro with a menu on a blackboard and carafes of rough red wine. 'Absolutely,' I said. 'A drink's a drink.'

We got out and went in. Pete opened the door for me, with a semi-bow and then, shrugging his arm over my shoulder, steered me to a table. We had our choice: it was almost empty. There were a couple of teenagers playing pool and an old man in a sheepskin coat at the bar. A big-screen television was showing MTV on one wall. It was still sunny outside, but it was dark in here as if it was underground. I sat down in the corner, next to a line of fruit machines flashing like Las Vegas. Pete went to the bar and came back holding a gin and tonic in one hand and a beer mug full of Coke in the other. 'Driving,' he said, chucking two packets of cheese-and-onion from his pocket onto the table.

'That's a shame,' I said. 'You should have got the Tube too.'

'Naaa,' he said, as if that would have been too complicated.

He opened one of the packets of crisps and started munching. He offered the packet to me. I shook my head and he delved his fingers back in again. Like a Big Mac, cheese-and-onion crisps are delicious in your own mouth, revolting in someone else's. I tried to ignore them. He said, sympathetically, 'So: your weekend? Bloody nightmare, was it?' I started telling him all about it, describing Ed and Pea and the others. He was smiling as if interested, but he was also tapping the table in time to the music. Britney Spears was miming to the song on the screen above the bar, her tiny headset mike buzzing in front of her mouth like a large insect. And the only comment he made was, 'She sounds a corker; bit of a goer, is she?' when I told him about Louisa.

'So how was your weekend?' I said. 'How was your *week*?'

He said, 'Fine, fine.'

There was a pause. Pete continued to tap his hands on the table. I said, 'There's a chill in the air, isn't there? We had a picnic today, Fergus and Dan and me, I mean, on the common, and . . . um, there was really quite a breeze.'

Pete shook his head, back and forth, rhythmically. There was a smile on his face, but I don't think he was listening.

'And we bumped into Lucinda, running in her new au pair. She told me, while the girl was poop-scooping after one of the dogs, that she'd looked "high and low" and this girl was "the best she could find".' I expected him to laugh, but he said soberly, 'She does seem to have her hands quite full with all those children.' And then he stopped drumming and opened his mouth wide to get a particularly large crisp in.

We didn't stay there very much longer. I finished my drink and would have had another, but Pete said if he had any more Coke, he'd be 'pissing all night'. Then I said we should go for dinner, but he gestured to the empty crisp packets and said he wasn't that hungry, so we idled back out to the car park and stood by the van wondering what to do. What did you do on proper dates? It had been such a long time. What did Jake and I used to do? I think we just used to talk. In fact, I think we'd sat in some pretty dingy pubs, but somehow . . . Well, that was then. This was a different kind of relationship.

Pete looked at his watch. He said some mates were meeting in Fiction at 10.00pm and if I . . .?

I said, feeling scared and shy and old, I didn't think so really, did he?

And he said, 'No, you're right. Sorry. So, er, what else then?'

He didn't want to drink. He didn't want to eat. I said, 'There's always late-night shopping at Sainsbury's.'

But he didn't laugh. He said, 'No, I've done my groceries this week.

Look . . . I think I might head off back to the flat. I'm pretty knackered and . . . But if you want to come, I'd be . . .'

It wasn't the most fulsome of invitations so I was going to say no, but Pete nipped away then to the other corner of the car park, to help a couple push-start their car. He was always kind like that, and when he came back, cheerful, shouting, 'All right, mate,' over his shoulder, I heard myself say yes, I would. 'Good,' he said, as if he meant it. 'Good.'

It was the first time I'd been to his flat. When we got there, Pete took the steps down to the basement two at a time and went straight in ahead of me, leaving the door open behind him. The hallway smelt damp and dark, musty like a cupboard that's been closed too long. There were pizza fliers on the floor, cab cards, a plastic bag to be collected by Mind and, on the wall, one of those depress-buttons that switches on a timer light. The timer light went out.

'I'm in the kitchen,' he called from a small galley off the sitting room. He was scooping Gold Blend into a couple of mugs. He chucked the spoon into the pile of washing up in the sink. 'You're supposed to be going, "brrrrnnggngng",' I said. Blank look. 'Like in the ad?' Incomprehension. 'It doesn't matter.'

He said, as if something had just occurred to him, 'Are you hungry?' He opened the fridge with a 'ha-ha', and brought out a boxed pizza. 'What do you say?' he said, already ripping off the cardboard wrapper and trying to squash it into the microwave.

I said, 'I thought you didn't want anything to eat?'

He said, 'Didn't I? Well, I guess I've got an appetite now.'

I took the pizza off him and cut it in quarters so that it would fit and stood back while he switched it on. He told me to go and sit down, to make myself at home, so I went into the sitting room. It looked like an unmade bed. There were papers on the chairs and cushions on the floor, mugs and dirty plates on the table, and towels draped over an exercise bike in the corner. I cleared a copy of *Loot* off the sofa, and sat down. There was something hard and knobbly under my bottom. I put my hand down and came up with some dumbbells, which I laid care- fully on my knee and stared at. Dumbbells and an exercise bike . . .

There was a ping and Pete came in, nudged the dumbbells onto the floor with his knee and handed me a plate. 'Tucker,' he said. 'Wrap your nostrils around that.' I took one chewy mouthful and said, 'Actually. It's a funny thing. But do you know, I find I'm really not that hungry.' Pete said he'd have mine then, putting the television on with his spare hand.

It was a very big television. I wasn't used to seeing Chris Tarrant so big somehow. He was coaxing a flight attendant from Bicester up to £4,000. 'In the famous quotation from Shakespeare's *Twelfth Night*, music is the food of what? Time, Appetite, Love or Ears?'

'Time,' said Pete.

'Love,' I said.

'Nah,' he said, wrinkling his nose. 'Are you sure?'

'Yes,' I said. 'Everyone knows that.' Then I caught his expression and added, 'Well, anyway, as Chris Tarrant's always saying; they're only easy if you know them.'

'Yeah, all right, clever clogs,' he said.

A little bit later, I said, 'So, Pete: what *are* your plans?'

Pete still had a mouthful of pizza. I waited, listening to the sound of his chews, until he swallowed. 'What plans?' he said, finally.

'Don't you want to travel? Isn't that what all Australians do?'

'Yeah,' he shrugged. He started another mouthful.

'And where would you go if you did?'

This time he didn't bother swallowing. 'Thailand?' he said through his pepperoni.

'Anywhere else?'

'Phuket? I don't know. Can I phone a friend? Ha, ha.'

'No, I'm being serious,' I said. 'I'm just trying to find out more about you. I don't even know if you plan to settle in England or whether you're about to go back to Australia. Are you?'

He put his plate down, wiped his mouth with the back of his hand and licked the remains of tomato off his fingers. He seemed to be giving it a lot of thought. 'Dunno,' he said finally.

I said, 'But do you think you'll go back some time?'

'Crikey,' he said. 'You and your questions. I dunno. Come on. Go fifty/fifty.' He wasn't talking to me now, he was talking to a sports instructor from Weymouth. I grabbed the remote control from under his plate. Chris Tarrant disappeared with a hiss.

'We never talked,' I said.

He didn't notice the change of tense. 'OK. OK. Sorry. Sorry.' He shifted slightly and put his arm round me. 'So,' he began, 'let's talk . . .' Then I realised one of his shoulders was easing me down onto the sofa, that a hand was climbing up my newly waxed leg.

'That's not . . .' I said, beginning to protest. His hands were inside my new taupe heels, slipping them off. '. . . what I meant,' I said.

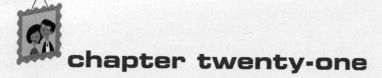

chapter twenty-one

OF COURSE I DID SLEEP with him in the end. It would have seemed churl-ish not to. Not after all the fuss I'd made about having a date in the first place. But it was over. I knew that now. I'd probably, in the back of my mind, known it for some time, but it was the dumbbells that finally did it for me. The cheese-and-onion crisps and the dumbbells. Our relation-ship had been all about sex, not because there wasn't time for it to be about anything else, but because that was all it was. And even the sexual attraction was based on a false premise. I'd thought he was so natural, so physically in tune with the elements, with the plants he tended, but it turned out even his muscles were artificially boosted.

I cried a little bit in the taxi on the way home, but the tears stopped as quickly as they came. The realisation in lots of ways made everything simpler. It was me and the kids now. Jake and Claire: me and the kids. I'd make a life for us after the separation, on our own. We could start again. There was no point mourning the past, I thought, opening the door of my sleeping house. I just had to get on with things.

Mel had flown home from France on Tuesday night, while I was with Pete. She had one last day off before going back to work, so we met in the park in the early morning. There was a chill in the air and the sun made striped shadows through the trees.

Milly and Fergus had run off to investigate some boggy ground near a tree trunk. They were poking about with sticks, squawking with laugh-ter every time they managed to fish a knot of brown foliage out of a puddle, whispering, daring each other to dip a sandalled toe.

'At least it's still warm enough not to mind,' I said, as we watched them venture in, bent double with pleasure and naughtiness. 'Soon, we'll be shouting, "No. Not in those shoes. You'll get cold feet."'

Mel said, 'So, come on. What's going on?'

We had talked all the way over, covering all the small, inconsequen-tial business that binds good friends, that tells you more about each

449

other's state of mind than any amount of soul-searching. She had told me about her holiday. Nice house. Good pool. Irritating sister-in-law. She'd missed Piers. I knew we'd get to me in the end.

I said, 'Do you think I can let Dan crawl around? He'll get very messy, but it seems unfair to keep him harnessed in.'

She didn't say anything. She sat down on a bench and waited. I undid the straps on the buggy and put Dan down on a drier piece of ground. He set off immediately, scrabbling across the grass on his hands and knees to join the other two in their home-made bog. 'Oh well,' I said. 'Doesn't matter. He'll dry off too.'

I sat down next to her on the bench. Someone had written 'Sue loves Pog' on the wood between us, only they'd written 'loves' in the form of a heart. I tried to rub the heart out with my finger as I filled her in. I told her I wasn't quite as mad as I had been, that I had the gardener in perspective, but that I did think things had got serious between Jake and Claire, and that he was probably on the verge of leaving me. It's like seeing a wall coming towards you, I told her: you know it's going to hurt, but there's nothing you can do except brace yourself. I also told her that I had to take a lot of the blame. I'd been awful. Brittle. Unapproachable. Worst of all, when I could have been fighting for him, I'd frittered away the time with some hunk from Down Under.

'Down Under being the operative words?'

'Well, maybe.'

'At least there's that,' she said.

We both laughed.

Milly and Fergus had run out of the trees and were heading away from us, elbows and knees and splashes of colour across the yellowing grass. Mel said, 'Do you think they'd make it to the border before we stopped them?'

'They'll come back,' I said. 'They always do.'

We watched them reach the pond, where they leaned against the railings, looking over their shoulders occasionally at us, taunting us with their daring. Grey clouds billowed across the sky, skudding like missiles towards the sun. The pond darkened and Milly and Fergus turned and started back, slowly, hand in hand, like an old couple.

Mel put her arm round me. 'I'm so sorry.' I could tell she wasn't sure what sort of thing I wanted her to say.

I said, 'You've got to tell me what to do. I'm in the middle of it. I can't see round it. I don't know what's what any more. Do I want Jake back even if he wanted to come? Do I want the gardener? No. Or should I be on my own? I've never been on my own. It would be good for me, wouldn't it? What do you think I should do?'

She took a deep breath. She said, 'Well. Maybe you should fight for Jake. If he can give her up, if you can forgive him . . . you won't be able to go back to how things were, but you can go on. You could make a life together, couldn't you? It might not be perfect, but you've got small children and they deserve some consideration in this. I mean, you always used to be so good together, so relaxed—no one else did cosy as well as you—and, I don't know, I don't think it's always a choice between being happy or being unhappy. I think if you make a decision to stay in a relationship and it seems hard, it doesn't mean you have to be unhappy for the rest of your life; you just have to try a bit harder to find happiness, root it out in the circumstances in which you find yourself. I don't think happiness is something that comes or doesn't; I think it's something you have control over.'

'But if he really loves her . . .'

'Well, maybe he does now. Maybe he doesn't. Who's to say how long it would last anyway? In a way, that's why I'm still with Piers. It's comfortable and comfortable only gets more comfortable as time goes by. Passion doesn't. Anyway, I have to say I always assumed Jake really loved you, Maggie. I know he didn't say much, but he was just one of those men. Carried it deeply, not on his sleeve, but in his heart, which is where it counts. And actually I can't believe that's changed. Not really.'

'I don't know.'

'This could be just an infatuation with Claire. Maybe you should see her for starters. Tell her to fuck off. Go round there. Cause havoc.'

'Maybe Jake and I need some time apart anyway.'

'Absolutely not!' Her eyes were bright. 'That's the worst thing anyone ever does. It's space that kills relationships. Once you have space, then all sorts of things start happening and none of them good.'

I smiled. 'OK. OK,' I said, 'point taken.' I got up to collect Dan, who had crawled over to the bin and was beginning to pull himself up to investigate its interesting-smelling contents. When I came back and had wrapped him up in the buggy, I gathered the V-neck of my cardigan into a bunch to protect my chest. It had got cold suddenly. 'And what about my Australian?'

'Dump him,' she said, standing up and brushing the bottom of her jeans. 'Now.'

I was cleaning out the bath a couple of hours later when the doorbell went. I peeled off the rubber gloves and jumped down the stairs.

'Coming!' I shouted.

Pete was standing on the porch looking doleful.

He said, 'You rushed off so quickly yesterday. I just wondered . . . I mean, are you cross with me for not having been around?'

'No,' I said. 'Not at all.'

He looked surprised. 'And I was a bit short with you yesterday. To be quite honest I wasn't really in the mood but—'

'No, really,' I said. 'It didn't matter.'

'Oh.' A look of relief came into his eyes, then he half closed them. 'I suppose I can't kiss you then, can I?'

I said, 'No.' I had Dan on one hip. Fergus was descending the stairs on his stomach. Head first. 'Look, I'm a snake,' he told Pete.

Pete ignored him. He said, head on one shoulder, 'When then?'

I said, 'How about never? How is never for you?'

He looked surprised.

'Sorry,' I said. 'That was a joke. Although . . .'

I didn't know what to say now. Mrs Allardyce was creaking by with her wicker trolley on wheels. She was wearing her mac and a plastic rain hat. Not my nemesis any more, my salvation. I waved. 'Any news?'

She smiled. 'Hello, dear. Well, it's not cancer. Old age probably. I've got a puffer.'

'I'm so glad,' I said. 'Cup of tea later?'

Pete didn't turn round during this exchange. When she'd gone he said, 'Aw, go on, let me in.'

I didn't have the heart to turn him away now. We went into the kitchen. Fergus had stopped being a snake and was hiding behind my knees, trying to prise them apart and peer through the middle. Pete, recovering himself, pretended to lunge at him, and Fergus giggled and clutched one of my thighs, twirled round my leg as if it were a Maypole. 'Steady on,' I said, almost losing my balance. 'Come on, Fergus, let's see if the Tweenies are on!' I said in a high, infectious pitch of excitement. 'Yes!'

Fergus, infected, echoed, 'Yes!' and ran through with me into the sitting room, where he snuggled down happily into the sofa cushions, like a guinea pig nestling into hay. I left Dan on the floor chanting 'bulubalubalu' next to a bucket of Duplo.

Pete's hands were waiting for me in the kitchen. 'Come here,' he said, kneading me and kissing my neck. 'I've missed this.'

I pulled away. I was all angles. It wasn't me he'd missed, it was the danger. 'Pete, I can't do this,' I said.

'I can,' he said, his voice husky, his eyes glazed. 'Come here,' and he pulled me towards him again and started kissing me. My knees weakened. I could hear the clatter of Duplo being emptied onto the boards; the Tweenie clock—'Where will it stop?'—Pete's hands were everywhere. There were alarm bells ringing in my head. This wasn't what I wanted. The alarm bells grew louder. More insistent. More ringing.

'Mummmeeee. Phone!'

'It's the phone,' I said, pushing him away. 'I've got to answer it.'

Pete rolled his eyes and stood crossly, looking out of the back door.

I grabbed the phone from under a tea cloth.

'Hello?' I said, breathlessly.

'Can I speak to Maggie Owen, please?'

'Speaking.'

'It's Dr Pulbrooke here, from Chelsea and Westminster Hospital.' Even as she was talking, I could feel panic starting at my toes and working its way up. 'I'm ringing on behalf of Fran Priton.'

'What is it?' I said. 'What is it? Is she all right? Is it the baby?'

'I'm afraid there's been an accident,' said the voice. 'Ms Priton is in theatre at the moment. She's going to be all right. Please don't panic. But she's been asking for you. Would it be possible for you to come in?'

'Yes, yes, I'll come now. Yes.' I was gabbling. I'd forgotten all about Pete. 'But the baby? What about the baby?'

'We're doing everything we can. We'll be able to tell you more when you get here.'

She gave me the details of where to go and I put down the phone and started throwing things into a bag—bottles, nappies, wipes. Pete said, his laid-back delivery a hundred miles behind me, 'Is everything OK?'

'No,' I said, 'it isn't.' I grabbed my car keys, switched off the television, drowned Fergus's cries of complaint with kisses, picked up both children for the sake of speed and started for the door. Pete trailed behind. Suddenly, I thought of something. 'Your mobile!' I said. 'I need to make some calls as I'm driving. Can I take it?'

'Er . . . Actually . . .'

'Thanks,' I said, before he could say anything more. I twisted him round and reached for it out of his back pocket. 'I'll ring you later.'

The children were muted in the car as if they sensed something was up. It had stopped raining but the traffic was still heavy for midmorning.

Queuing for the bridge, I fumbled with the phone until I got through to Jake's office. He was in a meeting, but I told his secretary it was urgent. When I said it was Fran, I registered a nanosecond of relief in his voice as he realised it was nothing about the children and then he sounded sick. 'I'll come now,' he said. 'I'll meet you there.'

The traffic was fine until the Fulham Road and then we inched along, stuck in single file behind a parked lorry. 'Come on,' I urged gutturally, like a businessman in a hurry. 'Come arnnnnn.' I put my foot down when I turned into the sliproad leading to the car park, a quick spurt of relief—and then I braked hard. There was a queue of cars in front, a Peugeot 205 with a fat man in the driving seat was trying to turn round, but a bus had come up on the other side of the road and was jamming his path. Everybody else was just sitting, patiently, some with their engines off, as the queue idled its way to the car park below. 'Shit,' I said, when I realised what was happening. 'Shit, shit. Bugger, bugger.' There were four cars ahead of us to the first bend. I looked at the clock on the dashboard. It was 12.40pm—forty minutes since the doctor had called. A sign on the wall next to us said NO STOPPING: OFFENDERS WILL BE CLAMPED. Why wasn't the road littered with clamped vehicles? This was a hospital, after all: a place for screeching brakes and crashing doors, and doctors hitting the decks running. But of course, outside of ER, hospitals are not places of urgency and panic. They are about boredom and interminable waiting . . . But not now, not for me NOW.

'Oh no,' I said through my teeth, as we entered the tunnel and I counted six cars in the flickering yellow light in front.

It was 1.00pm by the time the barrier had coughed us in, and ten past by the time we reached the lift. A heavily pregnant woman and her husband got in with us. She had her bag with her; he was carrying a bottle of Perrier. There were no obvious contractions between floors. I wanted to say in that irritating manner that women who've been there have, 'Go home. You'll only have to sit around and wait,' but the doors opened and I was out of there, scooting past the stall selling pastel, knitted rabbits, the sculptures hanging like shop window decorations in the atrium, past the cappuccino machine, and the 'café-style' caff, up in the Pompidou-style 'Bank D' lift to the ward.

Fergus said, 'Are we going swimming?'

'No, darling,' I said, pushing open the doors. 'We're going to see Fran.'

The sister, a petite brunette who looked about twelve, frowned at us when she saw us. 'Mother's own?' she said.

'Sorry?'

'We don't allow any other children!' she said sternly, but she melted when I told her who I'd come to see. 'Well, in that case, *one minute.*'

I said, 'I'm sorry. I was just in a hurry. I didn't have time to make arrangements.' A small, hiccupping kitten cry started up at one end of the corridor. 'How is she? How's the baby?'

'She's in here,' she said, leading us through a series of swing doors to a room at the side. 'In recovery.' She paused before letting me in. 'She's fine. She's a bit upset, and shaken up obviously. She's very sore. And she's had to have quite a lot of blood.'

'What about the baby?' I almost shouted. 'Where's the baby?'

'Sssh,' she said, too kindly. 'The baby is in the Special Care Baby Unit. She's very little. Thirty-two weeks is quite early . . .'

'So she's had the baby?' I said, one part of my brain saying, 'It's a girl!' the other dampening the hope down. 'Is she going to be all right? They say thirty weeks is OK, isn't it? I mean, it's fine, isn't it?'

She frowned. 'The doctors gave her a Caesarean,' she said, speaking slowly, as if this was something I was already aware of. 'The placenta, as you know, was damaged in the accident and so delivery had to take place as quickly as possible. The doctors are doing everything they can.' I must have looked stricken. She said more gently, 'She's in very good hands. Now . . .' And then she opened the door, and there was Fran lying on a high hospital bed with tubes coming out of her and drips hanging next to her and a strange oblong-shaped ridge under the sheet where her pregnant swelling had been. She looked very pale and very small. There was a nurse fiddling with a clipboard in the corner of the room. And next to her, looking very calm and comforting, was Jake. He was cradling her head in his arm and talking to her in a low voice and before he looked up and saw us, he had just put his finger on her cheek and said something that made her smile.

'Daddeeeee!' Fergus had leapt into the room. Jake looked up and nodded his head at me, telling me with his eyes how things stood, reassuring me and cautioning me, as he cushioned the blow of his careering son away from Fran.

'Sweetie,' I said. I abandoned the buggy in the doorway and went over to the bed. I bent down to put my arms round her. She flinched. There was a bruise on her forehead, a small cut above her mouth. Her eyes looked slightly odd, the pupils small. 'Maggie,' she said. 'Oh, Maggie.' And she started to cry and I was crying too and kissing her hair and saying I was sorry, so sorry, meaning sorry for all this and sorry for not having been there, for not having gone to Peter Jones with her, for not having stopped this from happening. And over and over I was saying, 'It's going to be OK. It's going to be OK.'

Fran was saying, 'It's so early. Is she going to be all right? Please tell me she's going to be all right. I really wasn't driving that fast. The van just sort of came . . .'

'Sssh.' Jake had put Fergus down and was stroking her hair again. He gave me another look, a serious look.

'I want to see her,' Fran said. 'Please.' She turned to me. 'Please, Maggie, ask them if I can see her now.'

Jake put his hand on her forehead. 'You'll see her very soon,' he said. 'As soon as you can be moved, you'll see her, I promise. And she's got Rain with her. She's not on her own.'

The nurse came over then. 'They're taking very good care of her,' she said. 'They're doing everything they can.'

Fergus was being very quiet. He was sitting on Jake's knee again, staring at Fran and the tubes coming out of her. But Dan was beginning to protest, unimpressed by the lack of attention coming his way, arching his back against the buggy straps, kicking his legs and crying crossly.

Fran said, 'Hello, Dan,' without moving her head and then closed her eyes. 'Hello, Fergus,' she said, opening them again. Fergus was pressing himself back against Jake's knees.

I said, 'I'd better . . .' But Jake said, 'Don't worry. You stay here. I'll take them downstairs to look at the fish.'

After he'd gone, Fran started telling me what had happened, going over and over it, as if she couldn't stop herself. 'It just came from nowhere, the van. It was a red van. I remember that.' She closed her eyes. 'One minute it wasn't there, the next . . . I was so excited to be getting all the nursery stuff, muslins, you know, so excited about getting there and I was taking that short cut, Maggie, you know, behind the Fulham Road, and we'd been stuck in traffic so I was sort of whizzing and then suddenly it was there, in the middle of the road. I tried to brake . . . but I went right into him. There was this horrible crunch. And I knew something was wrong, you know? I knew. At first I just thought, oh, and then I realised . . . It was really hurting in my back and here, this terrible pain, and Rain had put his arm out . . . and there was blood everywhere and I thought it was me . . . And then the ambulance came and . . .' She was crying again. I was wiping the tears away with my fingers, kissing her wet face. Two accidents in one summer, two vans.

'Sssh,' I was saying. 'It's OK. It's OK.'

'I'm so cold,' she said. 'I'm so cold.'

I asked the nurse if she could have a blanket and she went off to see what she could do.

'The doctor said we were lucky we were so close,' Fran said, tugging at the skin on her hand. 'But they don't know. Please, God, I wish . . . Oh God, if only I hadn't.'

The nurse came back in with a sheet and a towel, which we draped over Fran as well as we could. 'I'm sorry I can't find a blanket,' she said. 'There's a shortage of blankets.'

The door opened and Rain came in, his face calico-white against his rook-black hair. He looked lost and drawn. 'Hello, Maggie,' he said. I asked him if he was all right. His arm was in a bandage. There was blood in his fingernails. He shook his head and said he was fine as if he hadn't even noticed. I stood up so he could have my chair. He sat down and put his head on the pillow next to Fran and started telling her things about the baby. 'The doctor says her lungs aren't as mature as they could be at thirty weeks so she can't quite yet breathe on her own, but she's a good weight. She looks tiny but she could have been much smaller . . .'

'What do you mean she can't breathe?' said Fran.

'She's on a machine to help her breathe,' he said. 'So there's a tube going into her mouth, and there's something for her temperature, and something going into her stomach and there's a drip in her scalp, um, and that's for . . .' He looked anxiously at the nurse, who was doing something with the line in Fran's hand.

She said, 'That's to keep a vein open so they can keep testing her blood and oxygen levels. It looks awful, but it's all very necessary.'

'And she's under a light because she's a bit jaundiced . . .' His voice began to break up.

The nurse said, 'That's very common.'

But Rain's head was bowed. Fran was clutching him, and they were sort of rocking a little bit together. I felt in the way then and suddenly, with a pang, I wanted to see Jake again, and my children, so I said, 'I'll be back in a minute,' for the nurse's sake, because I knew they weren't going to hear me, and I left the room. First I went downstairs to the aquarium tank, but there was no sign of them. Then I went to the café-place, but they weren't there either. So I went through the big revolving doors at the front, and looked up and down the road outside. I thought perhaps he'd taken them to Starbucks, but they weren't there. I felt a little murmur of anxiety as I went back inside. I was on my way back to Lift Bank D, when I saw a familiar caravan coming towards me—not with Jake, but with my mother.

'Mum!'

'Oh hello, darling,' she said, as if I'd just bumped into her in Sainsbury's. 'Jake rang and asked me to pick up the children. We just went to say goodbye to you, but as you weren't there, we left a message with that lovely nurse. Now we're going to go back to Granny's house, aren't we, Fergus, and we'll have a lovely lunch and maybe a lovely walk and then Mummy will pick you up later.'

I was momentarily stunned by her tone of efficiency. 'What about—?' I began to say.

'Aqua-aerobics can wait!' she said. 'All that matters now is Fran.'

Then she turned the children round before they could complain and marched them briskly off in the direction of the front doors.

'Where are you parked?' I yelled after her.

'On a yellow line,' she called, without turning round. 'This is, after all, an emergency.'

I went back up to the ward when my mouth had fully closed, but turned round just before I got there. I asked the nurse for directions and took another lift up to the next floor. I couldn't work out where to go at first. The first room I peered into had a Beatrix Potter frieze along the walls, and mobiles hanging from the ceiling—it looked cosy and jolly, even the couple of small mites who were crying seemed to be doing so in a healthily demanding sort of way. Further along the corridor, I saw a man at the door, when I got to the right room, with his back to me, his face against the glass. He was wearing a suit, a familiar dark grey linen suit from Paul Smith, which was all baggy at the knees and crumpled across the bottom of the jacket. It needed to be dry-cleaned. Someone who cared about him should have taken it to be dry-cleaned. He moved so that his elbows were up against the door, his hands cupping his head.

'Hello,' I said.

He turned round and on his face was a gentleness I hadn't seen for a while. There was tenderness in his eyes and hope and desperation too.

'Hello,' he said. There was a catch in his voice. He moved aside. 'Look,' he said.

I stood next to him and with my head next to his looked into the room through the glass. There were a lot of people inside, and a bank of high-tech equipment, and seven or eight tiny incubators. The lights were on full. There was no crying here, just bleeping.

'She's over there,' he said. He pointed to the furthest incubator, over by the window. You couldn't see much, what with the wires and the plastic. You could just make out a shape really, an unimaginably small, bony shape in its artificial womb, a tiny squidge of life.

We stood there, with our heads resting together, for a long time.

chapter twenty-two

WHEN WE GOT BACK DOWN to the room where Fran was, she was sleeping. Rain was standing by the window, looking out across the roofs to the Chelsea football ground. He said he'd been waiting for us to come back so that he could go home and get some things, but Jake told him that we'd go, that he should stay in case Fran woke up.

On the way down to the car park, Jake said, facing away from me, 'Do you remember when Fergus was born?'

'Yes, of course.' I'd been thinking about it too. It wasn't in this hospital, with its light and its art, but in another nearer to us, a sprawling Victorian building with endless additions and corridors in which people seemed to wander about in constant confusion, amid a smell of fried food and bored relatives bearing feeble flowers in crimped plastic wrappings. We'd spent hours there, waiting for dilation, and then when things had speeded up, I vaguely remembered a room and a bed and a midwife, but most of all I remembered Jake gripping my hand, allowing me to dig into it with my nails, proffering water through a bendy straw, and then his face when the baby came and his face again, when I was too whacked to do anything but watch, when he rocked him, held this little bundle in his lap and sang.

'God, we were lucky,' I said.

'Yes, we were,' he said.

He took my hand for a moment and squeezed it. And then the lift doors opened and he walked out ahead of me into the car park.

When we got to Fran and Rain's building, we parked on a meter and let ourselves in with their key. There was something poignant about the state of their flat, about the fact that they'd let themselves out only that morning, not knowing they wouldn't be walking back in in a few hours' time. There was a half-empty cereal bowl on the kitchen table, and a carton of milk by the kettle. And the light had been left on—a weak beacon in a room full of slanting sun—as if they'd left when it was still dark. 'Oh God,' I said. 'Of course, it was raining.'

Jake said, 'The road was wet. She'd have braked in time otherwise.'

Together we cleared up the kitchen and tidied the sitting room, plumping up the cushions, emptying the ashtrays, straightening the copies of *My Pregnancy* into a neat pile on the floor by the sofa. There was a book of babies' names on the television. A sheet of A4 fell out as I picked it up to put it on the shelf. It was Fran's birth plan—the one Jake had defaced earlier that summer: 'Pethidine, Epidural, Emergency Caesarean', it said. 'Christ, Jake,' I said, showing it to him.

Jake looked grim. He shook his head and closed his eyes. 'I didn't know,' he said, sitting down on the plumped cushions.

I sat down next to him and put my arm round him. 'Of course you didn't,' I said. 'Anyway, it was my fault. If only I'd taken her.'

'It's just one of those things that happens,' he said.

We sat there for a bit and then I said, 'OK. Holdall, where do you think they keep it?'

And Jake said, patting his thighs, 'Stuffed under the bed . . . if I know my sister,' and we got on with the business of packing her a bag.

Before we left, I popped back into the kitchen where I'd noticed a packet of Hobnobs. I hadn't eaten since breakfast and was suddenly starving. When I got there, the packet was empty. 'Jake!' I called.

'What?' he called out from the bathroom where he was getting Fran's toothbrush.

I said, 'Where are the chocolate Hobnobs?'

'Ooh, it's funny you should mention them,' he said, poking his head round the kitchen door. 'I was in the kitchen about five minutes ago and suddenly I felt weird and when I came to, there were crumbs all over—'

'Yeah, yeah,' I said. 'All right.' But I laughed anyway.

When we'd finished, Jake went off to the police station to sort out Fran's car and I went to M&S to buy her fruit and biscuits and we arranged to meet later at the hospital. Fran had been moved to a bed on a ward when I got there. She was propped up in her cubicle, with the

460

curtains drawn on one side. There was a bit of colour in her cheeks, and her pupils looked more normal. She still had a couple of drips in her—glucose and morphine—and she still had her catheter tucked discreetly by the mattress, but they'd finished with the blood. She said, 'They said I can go and see my baby soon. When Rain gets back they're going to wheel me up in a wheelchair. I won't be able to hold her, but I'll be able to stroke her. Rain says there isn't much of her you can touch, what with the nappy and the bonnet, which she has to have to keep the thing on her and . . . and the lines. Do you think you could find someone, Maggie, and ask them? See whether I can go now? Oh, Mags, thanks. Did you bring a blanket? Oh brilliant. And my dressing gown.'

I made her some tea and sat next to her for a while until Jake came. She was calmer when he was there. She smiled at his jokes. And when he told her that everything was going to be fine, she seemed to believe him. And as we were leaving, he said, 'Oops, almost forgot this,' and took something out of his jacket pocket. It was the book of babies' names. 'Here you go, Fran,' he said, putting it on the bed by her. 'You'll need this.'

It was early evening by the time we picked up the children. My mother was still chirpy when we got there. She had the Scrabble out on the floor and was introducing Dan to the pleasures of the game. 'Look,' she was crying as we came in, 'Granny's spelt INGRATE. No, Dan. No grabbing.' Dan was trying to mash the rest of the letters into his mouth.

'That's my boy,' I said. 'You show her.'

There was a flash of lacy stocking top as she got up off the floor. 'You used to love Scrabble. Remember those lovely holidays in Cornwall?'

'Yes,' I said, extracting a wet P, fending off an image of a hotel lounge, with Crimplene chairs and a silent dining room. 'I do.'

I had picked Dan up and he was jerking up and down, salmonlike, with excitement. 'Umumamum,' he said. His hair was sticking up and I kissed it down. His head felt warm and smelt of kittens. He turned his mouth and held it open against my cheek. I wanted to hold him for ever.

Jake had wandered further into the sitting room. 'Christ,' he said. 'I mean, gracious. What's been going on here?'

The back half of the room looked like a bomb had been dismantled in it by disposal experts in a hurry. There was a big cardboard box on the floor, trailing white, polystyrene prawns all over the carpet.

'Ah!' said my mother, coyly flirtatious for Jake's sake. 'The new television. It arrived earlier. It's flat-screen. DVD.'

I left her showing him the finer points of Optimum Picture Control and went out through the kitchen into the garage where Fergus was helping Frank have a go at mending the old television. He had a big Phillips screwdriver in his fist and an expression of such knitted concentration on his face it was like suddenly seeing him grown up. He looked so separate. My heart contracted. I said, 'Hello, chaps.'

Fergus looked up, and bounced down off the wooden counter. 'It's my mummy!' he said to Frank, throwing his arms round me. 'It's my mummy.' Then to me, climbing up my body, using my arms as crampons, he said, 'We had lasagne. And I liked it!'

'Did you?' I said, kissing his nose, his eyes, his ears. I smiled at Frank. Frank in his overalls. Frank in his garage. Frank, surrounded by his tools and his clobber and his long-term projects. Frank who had been here, I realised, for really quite a few years now and who looked as if he was here to stay. 'Now, let's get you home.'

Both children, exhausted by an afternoon of board games and appliances, went to bed without a murmur between them. Jake and I made cheese on toast and sat and ate it outside in the garden.

It was dark and still out there. Occasionally I felt myself shiver as if someone had opened the door and let a draught in, but it wasn't cold. There were stars in the sky and a great big tangerine moon, an Edam without the skin. 'Harvest moon,' said Jake. 'Time to get the crops in.'

'Gather ye what ye sow,' I said. And then wished I hadn't.

The moon was casting limbed shadows that moved when the wind blew. There was a rustle in some far bushes. It was loud enough to be a person. But then next door's tabby streaked across the lawn, rattled over the fence and was gone. Not a cat burglar, just a cat.

Jake broke the silence. He said, 'Maggie, thank you for everything today. I know Fran appreciates it. And . . . um . . . I was glad you were there. It . . . um . . . made it easier for me having you with me.'

'Of course I was there,' I said. I touched his arm across the table. 'I had to be there.'

He'd changed out of his suit. He was wearing jeans and a soft, blue sweatshirt that he'd had since school, washed so many times it was as thin as felt. He didn't look that much older than when we'd first met.

I said, 'It just makes you think, doesn't it? Your life is just chugging along and you're in your own little bubble and something like this happens and it's just bang, you realise how vulnerable we all are, how thin the difference between safe and not safe. At least, they're both, they're *all*, alive.' I squeezed the wooden table.

'Thank God,' he said.

There was a pause. He said, 'I'd better go and ring Mum and Dad.' He got up to go, and then he leaned across the table and kissed me. 'Sorry,' he said, pulling back.

'It's all right,' I said, looking up at him.

There was a flicker across his mouth. 'For a moment there I forgot that we didn't kiss each other these days.'

'So we don't,' I said.

'Look.' He raked his hands through his hair. 'I'm sorry things have been so strained between us. I've had my head full of work and I know I've been irritable and distant. I shouldn't have let it come between us.'

'Maybe it hasn't come between us as much as Claire,' I said.

'Claire?' He looked taken aback. He sat down.

'There were clues,' I said calmly.

'Oh. Clues.' He still sounded more surprised than mortified.

I felt a wave of exhaustion. 'Well, let's not talk about it now. I'm too tired. We're both tired. But I just want you to know that I know. We can talk about it another time, OK? And there are things I have to tell you. I wish I didn't have to but . . .'

'I hated having secrets from you,' he said.

'Me too.' I was churning inside.

Jake bit the corner of his thumb. 'And there's something I've been meaning to ask you.'

He sat back, crossed his arms behind his head. 'Here goes . . .' he began. But he must have moved a fraction because a tendril from the albertine on the wall next to him caught in his hair. He moved to detach it. 'Ow,' he said, getting it tangled in his sleeve. 'Whatever happened to that gardener bloke you found?' There was a quizzical expression on his face. 'Did he disappear?' He turned away and was trying to extricate his jumper without further damage.

'Everything goes a bit mad in August,' I said.

He freed his jumper, inspected the little hole it had made. 'Anyway, where was I? Oh yes. What I wanted to ask you . . . What's that?'

'What?'

'That noise?'

I leaned forward with my ears straining. It was music, or a noise, like one of Fergus's broken tapes playing backwards.

463

We both got up and went to the kitchen door where the sound got louder. It sounded like an electronic musical box. I was still nervy about Jake's imminent enquiry or I suppose my reactions would have been quicker. Jake had bounded down the hall and got to the Sainsbury's bag I'd packed earlier that day to take to the hospital. Jake rummaged through the usual wrapping-and-juice-box detritus and I remembered what I should have remembered earlier: Pete's mobile. It was playing Vivaldi's 'Four Seasons'. The 'Four Seasons' by Motorola.

I leapt down the hall and grabbed it off him. 'What . . .?' Jake began.

I pressed green. 'Hello?' I said, turning my back on Jake so he couldn't see my face. A voice answered. It was a female voice, posh, anxious, asking for Pete. Jake was looking at me quizzically. 'He's not here,' I said. 'Try again tomorrow.' I pressed red. I was getting good at other people's phones now. And then I switched it off.

'Whose phone is it?' Jake said. He was standing right behind me.

'Oh.' I thought quickly. I said the first thing that came into my head. 'It's Rachel's. I borrowed it.'

'Oh. But you said "he". You said, "He's not here."'

'Guy. Rachel's husband.'

'Oh.' He must have been convinced because he seemed to forget all about it. He said, 'Oh God, I'd better ring Mum and Dad before it gets too late,' and went into the sitting room. I went to bed before he got off, but I lay awake for a while, running things over in my mind, thinking how to sort things out. Something else nagged at me too: the voice, the voice on Pete's phone. I recognised it, but I couldn't quite place it.

chapter twenty-three

IT WAS A WEEK BEFORE Fran and Rain's baby came off the ventilator. For three days one or other of us sat at the end of her incubator, stroking the square inch of flesh that wasn't covered in bruises or nappy. On the fourth day, Fran rang with the news that our niece was no longer 'critical', but 'stable'. She'd been moved to the room next door, where they switched off the lights at night—a gradual movement towards normality. Fran had given her some milk through a tube from her nose into her stomach and she had digested it. She had actually held her—albeit amid a tangle of wires. She also told Jake, who had answered the phone, that they'd finally chosen a name. I was standing next to him when she told him. 'Arabella!' he cried, rolling his eyes for my benefit. I let my jaw slacken in horror, but Jake started nodding his head, looking mollified. He put his hand over the receiver and mouthed, 'It's the name of the nurse.'

'Oh,' I said, and felt sheepish.

I'd gone in to see them every day. Fran was expressing milk for England and in need of much chocolate. Temporarily, she also seemed to have forgotten her principled belief in the right of all living creatures to freedom and dignity, not to mention her fear of BSE, and had developed a passion for Marks & Spencer's beef and horseradish sandwiches. So there was a catering job to be done, and also a chauffeuring one: the Pritons had come down to be near their daughter and were staying in Fran's flat. Stricken by my negligence during the Suffolk weekend, I was bending over backwards to make them happy, ferrying them from the flat to the hospital to our house for supper—nothing too spicy for Derek's digestion—and back to the flat.

Crisis, as ever, seemed to bring out the best, and the worst, in people. Rachel had been a brick. She brought round several ready-made meals: large casserole dishes awash with chicken and almonds (Claudia Roden), or saffron and cod (Jane Grigson), none strictly necessary in practical terms, but invaluable in terms of moral support.

'You're a good friend,' I said, giving her a hug at the door.

'Oh, it's nothing; I enjoy cooking,' she said, over her shoulder, nipping back to her car, which she'd left with its engine running in the middle of the road. 'You can fuck off,' she said to the man beeping her from behind. I liked her even more after that.

Lucinda had also revealed hidden depths—or hidden shallows. She rang the day after the accident in a complete state, caused, it turned out, by a missing member of staff. 'Maggie. Thank God I've found you in. Do you by any chance have another number for Russ?'

'Who?' I said.

'Russ. Russ the gardener. I'm desperately in need of him—the lawn is a total shambles and I cannot get through to him on his mobile.'

'Oh Pete,' I said. 'Er . . . Hang on . . . Sorry, we're having a bit of a time of it here.' And I told her what had happened. When I finished, she said, as if she hadn't even listened, 'Oh right. Oh dear. The number then?'

'Thanks for the concern,' I said, after I'd put the phone down.

Jake raised his eyebrows. 'Never liked her much,' he said.

Jake had taken the week off work. Things had eased since the Kyushi deal, and though there was trouble brewing at Pot Noodle—new flavour, new campaign—he'd decided to put all hot snacks on the back burner. 'Family comes first,' he'd said. He'd said it in a funny voice, as if self-conscious with the sentimentality, but I knew he meant it.

Fran wasn't the only person happy to have him around. His mother, Angela, who was delighted with her new granddaughter, seemed even more pleased to have unrestricted access to her son. His birthday was only three weeks away and she was knitting a sweater for him as a present. So every spare minute she spent pinning sections of knitting to his chest. 'Just make sure it's not too tight round the neck,' I heard Jake say once in a moany voice, 'or too itchy,' as if he was thirty-six going on eight.

I liked having him at home too. A lot of things were still unsaid between us. I didn't know whether he'd finished with Claire or not, but for the moment it didn't seem to matter. He was at home, or in the hospital, at my side or at Fran's, all week. He seemed wrapped up in us, in his children. He seemed happier than he'd been for months. There was no suspicious behaviour, no sneaking out to buy light bulbs.

Of course it was possible that while Fran was in hospital he had simply put the relationship on hold, and would pick it up with renewed vigour when she was out. I couldn't put this thought entirely out of my mind. Particularly in view of the phone calls. Someone was definitely trying to get hold of him—or me—or both. Pete rang once without leaving a message on the machine. I knew it was him because I heard the sound of a buzz saw before he hung up. But there were other calls too, which I didn't think were him because the phone went dead when I picked it up. I dialled 1471, but the caller had withheld their number.

I still hadn't dealt with Pete. I was dreading meeting him. I would have to confront my own foolishness as well as his possible anguish. I kept putting it off and it became more and more difficult as the days went by. Not least, because the last time I'd seen him, he'd seemed so very keen. But it had to be done. Also, I still had his phone.

So on a Saturday morning, almost two weeks after the accident, I told Jake I had some things to do. He didn't seem that bothered. His parents were coming round for coffee at 11.00am. It wasn't raining.

I drove to the other side of the common, along the row of beautiful

Georgian houses. When I got to the flat, I sat outside for a minute or two. There were battalions of small boys playing football on the common. It was quite warm but the sky hung low in a grey panoply as if the world had a false ceiling, their cries bouncing off the clouds.

I took Pete's phone from the glove compartment, where I had put it for safekeeping, got out and crossed the road, sticking my head out between Pete's van and a Mitsubishi Shogun, before I did so. The Mitsubishi looked familiar and there was a yapping and a mad scratching from its back windows, as a couple of Highland terriers tried to scrabble through the glass at the sight of me. They looked familiar as well, but I was too preoccupied to think anything of that then. There was a bus stop right outside the house and there were a couple of old men taking the weight off their feet on the step when I got there. The one who eased himself up to let me pass was wearing a stained tweed jacket and a spotted bow tie. They were remarking on each car as it went by. 'Toyota: they make a good car,' the older man on the step was saying as I clambered through. 'Absolute bloody sods, the Japanese,' said the man in the bow tie. 'Bloody awful what they did in the war. I couldn't buy Japanese because of that. Sorry, dear.'

Once past, I paused for a moment and then I went up the steps. I'd go down to see Pete later. I had to see Claire first. I had to talk to her. I rang the bell and waited, clenching and unclenching my fists, my toes curled in my plimsolls. And I heard footsteps, the jangle of the chain and then there Claire was. In her pigeon-coloured dressing gown.

'Oh,' she said.

Now she'd opened the door, my knees were trembling.

'Can I have a word?' I said, my voice unnaturally high.

'Er, yeah, hello, Maggie. Yes, come in.'

She went ahead into her flat and I followed. The curtains were drawn in the sitting room. There was an overflowing ashtray and red wine rings on the coffee table. A candle had been left alight on the mantelpiece and had dripped down onto the slate hearth below. There was a sweet cloyness in the air. Perfume and cigarettes and, to my nostrils, something danker, like other people's husbands.

Claire had gone into another room. She came out again almost immediately. 'How are you?' she said, closing the door behind her. 'I haven't seen you for ages. Not since the . . . er . . . swimming pool. Coffee?'

'Um, all right.' I felt my resolution weaken. She was on her way to the kitchen now, on the move as if to keep what I had to say at arm's length.

'It'll have to be instant,' she called. 'I've run out of real.'

She came back in after a bit and rooted around in the sofa next to me until she found a packet of cigarettes. She pulled one out, sat on the arm of a chair and tucked her dressing gown round her knees. But not before I'd caught sight of a web of broken veins on the inside of her thigh, like river tributaries on an Ordnance Survey map. She wasn't wearing make-up either and close to, she looked tired; there were dark smudges under her eyes. 'So, what's up?' she said.

I sat on my hands to stop them trembling. 'Look,' I began. I stopped. I cleared my throat. 'Look,' I said again. 'This is awkward I'm sure for both of us. I expect your heart sank when you saw me at the door.'

'Not really,' she said. She was so cool I wanted to scream.

'You must have some idea of why I've come.'

Claire was smoking. 'I have no idea,' she said. 'Though when we met at the swimming pool I could tell you felt some anger towards me.'

'Of course I feel anger,' I said. 'What do you expect?'

She was still smiling at me, her head politely cocked to one side. She was still smoking, but she seemed to be gripping the cigarette more tightly between her fingers. There was a click from the kitchen. 'I'm just going to go and make the coffee,' she said.

When she got up, I got up too and followed her in. She had her back to me. 'Fuck it,' I said. 'I don't want coffee.' The kitchen showed signs of a meal, only idly cleared away. I said, 'I just want you to tell me that you're not going to try and see Jake again.'

'What?' she didn't turn round. But she stopped what she was doing, which was pouring hot water into two Portmeirion mugs. Her grandmother's Portmeirion. Even Claire's mugs belonged to someone else.

'Yes, I know about it. I know about Jake and you. And I know something else too. It's over. OK? It's over between you. You may think he loves you, but he doesn't. I know he loves me. And I know he loves his children. And if you think for one minute that he's going to leave us you're very, very wrong. I will fight you all the way.' Even as I was talking, it struck me as odd how it's in moments of crisis that one falls back most readily on clichés, as if to force unwieldy emotions into something manageable. Claire turned, making a noise in her throat, but I carried on. 'I am not going to give him up. We've made something together, and if you think otherwise, you're . . .' I flailed for a moment, my arsenal of clichés temporarily exhausted, before I plucked something else from the ether, 'absolute bloody sods.'

Claire was clearly fighting to control herself. I had got to her. For the first time ever I had got to her. I had proved I wasn't mousy Maggie—I was a force to be reckoned with. She was biting the corner of her lip. 'Maggie,' she began. But I was unstoppable now, I had thirty years' worth of things to say. 'Of course men like Jake are going to fall for you,' I said, shaking my head. 'You're gorgeous and you're out doing interesting things so you've got interesting things to talk about. But it's not fair. It's not a level playing field. I'm boring and downtrodden because I look after children, Jake's children. And I've got no conversation because I've given up my life to do that. Not to mention my nights and half my brain. But this is what most people's lives are about. They're not about meetings with agents and weekends in New York. They're about muddling on, and finding shared pleasures in small things, like your child's first word, or a random unbroken night. They're about not getting on all of the time, and sometimes not getting on a lot of the time, but about growing old together, learning to fit together.'

Claire said, 'Maggie. Stop. STOP. You've got it all wrong. I am not seeing Jake. It's nothing to do with him. You've got the wrong man.'

'What do you mean "the wrong man"?' I was gripping the back of a chair.

She was looking horrified and yet slightly amused at the same time. 'Maggie. I don't know where you've got this from. I am having an affair, yes. But not with Jake.'

'Who then?' I screeched, still disbelieving.

'With Ed.'

'ED?'

She had started giggling. 'Sorry, sorry.' She straightened her face. 'I know it's not funny. It's just your expression. Maggie, I'm so sorry. I don't know how this has happened.'

I was staring at her. I could feel rushing in my ears. I was still holding on to the back of the chair, but to keep my balance now. I felt disbelief and confusion and something else glorious, which must have been relief. 'Ed?' I said again. 'Ed Brady? I don't believe you. You're lying.'

She was grinning. 'I'm not. He was here only a minute ago and you could have seen him with your own eyes.' She put her hand on my shoulder and guided me into the chair. 'Look, sit down.'

I said, 'I don't believe it.' Though I did now. There were just a hundred other things I didn't believe, like how I'd got it all wrong.

'I promise you, I'm telling the truth,' Claire said. 'Why would I lie?'

I just stared at her. 'I think you need that coffee,' she said. Claire tipped the mugs into the sink and began to reboil the kettle. She made a little 'tum-ti-tum' sound as she did so. Normal service had resumed for Claire; a minor misunderstanding had been mopped up. But what was minor to her was monumental to me. I sat, still unable to move, running through everything in my mind. How could I have been so wrong. How could I have misread the situation so badly? I realised I was crying. It must have been relief or shock or pity or guilt or all of those things. A couple of fat drops rolled down my face and fell onto some documents next to the dirty plates in front of me. I put my palms up to my eyes and then used my sleeve to dab at the paper. I saw then that it was estate agents' particulars. I picked the top one up: it was for a two-bedroom flat in Notting Hill.

'Are you moving?' I said.

'Well, Ed and I—'

'Ed and you?'

'Yes.' She brought the Portmeirion over and sat down next to me.

I said, 'But I don't understand. I saw you together . . . I—'

A door slammed and I didn't finish. There was the sound of hurried footsteps and a voice, getting louder, calling, 'Forgot my bloody squash kit! I'd forget my balls if—' and the door opened and there was Ed.

'If they weren't in a bag,' he said dumbly, seeing me.

'Ed,' I said, getting up.

'Hello, Maggie.' He grimaced, then shrugged. 'Caught in the act now, eh?'

'Ed,' I said again. Both my hands were clutching the top of my head, as if in a gesture of surrender.

He came and kissed me on both cheeks as if we were at a cocktail party. 'Lovely to see you,' he said. 'Sorry to hear about Fran . . .'

I couldn't concentrate on the small talk. I glanced at Claire and then back to him again. 'Ed, I don't understand.' I emitted a small, high laugh. 'You told me Claire was having an affair with Jake.'

'I told you what?' He pulled away.

'We had that conversation in Suffolk. About Claire and Jake.'

He looked over at Claire, who looked baffled. 'There is no Claire and Jake. There's only Claire and me.'

Could this be possible? 'But you did. You were so sympathetic.'

'I was sympathetic? *You* were sympathetic. You encouraged me to pack my bags.'

'I did?'

'Yeah.' He was frowning at me as if I'd gone mad.

I turned to Claire. I realised I was supposed to be feeling embarrassed now, but I was still too bewildered. 'I don't understand. You knew all about Jake's business trip—you knew about Kyushi. He knew all about what you were up to. I heard you on the phone to him arranging lunch. I followed you. I saw you together. I saw you embrace him.'

'You embraced him?' Ed said.

'You'd just fled the restaurant,' Claire said. 'He was comforting me.'

'And what about all the other things? All the coming round to our house, inviting us here, there and everywhere. I won't flatter myself that it was for my company.'

Claire had the grace then to look ashamed. 'Yes, I know. I used you and I used Jake. I used him to get to Ed when Ed wouldn't return my calls and when Ed's secretary, who had been my ally, suddenly developed a conscience—'

'And Jake didn't?'

'I don't think he liked doing it.'

'Yes, well, I'm very grateful to him now,' Ed interrupted. 'It was the right thing and I think he had my best interests at heart.'

'But not mine,' I said. 'He didn't tell me. If he'd told me, none of this would have happened.'

'I made him promise not to,' Ed said. 'I was just so petrified that Pea would find out and . . . well then anyway, you told me you'd guessed. But Jake said you didn't want to talk about it.'

'I didn't want to talk about *him* and Claire,' I said. I put my forehead in the palms of my hands and kneaded it. I stared at the table through the crack between my arms, overwhelmed by my own foolishness. I could see the corner of the estate agents' particulars. I picked them up again and held them out.

'Does Pea know?' I asked.

Ed said, 'Yes. She does. She's staying with a friend in Bath this weekend to think. She suspected something was up even before I told her. Actually,' he started laughing, 'she thought I was having an affair with you! In Suffolk anyway. She said we kept sneaking off!'

I smiled. I said, 'Yeah, well, stranger things have happened.' There was a pause. 'So you're leaving her?' I added.

Claire got up and was facing the sink.

'Yes.' Ed's face straightened. 'Yes, this time I am.'

'Poor Pea.'

'Yes and no,' he said. 'She's angry with me now. But she's always been angry with me. I was never quite what she wanted me to be, never successful enough. She thought she deserved more than me.'

'And what about . . .?'

'Clarice. It's awful. But I'll see her all the time. I won't let anything come between us. Actually,' he looked at his watch, 'I said I'd ring at lunchtime. If you'll excuse me, I'll just go into the bedroom and do that.'

Claire turned back from the sink after he'd gone. 'It's not true that I only go after married men. There were only ever two. Marcus—who told me he was single when we met and was a disaster anyway—and Ed. I would be lying if I said I hadn't known Ed was married. I knew right from the beginning. But we tried to stop it. And we split up for all that time. We did fight it.'

'But it was too strong for you?'

'Don't be mean, Maggie.'

'Sorry. I'm still stinging from my own mistake, still wondering what I would think if it was me.'

Claire sighed. She twisted her hair and tucked it into the back of her dressing gown. 'He wasn't happy, Maggie. I know some people think you should stay "for the children", but is that fair? Would you want to be Pea in those circumstances? Or Clarice? Knowing, or sensing, at any rate, that your father had given up everything for you?'

I said, 'My friend Mel thinks you make your own happiness.'

She shrugged. 'Who knows?' she said. 'Maybe you do, maybe you don't. Maybe Ed and Pea could have been happy. But he met me and they weren't. These things happen. Some relationships last. Some don't. Who knows why that is?'

She got up and started looking for something in the cupboard above the sink. One half of my brain was still flicking back. Something suddenly struck me. 'Why,' I said, 'when I bumped into you in Morton High Street, did you say that thing about Jake being boring?'

She turned round. 'What thing?'

'You made some reference to Jake being dull. Dullsville, you said. If you'd been seeing Ed you'd have known that Jake was with me, that he was the father of my children. Why did you say that?'

Claire smiled, as if amused by some private joke. 'Oh yes,' she said.

'Why?' I insisted.

'Look.' She bit the corner of a nail. 'It was cruel, I know. It was a moment of spitefulness. It's just there you were, with your two lovely children and your fresh-faced, outdoors radiance and your shopping bags full of meals for two. You were the woman who had it all, who had everything I wanted: children, a family to shop for, a house to go back to, a busy little bee making her own happiness, as your friend Mel would say, and I just wanted to dent it a bit. See that smug smile slip.'

'Smug?' I said, shaking my head. 'I was feeling desperate. I was at the end of my tether. I felt downtrodden and unloved. You were the one who shone. You were the one who looked smug.'

'Yes, well, things always look different from the outside.'

She was grinning at me now and I found I was grinning back. Ed came back into the room and Claire opened up a rusty Quality Street tin. 'Chocolate brownie, either of you?' she said. 'I made them myself.'

When I left the flat, the old men had gone and small, muddy boys were being shepherded into cars. Pete's van, along with the Mitsubishi Shogun and its yapping inhabitants, were still there.

I crossed the road and walked a little way across the common to a bench over by the railway line. I sat down. Pete's phone was in the back pocket of my jeans so I stood up again to take it out. I laid it in my lap and stared at my feet. I could hear people going by along the path next to me but I didn't look up.

There are very few moments in life when you see yourself for what you are. Not how you'd like to be, or how you think other people see you. These moments are very sobering.

I was the only one in our relationship who had been unfaithful. Everything that had gone wrong was my fault. I'd been selfish, self-obsessed, unimaginative. How could I have done what I had done? Jake had done nothing. Or if he had, falling for Claire's charm to the extent that he'd agreed to act as Pandarus, it was a trifle to what I'd done. To him. To my children. How could I have done that? How could I have lost touch with what really mattered?

I felt a surge of panic rise and stick like vomit in the back of my throat. Had I thrown it all away now? Would Jake forgive me? What would happen when I told him? (Because I would tell him, I *had* to tell him. How do you live with yourself otherwise?) The thought of the hurt on his face when I told him was almost unbearable.

I got up then, brushing away the tears on my face impatiently, walked back across the common and down the stairs to Pete's flat.

A strange man answered the door in his boxer shorts. 'You must be Lloyd,' I said clearly and firmly. 'Is Pete in?'

He paused, then said unconvincingly, 'Nnnnno. I don't think so.'

'Are you sure?' I said. 'It's just his van is here.'

'No, honestly he isn't.' His eyes widened in indignation.

'Do you mind if I check?' I said, manoeuvring past him into the darkness of the flat. 'Unlike him not still to be snoozing.' I was sure he'd be in: his van was here, the curtains to his room were still drawn, it was Saturday morning—where else would a single man be if not in bed? I had to make sure, because I wanted to get it over with now. I made for Pete's bedroom. Lloyd was behind me, making ineffectual noises. 'Hey,' he said. 'I wouldn't . . .'

I pushed open the door. A navy-blue court shoe was dangling from the post at the bottom of the bed. An olive-green Mulberry shoulder bag was lying, splayed open, on the floor; its contents, a Harvey Nichols diary, a Nokia phone, a pair of tiny, pink ballet shoes, were spilling out onto what I could tell from the door was a pair of Boden tartan checked pull-ons and a lamby half-zip. Pete was in bed. On top of him, her thick, curly locks not forced back in a band but tumbling down her back in an attitude of sweaty abandon, her broad shoulders arched in ecstasy, was someone to whom I had recommended his services and who was, at that very moment, making the most of them. Someone who for once had let her hair down.

'Oh, hello,' I said. 'Walking the dogs?'

Lucinda, hearing a voice, gasped and dived under the covers. Pete sat up quickly, tucking the bedclothes over her head and across his waist as if I was room service bringing breakfast in bed.

Pete said, 'It's not what it looks like,' which made the air escape explosively from the sides of my mouth. He must have thought it was a sob because he leapt out of bed, grabbed a grubby towelling dressing gown and hustled me out of the door and into the hall. 'She was feeling unloved,' he wheedled. 'She needed affection. I've been trying and trying to get hold of you and you're never in—or he is—and then when you answered I kept bottling out and . . .'

'What do you mean, bottling out?'

'I'd hang up.'

'So it was *you*? Why?'

He gave a pathetic shrug. 'I didn't know whether you wanted to see me or not. And also I needed my—'

'Your phone.' I reached into my pocket. 'Sorry I've taken so long to bring it back.' I held it out. I was whispering now. I didn't think Lucinda had seen me and I suddenly realised how much better it would be if she didn't hear my voice either.

Pete put out his hand to take the phone. 'Maggie,' he hissed. 'Please. I'll ring you. It's not what it seems.'

I took in his handsome, tanned face and his muscular arms and the golden legs poking out of his too-short dressing gown. I said, 'Honestly, it doesn't matter.' I gave him a peck. 'I should say thank you really.' And I turned my back, climbed the steps, and crossed the road to the car.

When I got home, Fergus was dive-bombing Dan in the sitting room. There was Lego all over the floor, and plastic cars all over the sofa and the animals from Dan's Alphabet Caterpillar had been scattered everywhere. Fergus appeared to have brought his duvet down too, and the television was on—but no one was watching; you could hardly hear it above their squeals.

Angela, Jake's mother, was in the kitchen, talking to my mother, who had popped round so as not to be left out. 'We saw a super play at the National last night,' my mother was saying when I walked in. 'It was part of the Irish season. Do you get to the theatre much? Oh, you don't.'

Derek, his father, was in the garden, studying a drainpipe with Frank, who was standing in the doorway to get a better angle. 'Think I might just pop home to get my tools,' he said, backing into the kitchen.

And there was Jake in the middle of it all. His dark hair tousled and pushed back from his face, his feet bare, pale after their summer in the office, an old blue jumper with the sleeves rolled up. He was standing by the oven with a saucepan of boiling water in one hand and an open tin of shiny tomatoes in the other, and he was smiling. He had the phone under one ear. 'Yes,' he was saying, tipping the tomatoes into a pan of sizzling onions, 'come round. The more the merrier. Maggie's just walked in. Do you want a word? No, no. Come straight round now.

'Mel,' he said to me, putting the phone down. 'She's bringing Milly to lunch.' He had picked up another pan to drain the pasta but he kissed me over it, a hot, steamy kiss. 'Then when we've had lunch I said we'd drive Mum and Dad to the hospital. The nurse said we could take Fran for a walk today, and Mum wants to go to Marble Arch M&S if there's time before catching the train. They want to take the five ten if they can. So I'll take her, shall I, or would you like to?'

Was I going to tell him? Was it the right thing to do? Would it destroy everything we had?

'Oh and,' Jake looked over his shoulder at our mothers, now happily discussing the Goya at the Hayward, and said in an undertone, 'Christmas. They want to know what's happening at Christmas.'

'But it's September!'

'Never too early,' he sang under his breath.

There was crying from the next room. 'I'll go,' I said, because Jake was already at the door. And I went through into the sitting room where Dan was sitting, sobbing with a bump on his head, with Fergus, who may well have been the perpetrator, sitting next to him trying to give him a kiss. 'Don't cry,' he was saying. 'Don't cry.' But Dan didn't want Fergus's kisses and was trying to push him off, which made Fergus cry too, so soon I was having to cuddle them both, trying to fit both on my lap, stroking their soft, baby hair, caressing their tears away. 'I only wanted to cuddle him sorry,' Fergus wailed, and I had to tell him that sometimes sorry was what people wanted and sometimes it wasn't. And I knew that I wasn't going to tell Jake about Pete, that *not* telling him would be my punishment. Maybe it was cowardly, or maybe it was brave. But to tell him would be to seek absolution, to beg forgiveness, and maybe that was the most selfish thing of all. No, it wasn't a case of kiss and make up. It was a case of carrying it along with me, proving to myself, day after day, that in the general, unruly, messy, dishevelled state of things, it really wouldn't matter that much.

'Come on,' I said, wiping away the last tears. 'Lunch.'

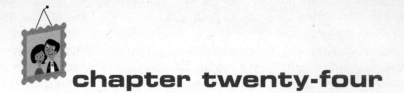

chapter twenty-four

IT WASN'T UNTIL SEVERAL DAYS LATER that I got round to asking Jake what it was he wanted to ask me that evening after we'd returned from the hospital. We'd put the children to bed after supper and were in the sitting room and Jake was reading the papers and I was sorting through some photographs. It was something I did from time to time, organise them into piles in preparation for putting them into a book. But I never actually got round to putting them into a book. It didn't matter. It was an excuse to flick through our life as much as anything.

I'd just come across a picture of Jake and me on holiday BC (Before Children). We had balanced the camera on a wall, on timer, and were crouched down, unnecessarily squashed together, with the Lake District stretching out on either side of us. 'Look,' I said. 'How young we were.' Jake looked up from his papers, said, 'Hm,' and went back to them.

I carried on staring at the picture. After it was taken, I remembered, we'd decided we'd had enough of scenery and we'd walked down to the car and gone back to the holiday cottage. And when we'd got back, we realised we'd run out of firewood and we couldn't be bothered to go out again, so we'd gone to bed instead. At 4.00pm in the afternoon and we'd stayed there until the next morning, and I remember thinking I had never been happier than that night and would never be happier again.

Jake looked up. I was still staring at the picture and I could feel my eyes pricking. 'Are you all right?' he said.

'I'm fine,' I said, slipping it back into the pile. 'But what was it you wanted to ask me? The night Fran went into hospital?'

Jake froze. He looked down. 'Er . . . oh, it doesn't matter. It can wait.'

'No, no. Tell me now. Now will do.'

I curled my legs up on the sofa, leaving the photographs on the floor. I had had a bath with the children and was wearing Jake's pyjamas.

'What, now?' he said.

'Yes now. Why not? Let's talk about whatever it is now.'

He put the paper down. He ran his hands through his hair. Suddenly, he looked terribly serious. For one thudding, piercing moment, I thought, He knows.

I said, 'Actually—'

He said, 'I've just been thinking and I know this summer . . . well, things weren't right . . . and I suspect—'

'What?' I said. I was gripping my toes.

'Well, maybe things would have been different if I . . . if I pulled myself together and—'

'What?'

'Well, whether you might like to get married.'

He was grinning at me now. I put my hand to my mouth to stop myself from bursting into tears. I could see it all. A white wedding: a white frock for the bride (skittishly ironic, of course), a black coat for the groom, and all our friends in rows, glasses raised, crystal catching fragments of light, and dancing, and small children twirled aloft by tipsy uncles and the maid of honour getting off with the best man and someone's cousin being sick in the loo, and bad speeches, and good ones, and a white pagoda cake, with tiers to shed tears of joy over, and drinking and merriment and, as Mel was always reminding me, lots of presents with my name on.

And I looked at Jake, sitting there next to me with a crooked smile on his face, the face I knew I could trace in my sleep, and I thought of the children asleep upstairs and I felt a great thud of joy in my heart. Because this wasn't an ending or a beginning. It was a continuation. I realised I didn't need to wait for something to happen. Something was happening all the time. I kissed his face, the rough bits around his chin and then his soft mouth. 'Let's not,' I said, switching off the television and wrapping my dressing gown around him. 'Let's stick with sin.'

SABINE DURRANT

When Sabine Durrant left Oxford University after reading English, she did not have any firm career plan in mind. 'I had a vague thought that I might get a job at some erudite literary publication, but I wrote loads of letters to anyone I'd ever heard of, or had any contact with, and the only person to reply was a wonderful journalist called Lucy Tuck who was running a free magazine called *The Magazine*. I worked for her for a year, doing a bit of everything: copy-editing, writing, commissioning. In fact, one of my very first assignments was to go undercover as an escort for an escort agency.' After this serious grounding in journalism, Sabine Durrant says she went on to work on the arts pages at the *Independent*, and then the *Sunday Times*, before landing what she calls 'a most brilliant job' working on the features pages of the *Guardian*. Sabine left the *Guardian* after she had her first son, Barney, but continued to write *The Sabine Durrant Interview* for them from home.

When asked who she had enjoyed interviewing the most in this feature, she replied, 'I loved interviewing everybody apart from comedienne Ruby Wax, who clearly took against me and wouldn't answer any questions— maybe because I spilt coffee on her carpet. Best of all I like the elderly men—Peregrine Worsthorne, Alan Clark, Robert Runcie, most of whom don't care any more what anyone thinks of them. Some of them tended to die after I'd interviewed them, but I hope it wasn't as a direct result!

'I loved doing *The Sabine Durrant Interview*, but it was always hard to guess which days I would need childcare, and the logistics of never knowing where I was going to be were a problem. When I was on maternity leave, I wrote the first three chapters of *Having It and Eating It* and intended to write the rest while doing my job, but I didn't find the time. So after a bit I sent the chapters to an agent, who found me a publisher on the strength of them, plus a synopsis which was completely different to how the book turned out—the characters just wouldn't behave . . . .'

Sabine Durrant lives near Wandsworth Common, South London, which, she tells me, 'is said to have the highest birth rate in Europe!' She and her writer and journalist partner, Giles Smith, now also have a second son. 'Being a working mother you feel torn in all directions, and spend most of your time feeling guilty. But having said that, I am also aware how different you feel if you have given up your job to look after your children. A full day with tiny children is more tiring and mentally gruelling than a day in the office. But I love being a mother: I love all the stuff that Maggie loves about her sons in the book—their affection and their physicality, their funniness. At times they drive me completely mad, but they are the centre of my life.'

Jane Eastgate